TEXAS BOARDINGHOUSE BRIDES

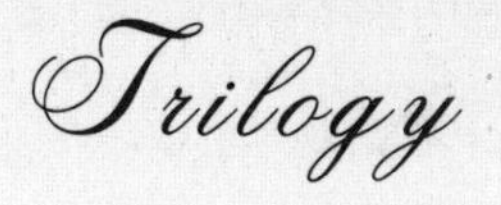

TEXAS BOARDINGHOUSE BRIDES

Trilogy

VICKIE McDONOUGH

ISBN 978-1-61626-700-1

Scripture quotations are taken from the King James Version of the Bible.

This book is a work of fiction. Names, characters, places, and incidents are either products of the author's imagination or used fictitiously. Any similarity to actual people, organizations, and/or events is purely coincidental.

For more information about Vickie McDonough, please access the author's website at the following Internet address: www.vickiemcdonough.com

Thumbnails of original covers by Faceout Studio, www.faceoutstudio.com

Published by Barbour Publishing, Inc., P.O. Box 719, Uhrichsville, Ohio 44683, www.barbourbooks.com

Our mission is to publish and distribute inspirational products offering exceptional value and biblical encouragement to the masses.

ecpa Member of the Evangelical Christian Publishers Association

Printed in the United States of America.

Anonymous Bride

Dedication/Acknowledgments

This book is dedicated to my editor,
Rebecca Germany; my copyeditor, Becky Fish;
and the wonderful staff at Barbour.
Thank you for believing in me as a writer and giving me
the opportunity to tell the stories of my heart.
You all are the greatest to work with.

Whoso findeth a wife findeth a good thing,
and obtaineth favour of the Lord.
Proverbs 18:22 KJV

Chapter 1

Lookout, Texas
April 1886

Sometimes God asked difficult things of a man, and for Luke Davis, what he was fixing to do was the hardest task ever.

Luke reined his horse to a halt atop the ridge and gazed down at the town half a mile away. Lookout, Texas—the place where his dreams had been birthed and later had died. He wasn't ready to return, to face the two people he'd tried so hard to forget.

"I'd rather face a band of Sioux warriors, Lord, than to ride into that town again." He sighed and rubbed the back of his neck.

Alamo, his black gelding, snorted, as if sensing they'd reached the end of their long journey. Luke directed his horse down the path to the small river that ran south and west of the town. A healthy dose of spring rain had filled the crater dug out by past floods where the river made a sharp turn. Local kids used it for a swimming hole, and a new rope had been added for them to swing on. Memories of afternoons spent there were some of Luke's favorite, but those carefree days were over.

He glanced heavenward at the brilliant blue sky, halfway hoping God would give him leave to ride away. When no such reprieve came, he dismounted at the water's edge and allowed his horse to drink while he rinsed three days' worth of dust off his face.

Alamo suddenly jerked his head up and flicked his ears forward. The horse backed away from the bank and turned, looking off to the right. Luke scooped up a handful of water and sipped it, watching to see what had stirred up his horse. Tall trees lined the life-giving river, and thigh-high grasses and shrubs made good hiding places. He knew that for a fact. How many times as a boy had he and his two cousins hidden there, watching the older kids swimming and sometimes spooning?

"Must have been some critter, 'Mo." He stood and patted his horse, finally ready to ride into Lookout and see up close how much the town had changed. How she'd changed.

Three heads popped up from behind a nearby bush. "Hey, mister," a skinny kid yelled, "that's our swimming hole, not a horse trough."

Rocks flew toward Luke, and he ducked, turning his back to the kids. Alamo squealed and sidestepped into Luke, sending him flying straight into the river. Hoots of laughter rose up behind him as cool water gushed into his boots and soaked his clothing. His soles slipped on the moss-covered rocks as he scrambled for a foothold.

"Foolish kids." He trudged out of the river, dripping from every inch of his clothing. His socks sloshed in his water-logged boots. Dropping to the bank, he yanked them off, dumped the water, and wrung out his socks. With his boots back on, he checked Alamo, making sure the horse wasn't injured; then he mounted, determined to find those kids and teach them a lesson. Playing childish pranks was one thing. He'd done his share of them. But throwing rocks at an animal was something else altogether.

"Heyah!" Alamo lurched forward. Luke hunkered low against the horse's neck until he cleared the tree line. He sat up, scanning the rolling hills. He didn't see any movement at first, but when he topped the closest hill, he found the rowdy trio racing for the edge of town. Luke hunched down and let his horse out in a full canter, quickly closing the distance between him and the kids.

All three glanced back, no longer ornery but scared. He'd never harm a child, but instilling a little fear for the law couldn't hurt anything.

The two tallest boys veered off to the left, outpacing the smaller kid. The boy stumbled and fell, bounced up, and shot for town. Luke aimed for that one as the older boys dashed behind the nearest house. The youngster pressed down his big floppy hat and pumped his short legs as fast as he could. The gap narrowed. Slowing Alamo, Luke leaned sideways and reached down, grabbing the youth by his overall straps. The child kicked his feet and flailed his arms, but Luke was stronger, quicker. He slung the kid across his lap.

"Let me go! I ain't done nothin'." The boy held his hat on with one hand and pushed against Luke's leg with the other hand. "You're gettin' me wet."

"Just lie still. And I wouldn't be wet if you hadn't thrown rocks at my horse." Luke held a firm hand on the kid's backside, but the boy still squirmed, trying to get free. "Don't make me tie you up."

Suddenly, he stilled. "You wouldn't."

"Whoa, 'Mo." Luke calmed his horse, fidgety from the child's activity. Alamo had carried him through all kinds of weather, fights with Indians in the Dakotas, and chasing down train robbers, but one skinny kid had him all riled up.

"My ma ain't gonna like you doin' this to me, mister."

Luke grunted, knowing the kid was probably right—but then his mama should have taught him not to throw rocks at strangers. The next man might shoot back.

Being sopping wet with a cocky kid tossed across his lap certainly wasn't the homecoming he'd planned.

Luke scanned Main Street as he rode in, noting the changes made over the past decade. Most of the buildings on this end of town, with the exception of the saloon, sported fresh coats of paint. The town hadn't grown nearly as much as he'd expected it would in the eleven years he'd been gone. With the new street that had been added after he left, the town roughly resembled a capital E: Bluebonnet Lane was the spine; and Main, Apple, and the new street served as the three arms.

Almost against his will, Luke's gaze turned toward the three-story Hamilton House that filled the end of Main Street. The house, no longer white with black accents, had been painted a soft green and trimmed with white. Rachel's influence, no doubt. If he kept going, he'd ride right up to her front door.

How much had she changed? Did she and James have a passel of children? A sharp pain stabbed his chest. They should have been his and Rachel's children, but the woman he'd loved had betrayed him. Married someone else—the town's wealthiest bachelor.

He shook his head. *Stop! You're here to put the past behind you. Once and for all.*

He couldn't allow himself to think about how Rachel had hurt him. He had to find a way to forgive her so he could move on, find a wife he could love, and start a family. Pushing thirty, he wasn't getting any younger. And why did returning home make him more nervous than he'd been the day he joined the cavalry a decade ago?

The boy he'd captured found new strength and bucked several more times. "My ma will take her broomstick to you, and I'm gonna laugh when she does."

Luke chuckled and shook his head. This kid needed his rear end tanned good, or maybe, beings as Luke was soon to be the town marshal, he should just lock the boy in jail for a few hours. That ought to scare him straight for a day or two.

A man exited the saloon, drawing Luke's attention to his right. The Wet Your Whistle had been enlarged and sported a fancy new sign in bright colors, which looked out of place against the weathered wood of the building. To his left, the livery looked to be well cared for. Was Sam still the owner? Or had his son taken over?

He rode past Polly's Café. The fragrant scents emanating out the open door reminded him that he hadn't eaten since his skimpy breakfast of coffee and a dried biscuit, leftover from dinner the night before. Maybe his cousins would join him for their noontime meal if they hadn't already eaten. 'Course, he had an issue of business to attend to before he could think of food.

Dolly, twin sister to Polly, evidently still owned the dress-maker's shop directly across from the café. The spinster had painted the small structure a ghastly pinkish-purple more suited to a saloon gal's dress. He almost felt sorry for the old building until he remembered that it sat next door to his cousins' freight office and they'd have to stare at it every day. He grinned. Served those rascals right.

He hauled the youngster up, slung him over his shoulder, then dismounted and tied Alamo to the hitching post outside of the Corbett Freight Office. A man and woman he didn't recognize approached on the boardwalk in front of the building. They gave him a quick glance, eyeing the child on his shoulder and his wet clothing. The man grinned and nodded, and they passed by, but the woman puckered up as if she'd sucked a lemon too long.

"Where do you live, kid?"

"None of your business." The boy kicked again and pounded on Luke's back. "Let me down, mister, 'fore I spew my breakfast all over your backside."

Luke chuckled and resisted smacking the boy's rear end. The kid had spunk; he'd give him that much.

"Ma! Ma! Help me!" The boy started bucking like a mule in a nest of rattlers.

A woman across the street halted and looked up, eyes wide. Her hand flew to her chest. She hiked her skirts and bounded down the boardwalk steps like a she-bear on attack. She quickly marched across the dirt street and stomped up the steps toward Luke. Her bonnet shielded her face, but for a woman with a child, she had a pleasing figure with curves in all the right places.

Luke lowered the kid but held on to the twisting boy's shoulders.

"Ma, he tried to kidnap me. Help me!"

Luke shook his head. "That's not the way of things, ma'am."

"Please let go of my daughter." The woman lifted her head and glared at him from under her sunbonnet.

Daughter? How had he missed that?

He glanced down at the kid again. The floppy hat hid the kid's hair and covered half her face. He yanked it off, and a matching set of auburn braids fell down against the girl's chest.

"Hey! That's my hat." She grabbed at it, but he held it high out of her reach.

What decent woman let her daughter run around dressed like a boy and playing pranks with older kids?

He clenched his jaw and stared at the woman again. Something inside him quickened.

The woman's irritated expression changed. Pale blue eyes widened, and her mouth gaped like a fish, opening and closing several times before anything spilled out. "Luke?"

A wagonload of gunpowder exploding right beside him couldn't have blindsided him more. "Rachel?"

She was older but still beautiful—still the woman he'd loved for so long. Luke straightened. No, he wouldn't give the thought a foothold. He'd known he would see Rachel when he'd decided to return to town, but this sure wasn't the meeting he'd expected. He'd faced all manner of dangers in his years in the cavalry, but as he stood there soaking wet in front of the woman who'd stolen his heart and then stomped on it, his brain plumb refused to send words to his mouth.

"You know this fellow, Ma? Make him give me my hat." The kid—the girl—stood as bold as you please with her hands on her hips, not looking the least bit repentant.

Luke captured Rachel's gaze, her light blue eyes looking big in the shadows of her navy calico bonnet. He forced himself to speak. "You should. . .uh, keep your daughter away from rocks."

Rachel's brows puckered. "What?"

Realizing how ridiculous that sounded, he tossed the hat at the girl, spun around, and stormed toward his horse. For years, he'd thought about what he'd say to Rachel if he ever saw her again, but he'd never envisioned it being something about naughty kids or rocks. He groaned and shook his head. She probably thought he'd gone plumb loco. And maybe he had.

Chapter 2

A horse in the street whinnied, drawing Rachel back to conscious thought. Luke Davis had returned to Lookout after eleven years. Why now?

"Ow, Ma! Let go." Jacqueline pried up the little finger of Rachel's trembling hand, and she released her death grip on her daughter's shoulder.

"Sorry, sweetie."

"Who was that man?"

The man who should have been your father—should have been my husband. Rachel watched Luke enter the livery with his horse following and forced some words through her dry throat. "Just someone I knew a long time ago."

"Well, he slung me over his saddle like I was a dead deer. Ain't you gonna do nothin' about that?"

Rachel took hold of her daughter's arm and forced her feet into action. She didn't want to be standing in the same spot if Luke suddenly exited the livery. On wobbly legs, she managed to make it two doors down, where a bench sat in front of the Lookout Bank. She plopped down, pulling Jacqueline with her.

This day had looked so promising when she'd first gotten up. Who could have dreamed that one man's return would change everything? Did he hate her for what she'd done? He didn't look happy to see her, but she understood why.

Dampness registered beneath her hand, and she glanced at her daughter. "Why are you all wet? Why are you dressed like that? And why aren't you in school?"

"I'm all wet because that yahoo was soppin' wet when he flung me across his lap."

"Why did he do that?" Rachel blinked, knowing she sounded like Jacqueline had back when she was four and asked *why* all the time. But she needed to know what had happened. What had Luke meant about her daughter and rocks? "Why was he all wet?"

"How should I know?" Jacqueline's dark blue eyes sparked, and she glanced toward the street. "Maybe he likes to take baths with his clothes on."

Pursing her lips, Rachel stared at her daughter. "Don't be crude, Jacqueline." She perused her daughter's flannel shirt, faded overalls, and boots —the clothes she was only supposed to wear when gardening. When had she changed out of her school dress? The girl was bound and determined to run with the boys of the town and skip school whenever she could. Rachel twisted her hands. If only she were a better mother, then maybe her daughter wouldn't run wild like a mustang. She sighed and stood. "Let's get home and get some dry clothes on you."

"I don't mind 'em. They'll dry soon enough." With her hands on her hips, she stared upward. "Who is that man?"

Rachel walked down the boardwalk toward Hamilton House. The big, three-story home she'd inherited when her husband died rose up at the end of the street like a monument to the Hamilton family. James wouldn't like how she'd turned the place into a boardinghouse to help support her and Jacqueline after he'd gambled away the Hamilton fortune.

"Ma–aaa. You're ignoring me."

No, not ignoring you. I just don't want to talk about Luke Davis. She stiffened her spine and glanced down at her daughter. "He's someone I went to school with many years ago."

"Why'd he come back here?"

"I don't know."

"Why are you so riled up?"

Rachel clenched a fold in her skirt and took a deep breath. She had to get control of herself. Guilt could be such a heavy burden, and seeing Luke again had brought it all rushing back as if the past eleven years had never happened. "I'm just surprised to see him again."

Jacqueline pursed her lips, studying her mother as if she didn't quite believe her. "Well, he'd better never haul me up on his horse again."

Rachel stopped in her tracks. "Just what did you do to him to cause that? I know Luke, and he's not the kind of person who'd manhandle a child without good reason."

Jacqueline's eyes grew wide as if she'd just been caught sneaking cookies from the jar in the kitchen. "Nothin'. I swear I didn't do nothin' to that sidewinder."

Rachel hiked up her chin. "We do not swear or call people names, young lady."

"Well, he's got no business treating a girl like that. Made my belly ache."

Rachel's gaze swerved down to her daughter's stomach. "I'm sure he didn't mean to hurt you, but you still haven't explained yourself."

Jacqueline shrugged. "We just yelled at him for watering his horse in our swimming hole."

That didn't seem such a bad thing. Why would Luke take offense to that? Maybe he had changed in the years he'd been gone. Gotten cranky as he'd aged. Still, she couldn't help thinking there was more to the story than Jacqueline was sharing. "Let's get home and have dinner; then it's back to school for you."

Jacqueline hung her head. "Aw, do I have to? I wanted to go fishing with Jonesy and Ricky this afternoon."

"We have extra guests staying with us since the mayor's family is in town to celebrate his and his wife's twenty-fifth anniversary. I could use your help. Besides, you know how I feel about you skipping school to fish and hang around with those older boys."

"You just don't like them because they're poor." Jacqueline glared up at her.

Rachel stopped on her front porch, noting that the white wicker rockers were all aligned neatly and the greenery in the potted plants was filling out nicely. Too bad she couldn't keep her daughter so orderly. "That's not true. My family was poor. Folks who don't have much are just as good and decent as anyone else. The reason I object is that you're ten, and you have no business running around with boys who are three years older than you."

Rachel held on to her daughter's shoulder to make sure she didn't bolt. Why couldn't children come with instructions? She hated the way Jacqueline challenged her constantly and dressed like a boy every time Rachel turned her back. She dearly loved her daughter, in spite of everything, but she wished that she was more obedient and ladylike.

Two boys dashed across the road toward them. "Hey, Jack, that was a close call, wasn't it?" said Ricky Blake. The tall, towheaded youth skidded to a halt, and Jonesy almost ran into his back.

"My daughter's name is Jacqueline, not Jack, and I'll thank you to remember that." Rachel narrowed her eyes, just realizing what the boy had said. What had been a close call?

Jacqueline scowled, and her gaze roved back and forth between the boys and Rachel. Her daughter was hiding something, but for the life of her, Rachel didn't know how to get at the truth.

The boys dashed past them, and Jacqueline suddenly jerked away and chased after them.

"Jacqueline, you come back here this instant!"

The trio disappeared around the corner. Ray and Margie

Mann and Thelma Jenkins all stopped on the boardwalk outside the bank and stared. Rachel ducked her head. Everyone in town knew her daughter ran wild, despite her efforts to control her.

And now Luke was back in town. Her troubles had quadrupled in a single day.

The bell over the freight office door jangled as Luke strode in. He couldn't shake Rachel's image from his mind. She'd seemed as stunned to see him as he'd been to see her again. She'd looked good, too good for someone he was trying to forget. But she was a married woman, and he'd best remember that. She'd made her choice a long time ago.

A blond man sitting behind the desk looked up with curious blue eyes, and Luke honestly couldn't tell which cousin he was. The gangly youth he'd left years ago was now an adult. "Garrett?"

The man's brows dipped. "Can I help you?"

"Yeah, I want to know when your next gold shipment is due in so I can steal it." Luke struggled to keep a straight face and was careful to keep his hands clear of his gun. Both of his cousins were crack shots.

"Pardon?" Garrett stood and walked around his desk.

Bold move for an unarmed man. Luke grinned. Evidently the confusion ran both directions. "Don't you recognize me, cuz?"

He scowled at Luke for a second; then his brows dashed upward. "Luke? Is it really you?"

Luke nodded, and Garrett let out a war whoop that brought Mark running out from the back room, holding his rifle. Though a good two inches shorter than Luke, Garrett grabbed him in a bear hug and lifted him clear off his feet. Mark obviously didn't know whether to shoot or join the ruckus.

"Welcome home, cuz." Garrett dropped him and slapped him on the back. "How come you're all wet?"

Mark's eyes widened. He laid the rifle on Garrett's desk and hurried forward, his hand outstretched. "Welcome home, Luke. It's great to see you again."

They shook hands. Luke's face hurt from grinning more than it had in a decade. Mark, too, gave him a slap on the shoulder but jumped back when he realized the state of Luke's clothing. Both brothers leaned on Garrett's desk, arms crossed. They had the same color hair—although Mark's was curlier than his older brother's—and the same robin's egg blue eyes, but that's where the similarities ended. Garrett had the chiseled jaw of his father, where Mark's features were more finely etched with the look of his mother's side of the family. Two tall, muscular men stared at him instead of the lean youths Luke had left behind.

Garrett glanced out the window and back to Luke. "It hasn't rained all week, so. . ." He waved his hand at Luke's clothing.

"Had a run-in with some of the local kids down by the swimming hole. Two adolescent boys and a girl about eight or nine." Luke chuckled, remembering what a handful Rachel's daughter was. "Spunky little thing."

The brothers exchanged a look. Luke figured it had to do with the girl being Rachel's daughter. Had one of the boys been hers, too? Mentally calculating the years, he decided they were too old. He leaned against the doorjamb, arms crossed. "I can't tell you how good it is to see you again."

"Are you home for good? Done with your wanderings?" Garrett always did get right to the point.

Luke shrugged. "I'm here for a while. I'm the new town marshal."

The brothers blinked in unison, their mouths dropping open. Luke smiled at taking them by surprise again. Twice in one day had to be a record.

"Well, that's good news." Garrett rubbed the back of his neck. "We haven't had a marshal since November, when the last one died of a heart condition."

"How'd you wrangle that job?" Mark asked.

"When I decided to leave the cavalry, I telegraphed the mayor to see if he knew of any jobs in the area, and he told me about needing a marshal and offered me the position. He figured my years in the cavalry qualified me."

"Yeah, things have gotten rowdy down at the saloon. I hope you can settle them down so us decent folks can get some sleep."

Luke bit back another smile and shook his head. "Since when are you two hooligans considered decent folk?"

Garrett stood. "Look around, cuz. We're upstanding businessmen now. We have to protect our reputation."

The brothers shared another look. One of Mark's brows darted upward.

Luke shook his head and chuckled. He couldn't help wondering how many days had passed since one of them had pulled a prank on the other or on some unsuspecting citizen of Lookout. "I'm starving. How about you two"—he lifted his hand to his mouth and faked a cough— "*upstanding citizens* join me for dinner?"

"You buyin'?" Mark asked.

"Sure, why not? I've got eleven years of cavalry pay burning a hole in my pocket."

Both men's gazes dropped down to Luke's trousers. He laughed out loud. "You're so predictable. C'mon, let's go grab some grub."

They crossed the street, shoulder to shoulder, like a trio of gunslingers looking for trouble. Luke's gaze swung toward Hamilton House. The three-story structure would have looked strangely out of place if not for the two newer mansions built to the right of it.

He imagined Rachel sitting on the inviting porch, knitting or mending at the end of the day. He hoped she'd lived a happy life with James. Her lifestyle certainly was better than it would have been if she'd married Luke. The best he could have hoped for back then was to have a small farm and a one-room shack. Yeah, Rachel had married for money, and it certainly paid off. She'd probably never given him a second thought after he left town.

So much for young love and promises of everlasting devotio. Clamping his jaw on that thought, he bounded up the steps to the boardwalk.

His heart jolted. A woman in a dark blue bonnet strode toward them, head down and looking at a list in her hand. Rachel? She glanced up, and dove gray eyes met his instead of Rachel's pale blue ones. He was both relieved and disappointed. The woman's cheeks flushed at his stare, and she looked down and walked past him.

Someone shoved him from behind, and he stumbled forward. "We ain't never gonna eat if you stand there gawking at every woman that passes by."

"Now, ease up, Garrett. He's been stuck out on the frontier with a bunch of smelly soldiers for the last eleven years."

Luke chuckled with them, not bothering to tell them that he'd seen women, but they'd all been married to officers, for the most part anyway. Besides, even though Rachel had married someone else, he'd never been able to consider starting life with another woman. That was one of his reasons for returning to Lookout—to get Rachel out of his system, once and for all.

They selected a table near the front window and placed their orders with a young man Luke didn't recognize. He stared out the window, trying to get a feel for the town and how much it had changed. How many of the folks that he knew from before still lived here?

"So, tell us what you've been doing the past eleven years."

Luke stared at his cousins. "You'd know if you read my letters."

Both men squirmed, but Garrett spoke up, "We read 'em. It's just been a long while since you wrote last."

"Been a lot longer since I've heard from you." Luke lifted his brow. Years had passed since he'd gotten a letter from either cousin, but he decided not to press the issue. Most men didn't like writing missives, and besides, his cousins had been hard at work developing their freight operation, from the looks of it. "Been busy rounding up Indians, cattle rustlers, and train robbers. Making the frontier safe for settlers."

"Sounds like you had your hands full." Mark grabbed a slice of bread from the basket in the center of the table and buttered it. "You must have spent plenty of time in the sun. You're brown as an Indian."

Luke chuckled. "Not quite." He snagged a slice of bread and slathered on butter. He closed his eyes, relishing the softness of the white center, the crispy crust, and flavorful spread. "Been a long time since I ate bread this good. It's a far cry better than hardtack."

He leaned back in his chair, enjoying the atmosphere of the small-town café. He'd missed this. Folks relaxed, not worried about Indian attacks. Silverware clinked, and in the doorway to the kitchen, he saw Polly waddling back and forth, dishing up plates of food.

"Yeah, Polly's cooking is the best. Why, if she was fifteen years younger and fifty pounds lighter, I'd marry her myself." Garrett grinned and grabbed a piece of bread.

"Why *aren't* you two married? I would have thought by now that you'd both have a ring around some pretty gal's finger."

Mark turned red. "Been busy. Starting up a freight business and delivering goods keeps us away from town for days at times. Most women want a man who's home every night."

"Speaking of women"—Garrett's eyebrows waggled up and down—"are you going to visit Rachel anytime soon?"

Luke halted the bread that was halfway to his mouth. "Now why would I do that? I don't reckon it would make James too happy."

Garrett and Mark exchanged a telling glance.

Why did they keep doing that? "What? Spit it out." Luke lowered his hand holding the bread, expecting some earth-shattering news from the looks on his cousins' faces.

"Uh. . .didn't we write and tell you about him?" Mark asked.

"About who?" All manner of thoughts skittered around Luke's

mind like insects swarming a lantern at night.

"James is dead," Garrett said, looking pointedly at him. "Died three years ago. Broke his neck when he got thrown from a spirited stallion he'd won in a poker game."

Luke opened his mouth, but all the thoughts that had scurried through his mind now fled.

Chapter 3

The kitchen screen door banged shut, and Rachel jumped. She pulled in a breath and forced her voice to sound steady. "Please do not slam the door, Jacqueline."

"I caught a mess of trout and bass." She dropped the smelly fish onto Rachel's clean kitchen worktable.

Rachel pursed her lips. How could Jacqueline just waltz in and pretend nothing had happened after defiantly disobeying her? "You know if you catch fish that you're supposed to clean them before bringing them in."

Jacqueline flopped into a chair. Auburn hair sprouted loose from her braids, making her resemble an old rag doll whose hair had seen better days. "Can't you do it just this once? I'm all tuckered out. Fishin's hard work."

Shaking her head, Rachel knew she had just the right ammunition for this argument since her daughter loved fried fish. "If you want me to cook those, you'll have to clean them."

Jacqueline sighed. "But I'm starving. Can't I eat something first?"

"Supper is nearly ready." Rachel used the end of her apron to pull a pan holding two baked chickens from the oven. Fragrant scents filled the room, making her stomach rumble. "Take the fish outside, put them in some water, and wash up. You can clean them after we eat, and I'll fix them up after supper. Set the table when you come back inside."

Clad in overalls and a blue plaid shirt, her child scowled, but then she scrambled out the kitchen door with the string of fish in tow. Rachel shook her head. James had always wanted a son, but only Jacqueline had lived to reach full-term. With an aching heart, she remembered the three infant boys she'd lost. Jacqueline tried so hard to be a boy when Rachel only wanted her to be a sweet little girl.

She mashed the potatoes with more force than necessary. Thoughts of James always stirred up a swirl of resentment in her heart. At least he could no longer make her feel helpless. She rolled her neck, trying to relax. She was thankful she no longer had to tiptoe around the house, worrying that she'd set James off; yet she felt guilty for her train of thought. *Forgive me, Lord, for thinking such things about the deceased.*

She dished up the turnips and sliced the chicken into pieces. Jacqueline tromped back inside, her face shiny with moisture.

"Run and change quickly into your green dress."

"Aw, do I have to?"

"You do if you want to eat, and I'm telling you right now, you're getting no pie and you will wash the dishes alone, afterwards; and you'll pen Colossians 3:20 thirty times."

Jacqueline's eyes went wide. "But why? I took the fish outside."

"How quickly you forget." Rachel tsked then shook her head. "You deliberately disobeyed me this morning when I told you that I needed your help for dinner, and you chose to run off with those boys when you should have gone back to school."

Jacqueline crossed her arms and frowned. "But I caught a whole mess of fish. You'll have extra meat to fix for supper, so I did you a favor."

The little manipulator. "It's no favor to disobey me, and in case you didn't notice, supper is ready now. Go get changed and hurry back. I've got to get the food served for our guests."

Jacqueline stomped off. Rachel hoped she hadn't been too hard on the child. Disciplining didn't come easy to her. She despised spanking even though she'd always heard, "Spare the rod and spoil the child." But after the way James had slapped Jacqueline in anger and spanked her repeatedly with his belt, she couldn't bring herself to lay a hand on her daughter, even if it meant the girl was a bit wild. Surely she would grow out of this stage as she got older. Maybe in a few years she'd think of boys as potential beaus and she'd like wearing dresses and looking pretty. *Please, Lord, let it be so.*

After serving the mayor's guests and eating, Rachel stayed in the kitchen and tinkered while Jacqueline washed the dishes. Normally, she enjoyed doing the dishes with her daughter. It was a time that the girl often dropped her guard and talked. Rachel wiped off her worktable and the stove. "Listen, sweetie, I appreciate the fish you caught, but I don't want you going off alone with those boys."

"Why?" Jacqueline crinkled her forehead. "They're my best buddies. Ricky dug up some great worms. Found a couple of fat, white grubs." Just that fast, she grinned. "Jonesy dared him to eat one, and he did."

"Ewww. That's disgusting." Rachel crinkled her lip. "You didn't eat one, did you?"

Jacqueline's eyes twinkled. "No, but if they'd dared me to, I would have."

"Don't let those boys talk you into doing something you don't want to do." Rachel stared at her child. How could such a pretty young thing be a tomboy? Why couldn't she love dresses and hair bows instead of pants and hanging around with rascally boys? She was young and naive, and Rachel had to protect her from the wiles of men—and boys. She pulled out a kitchen chair and sat down. "Sweetie, women have to be cautious around men. They're different than us. You can't relax and let down your guard with them."

Her daughter looked over her shoulder, innocent blue eyes staring at Rachel. "Ricky and Jonesy are my friends."

"Friends sometimes. . ." How could she explain that even friends could hurt you to get what they wanted? She sighed. That was no topic for a ten-year-old.

Rachel picked up a towel and dish and started drying. As soon as they were done, she could take her mending outside and sit down for a while.

"Ricky says there's a new marshal in town."

Rachel closed her eyes and willed strength back into her bones. So, her work wasn't over for the day. The marshal always took his meals at the boardinghouse, and in return for her work, which included cleaning the little house next door and doing the marshal's laundry, the town would pay her an additional forty dollars per month. The extra money would be a blessing, but it added to her busy workload. Why hadn't the mayor let her know a new marshal was coming today? "We'll need to go over and make sure the house is ready for him."

"Now? You cleaned it two weeks ago, and nobody's been there since. What's there to do?"

"Plenty. Dust, air out the place, put clean sheets on the bed. I wonder when he'll start taking his meals here." Rachel got a bucket and put a clean cloth in it. She'd have to run over and take care of things right away. Since the marshal was already in town, he'd probably be sleeping at the little house next door tonight. Her mending would just have to wait until tomorrow.

"You sure you don't want me to stay here so I can greet new boarders if we get any?"

Rachel smiled at her wily child. "Good try, but this won't take too long."

Jacqueline moaned but left her apron on and followed Rachel out the kitchen door.

At the Sunday house, as it was called, Rachel left the front door open. "Raise a few windows to let some fresh air in. I'll make the bed. You dust and then run outside and gather some wildflowers if you can find some nearby."

Jacqueline moaned halfheartedly but perked back up. "They say the new marshal is some kind of cavalry hero."

"Well, that's good. He should be well qualified to guard our little town if he's been a soldier." Rachel snapped open a clean sheet, enjoying the fresh, sun-kissed scent, and made the bed. She topped it off with a colorful bear's paw quilt she'd made the year after James had died.

The Sunday house, with its large, single room and the roof that slanted down on the back quarter of the house, giving it a lean-to look, reminded her of the type of home that she and Luke might have had if they'd married. The kitchen area had been turned into the bedroom, since the marshal didn't need to cook. If he was a tall man, he may have to duck to avoid hitting his head where the ceiling slanted over the bed. A parlor of sorts was set up in the main area with a settee, a rocking chair, desk, and table big enough for two people to eat at. The cozy place would be much better than staying in the jailhouse as early Lookout marshals had done.

Buying the Sunday house when the German owners moved farther south to be near their kinfolk and donating it to the town had been one of the nicer things the Hamilton family had done.

Footsteps sounded outside on the porch. Rachel's gaze darted around the tidy room. Everything was in place except for the flowers. She was glad that she'd come on over rather than waiting until tomorrow.

Jacqueline swiped the window sill and looked up. She tucked the dust cloth behind her and scurried over to stand by Rachel. "I saw the mayor."

"You'll find it's quite a nice home," the mayor's voice boomed through the open door. "A German farmer built it about ten years ago. His family stayed here when they came to market on

Saturdays. They spent the night and stayed for church before going home on Sunday afternoons. It's called a Sunday house, and it's the only one in this part of Texas, but I heard tell there are lots of them in the hill country."

Rachel wrung her hands together and resisted rolling her eyes. Surely the marshal had better things to do than listen to the history of the Sunday house. She wished there was a back door so that she and Jacqueline could slip out, but she needed to meet the man anyway since he'd be taking his meals at her boardinghouse.

The door squeaked, and Mayor Burke strode in. "Well, howdy there. I was coming your way next."

The marshal seemed to hesitate just outside the door. Finally, he stepped inside. Rachel grabbed hold of the bedpost; her pulse took off like a race horse at a starting line. Luke's eyes widened, and then he schooled his expression.

"*You're* the new marshal?" Jacqueline's voice rose to an abnormal pitch.

Luke eyed her daughter and then stared at Rachel. She shifted her feet, trying not to squirm. She had longed to see him again for so many years, and here he stood.

"I don't guess any introductions are needed since you two have known each other since you were in diapers." The mayor chuckled and glanced at Luke. "Guess you noticed there's no stove here. Did I mention you'll be taking meals over at Rachel's boardinghouse?"

Luke's eyes narrowed; a muscle ticked in his jaw. "That won't be necessary, mayor. I can fend for myself."

The skin on Rachel's face tightened at the irritation in Luke's voice. Her knees gave out, and she dropped onto the bed, then realized where she sat and jolted back onto her feet, clinging to the bedpost.

Mayor Burke raised his hand. "No need, Marshal. Meals are part of the deal, and Rachel is one of the best cooks around. She'll take good care of you."

Luke's lips pursed, as if he doubted the mayor's words.

"My ma's the best cook in this whole town." Jacqueline hiked her chin as if daring him to disagree.

"We should be going." Rachel's heart fluttered like a cornered rabbit's. How could she bear seeing Luke three times a day and dining with him? Evidently he didn't favor the idea either, since he looked as if he had eaten a sugarless rhubarb pie.

Eleven years ago, she'd pleaded for his forgiveness when she told him she had married James, but he'd said then he'd never forgive her. Over the years, she'd prayed for him and hoped he'd found it in his heart to pardon her for hurting him so much, but by the glare in his eyes and his hardened jaw, she knew the truth. He hadn't forgiven her, and he never would.

Ducking her head, she took Jacqueline's hand, and they skirted past the two men. At the door, she halted and forced herself to face Luke. She cleared her throat, hoping her voice didn't warble. "Breakfast is at six thirty."

Chapter 4

"Howdy, cuz." Garrett gave a welcoming nod.

Luke stopped next to the Corbetts' freight wagon and eyed several crates of supplies Garrett was tying down on the buckboard. "Looks like you're off again."

"Yep. We're taking this load to Snake River Ranch. Be gone a couple of days." He tossed the end of the rope across the wood to Luke. "You'll look out for things around here while we're gone, won'tcha?"

After securing the rope, Luke pulled to make sure it was taut. He grinned. "With you two hooligans gone, the town is bound to be as quiet as a funeral."

Garrett slapped him on the back. "Just keep thinking that way, and one of these days some real outlaw is gonna get the drop on you."

Luke shook his head. "Where's that rascally brother of yours?"

His cousin jutted his chin toward the other side of the street. "Over at the café. Polly's packing up a meal for us."

Luke walked around the stout draft horses, checking the rigging. He didn't need to, since both his cousins took excellent care of their animals, but it gave him an excuse to hang around for the moment. He hated seeing the brothers leave town again. Spending time with them helped keep his mind off other things.

Garrett lifted his hat and plowed rows in his blond hair with his fingers. His blue eyes stared back without the glint of amusement they often held. "How's it going with Rachel?"

Luke's gaze darted sideways at the unexpected change of topics. He hadn't told them how difficult it was being around Rachel. "Don't see much of her."

"Aren't you taking your meals at her boardinghouse?"

He shrugged, not wanting to admit the extremes he'd taken to avoid seeing her. "I usually take my plate home or to the jail."

Garrett shook his head. "James is dead, and Rachel's available again. What are you waiting for?"

Luke narrowed his gaze and clenched his jaw. Why couldn't Garrett leave well enough alone? "You know why."

His cousin's hat lifted as his brows rose. "All that happened a long time ago. She's a beautiful, young widow, and there's no reason you two couldn't get hitched now."

"There are a wagonload of reasons." Luke straightened.

"Well, if you're interested in her at all, don't wait too long. A local rancher named Rand Kessler has been comin' calling on her regularly."

Luke flinched at the thought of another man courting Rachel, but she was a beautiful woman of marrying age. It was to be expected. So why did it bother him so much?

"Y'all have a safe trip." He strode away, not giving Garrett a chance to say more. In the two weeks that he'd been home, both cousins had tried to get him to reconcile with Rachel. But they didn't know how much he'd loved her and how deeply her betrayal had gutted him, leaving him a shell of a man. If he couldn't trust the one woman he would have died for—the woman who was supposed to be his bride—how could he trust any others?

Joining the cavalry had been the only thing he could think of to keep him away from females. And it had worked for the most part.

He forced his jaw to relax. If he kept clenching it like he had the past few weeks, he'd need to visit a dentist soon. Maybe then he'd be worth his weight in gold. He chuckled and surveyed Main Street as he walked toward the boardinghouse. He lengthened his stride as he neared it, turning right onto Bluebonnet Lane. Next door to Rachel's home rose a huge white house with tall columns supporting the porch overhang. He'd heard that the banker who'd taken over after James Hamilton died lived there, and beside it, not quite so huge but still twice as big as any other house in town was Polly and Dolly's home. He shuddered at the pale pink color. What would entice a person to insult their home by painting it the color of a little girl's Sunday dress?

He shook his head. Who was this Rand Kessler fellow? Maybe he should make the rounds of the local farms and ranches and introduce himself. Yeah, that was a grand idea.

Turning right again, he made his way down Apple Street. The houses on this street were smaller, and many were not as well cared for as those on Bluebonnet Lane. He tipped his hat to a woman whose name he didn't know as she walked toward him. He recognized her as the wife of a local rancher. She was tall but not nearly as pretty as Rachel.

He uttered a growl and clamped his jaw down again. How was he supposed to get her out of his system when he saw her every day?

Forcing his mind on other things, his gaze shifted toward the end of the street where the old shack that he'd grown up in used to be. The vacant lot now served as a garden. At least someone was getting some use from the property. Just by looking at the land, you'd never know a fire had burned down his home and killed his mother. He should have returned then, but by the time he received the news, his ma had been buried a month. Maybe if he hadn't left home, she'd still be alive. He tried not to hold on to too many regrets. They rubbed blisters on his emotions.

A mangy dog darted out between two houses and limped across the street. Someone yelled, and a rock whizzed dangerously close to the poor creature. The two youths he'd chased from the creek the day he arrived in Lookout dashed across the street after the critter. Jack charged after them, trying to keep up.

Luke pursed his lips tight and marched toward them. The boys, so focused on picking on the poor dog, didn't notice him at first, but Jack skidded to a halt. Her panicked gaze zipped toward her friends, who, seeing Luke, ran off between two houses, and back at him. Suddenly her expression softened. A stick thumped to the ground behind her.

"Why. . .afternoon, Marshal Davis. Fine day, ain't it?" Jack's wide smile and lightly freckled nose made her look sweet and innocent.

The little imp. "Not so fine a day for that dog you and your friends are harassing."

"I wasn't chasing the dog."

Luke lifted his brows. "A lawman can generally tell when someone's lying."

Jack stomped her foot. "I was chasing those boys, not that dog. He cain't help it if he's hungry and muddles things up searching for food. People oughtn't be mean to critters." She lifted her pert little nose in the air.

This coming from the kid who tossed a rock at his horse? Luke squatted, giving her the benefit of height. "That's right. The good Lord gave animals to man to help him. It's our job to take care of them, and in return, they become our companions and make our jobs easier. He doesn't like it when we mistreat them, and neither do I. Stop throwing rocks and sticks, you hear me, Jack?"

"But I wasn't gonna throw it at the dog. Honest, Marshal."

Luke studied her pleading, dark blue eyes, so different from Rachel's. They begged him to believe her. Maybe she was telling the truth. "We don't throw things at people, either. You can hurt them, too."

The girl had the sense to look ashamed and nodded. "Can I go now?"

"Yeah." He wondered if his speech had done a lick of good. How could feminine Rachel end up with a girl who dressed like a boy and even wanted to be called a boy's name? He shook his head. What did he know about raising young'uns?

Tracking the dog, he found the mongrel sniffing at the trash barrel behind the saloon. The yellow mutt's ribs showed, and his skin hung loose. Luke needed a dog about as much as he needed a pink house, but he couldn't let the poor creature starve to death or be treated cruelly by others. "C'mere, you ugly thing."

The dog hunched down then trotted ten feet away. He looked as if he'd like a friend but was afraid to trust. Luke sniffed a laugh. "I know exactly how you feel."

Luke kicked through the trash, looking for something to tie around the dog's neck. Not finding anything, he marched up the boardwalk to the freight office. His cousins kept rope for tying down their freight and wouldn't mind if he helped himself to a few feet of it. Pulling out his knife, he whacked off a ten-foot length from a large roll. Hurrying back, he hoped the dog was still there and that the boys hadn't found him. He fastened a noose on the move and had it ready when he rounded the corner.

At first he didn't see the critter, but then he found him lying under one of the few trees in town. Luke tiptoed toward him, the rope ready. The dog sniffed the air, saw him, and stood, looking ready to bolt. Luke couldn't blame him after the way those kids had treated him. He tossed the rope and caught his target on the first try. The dog yipped and shied away, pulling up the slack and causing the noose to tighten around his neck.

Luke grinned. Maybe he'd just roped a new friend.

Garret drove the team away from Snake River Ranch. Without the weight of the heavy load, the wagon jostled more, but the horses were able to move faster. They should be home to Lookout by evening.

The morning sun broke over the horizon, chasing away all shadows of night. He pulled down the brim of his hat as his mind wandered to their next shipment. Maybe it was time to hire someone to help with the deliveries so they could keep the office open all the time. But that would mean not traveling with his brother, and he'd miss that. He and Mark shared a bond that many brothers didn't.

Garrett peered sideways. How Mark could read a book while the wagon dipped in and out of ruts in the road, he'd never know.

Too bad Luke had taken the marshal's job, or they could have hired him. He'd fit right in.

"Why do you suppose Luke decided to come home after all these years?" Garrett nudged Mark in the shoulder to draw him out of his book.

"Huh?" His brother glanced up, his mind obviously still in the story. After a moment, his gaze cleared. "What did you say?"

Repeating the question, Garrett took the novel from his brother's hand, knowing he'd be distracted by it.

"Hey!" Mark grabbed for the book, but Garrett held it out of his reach.

"Answer my question, and I'll give it back."

"I don't know. Maybe he got tired of riding all over the frontier, chasing Indians and outlaws, getting shot at, sleeping on the ground, and eating beans with dust in them."

Garrett grinned. "When you say it that way, it makes perfect sense."

Mark snatched back his book, found the page, and started reading again.

Garrett didn't care much for reading, except on a winter's night when there wasn't a whole lot else he could do. "I thought maybe he came back to fix things with Rachel, but I've changed my mind."

"Why's that?"

"Well, for one, he didn't even know that James was dead."

"Yeah, that's true." Mark rubbed the back of his neck. "I'm sure I wrote and told him, but he must not have gotten the letter. I feel kind of bad about that."

"It's not your fault. Besides, it's not like he'd come riding back if he'd known. He didn't even make it home for his own mother's funeral, what with mail being so slow and all." Garrett studied the landscape that had finally awakened from winter's chill. Colorful wildflowers dotted the valleys and rolling hills, and the grass was green again. The temperature was perfect, not like the deplorable heat of summer or chilly winters. Now that he thought about it, having a wife to cuddle up with on a cold winter's night didn't sound half bad. Neither did coming home to a hot cooked meal instead of having to scrounge up something after a full day's work. Maybe it was time to start looking for wives—for him and Mark—and one for their cousin. "I think Luke needs a wife."

Mark sighed and closed his book. "Trying to read with you gabbin' is as bad as trying to get a word in between Miss Polly and Miss Dolly."

"That *is* a hard thing to do." Garrett chuckled. "Do you think Rachel would make a good wife for Luke?"

"Don't be meddlin' where you haven't been invited." Mark's expression turned testy. "You'll only cause trouble. Besides, I heard Rand Kessler had his eye on her."

"That's all the more reason to find Luke a wife." Garrett held up a hand when Mark scowled. "Now, hear me out. I talked with him about Rachel, and I can tell that whole situation still bothers him. Don'tcha think it's rather ironic that he took the marshal's job in Lookout and didn't know that Rachel was a widow or that she was the one who'd be fixing his meals?"

Mark grinned. "Yeah, that is a bit funny. Though I don't think he's been spending any time at the boardinghouse. Half the time he eats with us."

The wagon tossed them from side to side as they turned off

the deeply rutted ranch trail and back onto the road to Lookout.

"Well, I don't think he'll be truly happy until he settles down and gets married. And if Rachel isn't the gal for him, then we ought to help him find the right one. He is family, after all."

"Meddlin'." Mark pursed his lips and shook his head. "Besides, who is there in town that would make a decent match for Luke?"

Garrett lifted his hat and scratched his head. He swatted away a horsefly that flew too close to his face. "There's that newspaper lady."

Mark's brows flew up. "I wouldn't wish her on my worst enemy, even if she ain't half bad lookin'."

Garrett lifted his hat and scratched his head. "Then who?"

"Luke's what? Close to thirty?"

"Yeah, pretty close, I imagine. He's about a year older than me, and I'll be twenty-nine this summer. I can think of some unmarried females, but they're all too young for him."

"I know some men marry much younger women. But personally, I think it's better to find a more mature woman, not one you have to finish raising."

Garrett held back a grin. Mark was beginning to get on the bandwagon, and he didn't even know it. Looking up, he studied the brilliant blue sky. A hawk circled high above, screeching now and then. Garrett moved in, ready for the kill. "You know how hurt Luke was when Rachel married James. We need to find him a good woman. One he can love who will help him forget Rachel once and for all."

Garrett rubbed his chin with his thumb and forefinger. "What do you think about the Widow Denison? She may be a year or two older than Luke, but she's not too bad on the eyes." He glanced at his brother.

"What about her five rowdy kids? You want to strap Luke with the job of caring for them?" Mark asked.

Probably not the greatest idea. "There's always Polly and Dolly."

Mark looked at him as if he'd gone loco then schooled his

expression. "I thought they were saving themselves for us."

Garrett stared at him for a moment then saw the corner of his brother's mouth twitch. "Ha! You almost had me there for a minute."

Mark hooted and bumped his shoulder against Garrett's. "Face it, brother, there's not a decent, marrying-aged woman in all of Lookout other than Rachel."

"We could always order up a mail-order bride."

Mark's eyes widened again. "You can't be serious. You wouldn't know what you were gettin'. Pretty or ugly. Nice or cranky. Old or young. She might not even be able to cook."

"I'm not the one marrying her."

"So you want our cousin to marry some woman who arrived on the stage, sight unseen?"

Garrett shrugged. "I don't know. It was just an idea. Besides, Ray Mann ordered Margie out of a magazine, and they seem happy."

"Sometimes I wonder about you. Ma must have dropped you on your head."

Garrett focused on the road ahead. Yep, Luke definitely needed someone to help him get over Rachel, and another woman would do the trick. Maybe he could check a few magazines or newspapers and see what kind of women were offering themselves up for mail-order brides. What could it hurt?

Chapter 5

A knock sounded on the jailhouse's open front door, and Luke glanced up from the wanted posters he'd been perusing. Jack leaned against the jamb, looking as if this was the last place she wanted to be. "Uh...Ma wants to know if you're gonna eat with us, or should she keep your supper on the back of the stove like usual?"

For a moment, Luke wished things were different, that he didn't feel as if he had to avoid Rachel. But until his emotions were less raw, this was best. Seeing her again had opened up a gaping wound he'd thought had healed, and being around her continually reminded him of what he'd lost. Why had God urged him to return? So far, it had only made things worse.

He shook his head, forcing away his melancholy thoughts. The truth was he wouldn't mind the company of her boarders. He'd had plenty of men to talk to when he was in the cavalry and missed the camaraderie. At least he could enjoy his cousins' company. "I'll get the food later and just take it back to my house."

Off to his right, the old mutt whined. Jack's eyes widened, and she stepped inside his office. "You put that dog in jail? Why? What did he do?"

"Stealing and being a public nuisance." Luke forced away a grin.

Jack's cute little mouth formed an O. "What did he steal?"

"People's trash. Food. Heard tell he snatched a pie right out of Myrtle William's kitchen window."

The girl's blue eyes swung from the dog to him and back. "You're joshin'."

"Nope."

Tonight she was wearing a dress, and her auburn hair hung down in two neat braids. It looked like Rachel had won the battle to tame the incorrigible child this evening.

"What will happen to him?" Jack moved closer and leaned against Luke's desk.

This was the first time he'd had a long look at her. She favored Rachel, especially in the nose and mouth, but in her expressions, he could see a touch of her father. His gut clenched. He didn't want to think of Rachel with another man. *God, how do I let go of this? Help me, Lord.*

"Marshal? What's gonna happen to the dog? You ain't gonna hang 'im, are you?"

Luke had to grin at that. "No, kiddo, I don't reckon we can hang him for being hungry. I figure he can make restitution by helping out around town."

She turned and leaned her elbows on his desk, looking at him with wide blue eyes. "He's dumber than a horse flop. How you gonna do that?"

"I imagine he's smarter than he looks." Luke glanced at the dog. One yellow ear flopped forward, while the other hung back. Scars mottled his snout, where gray hairs had started growing. "First, I need to get him fit. I've tended his wounds and figure some good food and rest should help him get back into shape."

"Don't forget a bath. Your jail stinks like dirty dog."

"Yeah, gotta tend to that tonight before I take him home."

"So you aim to keep him?"

Luke shrugged one shoulder. "Don't see why not. There's no law against a marshal having a dog."

"But he's just a mangy, ol' mutt. Homer Henry's got some pups he's givin' away. Reckon you could have one if you wanted it."

Luke couldn't help comparing himself to the dog. Alone. Unloved. He wasn't about to turn him away. "Every living thing needs somebody to love them, even an old dog like that one."

"Oh."

Luke straightened, an idea forming in his mind. "Maybe you could help me get him back in shape."

Interest danced in her eyes, but she did a good job of trying to hide it. "Don't see how."

"Maybe you could see if your ma could spare a soup bone now and then. Bring him the table scraps sometimes."

Jack smiled for the first time. "I could do that. What'cha gonna name him?"

Luke leaned back, and his chair squeaked. He placed his hands behind his head. "Hadn't thought about it. What if I let you name him, since you're going to help care for him?"

"Truly?" Jack's dark eyes flickered like blue fire, and her smiled widened. She was a cute little thing when she wasn't being a bully and trying to act tough.

He nodded.

Jack clapped her hands, and the mutt whined and ducked under the cot. Luke chuckled. Some guard dog he'd be.

Rachel set Luke's plate of chicken and dumplings and green beans on the back of the stove, hoping he'd arrive to eat before it cooled. She shook her head and sighed. In the weeks that he'd been home, he hadn't eaten with them once. Most mornings, he arrived early for coffee and a biscuit, then dashed out the door before she could finish fixing the rest of the meal. Nights, he'd slip in after she'd retired, grab his plate, and eat at his house.

She returned to washing the dishes. Jacqueline had scurried out the door after supper with a plate of table scraps and no explanation as soon as the guests were done. She'd probably taken up the cause to help feed someone's pig.

Her thoughts turned to Luke again. Though eleven years had passed, she still remembered the crushing hurt in his eyes the evening she'd told him she had married James. When he'd asked why, she couldn't tell him the truth. The shame of it all had made her sick for weeks. She'd avoided everyone and hadn't learned that Luke had left town until nearly a week after the fact. Her stomach swirled just thinking about how she'd wounded him. All he had done was love and trust her, and she'd betrayed him in the worst possible way. But what other choice did she have back then?

She washed the dishes, dipped them in the rinse bucket, and set them on a towel to await drying. After getting over the shock of seeing Luke again, she longed to talk to him, see where he'd been the past decade. But he'd barely spoken to her. Somewhere deep inside, she hoped for a second chance—that maybe God had brought Luke home so she could right a wrong—but it wasn't to be. Luke Davis wanted nothing to do with her.

She jumped when the kitchen door slammed shut. Jacqueline stood inside the door, her face bearing a pleasant expression instead of its normal scowl. She dumped the plate that had held the scraps into the sink and picked up a towel and started drying without being asked. She hadn't washed her hands, but Rachel wasn't about to mention that and stir up trouble.

"Where did you go, sweetie?"

Jacqueline glanced up, eyes sparkling. "The marshal's got a dog, and he's letting me help care for it."

Rachel closed her eyes at the turn of events. The only man she'd ever loved had formed an alliance with her daughter to care for a dog, but he wanted nothing to do with her.

"I get to name him." Jacqueline stacked the plates as she dried them. "I was thinking of something like Rover, or maybe Tramp, since he likes to dig in the garbage."

Rachel turned to face her daughter. "You don't mean he's adopted that ol' yellow dog?"

The girl grinned wide and nodded her head. "He had him locked up in his jail, Ma! Isn't that funny?"

Rachel smiled, enjoying the lighthearted freedom from the conflict that so often flowed between the two of them. "I can't imagine."

Jacqueline dried the last dish and tossed the towel over her shoulder like Rachel so frequently did. Mimicking such a little action shouldn't mean much, but it did. Perhaps if Rachel continued to lead by example, maybe her daughter would eventually model the more important things in life. She glanced out at the setting sun, wishing their time together didn't have to end, but tomorrow was a school day. "It's time for you to wash up and get ready for bed, sweetie."

"Aw...okay." Jacqueline tossed the towel over the top of a chair instead of putting it on the hook by the stove. At the hallway, she turned. "I kind of like Prince or King for a name, except that dumb mutt sure don't look like royalty."

"Don't call God's creatures dumb, please. He loves each and every one of us, even old dogs. And keep thinking. You'll find just the right name." Rachel put the towel back on the hook. "I'll come and pray with you after I get my pie dough made. Since the temperature has been so warm lately, I thought I'd bake them tonight instead of after breakfast."

"Good idea." Jacqueline spun around and headed across the hall into the bedroom they shared.

Rachel scooped flour from the fifty-pound bag in the pantry and dumped it in her big mixing bowl. After sifting out the weevils, she added some salt and sugar and stirred it together. She mixed in the water and one-third cup of lard, stirring until everything balled together. Just as she picked up her rolling pin, a knock sounded on the back door. Rachel jumped and turned, wielding the pin like a club.

Luke opened the door and lifted his dark brows. "You're not planning to whack me with that, are you? I did knock."

Hoping to hide her galloping heartbeat, she set a smile on her face and lowered her arm, hiding the rolling pin behind her. "Good evening."

Luke nodded and glanced at his plate of food.

Rachel peeked past him out the door in the waning light, wondering if he'd brought the dog with him. She hoped he could train that pest to stay away from her trash heap. "Where's your deputy?"

He glanced at the door. "Don't have one yet."

Her lips twitched, and she couldn't resist teasing him. "That's not what I heard. Or maybe I should say, 'Where's your prisoner?'"

Luke's brows lifted, and he casually leaned against the door frame, looking manlier than any fellow had a right to. "Rachel, I have no idea what you're talking about."

All humor flew out the door. Had her daughter been lying to her about the dog? What if she'd trapped a wild creature and was feeding it? Rachel clutched her hands to her chest, knowing that some critters carried the rabies. "Jacqueline said you had a dog locked up in your jail."

"Oh, that." For the first time since returning, Luke dropped his guard, and amusement danced in his brown eyes. "I tied that ol' dog up outside, but he kept trying to get away and was gaggin' himself, so I locked him in a cell. Jack thought it was funny."

Rachel straightened, turned her back to Luke, and started rolling out her dough. "Please don't encourage her with that name. She's Jacqueline."

"I figured if I called her Jack like she wants, maybe she'd warm up to me a bit. I'd like to help her change her ways before she gets hurt or into serious trouble."

Rachel cracked the spoon against the side of her bowl and spun around so fast Luke's eyes went as wide as biscuits. She wielded the spoon like a weapon. "Just what's wrong with my daughter's behavior?"

Luke bristled at Rachel's unexpected, stormy reaction. Surely she knew her daughter was gallivanting all over town with older boys. Rachel had been a near perfect daughter—sweet, kind, helpful, rarely disobeying her mother's wishes. How could she have ended up with such a wild child?

"I asked what is wrong with Jacqueline's behavior."

Luke straightened. "She's running with older boys, and I think they're causing her to do things she probably wouldn't do on her own."

Rachel's face paled, and she latched onto the back of a kitchen chair. "What kind of things?"

"The day I arrived, she and those boys threw rocks at my horse." He omitted the part about Alamo knocking him into the river. A man had his pride, after all.

Lifting her chin, Rachel glared and pointed her spoon at him. "I know Jacqueline's been with those boys, and I'm trying to stop it, but I don't for a second believe that she would throw rocks at your horse. She doesn't have a cruel bone inside her."

He thought about how he'd found Jack in the street with that stick in her hand. The jury was still out as to her true intentions. His gut said to believe Rachel, but there was a wildness in the child that could only be driven out by a loving parent who wasn't afraid to discipline. Rachel always had a soft heart, always saw the best in others. She was a peacemaker, a nurturer, and he could see where disciplining might be hard for her. "You're gonna have to be tougher than her, Rach."

Her eyes narrowed. "Just what do you know about raising children?"

He shrugged, hoping to look nonchalant. If she'd married him instead of James, he'd know plenty about raising kids by now. "Not much. I've been a soldier for the past decade, but I've learned that people rise to what's expected of them. They need rules. Boundaries. Especially children."

"Well, I have rules for Jacqueline. It's just difficult to enforce them at times."

"Try harder. You don't want to lose Jack because you're afraid she won't like you if you spank her."

Rachel puckered up like a raisin and crossed her arms over her chest. "I am not having this conversation with you. You don't know a thing about raising a girl. There's more involved than tanning her backside whenever she does the wrong thing."

" 'Foolishness is bound in the heart of a child; but the rod of correction shall drive it far from him.' "

Her brows lifted. "So you're quoting the Bible to me now?" Suddenly her expression changed from anger to despair. "I try to make Jacqueline mind, but she bucks me at every turn. I want her to be disciplined and to act like a normal girl, but I don't know how to make that happen." She swiped at the tears streaming down her cheeks. "I'm sorry I'm such a disappointment to you, Luke." She turned and fled the room.

He stood there looking at the empty doorway. Why had she gotten upset at him? He was just trying to help Jack. To encourage Rachel to be stricter.

He'd seen plenty of kids at the forts he'd been stationed at, and the ones who followed rules rarely got hurt or in trouble. The broken, bloodied body of a nine-year-old boy flashed before him. He'd told Thomas to stay away from the mustangs fresh off the plains, but the kid was stubborn. Determined to prove he was just as good a horse breaker as his dad. A brief encounter with a wild stallion had snuffed out the boy's life.

Luke snatched his plate off the back of the stove and stormed out the door, though his appetite had faded. Rachel had changed. When had she become so stubborn? Why couldn't she see that he was just trying to help her and Jack?

Chapter 6

Garrett sipped his coffee and studied the Dallas newspaper that a friend had sent him. He chuckled at the comical wording of some of the mail-order bride ads. He forked more of the scrambled eggs his brother had cooked into his mouth and peered over the top of the paper at Mark. "What do you think about this one?"

" '*Christian woman, 24, 5'7", thin, dark hair, seeking a father for her five children.*' "

"Five?"

Garrett nodded.

"Does that advertisement mean she's thin, or does she have thin, dark hair?"

Garrett chuckled and continued reading. " '*Has adequate house on 60 acres and $3000 in bank. Needs man willing to relocate and run dairy farm.*' "

"Sounds like she's wanting a hired hand more than a husband." Mark pursed his lips. "I bet she'll get lots of takers, but seems a bit risky to advertise that she has all that money." He shook his head. "I hope nobody takes advantage of her and runs off with it."

"Yeah. Many men would."

Mark picked up a thick slice of bacon. "Even if we found Luke a gal to marry like that one, I doubt he would want to leave Lookout when he just returned to town after being gone so long."

Garrett leaned back in his chair and glanced out the window. The overnight thunderstorm had left droplets on the panes and puddles in the street. "Yeah, I get the idea he wants to stick around here, but I don't know if he will."

"Because of Rachel?"

"Yeah. I tried to talk to him about her again, but he's touchy."

"Well, give him time. He hasn't been back all that long and has had eleven years to stew over the fact that his gal married someone else."

Garrett smeared strawberry jam on a slice of bread then licked the knife. "That's why we need to find him another woman. I mentioned that Rachel was now available, and you should'a seen how his hackles raised. Whoo-wee!"

"I still think you're messin' with fire."

"What could it hurt to write to a couple of these ladies? You might even decide to keep one for yourself."

"Me?" Mark's eyes went so wide that Garrett laughed. "What about you? You're the oldest."

Garrett shrugged. "Might be the only way to find a bride. This town's poorly lacking in females."

"Ain't that the truth? Let me have a look."

Smiling to himself, Garrett passed the newspaper to his brother and dug into the rest of his breakfast. He glanced around the kitchen of the house they had inherited from their parents. His mother would pitch a fit if she could see the unwashed dishes in the sink and the pile of dirty clothes on the floor of their bedrooms. "We sure could use a woman around this place. Maybe we ought to try to find someone to help out here a few hours a week."

"Yeah, it's filthy in here." Mark studied the room. "What kind of gal do you favor?"

Garrett shrugged. "Don't matter as long as she's pretty and not sassy."

"I kind of favor redheads." Mark's gaze remained on the paper as he took another bite of his toast. "You know, the color of a sorrel horse."

"You're comparing a woman's hair to a horse?" Garrett shook his head. "How romantic."

The paper dropped down, revealing Mark's clean-shaven face and sky blue eyes. He glared at Garrett then flung his toast through the air like a weapon. It hit Garrett on the nose. He jerked back his head, and after a moment of heavy silence, they both laughed.

"Okay, seriously, how about this one?" Mark tilted the paper as if to see it better. " '*Twenty-five-year-old woman seeks man to marry. Must be a godly man of high character and gentle heart. I have light brown hair, blue eyes, and no visible blemishes—*' "

Garrett looked up from his plate. "Wonder what that means? You think she's got a big mole on her back like a shooting target or something?"

Mark curled his lips. "I didn't interrupt you."

"Yes, you did."

Mark shook his head but continued reading. " '*I prefer a man who lives west of the Mississippi River.*' "

Garrett leaned back with one arm dangling over the back of his chair as he sipped his coffee. "Light brown hair, blue eyes, huh? Might be a good idea to order up a bride that has different coloring than Rachel."

"Aren't her eyes light green?"

Garrett shook his head. "Blue, like I imagine ice would be if it had a color."

"Oh, yeah. That's right. Hmm. . .how about a brunette? Here's one. '*Black-haired/black-eyed woman, age 18, seeks husband. Can cook and sew. Prefers to marry rancher. No soldiers.*' "

"Well, that puts Luke out of the picture." Garrett stood and took his plate to the sink and added it to the towering mess.

It wobbled but didn't fall. "A brunette is a good idea, though. Or maybe we could order him a choice: blond, brunette, and a redhead."

"You're loco, you know it? What would you do with the other brides? What if Luke didn't want any of them? Then you'd be stuck caring for a henhouse full of females. This is a bad idea, I'm telling you." Mark tossed the paper toward the middle of the table. He shoved back his chair, stood, and carried his plate to the counter. "One of us needs to do these dishes 'fore we get ants in here."

"I'll flip you for it. The winner needs to take the horses over to Dan's and get them reshod before he gets too busy."

Mark nodded, and Garrett tossed the coin in the air. It spun around, reflecting the morning sunlight coming in the kitchen window, then plunked onto the floor. It wobbled around before settling on *heads*. Garrett grinned. As oldest, he was always *heads*. "Better luck next time, brother."

Mark scowled but picked up the bucket. "Getting one of those brides for us sounds better all the time. I wouldn't mind having a woman around to cook and do the cleanin' and washin'."

"That would mean one of us would have to get married." Garrett bumped his brother's shoulder with his own. "You think you're ready?"

Mark looked up at the ceiling as if deep in thought. "Could be."

Garrett lifted his brows at his brother's confession. "I guess we aren't getting any younger, huh?"

"Not today."

The door creaked as Mark opened it, reminding Garrett he needed to grease the hinges. Things would change a lot if one of them was to marry. Would they lose the closeness they enjoyed as brothers? Still, being married did have its benefits. He glanced at the paper, formulating an advertisement for Luke in his mind as he walked toward the barn. He lifted his head, enjoying the crisp scent to the air after the overnight storms. In the barn, he fed the horses and grabbed the water bucket, stopping to lean on the fence rail. "Hmmm. . .let's see."

Town marshal wants wife who can cook, sew, and clean.

"Nah, better to not be so picky."

Town marshal wants wife who can cook.

He considered Luke's height. He was a good six feet himself, so that must have made Luke six feet two. He thought about his cousin's hair and eye color. Those things were important to women.

Town marshal, 6'2", dark brown hair and eyes, wants wife who can cook.

What else would a woman want to know? That he'd been a soldier? Thinking about that one ad, he mentally marked that off his list.

Maybe that was enough. Garrett didn't know if Luke had any money to his name after being in the cavalry for so long; and even if he did, it wasn't a cousin's place to advertise such information.

What else?

A woman's looks were important to most men, but character went a long way, too.

Town marshal, 6'2", with dark brown hair and eyes, wants pretty wife who can cook. Must be willing to move to Texas.

Garrett smiled. "That should do it."

Now he just had to decide where to place the ad.

Chapter 7

Southern Kansas

Carly Payton's stomach swirled so badly she thought for sure she'd retch any moment. Her mount trailed a few yards behind the two horses carrying her brother, Tyson, and Emmett, a member of her brother's outlaw gang. They slowly rode into a mid-sized Kansas town whose name she didn't even know. She scanned the rugged wooden and brick buildings for the bank and found it toward the end of the street.

She studied the town again, as Ty had taught her. Knowing the layout could well save their lives later on. Several horses stood tied to rails outside the saloon and the doctor's office, while a wagon sat in front of the only general store. Few people ambled down the boardwalks of the sleepy town in the heat of the noonday sun. Carly swiped at a trickle of sweat running down her temple.

A woman dressed in calico and wearing a straw hat held the hand of her daughter as they jogged across the dirt road in front of the riders. What would it feel like to walk so freely down the street of a town without concern that someone might recognize her brother as the leader of the Payton gang?

She shook her head. What a hoot to think she could ever be a lady. Why, she didn't even like wearing dresses anymore.

Ty swung around in the saddle and glared at her as if he thought she'd tuck tail and run. She'd tried that once, and Ty's threats to either shoot her or hand her over to the gang made her too afraid to run again. Sometimes she wondered if she'd have been better off if he hadn't come for her after Ma died. At least she didn't have an aching back from bending over a washtub all day like her ma had done—or cracked, reddened hands from hot water and lye soap, or blisters from chopping wood to heat the water.

"Quit hangin' back, Carly."

"I'm not." She kicked her horse into a trot and caught up. She wiped sweaty palms on her pants, wishing she were back at camp, cooking up a rabbit stew. If Clay hadn't gotten shot and killed last month, she might well be. But a man short, Ty expected her to take his place.

They passed the sheriff's office, and she yanked her gaze away, but not before she noticed half a dozen wanted posters tacked on the outside wall. Was there one on her yet? Or had folks even figured out that the Payton gang had a woman in it? She worked hard to disguise her feminine attributes during the two train robberies and the other bank heist Ty had forced her to participate in. From under her hat, she peeked back at the posters. She might end up famous with a bounty on her head like Jesse James or Belle Starr. How much would she be worth on her wanted poster? Fifty dollars? One hundred?

As much as she dreaded the robberies, there was a strange excitement to them. Yet afterward, guilt ate at her so badly she could hardly eat or sleep. Her brother said there weren't nothin' wrong taking from other folks that had so much. Even their pa had been an outlaw before U.S. Marshals had gunned him down.

They dismounted in unison, and Emmett held the reins. He hobbled between two of the horses and stooped down as if pretending to be checking its leg for injury. Getting shot in the foot two weeks ago made him too slow to go in the bank, so he was stuck tending the horses. "Make it fast," Emmett said. "I don't want anyone getting suspicious of me out here."

Ty glanced at her. His dark blue eyes looked cold as dusk in the heart of winter. His lips pressed together into a thin line. He was probably wondering if he'd be safe with only her at his side. He jerked his stubbled chin toward the bank. "Let's get this done."

She started toward him but stopped when he scowled. "Don't forget the bag."

Returning his glare, she snatched the burlap feed sack out of her saddlc bags. Making sure her hair was stuffed up under her hat, she followed him up the bank's steps, heart pounding and stomach churning. She would do her part, but she couldn't help being nervous.

Ty had taken her in after their mother died when no one other than the saloon owner had shown any interest in her. At fourteen, most folks must have assumed she could make it on her own, or more likely, they weren't willing to help the daughter of the town's laundress. Once he found out their ma was dead, Tyson had come for her. He let her cook for his gang of outlaws, although he'd nearly sent her packing after the first meal. She smiled, remembering Will, the oldest of the outlaws and former chuck wagon cook for a ranch. If he hadn't taken her under his wing, they'd all have starved. If only he hadn't been pumped full of lead during a train robbery last year.

What would it feel like to get shot? She knew it hurt, from the moans of the gang members injured during robberies. She swallowed hard, hoping nobody got hurt today.

Her brother was a cranky sort and often griped at her; but for years, he'd protected her from his gang members and vowed to shoot anyone who laid a hand on her—at least until the day she'd decided to leave.

She shoved back her shoulders and pushed aside all thoughts but the duty at hand. Daydreaming could get them all killed. Their boots echoed on the boardwalk, spurs jingled. As they entered the dimly lit building, Carly's eyes took a moment to adjust. The fresh scent of wood polish made her stomach roil, and well-shined boards creaked beneath their feet. At the counter on the right, two female clerks stood talking to each other. Carly bit back a smile. There were no barred windows on the counter and no guard. Obviously, this bank hadn't had trouble for a long while.

Ty leaned close to her ear. "This bank is ripe for the pickin'."

An empty desk to the left probably belonged to the manager. Ty had surveyed the town for ten days, watching people come and go, and had timed their entry with the manager's lunch break. Her brother might not be honest, but he was smart.

The two clerks turned toward them, and the taller woman stepped up to the counter. She smiled, revealing pearly whites with a wide gap between her top middle teeth. "May I help you?"

"Need some information on opening an account here." Ty flashed a wide grin that generally melted the hearts of any nearby females. With his black hair, blue eyes, tanned skin, and comely features, women would battle their best friend for his attention. He sauntered up to the counter, looking as if he had all day. He leaned casually on his elbows, grinning at the unsuspecting clerks, and shook his head. "I'm surprised this bank ain't overflowing with men, considerin' how pretty you lovely ladies are."

Carly rolled her eyes at the blush on both women's cheeks. The second clerk giggled behind her hand.

"I'm Miss Holt, and this is Mrs. Springer." She batted her lashes as if she'd been in a dust storm. "I apologize, but Mr. Wattenburger, the bank manager, is the only one who can open accounts. He's currently at lunch but will return soon."

Carly eased toward the wall, fascinated by the elaborate gold brocade wallpaper that blended well with the dark wainscoting. Never having seen anything so fancy, she reached out and touched the raised surface. Ty cleared his throat, pulling her mind back to their business. If she inched to her left a few feet, she'd be behind the counter.

"I'm only in town a short while. Maybe there's someone else here who could help me?" Ty glanced toward a back room where the vault was probably kept.

"I'm sorry, but Mr. Wattenburger is the only one that can help you." Miss Holt glanced at a watch pinned to the bodice of her stiff white blouse. "He should be back in less than a half hour. Could you wait?"

"Perfect. That gives me just enough time." Ty straightened and reached for his gun.

Her Colt ready, Carly did the same and slipped behind the counter.

"I'm sorry, but you can't come back—" Mrs. Springer slammed her mouth shut and frowned at them. Miss Holt gasped and stepped back.

Carly pulled the burlap sack out from under her arm and held it out. "Just fill this up, and make it fast. We don't want nobody gettin' hurt."

With shaking hands, the two women emptied the cash and gold coins from their teller drawers into the bag. They cowered together, all visible admiration for Ty gone.

"What about the vault?" he asked.

"I–it's closed." Miss Holt hiked up her chin.

Mrs. Springer gasped and nudged her friend with her elbow. "Tell him the truth. I don't want to get shot. I have two little ones, you know."

Ty narrowed his gaze and stalked to the back room, then reappeared in the doorway. "Get back here. Both of you."

Mrs. Springer whimpered but plodded forward, arms linked with Miss Holt. "Please don't shoot us. I've got children, and I'm a widow. They don't have anyone else to care for them."

Carly's heart went out to her, knowing her mother had been in the same situation.

"Hey, kid! Get that bag in here."

She jumped and hurried to the vault, coins clinking in the

bottom of the sack. Ty dumped in handfuls of money that were banded with a paper wrapping around the middle. Carly's eyes widened at the sight of so much cash. Robbing trains never brought in anything like this, although they had ended up with some nice watches.

Ty threw the bag over his shoulder. "Let's go."

Carly scurried out of the room, and Ty stopped, waving the gun at the two women. "You keep quiet until the manager returns. I'll have a gunman watching the door, and if you call out an alarm, he'll shoot you. Understand?"

Tears rolled down Mrs. Springer's cheeks, and she nodded. Miss Holt was slower to respond.

Ty stepped up to her. "You understand, Miss Holt? I'd hate for such a pretty little thing to end up with a hole in her chest."

He pressed the barrel of his gun to her bodice, and her eyes went wide. She nodded. Ty grabbed Miss Holt suddenly and kissed her hard on the lips. Mrs. Springer squealed, wobbled, and collapsed with a thud on the ground. Miss Holt looked as if she would join her any moment.

"C'mon. We need to get outta here," Carly yelled, careful not to say her brother's name. The clerks had already seen their faces.

Grinning wide, Ty stormed past her. She followed, glancing back at the door to make sure the women stayed where they were. Outside, they vaulted onto their horses. Emmett headed one way while she and Ty went the other. Folks were so busy tending to their own business that nobody noticed a thing. Bank robbing was as easy as picking clothespins off a laundry line—and a lot more profitable.

Just outside of town, Carly pulled her horse to a stop, leaned over, and spilled her guts.

Chapter 8

Rachel sat on the settee in the parlor sipping tea with her good friend Martha Phillips. "So, how has Hank been? Has he been very busy doctoring folks?"

"No, not too busy. With the warmer weather, there haven't been as many people taking ill." Martha nibbled on a sugar cookie then dabbed her lips. "I suppose you've heard by now that Louise Chambers had her baby a few days ago. Hank delivered their third son."

"No, I hadn't." Rachel shook her head, thinking of the three baby boys she'd lost. Still, she mustered some excitement for the kind lady she'd met at church. "They must be delighted. How is she doing?"

"Fine, last time Hank checked." Martha let out a sigh and looked down. "I wish that I could become with child. We've been married two years now."

Rachel watched a fly creep up her floral wallpaper as she considered her response. She knew that saying it was God's will didn't help one bit. "You're still young yet. Sometimes these things take time."

"Not for you. Guessing by the age of your daughter, you must have gotten with child on your wedding night." Martha's eyes went wide and her hand lifted to her mouth. "Oh dear. I beg your pardon. Hank talks freely to me of such things, and I tend to forget that such topics are not proper conversation."

Rachel forced a smile. Martha hadn't lived in Lookout back then, didn't know the circumstances around her pregnancy with Jacqueline—but then, neither did anyone else. Once again she breathed a prayer of thanks that her daughter had been so tiny at birth. Everyone assumed she'd been born early. "Think nothing of it."

"Hank is continually telling me to think before I speak, but I confess that I find it difficult. I tend to just blurt out whatever comes to mind." She lifted her cup to her lips and gazed out the window. Her eyes suddenly went wide. She stood and set the cup and saucer on the end table. "I'm afraid it's time I was going. I need to get Hank's supper on the stove."

Rachel peered out the window to see what could have disturbed her guest. Agatha Linus and Bertha Boyd barreled down the street toward the boardinghouse like a locomotive at full steam.

"Thank you for offering to make those pies for the church bazaar." Martha tied on her bonnet and reached for the screen door. "Next time, you must come to my house for tea."

"My pleasure." Rachel waved good-bye to her friend and waited on the porch for the busybody train to arrive. Visiting with Agatha and Aunt Beebee, as Bertha was better known, was always an experience, but she needed to get supper started for her guests soon. She'd have to make the visit with the two older women short, if that was possible.

"H'lo, dearie." Aunt Beebee waved her plump arm in the air as if she was at a hallelujah service. In her other hand, she balanced a pie. As she waved, the pie leaned precariously to the left. Rachel held her breath, but Beebee righted it before it could take a tumble.

Agatha smiled, looking embarrassed by her sister's outgoing display. Where Beebee was wide, Aggie was thin. Beebee was vibrant and gregarious, while her sister was prim, soft spoken, and proper. After losing both their husbands within a short time period, the two older women had sold their neighboring ranches and taken up living in town, much to the chagrin of the townsfolk.

"Good afternoon." Rachel smiled and held the door open to allow the two women to enter.

Beebee plopped the pie into Rachel's free hand. "That there's my prize shoofly pie." She leaned toward Rachel. "Made with our grandma's secret ingredient."

"Why, thank you." Rachel lifted the pie to smell it, wondering what it would cost her. Beebee always expected information in exchange for her treats, and Rachel doubted today would be any different.

Everyone in town knew Aunt Beebee's secret ingredient was rum, though folks never let on they knew. Rachel would love to eat pie other than her own, but she didn't partake of alcohol in any form. Her boarders would probably enjoy it though.

"Goodness me. Today must be the day to go visiting." Beebee huffed past Rachel into the house, bringing with her an overpowering scent of perfume. "I just saw the doctor's wife take her leave. Too bad she couldn't stay a bit longer."

Rachel nodded at Agatha as she came in. "Martha said she needed to get her husband's supper started. I must confess that I will need to do the same soon."

"No problem a'tall." Beebee barreled her way into the parlor, bumping the end table and rattling Rachel's hurricane lamp. "We only came for a short visit."

The hair on Rachel's neck stood on end. When Beebee and Aggie's visits were short—and they rarely were—it meant they came with a specific purpose in mind. What could they want?

Beebee backed toward the settee and dropped down. The couch creaked and groaned from her near three hundred pounds.

Rachel swallowed, hoping the antique that had belonged to James's grandmother could withstand the torture it was enduring. Beebee lifted her skirt a few inches off the floor and fanned it. "Whew! It's mighty warm for April."

Rachel glanced at Aggie, whose eyes widened at her sister's unconventional behavior. Aggie ducked her head, cheeks flaming, and stared into her lap. Sometimes Rachel wondered if the women had been adopted or had different mothers. No two sisters could be any more different.

"I'd have been here sooner but have been laid up with a sore foot. It's downright impossible to find decent shoes in this town." Beebee patted her large hairdo that resembled a hornet's nest. "I just had to come over and see how you were getting along now that Luke Davis is back in town. Seems he's been spending plenty of time with your daughter. And poor Rand Kessler. Whatever must he be thinking?"

Rachel's heart somersaulted. She'd known Beebee had had an agenda for visiting, but she hadn't considered it might be Luke. She set the pie on the parlor table and took a seat.

Aggie shook her head. "I told her to leave be, but she wouldn't listen."

Beebee frowned at her sister, and Aggie ducked her head again, fingering the fold of her matronly gray skirt. Beebee turned her gaze back toward Rachel and rested her plump hands on her skirt, the colors of a field of wildflowers.

Rachel swallowed hard, knowing whatever she said to Aunt Beebee would get around town quicker than a raging fire.

"It must be hard on you to have Luke back, I mean with you having to cook and clean for the man, what with him not even being your own husband." Beebee shook her head and swung her gaze toward her sister. "Don't you think that would be difficult, Agatha—to have the man you once thought you'd marry but didn't back in town and having to care for him? Why, James is probably rolling in his grave, bless his heart."

Aggie's gray eyes went wide. She reached up and pulled the collar of the stark white blouse away from her throat.

"Now that James is gone, surely you and Luke are gonna get back together. For the child's sake. That little scamp certainly needs a father, and I never thought that Kessler fellow was right for you."

"Bertha, that's none of your business." Aggie fanned her face with her hand. "And Rand Kessler is a fine gentleman."

Rachel jumped to her feet. "Oh, forgive me. I forgot to ask if you'd like some tea."

"Don't mind if I do." Beebee glowered at her sister and reached for the teapot still on the table beside the settee. She pulled off the lid and peered in.

"I could heat it up if you'd like." Rachel wanted to suck back the words as soon as she said them. Heating the water would take time and cause the ladies to stay longer.

"No need. As hot as it is, cool tea will be refreshing," Beebee said.

Rachel grabbed the pie Beebee had brought and hurried to the kitchen for extra cups. She glanced around, knowing all she needed to do, and breathed a prayer for patience. Back in the parlor, she filled a cup and handed it to Beebee.

Rachel offered another cup to Aggie, but she shook her head. "Thank you, but I just had some tea a short while ago."

Beebee drank nearly the whole cup, set it down, and reached for a cookie from the platter on the table. She lifted her brow at Rachel. "Well. . ."

Rachel didn't know what to say that Beebee couldn't construe the wrong way. She rubbed her thumb back and forth on the cording of her seat cushion. "Luke and I merely have a business arrangement. As a benefit of his job as marshal, I cook for him and any prisoners he has and clean the Sunday house, and I receive some additional income for doing so. There is nothing personal about it."

Aunt Beebee snagged the final cookie, looking less than convinced. She waved a beefy hand in the air, scattering crumbs. "All of us who were in Lookout back then know that you two young folks were as tight as a tick on a hound dog. Now that that worthless James is gone, there's nothing to keep you from marrying Luke."

Rachel and Agatha gasped in unison.

"Bertha, that's hardly any concern of yours," Agatha protested.

"It's nobody's concern." Rachel grasped the edge of her chair as if she were on a runaway wagon. "All that is in the past. I'm a widow with a daughter now."

Beebee's thick lips turned up. "That Luke Davis is a handsome man—and unmarried. If you don't snatch him up soon, someone else will, mind my words."

Agatha lurched to her feet. "Uh. . .thank you for your hospitality, but I'm afraid we must be going. Come along, Bertha."

"But I'm not done visiting yet." Taking up her cup, she sipped her tea and gave her sister a pinched look.

Rachel forced herself to stand. "I'm afraid I must head to the kitchen now, or I won't have supper ready on time for my guests."

"Well, if you insist." On the third attempt, Beebee managed to stand.

"Please come again sometime." The words nearly scalded Rachel's throat as she uttered them, but she refused to be inhospitable, even if her guests made her uncomfortable. "Maybe around two," she said, hoping the older ladies would be napping then. "That will give us more time."

Beebee nodded, making the rolls on her three chins jiggle like a turkey's wattle. "We'll just do that. Come along, Agatha. We best be getting out of Rachel's way so she can get her cooking done. Do enjoy the pie, Rachel, and have that girl of yours bring the plate back when you're done with it. Mind that she doesn't break it."

"Thank you," Rachel mumbled.

As Beebee lumbered out the front door, Aggie stopped beside Rachel. "I'm terribly sorry. She means well."

Rachel nodded and stood in the open doorway, watching the two women make their way down the street. The bank president had the misfortune to step outside the bank just as the ladies approached.

"Well, how do there, Mr. Castleby." Bertha was so close the banker took a step back.

Rachel held tight to the doorjamb. Had she kept her expression clear enough when Beebee had talked about Luke and her marrying? Would everyone in town expect Luke and her to get married? What would Rand think if he heard such talk?

She thought of Luke's cold expression the first few times she'd run into him and shook her head. Luke Davis no longer had designs on her. She was the last person he would consider marrying.

Chapter 9

The Bennett Farm near Carthage, Missouri

Leah Bennett dumped the last of the dishwater out the kitchen door and rubbed her lower back. Only nineteen, and she felt done in already. Shaking her head, she turned back into the kitchen to see what else needed cleaning before she could start working on the huge mending pile that never seemed to have an end. Mabel and Molly, her fifteen-year-old twin sisters, dried the last of the supper dishes with their heads together, giggling and talking about which of the town's boys they hoped to see at church on Sunday. The twins were the closest sisters to Leah in age, but they'd never needed her companionship.

"You two hurry up. The laundry needs to be taken down from the line and folded."

"But we wanted to walk out to the fields and see Pa." Molly drew out her words in a whine that made Leah want to cover her ears.

Leah shoved one hand to her hip. "Pa doesn't need you gettin' in his way."

"You're bossier than Ma." Molly stuck out her tongue while Mabel looked down, quietly drying the plate in her hand.

Leah turned away, not wanting her sister to see that her pointed words had hit their target. She never wanted to be the boss, but with so many children in the family and her being the oldest, she had to take over whenever Ma was tending to young'uns or something else that constantly demanded her attention.

Ten-year-old Sally shuffled in from the eating room, carrying a bowl of water and a wet rag. She placed it in the dry sink that Leah had just emptied. "The tables and chairs have all been washed down and straightened, and Ida finished sweeping the floor. Can we go out and play now?"

Leah shook her head. "Go weed the carrots first."

Sally scrunched up her face and leaned against the doorjamb. "Do we hav'ta? All we ever do is work."

Leah adopted the pose she'd frequently seen her mother use with one hand on her hip and her index finger wagging and echoed her words. "With eleven children in this family, there's always something that needs doing."

Sally stuck out her lip, and eight-year-old Ida sidled up beside her, bearing the same expression. "Andy says you're too bossy for your britches, and I agree." Sally hiked up her chin.

Leah sighed. Was a little respect too much to hope for? "I don't wear britches, young lady. You two get outside and weed the carrots. When that's done, you can play until dark."

The girls locked arms and marched out the back door, still frowning. Why couldn't they mind her like they did their mother? Because she wasn't their ma, and she hoped she never was one. Having children just meant extra work—and heartache if something happened to them. Nope, she never wanted to be a mother.

As long as she could remember, her ma was either pregnant or nursing and sometimes both. Not even forty yet, Alice Bennett looked closer to sixty. Leah washed out the bowl Sally had used and set it in the rinse bucket. Ma had probably finished tucking the youngest of her brood into bed already, but she hadn't come back downstairs. She'd most likely fallen asleep during the children's prayers.

Leah checked the bread rising for tomorrow. She punched down the first bowl of dough and then the second one, sending a yeasty odor into the room that reminded her grumbling stomach that she was still hungry. With so many mouths to feed, she never seemed to get enough to eat. Kneading dough always helped relieve her frustrations. She placed the frayed towel back over the bread and fingered a corner. Just one more thing that needed mending.

In the parlor, she sorted through the pile of clothing and picked out everything that needed to be repaired with blue thread. She grabbed the sewing kit and went outside to sit in her favorite rocker—the only one that didn't creak.

In the field next to the barn, Allan and Andy, her younger brothers, led the two cows toward the barn where they'd be fed and milked. There was plenty of work on a farm the size of the Bennetts', but there was a soothing rhythm to it. She selected a baby gown and found the place where her youngest brother, still a crawler, had snagged it on a loose floorboard. She cut a tiny patch from some scrap material and quickly stitched it over the tear.

Giggling preceded Mabel and Molly a short while later as they bounced out the front door and flopped down on the steps. "Tell her." Molly nudged her twin.

"Tell me what?" Leah folded the mended gown and laid it in the rocker next to her. She picked up a colonial blue shirt with loose buttons that belonged to three-year-old Micah. In the fields past the barn, she saw her father walking behind the huge draft horses, plowing.

"Nooo, you do it." Mabel shook her head and wrung her hands.

Molly grinned. "Sue Anne Carter is going to be a mail-order bride. She's got a magazine with ads in it, and she's studying them for a husband."

Leah blinked, and her mending dropped to her lap. There were advertisements where one could find a husband? "Why would she do such a ridiculous thing? Sue Anne could have any man she wanted."

Mabel piped up now that Molly had brokered the subject. "Maybe she wants to get away from her strict father, or maybe she wants an adventure."

The image of Sam Braddock rose in Leah's mind, as handsome and strong as any man she'd known. He'd been the only male to ever capture her heart, and he'd returned the attraction. But he died when influenza ravished the neighboring town, killing Leah's dreams. She placed her hand over her heart. Even after a year, the pain still felt fresh. She remembered her eagerness to marry Sam as the days to their wedding had drawn closer. Instead, Sam had been buried that day.

She shook her thoughts back to her best friend. Sue Anne hadn't mentioned anything to her about being a mail-order bride. And how could she consider traveling hundreds of miles to marry a man she'd never met? Seemed like a recipe for disaster.

The twins were huddled together, whispering, but Leah could still hear them. "Tell her the rest," Molly whispered.

"Nooo, we ain't supposed to know. Remember?" Mabel crossed her arms and flipped her long brown braids behind her.

Leah looked back at Molly and leaned forward. The little busybody never could keep a secret.

Molly glanced at Mabel. Guilt marched across her face, but her eyes twinkled with mischief. She stood up and swung her faded skirt back and forth as if she were dancing. "Mr. Abernathy is buying you from Pa."

"Mo–ll–y!" Mabel jumped up, her gaze darting to the field where their father worked. "Pa is gonna be furious with you for telling."

Leah's hands dropped to her lap like lead weights. Mr. Abernathy was. . .old. And fat. And had hair growing out of his nose and ears. "Wh–what do you mean, buying me?"

Proud that she knew something her big sister didn't, Molly puffed up like a toad. "Mr. Abernathy wanted *me*." She shuddered, as if the thought repulsed her. "But Pa said I was too young to marry and that he could have you instead. Pa said he had too many mouths to feed. Am I ever glad, for once, that I ain't the oldest."

"I don't believe you." Leah glanced at Mabel. Seeing the confirmation in her sister's brown eyes, her heart jolted, Molly might lie, but Mabel couldn't. Needing to get away by herself, Leah stood. "Did you two finish the laundry?"

Evidently realizing they'd said enough, the twins fled down the stairs and around the side of the house without answering. Pa was selling her like some. . .old cow? Shock pulled Leah back down into the rocker. He wanted to be rid of her because he had too many mouths to feed. Hadn't she proven her worth by taking up the slack when Ma needed help and working from before sunup to past dusk? How would Ma manage without her?

Tears stung her eyes. Hurbert Abernathy had to be forty. More than twice her age. He was an obese, smelly man, and the whole town knew he preferred gambling to working. How could her father agree to let her marry someone like that? Even if it did help the family.

Tears trailed down her cheeks. Once Pa made up his mind, he wouldn't be swayed. What could she do? She had no money. Nowhere to go.

Maybe she should visit Sue Anne and have a look at that magazine. Could marrying a stranger be any worse than being forced to wed Hurbert Abernathy? Funny, how an idea could sound outlandish one moment but seem perfectly sane the next because of desperation.

She stood, gathered the mending, and carried it back into the parlor. A lump the size of a goose egg made it hard for her to swallow. If she wasn't appreciated for all the work she put into this family, then she would leave. Tomorrow, she'd pay Sue Anne a visit.

Lookout, Texas

Shuffling sounded outside the open door of the marshal's office, pulling Luke's gaze away from the rifle he was cleaning. The yellow dog lifted up his head, sniffed the air, lumbered up from his spot near Luke's desk, and wagged his tail. The mutt whined and stepped forward as a girl stopped in the doorway.

Jack stood just inside the jail, dressed in a dark green calico dress with her braids hanging down the front. Her lunch bucket hung from one hand while she clutched a book to her chest with the other. The dog sniffed her pail and then stuck his head under her hand. Jack set down the tin bucket and scratched his head. Luke grinned as the old dog closed his eyes, looking contented and loved.

"Well, now, don't you look pretty."

Her cheeks turned red, but then she curled her lip and twisted her mouth up on one side. "Uh huh, and this ugly, ol' dog is purty, too." She crossed her arms over her chest, and the mutt looked up longingly. After a moment, he flopped down, lying his head on Jack's shoe, probably dreaming of the tasty table scraps the girl often brought him.

Luke studied Jack. What had happened to make such a young girl so jaded? He knew Rachel was a loving mother, so that only left her father. Or maybe she acted out because she'd lost her father. He leaned forward, catching her eye. "You *are* a pretty girl. Why I've known women who'd give just about anything to have auburn hair like yours."

Jack picked up one of her braids, looked at it, then dropped it as if it had burned her. "Yeah, then why do the kids tease me for having red hair? It ain't even red. More like brownish. Sort of."

Luke leaned his rifle against the wall, wiped his hands on an old towel, and stood. "Some kids always tease. When I was your age, I was real tall and skinny, and a boy in my class took to calling me chicken legs."

Jack looked on with interest, her blue eyes intent. "What did you do?"

Oops. He couldn't exactly tell her he'd waited after school and took that bully down a few notches. He shrugged. "Best thing to do is just ignore them."

Jack's lips curled again. "That's hard. Sometimes I just want to punch them."

"And is this person bigger than you? A boy?"

She nodded.

"Want me to talk to him?"

Jack's gaze sparked but then dulled. "No, but thanks. If you do anything, it'll make things worse. You can't be around all the time, and besides, you're not my pa."

She had no idea how much that comment poured salt into past wounds.

Luke sat on the chair across from Jack. "I was sorry to hear about your father dying."

Jack scowled. "I wasn't, so why should you be?"

Taken aback by her comment, he studied her as she stooped down to pet the dog. What would cause a child not to grieve over the loss of her father? Being the only child of a wealthy couple, James had been cocky and spoiled, but never cruel—although at times, he had bordered on it. Luke wanted to ask if her father had hurt her or Rachel, but it wasn't a topic to be broached with a child. Maybe his cousins could shed some light on that subject.

"I was wondering something." Jack kept her gaze down.

"What's that?"

She glanced up, nibbled her lower lip, then looked out the door. "Would you teach me to box?"

Luke tried to keep his expression straight. Wouldn't Rachel

love that? "Uh. . .I'm not sure that's a good idea."

"Why not?" She gazed up with innocent blue eyes, making him wish he could protect her from all the pains of the world.

"Because if you get in a fight, especially with someone bigger, you could get hurt."

"I get hurt anyway."

"Jack, you let me know if anyone bothers you, and I'll take care of it. All right?"

The girl studied him as if she didn't quite trust him, but she nodded. Relief washed through Luke. Some kids were just plain mean and wouldn't have a second thought about hurting a girl. He searched his mind for a lighter topic of conversation. "Have you thought up a name for this old dog yet?"

Jack lifted her head and smiled, revealing white teeth with a tiny gap between the middle two. "Took me a while. I thought about Prince or King, but those names just don't seem to fit him. Then I thought maybe we should call him Bandit since he likes to steal stuff from trash heaps."

"He's reformed his ways after being in jail for a few days."

Jack giggled and flopped onto the floor next to the dog. "Or maybe because you and me's feeding him every day." A wicked gleam entered her eyes. "I thought about maybe calling him Stinky, because. . .well, you know how the jail smells a while after he's eaten."

Luke chuckled and rolled his eyes. "Why do you think I leave the door open so often?"

Grinning again, Jack patted the dog, whose head now rested in her lap. She glanced up, vulnerability showing in her gaze. "I decided on Max. What do you think?"

"Max, hmm. . .I like it. Not too high and mighty, and not something he'd be ashamed of. Good choice."

She looked relieved. "Well, I suppose I should get along home. Ma probably has chores for me to do, though I'd rather go fishin' with Ricky and Jonesy."

Luke leaned forward, his elbows on his knees. "Those fellows are a bit old for you to be running around with, aren't they?"

She lifted one shoulder then dropped it down. "They're fun. Besides, the girls I know only want to play school or house."

"What's wrong with that?"

Jack's eyes went wide. "It's girl stuff. I like to fish and hunt and do what the boys do."

"Uh, has anyone told you that you *are* a girl?"

Jack stood, evidently not liking the turn of conversation. "Ma tells me all the time. I just wish. . ."

She didn't finish her sentence, and he sat still, hoping to learn what motivated her to dress like a boy and to run with them. "Wish what?"

Her eyes took on a sheen, and she batted them as if she had dust in them. "That God had made me a boy instead of a girl."

Luke opened his mouth to respond, but she tore out of the jailhouse as if a colony of wasps were on her tail. He flopped back in his chair. Max whined and stared out the door before coming over to sit by him.

Why would such a cute little girl want to be a boy?

Rachel opened the windows of the library, allowing the warm May breeze to flutter the curtains and air out the room. She looked forward to Tuesday afternoons when the ladies of town would gather just after lunchtime in her library. Since the huge house also had a parlor, she had gladly offered use of this room so that the quilt frame could remain up until the product was finished. The room was so large that her guests still had plenty of space to peruse the vast number of books that James's mother had been so proud of.

She removed the towels covering the raisin bread and sugar cookies and went to the kitchen to get the coffeepot. The ladies would start arriving anytime, and she wanted to have everything ready. As she entered the kitchen, a knock sounded on the front door, sending her spinning around to answer it. She pulled the door open and smiled. "Sylvia, Margie, I'm so glad you could come today." She stood aside, holding open the screen door to allow the pastor's wife and Mrs. Mann to enter.

Sylvia's gaze wandered up the showy staircase with its spindle balusters and wide steps. "You have such a lovely home."

"That Amelia Hamilton sure did know how to fancy up a room." Margie never failed to remind people that her good friend had once owned and decorated Hamilton House.

Ignoring the jibe, Rachel forced a smile. Though she'd redecorated the upstairs bedrooms and had the outside repainted, Margie seemed to take pleasure in reminding everyone that the older Mrs. Hamilton had first decorated the big home. "Would you care for some tea or coffee while we're waiting on the other ladies?" Rachel gestured toward the library's open french doors. Another knock sounded. Agatha stood on the other side of the screen door, fidgeting and looking over her shoulder.

"Is everything all right, Aggie?" Rachel looked past her but saw nothing except the normal activities of the peaceful town: a wagon rolling up Main Street, two cowboys talking outside the mercantile, Luke ambling along in front of the bank with Max trotting at his side. She pressed her hand to her chest where her heart had started galloping and forced her attention back to her guest.

Aggie wrung her hands and leaned forward as if preparing to share a big secret. "Bertha's down for her afternoon nap, and I slipped out. I'm hoping the door didn't wake her when the wind caught it and made it slam shut." The thin woman pressed her lips together and peered over her shoulder again.

"C'mon in. Sylvia and Margie are already here." Rachel's heart went out to the older woman. Having Aunt Beebee visit for an hour was almost more than she could cope with. She couldn't imagine how difficult it must be to live with the talkative, opinionated woman. She held her hand out toward the library. "Please find a seat while I get the coffee."

In the kitchen, Rachel removed her apron, wrapped a towel around the handle of the coffeepot, and carried it into the library. She poured three cups then set the pot on a trivet on the table in the corner where the lamp rested. "The coffee is ready, and I have some raisin bread and sugar cookies if you'd like some."

"That sounds delightful," said Sylvia, as she stood and made her way toward the table with the other two ladies following like ducklings.

Another knock pulled Rachel back into the entryway. "Martha! I'm so glad you could come today."

"Me, too. Hank didn't have any emergencies where he needed my assistance. He's just studying his medical books, so I told him I was going to the quilting bee. I brought some of Aunt Maude's oatmeal cookies."

"Thank you. It's always a treat to get to eat someone else's cooking." She stepped back to let her friend enter.

"I, for one, think you shouldn't have to provide refreshments other than coffee, which would be difficult for someone else to bring, since you host us each week and allow us to leave the quilt frame up. That makes the stitching so much easier."

Rachel hugged Martha's shoulders, grateful for a friend who was thoughtful enough to look out for her well-being. "Three ladies have arrived so far."

"That's a nice group."

Rachel set the plate of cookies beside her bread and helped herself to two of them. She took a seat on one of the chairs she'd pulled in from the dining room. Immediately, Margie Mann's gaze turned to hers, and the bite of cookie lodged in Rachel's throat. No subject was sacred with Margie around.

"So, how do you like having Luke Davis back in town?"

Aggie's eyes grew wide. Martha and Sylvia, who were fairly new to town, missed the ramifications of that question.

"I don't think that's a topic that should be broached here," Aggie said.

Margie swatted her hand through the air. "Oh, pish-posh. It's a perfectly fine subject. He seems to be doing a decent job as marshal, though we hardly need one as quiet as our town is."

Maybe Rachel could satisfy Margie's curiosity without venturing too far into deep waters. "I hardly see the man."

"Nonsense. You cook him three meals a day, clean his house, and do his laundry. How is that possible if you don't see him?"

It was hardly any of Margie's affair, but Rachel knew the woman would poke and prod until she was satisfied. "I do fix Luke's breakfast and dinner, but he prefers to eat at his house. I pack him a lunch, which he picks up at breakfast, and he eats that at the jail, as far as I know. I do my cleaning while he's away, so I only see him if I run into him walking around town."

Sylvia's gaze went back and forth between the two women, looking as if she'd missed something. "Why should Rachel care what the marshal does?"

A gleam lit Margie's eyes, and she leaned forward. "Luke and Rachel have a. . .past." She whispered the last word. "Everyone in Lookout thought for sure they'd marry up one day, but she jilted him for James Hamilton."

Sylvia glanced at Rachel, an apology in her eyes. Rachel wanted to talk to the minister's wife about Luke and her remaining feelings for him but hadn't had the chance yet.

Martha stood, helped herself to another cookie, and then stopped next to Rachel's chair. "I'm sure Rachel didn't jilt Luke. She's not capable of such an action."

"She married for money, that's what Ray's ma always said. Shucked that young Davis boy and broke his heart so badly that he left town." Margie paused to sip her coffee. "The thing is, I can't figure out why he'd come back here after so long. I bet that just irritates Rand Kessler to no end."

Aggie looked as if she were about to faint. The woman never

gossiped and had a heart as big as all of Texas. "I. . .I. . .uh. . .nice weather we've been having lately, isn't it?"

"Why, yes it is, Agatha," Sylvia rushed to pick up the new train of conversation. "Just perfect. Not too hot, not too cold, and the wildflowers are so lovely."

Margie looked as if she'd sucked on a green persimmon. Rachel stood to refresh the coffeepot, and Martha followed her into the kitchen. "The nerve of that woman," she hissed. "I'm sorry, Rachel."

Needing a moment to catch her breath and to allow her heart to slow down, she leaned back against the cabinet. "I should be used to folks' chatter by now."

Martha rubbed her hand down Rachel's arm. "I can tell Luke is still a tender spot for you. I don't know much about the situation except what I've heard around town lately." She glanced at the ground, and her cheeks reddened. "But do you think it's possible that you two might get a second chance? It is strange that he returned after being gone for eleven years."

Rachel's heart fluttered. If only Luke had come back because of her, but she knew the truth. She'd seen the disgust in his eyes, and he'd proven his feelings by the way he avoided her. He didn't even think she was a good mother. She took a moment to force the shakiness from her voice. "Honestly," she glanced at her dear friend. "I'm surprised he didn't return sooner. It's the only home he's ever had, even if the actual house is no longer there. His cousins are here, as well as many old friends. He shouldn't have to give that up just because I'm here, too."

"Well, the Lord works in mysterious ways. Maybe He's got a miracle or two up His sleeve."

Rachel stared at Martha's gleaming eyes, knowing that in Luke's case, nothing could be further from the truth.

Chapter 10

Carthage, Missouri
May 1886

Leah Bennett quickened her steps as the town of Carthage came into view. She was in no hurry to return home, but the sooner she'd finished her errands, the more time she'd have to spend with Sue Anne. She glanced down at her list of things to do, determined to finish them quickly. At the City Flour Mills, she entered the front office and rang the bell on the counter. A tickle in her nose made her sneeze, just as she always did whenever she entered the mill. Flour and dust motes floated in the air and coated her lips. A man she'd seen before entered from a back room, dusting off his hands.

"Good day, Miss Bennett. What can I do for you?" He wiped his hands on a dingy towel hanging from one front pocket. His tanned face was coated with white flour, as was his dark hair, making him look older than she suspected he was.

Leah refrained from grinning at him. "I need to have a fifty-pound sack of flour delivered to our farm next time you make rounds."

"I'm happy to oblige. We have a wagon heading out that way on Thursday." He smiled, wrote something down in a ledger book on the counter, and quoted her the price.

She paid him and marked that item off her list. Next stop, the apothecary. Hiking up her skirt, she crossed the dirt street, dodging horse flops. As she entered the apothecary, her nose wrinkled at the pungent scents in the small building, but the assortment of colorful bottles in different shapes and sizes never failed to intrigue her.

Mr. Speck looked up from his desk behind the counter and adjusted his wire-framed glasses. "Ah, Miss Bennett, a pleasure to see you again. I hope all is well with your family."

Leah nodded. "For the most part, but Ma has developed a cough."

"Is it a dry cough or a phlegmy one?"

"Thankfully, it's just a dry cough, but it's been persistent for half a week." She looked down, breaking his gaze. After her mother developed the cough, Leah found it hard to know how to pray. In her heart, she wanted her mother to be well, but if it took her ma a while to recover completely, Pa might realize how much he needed Leah to run the household and change his mind about forcing her to marry Mr. Abernathy. But she knew how stubborn her pa was once he made a decision. He wasn't likely to back down, especially if money was involved. He worked sunup to sundown, struggling to raise enough food for their big family, and would tell her she needed to do her part to help out, even if that meant leaving home and marrying a man she couldn't abide.

The tall, thin man moved from behind the counter and in three steps crossed the room. He picked up two huge glass containers, set them on the counter, and measured out some ginger and something she didn't recognize into two packets, then twisted them closed. After writing instructions on a paper, he handed them to her. "That should take care of your mother. Just follow the directions to make a tea that will help her cough get better, and make sure she gets plenty of rest."

She accepted the packets and put them in a cloth bag that she'd brought to help carry things, all the while wondering how a mother of eleven was supposed to find time to rest. Leah didn't mind doing more to ease her mother's load, but she couldn't do everything, and her siblings bucked her efforts to get them to help. "Thank you, Mr. Speck."

She closed the door, feeling sorry for the homely man. With his overly large eyes, buck teeth, and thinning hair, the poor fellow had never found a woman to marry. She knew he wanted to wed, because he attended the same church as her family, but sadly, the few eligible women shied away from him, including her. Was it wrong to hope to marry a comely man? Or should a woman be satisfied with one who was a good provider and kind to her? Or was even that too much to hope for?

Leah nibbled on her bottom lip, pondering the issue. She knew that you should judge a person by what was in his heart and not his features, but if you had to look at that face first thing in the morning for the rest of your life, shouldn't it be one that pleased you? She considered living with Mr. Abernathy and shuddered.

A jingling of harnesses pulled her from her thoughts, and she stopped to allow a wagon to pass. The driver touched the edge of his hat at her and smiled. Leah nodded back then scurried across the street before another buggy passed. At the mercantile, she needed to get several colors of thread, some coffee for her pa, and a bag of salt, and she wanted to talk to Sue Anne.

At the entrance of the store, she stopped and glanced at her thin calico dress. The gray with pink rosebuds had faded so that the flowers looked more like stains than roses. She glanced inside the store and breathed a sigh of relief when she found it empty of customers. Scents of all sorts assaulted her: the tang of pickles from the barrel near the counter, spices, leather, onions. She loved the variety of the store and seeing so many new things, even though she was rarely able to purchase anything except the everyday supplies they needed.

Sue Anne's father glanced up from a ledger book he'd been writing in and smiled. "Afternoon, Miss Bennett."

"Mr. Carter." Leah nodded. "Good to see you again. Would Sue Anne happen to be around?"

He nudged his head to the left. "She's in the supply room unpacking a new shipment. Feel free to go on back there and see her."

"Thank you." She reached in her bag, pulled out her list, and handed it to him. "Here are the things we need today."

He pushed his glasses up his nose and scanned the page. "How much coffee would you like?"

"Ma said to get two pounds."

He nodded. "I'm guessing you want to pick out your own thread."

"Certainly. I'll do that after I say hello to Sue Anne." Leah hurried toward the supply room, her insides twittering. Would her friend think her a copycat? With a wobbly hand, she pushed aside the curtain and stepped into the other room.

Sue Anne glanced up from the crate she'd been emptying, her eyes blank. Suddenly they focused, and a smile settled on her thin lips. She stood, shook off the packaging hay from her skirt, and hugged Leah. "It's so wonderful to see you." She smiled wickedly. "And I so need a break from all this work."

"I had some errands to run, which is why I'm in town. I was also hoping you might be free to talk for a few minutes."

"This is the last crate, and I'm nearly done with it. Could you wait a few minutes, or are you in a hurry to get home?"

"No hurry. All that awaits me is work." Leah offered a weak smile, knowing the truth of her comment. "I need to pick out some thread. I can do that while you finish here."

"Wonderful. That will give me an incentive to hurry." Sue Anne sat back down and rummaged through the straw for another tin cup to add to her growing stack.

Leah ambled through the crowded aisles, gazing at the stacks of ready-made clothing and shiny new shoes in various sizes. Then her eyes landed on the stacks of colorful fabric. She fingered a navy calico with small, yellow sunflowers. If only she had money enough to buy some fabric. "How lovely."

"That just arrived this week." Mr. Carter pulled a scoop of coffee from a large bag and poured it onto his scale. "It caught Sue Anne's eye, too."

Over the years, Leah had tried hard not to envy Sue Anne, but at times it was hard, even though she was her best friend. Being an only child of the store owner, Sue Anne had first pick of the beautiful, ready-made dresses and fabrics as they arrived. She had been generous to share her castoffs with the Bennett family, but they generally went to the younger girls since Leah was so much taller than her friend. Leah rubbed her finger over the blue calico again. If she married Mr. Abernathy, would he allow her to purchase pretty things? Repulsed at her train of thought, she shook her head and moved on to the thread rack. She selected white, black, and navy thread then laid them on the counter for Mr. Carter to add to her tally. How could Sue Anne consider leaving all of this to go west and marry a rancher?

Her friend popped out of the back room, looking bright and cheerful. "I'm finished, Papa."

He smiled. "Then I suppose you'd better go spend some time with your friend while you can. Your mother will need your help with supper."

Sue Anne grabbed Leah's hand. "Let's go upstairs. Ma's gone visiting."

They tromped up the steps in the back room, entered the second story where the Carters lived, and were met with the lingering scent of baked bread. Leah loved the inviting parlor with its pretty settee, needlepoint chair, and large wooden rocker. A colorful braided rug covered all but the corners of the wood floor. A blue floral hurricane lamp rested on a round wooden table.

Sue Anne turned before going into the kitchen. "Would you like some tea?"

Leah shook her head. "Water is fine, thank you." She sat on the needlepoint chair, enjoying being off her feet and the way the chair hugged her.

Sue Anne returned with a glass of water and a small plate of cookies. She set them on the table next to Leah and flopped onto the settee, making a whoosh and sending dust motes floating in the afternoon sunlight that gleamed through the large window. She leaned toward Leah, her blue eyes shining. "Have you heard the news?"

Leah nodded. "I think so, at least if it's the same as what Molly told me."

"I just have to show you something." Sue Anne jumped up and left the room again.

A rustling sounded from somewhere in the small home, and her friend all but skipped back, a wide grin on her face as she held up a newspaper. "I keep this hidden in my room." She sat down, opened the paper, and pointed to an ad. "I haven't told my parents yet, but I'm going to be a mail-order bride. That's the man I picked."

"So, it's true then?"

Sue Anne shrugged. "I hope so. I wrote to Simon—that's his name—Simon Stephens, and he wrote back. He owns a ranch in Nevada."

Leah grasped her friend's hand. "How can you even think of traveling so far to marry a man you don't know?"

"I won't marry him until I'm sure I know him well enough. Oh, Leah, he sounds so dreamy—curly blond hair, brown eyes, and over six feet tall."

Leah's thought drifted to Mr. Abernathy. That description fit him except for the height, but there was nothing dreamy about him.

Sue Anne sobered. "Don't you dare tell my parents. Pa would be livid and probably try to marry me off fast to someone in town."

"I won't tell them, but I learned about it from Molly, and if someone as loose-lipped as she knows, don't you think your folks will find out before long?"

"I just need to get another letter or two, and then I'll know for certain that Simon is the one." She stared into her lap. "Do you think it's silly of me? It just sounds so adventurous."

Leah shook her head. She couldn't very well scold her friend when she came wanting to have a look at the advertisements herself. "I. . .uh. . .no. In fact, I was thinking about maybe trying to find a husband myself."

Sue Anne's eyes brightened again, and she squealed, grasping Leah's hands. "You're thinking about becoming a mail-order bride, too?"

Leah nodded. At least it had sounded like a good idea last night. "Mr. Abernathy made an agreement with Pa to marry me, but I just can't."

Lifting her hand to her mouth, her friend stared back at her with wide eyes. "Oh, Leah, I'm so sorry. He's so—old."

Leah crinkled her lip and leaned forward. "And he has hair in his ears."

"And hanging out his nose." Sue Anne curled her lips inward, obviously fighting a smile. She lost the battle and giggled. "We can't have that, can we? Here, let's look at my paper."

Leah nodded, still wrestling inside. How could she marry a stranger? She'd only loved one man, but she'd lost him. She'd heard of people marrying who didn't know one another, but could love grow from such a union? Yet anyone would be better than Mr. Abernathy. Scooting over, Sue Anne patted the settee, and Leah slid beside her. They leaned forward, looking at the paper spread out on the coffee table.

"Do you want to marry a rancher? Lots of them need wives."

Leah considered that and shook her head. "No, I think I'd rather live in a town and preferably someplace that's not cold."

"Hmm. . ." Sue Anne tapped her chin. "How about this one. *'Bank clerk from Kansas City, Missouri, seeks wife. Has small house and regular income, 35, 5'6", brown hair and green eyes.'* " Looking hopeful, she glanced over at Leah.

"I don't know. He's rather old, though certainly younger than Mr. Abernathy, but Kansas City isn't too far by train. I'd hate for Pa to come find me and make me come back home. He's so stubborn, he just might do that."

"That's true." Sue Anne turned back to the paper. " *'Well-to-do saloon owner needs wife. Prefers a shapely woman who sings like a songbird.'* "

Leah gasped and swatted her friend's arm. "No, thank you. Some friend you are."

Chuckling, they searched the ads again. Suddenly, Sue Anne sat up straighter. "Here's a good one. *'Town marshal, 6'2", with dark brown hair and eyes, wants pretty wife who can cook. Must be willing to move to Texas. Travel money provided.'* "

Leah's heart leaped. She hadn't considered the cost of traveling.

"The address is Lookout, Texas. I don't know where that is, but Texas is such a big state that surely the town is far away. Clear across Indian Territory. Your father would never travel that far—and oh my, six foot two inches—how wonderful."

Leah leaned back, staring at the ad. She'd read a lot about Texas and its wild beginnings, but now it was a state, and things had settled down there. At least she hoped they had. The more she thought about it, the more she liked the idea.

Sue Anne nudged her arm. "I don't think you're going to find one better than a town marshal. Surely the man is honorable and trustworthy if he's a lawman. I wonder why he wants you to write him through a solicitor."

"Maybe he doesn't want the whole town knowing he's wife shopping." Leah leaned back, took a cookie off the plate, and nibbled it. Could she do this? Would he even want her?

Bouncing on the seat, Sue Anne squealed. "Say something, Leah. He sounds perfectly wonderful."

Leah looked at her friend. "Can I borrow some paper so I can write to him?"

Chapter 11

Shreveport, Louisiana
Late May 1886

Shannon O'Neil pulled open the tall double windows in the gentlemen's parlor and stared out at the dreary countryside. A cool breeze blew in, clearing the room's air of the stench of cigar smoke that had lingered overnight after the men's poker game. The damp weather and cloudy sky reminded her of her homeland. Ireland. Would she ever see the brilliant green grass and rolling hills again?

No, and 'twas best she put it from her mind. She would live the rest of her days in America, and though life here wasn't easy, 'twas far better than how her family fared as poor tenant farmers. If only her parents hadn't died so soon upon their arrival in New Orleans. Perhaps things would have turned out different.

"Miss O'Neil!"

Shannon jumped and spun around. Her hand clutched the paper in her pocket as if Mrs. Melrose could see the letter and knew her thoughts. A shiver ran down her spine.

The plump woman lifted up her chin and glared at Shannon. "Mr. Wakefield does not employ you so you can spend the day lollygagging. Have you finished cleaning and dusting this room? And why is that window open?"

Shannon's gaze ran swiftly around the gentlemen's parlor where each piece of furniture gleamed. "Aye, mum, the polishing is done, and I only opened the window to clear the air in here. 'Twas heavy with smoke from last eve's socializing."

"Fine, then see to it that the chamber pots are emptied while the family is at breakfast."

Stomach curdling at the nasty chore, Shannon dipped her head. "Aye, mum."

"Make haste now, and when you've finished that task, come find me downstairs in the kitchen or laundry." The head maid turned and strode out of the room, murmuring loud enough for Shannon to hear, "I declare, if I didn't keep a watch on each and every one of these girls, nothing would get done around here."

Gathering up the crate of empty liquor and wine bottles, Shannon made her way down to the kitchen. She set the crate on the rear porch and returned upstairs to close the window and retrieve the wine glasses. Back in the kitchen, she placed the dirty goblets in the sink to be washed. She hurried to the south wing of the huge mansion, dreading the duty before her. Though she'd worked at the Wakefield Estate for nearly a year, she was the newest servant, so the worst jobs fell to her. "But not for long."

She fingered the letter burning a hole in her pocket. Had she made the right decision to respond to that advertisement in the newspaper? He'd written twice and now sent her the money to come to Texas to be his wife. But could she actually marry a man she'd never met before? A town marshal, no less.

She'd dreamed of the six-feet-two-inch man last night. Dark brown hair and eyes. A marshal would be a man used to protecting people, but would she feel safe with him? Would he treat her kindly?

She emptied and washed out the pots for the master and mistress's room and their two daughters, but she dreaded entering their son's bed chamber. He was known for sleeping late and for forcing the female servants to please his every whim; but as bad as he was, he didn't have the cruel streak that his visiting friend and college roommate, Justin Moreland, had.

Shannon knocked hard on the door, waited, then knocked again. She wiped her sweaty hands on her apron. When there was no response, she pushed open the heavy door and peered inside. Morgan Wakefield's nightshirt lay in a heap on the floor, much to Shannon's relief. She hurried inside, fetched the pot, took it downstairs to be emptied and washed, and quickly returned it to the room, lest the younger Mr. Wakefield return and find her in his chamber. In the hall, she leaned against the wall and heaved a heavy breath. Just one more, and then the horrid deed would be done for the day.

She ventured out of the family wing of the home and into the north end where the guests resided. If the younger Mr. Wakefield was awake and at breakfast, he most likely had dragged his friend out of bed and downstairs with him. Shannon shook her head. How could anyone eat breakfast when it was nearly the noon hour?

She knocked loudly then shoved the door open, greatly relieved that Mr. Moreland was not present. Fifteen minutes later, the deed was done. She pulled the door shut as she was leaving.

"Well, well, what do we have here?" Justin Moreland leaned casually against the hall wall staring at her with lecherous eyes and a cocky smile. "Trying to sneak into my room, were you?"

Shannon jumped, her hand to her chest, and stepped back. "I was only tendin' to your—your room, sir." She curtseyed and stepped around him.

The tall, lean man leaped in front of her. "I've had breakfast, but alas, there was no dessert."

Shannon scowled, thinking of the delicious pastries with creamy filling that the cooks made for the family. Often the remaining ones were thrown away or fed to the swine rather than given to the lowly servants. She forced a smile and held her hands behind her back so that he wouldn't see them trembling. Though comely with his curly brown hair and blue eyes, something about the rogue scared her more than riding in the dark, smelly steerage on the ship that had brought her to America. "I'd be happy to fetch you a pastry, sir."

He stepped closer, grabbing her upper arms. "You're the only dessert I need. Give me fifteen minutes of your time, and I'll sweeten your pocket with a coin."

Gasping, Shannon struggled to pull free. Her virtue was not for sale at any price. "Nay, I cannot. I've duties to tend to."

"Come now, those other servants won't miss you for such a short while." Taller than she by a good nine inches, young and strong, he jerked her toward the bedroom door.

Praying hard, Shannon dug her feet into the carpet runner but slid forward as he turned and pulled her against him. *Father, help me.*

She shoved at the man's solid chest. "Nay, leave me be."

"Hey, Justin. What are you doing?"

At the sound of Morgan Wakefield's voice, Mr. Moreland halted. He scowled, then grinned and looked over his shoulder. "I'm just about to have some fun with this wench of yours. She's a comely thing, with all that dark red hair, don't you think?"

Morgan's gaze ran down Shannon's length. "She's a servant, for heaven's sake, Justin. Leave her alone. Did you forget that we're supposed to go hunting?"

Justin turned but held tightly to her with one hand. A leering grin twisted his features, and he waggled his brows. "I'm on the hunt for something else."

Morgan's lips curled. "I know of far better women to please your fancy than that one. Older and more experienced."

Justin's grip loosened. "Where, pray tell, would these lovely ladies be?"

Grinning, Morgan leaned one shoulder against the wall and crossed his ankles. "Stick with me, and you'll find out. But right now, the horses are saddled, and my father is awaiting us. Come."

Justin stared down at Shannon. Suddenly, he smiled and kissed her nose. "Tonight, my sweet tart. And next time, I'll not be dissuaded."

He released her arm so quickly that she nearly stumbled. Shannon swerved around him and ran past Mr. Wakefield, flashing him what she hoped was a grateful look. He scowled at her as if she were nothing but refuse to be scraped off the bottom of his boots. No matter, she would always be thankful that he had arrived when he had.

Hurrying down the stairs to the servants' quarters, she shoved her hand in her pocket and clutched the letter in her fist. Her decision had been made. In her room, she quickly changed out of her black servant's dress and hung it and her apron on the hook on the wall alongside its mate. She threw her few belongings into a worn satchel and donned one of her two dresses, saving the nicer one for when she'd arrive in Texas to meet her future husband, Luke Davis.

Shannon all but held her breath until she was out of the mansion, and she hurried down the lane lest someone see her and try to stop her. She had needed this job—until the day the letter arrived with enough money for her to take the train to Sherman, Texas, where she could then catch a stage to Lookout.

Her steps quickened as she reached the lane that would take her into town. "Please, Lord, let this be the right choice."

But what other choice did she have? She was alone in America with no hope of ever seeing Ireland again. She could only pray she wasn't jumping off the ship and into the ocean.

Southwest Missouri
June 1886

Carly shoved the last bite of scrambled eggs into her mouth, buttered another biscuit, and slathered peach jam on it. Normally, she had trouble eating before a robbery, but the restaurant's food was so much better than she made that she couldn't pass it up. "I wish I could fix biscuits this flaky. These are so good."

Her brother grunted an agreement and sipped his coffee, staring out the window at the small town of Decker. "Finish up. The stage is due in a half hour."

"I'm nearly done." She leaned forward, the high neck of her dress clutching at her throat. She tugged at the collar, fearing it would cut off her breathing. "This dress is about to kill me. I'd much rather wear pants."

Tyson looked her direction, blue eyes narrowed. "For what we have planned, you need that dress, so get used to it."

Thankful that no one else was in the dining room since it was well past the normal breakfast hour, Carly sighed and fanned the bodice of her dress to allow in some air. She hoped the stage robbery went well so they could lie low for a while. She was sick of stealing and constantly moving from one hideout to another, but after her brother had gambled away their share of the money from the bank robbery, he'd started planning another heist. Why couldn't she have been born into a decent family?

Ty stood. "Let's go."

Carly shoved the last bite into her mouth then downed the rest of her coffee. Standing, she gave the spacious hotel dining room a final glance. Each table was covered with a white tablecloth. Fancy chandeliers lit the room at night, but now sunlight reflected on the pieces of cut glass, making dancing rainbows on the walls. She'd miss feeling like a lady and being surrounded by such finery.

Tyson took her arm. "Don't forget your handbag."

"I don't like carrying it. That gun makes it heavy," she whispered. She'd taken to wearing a holstered gun partly to protect herself from the two newest gang members, but she couldn't very well do that or the stage operators might get suspicious. Now that they were heading toward their destination, her legs began to wobble. What if there were several men on the coach? Could she hold them at bay with her gun until her brother and the gang could take over?

She lifted her heavy bag, carrying it in the crook of her arm instead of letting it dangle. What if she had to shoot another passenger?

Licking her dry lips, she allowed Ty to tug her along. When he'd proposed the plan of putting her on the stage to help with the robbery, she'd fussed and fumed, but to no avail. How could he expect her to shoot an unarmed person looking her in the eye? She doubted she could. Maybe it wouldn't come to that.

"Hurry up. We need you on that stage." Tyson yanked her arm, and she jogged to keep up.

"I'm trying to hurry, but these confounded skirts keep tripping me."

Tyson slowed his steps as they rounded the corner and saw the stage still sitting there. "You'll keep your story straight? Watch what you say to folks?"

Carly rolled her eyes. "I ain't stupid. I'll just sit down and tell them all I'm an outlaw—a member of the infamous Payton gang—and if they give me any lip about it, I'll shoot them."

A brief smiled tugged at Tyson's mouth before he sobered. "Maybe it's best if you don't talk at all."

He didn't trust her to keep up her end of the deal. She knew the stakes—that Ty had learned a large payroll was on this stage and that there weren't going to be any additional guards so that nobody would suspect anything.

Tyson stopped behind the stage and handed Carly her ticket. "You have a good trip, sis, and tell Aunt Sylvie that I hope to visit soon."

She offered him a sweet smile for the sake of anyone watching. "Oh, I will. Time will fly past, and you'll be seein' me again before you know it."

Tyson scowled at her. Another man and woman stood in front of the stage office window. She was pretty with her black hair swept up in a net thing and her blue eyes glimmering. Carly guessed her to be in her late teens.

"Are you sure about this, Ellie? You know you'll always have a home with me." A short man about the same height as the woman stared at her with somber brown eyes. By the similarity in their features and coloring, Carly assumed they must be brother and sister.

"I'm sure, John. I've corresponded several times with my intended, and he seems a perfectly nice man."

John shook his head. "It just doesn't seem right for you to go off to Texas to marry a stranger. There are men here in Decker who'd be delighted to marry you."

The woman named Ellie patted the man's chest. "Don't worry, John. You have a new wife, and she doesn't need to share her kitchen with me. I'll be fine."

A stocky man dressed in denim pants and shirt and wearing a vest stomped down the steps to the street. He carried a Winchester rifle in one hand. His thick mustache twitched. "Load up, folks. We ain't got all day."

John helped Ellie into the coach and then moved back, looking worried. Tyson handed Carly up, and she stepped on the edge of her skirt, falling to her knees on the floor of the coach.

"You all right, sis?" Ty asked, sounding disgusted.

Carly bit back a curse and managed to wrangle the skirt out from under her shoes. Stupid dress. She hadn't worn one since shortly after Ma died and had forgotten how awkward they could be. Whoever invented them sure didn't give a hoot about how a woman was supposed to get around and do everyday stuff while managing the strangling fabric. She flopped onto the seat and rearranged the despised garment.

Ellie's eyes were wide, watching her. "Are you all right?"

"Fine." Carly crossed her arms over her chest and looked to see if Tyson was still there. At least she'd managed not to curse out loud.

Her brother lifted his brows and shook his head. "Safe trip, sis."

Carly merely nodded. What point was there in pretending

when she'd just see him again in an hour or so? Too bad she wasn't really going somewhere. She let her mind wander, trying to decide where she'd go if she could travel anywhere she wanted.

In a matter of minutes, the stage pulled out of Decker with no other passengers. She had never ridden in a stagecoach before and had been excited about the prospect, but as they bumped and shimmied down the road, she wondered how she'd manage until Ty and the gang intercepted the coach, several miles out of town. She watched the landscape speed by, thankful at least she wouldn't get bugs in her teeth like she sometimes did while riding.

"Sure is bumpy, isn't it?"

Carly glanced at the woman across the seat. "Yeah, sure is."

"My name is Ellie Blackstone."

Carly felt the blood drain from her face. They'd never discussed what to do if someone asked her name. "Uh. . .Carly. . .Payton."

The woman smiled, pulled some knitting out of her satchel, and started clicking her long needles together. All the while, Carly wondered if she should have given a false name. And how could that woman knit on such a bouncy stage? If Carly tried that, she was certain she'd end up stabbing herself. She set her handbag on the seat beside her, one hand on it so it wouldn't slide off and not be handy when she needed it. She hoped she wouldn't have to shoot Ellie.

"I'm a mail-order bride on my way to Texas."

Carly blinked and stared at the young woman. "You mean you're going to marry a man you ain't never met?"

Ellie giggled. "That's right, although I have received three letters from him. He's a marshal in Lookout, Texas. I've never been to Texas before. Have you?"

Carly shook her head. "No, but I'd sure as shootin' like to go some day."

"I'm excited about the trip, although my brother is worried about me. I just couldn't stand living under the same roof as him and his new wife." Ellie stopped knitting and lowered her hands to her lap. "Don't get me wrong. Charlene was nice enough, but I could tell she didn't like sharing the house with another woman, even if I did grow up there."

"How'dja learn about the marshal?"

Ellie smiled. "I placed an advertisement in a magazine, and a month later, I got a letter from a solicitor saying the marshal in Lookout, Texas, was interested in learning more about me. I wrote him, and he wrote back several times and then asked for my hand. I agreed, and then he sent me the traveling money."

Never having heard such a story, Carly sat back in the seat. "What if. . .what if he's old—and fat?"

Ellie giggled, brown eyes sparkling. "Luke is only twenty-nine, and oh so tall."

"That's gotta be a lot older than you are."

She shrugged and renewed her knitting. "Seven years. But lots of men are that much older than their wives."

Carly leaned back, staring out the window. She couldn't afford to take a liking to Ellie when she might have to shoot her in a half hour. She tapped her hand against the hardness of the gun in her handbag. How long would her brother wait to attack the stage? They should be far enough from town so that any shots fired wouldn't be heard back in Decker, but not too close to the next town. She jiggled her foot.

What would it be like to marry a stranger? A marshal, no less. Carly shuddered. But then she sat up straighter. A marshal would know when payroll shipments would be going out on the stage. If she could get close to such a man, she could learn about them herself and might be able to score a big enough heist that she could quit being an outlaw and live a respectable life. Course, a marshal might have heard of the Payton gang, but he would have no way of connecting her to it.

But there was the issue of Ellie. "Did you send the marshal a photograph of yourself?"

Ellie shook her head and looked out the window, nibbling on

her lower lip. "No, I was afraid he might not like what he saw." She patted her dark hair. "Men often prefer blonds."

So. . .the marshal didn't know what Ellie looked like. Thoughts spun through Carly's mind faster than the wheels of the stage turned. If only she could take the woman's place, but there was no chance of that. Tyson would appear soon with his gang, and she'd have to leave with him whether she wanted to or not. She thought of how Emmett leered at her across the campfire most nights. He'd tried to kiss her once, and even now a shiver ran down her spine. So far, her brother had kept the man away from her, but what if something happened to Tyson?

A shot rang out behind them, and Carly jumped, along with Ellie, even though she'd been expecting her brother.

"Robbers! No, this can't be happening." Ellie clutched her knitting to her chest. "I'm not even out of Missouri yet."

Above them, shots fired back toward the outlaws. A bullet hit the window frame, sending flying splinters of wood toward them. One hit Carly in the face, and she jerked her head to the side. Didn't the gang care that she was inside the stage?

She reached for her handbag as it slid along the seat. The coach hit a dip in the road, dropped down, and then back out. Carly reached for the edge of the window to keep from being flung to the ground. *If this thing doesn't stop soon, I'll be black and blue—if I even survive.*

The stage lurched side-to-side as the horses thundered down the dirt road in their effort to flee the outlaws. The coach groaned, and harnesses jangled. Dust coated Carly's lips. Ellie clung to the window frame with one hand and pressed her other hand against the seat, her eyes wide and her knitting forgotten.

Carly reached for her handbag again, but it slid onto the ground. She leaned forward, just as Fred, a new member of the gang, pulled even with Ellie's window. His gaze sought out Carly's, and then he fired toward the other passenger. Ellie slumped sideways just as Fred was blasted out of his saddle by either the stage driver or the shotgun rider. Carly jerked to the left and ducked, as if the shot had been meant for her. Why had he shot Ellie when she wasn't even armed?

Carly dropped to the floor and fumbled with her handbag, knowing how angry her brother would be if she didn't draw her gun. The coach lurched again, and Ellie fell on top of her. Carly's heart jolted clear up into her throat. With her bag in her hand, she attempted to rise, but Ellie's weight and the constant jostling held her down. She fought the panic blurring her vision and making her heart stampede. Was Ellie dead? Or just unconscious?

Behind the stage, she heard more gunfire.

Hoofbeats pulled even with the door. "Carly, you in there?"

Unable to catch her breath, she didn't respond to her brother's question. She tried to push up, but Ellie's limp body weighted her down. The stage swayed right and left, groaning and creaking, until she feared it would tip over.

Ty cursed. "Carly's down."

More gunshots echoed behind them.

"Soldiers! Let's ride."

Ty was leaving her? She had to get out of the coach or she'd be caught. But even as she struggled to get Ellie's dead weight off her, an idea formed in her mind. Did she dare go through with it?

She heard more riders pass the stage. "Get it stopped, Chet, and see if the passengers are injured."

The stage gradually slowed, but the other riders charged on ahead, probably after her brother. Would he fight for her or just keep running like the time a gang member had fallen under gunfire? A sudden thought blasted into her mind. She had no idea where to look for her brother now that they were separated. And she had no horse. They hadn't discussed this development.

Her breath came in ragged bursts as the stage squeaked to a halt. Footsteps marched in her direction, and the door opened. Carly's heart thundered, and she lay still. Since she'd have surprise on her side, she might be able to pull her gun and shoot the man.

He muttered a soft curse. "Looks like they shot two women."

Carly felt Ellie's limp body being lifted off of her, and she sucked in a deep breath and tucked her handbag underneath her. Should she continue to play possum or try to get up?

Before she could decide, steady footsteps brought the man back, and Carly froze. She felt herself being tugged toward the door then lifted into the man's arms as her handbag dropped to the ground. He smelled of sweat, dust, and leather. He gently set her down, and she moaned. Lifting her hand to her cheek, she pretended to be coming around after passing out.

"W–what happened?" She opened her eyes and saw a man with kind hazel eyes staring back.

"Just take it easy, ma'am. You was in a holdup."

Carly gasped and splayed her hand over her chest. "Oh mercy. What about the other passenger. Is she. . ."

"Passed out cold. Might have to do with the shot that grazed her head or the sewing needle piercing her side. And she's got another bullet in her shoulder." The man shook his head. "It don't look good for her. I doubt she'll make it, especially being so far from town. Joplin's the closest, so I reckon that's where you two will end up once the rest of my team returns."

"Returns?"

The man rose and took a canteen off his saddle horn. "They went after them outlaws. Killed one back a ways, but the others rode off." He stooped down, opened the canteen, and handed it to her. "What's your name, ma'am?"

Panic sliced through Carly as she slowly sipped the water, delaying her response. Ellie may not have recognized her real name, but a lawman surely would. "Uh. . .Ellie. Ellie Blackstone."

Chapter 12

Lookout, Texas
June 1886

Luke scanned Main Street, crowded with people from the town and nearby farms and ranches, all come to Lookout to celebrate his thirtieth birthday. At the far end of the street, music filled the air, and five couples danced to a lively tune. Tables filled with food served by the womenfolk lined one side of Main Street. Luke scowled as Garrett approached, knowing the shindig had been his idea. Max, lying on the porch, didn't bother lifting his head but wagged his tail.

Garrett laughed and wrapped his arm around Luke's shoulder in a friendly greeting. "Just relax and enjoy the festivities, cuz. You know these folks jump at any chance to get together for a celebration, especially those who live outside of town. Farming and ranching can be a lonely life."

"Maybe so, but I don't like being the center of attention."

Mark strode toward them carrying two cups, a grin widening his face. "Nice party, isn't it?"

He handed Luke a mug of something. Luke sniffed it, ignoring his question. Apple cider. He sipped the sweet drink, watching, looking for trouble. With so many people gathered in such a small spot, it was bound to happen sooner or later.

"So, how's it feel to be thirty, ol' man?" Mark lifted his cup to his lips.

"Where's mine?" Garrett stood with his hands on his hips. "I sent you off to get us a drink, and you give mine to Luke?"

Mark grinned. "He's the birthday boy. Fetch your own refreshment."

Garrett snarled his lip at Mark and muttered a phony growl, making Luke chuckle. His cousins were all the family he had left, and Lookout had been the only town he'd ever called home. He'd prayed long and thought hard before quitting the cavalry and returning to Lookout, but in the end, family and familiarity won out—not to mention he believed it was what God wanted him to do. His gaze journeyed to where Rachel was cutting pies at a table. Tonight the town was filled with women, and he only had eyes for one. He shook his head. How pathetic he was.

"Why don't you ask her to dance?" Garrett nudged Luke in the arm.

"What?" Luke shot a glance at his cousin, realizing he'd been caught staring.

"Go ask Rachel to dance."

"It may be my birthday, but I'm still on duty."

"Someone else will ask her if you don't."

At that very moment, Rand Kessler stopped at Rachel's table. He stood close to her and said something. Rachel offered a half smile and shook her head. Rand leaned closer. Luke's hackles lifted. Rachel nodded then waved to the doctor's wife, who came and took her place at the pie table. Rand offered Rachel his arm, and she took it, allowing him to lead her toward the dancing couples.

"If you still have any interest in Rachel, don't wait too long." Garrett gave him a knowing look. "Rand Kessler's been after her to marry him for a year now."

Luke ignored the comment, though it ate at him. "How big of

a ranch does this Kessler have?"

"Big. He's one of the more prosperous ranchers in this area."

Great. So Rachel was after another man with money. Even if Luke *was* interested in her, she'd never give a low paid town marshal a second look. He ground down hard on his back teeth. Maybe the best thing he could do was get married; then he'd have a woman who could help take his mind off Rachel Hamil—

A blast of shots rang out. Luke flung down the tin cup and yanked out his gun. Max lurched to his feet, whimpering, and disappeared into the jail office. Luke scanned the throng of merchants, farmers, and families gathered along Main Street. Where was the shooter?

His heart galloped. A shooter in such a crowded area could be a disaster. "Did you see the gunman?"

Beside him, Garrett held the same rigid stance. "No. It didn't sound too close, but it's hard to tell with all the noise here."

Luke searched the rowdy crowd. The townsfolk square-danced, chatted, and carried on as if nothing had happened. Had the band's music muffled the gunfire so they hadn't heard it? Couldn't they sense the danger?

The rapid pop sounded again. People on the fringe of the mass spun about, turning concerned stares toward the noise. A woman screamed and grabbed her husband.

"Over there." Garrett pointed toward the bank with his gun, and then he holstered it. "Stupid kids. Don't they know they can spark a blaze with those firecrackers?"

Shaking his head at the trio of adolescents, Luke pocketed his pistol. "I'll run 'em off."

Mark stepped forward. "Let me and Garrett do it. After all, it's your party."

"Yeah, but I'm the marshal. It's what I get paid to do." He glanced at the nearby table laden with desserts, where Rachel had been serving pie. "One of you could grab me a slice of Rachel's apple pie before it's gone."

Luke loped toward the bank. Truth be told, he appreciated the town's celebration of his birthday, but he hated having everyone's attention focused on him. As the marshal, he was more used to standing back, watching everybody else. He stopped in front of the mercantile and gazed across the road, watching the spot where the youngsters had been gathered. Two of the boys were gone, but a small shape huddled near the corner of the bank. The spark of a match illuminated the child's face.

Jack.

Not again. Luke strode around the corner, gritting his teeth.

The child glanced up, eyes widening. The match fell to the ground, and Jack took off like a rabbit freed from a snare. Luke stomped the flames that flickered to life on the dry grass, sending dust over the boots he'd polished for tonight's special occasion. No point chasing Jack now. She was long gone, and besides, he knew where to find her when the dust settled. Swiping the tops of his boots on the back of his pants leg, Luke heaved a sigh. Rachel didn't need this, but they'd have to talk about Jack's latest antic. She was going to have to face the facts about her ornery child before someone got hurt.

Fifteen minutes later, after taking a spin around the outskirts of town to make sure all was in order, Luke sat with his cousins on the steps in front of his office. He cut a large bite of golden crust and tender apple, shoved it in his mouth, and licked the cinnamon and sugar from his fork. "Rachel sure does make good pie."

"Too bad she can't control that kid of hers as well as she can cook," Garrett said.

"I'm tellin' you, Luke, you ought to marry her before Rand does; then you could eat all the pie you want." Mark's brown eyes flickered with amusement.

Luke nearly choked on his final bite. "You know I can't do that."

"All that was a long time ago, cuz." Garrett sipped a cup of coffee.

"Maybe so, but after the woman you love betrays you, a man thinks long and hard before risking his heart again."

"Then maybe you should consider marrying someone else. Have you thought about that?"

Luke stared at his cousins, wishing they'd pick another topic of conversation. "Maybe you should take your own advice."

Garrett grinned wide. "Maybe I will."

Luke sobered. He was ready to marry and start a family, but so far, no woman had been able to sear Rachel from his heart. Maybe one of these days someone would. "I guess I'd marry if the right woman came along."

Finished with his own pie, Mark reached over and ran his forefinger along the edge of Luke's plate, then poked it in his mouth. "Rachel sure knows how to cook. If you're not interested in her, maybe I'll see if I can turn her head away from that Kessler guy."

"That's not funny, Mark." Luke cast a sidelong glare to his right.

"You said yourself that you're no longer interested in her. What's wrong with me pursuing her?"

Garrett straightened, flicking a beetle off his brown vest. "Rachel's free to allow any man she wants to come courting." He looked past Luke to Mark. "But why would you want to marry her? She's got that pain-in-the-neck kid."

"Jack's not so bad. She just needs some guidance," Luke offered.

"But whoever married Rachel would never have to worry about food, and she is easy on the eyes." Mark grinned, an ornery gleam in his blue gaze that set Luke on edge. "She could do lots worse than me."

Having heard enough of his cousins' foolishness, Luke stood and walked toward the table where Rachel was again serving pies. He could no longer trust her with his heart, but how could he explain this fierce need to protect her, to be near her, when he didn't understand it himself? She glanced up and smiled, making his pulse gallop.

"Care for another slice? It is your birthday, after all."

He handed her his dirty plate. "No thanks. I'm good."

"Are you enjoying your party?"

Luke shrugged. "I guess so."

"It's nice having you back in town."

He shoved his hands in his back pockets, not knowing what to say to her now that he had her to himself. "Good to be back."

"Well, I hope you have a good time tonight."

Luke nodded, and Rachel's smile dipped as he turned back toward his office. Maybe returning to Lookout hadn't been such a grand idea. Why couldn't he get his head and heart to line up together? A part of him still cared for Rachel, but he would never again trust her with his heart. He'd done that once, and she'd tromped on it. His heart wouldn't survive if she did it again.

"You need a wife," Mark said as Luke approached him.

"Quit saying that."

"Maybe we'll just have to find one for you." Garrett chuckled and bumped his brother.

"No thanks," Luke called over his shoulder as he walked past them. Max trotted out of the jail and took a place beside Luke as he strode back to the bank to make sure the fire was still out. He returned to watching his town, hoping his hooligan cousins weren't planning another one of the many practical jokes they'd pulled most of their lives. But he had a bad feeling in his gut, as though he'd drunk soured milk. Those two were up to something; he could smell it.

Mrs. Fairland sat in the corner, listening to the first and second graders read. Jack glanced back at her list of spelling words. She should be studying them, but worry plagued her like a bad case of influenza. She took a deep breath and peered over her shoulder at Butch Laird. Even from across the room, she could smell the filthy scent of the Laird's pig farm. The thirteen-year-old stood nearly six feet tall and glared back at her with squinty black eyes. He pointed his finger like a gun and pretended to shoot her.

Jack spun back around in her desk, stuck in regret as thick as Texas mud after three days of rain. She should have kept her mouth shut. Shouldn't have yelled at Butch for picking on Jonesy at lunch. Shouldn't have screamed, "If you cook Butch Lard, he turns to Butch Fat."

She swallowed hard, tightly gripping the top of her desk, remembering how he glared at her and said his name was *Laird* not *Lard*. What had possessed her to do such a thing? What would he do to her?

He was between her and the door, or she'd light out the first chance she got. Maybe she could find some way to dawdle until he headed home. Tell the teacher she needed help with her schoolwork. But that left almost as sour a taste in her mouth as the thought of fighting Butch had.

Maybe her ma was right. Maybe she should think before she spoke. But her words always came flying out before she even thought about them. She hated Butch and couldn't help taking up for her friend. She pressed down on her knees to make them quit wobbling.

Jonesy looked at her from his seat across the aisle. His eye had nearly swollen shut. Mrs. Fairland had almost sent him home for fighting, but after Ricky and Jack's explanation of how Butch had started it, she'd let him stay. Everyone knew Mrs. Fairland was afraid of Butch, which was why she didn't send him home. Too bad she hadn't, and a fat lot of help the teacher would be if Butch jumped Jack after school.

Lifting her head to peer out the window, Jack tried to gauge how far it was from the school to her home. If only the jail was closer. Luke would save her.

Mrs. Fairland stood. "Very good, children. Practice reading the next three pages at home tonight, and we'll go over them in class tomorrow."

The four youngsters from the reading group scurried back to their desks and sat down.

At the front of the class, Mrs. Fairland looked pretty in her gold calico dress, even after a full day of school. "All right, students. We've had a good day of learning."

Jack glanced at the door and scooted to the edge of her chair. If she jumped over the desk to her right, she just might make it out the door and get away.

"Make sure you study your spelling words. The test will be before lunch on Friday, as usual." Mrs. Fairland's gaze traveled around the class, a pleasant smile lighting her pretty face.

Jack slid farther off the seat until her leg was halfway across the aisle. The other kids looked at her, but she knew most were used to her odd ways.

"Class dismissed."

Like a fire had been lit under her backside, Jack blasted off the seat and crawled across the top of Amanda Moore's desk, leaving the girl wide-eyed and mouth gaping. Jack raced for the door, fumbled with the knob, and yanked it open. Thudding like a stampede of Brahma bulls echoed behind her.

She bolted down the steps, heart thundering. Just as she leapt over the last step, someone snagged the back of her dress. It ripped and gagged her throat where it pulled taut.

"You didn't think ya was gettin' away from me that easy, did ya?"

Jack sucked in air and kicked her feet. Butch tucked her under his arm and lumbered around the back of the school toward the barn. Eyes blurring and throat aching from yelling, Jack kicked hard, trying to trip the big boy.

The children shouted behind her, but she couldn't tell who they were rooting for. Suddenly, Ricky stood in front of Butch, fists lifted. "You let her go. She's just a kid. A dumb girl, no less."

Ricky thought she was just a dumb girl? The pain of her friend's words took the fight out of her, and she went limp.

"Out of my way, Peewee." Butch shoved Ricky aside like he

was nothing more than an empty gunny sack.

"Ahhh. . ." Someone who sounded like a wild Indian charged them from behind. The force of the body colliding with Butch knocked Jack free. She fell to the ground, trying hard to catch her breath, and gazed up at the clear blue sky.

Her school friends stood around them in a circle, yelling hard. "Fight! Fight!"

"Children, stop this nonsense." Mrs. Fairland stood beside the group of onlookers as if she was afraid to move closer. "Stop that fighting right this minute."

Jack sat up. Ricky, Jonesy, and the Peterson twins were punching it out with Butch. Nobody liked the big, smelly bully, and that included her. Jack jumped up, righted her dress, took a running start, and latched onto Butch's back. She wrapped her arms around his neck and held on for all she was worth, holding her breath so as not to smell him.

Butch swung sideways, shoved the twins backward, then swung the other way. Green trees blurred into the white schoolhouse. Arms flew toward Butch as the younger boys rallied. He clawed at Jack's fingers, loosening them, then suddenly a fist collided with her eye, jerking her head backward with a snap.

Jack released her hold and felt herself falling. The screaming and yelling faded as she tumbled into a pit of black.

A brightness behind Jack's eyelids intruded into the black realm, pulling her from the dark pit of nothingness. She slammed into a wall of pain, radiating from her forehead over her eye and cheek. Jack froze. Moving caused pain.

She relaxed into the softness of a bed—her bed, if the delicious smells coming from the kitchen were any indication.

"This is all your fault."

The venom in her mother's voice took her by surprise. She lifted the lid of her uninjured eye and blinked to bring the room into focus. Luke stood just inside the door of the bedroom Jack shared with her mother, his arms crossed and his face scowling.

"How? What did I do to cause this?" he asked.

Her mother stepped forward. "You taught my daughter how to fight, didn't you?"

"What? No!" Luke lifted his hands as if surrendering.

Jack watched them. Whenever Luke came around, there was either a spark of light in her mother's eyes that wasn't normally there, or else the opposite—she seemed sad. How come Luke caused these reactions in her mother when no other man had? Dare she hope that maybe one day Luke could become her new pa? She'd take him any day over that rancher who didn't have the sense to stop calling on her ma. Did she even want another pa?

At least Luke wouldn't be mean like her real pa had been.

"I did not teach Jack to fight. I promise, Rachel."

That was another thing. Right from the start, they'd called each other by their first names, but whenever she asked about Luke, her mother only said he was someone she grew up with. Jack opened her eye a speck farther to see better.

Her mother scooted up close, wagging a finger in the marshal's face. "You must have done something. Just look at her! Why, she'll have a black eye for weeks."

Luke's gaze skimmed across the room to her. He looked sad and angry at the same time.

"Ah, ah, it's not nice to eavesdrop, young lady." The doctor leaned over the bed, and his face blurred as he moved in close and peered down at her. "It's good to see you coming to."

"Coming to what?" Jack asked.

Ma gasped and hurried to the other side of the bed. She sat down and clutched Jack's hand. "Jacqueline, oh, my baby, you gave me such a scare."

Jack stared up at Luke, who moved to the edge of the bed. She rolled her good eye, even though it hurt, and a smile pulled up one side of his mouth, though he still looked concerned.

"How do you feel?" Her mother laid the back of her hand over Jack's forehead. "Are you in much pain?"

"Luke didn't teach me to fight, Mama."

Her mother glanced up at the marshal but didn't seem convinced.

"Honestly." Jack squeezed her mother's hand. "I asked him to, but he said it wasn't a good idea because I might get hurt."

"Well, it's good to know he has some sense." Her ma looked as if it pained her to say those words.

"If'n he had taught me, maybe I wouldn't of gotten punched like I did."

Ma pressed her lips tight, giving Jack the look that told her a lecture was coming. "You wouldn't have gotten injured if you hadn't joined in that fight with those older boys. I told you they're nothing but trouble."

"That's not true." Jack bolted up, her head aching as if it might explode. She pressed fingertips against her temples and lowered herself back down. "B–but you don't understand. Butch—"

Dr. Phillips cleared his throat. "Perhaps the scolding could take place later? I need to examine Jacqueline now that she's awake. She was unconscious for a good fifteen minutes."

Ma looked well put in her place. "Of course. I'm sorry, Hank."

"I reckon I should go now that I know you're all right, Jack." Luke twisted the brim of his hat and watched her, making Jack squirm.

"Don't call her that," her mother growled.

"It's all right, Ma. I want him to."

Her mother crossed her arms, and her mouth looked as if it had been sewn up and the stitches pulled too tight. Jack didn't want to upset her more, knowing Ma was probably fit to be tied since her *little girl* had gotten hurt. But maybe she could twist things to her benefit. "My head sure hurts, and I'm getting hungry. Sure would like some shoofly pie after dinner tonight."

Her mother turned back toward her. "Oh, truly? Let me go

check and see if I have the fixings." Looking happy to have something to do, she scurried out of the room, her blue skirts whipping behind her.

Jack looked up at Luke. A wide grin covered his tanned face, and beside her, the doctor chuckled.

Luke shook his head. "Young lady, you're a stinker. You ought to get nothing but bread and water to eat tonight."

Relieved that Jack seemed to be fine except for some bumps, bruises, and a black eye, Luke left the room so the doctor could check her over without distractions. He stood in the kitchen doorway and watched Rachel rummage around inside her pantry. The lingering scent of baked pies filled the air, and his gaze drifted to the pie safe as he thought of the tasty treats. What kind would she serve with supper tonight?

She held up a jug with some thick, dark liquid in it. "What happened to all my molasses?"

Luke's gaze snapped back to Rachel. Her cheeks were flushed, and her blue eyes searching. She pushed some things around on the shelf, and Luke watched her, enjoying this time of seeing her relaxed and off guard. In spite of everything between them, he had missed her. Missed holding her close and making her giggle when he kissed her ear. Missed that look of adoration in her unusual eyes. Missed seeing her carefree like she'd once been.

The pretty girl he'd left eleven years ago had blossomed into a beautiful woman with pleasant curves and a voice that still stirred his senses. Something deep inside him wanted to protect her from the troubles of this world. Too bad they could never be together again.

Jack needed a father. But as much as he'd like the job, it wouldn't be him. He straightened. Would that job go to Rand Kessler?

He looked down at the floor. If he could manage to forgive Rachel completely, maybe they could be friends again. He'd heard a couple of sermons about forgiveness in the seven months that he'd been saved, but nobody ever mentioned *how* to do that.

Rachel turned around and gasped, splaying her hands across her chest. "Luke! I didn't hear you there."

He shrugged. "Doc needed to examine Jack, so I made myself scarce."

Rachel's face took on that pinched expression again, and she plunked the jar down hard on the table. "Why do you insist on calling my daughter by that hideous male nickname?"

"There's nothing wrong with the name Jack." He couldn't help grinning as he remembered a couple of rascally cavalry buddies with that moniker. "It's what she wants me to call her, and I figure it's a small matter if it makes her happy."

She shoved her hands to her hips. "It's not a small matter to me. She has a name. *Jac–que–line*."

Luke chuckled at how she emphasized each syllable. "I wanted you to know that I plan on walking over to the schoolhouse each day before and after classes. Maybe I can keep something like this from happening again."

Rachel's tense expression softened. "I'd appreciate that, but are you going to do anything to the boy who hurt my daughter?"

He rubbed his jaw with his forefinger and thumb and then scratched his neck, considering what the teacher had told him. It was probably just as well that Rachel didn't know Jack had jumped back into the fight after Butch turned loose of her. "Mrs. Fairland said that several kids were throwing punches at a big kid who tends to bully the younger ones."

"You mean that Laird boy, don't you?"

He shouldn't be surprised that she knew who he was talking about since Jack had probably told her about the kid. Luke nodded.

"What do you intend to do?" She hiked her chin as if daring him to argue.

"I'm going to have a talk with him and his father. You know his mother is gone, don't you?"

Rachel nodded. "She died about six months before James did. I didn't know her too well since she lived outside of town."

Luke clenched his fist at the mention of her deceased husband. He cleared his throat. "Well, Butch's father isn't exactly the nurturing type, if you know what I mean."

Her lovely blue eyes opened wide. For the first time, he noted the dark shadows under her eyes. Was the boardinghouse too much work for Rachel, combined with the stress of her unruly daughter?

He wanted to make things easier for her. "I'll let Murphy Laird know that if his boy causes any more trouble, he won't be allowed to come back to school. I'll also mosey around the schoolhouse during the times the children are at recess."

Rachel reached out and touched Luke's arm. The heat of her fingers nearly scalded him, and he could only stare at her small hand. Why did he always turn to cornmeal mush around this woman?

"Thank you, Luke. I'd feel much better knowing that you'll be keeping an eye on Jacqueline."

He didn't want to worry her by reminding her that Jack ran all over town and the outskirts. Just because Butch wasn't at school didn't mean Jack would be safe from him. But he would do his best to protect her. "I don't think Butch was the one who hurt her—at least I can't be sure. Could have been one of the others that hit Jack. Accidentally, I mean."

"Well, at any rate, I appreciate your help and that you carried Jacqueline home. I try hard to make her toe the line, but she still runs wild." Tears swarmed in Rachel's eyes. "I don't know what more to do to make her obey me."

Luke looked at the ceiling, noticing a spider web in one corner. He wanted to tug Rachel into his arms and ease her pain, but he couldn't. "I'll pray for her more, and you need to stick to your guns and make her mind you."

Rachel's sorrow ignited into flaming anger. "What do you

know about it? I tell her one thing, and she does exactly the opposite. I give her extra chores and make her write scriptures to help her see the error of her ways, but it seems to do no good. What else can I do?"

Luke shrugged. "Maybe she needs a good lickin' now and then."

Rachel sucked in a loud breath. "I will not spank my daughter."

"Why not? Spare the rod, spoil the child."

She spun around, leaning her hands on the edge of the dry sink. "I can't bring myself to spank her—not after. . ."

"After what?" Luke crossed the room and stood behind her, his hands aching to take her in his arms and drive away her anxiety.

"Nothing. Never mind."

"Tell me, Rachel."

She shook her head so hard, he thought sure the pins would fall out of her bun. "I can't. I don't want to talk about it."

Luke clamped down his jaw. What had happened to cause her to not want to discipline her child in the biblical manner? He didn't like where his train of thought was taking him. Knowing he shouldn't touch her, he reached out, placing his hands on her shoulders. As if he'd been struck by lightning, a fire surged up his arms and through his body. He closed his eyes, steeling himself against the desire to pull her close. He cleared his throat. "I'm here if you want to talk to me, Rach."

She stood stiff. Her sniffles made his heart ache. Made him want to take away her pain. *Father, help Rachel and Jack through this difficult time. Please heal Jack quickly and let there be no long-term effects from her injuries. Touch Rachel, and heal the hurting places in her heart.*

The doctor cleared his throat, and Luke stepped back. Heat swept up his neck at being caught nearly embracing Rachel. They both turned to face Dr. Phillips, and Rachel stepped in front of Luke, drying her eyes with her apron.

"How is she, Doctor? Will she be all right?"

The doc smiled and nodded. "Yes, she will. Keep her in bed for two days, and then let her get up and do things around the house. As long as she doesn't get dizzy and fall, she should be fine."

Rachel hurried forward and took the doctor's hands. "Oh, thank you, Hank."

"Don't send her back to school until next Monday, and just feed her soup and bread today, and some apple cider if you have any."

"So she shouldn't have any pie? I was going to make her that shoofly pie she loves."

The doctor glanced past Rachel to look at Luke, and he winked. "No, let's keep her on light things today. Give her eggs and biscuits in the morning, and if her stomach handles that without problems, she can go back to eating regularly."

Rachel nodded, and Luke grinned at the wily doctor. Wouldn't Jack be disappointed her little scheme hadn't succeeded?

Chapter 13

Her guests wouldn't like eating burnt pie tonight, but if the stage didn't arrive soon, that just might happen. Rachel checked the watch pinned to her bodice again and tapped her toe against the boardwalk. Seventeen minutes and no more. That was all she could wait. A vision of blackened pie crusts, burnt sugar, and a kitchen filled with smoke filled her mind. She glanced down the street in the direction the stage would arrive. A telegraphed message had informed her that the new lamp she'd ordered from a specialty shop in Sherman was on today's stage.

The bright sun gleamed down on the town, buzzing with its typical Monday morning activity. People ambled in and out of stores and offices, completing business and moving on to their next item of duty. She could hear the children at school squealing during recess. She shaded her eyes and searched for Jacqueline. Her daughter had been back to school for a week, and other than some teasing about her black eye, which the girl was quite proud of, there'd been no other problems. *Please, Lord, don't let her get in trouble today.*

Rachel swiped the sweat from her temple. Noon had yet to

arrive, and already the day felt as hot as August. Glancing around, she pulled the fabric away from her bodice and fanned in some air. Luke strode out of his office and crossed the dirt alleyway. She lowered her hand as her heart flip-flopped.

The birthday party the town had thrown for him several weeks ago had been one she'd remember for a long time, mainly because of her disappointment. She'd hoped Lookout's marshal would ask her to dance for old time's sake, but instead, he'd seemed content just to fill up on her pie and watch the town while chatting with his cousins. Rand hadn't had any problem asking her, though. He would have danced all evening if she had been agreeable. Oh, what was she going to do about him?

Before Luke's return, she'd toyed with the idea of marrying Rand. She would have a ranch house to tend but not the huge boardinghouse. Rand was a good man, even if he was a few years younger than her. But even though she found him a pleasant man to confer with, she didn't love him. And she couldn't marry another man she didn't love. She'd been working up her nerve to tell him just that when Luke had returned to Lookout.

Luke. Now that was another subject. Her throat tightened. She could never tell him that she still cared for him. Had cared, even when she'd been married to James. No wonder her husband had been so dissatisfied. Had he sensed that she didn't love him? But how could he expect love after what he'd done to her?

Her heart ricocheted like a bullet fired inside a stone house when Luke turned in her direction. Luke and James had been friends before she married. Oh, how she wished things had been different—that she could go back and rewrite her story.

"Morning." Luke tipped his hat and slowed his pace, but that wary look that had been in his gaze ever since he returned to Lookout still lingered. "Uh. . .what's for supper tonight?"

Rachel sighed inwardly, wishing he'd talk to her about something other than food or his laundry, but he seemed determined to keep her at bay. He'd let his defenses down the day Jacqueline had gotten hurt, but they were back in full force. Rachel should rejoice that he'd even bothered to say good day to her when he normally tried to avoid her. *Whatever happened to forgiving those who hurt you?* "Pot roast, your favorite."

"Sounds good." Luke nodded and headed into the stage office.

Too bad it was only her cooking he loved.

She checked her watch again. If she wasn't expecting that new lamp—the one she wanted to collect before the rowdy stagehands knocked it about any more than it already had been, she would return home. The pies would be done soon. At least she only had Mr. Sampson, a traveling salesman, staying at the boardinghouse and wouldn't need to fix an overly large meal.

Her heart quickened at the rumble of horses' hooves and the jangling of harnesses. The boardwalk shook as the stage rounded the corner, looking as if it would tip over, even though it never did.

"Whoa!" the driver shouted, pulling back on the reins. The coach slowed to a halt right in front of the Barfield Stage office amid a cloud of dust and the snorting and heaving of the four sweaty horses.

The shotgun guard climbed down, dropped the steps, and opened the door. A nicely dressed, albeit dust-coated gentleman stepped down then offered his hand to a pretty blond woman dressed in a blue calico. She accepted his assistance and exited the stage. The young woman glanced around, and when she spotted Rachel, she smiled and climbed up to the boardwalk, heading straight for her, straightening her bonnet. "Good day, ma'am. I was wondering if you might point me to Luke Davis's office. I do believe he's the city marshal—at least that's what he said in his correspondence to me."

Rachel's chest tightened. "Correspondence?"

The woman knocked the dust from her skirt and looked up. "Oh yes. I'm Leah Bennett, Marshal Davis's mail-order bride."

Rachel felt the blood drain from her face. Her mouth was suddenly as dry as a Texas creek bed in midsummer, and her knees quivered as her world tilted. She grabbed a post holding up the boardwalk roof to balance herself. "Luke's getting married?"

The woman's cheeks turned strawberry red. Eyes the color of a blue jay sparkled. "Well, that's the plan. At least that's what his letter said. So could you please point me in the right direction?"

Rachel glanced at the stage office, knowing Luke would come out at any moment.

Another woman who'd just disembarked from the stage also stepped up next to Rachel. Worried green eyes flitted between Rachel and the blond woman. Her pale face stood out against the curly curtain of auburn tresses that had escaped her chignon. A deep wrinkle creased one cheek, and she had that foggy look of just having awakened. "Uh. . .pardon me, but did you say city marshal Luke Davis is the man you are to marry?"

Miss Bennett nodded and smiled. "Why yes, I told you that right after we pulled out of Sherman depot, Miss O'Neil."

"Saints preserve us." She pressed her fingertips to her forehead. "I barely remember you sayin' you were to be married, but I must have fallen asleep. I never heard who 'twas you were to wed. What a dreadful mess." The woman's gaze flittered around the town as she wrung her hands. "Whatever will I do? I've nowhere else to go."

Confused at the woman's distress and intrigued by her lilting accent, Rachel put aside her shock at Miss Bennett's declaration and rested her hand on Miss O'Neil's shoulder. "What's the matter? Maybe I can help."

The auburn beauty glanced at Miss Bennett again. "I don't know how to tell you; truly I don't."

"Whatever it is, just spit it out." Leah Bennett hiked her chin and glowered like a schoolmarm scolding her students.

"I. . .oh, how is it something like this could happen?" Sympathy edged Miss O'Neil's green eyes. Wavy wisps of hair fluttered on the warm spring breeze. "I, too, have come to marry Luke Davis."

Rachel's battered heart endured another jab. What had Luke done? How dare he send for two strangers to marry when she had been there all along!

If he was the man of God he claimed to be, wouldn't he forgive her for betraying him?

Miss Bennett's blue eyes widened. "Why, that's preposterous. There must be some mistake."

"Nay, 'tis true. I assure you. I have Marshal Davis's letter right here." Miss O'Neil opened her tattered reticule and pulled out a crinkled page. She unfolded it and handed it to Miss Bennett.

Rachel couldn't help leaning over. She scanned the words, and her dread and confusion mounted when she saw Luke's name signed at the end of the letter. There was only one way to get to the bottom of this distressing situation, and that was to confront Luke. Fortunately—or not—he exited the stage office at that moment, pausing outside the door to look at a piece of paper he held.

"But I also have a letter, and I think you'll see that mine is dated earlier than yours." Miss Bennett quickly retrieved her missive and passed it around.

Rachel pursed her lips tight. This handwriting was different from that of the other letter. Couldn't the women see that? Somebody was toying with their affections, and that was wrong. But was Luke to blame?

He stood outside the stage office door, held a piece of paper up to the sun, and studied it.

"There's Luke now," Rachel said. Both women turned to face their intended.

"Oh my, he's quite handsome—in a rugged sort of way." Miss O'Neil's cheeks flushed, giving color to her pale complexion, and she fanned her face with her gloved hand. "And so tall."

Luke turned and walked toward them, paying no special attention to the women staring at him. "Ladies." He flashed Rachel a curious look, nodded, and proceeded to walk around them.

Rachel sidestepped into his path, barely able to keep a lid on her irritation and her disappointment. "Marshal Davis, it would seem we have a bit of a dilemma here."

Luke surveyed the two women; then he turned his innocent gaze on Rachel. "What dilemma? How can I help?"

Rachel clenched her fists. How could he be so naive? If he sent for a bride—or two—wouldn't he be expecting them? She hiked her chin. "It appears both of these ladies have come to town to claim you as their future husband."

"Pardon me?" Luke would have thought Rachel was joking if not for the anger in her voice and her pinched expression. He folded the payroll shipment information he'd been studying and stuffed it into his pocket, thinking he must have heard her wrong. "What are you talking about?"

"Oh dear. You tell him." The shorter, thinner woman with big green eyes and hair the color of a sorrel mare attempted to strangle the life out of the strings of her handbag.

Had they been robbed on the stage? Had some man acted inappropriately toward them? Luke gritted his teeth, ready to take action to defend them if necessary. But hadn't Rachel said something about marriage?

He cast a glance at her. Rachel's light blue eyes looked as cold as a January day in Colorado. What could have happened to turn her to ice?

The blue-eyed blond tossed her head like a mustang and narrowed her gaze. "It would seem there's been some kind of mistake, Marshal. I'm Leah Bennett. The mail-order bride you've been corresponding with."

The thinner woman sucked in a gasp. "But that simply cannot be the truth, for I have a letter right here, askin' me to m–marry you."

The Irish lilt in the woman's voice caught his attention, but his eyes widened as his mind grappled with what the women had said. "You're both here—to marry *me*?"

Rachel crossed her arms and frowned at him. "What have you done, Luke?"

"Nothing, I promise." He raised his hands, as if in surrender, and his gaze zigzagged among the three women. "I didn't write to either of these ladies."

The brides glanced at each other, apprehension evident in their eyes.

"Well, someone did. So what are you going to do about it?" Rachel crossed her arms and stared at him.

The trio of females, two steaming and one near weeping, standing side by side, created a unified barricade on the boardwalk; and around them, a crowd was gathering, casting curious looks in his direction. Luke's first thought was to flee, but he held his ground like a man and scanned his baffled mind, trying to make some sense of this. He knew he hadn't written to these women, but evidently someone had, and he aimed to find out who. Dallying with a woman's affections may not be a legal issue, but in his book, it was wrong, and now these ladies were suffering and inconvenienced because someone had pretended to be him. Besides, impersonating a lawman might just be a crime.

Luke lifted his hat and raked his fingers through his hair. "I guess you'd better get the women situated at the boardinghouse. Then we'll sit down and see if we can get to the bottom of this. I can assure both of you that I did not write those letters. But I intend to find out who did."

Chapter 14

Rachel grasped the folds of her skirt. How could Luke expect her to take responsibility for *his* mail-order brides? It was unconscionable. She sighed, pushing away her irritation, knowing none of this was the brides' fault. There was no other place in Lookout where a decent woman could spend the night, unless with a family. Smothering her anger and breaking heart, she faced Luke. "If you'll see to their luggage, I'll show the women to the boardinghouse. Ladies, please follow me."

Thank goodness she had a large enough roast to feed the additional people. She could add more potatoes and carrots, and the two pies would be sufficient for dessert. Rachel stopped in her tracks. "Oh, no! My pies."

She hiked up her skirt and dashed for her kitchen, not caring if the brides followed or not. She raced in front of a wagon, forcing the driver to yank back on the reins.

"Hey, watch it, lady."

Everyone probably thought her to be as crazy as a rabid skunk, but if she didn't save her pies, there would be no dessert for supper tonight. And with two women in the house, that would be a disaster.

Rachel stormed in the front door, through the narrow hallway, and into the kitchen. She stopped, a hand pressed to her heaving chest. No black smoke rose from the oven door. Instead of the stench of scorched sugar, the fragrant scent of apples cooked in cinnamon filled the heated kitchen. Her gaze landed on the perfectly cooked pies cooling on the counter. What was going on?

Someone clomped out of her bedroom at a quick pace. Jacqueline rounded the corner and halted wide-eyed when she saw her mother. Gratitude to her daughter for saving the pies flowed through Rachel, but the knowledge that the girl was supposed to be at school squelched her enthusiasm. "What are you doing home?"

Jacqueline shrugged and leaned against the doorjamb. The pretty dress Rachel had insisted she wear this morning had been replaced by a faded blouse with rolled up sleeves and black trousers. The ever-present western boots covered her feet, and her daughter's hair hung in straggly braids with a sprig of grass here and there as if she'd been wrestling on the ground. The deep purple and black that had surrounded her eye had given way to yellow and green. "I got hot, and I was still hungry after dinner, so I came home to change and get something else to eat."

"You know you're not allowed to wear pants to school. They are strictly for gardening, and if you keep wearing them, I'll burn them in the trash barrel." Rachel forced her voice to sound stern. Luke would be proud of her for standing up to Jacqueline, not that it mattered now that his "brides" had come to town.

Jacqueline's eyes went wide as biscuits, but she didn't comment.

"Did you ask Mrs. Fairland if you could leave the school premises?"

The girl shrugged again. She hadn't asked permission. She never did.

"Let me fix your hair, and then you need to change into a dress and get back to school."

"Aw, Ma, it's nearly over, and me and Jonesy's goin' fishing."

Rachel gasped in spite of her determination not to let her daughter fluster her. "Fishing! You most certainly aren't going anywhere with that boy. He's far too old for you to be hanging around with, and besides, you need to go back to school."

"Ah, Jonesy's all right, and Mrs. Fairland is just testing the little kids this afternoon. There's nothing for us big kids to do but practice cipherin' or read boring books."

Jacqueline hated reading, and it didn't seem right to make her sit still all afternoon if they weren't working. But she needed to be in school. And why did she always want to play with those older boys? It wasn't as if she was interested in them in a womanly way. Her daughter just wanted to be one of the gang—something that perplexed Rachel to no end. She shook her head.

"I'll bring home some bass you can cook for supper." Jacqueline's dark blue eyes twinkled. She strode to the jar and snagged two sugar cookies, bit off a chunk of one and stuck the other in her pocket.

She'd planned to fix roast beef for supper, but fish *would* taste good and didn't cost anything, and she did have a big issue to deal with immediately. Maybe it would be better if her daughter were not around until things with the mail-order brides settled down. Still, she couldn't abide by her missing school to go fishing. A knock sounded at the front door. The brides had arrived.

Jacqueline darted past her and out the back door. "I'll be home before supper."

"No, wait." Rachel spun toward the back door. "I didn't say you could go."

"You're welcome. I saved your pies, you know." Jacqueline yanked a fishing pole off the back porch and raced toward the river. A boy Rachel recognized as Jonesy stepped in beside her as she passed behind Luke's house.

"Oh, heavenly Father, what am I going to do with this mischievous daughter You gave me?" Rachel should go after Jacqueline and insist she go back to school, but she didn't want her daughter pitching a fit in front of the new guests.

"Rachel?"

"In the kitchen." Needing a moment to calm herself, she checked the oven to make sure the pies hadn't spilled over; then she hurried to the entryway, where Luke stood with his two brides. The thought of them living under her roof, eating meals she cooked, and asking her about the man they'd come to marry made her stomach swirl. Of course, they couldn't both marry him, but the idea of even one doing so made her want to cry.

The stage line's shotgun rider stood on the porch, holding a small trunk. Rachel forced a smile at the women, both young and pretty enough to snag the eye of any man. It was easy to see how Luke could prefer them over her. Pushing away her warring thoughts, she gave her guests a true smile. They didn't know her feelings and were innocents in this awful ordeal. She owed them her kindness and hospitality. "Follow me, please."

Luke's snort erupted behind her. "You said that already, just before you hiked up your skirts and made a mad dash through town as if your dress was on fire." He chuckled, and the man outside joined him.

Heat rose to Rachel's cheeks. "Yes, well, I remembered the pies I had in the oven. I was distracted by the unusual circumstances and had lost track of the time. You'd be sorely disappointed if they'd burned and you didn't have any dessert tonight." She glared at Luke, and he had the good sense to look chagrined.

Miss O'Neil cleared her throat. "They do smell delicious. And such a lovely home you have."

"Thank you. I apologize, Miss Bennett, Miss O'Neil, for running off and leaving you standing at the depot. My name is Rachel Hamilton, by the way. Let me show you to your rooms." Both women smiled, and Rachel felt as if they'd forgiven her. She started up the steps to the second floor, holding back a sigh at the spectacle she must have made. These women probably wondered if they'd be safe in her home.

Upstairs she stopped in the wide hallway. She pointed to a

matching set of doors on the far wall. "The door to the left is a washroom where I have fresh water each morning and afternoon. The door on the right leads to the back stairs, but I always keep it locked. There are four rooms on this floor that I rent out."

She stepped forward and opened the bedroom door to the left of the main stairway. "Miss Bennett, would this suit you?"

The woman stepped past her and glanced around the cheery room decorated in a soft blue and white. "Yes, this is very nice. Just have that man place my trunk along the wall, and please take care with that. It's my hope chest."

Rachel turned to the man and waved her hand toward the wall. "If you don't mind, please put the trunk where the lady indicated."

He lugged the chest inside the room and set it down. He nodded at the women and quickly took his leave. Halfway down the stairs on the landing, he paused. "There's a crate for you at the depot, Mrs. Hamilton. I'll fetch it and bring it to you."

Rachel smiled at the dust-coated man. "Thank you. I appreciate your assistance. And please take care with that. It's my new lamp."

The man nodded and continued down the stairs. Luke stood like a statue in the hallway, longingly watching him.

"Marshal." Miss Bennett cocked her head and batted her eyes at Luke. "My satchel, if you please. It's the one tucked under your arm."

Luke looked as if he were afraid to step into her room, what with the woman batting her lashes at him as if she'd been chopping onions. Rachel ducked her head to hide her frown. Would Miss Bennett win Luke's affections with her alluring ways? Though travel worn, both of the young women were lovely and didn't have the look of a haggard boardinghouse owner and mother of a precocious child.

Luke still stood at the threshold, holding three satchels and looking as if he'd like to tuck tail and run. She'd never seen a man so uncomfortable with women. Rachel let him off the hook and took the carpetbag he held tight under his muscled upper arm and set it on Miss Bennett's bed. She slipped past Luke, relieving him of a second smaller satchel, and opened the door across the hall.

"Miss O'Neil, perhaps you'd like the green room, as we call it." Rachel stepped inside, scanning the area to make sure all was in order, even though she already knew it was. She loved the pale floral wallpaper and the spring green curtains. The flower garden quilt on the bed also had green accents, as well as a pleasing variety of pinks, violets, and blues.

Miss O'Neil gasped. "I've never stayed in a room so lovely. 'Tis charming, it is."

"Thank you for your help, Marshal. We should probably let the women freshen up a bit before we discuss the—situation." Rachel lifted her brows at Luke. His ears reddened, and he handed her the final satchel and headed toward the stairs.

"Ladies, welcome to Hamilton House. Miss O'Neil, I'll have your trunk delivered as soon as that man returns with it."

The young woman's pale cheeks turned the color of an apple. "Um. . .this is all I have, mum."

Rachel hid her surprise at the young woman's lack of belongings. Maybe she planned to send more along later, after she got settled. Only she might not be settling here once all was said and done. "All right then. Please make yourself at home."

Miss O'Neil's gaze darted across the hall at Miss Bennett's room, and she stepped forward, wringing her hands. "How much is a room for the night?" she whispered.

"Two dollars, which includes your meals, or twelve dollars for a full week."

"Oh, blessit be, I uh. . .can only afford to stay two nights. I thought I would arrive and be married right away. Perhaps you might need some assistance here? I'm used to hard work."

Compassion for the woman surged through Rachel. The girl couldn't be more than seventeen or eighteen. Rachel couldn't afford to hire any help, but maybe someone else in Lookout could. "Don't worry about that now. Things will work out."

Rachel met Luke downstairs and motioned him to go outside. She paced the front porch, arms crossed over her chest, waiting on Luke to get his nerve up to talk to her. If her heart hadn't been split in two, she might have been tempted to feel sorry for the man.

He lifted his hat and slapped it against his leg. "Look, Rachel, I didn't write to those women. I knew nothing about them before you stopped me at the depot."

"Do you think this is some kind of sick prank? Those women have traveled who knows how far to marry you, and I've just learned that at least one of them has very little money." Rachel sighed and looked across the street. "If you're not responsible, who do you think is? Who would toy with two women like this?"

"I have my suspicions, but I want to do some investigating before I say anything."

Rachel nodded. "All right. Do you want to question the women?"

Luke shrugged. He'd probably never talk to them if he didn't have to. If Rachel wasn't so disturbed by the whole event and what it could mean to her, she might have found some humor in the situation.

"I'll try to get back before supper."

"Maybe we should talk after that. No sense in spoiling anyone's meal."

Luke nodded and walked away but suddenly stopped and turned back to her. "Oh, hey, Mrs. Fairland gave me a note earlier and asked me to pass it on to you."

Rachel puffed air into her cheeks and took the message. She knew what the schoolteacher had to say but opened the note anyway. Scanning the message, her frustration grew. That rascally child. She had been one of the children who was supposed to take the test this afternoon.

Wadding up the paper in her hand, Rachel watched Luke's

long legs take him away. Somewhere in the back of her mind, she'd hoped they could have a second chance. He'd seemed truly surprised about the two brides, but was that just for her benefit? None of it made any sense. If he wanted a mail-order bride, why would he order *two* of them?

The stagehand nodded as he passed Luke, carrying a crate on his shoulder. Her lamp. In all the hubbub she'd forgotten about it.

Rachel stepped aside and allowed the man to pass in front of her. "Where do you want this, Mrs. Hamilton?"

"Just set it on the parlor floor for now, and thank you so much for your help."

"My pleasure, ma'am."

He lowered the crate to her decorated rug, and the sound of clinking glass only added to her misery. Her new lamp was broken, just like her heart.

Chapter 15

Rachel finished sweeping the kitchen floor and glanced outside again. The sun had set, and darkness covered the land. She swept the dirt out the back door and stood listening to the crickets. Where was Luke? Had he gotten tied up smoothing out a disturbance, or was he simply avoiding the confrontation with the brides?

She shook her head. For a lawman, he avoided females like a mouse hid from a tomcat. With his gentle ways and soft-spoken demeanor, he was far different from James. That alone made him attractive to her.

She took the stack of dried dishes from the counter and set them on the shelf near the dining room door. Glancing around the tidy kitchen, a measure of satisfaction filled her. The flickering glow of the two lanterns mounted on the wall illuminated the room. Soft yellow walls looked cheery with the light blue gingham curtains. Every utensil had a place, and each item was in its place. At least it was as long as Jacqueline wasn't in the kitchen. The girl used things and set them down, never thinking to wash them or put them away.

Rachel shook her head, still tired from her battle with Jacqueline. When she'd told her daughter that she'd get no pie after supper because she had lied and skipped out of taking that test, Jacqueline had pitched a royal fit. Both the brides had declined pie themselves and had quickly disappeared into their rooms. Mr. Sampson, one never to refuse dessert, had taken his slice and eaten it on the porch to avoid the girl's ranting. Glancing down, Rachel noticed her white-knuckled grip on the back of the chair. She released her hold and glanced at the ceiling. "Lord, help me raise this child You've given me."

Three quick knocks sounded on the kitchen door. Rachel jumped as Luke slipped in.

"About time you showed up. The brides went to bed an hour ago."

"Sorry. I got busy." He studied the floor for a moment then glanced up, the lantern light shimmering in his coffee-colored eyes. "I have my suspicions as to what happened, but I haven't been able to confirm them yet."

"Care to share?" Rachel crossed her arms and leaned back against the worktable.

"Not till I know for sure. I could be wrong." He captured her gaze, sending her stomach in a tizzy. How could he affect her so when she was still upset with him?

He glanced at the stove where she kept his dinner warm whenever he missed a meal. His features relaxed when he saw the meal covered with an inverted pie plate. Had he thought she wouldn't feed him because she was irritated?

"Have a seat. You must be starving by now." She retrieved his dinner and placed it on her worktable.

For once he didn't snatch his plate and disappear out the door. Luke washed his hands in the bucket of water sitting in the sink and dried them with a towel. He removed his worn Stetson, revealing a sweat ring that had darkened his brown hair, making it look black. He hung the hat on the edge of the ladder-back chair, sat, and picked up his fork.

Rachel resisted the urge to sigh. As an adolescent, she'd dreamed many nights of Luke and her sharing a meal together in their own kitchen. But all of her girlish dreams had been dashed in one horrible afternoon. Luke avoided looking at her and put away his food as if it were his last meal. If he wasn't willing to let her in on his thoughts about the brides, she might as well go to bed. Tomorrow would be a long day, and dawn came early. She walked toward the hallway. "I'm plumb tuckered out. See you in the morning."

"Rachel. . ."

She stopped but didn't turn to face him. How could he put such pleading into her name?

"Look at me, please."

She took a deep breath, gathering strength, and then spun to face him, bracing her shoulder against the doorjamb. His miserable expression made her want to wrap her arms around him and tell him things would be all right. But would they? There was only one Luke Davis, and two women had set their hearts on marrying him.

His lips pressed together so hard they turned pale. "I hope you know that I had nothing to do with this. I could never toy with a woman's affections in such a manner."

That's what her heart believed, but her mind wasn't so sure. Someone had written to the women, probably even sent money. If some man had wanted a bride for himself, why pretend to be Luke? Everyone knew the city marshal's pay wasn't that great. Why, a woman would either need to be self-sufficient or very desperate to want to marry a low-salaried lawman who put his life on the line everyday. Or be in love. She glanced at him again, sitting there, wanting her support. He'd once supported her, helped her whenever things had gone bad. His had been the shoulder she cried on for so many years—when her pa died, when things were difficult—but that was a long time ago.

She sighed heavily and tugged out a seat across from him. "I believe that you wouldn't purposely dally with a woman's affections, Luke." Heaven knew she wished he'd toy with her affections, but he no longer looked at her with love in his eyes. At least he was talking to her now.

"Thanks, Rach." A soft smile tugged at Luke's lips, sending Rachel's heart pounding. He picked up his fork and attacked the pot roast, potatoes, and carrots. It was a good thing she'd gone ahead and fixed the meal, because Jack had returned home without any fish.

"Would you like me to heat up your coffee? I was heading to bed, so I banked the fire and put the pot on the back burner."

Luke shook his head. "It's plenty warm. So. . ." He glanced up. "How are the women faring? Are they terribly upset?"

Rachel gave him a stern look. "Of course they are. Both had their hearts set on marrying you. They left their homes and traveled hundreds of miles, only to find out the man they planned to marry knew nothing about them. Oh, and did I mention there was instant competition for your attention, being as there were two brides, not one?"

"It's a fine mess, all right. When Gar—" Luke shoved another bite into his mouth, as if he'd said something he hadn't intended on saying.

"What?" Rachel's mind raced as she tried to figure out what he'd almost said.

"Never mind." For the next few minutes, he wolfed down the rest of his food; then he leaned on his elbows, staring into his coffee cup. "I have a little money. I've been saving to buy a house. I suppose I could give each of the ladies enough cash so they could get back to wherever it was they came from."

Luke was going to buy a house? Rachel's mouth dropped open. Could he have accumulated that much money on a soldier's salary? Having a house meant he'd be staying in town. How could she spend the next twenty or thirty years living in the same town as Luke, watching him one day marry another woman and then raise their children? Dread melded her to her chair. She thought of the letters from her aunt, asking her to bring Jacqueline and move to Kansas City. Maybe now was the time to finally consider her offer.

Luke glanced up, his forehead creased. "Do you think that's a good idea, Rach?"

"Hmm?" What had he said before tilting her world off its axis? "Oh, um. . .I don't know. I'm not sure either woman wishes to return where she came from. And if you weren't the one to send for them, it isn't your duty to provide for them. Why would someone impersonate you?"

Luke's guarded expression revealed nothing. "I don't want to say until I'm sure."

Rachel scanned her mind, trying to think who might be out of town that he would suspect. The Ralstons had gone to Dallas to care for her elderly mother. Garrett and Mark Corbett were on a run, delivering freight for the company they co-owned. The mayor was at a convention in Dallas.

Wait a minute! She slapped her hand on the table, receiving a curious stare from Luke.

That was it! Rachel stood so abruptly her chair fell back and banged against the floor. Luke jumped up and spun toward the door, his hand reaching for his pistol. Rachel might have smiled if not for her building anger.

He twisted back around, his diligent gaze checking the other doorways then finally settling on her. "What's wrong?"

Rachel scowled and heaved angered breaths out her nose. "It was *them*, wasn't it?"

"Who?"

"Garrett and Mark. Those two hooligans have been pulling pranks for as long as I've known them. They were the ones who ordered the brides." Rachel picked up her chair and set it aright. It was a good thing those men were out of town, because she wasn't sure what she might do right now if they weren't. "I'm a little surprised at Mark doing such a thing, or maybe Garrett did it on his own. I wouldn't put it past *him*."

Luke's gaze found something interesting on the floor, his ears turning red. "I told you I'd rather not say until I can confirm it."

She marched around the table and stopped a foot from him. "So, you *do* suspect them. They've done a lot of ornery things in their lives, but this takes the cake. It would serve them right if you made *them* marry those poor girls, except I'd hate for either one to get strapped with the likes of those two yahoos."

A tiny smile tugged at Luke's lips. "It would serve them right, wouldn't it?" He chuckled.

Rachel was tempted to smack him, but a tiny giggle swelled up inside her, begging to be set free. She could imagine the pinched expressions on Mark and Garrett's faces when Luke forced them into shotgun weddings. She pressed her lips together, but a little snort erupted, making Luke laugh. Rachel joined him, feeling a release of tension for the first time that whole day.

Luke's laugh deepened, and Rachel shoved her hand over his mouth. "Shh. . .you're going to wake the whole house."

Humor still glimmered in his eyes, but he pulled her hand down, keeping quiet. "My cousins should be back tomorrow, and then we'll see what they have to say about all this." He shrugged. "Could be they aren't even involved."

"Uh-huh, and it's going to snow in July in Texas."

Luke tightened his grip on her hand, sending pleasant shivers up her arm. What he meant as a friendly gesture made her want to lean in and hug him. Pulling her hand from his, she stepped back, knowing that he wasn't aware he'd let his guard down around her for only the second time since coming back to town. "It's late, and tomorrow will be a trying day. Best we get some sleep."

Luke nodded. He claimed his hat and walked toward the door. "Sleep tight, sweet Rachel."

She watched in the moonlight as he strode toward his house,

and then she closed the back door. Had he purposely used that endearment, or had it just slipped out? Rachel scraped his plate and set it in the sink along with his cup. She turned down the lantern and ambled toward the downstairs bedroom she shared with her daughter. Her hand caught the doorknob, and she paused, thinking how warm and soft Luke's lips had felt against her fingertips when she'd covered his mouth. A sudden thought sent warm hope traveling through her being. If Luke had no intention of marrying the brides, maybe there was still hope for her.

The next morning, Luke rode Alamo back into Lookout after a brisk ride. With most of his duties in town, he'd neglected to exercise his horse. Both he and his mount had benefited from the long ride. He breathed in a deep breath when he saw his cousins' wagon parked outside the freight office. He didn't care for confrontations, and having been a cavalry officer, he'd had his share of them, but this was different. Innocent females had been given false hope—their emotions toyed with, their dreams smashed. "Help me not to lose my temper, Lord."

Luke tied his horse to the hitching post outside the freight office and stormed inside. He shoved his hands to his hips and eyed both men. Mark and Garrett looked up from their desks where they'd been working and exchanged a glance. "I reckon you heard what happened yesterday."

Both men had the audacity to grin.

"Good morning to you, too." Mark chuckled.

"This isn't a laughing matter." Luke crossed his arms and glared at the two. "I can't believe you would do such a low-down thing."

"What thing is that?" Garrett leaned back in his chair, hands crossed over his stomach, obviously trying to look innocent.

"You know good and well what I'm talking about." He paced the room, casting glares at his cousins. Too bad this wasn't a legal offense or he'd haul them both of to jail and see who had the last laugh. Then again, maybe he could arrest them for impersonating a lawman.

Mark tapped a finger on his desk, his blue eyes gleaming. "Well, you did say you'd marry if the right woman came along."

"When did I say that?"

"The evening of your birthday," Mark said.

"That's right. We just figured you needed some help finding her." Garrett nodded as he straightened a stack of papers on his desk. "We wrote to several women who had advertisements in the newspaper but sure didn't expect more than one would be willing to travel all the way to Lookout." Garrett leaned back in his chair and put his feet on his desk, crossing his hands behind his head. "We didn't know the brides had arrived until we got back in town this morning and stopped at the café for breakfast. Weren't sure any of them would show up."

Mark nodded. "Everyone was talking about it."

"Them? Just how many did you write to?"

"Five." Garrett stretched, holding up all the fingers on one hand. "But a couple weren't interested in moving to Texas." He stroked his chin with his index finger and thumb and waggled his brows. "Two did, huh? Guess you get to pick which one you like best. Are they pretty?"

Luke couldn't believe his ears. What were they thinking? Mark and Garrett had always been rascals, but they'd never been purposely hurtful. "How could you trifle with those women? Don't you realize they've left their homes and families and traveled hundreds of miles in hope of marrying me?"

"Well, you can make dreams come true for one of them at least." Mark grinned. "So, are they pretty?"

Grinding his back teeth, Luke spun toward the window and checked to make sure things were still quiet outside. It wouldn't do to let his cousins know both women were pretty enough to catch any man's eye. "They're nice enough, I suppose."

"What do they look like?" Garrett's chair squeaked.

Luke shrugged one shoulder. He might as well tell them, or they'd just hurry out the door and go see for themselves. "They're very different. One's blond with blue eyes. The other is shorter and has reddish brown hair and green eyes."

Mark chuckled. "I thought you weren't interested. Sounds like you looked them over real good. Mmm. . .I always imagined falling in love with a redhead. If you don't want her, maybe I'll try my hand at wooing her."

Luke turned back to face the two scoundrels. "These are people we're talking about, not horses or cattle. You can't play with a woman's emotions. They're not like us. They're sensitive."

Mark grinned. "I had no idea you knew that much about females. Is that why you avoid them?"

Luke studied the dirt on his boot tips. Did he avoid women? Maybe one in particular. "I see women all over town every day."

Garrett dropped his feet to the floor with a loud *thunk*. "Married women don't count. When was the last time you showed interest in a gal of marrying age?"

Luke glanced at the walls of the freight office as he contemplated Garrett's question. A large area map hung on one unpainted wall with pins stuck in it indicating the smaller towns that his cousins delivered freight to. Papers littered Garrett's desk in haphazard piles while Mark's were neatly stacked. Boxes and crates waiting to be shipped filled one wall.

His cousins didn't understand the position he was in. "If I show attention to anyone past school age, I'll have all the mamas in the county wanting me to come for dinner and court their daughters."

"Oh, to eat good food with a pretty woman. What a cross to bear." Mark folded his arms over his chest and leaned his hip on his desk. "I might believe that if there were any marriageable women in Lookout."

"We've provided the perfect solution," Garrett said. "Pick one of the brides, marry up with her, and then all the mamas will turn their eyes on someone else."

Luke smiled for the first time since entering the freight office. "Yeah, like you two yahoos."

"Hey, I don't mind a home-cooked meal and a pretty woman to share it with once in a while. It's just too bad there aren't some in this town." Garrett picked up a pencil and started shaving the end with his pocketknife. Mark scowled at the mess he was making on the floor.

"I think the best thing would be for you two to marry the brides." Luke held back his grin and tried to appear stern.

Garrett stood and pointed a finger at Luke. "Now hold on a minute. We ordered those brides for you, not us. I'm sorry that two of 'em showed up. I figured when it came right down to it, they'd back out. I never expected to get so many responses to my advertisement."

Luke stiffened. "You posted a notice about *me*?"

"It sounded like a good idea at the time," Mark said.

"What did you say? That I'm a desperate marshal who needs a wife? I don't even own a home, for Pete's sake."

Garrett shrugged and tried to keep a straight face, but it wasn't working. "Just that you were handsome, well established, friendly. Stuff like that."

"Well established? Did you also tell them that I live in a one-room cabin next to the boardinghouse where I take all my meals? I don't even own a cookstove. What woman would want to live in a cabin with no stove?"

Mark grabbed a cup off his desk and filled it from the coffeepot he picked up at the café each morning. "Want some?"

Luke scowled at him. "No, I don't want coffee. This is serious business. We need to decide what to do with those women." He fingered his pistol handle. "I'm still of a mind to march you down to the boardinghouse and make you two marry those gals."

Mark sat and took a sip from his cup. "Have you spent any

time getting to know them?"

Luke stared at the ceiling. This conversation wasn't going as planned. Perhaps he should have let Rachel join him as he confronted his cousins, but he'd told her he could handle them. Could be he'd overestimated his abilities. "No, I haven't. They just arrived yesterday while you two were conveniently out delivering freight. I got them situated at the boardinghouse while I tried to figure out what in the world was going on." He picked a paper off of Garrett's desk and examined the script, receiving a scowl from his cousin. "Once I recognized the handwriting in the letters those gals showed me, I knew pretty much what had happened."

Garrett squirmed and looked at Mark. "We were just trying to help you. Like get you a bride for your birthday."

"My birthday was weeks ago."

"Yeah, well, it takes time to communicate with a woman. You can't hurry them, and you have to answer all their nitpicky questions 'cause they're suspicious," said Mark.

"I wonder why." Luke shoved his hands to his hips and glowered at them.

"What you need to do is get to know the women. You can't be certain one of them isn't the gal for you unless you spend time with them. Why not take each one to the café for dinner or supper?" Garrett's gaze lit up as if he'd just solved the dilemma.

"And have the whole town talkin'?" Luke rolled his eyes. The town was already talking. All yesterday afternoon and evening people had stared at him and whispered as he walked along the street.

"Look, you two are the reason those women came to town. I'm going to talk to Rachel and see when's a good time, and you two are coming to the boardinghouse to apologize and make amends. Is that clear?"

His cousins shared a glance, but both men nodded. Luke stared each one in the eye, making sure they understood he was serious. "I'll let you know what time the meeting is."

He shoved open the door, and several people on the boardwalk gawked at him with curious expressions. He liked small-town life except when he was the main attraction, and he didn't want to admit that he enjoyed the time he'd spent chatting with Rachel last night. It was almost as if they were friends again, without their troubled past. He wouldn't likely get to do that again if he was with another woman. In spite of all that had happened between him and Rachel, she was the only woman he'd ever known as a close friend. A part of him longed to rekindle that relationship, but could they do that? Just remain friends?

They'd have to, because that was all he was willing to be.

Chapter 16

Rachel, Jacqueline, and the brides sat at one end of the dining table while Mr. Sampson ate at the other end. Rachel sighed inwardly. You'd think the middle-aged salesman wouldn't mind eating with a couple of pretty women, but he almost seemed afraid of them. Maybe he feared one of them would set her sights on him. She smiled and ducked her head.

He wolfed down the last of his eggs and stood. "Thank you for another fine breakfast, Mrs. Hamilton. See you at supper tonight." His gaze danced toward the two brides, and he nodded. "Ladies. Miss Jacqueline."

Rachel shook her head and buttered her biscuit. She hoped he did better talking to women as he hawked his wares than he'd done with the two brides.

Miss O'Neil cleared her throat and laid down her fork. "Will we be able to talk to Marshal Davis this morning? I. . .uh"—she glanced at Miss Bennett—"need to make some decisions as to what to do very soon."

"I, for one, plan to marry the marshal, so I suppose you do need to make alternative plans." Miss Bennett dabbed her lips with her napkin and eyed Miss O'Neil with disdain.

Rachel swirled more sugar into her coffee then took a sip of the hot liquid, hating that the women were fighting over Luke. How had things gotten to this point?

Jacqueline shoved another slice of bacon in her mouth. "Luke's gonna marry my ma."

Rachel choked as she swallowed. She coughed as she tried to clear her clogged throat. Tears blurred her vision. Both brides stared wide-eyed at her. Rachel turned her attention to her daughter. "Wherever did you get that idea?"

Jacqueline plowed rows with her fork lightly across the lukewarm gravy covering half of a biscuit. "It just makes sense. He nearly lives here. You feed him and do his laundry already. You need someone to take care of you. But I don't hav'ta mind him." She dabbed some peach jam onto her biscuit and took a bite.

"Saints preserve us." Miss O'Neil held her napkin to her chest and squeezed it fiercely.

"Luke does not live here. He lives next door." Rachel tried to apply salve to the wound her daughter had just inflicted.

"Same thing." Jacqueline shrugged.

Rachel closed her eyes and shook her head. "I'm not marrying Luke."

Especially now.

Desperate to change the subject, Rachel turned to Miss Bennett. "Why don't you tell us a little bit about yourself?"

The young woman took a sip of her coffee then touched her napkin to her mouth. "I have lived just outside of Carthage, Missouri, for the past twelve years, but I was born in Boston. My father got it in his system to travel west when I was a child, but Carthage was as far as Mother would go. She simply wouldn't tolerate moving to the frontier. Father owns a farm, and I'm the oldest of eleven children." Miss Bennett stared at Miss O'Neil as if saying it was her turn to share.

Eleven children! Was that why she decided to become a mail-order bride? To get away from such a large household? Rachel couldn't imagine the responsibility that must have fallen on Miss Bennett's young shoulders. Why, she doubted either woman had reached her twentieth birthday yet.

Suddenly, she felt old. She was twenty-eight and still two years younger than Luke, but maybe he was now looking for a much younger woman to marry.

Miss O'Neil cleared her throat. "I came to New Orleans from Ireland with my parents, but they both died shortly after we arrived. I uh. . .met a couple from Shreveport who took me there to work on their estate just outside of town." She fingered the handle on her coffee cup and stared at it, looking apprehensive. "I was a h–housemaid."

Rachel's heart ached for the girl. She'd lost her parents, was all alone in a foreign country, and now had to deal with competing for Luke's affections. No wonder she was so desperate. She couldn't have made much money working as a servant, which explained why she only had the funds to stay two nights.

Rachel tapped her finger against her plate, thinking. When a close friend or distant relative visited, she would often offer them a room for free, but she hesitated doing that with someone she barely knew since the boardinghouse was her sole source of income. And it would hardly be fair to give one bride free room and board and not the other bride. Still, she couldn't just toss the woman out on the streets.

Miss Bennett stood. "I'm going to my room to freshen up. I imagine the marshal will be here soon."

Rachel watched her sashay out of the room. The woman put on airs for some reason, though her clothing was faded and thin. She seemed bound and determined to become Luke's bride, but why? Had something driven her away from her home, other than her numerous siblings?

Jacqueline jumped up. She disappeared into the kitchen and

returned with a bowl filled with the contents of the scrap bucket. "I'm running this over to Max."

Rachel stood and gave her a hug. "All right, but you come right back. Just because it's Saturday, doesn't mean you can play all day. We need to weed and water the garden before it gets too hot."

Jacqueline nodded and tugged loose from the embrace, then swaggered out of the dining room, walking like a boy. She'd even requested that the brides call her Jack. Rachel couldn't understand the changes in her once sweet child. Were they because her father had died? Or just a natural part of growing older?

"Um. . .excuse me, Mrs. Hamilton, but have you by chance thought of a place I might find employment?"

Rachel turned her attention back to Miss O'Neil. Her curly auburn hair looked as rebellious as Jacqueline as it fought against the confines of its hairpins, and her green eyes looked large against her fair complexion. Her Irish accent only enhanced her beauty.

"Oh no. I haven't thought about that, but let me do so now." She took a minute to consider the establishments and then the families in the area. "Um, well, there's a family just outside of town that has a new baby. They already have two other small children. Perhaps they could use some help, or they might know of someone else who does. Why don't we start there? I've been meaning to go visit them anyway."

Miss O'Neil smiled. "'Twould be nice, as long as it won't inconvenience you."

"No, not at all. Just let me get the dishes cleaned up." Rachel stood and placed Miss Bennett's plate on top of her own. Miss O'Neil set Mr. Sampson's plate on top of hers and followed Rachel into the kitchen, putting them on the worktable. Rachel looked at her boarder. "Thank you for bringing those in, but you go and relax."

"I don't mind helpin'. I'm used to staying busy. When I'm idle, I worry too much."

"If you're sure, I'd be happy for some help."

"I shall finish clearing the table, if'twould be all right."

Rachel nodded. She took some hot water from the stove's reservoir, poured it into the sink, and then scraped the plates into the scrap bucket for Max. Miss O'Neil brought the salt and sugar bowls in, set them down, and then darted back into the dining room. The two women were so different. Miss O'Neil, while lovely, was quiet and seemed quite insecure. Miss Bennett's clothing indicated someone who also had little money, but she seemed sure of herself. How did they end up becoming mail-order brides?

Luke was certainly handsome, but they hadn't known that before coming to Lookout. And they knew nothing of his personality. What if he changed like James had after he married? Her husband had been charming—except for when he grew angry or drank or lost at gambling, which happened more and more often toward the end. Rachel shuddered at the memory. But Luke wasn't like James. He'd never hurt someone, no matter how angry he might become.

The chair behind her banged against the table, and she jumped. Just thinking about James had set her on edge.

"Sorry. I accidentally kicked the chair."

Rachel peered over her shoulder, her heart still thudding. "It's all right. I was just lost in thought, and the noise startled me."

Half an hour later, Rachel and Miss O'Neil headed out the front door. Miss Bennett sat in a rocker on the porch, reading a book. Rachel lifted her basket over one arm, stopped, and turned to her. "We're off to visit a friend and see her new baby. Would you care to come with us?"

Miss Bennett stuck her finger in the book to mark her place and looked up. "No, thank you. I've had my fill of babies. I believe I'll sit right here and wait for the marshal to show up."

Miss O'Neil's gaze darted up Main Street. "I'd hate to miss Marshal Davis's visit. Should I be staying, too?"

Rachel shook her head. "Luke is easy enough to find if you

want to talk with him. You need to come with me so we can attend to that other business you asked me about."

Miss O'Neil nodded. "Aye, you're right. 'Tis most important."

Rachel and her guest crossed the dirt road, walked toward the stage depot, and stayed to the north side of the street so they wouldn't have to walk past Luke's office and risk running into him. What would the brides say when they learned he wasn't the one who had contacted them? It would be better for Miss O'Neil to accept the fact that Luke wasn't likely to marry her and for her to find gainful employment. She obviously didn't have the money to return to Shreveport.

"I suppose Marshal Davis will wed Miss Bennett."

Rachel looked askance at the young woman. "Why would you think that?"

Miss O'Neil shrugged one thin shoulder. "She's quite pretty and so self-assured."

"That's true, but you're every bit as pretty as she." Rachel couldn't help wondering if the girl had been mistreated at some point in her life. She was as skittish as an abused animal and didn't like looking people in the eye. Rachel remembered acting the same way after experiencing James's outbursts when he lost at the gambling tables.

On a whim, she wrapped her arm around the young woman's shoulders. "Lookout is a nice little town. People here are friendly and treat each other with respect. Whether or not you marry the marshal, this is a place where you could start over."

" 'Twould be wonderful if I could. There's nothing for me to return to, either in Shreveport or in Erin—Ireland, as you call it."

They passed the banker's house and the Dykstra sisters' home as they ambled down the dirt street. Rachel shaded her eyes from the bright morning sun and gazed at the one-room schoolhouse, where church was also held. Was Jacqueline behaving herself? Rachel had heard tales from the church women about children reaching their adolescent years and acting out, but Jacqueline was only ten. Was she just an early bloomer, or were other issues troubling her?

A small cottage about a half mile from the schoolhouse sat nestled among a copse of pines and oaks. Diapers and children's clothing in various sizes flapped in the warm breeze on a line strung between two trees. A lazy hound lifted its snout, sniffed, and glanced at them, then dropped his head back onto his front paws.

Louise Chambers sat on the front porch rocking a squalling baby. She raised one hand in greeting and resumed patting the infant's backside so roughly Rachel wondered if that was why the infant was wailing. "Have a seat, if you can find one. Cyrus must be colicky. He's normally a good baby, but he's fussy today."

Rachel accepted a rocker next to Louise's and set her basket on the porch, while Miss O'Neil took the chair beside Rachel.

"I'm so glad you came to visit. I'd let you hold little Cy if he wasn't so cranky."

"How have you been feeling?" Rachel asked as two blond toddlers ran past them hollering like Comanches.

"Hush up, Sam. Ethan. I'm trying to get Cy to sleep." The dirty children instantly quieted and ran toward the hound dog sleeping under a persimmon tree.

Rachel wondered what the secret was to getting children to obey so swiftly and without arguing. Maybe she should return alone and talk with Louise sometime soon.

"I brought you some of my cinnamon bread." Rachel uncovered her basket and held up the loaf.

"That's right kind of you. I know we'll all enjoy it." Louise leaned forward and glanced around Rachel to Miss O'Neil. "My name's Louise Chambers. Them two youngsters over there are my two oldest boys. Cy, here, is the baby. Jarrod, my man, is out working somewhere in one of his fields."

"This is Miss O'Neil. She's staying at the boardinghouse for a while." Rachel wondered if Louise had heard what had happened yesterday. Perhaps they could simply avoid the uncomfortable topic. "Miss O'Neil is in need of employment, and I thought perhaps you could use some help or might know of someone else who needed the services of a nice young woman."

Louise looked past Rachel as she rocked forward. "It's a pleasure to meet you."

Rachel's boarder nodded, her cheeks a bright pink as she fiddled with the edge of her sleeve.

"I won't argue that I could use some help, but sadly, I cain't pay no one, and I don't have a spare foot in the house, or I'd offer room and board. I'm sorry, I wish I could help, but nothing comes to mind at the moment."

Carly Payton held tightly to the window frame as the stage rounded the sharp turn into Lookout. She'd never been to Texas before this trip, which was one thing in her favor. If all went as planned, she would find the means to start over somewhere far away like Colorado or California, somewhere her brother would never find her, but first, she just might have to get married.

She pulled Ellie Blackstone's letter from her reticule and reread it. She could do this. Hadn't she done far worse?

Closing her eyes, she memorized the name that the letter had been addressed to: Ellie Blackstone. Once she arrived in town, she was to see a man named Garrett Corbett, who was the marshal's solicitor—whatever that was. Then again, maybe she'd bypass him and just go find her future husband on her own.

"Whoa!" The stage driver's loud voice echoed through the open windows, and the coach shimmied in a series of jerks as it slowed to a halt amid a cloud of dust and high-pitched creaks. The door opened, and the shotgun rider reached in with a smile to help her down. She accepted his hand as a lady should and allowed him to assist her. Once on solid ground again, she dusted her skirts with a fervent shake. The neck of the high-buttoned shirtwaist pressed uncomfortably against her throat, and the long skirts threatened to trip her as the stiff breeze trapped them around her legs. Oh for a soft flannel shirt and trousers.

As she waited for her satchel to be unloaded, she scanned the town and took a deep breath to settle her nerves. What was the name of this place? She pulled the creased letter from her pocket and peeked below the signature. Lookout, Texas. She knew it was something odd, and she hoped that wasn't a warning. Lookout where you're going. Lookout, we'll catch you if you do wrong. Lookout for the law!

The town was just like so many others that she'd traveled through with her brother, but she hoped this one was far enough off the beaten track that he wouldn't find her, at least until she'd accomplished her goal in coming here.

If not for Miss Blackstone's timely injury and her bleeding all over Carly's dress, making her brother think she was dead, who knew where she might be? Still robbing banks and trains and anyone with money, most likely. Everything had worked unbelievably in her favor. Even Ellie's clothing had fit her fairly well; but would the townsfolk be able to tell she was a sham?

The shotgun rider set her satchel on the boardwalk among the crates they'd just unloaded. Carly cleared her throat, and the man glanced her way. "Pardon me, but do you know if there is a decent hotel in this town?"

"Nope." He shook his head. "No hotel a'tall. But you might find a room at Miz Hamilton's boardin'house. Don't know if she has any rooms available, though, what with all the brides that arrived the other day."

Carly didn't bother trying to make sense of his words. "Which way do I go?"

He grinned and yanked off his hat. A layer of dust cascaded down like a waterfall. "See that big green house at the end of the street?"

Carly held on to the sunbonnet that made her head sweaty

and blocked her view of most everything and spun in the direction he was pointing. She tilted her head up. "Yeah. . .uh, yes, I see it."

The man chuckled. "That's it right there."

"Oh. Good." She grabbed her satchel off the pile of crates the stage had delivered and walked toward the boardinghouse. The light green, three-story house looked homey with its white shutters, wrap-around porch both downstairs and up, and numerous rocking chairs. At least she would get to sleep in a real bed, which would be much more comfortable than the hard ground she normally slept on. And she could take a bath. While traveling with her brother, she'd pretty much given up hope of ever being clean and sweet-smelling again. At the time, it was just as well that she wasn't. Helped deter any unwanted male attention.

As she approached the house, two women who sat in rockers on the porch snapping green beans looked up at her. She wiped her sweaty palms on her skirt and forced a smile. Being around normal people would tax her to her limits, but she could do this. It could mean starting over fresh instead of living with her brother and being an outlaw for the rest of her life—which might not be all that long if Tyson discovered she was alive and caught up with her.

The older of the two women smiled. Though pretty in her own right, her average brown hair and pale blue eyes made her look plain next to the younger woman with the wild, sorrel-colored hair.

The older woman set her bowl on the porch and stood, smiling. "I'm Rachel Hamilton. Can I help you?"

Carly nodded. "I'm Ellie." Oh, what was that name? "Uh. . . Blackstone. Ellie Blackstone. I need a room for a few days—just until I can make arrangements to marry Marshal Luke Davis."

Chapter 17

Rachel clutched the nearest porch post as her mind swirled with disbelief. Not another bride! Whatever was going on?

"Saints preserve us." Miss O'Neil muttered something in Gaelic, and she leaned forward, holding her face in her hands. Suddenly, she jumped to her feet, the bowl of beans falling to the floor and scattering all over the porch. With the back of her hand against her mouth, she dashed into the house.

Miss Blackstone's light brown eyes widened. "Goodness! Does she always react to strangers like that?"

Hating to be the one caught in the middle of all this, Rachel stooped down and gathered her thoughts along with the beans. *How could this happen? How do I tell her, Lord?*

"Well. . .you gonna answer me?" Miss Blackstone tapped her foot on the ground. "Evidently something I said flustered her, but I cain't figure out what."

Setting the beans aside, Rachel held out her palm. "Please, won't you have a seat for a moment?"

"I'm tired and would like to freshen up in my room before I meet the marshal. You do have a room available?"

"Yes." Rachel forced a smile. "That's not the problem."

"Then what is it?" Miss Blackstone flopped down, albeit reluctantly. "Spill the beans."

If the topic hadn't been so serious, Rachel would have laughed at the women's obvious effort to lighten a tense situation. Sucking in a steadying breath, she stared up at the soft blue sky. "There's been a horrible mistake."

The young woman straightened. "What do you mean? Marshal Davis ain't already married, is he?"

Rachel clenched her hands together. "No, not exactly."

"How can a body be not exactly married?"

"He's not, but two other women have recently come to town expecting to marry him."

"What!" Miss Blackstone lurched to her feet and kicked her satchel. "How is that possible? I came a long ways and won't have some namby-pamby stealing my place as the marshal's bride. He is an honorable man, ain't he?"

Rachel stood. "Oh yes, he surely is, but it seems his ornery cousins played a trick on him."

"But I've set my sights on marrying up with him."

Reaching out, Rachel touched Miss Blackstone's shoulder, but the other woman sloughed her hand away. Miss Blackstone narrowed her gaze, and her light brown eyes glinted.

"I'm terribly sorry for your inconvenience," Rachel said. "I'm hoping Luke will demand that his cousins make restitution for any expenses you've incurred and for your inconvenience."

Her visitor hiked up her chin. "I ain't come all this way just to be turned out. Where *is* the marshal? I got me a few words for him."

"Like I said, it wasn't his fault. Luke knew nothing until the other brides showed up."

Miss Blackstone studied her. "That's twice you've referenced my future husband by his given name. Just what's your stake in all of this?"

Rachel clasped her hands together and tried to hold her ground.

She was a peacemaker— didn't like conflict—and Miss Blackstone seemed more determined to acquire Luke for her husband than even Miss Bennett. "We grew up in Lookout together. I've known Luke most of my life."

The newest bride pulled off her bonnet, revealing glistening black hair, and fanned her face. With her lightly tanned complexion and snappy eyes, she was a lovely girl if one didn't take into account her pushy attitude. "That stage driver called you *Mrs.* Hamilton, so that means you're married, right?"

"Was married," Rachel said. "I'm a widow."

Rather than saying she was sorry for her loss, Miss Blackstone narrowed her gaze and stared at Rachel as if she, too, were a competitor for Luke's affection.

"Have you set your cap for him?"

Rachel thought back eleven years to when she'd been seventeen and had eagerly looked forward to marrying Luke. She'd loved him so much and never had eyes for any other man. If only. . .

Rachel shook her head. "No, that's not an option."

Miss Blackstone stared down Main Street. "Could you take me to talk with the marshal?"

"Don't you want to get settled in your room first?"

She shook her head. "No. I need to know where things stand."

Rachel sighed inwardly. "Let me put these beans away and set your carpetbag inside. Would you care for a drink of water?"

"Afterwards."

Rachel hurried to the kitchen, wondering about Miss Blackstone. Her speech and manners seemed gruff, but she dressed nicely. She set the bowl of beans on the counter and thought about the other two brides upstairs. How could things have gotten so out of control? What were those Corbett brothers thinking?

"They weren't, and that is a fact," Rachel mumbled. Those two had done many foolish things in their lives, but this one took the cake.

Maybe she and the new bride should pay the Corbett brothers

a visit, since the low-down hooligans had yet to come and apologize or make restitution. Rachel reached out and clutched the door-jamb at the new thought that struck her weak-kneed. If there were three brides, could there be more to come?

Outside, Rachel crossed the street with Miss Blackstone beside her. She didn't know what else to say to calm the woman. Her new boarder was obviously upset. Who wouldn't be? How would Rachel respond if she found herself in a similar situation?

Her mind swirled with thoughts as her quick steps ate up the ground. She stomped up the boardwalk steps and ran smack into a solid body coming out of the bank. She was shoved sideways, colliding into Miss Blackstone, who grabbed a post, or she would have fallen into the street. The man grabbed Rachel's arm before she, too, fell, and righted her.

"Where's the fire, Rachel?" Luke stared down with a half grin on his handsome face.

She spun back toward him, irritated that her heart pounded from having rammed into him. Max squeezed out the door and past Luke's long legs. The mutt sniffed her hand, looked up and whined, then scurried back into the bank. Rachel's frustration burned like the heat of a flat iron and had probably scorched the poor dog's snout. She stepped forward and wagged her finger under Luke's nose. "There's no fire, but there's about to be a murder."

The humor left Luke's face, and his gaze dashed past her, probably to Miss Blackstone. Rachel noticed the bank teller and president staring at them from inside the bank, and she grabbed Luke's arm, pulling him out of the doorway. "Marshal Davis, meet Ellie Blackstone, your third bride."

Confusion wrinkled his brow. He opened his mouth but nothing came out for a moment. "What?"

"This woman has come to town to marry you. Imagine that."

Miss Blackstone smoothed her dress and squared her shoulders, eyeing Luke with a mixture of apprehension and the determination of a hungry huntress suddenly spotting an eight-point buck. Her expression softened, and she scurried up close to him, smiled, and held out her hand. "A pleasure to meet you, Marshal."

Luke, ever the gentleman, tipped his hat to her and shook her fingertips. "I'm right sorry about all this, ma'am." His gaze turned to steel as he glared at Rachel. "Lawman or not, I just may help you string up those two scoundrels. Let's go see what they have to say about this."

The glass in the window rattled when Luke yanked open the freight office door. His irritation nearly bounced off the wooden walls, and his cousins were lucky he hadn't jerked the door clear off its hinges. He allowed the two ladies to enter before him. The new bride—Miss What's-Her-Name—brushed up against him, stared unabashedly into his eyes, and gave him a sultry smile.

She was pretty all right, like the other two brides, but this one had a worldly quality that set the lawman in him on alert. Or maybe he was just fearful for his bachelorhood. Even though she looked no older than the other brides, this woman's expression spoke of experience—but just what kind of experience, he wasn't sure.

Luke rubbed the back of his neck and for the first time wished he'd never quit the cavalry and returned home. Life had gotten so complicated. *I could use some help here, Lord. What's to be done about all these brides?*

Max lumbered in after the ladies, and Luke shut the door. The dog flopped down near his feet. Mark stared up from his desk, where he'd been doing paperwork. The color drained from his face as his gaze landed on the stranger.

"Where's Garrett?" Luke asked.

Mark nudged his head sideways. "Out back, packing up the wagon. We're getting ready to head out on a delivery run again."

"Get him," Luke ordered.

"You're not going anywhere, Mark Corbett." Rachel pressed

her hands flat on his desk and leaned over, glaring at him. "You and that up-to-no-good brother of yours are to come over to the boardinghouse right now and discuss what you to intend to do about this disastrous situation."

"But we're just about to leave to make deliveries."

"Not until we get some answers."

Luke nearly chuckled at the stunned look in Mark's eyes as mild-natured Rachel turned into a she-bear. Luke strode into the back room, out the open rear door, and onto the porch. Garrett set a large crate onto the buckboard that already had a team hitched to it. A copse of trees shaded the area, giving it a serene setting totally at war with the fire raging within him. Did the brothers think they could make a quick escape and get out of talking with the brides?

Garrett smiled. "Come to help?"

Luke snorted. "Not hardly. You'll never guess who just showed up in town."

His cousin's eyes lifted as if he were deep in thought; then he refocused on Luke. "That pickpocket you were after?"

"No, but I've got something else that might interest you."

Garrett pulled a bandanna from his rear pocket and wiped his face and the back of his neck. "No foolin'? What is it?"

"Another bride."

His cousin's blue eyes had a blank stare for a split second before they widened. Red crept up Garrett's neck to color his cheeks and ears. "Uh. . .you don't say."

Luke rammed his hands to his hips. "I do say. Now get in here. We're going over to Rachel's to discuss this situation."

"But we've got deliveries to make."

"They can wait," Luke ground out each word, making sure Garrett realized the seriousness of the situation.

His cousin nodded and climbed the stairs. He grabbed another crate, and Luke glared at him. "I've got to at least get the wagon loaded and tied down, or I'm likely to lose all of this freight to some kids or a bum."

Luke wanted to argue, but although Lookout was a peaceful town and most folks were the decent sort, there were always a few families that were hard up and wouldn't mind stealing to put food on the table. He grabbed a crate, descended the steps, and slung it onto the buckboard.

Garrett hauled another crate off the porch, and after a few minutes of working in heated silence together, he tossed a rope across the top of the wagon to Luke. "So, is this one as pretty as the others?"

"Black hair and unusual, light brown eyes." Luke didn't mention his concerns about the woman. Maybe he was overreacting. Could be she just looked hardened because she was angry over the situation.

"That doesn't tell me much." Garrett grunted as he pulled the rope taut and tied it.

Luke dusted off his hands and rested them on his hips. "Guess you'll find out soon enough."

"Yep."

Garrett walked in front of his horses and patted each one on the head. "I'll be back soon, girls." He strode toward Luke and hopped up the steps. "You know, that means there's enough of them brides for each of us to have one."

Luke gave his cousin a playful shove but couldn't help grinning when Garrett walked into the office in front of him. He shook his head. This was no laughing matter, but his cousins had a way of seeing the up side of every situation. Why couldn't he be less serious and more like them?

Rachel glared at Garrett then Luke. "Took you long enough. Did you have to chase him down and haul him back?"

"Nope, he came of his own free will." Luke lifted his hat, swiped his hand through his hair, and glanced at the new bride. "These two yahoos are my cousins, Garrett and Mark Corbett."

"And this is Ellie Blackstone," Rachel said. "Now, let's head back to the boardinghouse and sort through this mess."

Garrett grinned at Miss Blackstone and opened the door. Mark hurried around his desk and offered her his arm. She glared at the two men then marched past them and took hold of Luke's arm. "I traveled here to marry the marshal, and that's what I aim to do."

Luke swallowed the cannonball-size lump in his throat. "But I—"

Rachel held up her palm. "Save it for the boardinghouse. You can tell all the brides at once, and that way you won't have to keep repeating yourself."

Suppressing a sigh, Luke followed Rachel to the door with Miss Blackstone attached to his arm. He held his hand out, indicating for the third bride to go first. She released her hold and, with a flounce of her head, strode out the door.

He dreaded the confrontation ahead. Why couldn't things have gone along nice and quiet like when he first arrived? Being around Rachel again had been hard enough, and they seemed to be moving toward a passable friendship, but now she was angry with him, and he didn't like how that felt. He glanced at his cousins, and his own anger simmered. How could those ornery brothers put him in a situation like this? What could they have been thinking when they wrote to so many women?

He was knee-deep in turbulent female emotions and had no clue how to get free of the muck. He moved closer to Rachel. She had a good head on her shoulders and didn't buckle during hard times. Maybe she could be the voice of reason in this trying ordeal.

Luke ran his gaze around town, making sure all was quiet. As he'd expected, several groups of people had gathered, and he knew exactly the topic of their conversations. Everyone watched Luke, his cousins, and the ladies like a group of Indians surveying a blanket full of beads and trinkets. They were the news of the day. Shoot, three brides coming to marry one man was probably the hottest news they had all year. No wonder they were curious.

Jenny Evans, the newspaper editor, exited her office door just as Luke passed by, as if to emphasize his point. She fell into step with him, albeit taking three steps to his one.

"So tell me, Marshal, how does it feel to have so many women wanting to marry you?" She held her pencil poised above a pad of paper, awaiting his response.

He grunted.

"Am I to take that to mean you're not happy with the situation?"

He kept his face straight, watching the bank president step out the door of his establishment. He nodded to the man he'd just spoken to a short while ago. "Mr. Castleby."

"Ignoring me won't change a thing, Marshal. I intend to get my story." Miss Evans hurried to keep up, her breath running short.

"There's no story here, ma'am."

"I beg to differ. What's going to happen to those brides? There are three of them now—am I correct?"

Miss Blackstone tossed a snappish look over her shoulder.

Luke shook his head. News traveled faster than a prairie fire in the small town. His footsteps stopped echoing as he stepped off the boardwalk onto the dirt street. "That's right," he finally answered.

"Did you write to all three of them, hoping one might come here?"

Luke halted, and she sped past him, slid to a stop, and turned back. He might not want to comment on the situation, but neither did he want his character defamed. "For the record, Miss Evans, I didn't write to any of the brides. I knew nothing about them before they arrived in town."

Her wide gray eyes stared up at him. "Well, someone must have. How else would they have known about you or known to come to Lookout?"

"I'm not at liberty to say just yet."

She licked the stub of her pencil. "Will you tell me when you are?"

He shrugged. “It’s nobody’s business.” Luke eyed his cousins as they slinked around behind the journalist like two kids hiding from an irate neighbor after they’d pulled a prank. He was tempted to turn the rabid reporter loose on them, but he wanted to see how things played out first.

“It’s a great story, Marshal.”

He crossed the street and followed the others inside the boardinghouse, and turned, blocking the entrance. “The matter is private, ma’am.”

“But—”

He stepped back, hand on the door knob. “Good day, Miss Evans.”

Chapter 18

Rachel escorted her small group to the parlor. The scent of chicken baking in the kitchen filled the air and reminded her of all that she needed to do to get dinner ready on time. "If you men will have a seat, I'll show Miss Blackstone to her room and have the other ladies come downstairs."

Jacqueline must have heard them enter, because she ambled out of the bedroom and up the hall. "What's goin' on, Ma? Why's everybody here?"

Rachel turned to her new guest. "Miss Blackstone, this is my daughter, Jacqueline. She and I have a room downstairs, and if you ever have need of me during the night for any reason, you can find me there."

"Pleased to meet you, ma'am." Jacqueline squinted at the new boarder as if something was wrong, but thankfully, she used her manners.

"Same here." Miss Blackstone nodded. She lifted her head and sniffed. "Somethun sure smells good."

"That's baked chicken. Mom's is the best in town. Even better than at Polly's Café."

A blush heated Rachel's cheeks at her daughter's rare compliment. "Why, thank you, sweetie. That's very kind of you to say. Speaking of chickens, have you fed and watered ours today?"

Jacqueline scowled but turned and headed for the back door. Feeding the hens wouldn't take her long, and Rachel didn't want her daughter around to hear what was certainly to be a heated debate. "Wait just a minute."

Jacqueline stopped near the kitchen door, eyeing her with a suspicious gaze as if she expected her mother to give her more chores to do. Rachel looked at her guest. "Miss Blackstone, would you excuse me for a moment?"

The young woman nodded and shifted her satchel to her other hand.

Rachel motioned her daughter to follow her into their bedroom. She searched her unmentionable drawer for the little bag where she kept her cash. She pulled out two coins and handed them to Jacqueline. "After you feed the chickens, go to the mercantile and get yourself a treat."

The girl's deep blue eyes widened. "Oh boy! Thanks, Ma." Jacqueline snatched the coins as if she thought Rachel might change her mind and hurried out the back door. Its loud bang made Rachel cringe.

She forced a smile and returned to the entryway, where her newest guest waited. She pointed back to her right. "That's my kitchen back there. You've already seen the parlor, and the dining room is right next to it. The only other room downstairs that's available to guests is the library. We have a large assortment of books if you enjoy reading."

"I don't read much." The woman's gaze darted around the kitchen as if the room interested her. She looked refined in her cornflower blue and white blouse and dark blue skirt, but she tugged at the sleeves and kept pulling at the high collar as if it were too tight. She watched everyone intently.

"If you're ready, I'll show you to your room."

The woman nodded and followed her back through the hall and toward the stairs. The quiet rumble of male voices echoed from the parlor, and Rachel glanced inside as she passed the doorway, capturing Luke's gaze. Her heart flip-flopped. How could the man still move her after so many years?

She placed a hand on her chest as a thought hit her. Luke had been looking at her, not the new bride. Was he hoping to find a friendly face in the midst of such a horrendous event? As she climbed the stairs, she tried to consider how she'd feel if the situation were reversed. What if three men had come to town to marry her when she'd known nothing about them? The awkwardness of the situation would be unbearable.

At the top of the stairs, she noted that both brides' doors were shut. Had Miss O'Neil mentioned the new bride's arrival to Miss Bennett?

Rachel opened the door to the yellow room and stepped aside to allow Miss Blackstone to enter. The woman's eyes widened, and her mouth formed an O.

"I ain't—uh. . .never stayed in a place this purty." She slowly turned, as if taking in everything in the pale yellow room. The log cabin quilt, with its light yellow accents, matched the wall and added a splash of color.

Women always loved Rachel's rooms, while the men sometimes grimaced. But at least the beds were comfortable and the rooms clean. If the men didn't like the slightly feminine decor, they could stay in the community room above the saloon.

"Take a few minutes to refresh yourself, and then please join the rest of us in the parlor so we can get this mess sorted out."

Miss Blackstone nodded, her lips pursed. No doubt she dreaded confronting the men as much as Rachel. The third bride closed her door, and Rachel stood in the wide upstairs hallway. A small table covered with an embroidered cloth held the hurricane lamp that she lit each night to help her guests see in case they needed to go to the necessary. The striped, cream-colored wallpaper brightened the area and blended well with the floral carpet runner that covered the middle of the floor.

She looked at the three closed doors, knowing she couldn't put her task off any longer. How had she become the mediator of this mess?

She clutched her chest as a thought slapped her across the face. Three brides, each lovely in her own way, were now available, which meant that each man—Luke, Garrett, and Mark—could possibly marry one of them. If that happened, any hope of getting back with Luke would be dashed.

Remaining a widow and unmarried had never bothered her until Luke had come back to Lookout. Even Rand's frequent attentions hadn't swayed her to want to marry again. But with Luke's return, she'd begun to hope—hope he would forgive her and they could have a second chance. She clenched her fists. What could she do? She could hardly force Luke to forgive her for marrying another man, even though she'd been so in love with Luke. He didn't know the truth of the situation, and she could never tell him.

Heaving a sigh, she lifted a hand and knocked on Miss O'Neil's door. Rachel studied the floor. Why would Luke even consider her again—a tired, aging woman with responsibilities and a rambunctious child—when he could have his pick of these three pretty, young ladies?

Miss O'Neil opened the door a slit and peered out as if she were frightened of who might be on the other side of the door. "Oh, Mrs. Hamilton." She pulled the door open, offering a half smile.

"I wonder if I might have a word with you and Miss Bennett for a moment."

The young woman glanced across the hall and scowled. Rachel wondered if the two brides had suffered an altercation of some sort or if she was just concerned about losing Luke to Miss Bennett.

"Aye, of course you can." The younger woman straightened her skirt and stepped out of her room.

Rachel knocked on Miss Bennett's door, and after a moment, the woman flung it open, staring with curiosity at the two women in the hall. "I need to speak to you and Miss O'Neil, if I may."

Miss Bennett nodded and stepped into the hall, closing the door behind her. "What is it?"

Rachel licked her lips, wishing she could be anywhere but here. "The men are downstairs, ready to discuss the. . .uh. . .situation."

"Finally." Miss Bennett crossed her arms over her chest, but the worry in her gaze belied her tough demeanor.

"Yes, well, there's been. . .uh. . .a new development."

"What sort of development?" Miss Bennett asked, her eyes wary.

Rachel glanced at the door to the yellow room. "I'm afraid another bride has arrived."

Miss O'Neil looked down, wringing her hands, still upset over meeting Miss Blackstone earlier.

Miss Bennett's blue eyes widened, her nostrils flared. "Why, that is utterly preposterous. What kind of game does the marshal have going? I left my home and family to come all this way to marry, and I intend to do so."

The door to the yellow room slowly opened, and Miss Blackstone stepped into the hall. All eyes turned in her direction as each woman sized up the other. Rachel wondered what they were thinking. What would she think if she were in their situation?

A verse from Psalm 82:3 popped into her mind. "*Defend the poor and fatherless: do justice to the afflicted and needy.*" In spite of the possibility of losing Luke again, sympathy filled her heart. None of this was the brides' fault, and as a Christian woman, she was obligated to make things as easy for them as possible, no matter the cost.

Miss Blackstone lifted her chin and glared at the other two

brides. "Maybe I was the last to arrive, but I'll tell y'all here and now that I plan on winnin' the marshal's hand."

Jack tossed a handful of feed in the air and grinned as the chickens flapped their wings and raced to be the first to catch one of the tasty morsels. She didn't like tending the dumb, smelly birds, but she sure enjoyed eating them. She sprinkled another scoop of feed on the ground and then poured water from the bucket into two water bowls.

The two coins her mother had given her clinked in her pocket. Jack left the pen, set the bucket by the well, and fingered the coins. Ma must have really wanted to get rid of her since she'd given her so much money. Her mind raced with all the things she could buy with it. Twenty pieces of penny candy. Or maybe she could get a dime novel *and* a sweet treat. Or a dill pickle from the barrel—those never failed to make her mouth water.

She rounded the corner of the house just in time to see someone duck behind the Texas azalea bush that grew almost below the parlor window. Jack darted back against the rear of the house and then peeked around the corner. She had planned to stop and listen in that very spot before getting her treat. No bribe was going to make her miss out on hearing the hullabaloo that was sure to occur now that another bride had arrived.

Jack hunkered down and scurried around the corner of the house. Keeping low and behind the bush, she tiptoed to the edge of the shrub. Looking through the leaves, she recognized Jenny Evans, the lady newspaper owner. She must be out to get a story, and Jack knew she was about to get a good one. The brides had been the talk of the town when there were only two of them. What would people say now that another one had arrived?

Her ma's lacy curtains fluttered through the open window. If she stayed on this side of the bush, she was certain to miss out on most of the conversation that was sure to drift out. Miss Evans peeked up and through the window, then ducked back down and scribbled something on her pad of paper.

Jack scowled and bit the inside of her cheek. “Humbug.”

Well, if Miss Evans could spy on the brides, so could she. As quick as a greased pig, she dashed around the bush and slid up against the house. Miss Evans gasped and covered her mouth with one hand while holding her notepad against her chest with the other. Her flaring nostrils and wide eyes reminded Jack of a spooked horse.

She leaned toward the woman and whispered, “What’cha doing?”

Miss Evans’s mouth worked as if she’d swallowed a bug, but nothing came out. She patted her chest and seemed to be trying to breathe normally. Jack grinned, knowing she’d scared the woman half to death.

After taking a few moments to compose herself, Miss Evans leaned toward Jack. “I’m just trying to get a story for my paper,” she whispered. “I asked to sit in on the discussion between the men and the brides, but the marshal refused. What else could I do?”

The woman’s soft breath tickled the edge of Jack’s ear, and she rubbed it. “Spy on them, I guess.” She grinned, and Miss Evans smiled back.

“I won’t tell if you won’t.” Miss Evans held out her hand. “Deal?”

Jack pressed her back against the side of the house and eyed the woman. “I won’t tell if you give me twenty cents,” she whispered.

Miss Evans’s brows shot up, and her mouth twitched. Jack frowned. Was she laughing at her?

“I like enterprising people.” She dug around in her skirt pocket, pulled out two dimes, and handed them to Jack. “Deal.”

Luke paced the parlor, waiting for the women to come downstairs while his cousins argued over the event.

"I told you this was a bad idea when you first thought it up, didn't I?" Mark glared at his brother.

Garrett curled his lip. "If you were so all fired against it, why did you write to those two brides?"

Mark fell back against his chair and ran his hand through his curly blond hair. "I don't know. You made it sound like such a good idea that I got caught up wanting to find Luke a wife."

"I don't need any one bride shopping for me. When I'm ready to marry, I'll find my own." Luke muttered a growl and turned toward the side window, arms crossed. He stared outside. Whatever made them think he needed their help in finding a wife?

A noise outside snagged his attention. He stepped to the side of the window, pressing his back to the wall, and peered down. The bushes rustled, and then he saw the top of a head—Jack's head. He bit back a smile, knowing the girl was listening in. He probably should shoo her away, but given the same situation when he'd been a boy, he would have eavesdropped, too. Besides, she'd know everything soon enough.

Rachel cleared her throat. Garrett and Mark shot to their feet, looking like schoolboys who'd pulled a prank and were now sitting in a meeting with the teacher and their parents. Luke shifted his attention to Rachel and the three brides coming into the room. He'd always figured mail-order brides were homely women who couldn't find a husband, but that wasn't the case with the trio of females in the parlor.

His gaze was drawn to Rachel. Though she was probably close to ten years older than the other women, she was still willowy and pretty, with her pale blue eyes and soft brown hair. He couldn't help wondering why Rachel hadn't remarried. That Rand Kessler sure seemed interested in her.

He scowled at the thought. If he didn't want her, why did it bother him to think of her marrying some other man?

"Ladies, if you will please have a seat, we will get things started."

Rachel held out her hand, and each of the women scurried past her and sat.

Rachel introduced everyone and looked at Luke and then his cousins, as if she didn't know where to start. Maybe he should help her out. He stepped forward. "First off, let me say that I'm sorry about this mess. I knew nothing about any of this and didn't write to any of you."

Miss O'Neil sucked in a loud breath that sounded like a hiccup and held her hands in front of her mouth. "Blessit be."

Miss Bennett and Miss Blackstone exchanged glances but kept silent.

"What Garrett and Mark did was inexcusable." Rachel cut both men a scathing glance. "But I also know they meant well when they tried to find Lu—uh. . .the marshal—a wife." Rachel picked up a Bible off a nearby table and held it to her chest, as if drawing strength from it. She faced Luke's cousins again. "Do either of you have anything to say?"

Garrett glanced at his brother and then stepped to the center of the room. "We had good intentions, but we never expected to get the results we did. I'll admit that I wrote letters to two of you, but I really didn't think any woman would be willing to travel clear to Lookout to marry, and I only sent money for traveling expenses to Miss Bennett."

Mark cleared his throat, his neck and ears flaming red. "I, uh. . . sent travel money to Miss O'Neil."

"You were wrong about us not wanting to come here." Miss Bennett squared her shoulders as if daring Garrett to argue with her.

"That's right," Miss Blackstone said, lifting her chin in the air.

"Well, be that as it may," Rachel said, "the only proper thing to do would be to pay the ladies' ways back to wherever they need to go."

"No!" The three women shouted in unison.

Miss Blackstone shot to her feet. "There ain—uh. . .there's

nothing for me back in Missouri. I came here to marry the marshal, and that's what I intend to do."

Miss Bennett jumped up and faced her opponent, blue eyes flashing. "I was the first to arrive, so it only seems fair I should marry Marshal Davis. I have no intention of returning home, either."

"Oh, saints preserve us."

Luke stepped back. How could something like this have happened?

"Please, everybody, let's remain civil." The women sat down at Rachel's gentle admonishment. "Do any of you wish to return home?"

The trio of brides shook their heads.

"All right then, let's see if we can come up with a different solution." Rachel turned to face the men. "I suppose you men could pay the women's room and board until they found work or uh. . .someone else to marry."

"Or maybe they should just marry the brides." Luke grinned at the thought then sobered as he realized that still left one bride.

Garrett shook his head. "I'm not ready to marry."

"Me either." Mark leaned back in his chair and crossed his arms.

"Then what do you suggest we do?" Rachel stood in the parlor entryway looking like a warrior matron ready to fight for her young charges. "It would seem we have a stalemate."

Suddenly, Jenny Evans strode through the parlor doors with Jack fast on her heels. "A breech of promise is grounds for a lawsuit." Miss Evans's eyes shone bright. She held her notepad to her chest and looked at the brides. "I know a good attorney who will sue the britches off those three men for falsely luring you to town under the guise of marriage."

Luke stood stunned to silence like the rest of the group. Even the brides appeared shocked at Jenny's declaration.

"You've forced these poor women to leave the comforts of their home and travel hundreds of miles, and now you refuse to marry any of them?" Jenny glared at Luke. Why should her accusations make him feel guilty when he had no part in this loco scheme?

Rachel took a step forward. "I'm sure we can come to some sort of solution without something as drastic as a lawsuit."

"No, I think these women should sue the marshal and the Corbett brothers as accomplices. Of course, the suit could always be dropped if the marshal agreed to marry one of the women."

Miss Bennett stood and scurried over to stand beside Miss Evans. "I believe this woman has a point. Marry one of us, me preferably, or we'll sue you men. Don't you agree, ladies?"

The other two brides glanced at each other. Miss Blackstone shoved up from her seat and joined them. Miss O'Neil was slower to follow and seemed to do so only to avoid being left out.

Jenny smiled. "There you have it, gentlemen. What will it be? A wedding or a lawsuit?"

"This is ridiculous." Garrett jumped up. "A lawsuit could ruin us and put us out of business. We've worked hard to make a go of our freight line, and this town needs our services. Luke would probably lose his job as marshal, and how would he support a wife then?"

Miss Evans shrugged. "I'm sure he'd find a way to get by. He's big and strong and could do about any kind of work he put his shoulder to."

Luke wrestled with the thoughts bombarding his mind. He didn't want to be responsible for his cousins losing their business, yet none of this was his fault. How had this fiasco turned into a shotgun wedding with the sights set on him?

"Even if the marshal is agreeable, how will he be choosin' *who* to marry?" Miss O'Neil asked.

Garrett sat on the vacant settee and held his chin in one hand while he tapped his index finger against his cheekbone. "I have an idea. Why not have some type of contest? See which gal is the best cook or seamstress. Which one would make the best wife."

Mark leaned forward, steepling his fingertips together. "That's not a half bad idea."

"It's a stupid idea." Luke rolled his eyes. Would these fellows never grow up?

"That's preposterous," Rachel cried. "There's more to being a good wife than domestic abilities."

Miss Blackstone stamped her foot. "I got me a letter stating the marshal wants to marry me. I won't vie for him like some prize at a carnival."

Miss Bennett shoved her aside with her elbow. "I'm not giving up without a fight, and if we have to have a contest to find the winner, I'm game."

The young Irish woman looked as white as milk and remained silent.

"This is a bigger mess than you'd find at a stockyard." Miss Blackstone plopped back onto her chair, arms crossed.

"Well, you only made things worse when you showed up," Miss Bennett said. "Two brides wanting the same man was bad enough."

Miss Blackstone puckered her lips and glared at the young blond. Luke wondered if he might have to separate the brides to keep them from throwing punches. He could hardly blame them for being disconcerted. He certainly was.

"I really like the contest idea." Mark leaned back with his fingers laced behind his head. "It could solve our problem, and we could get the whole town involved. The women could make you dinner, maybe sew you a shirt or something—I don't know."

"And just where are they going to cook this dinner?" Luke shook his head at the absurdity of the idea.

"Rachel would probably let them use her kitchen, beings as it's for such a good cause." Mark grinned.

"What good cause? And there's not a kitchen in town big enough for three feuding women to cook in." Rachel crossed her arms over her chest, a frown marring her pretty features.

"We could charge people to sample and judge the food, and the money could go to the church." Garrett stood with his hands on his hips, grinning, as if he'd just solved everyone's problem.

"No, wait. Not a dinner. How about a pie-making contest? And we can help judge it." Mark licked his lips and raised his brows.

Luke shook his head. "I'm not about to ask these women to spend what little money they may have left cooking for me."

Mark drew his eyebrows down. "Of course you won't. You'll provide the supplies, and they'll do the work."

Luke scratched the back of his neck and half admired his cousins for their ingenuity, even though it was going to cost him more than money, he suspected. He glanced at Jenny Evans to see what she thought of the idea and found her scribbling notes as fast as she could write. Jack sat off to the side, behind her ma, watching the whole ordeal with wide-eyed excitement. His gaze swung over to the ladies. "What makes you think these ladies would even agree to such a harebrained idea?"

Garrett turned to face the women. "If you're serious about marrying the marshal, you'd be willing to fight for him, wouldn't you?"

Each bride slowly nodded but looked skeptical.

"Besides," Garrett said, "a contest would be a good way to see which of you would make the best wife for Luke, and the whole town could get involved."

"Now hold on. I didn't even say I wanted to marry one of 'em."

Jenny looked up from her pad and quirked a brow. Luke fidgeted, knowing he wanted nothing to do with a lawsuit.

Mark strode to the front window and looked out. "Well, you won't know for sure unless you spend some time with them—see how good they can cook. You just might fall head over heels in love, and then you'll be in debt to us for the rest of your life."

"Just where I've always wanted to be." Luke shook his head. All three women were comely enough that a man wouldn't tire of looking at them over the years, but was marrying one of them the right thing to do? Hadn't he asked the good Lord on occasion to send him a mate? But a stranger—a mail-order bride that he hadn't ordered? What would God have him do?

The Lord moved in mysterious ways, he knew, but this situation seemed too outlandish to be the hand of God.

"Personally, now that I've had time to ponder the idea, I think it's excellent." Miss Bennett curled her finger around a tress of loose blond hair.

"B–but what happens to the l–losers?" Miss O'Neil's eyes looked as wide as silver dollars.

Rachel glanced at Luke's cousins. "Since you and Mark caused this situation, it's only fair that you pay for the ladies' room and board until they can find employment or marry."

"What if that takes a while?" Mark straightened and crossed his arms over his chest. "Jobs aren't readily available for females."

Rachel shrugged. "You should have thought of that before writing to so many women."

"Maybe the contest will show off the ladies' talents, and the other bachelors in the area will be swarming for their attention." Garrett grinned.

"I'm not much of a cook, b–but I can sew." Miss O'Neil gazed up, a wary look engulfing her fair face.

"That's why we'd need to have several categories—to make it fair for all entrants." Garrett paced the room, his eyes dancing. "This could be the biggest thing to happen in Lookout in a decade."

Luke couldn't help wondering if the last big news story in Lookout had been Rachel's marriage to James Hamilton when the whole town had expected her to marry him.

"Yeah, I bet everyone for miles around would like to get in on the fun." Mark leaned forward in his chair, his elbows on his knees and his eyes livelier than Luke had seen them since his homecoming.

"I don't know. It seems rather. . .unconventional," said Rachel.

"But it would solve one bride's dilemma, providing the marshal was willing to marry the winner." Miss Evans looked at Luke, all but daring him to say no.

He swiped at a trickle of sweat on his temple. Was he ready to marry? Could he make a life with one of these women?

His gaze drifted to Rachel. Marrying would sure solve one problem—it would get Rachel off his mind. The Lord did work in peculiar ways at times, but was this the Lord's provision? Or just another of his cousins' crazy stunts?

He thought of the lawsuit. Jenny Evans was tenacious enough to actually sue his cousins. He couldn't stand by and watch them lose their livelihood if he had it within his power to help them. He felt his head nodding in spite of his reservations.

Rachel's eyes went wide; then something that looked like disappointment crossed her pretty face. Would she begrudge him marrying, having a family, and finding some happiness like she had?

"Was that a yes?" Jenny asked.

Luke shrugged. "Yeah, I reckon so."

Garrett and Mark let out a whoop in unison that made the brides jump. Luke wished he could be that excited instead of feeling like he'd just stuck his head into a hangman's noose.

Chapter 19

Luke sipped his morning coffee and studied the newest batch of wanted posters that had come in on yesterday's stage. He didn't recognize any of the men, nor had there been any illegal activity in the region since he'd arrived other than a pickpocket who seemed to have moved on to better pickings. The peaceful little town hardly needed a marshal, except maybe on Friday and Saturday nights when the cowpokes came in.

Max looked up at him with big brown eyes, and Luke realized that Jack hadn't come by with the bucket of breakfast scraps that she normally brought each morning. He gazed out the window and watched the citizens of Lookout as they went about their daily business. Maybe he and Max should wander over to Rachel's and see what the holdup was. But then he might run into one of the brides.

Rachel hurried past his window and charged through his open door with a scowl on her normally happy face. What now?

He rose and nodded. She sure was pretty when she had a bee in her bonnet.

"Have you seen this morning's paper?" She set the scrap bucket down in front of Max and slapped the *Lookout Herald* on his desk before he could respond.

Luke picked up the paper and read the headline. "THREE BRIDES BATTLE FOR ONE MAN'S HEART." Grinding his back teeth, he slammed the newspaper against his desk and paced the small office. Was nothing sacred?

"What are we going to do?" Rachel stared up at him, her soft blue eyes looking vulnerable.

Luke didn't like her fretting. He wanted to fold her into his arms until her frown turned into a smile. To avoid doing just that, he picked up the paper again and started reading: *"Lookout, Texas, to host bride contest. In hopes of helping their cousin, Marshal Luke Davis, find a wife, Garrett and Mark Corbett wrote to several mail-order brides. Imagine their surprise when not one, but three women arrived in town to marry the same man."*

Luke clenched his jaw. This whole situation was getting out of hand faster than a drunken brawl at the Wet Your Whistle. He continued reading about the pie-making contest that would be held in three days and how people could participate and raise money for the church by paying five cents for a small taste of each pie. Then they could vote for their favorite. At least the newspaper lady had told the truth about the contest and hadn't added a slant to the story. Nor had she mentioned blackmailing him with threats of a lawsuit.

He laid the paper back on his desk, slid his hip onto the corner, and crossed his arms, wishing this whole thing would go away.

"Are you really going to marry one of those women?" Rachel nibbled her lower lip, and he couldn't help watching. She'd always done that when she was nervous, and it never failed to intrigue him. Her lips looked so soft. No, he *knew* they were soft.

He shook his head to steer himself away from such disastrous thoughts. Why was Rachel so anxious?

"I reckon I will get married since I said I would. A man has to keep his word."

"I can't believe that." Her nostrils flared and eyes sparked, doing odd things to his insides. He held her gaze, and after a moment, she ducked her head and seemed to be watching Max, who'd nearly finished his breakfast. The dog glanced up, licked his lips, and burped.

Luke grinned. With Max, all was good as long as he had food and someone to love him. Was *he* all that different? What more did a man need?

He tried to imagine what life would have been like if he'd been married to Rachel all this time. He'd never have been in the cavalry and probably wouldn't be the marshal now. How would he have supported a wife and family?

He'd been so young and naive when he'd lost his heart to her. Now that he was older and had hindsight, he realized how ill prepared he'd been to marry back when he was eighteen. He and Rachel would have had next to nothing, but somehow that would have been enough. All he really needed was her—and the Lord. But he hadn't known much about God back then.

Rachel peered at Luke without lifting her head. "Could you actually marry a woman you don't. . .love?"

Filled with a sudden desire to shove away his melancholy thoughts, Luke snorted a sarcastic laugh. "Loving a woman doesn't guarantee a happy marriage. It doesn't guarantee a marriage at all."

"I'm truly sorry, Luke." She reached out and laid a hand on his arm. Her eyes glistened as if she might cry. "You have no idea how much."

He shook off her hand and strode over to stand in front of the window, not wanting to see her sad expression. How could a man stay strong and determined in the face of a woman's tears? Females never played fair. He ran a finger down the window. One of these days he needed to clean the dingy glass.

"I heard that you became a Christian. Surely you've learned that God expects us to forgive one another for our misdeeds. Can't you forgive me for what I did?"

He flinched as if she'd punched him in the gut. Didn't she know that she hadn't just broken his heart but that she'd crushed it into so many pieces it would never be the same? Left it so shattered that he'd never love again? He wanted to forgive her, but he didn't know how. *Lord, help me.*

"You'll never know how sorry I am that I married James."

"Why did you?"

"I–it's not something I can talk about."

"Don't you think you owe me that much?"

"Yes." Rachel's soft whisper almost made Luke turn around, but he held himself stiff, as if at attention. He couldn't help being intrigued. Why would she regret marrying the richest man in town? Had she learned that true love meant more than money?

He'd never considered that James and Rachel's marriage might not have been a happy one. James was a charmer who most people liked. Yeah, he could be selfish, having been the only child of a wealthy couple, and he liked to gamble more than the average fellow, but he was friendly, funny, and generous with his money.

Max whined and nosed Luke's hand. Even the dog could sense the tension in the room. Luke hated causing Rachel pain, but after all he'd suffered, the least she could do was explain why she'd dropped him so suddenly and married James.

Rachel made a noise that sounded like a strangled sob, and she dashed out the door. Luke's first impulse was to run after her, but he held his ground. He was empty—had nothing to say that could ease her pain.

He thought of a verse from Mathew that he'd read last night before going to bed. *"For if ye forgive men their trespasses, your heavenly Father will also forgive you: But if ye forgive not men their trespasses, neither will your Father forgive your trespasses."*

Luke returned to his desk and dropped down onto the chair, his fingers forking through his hair. Max rested his head on Luke's thigh, and he reached out to pat the dog. "How do I excuse what she did, Max?"

But God's Word was clear: if he didn't forgive Rachel, then God couldn't forgive him.

Luke hung his head. Without God's love and pardon from sin, he would still be a lonely sinner, lost and unsaved. Somehow, he had to find a way to get over Rachel, to forgive her, and to turn loose from his pain.

But how?

The mayor appeared in the doorway and leaned on the jamb, pulling Luke from his perplexing thoughts. Mayor Burke's dark hair, slicked down and divided in the middle, gleamed like a raven's wing. Luke could smell the odor of pomade clear over at his desk. "Mrs. Hamilton sure left in a hurry. Looked like she was kind of weepy."

Luke drew a deep breath in through his nose. He wasn't in the mood to deal with the pompous mayor just now.

Titus Burke tugged on his fancy vest. "She's a fine woman, and I don't like seeing her hurt."

The man's words ignited a flame of irritation. "I don't like it, either, and honestly, Mayor, it's none of your affair."

The man sniffed and looked over the top of his wire-rimmed glasses at Luke. His eye twitched, reminding Luke of a long-lashed mule that he worked with back at the fort. "Well, this hoopla you're causing with all these boardinghouse brides *is* my concern. Lookout can't afford a lawsuit."

How had he heard about that? Luke stood, giving himself the advantage of height. "Nobody's going to sue the town."

The mayor scowled and looked up. "I certainly hope not. This bride contest is the biggest thing since James Hamilton gambled away his family's fortune. It's the kind of thing that could put Lookout on the map."

Luke blinked, stunned by the mayor's declaration. He couldn't imagine James Hamilton broke, but that explained why Rachel had turned Hamilton House into a boardinghouse. How had she taken the news of her husband's poverty when it had come? Must have been difficult to go from having next to nothing to being the richest woman in town, and then back to nothing again. But then, Rachel had always been one to roll with the punches, except where her child was concerned.

"This bride thing is big news. We could have folks from all over the county coming here to participate."

Luke hooked his thumbs into his belt. "So?"

"The point I'm trying to make is that I. . .uh. . .the town council expects you to do your part and marry up with one of those women."

Luke lifted one brow. "Or what?"

Mayor Burke pulled off his glasses and busied himself cleaning them. He took his own sweet time putting them back on and adjusting them to fit. "Or you may find yourself out of a job."

Luke straightened, hands on his hips. "That's ridiculous. A man can't be fired because he chooses to marry or not."

"You need to do the right thing by those women."

Luke leaned forward, glaring at the mayor. The man took a step back and swallowed hard. "Look, I didn't have anything to do with their coming here. That was all my cousins' doing. Maybe you should be forcing them to marry."

"You're the one in the limelight now, and the one who can make this town look bad. Folks won't want to move here if word gets out that we don't treat our women right."

Luke clamped his back teeth together and swallowed a growl. This was ridiculous. He'd be better off leaving this hole-in-the-wall town and rejoining the cavalry. *Lord, give me patience.*

"Even if I do marry one of them, that still leaves two disappointed women."

The mayor shrugged. "We'll think of something. Maybe have a contest to find grooms for them." He chuckled.

Luke rolled his eyes. "I may regret doing so, but I gave my word to marry, and I will—unless the good Lord makes it clear that He doesn't want me to."

The mayor puffed out his chest. "Good. Things should be just fine." He stared at Luke for a moment then ambled out of the office.

Luke strode to the porch and studied the town. He had a strange feeling that things would never be fine again.

Jack paced alongside the river, picked up a rock, and flung it as far as she could. If only she could be rid of the brides so easily.

"What's got your dander up?" Ricky leaned back against a boulder, relaxing in the shade.

"Whatever it is, stop chuckin' them rocks in the water. You're scarin' the fish away." Jonesy cast a glare in her direction then went back to staring at the water where he'd dropped his fishing line.

Jack stomped closer to her friends. "The marshal has agreed to marry one of those brides."

"So? He's gettin' long in the tooth," Jonesy said. "If'n he wants to marry, I reckon he should do it before he gets much older."

Jack shoved Jonesy in the shoulder. "Luke's not old."

"Well, he's way too old for you to be frettin' over." Ricky yawned, crossed his arms behind his head, and closed his eyes.

Irritation welled up in Jack like steam building in a locomotive. "Oh! You two are dumber than all them grown-ups runnin' that stupid bride rodeo."

Ricky sat up and glared at her, his eyelids heavy with sleep. "Watch who you call names, or we won't let you hang out with us anymore."

"Fine, then I won't give y'all any more of my ma's cookies." Jack crossed her arms and marched back to the water's edge.

"Aw, leave her be, Ricky. You know how good her ma's baked goods are." Jonesy winked at her as their friend dropped back down on the boulder.

The water lapping against the river's edge and the whispering of the trees above as they cast dancing shadows out over the water failed to soothe her as they normally did. All she could think about was Luke marrying one of those brides instead of her ma. She'd hoped so much that Ma and Luke would fall in love and that the three of them could one day be a family. Her ma cared for Luke, Jack was certain of that, but he didn't seem to return the affection.

She kicked at a small rock, sending it sailing into the water. Oh, she'd seen Luke look at her ma on occasion as if she was the prettiest lollipop in the jar, but then his expression would sour, as if she'd done something bad to him. She dropped onto the creek bank and pulled up her knees, resting her arms and head on them. Her eyes stung as tears threatened, and a big lump in her throat made it hard to swallow. Why did all those dumb brides have to show up and ruin things? If she'd only had a bit more time, she might have figured out a way to get Luke and her ma to fall in love.

Jonesy heaved a big sigh, dragged his line through the water, and sat down beside her. "You ain't cryin', are ya?"

"No! I just got somethin' in my eyes." Maybe that was stretching the truth, but her friends would think she was a crybaby if they ever caught her weeping. She turned her face to the side and wiped the moisture from her eyes.

"Then what's got you so long-faced? You remind me of my pa's mule."

Jack gasped and punched him in the shoulder. "I don't look like a mule."

He rubbed his arm and scowled back. "I didn't say you looked like one. Why are you in such a foul mood?"

Jack turned back to stare at the water. "All those brides."

"What about 'em?"

She pressed her face into her arms. "You wouldn't understand."

"Understand what?"

Jack shook her head, heaved a sigh, and rested her head on

her arms again. "I want Marshal Davis to marry my ma, not those other women."

Jonesy gasped. "Why in the world would you want the marshal for a pa?"

She didn't look up but could imagine Jonesy's green eyes going wide, like they did when he was scared or surprised. He didn't understand any more than the chirping birds overhead. "I like Luke. I don't think he'd be mean like my other pa was."

"Aren't all fathers mean?"

Jack shook her head. "I don't think so. I've seen men at church smile, even when their kids acted up. I've seen them stroke their child's head, like Luke did mine once, and even kiss their children."

"Well, I don't think stroking heads is much of a reason to want someone to be your pa."

"It's not just that. He took Max in and gave him a home when nobody else gave a hoot about him."

Jonesy gazed out where his line was in the water. "That dog was just an old stray."

She scowled and lifted her head. "He's a good dog that just needed someone to love him."

"If you say so."

"I do." She bumped Jonesy's shoulder, a little less hard this time. "So what do I do about those brides?"

"How would I know?"

She rested her chin on her arms and stared at the water. The sun glistened in spots where it managed to break through the thick layer of leaves overhead, looking like swirling stars. She had to do something to make the brides leave before Luke could choose one to marry. But what?

"Maybe we could do something to scare them off. Like make up a story about a ghost haunting the boardinghouse," Jonesy offered.

"Yeah," Ricky bolted up, even though Jack thought he'd fallen asleep. "We could even dress in a sheet and sneak into their rooms at night and scare them."

Jack felt their excitement growing but shook her head. "We can't do anything to give the boardinghouse a bad reputation. That's how Ma makes a living for us."

"Then let's think up something else."

The boys were silent for a few moments, each lost in their own imagination, just as Jack was. Sadly, she drew a blank the one time her own future was at stake.

Jonesy snapped his fingers. "I've got it. We could sabotage the pie contest."

A wide grin pulled at Ricky's face. "Yeah, that could be funny, since the whole town seems bent on buying pieces of the pie so they can vote on them."

Jack smiled. "It wouldn't be too hard to do. Just dump some extra salt into the pies before they're cooked."

"Remind me not to sample them," Jonesy said.

The boys laughed, and Jack joined in, feeling better for the first time in days. She had a plan, and surely it would work. She just hoped her mother didn't find out.

"Hey!" Jonesy jumped up. "I got a bite!"

Chapter 20

Shannon ventured out of her room and made her way downstairs. For two days, she'd chewed her fingernails worrying about making a pie and had finally worked up her nerve to ask Mrs. Hamilton for help. No doubt the other brides had already decided what they'd be baking, but she'd never made a pie before.

Back home in Ireland, her mother had barely put enough food on the table for them to survive, much less made desserts. Shannon hadn't tasted her first pie until she'd started working at the Wakefield estate, and while she thoroughly enjoyed them, especially the apple pie with cinnamon added to it, she'd been a maid, not a cook.

At the foot of the stairs, she noticed Miss Bennett and Miss Blackstone in the parlor, both studying thick books. Cookbooks would be her guess. Maybe she should try that, but then she knew nothing of measuring or cooking terms.

Miss Bennett didn't acknowledge her and kept studying the page before her, but Miss Blackstone glanced up and scorched her with a glare.

Shannon lifted her skirt and dashed down the hall, away from the heat of the other bride's stare. She had hoped to make friends with the women, but both only saw her as competition, which she was, even though she doubted she stood a chance at winning the marshal's heart. If she had any other option, she'd willingly give up her chance to marry him. Not that he wasn't a fine man, but she'd prefer to be courted and wooed by a man she knew at least a wee bit. Yet who would want to court her? Other than keeping a clean home, what did she truly have to offer a man? Hadn't her da told her on many occasions how useless she was?

She walked past the dining room to the kitchen. Mrs. Hamilton stood with her back to Shannon as she reached the doorway. The pale yellow walls looked so cheery, and everything had its place, making the room tidy and organized. She'd never worked in a kitchen before. She was kept too busy at the Wakefield estate, and by bedtime, she was so tired she could almost fall asleep on her feet.

If she ever hoped to have a fair chance with the marshal, she had to learn to cook. At least to bake a pie. She cleared her throat, and Mrs. Hamilton pivoted.

Her hands were covered in flour from the dough she was working with. She held one hand to her chest, leaving white powder on her blue apron bib. "Oh, you startled me."

"Beggin' yer pardon, mum. I was wondering if I could ask for yer assistance in an important matter."

"Of course. How can I help you?"

Shannon twisted a strand of hair and stared at the ground. Why should asking such a small thing be so hard? Maybe because she'd never asked for help before? She had made her way as best she could after her parents died and had nothing to be ashamed of. She'd even gotten that job at the beautiful Wakefield estate, although little help that would be now since she left in such haste without obtaining a referral letter. Gaining employment could prove difficult. At least she didn't have to worry about paying room and board for the time being.

"Do you mind if I keep working while we talk? I want to be sure to have supper ready on time." Without waiting for a response, Mrs. Hamilton spun around and went back to cutting out biscuits with the edge of a glass dipped in flour.

Shannon moved into the overly warm room to stand next to her hostess. "Is there anything I could help you with?"

"You might peek at my pies and see if they are browned yet."

Shannon took the towel lying on the worktable and opened the stove door with it. "They're a wee bit brown, but I'm not sure if they're done yet."

Rachel looked over her shoulder. "Go ahead and take them out, if you don't mind. Then close the door so the oven can reheat. I'll have the biscuits ready to go in soon. So, what can I help you with?"

"I. . .wondered if you might. . .uh, help me to bake a pie—for the contest, I mean. A pie that would win the marshal's heart." Shannon's cheeks grew warm. "I've. . .uh. . .never learned to cook."

Rachel's grip tightened on the glass. This was too much to bear. She'd housed the brides, cooked meals for them, kept their rooms clean, and put fresh sheets on their beds, but to help them bake pies that would steal Luke's heart away from her was too much to ask.

She blinked away the surprising tears stinging her eyes. How could she respond to such a question?

Stiffening her back, she considered what the Lord would have her do. Obviously, it wasn't His will for her and Luke to marry. A pain clutched her heart, almost as if her butcher knife had slipped and stabbed her chest. She didn't deserve Luke, but she couldn't help loving him. She'd never stopped, even though she'd tried hard to squelch any thoughts or feelings for him while married. But his return had reopened a deep wound she thought had scabbed over.

Miss O'Neil still awaited her answer. Rachel took a fortifying breath, forced a smile, and looked over her shoulder. "Of course

I can teach you to bake a pie."

Miss O'Neil gazed at her with uncertain eyes. "You're sure 'twouldn't be a bother?"

Rachel's chin quivered, and no amount of willpower could stop it. She spun back around to her biscuits and forced her voice to be steady. "No trouble at all. I bake pies most days, anyway. How about tomorrow after breakfast?"

"Aye, tomorrow then. Thank you ever so much, and I'd be happy to help you as repayment, if you could just let me know how."

Rachel's lips trembled, and tears blurred her eyes. "No thanks needed."

Miss O'Neil padded away, and Rachel lost her composure. She dropped the glass on top of her dough and rushed outside. Tears that she'd tried so hard to conquer spilled down her cheeks. She trotted past the woodpile, where she'd often seen Luke shirtless, his skin gleaming with sweat, his arm muscles bulging as he lifted the ax. A deep sense of loss nearly knocked her off her feet. How could she go on knowing he was married to another woman? Was this piercing pain what he'd felt when she'd married James?

She dropped to her knees behind Luke's little house and out of view of anyone looking out her back door. Gazing up at the sky, she sought God for strength. "How do I do this, Lord? How do I help these women prepare to battle for the man I love?"

Only a few weeks had passed after Luke's return before she realized the depths of her feelings for him. But what did that matter when he refused to forgive her? And enduring the ache of his rejection had opened her eyes to how he'd suffered. New tears spilled for the pain she'd caused him. If only she hadn't trusted James. Hadn't dawdled at the river when she'd learned Luke wasn't coming. Hadn't allowed herself to be alone with James that one time. She faced the truth: She didn't deserve Luke. He was a good, honest man who'd loved her with his whole being—and she had betrayed that love.

She cried until her throat ached and her nose was stuffy. Using her apron for a handkerchief, she wiped her face and sat on the warm ground, empty and barren. "Help me, Father. Give me strength."

She glanced up at the brilliant blue sky showing through the canopy of trees. The leaves swished in the light breeze, and the warmth of the sun dried her tears. "Show me what to do. *Please.*"

After a short time of sitting and praying, a calm spread through her limp limbs and peace again reigned in her heart. If she couldn't have Luke, maybe she could help him find the best bride. She wouldn't be vindictive or allow selfishness to keep her from helping them. She didn't know which woman would be the best fit for Luke, not that it was her choice, but at least she could teach Miss O'Neil to bake a pie.

Standing, she dusted the back of her dress and wiped off her face again. As she ambled back to Hamilton House, her aunt's letters came to mind. For years, her Aunt Millie, her mother's sister, had tried to get Rachel to move to Kansas City to live with her. Rachel had never seriously considered the woman's offer. Lookout had always been her home, and she had the boardinghouse to support her and Jacqueline. But if Luke married, she didn't think her heart could take seeing him happily wed to another woman and raising children. Her lip wobbled, and fresh tears stung her aching eyes, but she batted them away. At the well, she drew up a fresh bucket of cool water and rinsed her face.

The mayor had offered to purchase Hamilton House several times since James's death. Kansas City was a bigger city than Lookout and would most likely have a school that ran higher than eighth grade, giving more educational opportunities for Jacqueline and plenty of ways for Rachel to earn some income, should she need it after the sale of her home.

She heaved in a raggedy sigh. Maybe it was time to consider leaving Lookout.

Leah dipped her pen in the ink bottle, then blotted the point and continued her letter to Sue Anne:

I envy your being engaged to that rancher. I never thought when I traveled so far from home that I'd have to battle two other women for the marshal's heart. Can you even imagine such a fiasco? Now there's to be a contest to determine who will make the best bride for him. Whoever heard of such a thing? The first round is a pie-baking contest.

Leah grinned, thinking of the second place ribbon she'd won in last year's county fair for her rhubarb pie. She'd been baking since she was a young girl and would surely win this round.

Have I told you how charming Luke Davis is? Oh my. So tall, and ever so handsome with his deep brown eyes and pecan-colored hair. He walks so straight and with such authority, although I do delight in seeing him flustered. With all the brides arriving to marry him, he's been more frustrated than a man whose wife just birthed him his seventh daughter.

I intend to win. I have no other option. What is to become of me if I should fail? I can't return home. Pa surely wouldn't allow me to after I refused to marry Mr. Abernathy and ran off without so much as a good-bye.

Losing is not an alternative I can bear to think about. I simply must win.

How is Ma? The children?

Have you received any more letters from your Simon?

I want you to know that the money you gave me just before I left town was a lifesaver. You'll remember how I didn't want to accept it, but I'm thankful now that I did. I was able to pay room and board at the boardinghouse the first few days I was here. The marshal has ordered his cousins to foot our bills until things are settled. I don't like that, but there's little I can do about the situation.

And thank your brother again for helping me with my trunk that night I snuck away and for driving me to Joplin. I couldn't bear to leave it behind since Sam made it for me.

Leah finished the missive and sat back in her chair. She would mail the letter tomorrow morning, but tonight she had to decide which pie she would bake. It needed to be something that would please the marshal's palate and stand out from the others. The contest was only two days away, and she could not fail.

She unfastened her high-topped shoes and sat on the edge of the bed, considering her competition. Miss O'Neil, looking shy and fearful all the time, surely wouldn't turn the marshal's head; but then again, who needed to cook and sew when she had such an intriguing accent and such luscious auburn hair and fair skin. Shannon really was a lovely girl.

Leah reclined on the comfortable bed. She loved the pretty room painted a pale blue, almost the color of Mrs. Hamilton's eyes. Leah scowled at the memory of how the woman had looked at Luke with such longing in her gaze. She obviously knew the marshal well. But just what their relationship was, Leah wasn't sure. It seemed much deeper than Mrs. Hamilton simply providing his meals. Why, she'd bet her grandmother's cameo that they had an intertwining past of some sort.

Turning over, she stared out the window, watching the sunset. A bird chirped in a nearby tree, trying to outdo the crickets in the grass below. She should probably put on her nightgown. All the stress of the contest and being around the other brides daily wore on her. Made her tired, even though she'd done very little work that day. Who would have thought idleness could exhaust a person?

Maybe she should ask Mrs. Hamilton if there was some work she could do to pass the time. After working her fingers to the nubs at home, she had enjoyed having little to do, yet that was getting old. Maybe she didn't mind working as long as she had a choice in the matter.

The sun sank below the horizon, painting the undersides of the clouds a breath-stealing pinkish purple. A brisk wind snapped the white curtains like flags. She actually liked the wide-openness of Texas. Something about the place pulled at her, made her never want to leave. But if she lost the bride contest, she'd have to seek employment somewhere or return home—and that was something she was unwilling to do.

Forcing herself up from the bed, she unfastened the buttons on her dress and let it drop to the floor. Miss Blackstone's calculating stare entered her mind. The woman had a perpetual scowl and talked very little, yet she was quite pretty in an unfinished way. She tried to hide her roughness, but Leah saw right through her. If the lady could cook well, she would surely be her toughest competitor. Maybe it was time to look at her more closely.

Chapter 21

The night before the bride contest, Rachel sat in her bedroom, brushing her long hair for one hundred strokes. Jacqueline was in bed, but the girl fidgeted, unable to lie still. Something was bothering her, but she'd been tight-lipped and scarce the past few days.

Rachel reached out to set her brush on the vanity when a shrill scream broke the silence. Jacqueline bolted up in bed as Rachel vaulted to her feet. Their gazes locked. "Stay here."

She grabbed the rifle that always sat behind the door and ran up the stairs. Miss O'Neil's door opened, and bright light from her lantern flooded the hallway. Miss Bennett stood immobile at her door, her wide blue eyes gleaming in the light. Mr. Sanderson, a new guest in town with his wife for the contest, stood at the open door of the fourth bedroom, a pistol wobbling in his shaky hand. "What's going on, Mrs. Hamilton?"

"I don't know, sir, but I'll find out."

"Do you need my help?" The man lifted one brow.

Rachel glanced at Miss Blackstone's door. "Perhaps you could stay in your room and watch—just in case?"

"This is highly irregular," said Mrs. Sanderson. "Harvey, come back inside and shut the door. I'm sure Mrs. Hamilton can handle the disruption without your assistance."

He harrumphed but didn't close the door. He winked at Rachel and motioned her forward with his gun just as another squeal erupted from Miss Blackstone's room.

Rachel hurried over and knocked on the door. "Is everything all right, Miss Blackstone?"

"N–no, there's a snake in here." At the other bride's declaration, Miss O'Neil scurried back into her room and slammed the door.

Rachel opened Miss Blackstone's door and peered around the room. How in the world could a snake have gotten up to the second story? A dim light from her lamp left the room in a contrast of light and shadows. Watching her step, Rachel crossed the room and turned up the flame. "Where did you last see it?"

The woman who'd always seemed tough as overworked dough huddled in a tight ball on her bed, arms locked around her legs. "U–under the d–dresser."

"Do you know what kind of snake it is?"

Miss Blackstone shook her head; a thick curtain of black hair fell around her shoulders. Her eyes were wide, and her lips pressed tightly together.

Rachel didn't care for snakes, but she wasn't frightened of them, except for the cottonmouths that sometimes frequented the river tributaries. Growing up in Texas and working in her ma's garden, she'd seen her share of snakes. She lifted the lamp and stooped down. Sure enough, something was under the wooden chest of drawers. She used the muzzle of her rifle and flipped the intruder out onto the rug. Miss Blackstone screeched, making Rachel jump.

"It's just a harmless garden snake."

Miss Blackstone cowered on the bed. "I hate sn–snakes of all kinds. My brother used to torment me with them."

"I'm truly sorry for your discomfort. I can't imagine how it got up here unless it somehow crawled into my laundry basket while I was gathering things off the line." She picked up the harmless foot-long snake by the tail.

Miss Blackstone squealed and dove under the covers. Rachel shook her head and left the room. "Please try to relax and get some rest. Tomorrow is a busy day." Juggling the rifle and snake in one arm, she closed the door.

Rachel glanced at the Sandersons' door, and Mr. Sanderson lifted his brows. She held up the snake. "Nothing but a little intruder, sir. Nothing to be concerned with."

He nodded and closed the door.

Miss Bennett leaned against the door frame of her room, her lip curling. "That's what all the ruckus was about?"

Rachel battled her grin. "I can't imagine how it got up here."

"I didn't think Miss Blackstone was afraid of anything. I mean, she seems so tough."

Rachel nodded. "I suppose there's something that frightens each of us. Good night, Miss Bennett."

As Rachel plodded down the stairs, she considered what frightened her most—Luke marrying another woman. She tossed the snake outside and closed the front door. Suddenly, she realized that her daughter hadn't made an appearance upstairs, and that was highly uncharacteristic of her.

With suspicions mounting, Rachel hurried to their bedroom, but much to her relief, the girl was still in bed. Miracles happened after all.

Jack's heart pounded like she'd run all the way to the river and back. She'd barely made it back into bed when her mother closed the front door. Did she suspect her of putting the snake in Miss Blackstone's room?

Jack worked to slow her breathing, thinking of the open door to the pie safe. She'd hoped to stir something into the pies that would ruin them before they were cooked, but there'd been no opportunity. She might not get dessert for supper tomorrow if the mice invaded the pastries, but at least Luke couldn't pick a bride if the pies weren't edible. She grinned into her pillow, just imagining the howls of the brides when they saw their ruined entries.

A tiny measure of guilt wafted through her, but she shoved it away. Luke was worth fighting for, no matter the cost or how many years she'd be punished and sent to her room if her mother learned what she'd done.

She could hear her mother moving around the room, settling the rifle behind the door, and the click of the latch as the door closed. The double bed creaked and dipped on one side as her mother sat down. A sudden thought charged into Jack's mind—if her mother married Luke, she would get a room of her own. She smiled and wondered which one she'd choose.

Her mother heaved a big sigh and relaxed against the pillow, sending the odor of lavender her way. "Don't you want to know what happened? I know you're not asleep. And thank you for obeying me and staying in the room."

Jack cringed, knowing she'd done the opposite. Why did disobeying feel so awful?

Turning onto her side, she stared at her mother's face, illuminated by the faint moonlight shining through the open window. "Do you know what folks are calling those brides?"

Her ma shook her head. "What's that?"

"Boardinghouse brides." Jack flopped onto her back and stared at the dark ceiling. "Are you gonna let Marshal Davis marry one of them without so much as a fight?"

Her mother's heavy sigh warmed the side of her face and fluttered her hair. "There's nothing I can do about the situation. Luke agreed to marry one of them."

Jack sat up, fighting back tears. "But you have to do something. I want him to be my pa."

Rachel pulled her down into her arms, and Jack reveled in her ma's softness and sweet scent. "Oh baby, I'm sorry. Why didn't you tell me how you felt?"

"It didn't matter until all those dumb brides showed up. I figured we could take our time, and eventually he'd fall in love with us."

Rachel tightened her grip. "I'm sure he loves you, honey. How could he not?"

Jack wrapped her arm around her ma's trim waist. "But I want him to love you, too."

Her ma smoothed Jack's hair from her face. "Oh sweetie, you can't force someone to love you. It has to come natural."

"But I heard that Luke used to love you—before you married my pa. Can't you make him love you again?"

Rachel winced as her daughter's words pierced her heart. If only Jacqueline knew how badly she wanted Luke to love her. But she'd done all she knew how to get him to forgive her. She had to leave it in the Lord's hands now.

Tears burned her eyes and ran down her temples into her ears. If only there was something she *could* do.

Jacqueline tugged away from her and sat up. "I have an idea."

Rachel wiped her eyes, hoping her daughter couldn't see her tears. "What's that?"

Jacqueline clutched her hand. "Why don't you enter the bride contest?"

She opened her mouth, ready to give a dozen reasons why she couldn't, but her voice refused to respond.

"Really, Ma. Why don'tcha?"

"Well, because it's a contest just between the brides."

"But don't you care for Luke?"

Rachel nodded, unable to deny the truth. Somewhere over the past few weeks, her love for him had rekindled and flamed to life like a rampant prairie fire. "Yes, I do, but—"

"No buts. You *have* to enter that contest."

"I can't. It wouldn't be fair to the brides."

Jacqueline shook her arm, her voice sounding frantic. "If you love him, you have to. Otherwise, we're going to lose him."

Rachel considered the wisdom of her daughter's words. It was true. If she passively did nothing, Luke would choose one of the brides and marry, leaving her to endure the rest of her life alone and filled with regrets. Still, if by chance he did pick her, all the brides would be left unmarried. How could she do that to them? "I don't think it's fair for me to enter. Luke already knows me, and that might sway his choice."

"Well, enter anan. . .anon—what's that called?"

"Anonymously?"

"Yeah! That."

Rachel sat up, her heart taking off like a caged bird finally set free. Could she do it? Enter the contest anonymously? At some point she'd have to admit the pie was hers, but maybe, just maybe in the meantime, Luke would realize how much she still loved him. Excitement drove away her sadness. Maybe she still had a chance. Grinning, she pulled her daughter into a warm hug. "I think that's a brilliant idea, sweetie. But it will be a secret, and we can't tell a soul."

"My lips are locked shut." In the moonlight, Jack twisted her hand in front of her mouth as if turning a key in a lock. She bounced on the bed, grabbing Rachel's shoulders. "Oh Ma, this will be such fun. The whole town will be wondering who the pie is from."

Rachel laid back down, smiling to herself. Why hadn't she thought of the idea? Maybe because she was too busy mourning her loss of Luke. *Oh, please, Lord, let this work. Help me to win back Luke's heart.*

She turned onto her side, thinking of all the pies she'd served Luke since he returned. To make things fair, she needed to bake a different pie—something he wouldn't recognize as hers. Jacqueline fidgeted for a while; then her breathing deepened as sleep claimed her. But Rachel's mind raced. She had to find a special pie to woo the man she loved.

Chapter 22

Marshal, they're ready for you to come and judge the pie contest." Mayor Burke stood inside the jail door, all but bouncing. He grinned. "And there's a big surprise for you."

Luke stood, dreading the task ahead. If he chose a winner, the losers would be disappointed, but then contests were always like that. They just didn't normally have your whole future riding on them.

He followed the mayor outside, where a crowd filled the street and boardwalks. His cousins had rigged up a table in front of the freight office, and Rachel and the ladies had decorated it with a white tablecloth, ribbons, bows, and other frippery. Atop it sat not three pies, but four.

"How in the world could something like this happen?" Luke's gaze swerved toward the mayor, who stood to the left of the table.

The man grinned and shrugged. "Nobody seems to know. One minute it wasn't there, and the next it was."

Luke lifted his hat, ran his hand through his hair, and slapped the hat back down. Picking a wife by sampling three pies was enough of a chore, but now there were four—the last, a golden-colored one that looked like a custard pie, with a sign beside it reading Anonymous Entry. The fragrant scent of the pies made Luke's mouth water. But warning bells clanged in his head. That pie could be from any unmarried woman for miles around.

"Hey, Marshal, how's it feel to have all them gals wantin' to marry up w'ya? Maybe some of us bachelors could have the leftovers." Dan Howard laughed, and the crowd filling Main Street joined in.

"Yeah, Marshal, share the wealth," someone cried.

Luke shook his head at their good-natured teasing but focused a glare on Garrett. None of this would have happened if not for him. "Are you sure no new brides have come to town?"

"Not as far as I know," Garrett answered.

Standing beside his brother and the mayor on the left side of the table, Mark also shook his head and shrugged one shoulder.

Luke scanned the crowd for Rachel. She could confirm if another bride had arrived in town, but he didn't find her. He could hardly blame her for not attending the contest, considering their past and how she'd begged him for forgiveness. He studied the ruffled edge of the tablecloth covering the pie table and sighed. He couldn't give her something he didn't have. So why did he feel guilty about the whole situation?

"This is outrageous." Miss Bennett, standing to the right of the table with the other brides, stomped her foot and hoisted her chin in the air. "That last pie ought'a be tossed out."

With her hands planted on her hips, Miss Blackstone stepped forward. "Yeah, I thought this contest was just between us three."

Miss O'Neil fiddled with her sleeve, her eyes looking as wide as dinner plates.

Luke pinned his stare on the brides. "Has someone new moved into the boardinghouse? Another bride, I mean."

All three gals shook their heads in unison—blond, brunette, and redhead. They would certainly know if another husband-seeker had come to town.

He studied the table holding the contest entries. Each one

had a label made from a folded paper, and they read BRIDE #1, BRIDE #2, BRIDE #3, AND ANONYMOUS ENTRY, but the last sign was in a different handwriting than the others. The four pies sat, begging to be cut, although one of them looked a bit charred, and two had notches out of them that looked as if a varmint had feasted on them. The pie from the anonymous bride was by far the best looking. His stomach gurgled, reminding him that he'd been so nervous this morning he'd skipped breakfast.

His gaze wandered back to the fourth pie. What if it tasted the best? If he chose that one as the winner, he might well end up marrying Bertha Boyd. A shiver snaked down his spine, and he scanned the crowd to see if she was there. Sure enough, the wagon-sized woman sat on a sagging bench on the boardwalk across the street, fanning herself with one of those cardboard advertisements on a stick that a mortuary office from a neighboring town had handed out. The crowd in the street in front of the freight office, watching and waiting to help judge the event, had tripled in size from what it had been earlier.

Max crept up beside Luke and licked his hand then trotted back into the jailhouse. The dog hated crowds, probably because most of the "kindly" townsfolk had chased him away from their trash heaps at one time or another. Luke wished he could hide out like his dog, but he straightened his shoulders and turned back to the mayor. "What do you make of this additional entry?"

The mayor sucked in his overly large belly and grinned. "I haven't a clue, but it will make a great headline: ANONYMOUS BRIDE COMPETES FOR MARSHAL'S HAND IN MARRIAGE." He chuckled and shook his head then scanned the crowd. "Where's that newspaper woman? Someone get Jenny up here," he yelled, "and tell her to bring her photographic equipment."

"I'm here, Mayor." Jenny Evans peeked her head between two beefy men. "Let me through, you big belugas."

Both men turned sideways, looking as if they were trying to figure out if she'd called them an offensive name, and Jenny shot through the opening carrying her big camera. Jack followed right on her tail with her arms filled with photographic plates. Jenny was one gutsy lady to entrust Rachel's daughter with something so fragile.

"You brides line up behind the pie you made." Jenny set down the long legs of the tripod and arranged them the way she wanted, then set the boxy camera on top. Jack handed her a film plate, and Jenny inserted it. "All right, ladies, look up here. Hold your expressions steady."

Luke was amazed the three mail-order brides did as ordered without complaint, although Miss Blackstone hung back a bit, as if she didn't like being photographed. He now knew who made which pie. Not that it mattered, because he didn't favor one gal over the other, except he maybe liked Miss O'Neil the least because she was so skittish. She was a lovely thing with that mass of copper hair and intriguing accent, but she didn't have what it took to live in Texas.

That would have left two brides to pick from if not for the anonymous entry. He searched his mind, trying to figure out who might have made it. There weren't many marriageable women in Lookout, which was why his cousins had concocted this whole scheme. But someone from another town might have read of the event and entered, or someone from a family he hadn't yet met.

"Thank you, ladies. You can move now." Jenny waved her hand, setting the brides in motion.

"Now, Marshal," Miss Evans said, "if you'd be so kind, I'd like a picture of you in front of that mystery entry."

Luke shook his head. He'd never had his photograph taken before and wasn't going to start today.

"Go on, Luke. Don't be shy." Garrett's cocky grin made Luke want to knock it off his face. "You gonna let those brides show you up?"

The crowd joined in cheering for Luke to get his photo taken. He sighed and took his place behind the table. Holding a hooded glare on his face, he hoped he made everyone squirm. This whole shebang was getting out of hand. Whatever made him agree to marry was beyond him. Even a lawsuit sounded half good at this point.

Jenny took the photograph, and the mayor quickly stepped in front of the table, facing the crowd. Jack slipped in beside him and tugged on Luke's pants. He leaned down. "I like that surprise pie best, don't you?"

He studied her expression for a minute but decided she knew nothing about the owner of that particular entry. Either that, or she sure could keep a straight face.

"I probably should reserve judgment until I taste them." He grinned and tweaked Jack's button nose.

Mayor Burke lifted his hands, and the crowd quieted. "All right, let's get this show on the road, and maybe we'll have a wedding tonight."

A cheer rang out from the crowd at the same time a lump the size of a turkey egg formed in Luke's throat. Nobody had said anything about an immediate wedding. Weren't there other parts to this contest yet to be held? He ran his hand over his jaw. If only he hadn't given his word to marry.

"First, we'll let the marshal taste the pies. I'll go next, and then the Corbetts. After that, it will cost you five cents for one spoonful of each pie until they are all gone. There's a jelly jar in front of each pie plate. When you pay your money to my wife over there," he motioned his hand to the right, "you'll get a dried bean. Taste the confections, then drop your bean into the jar you feel is the winner. All funds received will be donated to the church, so if you feel inclined to give more than required, I'm sure the reverend would be appreciative. And of course, Luke doesn't have to marry the gal who gets the most votes. He has the final say as to which pie he thinks is the best. If he's ready to pick a bride, I reckon we could have a weddin' tonight."

The mayor glanced at Luke, as if expecting him to object,

but Luke clamped his mouth shut. He just wanted to get this over with.

"All right," the mayor said. "Let's get started."

People pushed forward, as if each wanted a chance to sample the pies before they were all gone. The noise of the crowd grew louder. Many of the folks who lived around Lookout were farmers or ranchers who worked hard and lived a lonely existence. These social gatherings were few and far between, but Luke knew that each person would be encouraged just because they came to town to enjoy the fun and were able to forget their own troubles and visit with their neighbors for a short while.

"Just wait until you bite into this, Marshal Davis." Miss Bennett grinned and batted her lashes. She served him a large slice of her pie, which was the one with the bite gone. Luke was glad she cut his slice from the other side of the pie, not that he wouldn't eat it just because of that, but he'd had his share of eating food that critters had gotten into during his cavalry days. The other brides also served him generous portions of their pies. Miss Blackstone's and Miss O'Neil's were the overly cooked ones, but they still looked juicy inside. Maybe all wasn't lost for them. He stopped in front of the fourth pie, but nobody stepped up to serve it.

"I can help." Jack, her hands now empty, scurried behind the table and reached for the knife.

Miss Bennett hurried past the front of the table and held out her hand. "You'd better let an adult handle that."

Jack scowled but dropped the knife and stepped back, arms crossed. Miss Bennett deftly cut a rather thin slice and dropped it onto his plate. She grinned. "Here you go, Marshal Davis."

Eager to get away from the staring brides, Luke took his plate back into the jail and shut the door. He didn't want people gawking at him while he ate and decided which pie he liked best. His mouth watered at the scent of cinnamon, apples, and peaches, but his fork went to the custard first. It had always been a favorite of his, and he hadn't had any since he'd left the cavalry. The sweet, buttery flavor tickled his taste buds, and his eyes dropped shut as he ran the confection over his tongue. This wasn't custard at all, but something different. Something even better. And it was a chilled pie, something he'd very rarely had. Too bad he hadn't gotten a larger slice of that one.

Garrett kicked the door open and stormed into the room, carrying his plate. "Whoowee! Can you believe all the people who came to town today? Must be a couple of hundred."

Mark followed, already chewing. His blue eyes widened, and he spit out the bite of pie. His wild gaze searched the room, then he grabbed Luke's coffee cup off the desk and downed the last of the cold coffee. Garrett lifted up an edge of the apple pie as if wary of it.

Mark spun around, one hand lifted up, palm outward. "Don't try that. Something's wrong with it."

Garrett sniffed it. "Smells fine."

"By all means, if you don't believe me, go ahead and take a bite."

Garrett eyed it again. "Guess I'll try the peach one." He cut a slice with his fork and shoved it in. His eyes closed for a second but then went wide just as Mark's had. He wagged his hand in front on his mouth. "Water!"

Mark shook his head and grabbed Luke's coffeepot. Garrett downed the mug in one long gulp then glared at this brother. "I thought you said it was the apple pie that tasted bad."

"I did."

"Well, so does the peach. Miss O'Neil must have grabbed the salt instead of the sugar."

Luke stared at his plate, wondering if the nut pie would also be bad. He glanced up at his cousins. Mark dropped down onto a chair, arms crossed, and grinned at him. Garrett set his plate on the desk and watched. Luke now dreaded having to taste the last pie, but he figured it was only fair to try each one. He put a tidbit of the nut pie on his fork and licked it. Burnt sugar assaulted his senses.

"I can tell that one's just as bad." Garrett said. "What do you think happened?"

Luke swallowed hard and set the plate down. "I don't know. This one's not salty, but the inside tastes burnt. As for those other two, I can understand *one* person accidentally grabbing the salt instead of sugar since they look just the same, but for two of them to do that?"

Mark's head jerked up. "Two?"

"Yeah, that custard—or whatever it is—tastes great." As if needing to confirm it, he retrieved his plate and finished off the last of his slice while his cousins dug into theirs.

Mark's eyes rolled upward. "That was delicious."

"Yeah, it's great," Garrett said around a mouthful. "But who made it?"

Luke shrugged. "I have no idea."

"Seems strange for a woman to enter a pie-baking, husband-getting contest but not give her name."

Garrett shrugged. "Maybe she's as ugly as the backside of a mule."

Luke didn't care for his cousin's crude comment. "So, what do I do about it?"

Mark licked the section of his plate where the custard had been. "If everything she cooks tastes like this, I'll marry her myself."

The men chuckled, and Luke shook his head. The outer door opened, and the mayor stomped inside and glared at Luke.

"What a disaster. The whole town is upset. Half the people are fussing for a refund because the pies were so bad. Only one of them was edible."

Luke walked to the door and looked out. "Guess I should go see if I can soothe everybody."

"This is a nightmare. That's what." The mayor huffed and puffed like a wild turkey trying to impress its mate.

"It's a setback, not a disaster, Mayor." Mark always was the diplomat of the group. "It will just serve to increase interest for next week's contest."

The mayor tugged his vest down and pushed his glasses up on his nose. "How so?"

Garrett flashed the grin that Luke knew would make the mayor see his side of things. "Everyone will wonder if those brides can sew better than they can cook. If Luke postpones making a decision, I reckon most folks will come back next week to see if he chooses one then. Also, everyone will be talking and trying to figure out who the mystery bride is."

"Maybe you could somehow play it up to benefit the town," Mark said. "Have a potluck and dance afterward."

Mayor Burke rubbed his chin with his index finger and thumb. "Yes, I do see your point. Perhaps this wasn't quite the disaster I thought. Although most of the men who were asking about the leftover brides took to the hills when they learned the women couldn't cook." He chuckled, and his whole belly bounced.

Luke stepped away from the door now that he was sure things were all right outside. "It's odd that three of the four pies would be so bad."

"You think someone sabotaged the contest?" Garrett asked.

Luke shrugged. "I don't know, but it is a possibility."

"But who, and why?" Mark asked.

Since the pies were cooked at Rachel's, Luke could well imagine Jack playing a prank and swapping the salt and sugar containers, but for what purpose?

Could it be the girl was jealous and thought she'd lose his friendship if he married? Maybe he needed to reassure her that such a thing wouldn't happen.

Rachel stirred the pot of potato soup then set the spoon on her worktable. The sandwiches and pumpkin pudding were ready for lunch as soon as the brides and other guests returned from the pie contest. She'd stood in her doorway, watching the crowd, but couldn't bring herself to walk down there. If Luke selected a bride today, she didn't want to be there.

It was foolish of her to have entered, and if not for Jacqueline's help, she would have been discovered. Her gaze darted toward the pie table. Had Luke liked hers the best?

A figure parted from the crowd and strode in her direction. Rand. Rachel clutched the door frame, not wanting to face him today with her emotions all in a tizzy.

"Afternoon, Rachel." Rand removed his hat and held it in front of him.

She forced a smile, almost wishing she did have feelings for the kind rancher. "Rand."

He glanced back over his shoulder. "That's some to-do they're havin'."

"Did you sample the pies?"

He shook his head. "Nah. I thought about it, but I don't like being caught up in a crowd. Been out on the open prairie too long, I reckon. Anyway, I heard none of them were any good except that mystery pie."

Rachel's heart somersaulted. "What was wrong with the others?"

"Two of them were too salty, someone said. Not sure about the third one."

Her grip on the door frame tightened. "So, the marshal didn't pick a bride?"

"Nope. There's to be a shirt-sewing contest now."

Relief that Luke hadn't chosen a wife yet made her knees weak.

"You wouldn't want to accompany me to the judgin' next Saturday, would ya?"

Rachel closed her eyes. She didn't want to hurt Rand, but he needed to know she had no interest in him.

"Never mind. I can tell by your expression that's a no." He

hung his head and curled the edge of his hat.

"I'm sorry, Rand. I like you a lot. You're a good friend, but friendship is all I have to offer you."

His mouth pushed up in a resigned pucker. "I reckon I've known that for a while, but I just didn't want to accept it."

Rachel laid her hand on his arm. "You're a good man, Rand. You deserve a woman who will love you with all of her heart."

"Thank you for your honesty." He nodded and shoved his hat on. "I won't pester you anymore."

She watched him stride back toward the dispersing crowd, her heart aching. But she'd done the right thing. She wouldn't marry another man she didn't love.

She returned to the kitchen, and her hands shook as she carried the plate of sandwiches to the buffet in the dining room where she set them beside the individual bowls of pudding. She just needed to ladle up the soup, and all would be ready.

"Who would do such a thing?"

"I've never been so humiliated in all my life."

Rachel hurried into the entryway at the distressed sound of the brides' voices.

Miss O'Neil held her handkerchief in front of her red face. "Oh Mrs. Hamilton, everything was such a—" The girl lapsed into a phrase in Gaelic.

"My thoughts exactly." Miss Blackstone's face scrunched up, and she kicked at the bottom step of the inside stairway. "The whole thing was a disaster."

Miss Bennett anchored her hands to her hips. "I want to know who would trick us like that."

"Please, won't you sit down to lunch and let us sort this out?" Rachel held out her hands, hoping to calm everyone.

"I. . .I don't believe I can eat." Miss O'Neil dropped into a chair and rested her chin in her hand, elbow on the table. The poor girl looked so forlorn.

Miss Blackstone rolled her eyes, while Miss Bennett claimed

her seat at the dining table.

Rachel laid her hand on the Irish girl's shoulder. "Some warm soup will make you feel better."

While the women waited, Rachel quickly ladled the soup into the tureen and placed it with the other food on the buffet. By now, the other guests had entered and also seated themselves. She stood at the head of the table, curiosity nibbling at her. She knew about the mice getting into the pie safe and damaging a couple of the pies, but how had two of them turned out too salty? "Shall we pray?"

Miss Blackstone made a snorty sound that resembled a laugh, but everyone else ducked their heads. "Heavenly Father, we thank You for Your bountiful blessings and pray that You will work out things for each of the young women seated here today. Bless my other guests, too, and keep them safe in their travels."

Conversation was kept to a minimum while her guests served themselves. Rachel walked to the front door, wondering where Jacqueline was. She rarely missed mealtimes. Just then, she saw her daughter exit the marshal's office, hike up her skirt, and make a beeline for home. Rachel pursed her lips. Would that child never learn proper manners?

Jacqueline skidded to a halt on the porch when she saw her mother watching her. "You missed all the excitement, Ma! I just gotta go wash up. Sorry I'm late for lunch, but I was talking with Luke."

Rachel stepped outside. "Jacqueline, ladies do not run—and don't refer to the marshal by his given name."

"Sure, Ma." Jacqueline waved her hand as she hurried around the side of the house toward the back where the water pump was.

Shaking her head, Rachel walked back inside, suddenly remembering the day the brides had arrived. She'd done the very thing she'd chastised her daughter for doing when she'd remembered the pies she'd left in the oven. She sighed and went to the buffet and dished up Jacqueline's soup.

When they were all seated again, Rachel looked around the table. "So, what happened? Mr. Kessler mentioned something about the pies being too salty."

The three brides looked suspiciously at one another. Miss Bennett hiked up her chin. "It seems someone must have switched your sugar for salt. My pie and Miss O'Neil's were both overly salty and inedible. We made our pies at the same time, remember?"

"Maybe you just grabbed the wrong container," Jacqueline said, helping herself to a bowl of pudding off the buffet.

Miss Bennett frowned at her. "I've been cooking all my life and have never made that mistake."

"That nut pie tasted as if the inside mixings had been burnt," Mr. Sanderson offered.

"I guess I cooked it too long." Miss Blackstone stirred her food on her plate. "I didn't normally cook on a stove, so I didn't make many pies."

Rachel wondered about her comment. Where had she lived that she had to cook without a stove?

"The fourth one was the best," Jacqueline interjected as she took her seat. "It was better than perfect."

If the other three pies had turned out bad, that meant Luke probably liked hers the best. Rachel ducked her head to hide a smile.

"You didn't by chance get the salt and sugar in the wrong containers, did you?" Miss O'Neil asked.

Rachel shook her head. "If I had, we'd have noticed. Most things I cook have either sugar or salt in them. I don't understand how such a thing could happen. I keep my containers clearly marked."

Miss Blackstone shook her head and slurped her soup. "Sure seems odd that all three of ours turned out bad. It's almost as if someone did it on purpose."

"Uh huh, like that anonymous bride," Miss Bennett muttered.

Rachel winced and stuck a spoonful of soup in her mouth. Her gaze drifted to Jacqueline. The girl didn't want Luke marrying one of the brides, but would she go so far as to ruin the other entries?

Jacqueline looked up and smiled with innocence. Wouldn't she look guilty if she'd done such an unconscionable thing?

"I'm certainly curious who that fourth entry was from," Mrs. Sanderson said.

Her husband grinned. "That sure stirred up a lot of interest. Everyone's speculating who it belongs to."

"Well," Mrs. Sanderson said, "the marshal is a handsome man. I can see why an unwed woman would want to throw her hat into that contest and win him for a mate."

Mr. Sanderson's spoon stopped in front of his mouth, and he scowled. His wife patted his arm. "Now, Harvey, don't let such a little comment spoil your dinner. The marshal is a comely man, but you're the one who's held my heart all these years." She smiled sweetly at him, and he nodded and resumed eating.

Rachel's heart ached. Would she ever know the love of a good man again? Her thoughts flashed to Rand, but she knew he wasn't the man for her. She'd only ever imagined herself married to Luke. With him out of the picture, could she love someone else?

She shook her head and stared into her soup. No, Luke was the only man she'd ever love. Oh, she'd tried to care for James after they were married, but he pushed her away with his cruel streak. And on the day he first slapped Jacqueline and knocked her down, Rachel knew she could never love him. If only she'd never married him.

Her mistake had been to allow James to comfort her that day at the river. She hadn't spent time with Luke in over two weeks because he'd been working so much. When she learned he wasn't coming, she'd gotten teary-eyed. James had hugged her. Told her he'd never neglect her like Luke had.

She shivered, remembering how he'd kissed her temple. How his hold on her had tightened. "I love you, Rachel. I have for a long time." He kissed her lips, and for the briefest of seconds, she'd felt like a princess because the most eligible bachelor in town cared for her. But then she saw Luke's face in her mind and knew where her heart belonged. She struggled—told him to stop—but James, carried away by his passion, shoved her down. She'd tried to fight him off, but he was too strong. And afterward, he'd told her that Luke would no longer want her since she was a fallen woman. James offered to marry her, but now she realized that she'd only been a pawn.

James had been spoiled as a child, and as an adult, he took what he wanted. Somewhere along the line, he'd decided he wanted her and was determined to steal her away from Luke. When he realized he couldn't overcome her love for Luke, he stole the most special gift she had to give her husband, her purity.

"Something wrong, Ma?" Jacqueline stared at her with worried eyes.

"Uh. . .no baby, I just need to get more soup." Jumping to her feet, Rachel hurried to the buffet, grabbed the tureen, and hustled into the kitchen where she slowly refilled the big bowl. She hung her head. Did Luke know what James had done? Did he know why she had to marry James?

No wonder he couldn't forgive her. She could hardly forgive herself. Tears burned her eyes, but she blinked them away lest they fall in the soup or her guests notice. Somehow she had to find it within herself to keep going until Luke chose a bride. She'd been foolish—hopeful—to enter the contest, but she wouldn't do it again.

Chapter 23

Jack hurried through her morning ablutions and dried her face with a once-blue towel, now faded to a soft gray, that smelled of sunshine and the outdoors. She always felt more awake after washing her face in the cool well water.

The house smelled of fried bacon and eggs, making her tummy squawk. She slipped the hated dress over her head and buttoned up the front. Whoever made the rule that girls had to wear dresses should have been forced to wear one himself. It was hard to run in them—not that ladies should run—but who wanted to be a lady?

Boys had all the fun. They got to work with horses, fish, even chop wood while women had to cook, clean, wash, and sew. How was that fair? She ran the brush through her hair and braided it. If her ma would let her, she'd cut it all off short; but according to Ma, a woman's glory was her hair. Men liked women to have long hair, she said.

Jack smacked the brush down on the vanity, wincing at the loud noise. If her ma heard that, she would lecture her about taking care of what they had and have Jack polishing every piece of furniture in the whole house as punishment.

She rubbed her hand over the dark wood, thankful that she hadn't scratched the vanity that her grandmother Hamilton had shipped from New York. Jack appreciated having nice things, because she knew that most of the kids at school didn't enjoy such luxuries.

She glanced at herself in the oval mirror, grimacing at how girlish she looked. Why couldn't she have been born a boy? Then she could have protected her ma from her father.

Yesterday had been Sunday, and her ma hadn't said anything about the pies, probably because it was the Lord's Day. Jack was sure she would today, and she couldn't wait to tell her again how much Luke had liked her pie. She had no idea how the salt and sugar had gotten mixed up when the brides were baking their pies, but she sure was glad it had.

Jack walked into the kitchen. Her ma bent and removed a pan of biscuits from the oven. She smiled when she saw Jack. "I was just coming to make sure you'd gotten up and that you hadn't taken ill. By the way, the Sandersons are leaving today."

Jack sighed. School had ended on Friday, and she'd hoped to go fishing today, but with the boarders leaving, she and her mother would have extra work cleaning the empty room.

"Put these on the buffet." She slid the bowl of biscuits toward Jack. "And please set the table and put out a plate of butter. I'm running a bit late myself."

Wondering if her ma had overslept, too, Jack carried the bowl to the buffet, then pulled cloth napkins from a drawer as well as silverware. She set the table, thinking how her ma had looked tired rather than rested. Maybe she was upset about Saturday's events. Jack had expected questions about the pies, but Ma had been especially quiet last night.

Shouldn't she have been happy that her pie was the only edible one?

Breakfast was a quiet affair. Miss O'Neil didn't come downstairs. Jack glanced over at Miss Bennett. The pretty blond slathered peach jam onto her biscuit and took a bite. Miss Blackstone ate with her face almost in her plate, as if she feared someone would take the food away from her. Jack's ma would never let her get away with that kind of behavior.

"I'm finished, Ma." Jack placed her silverware on her plate.

"Very well. Take your dish to the kitchen, please."

Jack looked at her ma's plate as she passed her, surprised at how little she'd eaten. Something was certainly bothering her.

She dumped her food scraps in the bucket for Max and set her plate in the sink, just as her ma entered the kitchen. Jack grabbed the partially filled scrap bucket and hurried to the door, hoping to make a quick escape.

"Wait. I need to ask you something."

Ack! Too late. "I gotta get these scraps to Max. You don't want him goin' hungry do you?"

Her ma followed her outside and grabbed her shoulder. "Just a minute, missy."

That stopped her. If her ma said "missy," she meant business. Jack swallowed the lump building in her throat.

"Did you swap the sugar and salt containers the day the brides were baking their pies? I want a truthful answer."

Jack felt her eyes widen. She'd thought about doing that very thing, and guilt wormed its way through her, even though she was innocent. Her remorse shifted to anger. Why did she always get blamed when something went wrong? "No Ma. Honestly, I didn't. I swear."

"Don't swear." Rachel crossed her arms. She lifted her eyes to the heavens as if she were praying. "Just tell me the truth. Did you do it so I might win?"

Jack flung her arms up. "I told you. I didn't do that."

"If I can't win fair and square, I don't want to win at all. Can you understand that?"

Jack shrugged. "I guess so. But if you don't win, we'll lose Luke."

Her ma closed her eyes as if the thought pained her. "Luke

was never ours to win. And I won't win by cheating, no matter what the cost."

Jack thought of a few times she'd cheated and won. It felt good to win, but afterward guilt had eaten away her joy, except for the time she'd beaten Butch Laird in a spelling contest. A light breeze lifted a lock of hair and blew it across her face, bringing with it the scent of wood smoke. Her ma reached down and tucked the wayward strand behind her ear. Jack studied her ma. Why couldn't Luke just pick her? She was every bit as pretty as the brides, although she was older than them. But didn't someone say *older was better*?

"Sweetie, I appreciate that you wanted to help me, but you were wrong to tamper with the pies."

"But I didn—"

Rachel lifted her hand. "I just wish you'd be honest. Other people were affected by your actions, and you'll have to be punished."

"But Ma—"

"I've decided not to enter the next round."

Jack's mouth fell open. Her ma still believed she was responsible, but even worse, she was giving up on the contest. "You can't quit." She tugged on her mother's sleeve. "I want Luke to be my pa, and you gotta marry him for that to happen."

Her ma looked up again, and Jack searched the sky to see what was so interesting up there.

After a while, her mother released a loud sigh. "Go feed Max, but when you get back, I'll have a list of extra chores for you to do as punishment."

Jack scowled and stomped off. Getting punished for something she'd done was bad enough because she deserved it, but knowing her mother didn't believe her made her stomach ache. Yeah, she'd opened the pie safe doors, but that's not what her ma had asked her about.

The thought of her ma quitting the contest brought tears to

her eyes. She swatted at them. She'd promised herself she'd never cry, because crying was a weakness. Boys made fun of kids who cried and picked on them.

She thought again of her ma not entering the other contests, and the idea sobered Jack. Somehow, she had to make sure her ma had an entry. She couldn't quit.

A few minutes later, she stopped at the marshal's office. Luke was gone, but Max lay sprawled on his blanket as if waiting for her. He lumbered up and wagged his tail. The old dog licked the gray whiskers around his nose and looked up eagerly. Jack set down the bucket, and Max started eating.

"I wish you could talk, old buddy." She scratched his back while he ate. "I'm sorry for being mean to you before. I didn't know what a good dog you were."

She thought of the many times the townsfolk had shouted at Max and chased him away from their trash heaps. Why should they care if a hungry dog helped himself to what they no longer wanted? Ricky and Jonesy had liked to chase Max and throw sticks at him, but she always tried to make them stop.

She knew what it was like to have someone yell at you and threaten to hurt you. She shivered just thinking about the evenings her pa would come home drunk or having lost at gambling. He'd holler at her ma like it was all her fault, shove her, and sometimes even slap or hit her. He hadn't been much of a father and never seemed to like her. Many times, he said he wished she'd been a boy.

Tears stung Jack's eyes again, and she swiped her sleeve over them. Max whined as if sensing her frustration and licked her cheek. "Oh Max, why can't Luke marry my ma and be my pa?"

Luke crossed the dusty street, waving to Simon O'Malley as he drove by with a load of hay in his wagon. The man kept Dan Howard, the livery owner, well-stocked in hay and feed. Luke could see Jack sitting on the floor, patting Max. As he neared, her words about wanting him for a father nearly made him stumble. He righted himself, looked around to see if anyone had noticed, and then stood outside his door. Luke's heart ached for the child, but he wasn't the answer to her prayers.

Jack didn't say anything else, but she suddenly jumped up. "Gotta go, boy."

She ran out the door and straight into Luke. He grabbed her shoulders to steady her, and she gasped and peered up. Her wariness changed to delight, warming his insides.

"Howdy, half bit. I just heard your ma holler for you."

She frowned and plodded back toward home.

What was wrong with her? If he wasn't mistaken, her lashes had looked damp from tears—and Jack never cried. Halfway home, she turned while walking backward and waved. "See you later."

His gaze followed her to the end of the street to make sure no one bothered her. She was a cute kid and reminded him of himself when he was young. Ornery, feisty. If only she were his child.

He scowled. Better not to think such thoughts. Spinning around, he marched back to his office, scanning the town and thinking about the wanted posters he'd looked through earlier. If he could capture one or two of those outlaws, he would get enough reward money so that he could order lumber for a house. He already had a lot picked out with a view of the river and could imagine a white clapboard house sitting on it.

He stopped and leaned against a hitching post. If he *were* to marry, he'd need a bigger house. The one the town provided was fine for him alone, but a wife would want to cook, and that Sunday house had no stove. He supposed he could build an outdoor kitchen. Lots of homes in Texas had them, usually on ranches and farms rather than in-town houses. That would be much easier, and maybe it would solve his problem for now.

The bigger problem he had was envisioning a woman other than Rachel in his home. Maybe because she cooked his meals now and did his laundry. He'd run into her a few times when she'd come over to clean or return his clothing. He shook his head. Somehow he needed to rid his mind of such images.

Forcing himself to focus on the brides, he stared across Bluebonnet Lane at the boardinghouse and tried to decide which woman would make the best wife. They were all pretty, but he wasn't attracted to any one of them in particular. He sighed and thumped the railing. That pie contest sure hadn't helped.

Who was the anonymous entry from? He'd racked his mind, trying to figure out who she was, but had no luck. He turned around and moseyed into Foster's Mercantile, nodding at Trudy Foster. "Everything all right in here?"

"Yes sir, Marshal. We're fine and dandy." Trudy smiled and continued sorting skeins of colorful thread.

Luke looked around for a few minutes, thinking about all the things he'd need to buy if he did get a house of his own. Finally, he exited the store. As he turned right, a woman's shapely body appeared in the doorway of his office. Miss Blackstone.

She looked down the street right at him and waved. "Morning, Marshal Davis. How are you this fine day?"

He'd been fine—until he saw her. Now his neck felt as tight as if he were dressed up in his church clothes. He pushed away from the hitching post and shoved his hands into his pockets as he walked toward her. Just what had she been doing in his office? And how had she gotten in there without him seeing her?

She looked pretty in her pine-colored calico, which made her brown eyes look almost hazel. Her hair was always a bit disheveled and tended to just be tied behind her with a ribbon, as if doing anything more to it was a chore. Something wild sparked in her eyes on occasion, making him wonder about her past.

He walked up to her and stopped since she blocked his doorway. "What can I do for you today?"

"I noticed that you never eat at the boardinghouse and thought you might be hungry." She stepped back into the office and motioned to something on his desk. She removed a towel from a plate, and the scent of bacon and eggs filled the room. His mouth watered.

"You made this?" he asked, walking over to look at the plate. His stomach rumbled.

She shifted her feet and looked around his office. "Well, uh... nope, but Mrs. Hamilton let me bring it to ya. I couldn't very well cook up somethin' else when she had all this left."

No, he didn't figure she could—and somehow didn't think she would have even if Rachel had allowed her use of the kitchen. Still, he sat down and tucked into the food since he hadn't had time to get over to the boardinghouse for breakfast this morning.

Miss Blackstone looked at a map on his wall. Luke noticed her hands trembling. Was she nervous being alone with him?

"Do you catch many outlaws in this little town?"

He shook his head. "No, but I run a tight command here and don't let things get out of control."

"Well, that makes me feel safer." She stared at him with her head cocked to one side until he looked away.

The hairs on the back of his neck lifted, and he couldn't for the life of him figure out why. A horse whinnied outside, and Miss Blackstone turned to look out the door. Luke studied her profile. Yeah, she was pretty, but something about her set him on edge.

He leaned back in his chair, holding his lukewarm coffee. Miss Blackstone pivoted back toward him and smiled. She looked softer, more approachable when she was happy. Maybe he was overreacting. Or just touchy, since she could be his wife one day soon. A shiver charged down his back.

He turned back to his food and noticed one of the two desk drawers was off kilter. He ignored it for the moment but knew it hadn't been like that when he'd left his office earlier. He took several more bites of food, hoping she hadn't noticed him looking at the drawer.

Had Miss Blackstone gone through his desk?

And if she had, what had she been looking for?

Carly resisted tapping her foot while the marshal ate. Just being in the jail office around a lawman made her itch to leave. Did she look more casual than she felt? Or could he tell she was nervous?

She cast a glance at the two cells in the shadows at the back of the room, and her throat threatened to close up and choke off her breath. One door was open, as if daring her to enter. If the law ever caught up with her, she would be locked up in such a place. A cold shiver snaked down her spine.

She forced her gaze back to the marshal. There hadn't been any information about payroll shipments in his desk. Tyson had said that town marshals always had that kind of information, and without it, she was stuck in this dinky town. Maybe she needed to come up with a better plan. Besides, how could she pull a payroll heist alone?

Trying to sway the marshal in her direction by flirting and taking him breakfast had probably been a dumb idea, but she had to do something to make herself stand out from the others. The marshal's fork scraped against his plate. He ate the last of the eggs and took another sip of his coffee.

"Could I freshen that up for you?"

He shook his head. "No thanks. I'm about done." He shoved the last third of a biscuit into his mouth.

The marshal was a fine-looking man with his lean, muscular body, handsome face, and dark hair and eyes. She had hoped he might like her nut pie better than the others, but that had hardly been the case. She had switched the salt and sugar before the other brides mixed up their pies, but she hadn't counted on burning hers.

Her gaze swerved toward the cell again, but she yanked it back. A stack of wanted posters on the side of the desk caught her eye. "Mind if I have a look at those?"

The marshal shrugged. "Suit yourself." He leaned back in his chair, holding his coffee cup and watching her.

She picked up the thick stack of posters and sat in the chair across from the marshal's desk. Slowly, she thumbed through each one. A hand-drawn picture of each outlaw looked her in the face. She didn't know most of the rough-looking men but did see two that she recognized—Wild Willy Watson and Hank Yarborough. Both men had run with her brother for a few months.

Pressing the posters to her chest, she stared at one lying in her lap and saw her brother's face. Her heart took off like an outlaw being chased by a posse.

The marshal's cup thunked as he set it down. He stared at her, brows lifted. "See someone you recognize?"

Carly forced a laugh. "Only someone who looks like someone I know."

Marshal Davis's eyes glanced toward the papers, and Carly quickly dropped the stack of posters back on top of her brother's likeness. She stood, and the whole pile slipped from her hands. "Oh goodness."

She squatted down, snatching up poster after poster, all the while her heart thudding as if she might be arrested. The marshal had noticed her reaction to Ty's poster. While she resembled her brother in some ways, she didn't look enough like him for the marshal to put two and two together. Too bad she hadn't had time to read the writing below Ty's likeness. Did it mention anything about him having a sister? If only she could get rid of Tyson's poster somehow.

The marshal stood and came toward her. "Let me get those for you, ma'am."

She forced herself up on wilting legs and handed him the stack. "If you're finished, I'll just take the plate back to the boardinghouse."

"Thank you kindly for bringing my breakfast." He nodded.

Carly picked up the plate, but the fork clattered to the floor. The marshal bent easily and handed it to her. She forced a grin and was half a block away before she could suck in a breath. Her gaze roamed over the town as she forced herself to relax. There was nothing to connect her with Tyson, but the marshal was a smart man. Could he tell she was lying? Whatever possessed her to do such a foolish thing as to visit him?

She continued on toward Hamilton House. Had it been a mistake to assume Ellie Blackstone's identity? Now that she was in Lookout and had seen the one-horse town, she doubted many payroll shipments passed through here. Yep, she needed another plan.

Maybe things would have been better if she'd never crossed paths with Ellie Blackstone.

Luke stood at his door and watched Miss Blackstone scurry away like a rat caught in a feed bag. She was hiding something. And if he wasn't mistaken, she was lying, too. But about what?

He sat down at his desk and slowly studied each poster. He was certain she'd recognized someone, but there were nearly twenty likenesses of outlaws, and he hadn't gotten a good look at the one she'd stumbled over. None of the wanted men were named Blackstone, but a name was a simple thing to change.

The hairs on the back of his neck stood on end. Did Miss Blackstone have other business in town besides landing a husband?

Chapter 24

Rachel stood in the backyard with her hands on her hips, staring down at her precocious daughter. The sun sprinkled through the trees, dappling Jacqueline's upturned face, casting shadows on the smattering of freckles on her nose. "I'm sorry, sweetie, but I've told you before, I'm not entering the bride contest this time around."

Jacqueline clutched Rachel's arm. "But Ma, you've gotta. You can't let Luke marry one of them brides."

Rachel closed her eyes for a moment, steeling herself against her daughter's pleas. Jacqueline was too young to understand all that had happened between her and Luke. "No. I can't enter."

Tears filled Jacqueline's blue eyes, piercing Rachel's heart. Her tough daughter rarely cried, and seeing her do so now made Rachel waver. Should she compete in the contest's next round? Even if she happened to win, there was still the issue of Luke's unwillingness to forgive her. She straightened her back and her resolve. "I can't."

"You mean you won't." Jacqueline stomped her feet. "You're ruining everything."

Rachel sighed and took her daughter's hand, pulling her over to sit in the double rocker that rested under a tall pine. She hugged the stiff girl. "Just because I enter the contest doesn't mean Luke would pick me anyway. He doesn't know my pie was the anonymous entry, and he's sure not going to agree to marry the winner if he doesn't know who she is. Besides, there are things you don't know about Luke and me."

Jacqueline rubbed her sleeve over her eyes. "What kind of things?"

Nibbling the inside of her lower lip, Rachel considered how much to tell her. "I was engaged to Luke before I married your pa."

The blue of Jacqueline's eyes intensified. "You nearly married Luke? What happened? Why didn'tcha?"

Rachel pressed her lips together. What a can of worms she'd just opened. It would have been best to keep quiet. A blue jay screeched overhead as if agreeing and letting her know she was intruding in its territory. She stroked her daughter's head. "It was a very long time ago, and I don't want to talk about it. I just thought if you knew about the engagement you'd understand why I can't enter the contest."

"No! I don't." Jacqueline shot to her feet. "If you were engaged once, why couldn't you be again?"

Smoothing out her dress, Rachel prayed for the right response. "Because it ended badly. I married your father, and Luke left town and joined the cavalry."

"So? He's back now, and you're not married anymore."

She made it sound so simple. But Rachel couldn't think of a way to explain without mentioning Luke's inability to forgive her, and she wouldn't make Luke look bad in her daughter's eyes. "That's all in the past. I'm not entering the contest, and that's final."

Jacqueline flung out her arms. "Why do you always have to ruin things? I hate you." She spun and ran toward the river, her braids flying behind her.

Rachel clutched her upper arms, her heart aching. She knew Jacqueline didn't hate her, but the words still inflicted pain, as they were meant to. She stared up at the sky. "Lord, I know You control all things, but I don't understand why You had to bring Luke back to town. Maybe things wouldn't hurt so bad if he'd forgive me, but to see him each day and to always have this past between us is so difficult. Is it my punishment to watch Luke marry one of the mail-order brides? Is that what You require from me as penance for what I did?"

She dropped her head. God didn't work that way. She knew that. But she wanted Luke for a husband as badly as Jacqueline wanted him for her pa. The truth was she still loved him. She sat for a while, praying and seeking God, but no answers came. Blinking the tears from her eyes, she saw the back door open. Miss Blackstone looked out and saw her then started forward. Rachel straightened her back. For some reason, God had sent the brides to live with her for a time. Maybe it was so she could speak His Word into their lives. *God, help me. Give me the fortitude to do what You've set before me, and please watch over Jacqueline. Comfort her and keep her safe while she's away from me.*

"Could I. . .uh. . .talk with you for a minute?" Miss Blackstone looked hesitant to interrupt her.

"Certainly." Rachel sniffed and patted the chair beside her, hoping her face wasn't red and splotchy from crying.

Miss Blackstone sat and glanced sideways. "You all right?"

Rachel forced out a little laugh. "Yes, I just had a confrontation with my daughter."

"Oh. Well, I was. . .uh. . .wonderin' if you could show me how to stitch a shirt for the next bride contest." She wrung her hands. "I mean, I can sew—some. I ain't never made a shirt before."

Part of Rachel wanted to shout no. To jump up and run away like Jacqueline. She already housed and fed the mail-order brides, but they wanted her to help them win Luke's heart. She simply couldn't do that. "Of course I'll help you."

Miss Blackstone smiled, looking younger than she normally did. "Thanks. That's right nice of ya."

Rachel fingered the long hair hanging down the young woman's back. "I don't want to offend you, but if you'd like, I could show you some ways to style your hair—so you'd look extra nice for Saturday's contest, I mean."

Surprise flashed in Miss Blackstone's eyes. "Thank you, kindly. I'd like that." She looked down and seemed to be studying the ground. "My ma died when I was young. I lived with my brother for a while, but he didn't have time or patience for things like fixin' hair."

"I'm sorry about your mother. I lost mine, too. If not for the Lord, I don't know how I would have made it without her."

Miss Blackstone gave her an odd look.

Rachel jumped up. "I have about a half hour before I need to start supper. Would you care to get started on the shirt now?"

Miss Blackstone nodded and followed Rachel through the kitchen and into her bedroom. As she reached for the dresser knobs, Rachel's hands shook. She hadn't looked at James's things since she put them away, shortly after his death. She pulled out the bottom drawer and scanned the garments. Several shirts lay next to the stack of store-bought silk handkerchiefs that James had preferred to her homemade ones. She really should get rid of all these things. Why had she kept them so long?

"These were my husband's." She laid the four shirts on the bed and rifled through them, finding the one she wanted. "This is a simple design. We'll need to choose some fabric. I. . .uh. . .have a small supply."

Miss Blackstone shook her head. "The marshal's supposed to give us money to buy cloth and supplies, so I won't need yours."

The young woman fingered the edge of the top shirt, a tan one. "Mine won't look near as nice as yours."

Rachel forced a smile as she gathered up the shirts. "But mine won't be in the contest."

Jack's heart pounded as she shut her bedroom door. Her mother was across the hall, busy with supper preparations, but if she noticed the closed door, she'd surely come to investigate. Jack had told herself that what she was doing wasn't wrong. In a way, her father's belongings were partially hers, weren't they?

Standing in front of the chest of drawers, she forced her hands to stop shaking. It only worked for a second before the trembling started again. She knelt down, slid open the bottom drawer, and scowled. Even after three years, she could still smell her pa's scent on his clothing, and it was all she could do not to retch in the drawer.

She quickly thumbed through the shirts that lay with his socks and the fancy hankies he'd liked. A soft blue one stood out among the others, and she picked it up and examined its stitching. Perfect, just like all her ma's sewing. If Jack put her mind to it, she could probably sew as well one day, but the thought of sitting in one spot long enough to make something this nice made her shiver. How did women do it? Sewing hours and hours at a time? They even seemed to have fun at quilting bees, but of course, they chatted with the other women and had food to eat.

Jack shoved the drawer shut and held the shirt in her hand. Luke liked blue. She knew that because he wore that color a lot. But would it fit him? She tried to remember how big her father was, but Luke seemed so much larger. Well, there was nothing she could do about that.

She heard a sound just outside the door and jumped. Grabbing her skirts up, she dove between the bed and the wall. The handle jiggled, and the door opened. Jack stuffed the shirt under the bed and tried to calm her shaking.

"Sweetie?" Footsteps followed her mother's voice into the room. "Hmm. . ."

Jack held her breath. The room was small, and if her ma

walked much farther, she was sure to see her hiding—and what excuse could Jack give for being on the floor? That she was asleep and fell off the bed?

Footsteps carried her mother away, and Jack waited a few minutes for her heart to stop banging before she peered over the bed. She nearly gasped out loud when she saw the door was left open.

"Jacqueline?" Her mother called, sounding as if she were yelling out the back door.

Ducking down again, Jack considered how she might get the shirt onto the table with the other brides' entries. Surely Luke would like her mother's the best. Nobody could sew like her ma. Jack looked down at her dress, and in spite of hating it, she thought of all the hours her mother had put into sewing it for her. She always had nice clothes made from pretty fabric and had never worn a scratchy flour-sack dress like several of her schoolmates.

She peered over the bed again, keeping watch, and every few minutes, she'd see her ma cross from the kitchen into the dining room, carrying bowls and trays of food. She ought to be helping instead of hiding like some thief. And it wasn't stealing to take something that belonged to your family, especially if you were going to put it back after the contest, was it?

Her legs had finally quit shaking, and she drew up her knees to stand. If she got up just as her ma went into the dining room, she'd have time to hurry out of the bedroom and into the kitchen. She started to stand when she heard a shuffling sound and dropped back down. Her heart set off like a wild mustang again.

It sounded as if someone else slid into the room, and she held her breath. Sure enough, she could hear rough breathing. The person's shoes tapped out a quiet repetition and then stopped. A drawer squeaked open. Someone muttered a curse, and then the drawer squealed shut again. The bottom drawer was the only one that made a noise like that. Who could be in it, and what was it the person wanted?

She longed to peek but was too scared to move. Her breath

turned ragged, almost as if she'd run a long race. After a few minutes of not hearing anybody nearby, she peeked over the bed's quilt and saw her ma zip into the dining room. Jack jumped to her feet and hurried into the kitchen.

Her ma rushed back in the room. "Oh, there you are. Supper's finished, and I need your help. I was looking for you."

Jack ducked her head so her mother wouldn't see her guilt and grabbed the bowl of biscuits. She hurried into the dining room and set them on the table. None of the brides were there yet, and she wanted to run upstairs and look around to see if one of them had taken something from the dresser. Her mother hadn't, because she never opened that particular drawer. Jack tiptoed past the kitchen door and dashed into her bedroom. She needed another look, and she didn't like the thought worming its way into her head. She yanked the drawer open and knew right away that the tan shirt was gone. Someone staying in their home was a thief.

"Finish drying the breakfast dishes and you can go outside for a little bit." Rachel looked around her kitchen, glad that for the moment it was clean again. All too soon she'd have to start dinner.

Jacqueline wiped a dish with a towel and set it on top of the pile of clean dishes. "I'm so glad I don't hav'ta go to school for a while."

Rachel enjoyed her daughter being home more, but at times she could be trying. "I'm going out on the porch to mend the red checkered tablecloth. Make sure you come back in time to help with dinner."

Her daughter nodded, and Rachel left the kitchen, ready to sit down for a while. As she reached the parlor, she heard raised voices.

"I'm going over there right now and take his measurements. How are we supposed to make a shirt for him when we don't even know what they are?" Miss Bennett asked.

" 'Tisn't proper for an unmarried woman to measure a man." Miss O'Neil sat in one of the parlor chairs, hands clenched together.

Rachel stood in the doorway, suddenly realizing their dilemma. The women had less than a week left to fashion a shirt for the marshal, yet they didn't have his measurements. She dreaded the thought forming in her mind, but there was no other option. "I'll go take the marshal's measurements. And you're welcome to use the dining table to lay out your fabric, as long as it can be cleared by dinnertime."

Miss O'Neil smiled. "Aye, a grand idea to be certain."

Miss Bennett scowled. "I was just heading over to the jail to do that very thing."

Rachel shook her head, knowing the young woman would use the time alone to flirt with Luke. "I've been married before. I don't think it's appropriate for you to tend to such a task."

Miss Bennett harrumphed, grabbed the pile of dark blue fabric she'd purchased, and marched into the dining room.

Rachel returned to her bedroom, found her measuring tape, some paper, and a pencil, and headed to the jail. The breakfast she'd recently eaten churned in her stomach. She thought of being so near to Luke and yet so far. Maybe he wouldn't even be there, but even as the idea entered her mind, she saw him leaning against the doorjamb, watching the town as he frequently did.

The streets were quiet for a Monday morning. The shops were open, but many folks did their business on Saturday. She waved at Aggie, who walked down the other side of the street and entered the bank.

As Rachel neared the jail, her hands started trembling and her legs felt as solid as melted butter. Luke saw her coming and stood looking out from under his hat like a cougar eyeing its prey. He straightened as she drew near. In the years that he'd been gone, he'd changed from a lithe youth to a tall, broad-shouldered man. Rachel licked her lips, but her mouth felt as dry as flour.

Luke nodded at her. "Come to fetch my breakfast plate?"

"No, I've come to take your measurements so my boarders can start sewing your shirts."

He shook his head. "Don't know what I'll do with so many."

"Wear them, I guess. Although the woman you marry may not care for you to be donning the ones the other ladies made."

Luke quirked a brow. Rachel wanted nothing more than to tuck tail and run back home, but she forced herself to stand still. "Could we go inside? Or would you prefer staying out here?"

Luke stepped back and allowed her to enter in front of him. Rachel hesitated then walked into the jail with him following. She set her basket on the table, pulled out her supplies, and motioned for Luke to turn around.

"Hold out your right arm." Luke did as told, and she held the measuring tape against his shoulder, stretching it out to his wrist. The heat of his body burned her fingertips, and she longed to caress his arm. She forced her hand away and wrote down the length, then determined the width of his shoulders and the span from his collar to his hips. She ducked under his arm and stood in front of him. How many times in the past had she been this close to him? Had the right to touch his face or to hug him without giving it a second thought? Now her hand quivered, and she tried to finish her task without touching him again. She swallowed hard and dared to look up. Luke's brown eyes watched her, almost with—dare she hope?—longing.

"I. . .uh. . .need your help for this last measurement."

He nodded, and she handed him one end of the measurer. "Hold that against your chest, please."

She slipped behind him, wrapped the length around his chest, and pulled it tight, stopping again in front of him. Her breath caught in her throat. Luke smelled of leather and fresh soap and a scent all his own. If she didn't finish this task soon, she might swoon at his feet.

How bittersweet. If things had been different, she might well be preparing to sew a shirt for Luke herself, as his wife. Through stinging eyes, she noted the number and tugged on the tape, but when it didn't fall free, she looked up. Her gaze collided with Luke's.

He stared at her with an intensity she hadn't seen in years. His breath tickled her forehead.

"Rachel. . ."

For a fraction of a second, she thought he might kiss her. His gaze roved her face like a starving man eyeing a Sunday potluck picnic. Suddenly, he blinked, his expression hardened, and he stepped back.

Rachel caught her measuring tape as it fell free and snatched up her notes. "Um. . .thank you. I'm sure the brides will find this most helpful."

She spun around and hurried out the door.

"Rach—"

The jangling of a wagon passing on the road drowned out whatever Luke had said. Rachel's heart plummeted so low she thought certain she would trip on it. Those brides had no idea how much this little deed had cost her.

Carly handed the mayor her entry. The tan shirt with dark brown stitching hadn't been her first choice, but the blue one was gone from the drawer.

"Why, that's lovely stitchery, Miss Blackstone. I wouldn't be surprised if the marshal picks your shirt as the winner."

She straightened tall at the mayor's compliment, pretending his words pleasured her, but in truth, they meant little. She hadn't done the sewing, had instead stolen the shirt that had belonged to James Hamilton from Rachel's bottom dresser drawer—and filching from the kind woman had left a bad taste in her mouth. But she'd never be able to sew a shirt as nice as the ones Rachel Hamilton had made.

If only Mrs. Hamilton hadn't been so nice to her, then she wouldn't be feeling this regret. But a person did what she had to do. She needed Luke to pick her. Since her plan to find the payroll information hadn't worked, she needed some way to survive, and marryin' seemed better than stealing from decent folk. Besides, the marshal was a comely man, and being his wife wouldn't be so bad.

She stepped outside the jail and surveyed the table that had once again been set up for the contest. Four new signs indicated where the entries would be laid. She curled her lip and surveyed the growing crowd. Would there be a fourth entry today? Who could be the mystery bride?

Carly walked to the railing and stared down Main Street. She hadn't expected as large a group this Saturday since there was no food to be judged, but there looked to be about the same number of folks. Most likely, everyone was just curious as to who the marshal would pick for his bride.

A shuffling sounded behind her, and she spun around. Her hand reached for her gun, but she lowered it, remembering she was unarmed—that she was dressed as a lady and not an outlaw. She blinked and stared at the table. Somehow while her back was turned, somebody had placed a blue shirt on the table behind the Anonymous Bride sign.

Carly stepped closer to inspect her competition. She bent down and looked more closely at the anonymous entry. It looked just like the cornflower blue one Rachel Hamilton had shown her that day she'd asked her for help. But it couldn't be. Mrs. Hamilton hadn't even attended the first competition. Carly spun around and studied the crowd. She wasn't here today, either. Pivoting, Carly looked at the blue shirt again. That one had to be Rachel's. It had been missing when she'd sneaked in to steal it.

She thought about the times she'd seen Mrs. Hamilton and the marshal together, talking or arguing—watching each other. Now all those covert looks Rachel had sent the marshal's way made sense. She was in love with him, and he had no idea that was the case.

That meant Rachel Hamilton was the anonymous bride—and she was out to win this contest.

Chapter 25

Jack's heart still pounded as she thought about how she'd walked right behind Miss Blackstone and dropped her ma's shirt on the table. She'd spun into the marshal's office, past the mayor and his wife, and slipped into the cell where Max was hiding under the cot. Her heart pounded like a Comanche's war drum, and she sat on her hands to keep them from shaking.

Why was she so nervous? She hadn't done anything wrong, unless it was taking one of her pa's old shirts that nobody ever used. Just because her ma didn't want to enter the contest didn't mean Jack couldn't enter for her.

Max crept out of his hiding place and sat up, dropping his head on her leg. She scratched him behind the ear, enjoying how he lifted his head and looked as if he were smiling. She was half surprised the dog wasn't with Luke. He must be out on rounds, because she hadn't seen him since dropping off Max's food this morning. Either that or he was hiding from the brides. That thought brought a grin to her face.

Miss Bennett and Miss O'Neil both came in and handed their entries to the mayor, but she couldn't see them from so far away.

"Are you going to allow that mystery bride to enter again?" Miss Bennett lifted her chin. "It's highly irregular."

"I don't guess it matters since she hasn't submitted an entry." Mayor Burke scratched his jaw with his thumb and forefinger. He glanced at his watch. "And the time limit to do so just expired."

"Saints preserve us." Miss O'Neil held her handbag below her chin as if she were praying.

"What's the matter?" asked Mrs. Burke.

"There's already an entry on the table."

The mayor and his wife exchanged a look and hurried outside, followed by the two brides. Jack jumped up and ran to the door.

"Oh, my, that's very fine work." Mrs. Burke fingered the collar of the medium blue shirt then slid her hand down the buttons, admiring it.

Jack's hopes shot upward like a firecracker.

Mayor Burke cleared his voice. "Did anyone notice who submitted this entry?"

Jack moved past him so she could see, but relief washed through her when the townsfolk stared back with blank looks.

"Surely, you ain't gonna allow that fourth shirt in the contest? Ain't it supposed to be between us three?" Miss Blackstone wagged her finger between her and the other brides.

"We allowed it last time, so I don't see how we can exclude it now." Mayor Burke handed the shirts the brides had made to his wife. "Please distribute those, and we'll commence this competition."

His wife accepted the entries and laid each one behind a numbered bride sign. "How can we start without the marshal?"

"He's probably hidin' out somewhere so's he don't hafta get hitched to one of them brides." The comment from a bearded man standing in the street brought hoots of laughter from the crowd.

Jack smiled, but her eyes were drawn to the second shirt. She slipped around the mayor's wife to get a closer look and nearly gasped out loud. On the table lay a tan shirt with brown stitching—

the very shirt her ma had made for her pa. She glared at the brides.

One of them was a thief and a cheat.

Luke rode back into town after spending several hours in prayer down at the river. For the past few days, he'd thought about the brides, stewing over them and praying about which one to marry, but so far, God wasn't answering.

Even before he reached Lookout, he encountered dozens of buggies, wagons, and saddled horses lining the outskirts of town. Some folks had set up tents and made campfire circles, probably planning on overnighting and attending church tomorrow.

He wove his way through the mess, half dreading the shirt contest. No matter what, several of the brides would end up disappointed. He shook his head and rode into town.

People lined the streets like a cattle drive, in spite of the warm day. The sky had still been dark when he'd first ridden out this morning, but now the sun glimmered bright above the horizon with the promise of a perfect day—a complete contrast to the nervousness sending his belly in a tizzy and causing pain between his eyes.

He rubbed his fingertips in small circles on his forehead. Last week's measuring session had nearly driven him loco, with Rachel moving around him, leaving her scent, touching him like a wisp of wind. Was it possible that he still had feelings for her?

He reined Alamo to a stop. What was he going to do?

If only he hadn't given his word to marry.

His prayers seemed to have fallen on deaf ears, even though he knew that wasn't true. He'd pleaded with God to show him which bride to choose, yet here he rode back toward town, with no leading one way or the other and thoughts of Rachel filling his mind. All he knew to do was to pray more and wait until God revealed His will to him.

If only the mayor wasn't pressing him for a decision. And that newspaper lady. He halfway wondered if she wasn't thc anonymous bride. Maybe she added the mystery entry just to beef up interest in the contest and to help sell her papers. Maybe there wouldn't be a fourth entry today.

"Hey, there's the marshal," a man from the crowd hollered.

All eyes turned toward Luke, and for the briefest of moments, the town was silent except for a baby's wail. Suddenly, the crowd erupted in cheers. Alamo jerked up his head at the roar and pranced beneath Luke. There was no getting out of this contest, so he'd best just get it over with.

He looped Alamo's reins around the hitching post outside the livery where three other horses had been tied and made his way toward his office.

"Who ya gonna pick?"

"I like that Irish gal. Don't choose her."

"You getting married today?"

The questions fired from all sides. Luke shook his head and pushed his way toward the mayor.

Jack stood behind the man and raced forward when she saw him. "Luke, I gotta tell you somethin'."

Mayor Burke shoved his way in front of her. "Not now, kid. We've got to get this judging started."

"But—" Jack reached for Luke as the mayor pushed her back.

Luke scowled, not liking how the mayor was treating the girl, but the man was right. Whatever she wanted to say could wait.

The boardinghouse brides huddled together at the far end of the table, each one looking as if she'd worn her Sunday best. Even Miss Blackstone's hair had been pulled up and pinned on top of her head. Just then, the woman scowled and reached up to scratch her head with her index finger. Luke smiled. For some reason, she didn't seem comfortable all gussied up.

Miss Bennett batted her lashes at Luke and smiled at him with her head cocked sideways. Miss O'Neil looked everywhere but at him. He bet if he were to pick her she'd faint dead away.

Garrett walked out of Luke's office with Mark on his heels. " 'Bout time you got here."

"Yeah," Mark said, "we were just about to round up a posse to go hunt you down."

"Well, I'm here."

The mayor nodded and turned toward the crowd, beefy hands lifted. "All right, now that Marshal Davis is here, we'll get things started. I imagine Luke will want to try on each shirt before deciding on the winner." Mayor Burke gave Luke a shrewd glance that set his nerve endings tingling, then faced the crowd again. "And if he's ready to make an announcement, could be we'll have a wedding today."

Cheers erupted. Luke frowned and bit back a growl. He was getting tired of being manipulated.

"Gather 'round the table, Luke. Look at all these fine shirts." The mayor shook his head. "Don't know how you're going to pick just one as winner."

Luke gazed at the table, his heart dipping into his boots. There were four entries.

People crowded the tables, pushing and shoving. "I cain't see," an old cowboy yelled.

The brides were crowded from behind and moved toward Luke as if part of the herd.

"Hold on, hold on!" Mayor Burke held up his hands. "Y'all just back up right now 'fore I have the marshal get his rifle."

Mumbles and murmurs surrounded them, but the swarm slowly backed up.

"Now, the marshal will stand here and try on each shirt." The mayor waved him toward the railing.

Luke shook his head. "I'm not shedding my shirt in front of all these folks."

"Aw, don't be shy, cuz." Garrett nudged Luke in the back.

Enough was enough. Luke spun around and glared down at Garrett. After a few seconds, Garrett held up his hands. "Sorry."

"Maybe you should try the shirts on in the jail?" Mark offered loudly, over the buzz of conversation.

Luke nodded, snatched up the four shirts, and strode into his office. The crowd voiced their objections while the mayor tried to pacify them as if it was his idea to use the jail. "Now it isn't proper for a man to undress in front of all you pretty ladies."

Jack squeezed in between Garrett and Mark. "I gotta tell you somethin'."

Luke tossed the shirts onto his desk. "Make it fast."

She nodded her head up and down. "One of them brides is a cheat. That brown shirt belonged to my pa. Ma's the one who sewed it."

Garrett and Mark stood behind her. Both sets of eyebrows shot up at Jack's declaration.

Luke frowned and tugged out the tan shirt. "This one?"

"Yeah."

"How can you be sure?" Garrett asked.

"It was in Ma's bottom dresser drawer a few days ago. I know it by that dark stitching."

"It's possible someone else just happened to sew a similar one." Mark rubbed the back of his neck.

Jack shook her head. "I know it's my ma's."

"What's going on in here?" Mayor Burke squeezed in the crowded office and looked around. "Get along, Luke. We've got a whole town of folks waiting."

Luke bent down and looked at Jack. "Keep this to yourself for now. I'll check into it though."

Jack stared at him with her big eyes and finally nodded.

"All right, half bit. Scoot outside with the rest of the ladies."

"I ain't no lady," she called over her shoulder as she left and closed the door.

"That's the honest truth. That kid is as wild as they come." Mayor Burke shook his head. "How did Rachel end up with such a hooligan child?"

Luke narrowed his eyes, halfway ready to knock the mayor on his backside. He oughten to talk about Jack like that. She was just a little girl who needed a firm hand.

"So, which shirt do you like best?" Garrett laid each one out across the top of Luke's desk.

"Pick a shirt; pick a wife." Mark chuckled.

"This is just plain loco. How am I supposed to pick a wife by choosing the best shirt?" He shook his head. "You and your crazy schemes. I don't know how I got caught up in this one."

Garrett ignored him and sorted through the entries. "Which one you want to try on first?" He held up the blue shirt and fingered the collar. "This one's nice."

Luke shrugged and crossed his arms, wishing he was anywhere else.

"You know you've gotta do it, so get going." Garrett shoved the shirt toward Luke. "Put it on."

He heaved another sigh but shucked his shirt and pulled on the cornflower blue one. It fit like a gun sliding into a perfectly made holster. He adjusted the shoulders and buttoned it up. Holding out his arm, he eyed the sleeve. "Fits well enough, but the sleeves could be a tad longer. I do like this color."

Garrett held up the dark blue shirt and waggled his brow.

Luke removed the medium blue shirt and tried on the indigo one. It, too, fit well, and the sleeves were longer, but the seams under his arms were too small and restricted his movement.

"This one's got a little stain on it. Maybe one of them brides poked her finger while stitching it—or maybe the kid was right." Garrett rubbed at the spot and unfolded the tan shirt. "I like how it has this brown stitching on it. That's different."

"That's the one Jack claimed was stolen." Luke looked it over, but the tan garment revealed no clues as to who had made it. He tried it on, trying to imagine Rachel's hand sewing it. But if she had, she'd been making it for James, not him. He shucked it off and tossed it on the desk. Garrett held up the final entry. Luke resisted rolling his eyes. What sane man tried on four shirts in a single day?

He shoved his arm in the white shirt, but when he tried to get his second arm in, he couldn't. The shoulders were too narrow. A rip sounded, and one of the sleeves tore off.

"Oops." Garrett grinned. "Guess that's not the winner."

Luke tossed the ruined shirt on the pile and pulled his comfortable chambray back on.

"So, which one did you like best?" The mayor drew in closer and leaned over the desk.

"I don't know. The stitching on the tan and the cornflower blue was the nicest, I guess, but I like the dark blue color best."

"So the dark blue is the winner?" Garrett asked, picking it up again.

Luke studied it, then shook his head. "No, it's too tight in the underarms and reminds me too much of my cavalry uniform. I wore that color for ten years."

Garrett held up the tan and medium blue shirts and wiggled them in front of Luke.

"The cornflower blue's my favorite."

"Do I hear a but coming?" Garrett lifted his brows.

Delaying his response, Luke looked out the window. Dozens of people stared in at him. Finally, he turned back to his cousin. "What if that anonymous bride made that one?"

Garrett shrugged one shoulder. "You have a three-in-four chance of it not being hers.

"Yeah, but that still bothers me." Luke snagged his hat off the back of the chair and put it on. "Seems like I have a right to know whose competing, being as I'm supposed to marry the winner of the contest."

Garrett grinned. "Now that would take all the fun out of the competition."

Luke leaned forward and glared across the desk. "This isn't a game, Garrett. This is my future, my life we're talking about."

His cousin sobered. "I know. Sorry for making light of things." Garrett stood and set his hands on his hips. "Look, Luke. Mark and I didn't know all this craziness would happen when we ordered those brides. We were honestly just tryin' to help you."

Luke pinched the bridge of his nose with his thumb and forefinger. "I know, but what you did was really dumb. You took those gals away from their homes and families. Gave them hope that they could start over here and get married. Even if I choose one, that still leaves two without husbands."

"Leave them to me and Mark. We'll figure out something."

Luke shook his head. "I don't know what, unless you plan to marry them yourselves."

Garrett made a choking sound as if his neck were in a noose.

Luke grinned. "How do you like it when the tables are turned?"

"They aren't exactly turned, are they? I didn't promise to marry anyone." Garrett's mouth cocked sideways in a teasing grin.

"I sure wish I hadn't either." He shouldn't have yielded to the pressure everyone put on him. A man should marry the woman he loved. A woman who was his friend. Rachel immediately came to mind.

Maybe he had it all wrong. Men in the West married women they'd just met all the time. The only way to truly get over Rachel would be to marry someone else. So why did that sit so badly with him?

Mayor Burke reached out and grabbed the blue shirt. "Well, let's get back out there and see who made this shirt."

"Hold on a minute. I'm going to have to figure out who stole that tan shirt."

"That kid's probably just making up that story." The mayor tugged on his vest.

"Jack didn't have any idea?" Mark asked.

"No, but I don't mind telling you that I've had suspicions about one of the brides for a while now."

"Which one?" Mayor Burke's fuzzy brows lifted.

Luke shook his head. "I'm not ready to say just yet."

Garrett looked as if he was staring out the window in deep thought. He glanced back at Luke, a worried expression on his face. "Could Jack and Rachel be in any danger?"

Luke shook his head. "Don't think so, but I'll keep a closer watch on them."

Outside, the crowd started chanting for Luke. "Marshal! Marshal!"

Holding the winning shirt, the mayor headed for the door but suddenly turned back and collected the other shirts. "If I go walking out with just one, everybody will know that's the winner."

"Makes sense." Garrett nodded.

"After I announce the winner, I'll put the shirts back on the table. Maybe one of you can keep an eye on them and see if the person who brought the tan shirt will reclaim it."

"That's not likely if it was stolen." Luke pursed his lips.

Mark straightened. "Unless they feel the need to return it so Rachel doesn't know it was ever gone."

Luke grinned and slapped his cousin on the shoulder. "If I ever need a deputy, you've got the job."

Mark's response was lost as the mayor opened the door. The crowd roared with excitement. Luke followed his cousins outside and glanced around, hoping to see Rachel. It looked like everyone in the county had shown up but her.

The mayor lifted his hands, two shirts in each one. "Quiet down. Hush up, now. We have a winner, although I want to say the competition was stiff." He looked over his shoulder at the brides. "Nice job, ladies."

His announcement sent the crowd into another frenzy. After a few moments, the noise settled, and the mayor continued. He held up his left hand again—the hand that held the tan and white shirts. "These two are not the winners."

Luke watched the brides' expressions as the mayor tossed the shirts back onto the table. Miss O'Neil ducked her head and wrung her hands. Miss Bennett's eyes gleamed, and Miss Blackstone puckered up her lips and shoved her hands to her hips. He was certain he knew who'd taken the tan shirt.

With a blue shirt in each hand, the mayor waved them around. "One of these is the winner."

The crowd silenced as if they were awaiting a life-changing announcement—and well it could be, for one woman. Mayor Burke held up the dark blue shirt. Miss Bennett's hands flew to her chest, and she leaned forward.

"This one here," the mayor said, "is not the winner."

Miss Bennett blinked and fell back against the side of the jail, disappointment dulling her countenance. Something twisted in Luke's gut. The last shirt must be from the anonymous bride. Bile churned, and thoughts of all the unmarried women in the area, from Bertha Boyd to the Widow Denison with her five kids, raced across his mind.

"Here's our winner, folks." Holding the cornflower blue shirt by the corners, the mayor peered back over his shoulder again. "Which one of you ladies does this belong to?"

No one moved, just as Luke knew they wouldn't. The mayor scowled and turned to face the brides. "This doesn't belong to one of you gals?"

All three shook their heads.

"Well." The mayor faced the crowd again. "Looks like the anonymous bride is our winner again. If you're here, ma'am, would you please step forward?"

Other than the playful shouts of some children, total silence reigned. Heads turned left and right as each person seemed to be looking for the anonymous bride.

"She's not coming. Just like last time." Miss Bennett stepped forward. "If she can't bother to show up, seems like she ought to be disqualified."

Luke knew her plan. If the winning entry was thrown out, she would be named the winner. He wasn't sure how he felt about that. The blond wasn't hard on the eyes, but he didn't care for her tendency to boss others around. He preferred a woman who was quieter—and sweeter.

Mayor Burke surveyed the crowd. "What do y'all think? Should we toss out the winner?"

*Yea*s and *nay*s sounded all around, until the mayor held up his hand. "Let's take a vote. Who all thinks the anonymous bride should be disqualified?"

"Yea!" The loud cheer filled the air.

"All right now, who's opposed?"

An even louder roar rumbled down the street. Luke's heart sunk. He'd halfway hoped the anonymous bride would be eliminated. But that would mean he'd have to marry one of the boardinghouse brides. Somewhere, deep in his heart, he was holding out for someone better suited to him. He just couldn't let his brain—or his heart—wrap around who that was.

He stared out at the many faces in the crowd. So many he knew, and others he didn't. Could the anonymous bride be standing right there in the road but not have enough nerve to step up and announce herself?

"All right, the nays have it. Here's what we're gonna do," Mayor Burke said. "I'm giving the marshal two weeks to take each of the brides to dinner one night so he can get to know them better. If the anonymous bride doesn't reveal herself in a fortnight, she'll be banned from participating further."

People swarmed Luke once the mayor dismissed them. He fielded comments and questions and an interview from Jenny Evans. When the music started, the townsfolk drifted back to their friends and families.

Luke turned around, and his gut twisted. The tan shirt was no longer on the table with the other shirts.

Monday morning, Luke strode into the freight office with Max at his side. The whole town was buzzing over the mysterious bride, and he was sick of fending off questions from folks who wanted to know if he knew who she was. He needed some advice. He was feeling more and more that he couldn't marry one of the boardinghouse brides.

Garrett looked up from his messy desk. "Well, howdy there, cuz."

Luke nodded. "Where's Mark?"

"Gone to fetch some coffee. Want some?"

"I could use a cup. Been several hours since I had some at the boardinghouse."

Garrett leaned back in his chair. "So which of them brides are you gonna ask out first?"

Luke crossed the room and leaned against Mark's tidy desk. "I don't know. I've been trying to figure a way to get out of taking them at all."

"The mayor won't like that."

"Nope, I don't guess so. But I've been praying hard about what to do, and I haven't gotten leave from the Lord to marry any of those gals."

"I reckon He'll give you guidance if you keep praying. Maybe you outta go talk to the reverend. He might could offer you some good advice." Garrett leaned his chair back against the wall and put his feet on his desk. "Then again, you could walk right out the door and marry the first bride you see."

"You might be onto something there." Luke ran his hand over his bristly jaw. He hadn't even taken time to shave before he rode out.

"Right about what?"

"Talking to Reverend Taylor." Luke should have thought of that sooner. He was still a fairly new Christian and needed the wisdom of a man more schooled in God's way. As soon as he left here, he'd pay the parson a visit.

"And here I thought you meant that you were gonna marry

the first woman you saw when you left here. But then again, it just might be Bertha Boyd."

Luke grinned and shook his head. His cousin was ornery all right, but he sure could make him chuckle.

Luke left the freight office, made his rounds through town, and headed toward the parson's house. At the end of Main Street, a motion snagged his attention, and he stopped and leaned against a post. Rachel was sweeping her front porch, but the way her hips swayed, she could be dancing.

Suddenly what Garrett had said came to mind. *Why not marry the first woman you see?*

A lump lodged in his throat. Marrying Rachel didn't sound as distasteful as it had when he'd first returned home. Had he gotten used to seeing her? Being around her? His clothes often held her scent as if she'd held them against her chest while returning them to his home. Her tasty meals had filled his belly three times a day. But he'd once trusted her completely, and she'd stabbed him in the back in the worst way possible. How could he ever trust her again?

Pushing away from the post, he walked down the street. Rachel saw him and stopped sweeping. Her gaze looked worried, apprehensive, but why should she be uneasy around him? He touched the end of his hat and dipped his head at her. She acknowledged his greeting by nodding once.

He should have kept on walking, but something drew him to her like a moth to a lantern. Maybe she could never be his, but he could be polite. Sociable. "How are you today?"

"Fine, thank you." She studied the porch floor rather than looking at him. "I thought I'd get out here and do the sweeping before the day heated up."

"It's a lovely day." She'd once been his best friend, the one person he shared his hopes and dreams with, and now they were reduced to talking about the weather.

She glanced up at the sky, avoiding his gaze. "Yes, it's near perfect, although I wouldn't mind a summer thunderstorm to blow through and cool things down."

"It would probably just dump more moisture in the air and make us all sweat." Luke winced at his dumb remark. Goodness, couldn't he even talk normal with her?

"I suppose that's true." She glanced at her front door. "I'd better get back inside and start breakfast. I imagine you're getting hungry, and my guests will be up soon, wanting to eat."

"Don't hurry on my account."

Rachel's cheeks turned a soft rose color. "I'll see you in about an hour, I guess."

Luke nodded and watched her go inside. He hadn't noticed before, but she looked as if she'd lost weight recently. Her dress hung looser and looked a bit bunched up at her waist. Was caring for the brides too much for her? But owning a boardinghouse, she was surely used to having guests much of the time.

Concern for her nagged his steps as he headed toward the parson's place.

Rachel watched Luke walk away. She hated the awkwardness that existed between them, but with him close to choosing one of the brides to marry, she had to distance herself from him, had to protect her heart.

There was no sense mooning over what could never be, even if her heart was breaking. She'd prayed for Luke's forgiveness ever since he returned, but she couldn't force him to pardon and forget what she'd done to him.

Back in the kitchen, she washed her hands and tied on her apron. She wondered who he would choose, though she'd decided Miss Bennett would be the best choice, even if she was as prickly as a cactus at times. Rachel hugged her mixing bowl to her chest. The young woman was a farm girl, surely a good cook and seamstress, and would make any man a decent wife so long as she held her attitude in check. Miss Blackstone was too rough and seemed unsettled. Rachel couldn't help feeling as if that woman was hiding something. And Miss O'Neil wasn't much of a cook and didn't seem to have the stamina needed to survive the rugged lifestyle a Texan lived, although she sure kept her room tidy.

Truth be told, none of the brides were the perfect match for the marshal. But then, was there even such a thing as a perfect match between a man and a woman?

Standing at the counter, she stared at the rounded bread dough that was ready to go in the oven. She'd once thought that she and Luke were a match made in heaven. But she had to go and ruin it. Tears burned her eyes and made her throat ache. If only she could go back and do things over—but then she wouldn't have her daughter. *Give me strength, Lord, to do the right thing.*

She reached into her pocket and touched the letter from her aunt. Millie had written again, asking her and Jacqueline to come to Kansas City and live with her and help work in Millie's mercantile. The move might be good for Jacqueline. It would get her away from those ruffian boys, but she wouldn't like moving and would most likely throw a fit at leaving Luke and Max. But once Luke had a wife and children of his own, he would no longer be interested in her daughter.

Rachel's chin wobbled. She had to get hold of herself before either Jacqueline came to help or someone else noticed. With the oven properly heated, she placed the two loaves of bread in it and cracked the eggs for breakfast.

An hour and a half later, after she'd sent Jacqueline out to weed the garden, she donned her bonnet and headed to the mayor's office. She had a hard time imagining living anywhere other than Lookout, but she knew her days in the small town were numbered. Living here with Luke married to one of the brides was out of the question. She hoped that the income from the sale of the boardinghouse would be all the money she and Jacqueline needed for a long while with her aunt providing room and board.

Before entering the mayor's office, Rachel turned and looked at Hamilton House. She loved the soft green with white trim and the wraparound porches that looked so inviting with all those rocking chairs just waiting for people to sit in them. But Hamilton House would soon be part of her past.

Sucking in a steadying breath, she opened the door and went inside. If things went as planned, she and Jacqueline could be on the train to Kansas City in a week or two.

Chapter 26

Luke stared into his coffee cup as Mrs. Taylor finished up the breakfast dishes. "Thanks, ma'am, for that fine meal."

The preacher's wife looked over her shoulder and smiled. "You're very welcome. We're happy to have you anytime, but it's the least we could do after all the wood you helped Thomas chop and stack. Why, we shouldn't need any for a month, I would imagine."

Luke nodded. "My pleasure."

"I helped, too, Ma."

Mrs. Taylor smiled at her son. "I know, Sam. I saw you out there stacking wood. You did a fine job."

The boy puffed up his chest and glanced between his pa and older brother.

"Boys, you head on out to the barn and muck the stalls." The pastor turned to his daughter, a cute blond around six years old. "Emily, help your ma finish cleaning up, and watch the baby when she wakes up."

"Yes, Pa."

The boys carried their dishes to the cabinet beside the dry sink and rushed outside. Emily scraped the plates and stacked them beside the basin where her ma was washing. Luke watched the activities around him. What would it be like to have a home with a mess of children?

The pastor couldn't be more than five years or so older than him, but he was way ahead of Luke as far as starting a family. Pastor Taylor downed the last of his coffee and stood. "Shall we adjourn to my study?"

Luke followed the man out of the cozy kitchen, down a short hall, and into a nook across from the parlor. The small room painted white held a desk on one wall, a bookcase filled with reference books, and a small settee. In front of the desk was a chair. Pastor Taylor motioned for Luke to have a seat on the settee and grabbed the top of the chair and swung it around to face the couch. Then he closed the door to the room and opened both windows. A light breeze fluttered the blue curtains as the pastor took a seat.

With short brown hair and wire-rimmed glasses, he looked more like a bank teller than a minister of the gospel. He crossed his hands over his light blue chambray shirt and stared at Luke. For a moment he refrained from speaking, and Luke sat still, resisting the urge to wiggle like a schoolboy in trouble. Was the man praying?

Luke cleared his throat. His nerves had settled during the hour and a half that he'd chopped wood and eaten breakfast, but they were on the rise again. He jiggled his foot and stared out the window. Why had he felt such a need to speak with the pastor?

"So. . .something on your mind today?"

Luke nodded, relieved to be starting yet unsure where to begin. The pastor wasn't a native of the town and probably didn't know about Luke's previous relationship with Rachel.

"You nervous about picking a bride?"

"Uh. . .no, well yes. But that's not the main reason I needed to talk to you."

"All right. Just take your time. I'm in no hurry."

Luke ran his fingers through his hair. Sucking in a steadying breath, he stared at the preacher. "I. . .uh. . .guess you could say I'm having trouble forgiving someone for a past offense."

"Ah, I see. And have you prayed about it?"

Luke's hand clamped onto the arm of the settee. "More than you can imagine."

"Is it something that's happened recently or a while back?"

"A long time ago—more than a decade, actually."

The pastor's brows lifted. "That's a while to carry an offense. Must have been a big one."

Luke pursed his lips and stared out the window, remembering Rachel's words. She'd looked at him, the whites of her eyes and her nose red from tears, and that alone had nearly done him in. *I've married James Hamilton.*

A gunshot point blank couldn't have hurt any worse. He'd been working for a year to make enough money for a down payment on a little house and to support Rachel. She'd been the love of his life, the only girl he'd ever had eyes for. But she dumped him to marry the richest man in town.

"Luke," the pastor's soft voice drew him out of the past. "I know you're a Christian, but how long have you been one?"

He shook his head. "Not long. Less than a year."

"I can tell you that forgiving isn't an easy thing, even for a man who's been a believer for most of his life." He leaned forward, head down for a moment. "If you've read your Bible, you know that it says in Mark, 'But if ye do not forgive, neither will your Father which is in heaven forgive your trespasses.'"

Luke faced the pastor. "I know that, but it doesn't tell me *how* to forgive. Just that I need to."

"I can tell by your expression how you've struggled with this. Forgiveness is a choice, Luke. We must choose to forgive and turn loose of our hurts. Nobody can do that for us."

"But how do you do that?" Luke leaned forward, his elbows on his knees.

"You have to make a conscious effort to do it. Say 'I choose to forgive you,' and then let go of the hurt. Give it to the Lord to carry."

Luke looked down at the pastor's boots. "I don't know if I can do that. I've carried this hurt for so long."

"And look what's it's done to you."

He glanced up. "What's that?"

"It has you all torn up inside. Jesus died to set us free from our sin. He wants us to live a victorious life, not one weighed down by sin and an unforgiving spirit. If you believe Christ died for you and have given your heart to Him, He'll help you with your struggles. But that doesn't mean He doesn't expect us to do our part."

"So I'm just supposed to turn loose of my pain, just like I turn my horse loose in a pasture?"

Pastor Taylor nodded. "Pretty much. You let it go and make the choice to forgive. When negative thoughts come back to pester you, mentally you have to chase them away and not dwell on them." He turned and grabbed his Bible off the desk and thumbed through some pages. "In James, the scriptures say, 'Submit yourselves therefore to God. Resist the devil, and he will flee from you. Draw nigh to God, and He will draw nigh to you.'"

He glanced back at Luke. "Once you've forgiven, continue to resist Satan and don't allow thoughts of bitterness or hurt to creep back in."

Luke considered all that the pastor said. He could see his problem had been continuing to dwell on the situation with Rachel when he should have given it over to God. He just had to choose to forgive her and then refuse to think about the offense again. Could he do that?

What choice did he have? If he wanted God's forgiveness—and he did more than anything—then he had to forgive Rachel.

"I understand now. I may have forgiven in the past, but I kept thinking of how much I was hurt—and that made me angry."

The pastor nodded. "You kept taking the offense off God's

shoulder and putting it back on yours. Give your burden to him, and then forget about it. Don't let the enemy talk you into shouldering it again."

Luke smiled. "You make everything sound so easy."

A melancholy look draped the pastor's face, making Luke wonder what he struggled with. Pastor Taylor shook his head. "It's not easy, but God gives us the grace to do it. And remember, refusing to forgive hurts you more than the people you're upset with."

Luke nodded, and for the first time, he felt he had the power to conquer his pain.

"Would you like me to pray with you?"

"Yep, I would."

Ten minutes later, Luke walked out of the pastor's house feeling freer than he had in years. He still wanted to get alone with God, but he knew now that he could forgive Rachel and let go of the past.

Carly followed the other brides upstairs. She'd miss Mrs. Hamilton's cooking when she left here—that was for certain. Her stomach ached from chicken and dumplings, green beans, applesauce, and rolls that the boardinghouse owner had made for supper. And then there was the peach pie. Mmm. . .

At the top of the stairs, Miss Bennett stopped suddenly and pivoted, crossing her arms over her chest. Miss O'Neil almost ran into her but sidestepped in time to move past her.

"I'm telling you both now that I'll be marrying the marshal, so you'd better decide what you're going to do." Miss Bennett lifted her chin to emphasize her point.

Carly walked up the two stairs to the landing, not wanting to give the snooty woman the benefit of looking down on her. "Just what makes you think you'll win?"

"I can cook and sew better than the both of you put together, that's why."

"Aye, 'tis true. I can't cook a'tall." Miss O'Neil backed toward her bedroom door. "But you can't know who the marshal will choose."

"That's right. I noticed he didn't pick your shirt." Carly glared at the blond, wondering why she was siding with the Irish girl. "Maybe the marshal don't even like blonds."

"Well, we shall see. I'm just giving y'all fair warning. I do not intend to lose this competition." Miss Bennett's countenance changed swiftly, and it looked as if a wave of uncertainty washed over her face. "I simply can't lose." She spun around, skirts swishing, enveloping Carly and Miss O'Neil in the scent of lilacs. She hurried into her room and slammed the door.

Miss O'Neil jumped. The paleness of her face matched the white wall trim. Her green eyes looked as big as the buttons on Bertha Boyd's dresses. Carly felt an uncharacteristic desire to comfort the girl. Though they were both competitors for the same prize, she felt an odd kinship to the other brides in spite of Miss Bennett's outburst. "Don't pay her no mind. We got ever' bit as good a chance at winnin' as her."

Miss O'Neil nodded, but the look of concern didn't leave her eyes. "Good evening."

The bedroom door shut quietly, and Carly continued down the wide hall to her room. Mrs. Hamilton had done a nice job decorating the boardinghouse, giving the place a homey feel. A hurricane lamp sat on top of a lacy tablecloth, bathing the dim hall in a soft light. The scents of the delicious meal still lingered, even upstairs, reminding her she'd eaten too much. This was the nicest home she'd ever been in. If only she never had to leave this place.

She reached for her door and paused, knowing her thoughts were foolish. This was a temporary stop. But she'd grown to like the little town and its people. If only she could somehow find a job, maybe she could stay here awhile. Grinning at the thought, she stepped into the room, and a whiff of something odd hit her in the face. Smoke?

Her gaze dashed around the room for the source. The door slammed shut behind her, and she whirled around, her heart jumping into her throat.

"Howdy, sis. You're a hard gal to track down."

She glared at her brother. How in the world had he found her? She tried to look relaxed though she felt anything but that. "What are you doing here, Ty?"

He sucked in a puff of his cigarette and then leaned casually against the wall and blew smoke rings. "Lookin' for my sister. I *am* responsible for ya."

"Not anymore. You left me for dead after that stage robbery."

He shrugged. "What was I s'posed to do if you were dead? Didn't see no reason to get caught tryin' to fetch your body."

She huffed out an angry sigh. "I can see how much I mean to you. I ain't even worth a decent burial."

Tyson gave her the charming grin that made many a naive woman swoon, but it was wasted on her. "Now, what'cha gettin' your petticoats in a twist for? You ain't dead."

She narrowed her eyes. "I'll thank you not to mention my unmentionables. And what if I had been lyin' in that stage, bleeding and in need of a doctor? You didn't bother to check."

He pushed away from the wall with a menacing glare and flicked the cigarette onto the carpet. "You ain't dead, so just hush up all this chatter before someone hears." A twisted grin pulled at his mouth. "And don't you look purty all gussied up like some schoolmarm."

Carly stomped on the cigarette butt before it could burn the carpeting that covered the center of the floor. She picked up the stub, stalked to the window, and flicked the butt outside. Marshal Davis stood on the street beside the bank, talking to two women. If only she could get his attention—but then what? She may not like her brother, but she didn't want him shot, and if the marshal jailed him, Ty would for sure rat on her. On the other hand, her brother was a keen shooter, and if the marshal got mortally wounded, it would ruin all her plans. How was she going to get rid of Ty before he spoiled everything?

"The marshal has a wanted poster with your likeness on it." She crossed her arms and pivoted back to face him. "You cain't stay here, you know."

He strode past her and flopped on her bed, making it creak under his weight. He didn't bother to remove his dirty boots from the quilt that Mrs. Hamilton had probably spent months making. "I can do anything I want."

Carly bit the inside of her cheek, battling both anger and desperation. "You're not concerned about the poster?"

He shrugged. "Those drawings ain't too good."

"How did you find me?"

"Pretty slick move of yours, pretending to be that other gal on that stage."

Carly tensed. If Ty knew she was impersonating Ellie Blackstone, who else did? "How do you know about that?"

"Read the story in the Joplin newspaper. It said Ellie Blackstone had survived and was traveling on to Lookout, Texas, to be a mail-order bride, but another unknown woman was near death. I 'membered that name from when I put you on the stage, so I snuck in the doctor's office one night to get you." A smirk tugged at his lips. "Imagine my surprise when it weren't you but that other gal. I put two and two together, and here I am."

Carly's heart jumped like a horse clearing a creek. How had the paper known where she was going? She didn't remember telling the lawman anything but her name. Then she realized what her brother had said and felt the skin on her face tighten. "Ellie Blackstone is alive?"

Ty shrugged. "Don't know. She was wounded bad. I imagine she's dead by now."

Sinking down on the vanity stool, she considered what it would mean to her if the woman wasn't dead. She could show up here any day.

"I don't know what your game is here, but I noticed this little town has a nice-sized bank—and only one lawman. We could make off with a haul."

So Ty had been scoping out the town. That didn't surprise her. He might not be the sharpest knife in the drawer, but she couldn't fault his thorough planning before a robbery. "I'm not helpin' you rob that bank."

He sat up and stared at her, brows lifted. "Don't sass me. You know I don't like it."

Carly's gaze drifted toward the door. She could probably get there before him, but then what? Ty wasn't beyond hurting anyone to get what he wanted—and that included her. He might act the caring brother, but he only had one goal: to take what he wanted. She couldn't stand the thought of something happening to Mrs. Hamilton. The woman had been kind, and Carly had begun to actually like her.

"Don't even think about crossing me, Carly. I don't like hurtin' ya, but I will if'n ya force me to."

She squeezed her eyes shut, trying to form a plan.

"Tell me what your scam is. I want in on it."

"My plan hasn't exactly succeeded." Otherwise she would have been long gone, and he'd never have found her.

Ty grinned and leaned back against her pillow with his hands behind his head. "That's because I'm the brains of the Payton gang. You need me."

"We're not a gang. At least I'm no longer part of it."

Ty pursed his lips and stared at the ceiling as if something was on his mind.

Carly walked over to the bed and leaned on the bedpost. "Did something happen to Emmett and Floyd?"

Ty sat up cross-legged on the bed. "Emmett got himself killed in that stage robbery, and Floyd found out his ma was dying and went home."

"You let him go?" Carly found that hard to believe, knowing

all that Floyd knew about her brother's shenanigans.

Ty shrugged. "I thought about shooting 'im for leavin' me, but he's the only man I trust. I reckon once his ma dies he'll come back. What else could he do? He ain't done an honest day's work his whole life."

"Well, he'll never think to look for you down here in Texas."

"Neither will them lawmen what's after me." He chuckled. "Gotta hand it to you, I never expected you was smart enough to take care of yourself."

Carly scowled at him. No, she could cook and do his gang's wash and even help in a robbery, but she wasn't smart enough to fend for herself. She'd forgotten how much she disliked being with her brother. How he continually belittled her as if she were nothing more than a maggot.

She strode to the window again and saw Jack outside, throwing a stick for that ugly yellow dog to fetch. If she could just get her attention—

"Whatever you're thinkin', don't. I've seen all the pretty gals what live here and that lady and her kid. I'd hate for any of 'em to get hurt because ya did something stupid."

"What is it you want?"

"I want to know what you had planned when ya came here."

Carly sighed. What did it matter now? Her plan had failed. "I came here pretending to be Ellie Blackstone. She told me on the stage she was comin' here to marry the town marshal. I thought if I took her place, I might weasel up close to the marshal and find out about payroll shipments."

A glimmer sparked in Ty's blue eyes. "And?"

She shrugged. "And nothin'. I even searched his office once when he was gone. Nothing. No payroll shipment information of any kind."

"That sounds a bit odd with him being the only protection in this town."

"Either he doesn't know about any, or there aren't any in this area, or. . ." She wasn't sure if she wanted to share this thought.

"Or what?" He slid off the bed and crossed the room, standing off to the side of the window.

She shrugged. "It's just a guess, but maybe he keeps them in his pocket or at his house."

"Hmm. Could be." Ty leaned against the wall and crossed his boot over his ankle. "Reckon it wouldn't be any trouble to search his house. Where's it at?"

Carly pinched her mouth shut. Hadn't she told him enough? If Ty didn't find the information in the house, he might shoot Luke to get it—and she didn't want that to happen. Sometime, somehow, she'd started liking the people of Lookout. She knew Luke was suspicious of her, but he was so kind to Jack and that dumb dog. She never should have let her defenses down, because now her brother could use them against her.

Ty suddenly grabbed her shoulders and shook her. "Where's the marshal's house?"

She glanced out the window, hoping someone had seen him. Ty must have realized the same thing, because he let go and stepped back, but his hand slid to his gun handle, letting her know he meant business.

"It's next door. That little house just west of the boardinghouse."

"I'll scout it out tomorrow." Ty pulled his gun and waved it in Carly's face. "You just keep quiet about me. If word gets out I'm here, someone's gonna get hurt. Maybe that cute little kid."

Carly glanced out the window again, and her heart jolted. Jack was staring up at her.

Chapter 27

Jack threw the stick and stared up at Miss Blackstone's window again. She was sure she'd seen someone in the room—a man to be exact.

But having a man in a woman's room was against her ma's rules.

Max trotted back with the stick in his mouth, looking happy. She took it from him, tossed it away again, and wiped the dog slobber on her skirt. Peering over her shoulder, she saw that Luke was still talking to Polly and Dolly Dykstra.

Max grabbed the stick and hurried back to her. He dropped it at her feet then stared up at her, looking as if he were grinning. He waited, wagging his tail, ears alert. She backed up a few feet so she could get a better look at the window and tossed the stick. A person stepped up close to Miss Blackstone and then quickly jumped back into the shadows. There *was* someone in her room, and that person wore a man's plaid shirt. That left only one possible solution—there really was a man in that room.

And currently, they didn't have any male boarders.

The front door opened, and her ma stepped out. "Time to come in, Jacqueline."

This time, Jack didn't argue. She had to find out what was going on. Max walked back, head drooping. The stick fell from his mouth, and his tail wagged. She bent down to scratch his ears. "Gotta go, boy. There's something strange goin' on at home."

The dog whined as Jack jogged toward her mother. How could she get upstairs without making her ma suspicious?

"Go wash up and get ready for bed, sweetie." Her mother stood in the doorway, looking down the street.

Jack gazed back over her shoulder. Was her ma looking at Luke? As much as she hoped so, she had a problem that needed investigating. "Don't you need me to take some fresh water upstairs to the boarders?"

Her ma's brows lifted. "Uh. . .thank you, but no. I did that before I fixed supper."

Jack searched her mind for another excuse. "Well, maybe they need some clean towels."

"What's going on?" Her mother glanced up the stairs.

Jack leaned forward to close the space between them. Maybe confessing was the best alternative. "I saw a man in Miss Blackstone's room, Ma."

"What? When?" She placed her hand over her heart like she often did when she was worried.

"Just now when I was playing fetch with Max. I saw him twice through the window. Honest, Ma."

Different expressions flitted across her mother's face until she settled on one—and Jack knew then that she didn't believe her.

"Just get inside and get ready for bed. I'm too tired to deal with your nonsense tonight."

"But—"

Rachel held up her hand. "No 'buts.' It's time for bed."

"You never believe me." Jack scowled and stomped past her mother. "Why would I lie about something like that? Even I know your number one rule for unmarried women—never have a man upstairs."

In the bedroom, she slammed the door. She'd told her ma about thc stolen shirt, too, but she hadn't believed her enough to even look to see if it was missing.

Jack tore off her clothes and yanked on her nightgown, not even taking time to wash. Tomorrow she'd tell Luke about the man. She might just be a little kid, but she knew what she'd seen.

A leaf floated on the river's current as the water rippled along on its way to join the waters of the Red River. Luke stood by the river's edge, feeling as if all his troubles and worries had drifted away. The pastor had been right. Once he'd made the mental decision to forgive Rachel, his spirit had risen like a caged bird set free. He felt like a prisoner whose shackles had been removed for the last time. Free to move on. Free to admit he still loved Rachel.

But had he driven her away with his hard-nosed refusal to forgive for so many years? He ducked his head and kicked a rock. Rachel was so tenderhearted that his attitude must have broken her heart—just like she'd broken his.

No! He held up his hand as if shoving the enemy back. "I will not take up that offense again. I've forgiven her, once and for all."

He breathed in a cleansing breath through his nose. He needed to tell her—needed to ask her to forgive him for being so obstinate. And she would—in a heartbeat, because that's the kind of woman she was. Unable to hold an offense against anyone. A loving nurturer. No wonder she found it hard to discipline her daughter.

Luke mounted Alamo, knowing he'd spent enough time away from town. Not that much ever happened there. As he headed toward town, he watched the remains of the sunset. Bright pink, the same color as Rachel's Sunday dress, painted the belly of every cloud in the sky. Like a ripe peach, orange mixed with the pink to create an amazing sight that only the Creator of this world could have designed.

He thought about the final leg of the bride contest. The mayor had let him know that he was to take each bride out to eat and get to know her better—all except that anonymous bride, of course. That had been a decent idea until he'd forgiven Rachel, and then like a dam breaking, his heart was flooded with love for her again. Had he ever truly quit loving her?

God was giving them a second chance—and he was sure going to take advantage of it.

Max lay under the bench in front of his office, exhausted from chasing all the sticks Jack had thrown him earlier in the evening. The lights were off in the freight office, so Luke turned his horse between the livery and Polly's Café to Oak Street.

"Marshal, wait!" Jenny Evans jogged toward him, holding her skirt up to avoid tripping. "Might I have a word with you?"

Luke sighed and dismounted. What did she want now?

She opened her pad of paper and turned so the fading twilight illuminated it. "The mayor mentioned that you're going to be taking the boardinghouse brides out to supper separately so you can get to know each one better. Can you tell me where and when? Which bride will you invite first?"

Luke worked to keep a cap on his irritation. "No, I can't tell you. But I will say that I'll make the announcement of my choice of bride tomorrow night."

"Tomorrow?" Jenny's eyes widened. "Why, you can't do it tomorrow. That's Wednesday. I've got to have time to get the announcement out in the paper so folks around here will know about it. Everyone will want to come to town for that. It's the best fun anyone's had since those kids hauled Simon Jones's plow horse up into his hay loft."

Luke tried hard to remember the time of prayer he'd just finished. *Breathe. Don't let her get to you.* "Tomorrow night. Whoever is here is here. And that's final."

She worked her mouth as if trying to get something unstuck from her teeth. "The mayor might have something to say about this." She spun around and marched off.

Luke sighed. He probably should expect a visit from Mayor Burke before long.

He stopped in front of his cousins' house and noted only a faint light glimmered in the parlor. Maybe he should wait until morning, but he ached to share his news with someone. He dismounted, tethered Alamo to the porch, and knocked on the door.

Mark opened it and grinned. Shirtless, he scratched his belly and then waved Luke inside. "Didn't expect to see you at this hour."

"Is it too late?"

"Nah, come on in." Mark combed his curly hair with his fingers. "I'd offer you some coffee, but we've already dumped the dregs."

"I don't need anything. Just wanted to tell y'all something." Luke stepped inside and studied his cousins' home. Since he normally met with them in their office, he'd only been here a few times. Books stood in stacks on the floor beside the small settee and the table in front of it. Dust balls littered the floor like tumbleweeds, and piles of papers were everywhere. "Is this where you file your paperwork?"

Mark chuckled. "It's an organized mess. Trust me."

Luke shook his head. "You need a housekeeper—or maybe a wife."

Garrett walked into the room barefoot and dressed in his nightshirt. He yawned and scratched his chest. "What are you doin' here?"

Maybe this wasn't such a good idea. "I'll just wait till morning. I can see you're both ready for bed—unless you're accustomed to wearing dresses at home."

Garrett perked up, obviously not taking offense at Luke's joke and not wanting to wait for news. "No, you're here now, so spill the beans. What's going on?"

Mark turned up the lantern and motioned for Luke to sit down in the only empty chair. Luke obliged. Mark shoved aside a stack of papers, and he and Garrett perched on the edge of the settee.

Luke grinned, and both brothers lifted their brows. "I've finally forgiven Rachel."

Garrett smiled and slugged Mark in the shoulder.

Mark scowled and rubbed his arm. "That's great news. How'd she take it?"

Luke shook his head. "Haven't told her yet. It just happened—down by the river."

"I guess you had that talk with the pastor?"

"Yeah. Thanks for suggesting that."

"So, what are you gonna do now?" Mark asked.

"He's gonna stop the bride contest and marry Rachel, that's what." Garrett grinned and leaned back, arms crossed over his chest as if he were responsible.

Luke stared at his cousin. Was he that transparent?

"Oh, come on, we both know you're still in love with Rachel. That's the only explanation for you still being upset at her after all these years," Garrett said.

Luke stared at the floor, trying to make sense of his thoughts. A mouse ran out from under his chair, sniffed the air, and dashed back to his hiding spot. "If you knew I was still in love with Rachel, why did you order all those brides?"

Mark sat forward, elbows on his knees. "We didn't know then, and if we had, it would have saved us a lot of trouble."

"Yeah, but on the other hand, maybe it took some competition for your affections to make you realize where your heart belongs." Garrett looked so proud that he nearly beamed.

Luke leaned back, not wanting to admit there might be some truth in Garrett's comment. "I've forgiven Rachel, and I sincerely hope she still cares for me and will be willing to forgive my stubbornness."

"Let's hope it doesn't take another eleven years." Garrett chuckled. "We're all getting a bit long in the tooth."

Mark elbowed his brother. "Speak for yourself."

Luke smiled at his cousins' horseplay. "Do you think I still have a chance with her? Am I needlessly getting my hopes up?"

"Rachel has only had eyes for you. It was true back then and true today."

Luke ground his back teeth together as a fraction of the old hurt shoved its way to the surface like a boil. "Then why did she marry James?"

His cousins glanced at each other.

Luke stood and paced the small room. "What are you not telling me?"

Garrett ran his hands through his hair. "What did she tell you back then?"

Luke threw up his hands. "Nothing. Just that she couldn't marry me because she had already married him. I figured she wanted an easier life than I could have given her."

"You figured wrong," Garrett said. Both cousins stood, still casting odd glances at each other and back at Luke.

A knot twisted in Luke's gut. Had there been more to her decision than he thought?

"What are you not telling me?" He rubbed his nape, his peace fleeing.

Garrett ran his hand over his jaw. "It's not our story to tell. You need to ask Rachel about it."

Luke stopped in front of his cousins. "I tried that once, but it didn't work."

"Try again." Garrett crossed his arms.

All manner of thoughts assaulted Luke, none of them good. His cousins were right; he'd put off this discussion long enough. He said his good-byes and strode to Rachel's house. From the front, all was dark. He rounded the side of the house and was glad to see the kitchen light still on.

Because of the lateness of the hour, he knocked on the back door and waited instead of entering like he normally did. Rachel opened the door a smidgeon and peeked out. She looked tired, and he almost changed his mind. "I need to talk with you for a minute."

She hesitated a moment then nodded and opened the door. "I need to close the bedroom door so our talking doesn't disturb Jacqueline."

He touched her arm to stop her. "Could we take a walk outside?"

Rachel studied his face and must have seen something worthy, because she nodded. He held the door open, and she followed him out. His hand shook as he closed the door. They walked toward the back of her property, silencing the crickets with each step.

He needed to tell her that he forgave her, but now his bitterness seemed petty. Why had it taken him so long?

Rachel walked beside him, wringing her hands together. Did he make her nervous?

He sighed and faced her. "I want you to know I'm sorry."

She shook her head. "You have nothing to be sorry for. I'm the one at fault."

"I wish you'd explain to me what happened."

She turned away, fidgeting. "I should have told you right away, but I was afraid."

He clutched her shoulders, forcing her to face him. "Afraid of what?"

Her head hung down, and her hands refused to be still. "That I'd lose you."

"You lost me anyway. It's time you tell me what happened. It will help us both. Take a load off our shoulders."

The crickets resumed their chirping all around them, blending with the noise of the tree frogs. A full moon shone bright, illuminating Rachel. He tipped her face up. "Please tell me, Rach."

She shuddered, as if carrying the weight of the world. "I

married James because I was pregnant with his child."

Luke staggered, his hand going to his chest. Never once had he considered she might have been unfaithful. All these years he'd pined for her, and now he allowed his hopes to rise again, only to be dashed on the rocks once more. She'd been with another man. Before marriage.

Rachel stared up at him with tears charging down her face. "I'm so sorry, Luke."

He paced away, putting some distance between him and Rachel. *God, how could this happen?* His heart ached as if someone had plunged a sword through it. "I loved you like no man has ever loved a woman. I'd have done anything for you, and you betrayed me with another man—my friend, no less."

Tears burned Luke's eyes as Rachel's betrayal burned deep. The rage of his unforgiving spirit shot up like the force of a dark angel fleeing hell. He ground his back teeth together and clenched his fists.

"I tried to f–fight him off, but he was too strong." Rachel's voice sounded far away, as if she'd fallen in a well.

Suddenly his rage fled, and something worse wormed its way into his heart. Had he heard correctly? "What?"

"I told him no. I tried to get away, but we were alone, and h–he always took what he wanted."

Luke closed his eyes, hating the truth. James had his way with the woman Luke loved.

"If he wasn't dead, I'd be very tempted to kill him." Luke grabbed Rachel's shoulders. "Why in the world did you marry him after that? Didn't you know I'd take care of you?"

Rachel ducked her head. "I went to visit my aunt after the attack for six weeks. By the time I returned, I knew I was pregnant." Rachel's chin quivered. "You were out working on the Carney ranch by then. I saw James one day, and he convinced me that you wouldn't want me anymore. That no decent man would." She heaved in a breath that made her shudder. "He offered to do right by me, and we married the next day."

Luke stared up at the dark sky. *Why didn't You protect her?*

"I was also afraid if you knew the truth that you'd do something to James. His father would have made sure you went to prison—or worse—if you'd retaliated."

She was right. He knew that. But he felt robbed of the chance to vindicate Rachel. He would have back then if he'd known the truth, and that could well have ended in his death.

"Is Jack the child you had?"

Rachel nodded. "Garrett and Mark spread word that she was born early, since she was so small. I never liked what they did, but I know it was to protect my reputation. I'll always be grateful."

"How did they know to do that?"

"They found me at the river. They knew you and I were supposed to be there, and they came to swim, but t–they found me instead. I pleaded with them not to tell anyone, and for once, they did as asked."

Luke forked his fingers through his hair, hating himself for choosing work over Rachel that day. If only he'd gone to the river. "I appreciate your telling me this. I know it wasn't easy."

Rachel didn't respond. She wiped her eyes and fiddled with a fold in her skirt. Luke didn't know what to say. His cousins had lied to protect Rachel, and wrong as it was, he'd be eternally grateful. A woman had nothing if she didn't have her reputation.

All manner of thoughts swirled through his head. He'd blamed Rachel for wanting a better life—for marrying James because of his money—when the truth had been far different. He squeezed his eyes shut. Oh, how he must have hurt her by his refusal to forgive. He'd been stupid. Ungrateful for the changes God had made in his own life. Rachel had been a victim, but he'd blamed her for his own pain, when hers must have been unbearable.

"I want you to know that I'm sorry for everything—for not showing up that day—for what James did. For not being there when you needed me." He took hold of her and pulled her into a hug so quickly she gasped. She stood there woodenly, not responding, and he could hardly blame her. She probably hated him for how he'd treated her. "C'mon, I'll walk you back."

At the door, she stopped. "I don't blame you for any of this, I hope you know that. You were just trying to work hard to get us a start."

"I need some time to think and pray; then I'd like to talk to you again, if that's all right."

She nodded, and a faint smile tugged at her cheeks. The door clicked shut, and he leaned against the house, digesting all he'd learned. Never once had he considered such a scenario.

He allowed himself to think back, and the memory of that day came into focus. He'd been whipping through his chores at home, anxious to meet Rachel at the river as they'd prearranged. He'd been busy working for weeks and missed her terribly, and he had looked forward to sweet talking her and stealing a few kisses. She'd set aside an hour to sit and talk with him at the river before her mother expected her back home to help with supper. He'd been on his way to meet her when a local rancher had waylaid him and asked him to deliver a load of supplies he'd just bought to his ranch.

The choice had been hard. Everybody in town knew he'd do any kind of honest work to make money—and the rancher had offered him a fair amount. Luke needed only about fifty dollars more before he could put a down payment on a house for Rachel and him to live in after their wedding. The pull to spend time with her had been strong, but in the end, the chance to make money won out. After all, once they were married, they'd have all the time in the world together.

He remembered looking for his cousins as he drove out of town but finding James instead, lounging outside the bank with a friend. James had more than willingly agreed to deliver a message to Rachel that Luke had found work and wouldn't be able to meet her.

Luke's stomach swirled with sudden realization. His limbs trembled, and he leaned forward, hands on his eyes, sure that he would retch at any moment as the truth dawned.

It's my fault James took advantage of Rachel.

Chapter 28

Rachel leaned back on the chair in her bedroom, eyes closed, relishing the moments she'd spent with Luke. He hadn't said he forgave her, but he had said he was sorry. He'd barely reacted to all that she'd revealed, but he'd been right: she felt better for having finally told him the truth. Only time would tell how he would respond, and she was afraid to hope for too much. But she could still pray for him—pray that he wouldn't feel responsible for what James had done. Luke had always tried to protect her when they were young. Now that he knew the truth, would he blame himself for not showing up that day at the river?

She sighed. Her legs ached from standing much of the day. She loved tending the boardinghouse and her boarders, but by evening, she was exhausted. Maybe selling the place wasn't such a bad idea. She stretched and sniffed her fingers. In spite of the scrubbing with lye soap she'd given them, she still caught the faint whiff of the onions she'd cut up to go with the fried liver she'd made for supper.

Her gaze traveled across the room, and she watched the rise and fall of her daughter's chest as she slept. This was about the only time her child was peaceful and not running about or causing trouble. She blew out a heavy sigh. Why was raising children so difficult?

Jacqueline had said a man was in Miss Blackstone's room, but Rachel didn't believe her. The young woman had made it clear that she planned on marrying the marshal, so why would she risk her chances by inviting a man to her room?

She wouldn't. Besides, Rachel didn't know of a single man in town who'd lower himself to steal another man's potential wife or sneak into her boardinghouse. Most of the men in Lookout were good, decent sorts. She shook her head. If only Jacqueline wouldn't tell falsehoods. It surely made it hard for Rachel to tell when the girl was being honest.

She pulled her high-top boot up on her knee and untied the laces, thinking about her visit with Mayor Burke. Though a bit less than she'd hoped for, he had made her a fair offer for the boardinghouse, but was it enough to start over in a new town? Could she really leave her hometown and move in with her aunt?

The thud of heavy footsteps above her head drew her gaze to the ceiling. Why would Miss Blackstone be stomping around like that?

Who knew what that young woman was doing? Something about her made Rachel wary, but maybe it was just that she was competing for Luke's affections. Rachel's lip wobbled at the thought of him picking one of the boardinghouse brides, but she'd done all she could to get him to forgive her. She must have hurt him much more than she realized.

Rachel worked at the laces, stretching them apart so she could get her foot free from the boot. Overhead, a softer set of footprints walked in the same direction as the heavy ones. The floor creaked above her head, and she thought she heard voices. Rachel froze.

What if Jacqueline had been right?

Pulling her boot back on, she hurriedly tied the laces and tiptoed to the open window. Miss Blackstone's window was right above hers, and she listened hard for the sound of people speaking. The darkness of night had wrapped the house. The lights were already out in the Castleby house next door, and only the faint glow of the lantern on the dresser held the darkness at bay. Crickets battled tree frogs, but she couldn't hear any voices.

Still, there were those footsteps.

The thought of a trespasser in her home flooded her limbs with strength. Maybe Jacqueline hadn't been lying.

Guilt needled her, but the desire to know the truth pushed her forward. She crept to the entryway and paused at the staircase, her heart thundering. Maybe she should get her rifle—or Luke.

Maybe she was making a big deal out of nothing.

With her hand shaking, she held on to the railing and climbed the stairs to the second floor, being careful to miss the squeaky steps. No light shone from under either Miss Bennett's door or Miss O'Neil's, but a faint glow illuminated the floorboards around Miss Blackstone's. Rachel tiptoed forward across the wide hall, wincing when a board creaked. At the door, she stood, her breath sounding like a locomotive chugging uphill. Was she overreacting?

She heard a thump in the room, and suddenly, the door flew open. A large stranger stood in the doorway, grabbed her wrist before she could react, and yanked her into the room. A gasp fell from her mouth as he kicked the door shut with his foot and pressed her up against the wall in one swift motion. His arm against her throat cut off Rachel's breath, and she shoved against it.

"Be still, and I'll loosen my hold." His hot breath smelled like smoke.

"Let her go, Ty." Miss Blackstone's voice sounded from behind the man, but Rachel couldn't see her.

He stared into Rachel's eyes. "You gonna cause me any trouble? I know ya got that purty little girl downstairs."

Fear she hadn't known since the day James had his way with her flooded her whole being. Her body shivered as if it had been caught up in a tornado. *Dear Jesus, help me.* "W–what do you want?"

"Well, now, that's none of your businss." He loosened his hold just enough for Rachel to catch a deep breath. "You're an unexpected development. You should've stayed downstairs."

"Just let her go, Ty. She's not part of this." Miss Blackstone grabbed the man's arm.

He shoved her back, and she lost her footing, falling to the floor. "Don't be tellin' me what to do."

Rachel's mind raced for a way of escape. If she could get away and run for Luke, this man would get to Jacqueline before she could return. But if she got loose and ran to her bedroom to get her daughter, surely the man would catch up with her. She had the other two brides to be concerned about, as well.

The man turned back to her, his leering gaze running over her face and down her body. "I'll let ya go if you promise to behave, although I'd like it even better if you chose not to." He licked his tongue across his lips.

Rachel turned her face away as a shiver wormed its way down her spine. "I won't cause any trouble. I promise."

He backed away nearly as quickly as he'd captured her and leaned against the door, resting one hand on the butt of his revolver. Rachel hurried across the room and stood next to Miss Blackstone, who'd managed to untangle her skirts and get back on her feet. "Do you know him?"

Her boarder nodded. "Unfortunately. He's my brother."

Rachel noted the resemblance in their black hair and some of their features, although their eye color was different. The man chuckled and touched the edge of his hat. "Tyson Payton, ma'am. A pleasure to meet ya."

Frowning, Rachel swung her gaze back to the young woman. "Did you have different fathers? I mean, since your last name is Blackstone." A sudden thought bolted across Rachel's mind. "Or have you been married before?"

"Wrong and wrong." Tyson chuckled and crossed his arms over his wide chest.

Truth be told, he was a handsome man, even in the pale light from the hurricane lamp. But his response confused Rachel. "What do you mean?"

"Ty, please. . ."

He snarled at Miss Blackstone. "I mean her name ain't whatever she told ya. It's Carly Payton."

Rachel gasped and clutched her bodice. "You've been lying? Why?"

"Never mind all that." Ty scratched his jaw and eyed her. "The question is, what are we gonna do with you?"

Rachel had dealt with stubborn, troublesome men before and drew in a fortifying breath. "Why don't you just leave and let the rest of us get on with our business?"

Tyson chuckled again. "I kinda like your spunk." Suddenly, his countenance changed. "But spunky or not, you've gotten in the way of my plans. I'm gonna have to do somethin' with ya."

Miss Blackstone—no, Miss Payton—crossed the room. "Ty, she's not part of this. Let's just cut our losses and leave this dumpy town."

While the brother seemed to be considering her suggestion, Rachel's mind raced. Had they come to town with some kind of nefarious scheme?

She wrung her hands together. *Heavenly Father, please help me.*

"No, I think it's best if we get rid of her."

Rachel's heart bucked in her chest. He was going to kill her? What would happen to Jacqueline? *Lord, no.*

He pulled out his pistol and pointed it at her. She took a step back. Surely he wouldn't shoot her here, not with Luke and the whole town so close by.

"You can't kill her, Ty. She's got that kid to care for." Miss Payton turned to face Rachel, worry etched in her face. "I'm so sorry. I never meant for him to find me here." She broke her gaze and looked down.

"You got a key to the door leading to those back stairs, lady?"

Rachel nodded and reached into her apron pocket. Thank the Lord she hadn't left the key in her bedroom.

"You go first. Quietly. Unlock the back door, then Carly next, and I'll follow. If you try anything, I'll shoot ya and then come back and finish off your kid and the rest of those gals."

Rachel searched her mind for a way of escape, but she didn't want her daughter or the brides to get hurt. If she followed along, maybe she could find a way to overpower the man and get free. *Please, Lord.*

"You got a scarf or bandanna, sis?"

Miss Payton scowled at her brother but nodded. She pulled a red bandanna out of a drawer and held it up.

"Gag her so she don't make no noise."

Rachel winced as the cloth cut between her teeth and pinched her cheek. Miss Payton tied a knot, pulling Rachel's hair.

"Sorry," the girl whispered.

Tyson slowly opened the door and peered out. He waved his gun at them. Rachel breathed a sigh of relief when she entered the hall and found the other doors still closed. In the light of the hall lamp, she located the right key and unlocked the back door, taking one last glimpse at the hall she'd so carefully decorated to be pleasing to her guests. Would she ever see her home again? Or her daughter? Swallowing hard and forcing back the tears burning her eyes, she hurried down the dark stairs that wrapped around the back side of the house, praying Luke would find them.

Yet a part of her hoped he wouldn't. She couldn't bear if he got mortally wounded.

At the back of her lot, two horses were tied in the trees, out of sight of anyone who'd pass by. How had she and Luke missed them earlier when they were in the yard? Ty grabbed her waist and hoisted her onto one horse. "Get on behind her, sis."

Miss Payton clawed her way up and managed to climb on behind her. "It wouldn't have killed you to help me," she hissed at her brother.

He took the reins of their horse and mounted his own. Tears she'd fought to keep at bay charged down Rachel's cheeks. The light still glimmered in her bedroom, waiting for her return. She thought of her daughter sleeping there so peacefully. Would she ever see Jacqueline again?

Jack covered her head with her pillow to drive away the cheerful chirps from the birds welcoming the new day. If only she could sleep another hour. Bad dreams had pestered her all night. Dreams of Butch pulling her hair. Of him throwing her in the lake when she had her Sunday dress on. Dreams of her marrying him.

"Ick!"

She tossed the pillow aside at the disgusting thought.

Her body let her know that she'd get no more sleep until she visited the necessary. Sighing, she stood and stretched. She turned around and froze. Her mother's side of the bed looked as if it had never been slept in. And the lamp still burned. How odd.

Now that she thought of it, no fragrant smells greeted her this morning or the familiar sound of her ma clattering in the kitchen. She glanced at the clock on the fireplace mantel. Eight o'clock?

Jack hurried out the door and into the kitchen. She struggled to make sense of what she saw. First thing every morning, her ma cooked biscuits and made coffee. The kitchen looked just as clean as it had been last night before bed, while the coffeepot was as cold as a winter's night.

She opened the back door and stuck her head out. "Ma?" When she got no response, she hurried to the necessary and ran back inside, racing from room to room downstairs but finding no sign of her mother. Where could she be? Had there been some emergency in town?

Jack raced to her bedroom and found her shirt and overalls. Once dressed, she ran upstairs and pounded on Miss Bennett's door.

The woman opened it and scowled down. "Is breakfast ready? I haven't smelled a thing this morning."

"Have you seen Ma?"

"You mean today? Uh, no I haven't. Why?"

Jack spun around and pounded on Miss O'Neil's door. It fell open but the room was empty. Could her ma be somewhere talking with the Irish lady?

"Try the washroom," Miss Bennett offered.

Jack jogged to the back of the second story, noting that Miss Blackstone's door was open and the room also empty. Suddenly remembering the pastor's sermon about being ready for the rapture, Jack halted. She thought about how much trouble she'd caused her mother. Was she such a heathen that the rapture had come and she'd been left behind?

Her heart pounded like the blacksmith's hammer. The washroom door handle jiggled, and she looked up. Miss O'Neil came out, her face looking pink and freshly scrubbed. If Miss O'Neil was still here, Jack felt certain that the rapture hadn't come. God might leave snooty Miss Bennett, but surely He'd have taken the kind Irish woman.

"Top o' the mornin' to you. Would it be breakfast time?" Miss O'Neil lifted her head and sniffed, and then her brows dipped down.

"Have you seen my ma?"

"Nay, I have not."

Jack started to turn, but the back door caught her eye. "Did one of y'all unlock that door?"

Both brides shook their heads. "We don't have the key," Miss Bennett said.

Jack spun around, worry for her mother rising like the summer temperature. "Ma's missing, and I've gotta find Luke."

Chapter 29

Luke scrubbed the sleep from his face in the warm river water. The whiskers on his jaw bristled as he ran his hand across his face. He hadn't planned to be out all night, but after crying out to God and praying like he never had, he'd fallen dead asleep near the riverbank just before sunrise. He yawned. A few more hours rest would be nice, but he needed to check on the town, and then he had to see Rachel again.

Now that he'd wrestled with his unforgiving spirit and his guilt over what had happened, he was eager to see what God would do. The blinders on his eyes had been removed, and he saw things clearly for the first time in years. He stood and looked toward town. Excitement battled regret. Alamo nickered to him and walked away from the patch of grass where he'd been grazing.

Luke patted his faithful horse, bridled him, and mounted. He'd have to eat a lot of crow with Rachel, but she wasn't one to hold a grudge. And if he wasn't wrong, she still had feelings for him. He'd just spent the last few weeks denying them, but in his heart, he knew she still cared just as he did.

Last night, once he'd let go of his anger at James, he'd wallowed in guilt for an hour or two. Good thing he wasn't a drinking man, because he wouldn't have been sober for a week after he realized how he'd failed Rachel. Instead, he had to face the facts. He *was* responsible for what happened to her, but his intentions had been good. He was just trying to get enough money to get them a home so they could get married.

Then why did he still feel bad?

As he drew near the town, he surveyed the serene scene before him. The business folks were opening up their shops. The clink of a hammer could be heard coming from the livery, and fragrant scents from Polly's Café filled the air, making his belly rumble.

The boardinghouse drew his gaze, and he hoped to see Rachel outside sweeping. But then at this hour, she was more likely cleaning up the breakfast mess. At least he knew there would be a plate of her fine cooking waiting for him.

The mayor walked out of Luke's office, hands on his hips, and looked around. When his gaze latched onto Luke, he strode toward him. Dismounting, Luke met the mayor in the street. What could he want at this early hour?

"Jenny tells me you're going to announce who you want to marry tonight. That right?"

Luke suppressed a chuckle. The mayor sure didn't waste words on greetings. Luke nodded, but a twinge of uncertainty wiggled its way through his composure. Was he doing the right thing by making a public announcement? What if she turned him down flat? What if *she* refused to forgive *him*?

"That's right, I am."

The mayor puffed up his chest. "What about the next contest?"

Luke searched his mind but drew a blank. "What contest? I thought the next thing was for me to have supper with each of the gals."

Mayor Burke nodded. "So you can get to know them better. I was thinking maybe we should have the brides cook you something else since the pie contest didn't turn out well." He tapped his thick mustache as if considering the idea then studied Luke's face. "How is it you already know which one you want?"

"I just do. And I need to get my announcement made so the other gals can make some plans. No sense leaving them hanging."

"True, but I think we should wait until Saturday when most of the folks come to town. A lot of folks will be disappointed if you do it midweek."

Luke shook his head. "Too late. I told Jenny yesterday to post an announcement in the paper. Knowing her, she's probably already got them made up and ready to distribute."

The mayor's mustache twitched, and he leaned forward. "So... which one is it?"

Luke should have expected this, but the mayor surprised him. "Surely you don't expect me to tell you when I haven't even told her?"

"I guess not." He looked put off but shook his head. "Well, if we're going to have the announcement tonight, I've got a lot to do. Have you seen Rachel today?"

"Not yet. I'm headed there now to get my breakfast."

Mayor Burke walked toward the café. "Tell her I need to see her right away. I'll be at Polly's for the next half hour or so."

Luke quirked his mouth. If the mayor wanted to see Rachel, he could go to her house. He tied Alamo to the hitching post outside the jail and glanced around. Few people were out this early. Birds chirped in the tree beside the jail, and the sun shone full in the cloudless sky, promising another scorching day. But this day was filled with hope. Hope for love. Hope for the future. Hope for a family. Luke couldn't help grinning.

He whistled, and Max ambled out the jail door, wagging his tail. Luke stuck his head in his office to see if Jack had brought the scrap bucket yet, but it wasn't there. Hmm. Where was that gal? She usually headed to see him first thing after breakfast.

He took Alamo to the livery, rubbed him down, and fed him before tending to himself. A man who didn't take care of his animals first wasn't worth much. Reaching down, he scratched

Max's ear. "Right, boy?"

As he neared the boardinghouse, Luke's steps quickened. He had a lot to repent for, but for the first time in over a decade, he had a clear hope for the future—and that future included a pretty brunette with blue eyes as pale as—

The front door of the boardinghouse flew open, and Jack galloped out the door. She jumped off the porch and raced toward him. "Luke, help!"

What in the world? He burst into a run, stopping as she skidded to a halt in front of him. His gaze scanned the house for signs of trouble. "What's wrong?"

"It's Ma. She's gone."

Luke's heart all but stopped. Was this just another of Jack's tales? "What do you mean?"

"She never came to bed last night, and she hasn't even started breakfast."

Luke's jaw tightened. What could have happened? She'd been fine when he last saw her. "Are there any signs of anything disturbed in the house?"

Jack shook her head, her unbound auburn hair swinging side to side. "No, except the back door upstairs was open—and Ma always keeps it locked to protect our guests."

"All right. Calm down and let me have a look inside."

"Where could she be? She never leaves without telling me where she's going." Jack's deep blue eyes carried too much concern for a child. Max whined and stuck his head under her hand.

Luke pulled her to his side. "Don't worry, half bit. I'll find her."

Of all the nights for him to be off licking his wounds.

What could have happened? Rachel was a very responsible person and mother. She'd never go off without her daughter or leave her guests to fend for themselves.

Jack pulled him through the house and into the kitchen. She waved her hand toward the empty room. "See. No food. She hasn't even made coffee."

Luke's concerns mounted, knowing Rachel always did that first thing each morning. Jack yanked on his arm and dragged him to the bedroom. Luke stopped in the doorway, not wanting to intrude into Rachel's most private area.

"See. Her side of the bed is still made, and her nightgown is still on its peg." Jack pointed behind the door.

"Could she have made up her side of the bed and then gotten dressed?"

Jack shook her head. "No, we make it together right after breakfast most days."

The hairs on the back of his neck stood at attention. Something must have happened to Rachel after he left. But what? He hadn't had any reports of trouble. Yeah, he was down at the river, but he would have heard any gunfire, and the mayor would have said something if there'd been any trouble. He forced himself to step into the room. He didn't want to miss any evidence—if there was some.

"Miss Blackstone is gone, too."

Luke spun around and stared at Jack. "What?"

"I noticed when I was upstairs looking for Ma that Miss Blackstone's door was open and she wasn't in her room. Do you think they could have gone somewhere? Did something happen in town last night?"

Luke shrugged, not willing to admit that he'd shirked his duty. He might have seen something suspicious if he had been working. Maybe Rachel had gone out to help a friend. His conscience told him she'd never leave Jack or her guests unless forced. He placed his hand on his pistol, not liking the thoughts chasing through his mind. "Show me Miss Blackstone's room."

He followed the child upstairs and first checked the back door. "No signs of forced entry. Whoever came or went this way must have had a key."

"Ma's got the only one. Keeps it on a ribbon in her apron pocket."

Luke's thoughts raced around his mind like a bumblebee caught in a jar. Had someone broken in and taken Rachel and Miss Blackstone? But why those two? If someone had come upstairs, why not take the other brides, too? Why Rachel?

He had to find her. After he left last night, he realized he still hadn't told her he'd forgiven her. He had to tell her—had to let her know that he still loved her.

How could he go on if something happened to her?

One of the bedroom doors opened. Luke grabbed Jack and flung her behind him at the same time he drew his gun.

Miss Bennett yelped and lifted her hands, her blue eyes wide.

Luke relaxed and holstered his weapon. "Sorry to frighten you, ma'am. Did you see or hear anything unusual last night?"

She shook her head. "Not really. Maybe just a thump or two."

Miss O'Neil's door flew open, and Luke turned toward it, hand on gun. The young woman took a step back when she saw him. "I heard voices last night. It sure enough sounded as if Miss Blackstone had someone in her room, but I wasn't certain, because we often hear noises from the street. Right after that, I went to bed and fell asleep."

If someone had been in Miss Blackstone's room, he—or she—could have taken Rachel and the young woman somewhere. But why?

He was going to need some help. "Jack, could you go fetch my cousins?"

She nodded but seemed reluctant to leave his side. He squeezed her thin shoulder and bent down. "I promise I'll find your mother."

Jack's chin and lower lip wobbled, but he gave her credit for not crying. "All right."

Luke offered her a smile; then she spun and raced down the stairs. He looked at the brides. "You're sure you didn't hear anything else last night? See anything out of the ordinary?"

Miss Bennett shook her head, but at the glint in the Irish girl's eyes he lifted his brows.

"'Twas smoke I smelled—before I heard the voices. I stuck my head out the window and looked around but didn't see anything a'tall. The scent didn't get any stronger, so I didn't worry about it."

"Thank you. I'm sure Rachel would want you to help yourselves to breakfast, if you don't mind fixing it. I could use a cup of coffee to help me think."

Both women nodded and headed downstairs. Luke studied the back door again but still found no signs of forced entry. Rachel must have unlocked the door.

Luke pushed open Miss Blackstone's bedroom door and surveyed the room. The bed was slightly rumpled but didn't look as if anyone had slept in it. He checked for signs of disrupted things, but all looked in order. He started to leave, but his gaze fell to a black spot on the rug. Squatting, he touched the spot and sniffed his finger. Ashes?

So, someone *had* been smoking, and that would most likely be a man. Someone Miss Blackstone knew, perhaps?

His gut twisted. Had Rachel smelled the smoke and come upstairs to investigate? That could explain why she was upstairs.

Down at the bottom of the back stairs, he checked the dry ground for footprints—there were several. He knew Rachel kept the door locked, so these prints had to have been made last night. There were two narrow sets and a larger set about the same size boot print as he made. He clenched his jaw. Was this a kidnapping? For ransom?

Please, Lord, keep her safe until I can find her.

"Luke!" Garrett yelled.

"Down here."

His cousins trotted down the stairs and joined him with Jack following on their heels. "What's going on? Jack just said you needed us fast." Garrett looked around the backyard; then his gaze landed on Luke again, while Mark held his rifle, waiting with a concerned expression on his face.

"Rachel and Miss Blackstone are missing. I think—" He glanced at Jack.

"What?" she asked, brows dipped as if she dared him not to tell her.

She'd know soon enough as it was. He would need the whole town's help to find Rachel. He squatted down and pointed to the prints in the dirt. "See here. There are two sets of women's prints, and a larger set. I think a man took them."

Jack gasped and covered her mouth with her hand. "I just remembered. I saw a man in Miss Blackstone's window last night. I told Ma." She ducked her head and frowned. "But she didn't believe me."

"I believe you." Luke pulled her to him. He stared at his cousins. "Gather the town outside my office—and fast."

His cousins nodded. "You take Main and Oak streets," Garrett said, "and I'll take Bluebonnet and Ap. . ." His voice faded as both men jogged around the side of the house.

"I want to help." Jack yanked on Luke's vest and stared up at him. Her vulnerability made his heart ache.

He shook his head. "I need you to stay here and watch over the brides."

Jack puckered her lips. "They don't need me. They don't even like me."

"Well, your ma will want to see you the moment I bring her home. You don't want her to get here and you not be here, do you?" Luke hoped she'd take the hint and stay out of trouble.

She toed the dirt with her bare feet. "I guess not."

"Good." He placed a kiss on the girl's head. "Say a prayer that we find them fast, all right?"

Jack nodded and looked on the verge of tears. He wished he had someone better than the remaining brides to entrust her care to, but he supposed they'd do. He hugged her tight then turned her away. "Go on, now."

As soon as Jack had traipsed in the back door, Luke started

following the tracks. They led to the rear of Rachel's property and to hoof prints. Luke ground his teeth together.

"God, I need help here. Help me find Rachel, and soon. Keep her safe until then."

Spinning around, he headed back to his office. He needed his rifle. Needed his horse. And he had a rescue to organize.

Chapter 30

Jack hurried through the house and out the front door, then slipped back around the side, her heart pounding. She waited a few minutes and then peeked around the corner. Luke was at the back of their property, studying the ground. She'd seen the footsteps he'd shown his cousins. They were clearly marked in the dirt, and if Luke could follow them, so could she.

Something wet touched her hand, and she jumped and yelped at the same time. Max cowered beside her, staring up with questioning eyes. She knelt and patted his head. "You scared the dickens out of me."

She sneaked another glance at Luke and then ran to the nearest oak and hid behind its large trunk. Max followed at a jog. Jack tried to wave him away, but he didn't take the hint. She feared he would draw Luke's attention her way. Peering around the trunk, she watched Luke walk behind the Sunday house and stare off with his hands on his hips. He looked up at the sky, and she wondered if he was praying. Suddenly, he turned left and strode away.

Jack jogged to the shed that held the garden tools and watched Luke march past his house and down Main Street. A small crowd had already gathered outside his office. She waited for a few minutes as the crowd grew, debating whether to follow the tracks or do as Luke had ordered.

There was only one thing she could do to help her ma. She spun around and ran back into the house, leaving Max whining at the back door. She hurried past the two brides, who had made themselves at home in her ma's kitchen. Scowling, she scurried into the bedroom she shared with Ma. She opened the last drawer and pushed aside her pa's old shirts. A black pistol lay in the bottom, and next to it was a round tin can. She pulled out both the gun and the can of bullets. She might need them to save her ma.

"Jacqueline, where does your mother keep her bacon grease?"

Jack jumped as Miss Bennett appeared in the doorway. She slammed the drawer shut, heart pounding, and stood, keeping the gun behind her. "Uh. . .in that Elkay loganberry can beside the stove."

The woman eyed her with suspicion but nodded. "Thank you. Breakfast will be ready in about twenty minutes. You should get cleaned up." She turned, and Jack allowed the tension to drain from her shoulders, but then Miss Bennett spun around again. She nibbled on her lip. "I'm sure the marshal will find your ma."

Jack nodded. If she didn't find her first.

The woman left, and Jack nearly collapsed on the bed. If Miss Bennett had seen her with the gun, what would she have done?

She waited until both brides were busy then ran down the hall and out the front door. Max greeted her in the backyard, wagging his tail. She stuffed the small tin of bullets into her pocket and shoved the heavy gun between the bib of her overalls and her shirt. At the rear of the yard, she found the hoof prints and started following them. Max trailed alongside her, looking as if he had every intention of helping her. Grateful for the dog's companionship, she patted her thigh. "C'mon, Max. We have to rescue Ma before something bad happens to her."

"No, don't." Rachel tried to run, but her feet felt as if they were stuck in quicksand. She fought the swirling haze and tried to get free from James's groping hands, but the tight grip of his arm held her immobile. She'd thought him a charming and comforting friend, but in a moment, he turned on her. Tears ran down her cheeks, and her stomach churned. He stole the most precious gift that she'd had to give Luke. "No!"

She jerked awake and felt herself falling. Her head collided with the hard wooden floor, and she sucked in a breath, allowing her vision to clear. But when she tried to move her hands, the bristly rope cut into her wrists. She'd been dreaming, but the reality of her situation was just as dreadful.

Ignoring her head, she wrestled herself into a sitting position and studied the small cabin. Fingers of sunlight clawed their way through the gaps where the chinking had eroded between the logs, giving the room a striped look. Dust coated her lips, and she longed for some water.

Sitting was difficult with her hands tied behind her back and her ankles bound together. At least the bed had been slightly soft, though it was dusty and smelled like it had been used as a carpet for a privy. She shuddered and scooted sideways. Miss Blackstone was still asleep on the small bed. At least she was against the wall.

Rachel struggled with the ropes, but they wouldn't yield. She leaned her head against the side of the bed. What had Jacqueline done when she'd awakened and hadn't found her?

Had she been worried? Scared? Gone to Luke?

And where had Miss Black—no, Miss Payton's—brother gone? What did he intend to do?

She had to get free. To find her daughter and get her somewhere safe. To warn Luke about Ty Payton.

She searched the room, looking for something, anything she could use to cut the ropes. But there was little in the cabin. It must have been abandoned years ago. Or maybe it was a line shack some rancher no longer used.

One chair lay on its side, halfway under the small, warped table. The fireplace was filled with debris—the remains of a bird's nest, charred wood, ashes, and leaves that had fallen down the opening. On the wall sat two shelves that held three cans. If she could get free, maybe she'd find one of them held something edible.

She scooted across the floor, trying hard to ignore the filth and the pain in her shoulders from having her arms pulled back for so long. Up close, she noticed one of the chair legs was broken, leaving a pointy end. Maybe she could cut her bindings with it.

She squirmed around until the chair was behind her and started sawing the rope back and forth against the point. Miss Payton rolled over onto her side, and Rachel stared at her. She'd been irate at her brother for tying her up and leaving her. At first, she'd tried to reason with him to let them go. But her brother was a hard case. He slapped her and told her to shut up. Rachel could see that the young woman's lip had swollen overnight.

Rachel's hands slipped, and the sharp point bit into the tender flesh of her wrist. She cried out, and Miss Payton's eyes flew open. The young woman looked around, and Rachel knew the moment she remembered her circumstances, because her eyes widened.

She struggled for a few minutes and managed to sit up on the bed. Rachel froze. Should she continue to try to free herself?

"I'm gonna kill Ty for doing this."

How would she go about that, trussed up like a turkey? "Why did your brother do this? What does he want in Lookout?"

Miss Payton sucked her lips in for a moment. "At first all he wanted was me. But now, I'm not so sure."

"Why would he come to get you?"

Miss Payton stared at Rachel so long she thought the girl would remain silent, but she must have found Rachel worthy, because she started talking.

"My brother is the leader of the Payton gang, out of Missouri. Maybe you've heard of them?"

Rachel shook her head.

"Well, that wouldn't please Ty. He wants everyone to know who he is."

"Were you part of his gang?"

"In a way. My ma died when I was fourteen, and I didn't have no pa. Nobody in town would help me, so Ty let me live with him and his gang. I cooked and did their laundry for years."

"I'm sorry about your mother. Mine is also gone."

Miss Payton nodded. "I hated the way the gang members gawked at me, especially as I got older. Gave me the shivers."

Rachel's heart ached for the young woman. She understood how hard it was for an unmarried woman with no family ties to make it alone. She turned away, watching the dust motes floating in the air. James had convinced her that Luke would no longer want her once she was sullied. He'd talked her into marrying him so her child would have a father. She shook her head. Some father he turned out to be. Once he realized she'd had a daughter instead of the son he'd longed for, he had lashed out and hit Rachel for the first time.

"I ran away the first chance I got. Came here, hopin' for a fresh start and that Texas was far enough away that my brother wouldn't find me. Guess I should have gone to Mexico."

Now that her shoulders had relaxed a bit and the pain in her wrist had eased, Rachel started sawing again. She doubted that Ty Payton would let her live. Her only chance was to get away.

Had he found Jacqueline? Had he hurt her? She had to get loose—had to protect her daughter.

"What are you doing over there?" Miss Payton scooted to the edge of the bed.

"Trying to get free. I've got to get back to my daughter."

Miss Payton gazed around the room. "There's not much here." She sniffed the air and then her shoulder, and wrinkled her nose.

"Eww, this place stinks."

Rachel suspected some varmints had used the bed as a nest a time or two. She shuddered at the thought of lying on that nasty mat. Her clothing also carried the foul stench.

"I met Ellie Blackstone on a stage my brother was plannin' on robbin'. He set me up as a passenger so I could hold a gun on the travelers while he robbed it." She bit her lip and looked away. "I didn't wanna do it."

Her anxious eyes turned to Rachel. "But I was scared if I didn't he might let the gang have me. The way they looked at me made my skin crawl as if I had fallen into a crate of spiders."

Rachel's heart went out to the girl, and she could understand her overpowering desire to get away. She'd once felt that way herself. "Miss Payton—"

"Do think maybe you could call me by my given name—Carly?"

"Yes, and you must call me Rachel."

Carly nodded.

"There's something I don't understand. Why did you assume Miss Blackstone's identity?"

"She told me about coming here to marry the marshal. She was all excited about it, but then she got shot. I thought she was dead and took her identity." Carly looked away and stared out the lone dingy window. "Wouldn't she have been in for a surprise once she got here?"

Rachel almost grinned. "That mail-order bride debacle sure got out of hand, didn't it?"

"You like him, don't you? The marshal, I mean."

Rachel's gaze collided with Carly's. Was her affection for Luke obvious to others? She tried so hard to hide it. "We were engaged a long time ago—when we were even younger than you are now."

Carly leaned forward until Rachel thought that she, too, might fall headfirst off the bed. "What happened?" she asked in a hushed voice.

Rachel grimaced. "It's a long story."

"We're not going anywhere anytime soon."

"We are if I have my way. You ought to see if you can find something sharp and try to cut your bindings. We need to get away from here before your brother returns."

Carly nodded and eased to her feet. She hopped around the room, searching, and with each bounce, Rachel thought for sure she'd get tangled in her skirts and fall. Carly's foot bumped something, and it clinked. Rachel's heart leaped as Carly looked up, eyes wide. "There's some glass here that must have fallen out of the window."

Rachel eased onto her knees. "Can you get it?"

Carly stooped down, trying to get her hands low enough to pick up the broken pane. Suddenly, she wavered and fell over backward. She winced, but as soon as she hit the floor, she scooted back toward the glass. Rachel held her breath. *Please, Lord.*

"Ouch!" She jumped and grimaced; then her gaze lit up. "I've got it!"

Hope surged through Rachel's heart. "Praise the Lord. Can you work it so you can cut the ropes?"

"It's awkward, but I think I can."

Rachel went back to sawing her ropes against the chair.

"So, are you gonna tell me why you didn't marry that handsome marshal?"

"He wasn't a marshal back then, just a poor youth who did every job he could trying to make enough money to get us a place to live so we could marry."

"Why didn't you?"

Rachel didn't want to tell her what had happened. Didn't want her to think less of her. Was it just pride? No, it was to protect her daughter. If the townsfolk knew that she was already pregnant when she married James, they would look down on Jacqueline, and the poor child had enough troubles as it was. "It just wasn't meant to be, I suppose."

"You mean you don't think it was God's will?"

Stopping her sawing, Rachel stared at the young woman. "I used to think marrying Luke was God's will."

"But if you'd married him, you wouldn't have that kid of yours." Carly flinched and cursed. "Sorry. I cut myself again. Don't know if this is such a good idea."

Rachel thought about what Carly said. "That's true. My marriage to James wasn't. . .um. . .a love match. But God did use it to give me Jacqueline. The Bible says, 'And we know that all things work together for good to them that love God, to them who are the called according to his purpose.' "

"And you believe that?"

Rachel nodded, seeing for the first time that something good had come from her marriage to James. He'd given her a daughter. She smiled at Carly. "Yes, I do believe that God can bring good from any situation."

Carly looked at her as if she'd gone loco. "How could good come from us gettin' kidnapped and tied up? You know my brother will probably kill you—and maybe even me, too."

Rachel swallowed hard. "That's why we can't be here when he returns. Luke will be looking for us by now. Jacqueline would have gone to him when she couldn't find me."

At least she hoped that had happened and that Carly's brother didn't have her child.

"How can you believe in God when so many bad things happen?"

Rachel felt her ropes give way a little, and she renewed her efforts to get free. "It's a matter of choice. I choose to believe. I know God's nature from reading the Bible and listening to the preacher. He's a God of love and wants nothing more than to have His children love and worship Him."

Carly ceased her efforts and wrestled her way into a sitting position. The side of her face that had been against the floor was coated in dust. "Who gets to be God's children?"

Rachel smiled. "God wants every person on earth to become one, including you."

The young woman's eyes widened with awe, and she sat up straighter. "Me?"

"Yes, it's true. But God gives us a choice whether to serve Him or not. Sin separates us from God."

Carly ducked her head. "I've done some bad things."

"We all have."

"Not you." Carly shook her head. "You're as good a person as I ever met."

The compliment warmed Rachel's heart. "Thank you, but I'm a sinner, too. God made a way for sinners to come back to Him, though. He sent His only Son, Jesus, to earth. Jesus lived here among us, but He was the sacrificial lamb, and His death on the cross meant that we could again be one with God."

"Truly?"

Rachel nodded. "All you have to do is believe that Jesus Christ is God's Son, and ask forgiveness for your sins."

Carly's face crumpled. "My brother and I have done too many bad things. It's too late for us."

"No, it's not. As long as you're still breathing, there's hope."

"Even for bank robbers?"

Rachel held back a gasp. She knew Carly harbored secrets but never suspected that she, too, was an outlaw. She cringed at the memory of her daughter interacting with the young woman. They'd had an outlaw living in their home.

"See, even you look at me different, now that you know. I only did it because Ty said I had to. I didn't never shoot nobody." She hung her head but continued to saw at the ropes.

"I'm sorry. You just surprised me is all. But whatever you've done, God will forgive you if you ask Him—even for bank robbery."

Carly remained silent, and they both worked to free themselves. Rachel still worried about their situation but marveled that God could have put her here—just like Queen Esther in the Bible—for such a time as this. And if He had, He would see her safely returned to her daughter.

She bowed her head. *Help us, Lord. Keep Jacqueline safe. Help Carly to understand that You love her no matter what she's done.*

Chapter 31

Luke walked his horse toward Lookout, feeling as if a five-hundred-pound weight was pulling him down. He'd searched for hours and found no sign of Rachel. The tracks had simply disappeared when they blended with other hoof prints on the road.

The hot July afternoon sun beat on him, sending rivulets of sweat down his temple and back. He stopped and took a drink of the lukewarm water from his canteen as he studied the countryside. Not even a bird dotted the pale blue sky that reminded him so much of Rachel's eyes. He wanted to see those eyes spark with laughter. To see them darken with love for him again.

He longed to hold her close and never let her go. Why had he been so stubborn? Why hadn't he realized sooner that he was at fault?

His gaze searched the rolling hills whose green was turning to dried yellow from the heat and lack of rain. He'd been barren like that before God entered his life. He'd wasted so many years, wallowing in self-pity and a refusal to forgive. But now he had a chance to start over, if only. . .

Where was Rachel? Did she have water at hand? Was she

somewhere sweating in a stuffy, little room? Was she still alive?

No! He couldn't allow that thought to creep into his mind. To give him doubts. God wouldn't bring him home and finally remove the shroud of resentment and bitterness from his heart only to take Rachel away before he could tell her he still loved her.

"God, please. Help me find her. Give me a chance to make things up to her. To show her how much I love her." He lifted his hat and ran his hands through his sweaty hair. "Show me where she is."

Rachel's shoulders ached from her efforts to get free. Hours of rubbing the rope across the wood spike had yielded little. She had more movement in her hands, but they were still lashed together. Her stomach complained of the lack of food, but what she craved most, next to her freedom, was a drink of cool water—and to know Jacqueline was safe.

The hot sun beat relentlessly on the little shack, heating it to unbearable temperatures. Her hair and clothing were soaked with sweat, and she longed to close her eyes and sleep. But she had to get free before Carly's brother returned. She couldn't let herself think what would happen if she didn't.

Carly gasped. "I broke through another thread. Just a little more and I should be able to get loose."

"Oh, thank the Lord." Rachel renewed her efforts. Even if Carly got free, she wasn't sure if the young woman would release her, too, or just take off without her.

They continued sawing in silence for a while, then Carly suddenly looked up. "So you gonna tell me what happened between you and the marshal?"

Rachel blinked. She'd hope Carly wouldn't bring him up again. "That was a long time ago."

Carly shook her head and grinned. "I don't think so. I've seen the way you look at him."

"What do you mean?"

"You look like a woman in love—at least what I'd expect a woman in love to look like. Not that I've ever known any." She blushed and looked over her shoulders as if trying to see her hands.

Rachel sat back a moment. "Was it really that obvious?"

Carly shrugged. "Maybe not to everyone, but I also saw how the marshal watched you whenever the two of you were together. Me and them other brides never stood a chance. Don't know why his crazy cousins thought Marshal Davis needed help finding a wife when he was already head over heels for you."

A warmth flooded Rachel's chest before she threw a cold bucket of reality on it. "You're wrong about Luke. He may have loved me once, but no more."

A man who couldn't forgive a woman for a past hurt certainly couldn't be in love with her. Yet he'd said he was sorry. Sorry for not forgiving her? Sorry for giving her the cold shoulder? Sorry for something she didn't yet know about?

"I ain't mistaken about him, but I wanna ask you somethin' else. Were you the anonymous bride?"

Rachel knew the color on her cheeks gave her away, and she nodded. "That was foolish of me. I just didn't want to let Luke go without at least trying to win back his favor."

"Your pie was the only one worth eating. All of ours were too salty or burnt." Carly scowled. "It was a waste of time to mess with those pies."

Rachel's head jerked up, a sick feeling of regret churning in her stomach. "What do you mean?"

Carly nibbled her lower lip. "Guess it don't matter no more. When them two brides was fixin' to make their pies, I switched the salt and sugar."

A shaft of guilt speared Rachel. She'd blamed Jacqueline for that little stunt. No wonder her daughter had gotten so mad. She'd been innocent, but Rachel thought her daughter had tried to fix the contest so that she would win. She leaned her head against the chair leg and closed her eyes. *I'm sorry, sweetie.*

"I knew it was you when I saw that blue shirt. I. . .uh, saw it when you showed me all them shirts. Later I snitched the tan one from your drawer."

Rachel's eyes popped open. "You stole one of James's shirts?"

Nodding, Carly turned back toward her. "I'm right sorry for doin' that, Rachel. I just knew I'd never be able to sew nothin' that could equal what them other brides was makin'. I'd hoped to borrow it and put it back, but after the contest, all of them was gone."

Rachel felt violated. Someone living in her home had stolen from her. Granted, the shirt held no value to her, but just the thought of Carly snooping around her room gave her the shudders. Had she noticed the gun in the bottom of the drawer?

And Jacqueline had told her that one of the shirts had been stolen—but she hadn't listened. Rachel hung her head, feeling guilty for not believing her daughter. She prayed she'd get a chance to apologize.

"I know you're probably mad at me now, but if I had to do it over, I wouldn't take it."

A part of Rachel wanted to stay angry. Angry at feeling so helpless. Angry at Luke for his stubborn refusal to forgive. And angry at Carly for violating her trust.

But she knew this could be a pivotal moment for the young woman. Shoving aside her hurt, she forced herself to smile. "It was just an old shirt, Carly. I wouldn't let that affect our friendship."

Carly sniffed. "It was more than that, and you know it."

"God has forgiven me a lot. How can I not forgive you for something so small?"

Tears made Carly's eyes glisten, and she dipped her head and tried to wipe them on her shoulder. "Oh! I'll kill my brother for this. I can't even blow my nose."

Rachel winced at the harsh words.

"No, wait. That's just a figure of speech. I've never killed anyone, and I'm not gonna start with Ty, even if he deserves to be shot for what he did to us."

Rachel just hoped he didn't return and do more to them. " 'Vengeance is mine; I will repay, saith the Lord.' "

"You really believe that?"

"Yes, I do."

"I hate to think what Ty will have to suffer if that's true. He's done lots of bad things." Carly shuddered, and her face went pale. She looked at Rachel. "What will God do to me?"

This was the moment Rachel had waited for. *Give me Your words, Lord.* "God will forgive you, if you only ask Him."

She shook her head. "I ain't never killed nobody, but I've done some real bad things."

"It doesn't matter to God. If you believe that Jesus Christ is His Son and that He died on the cross for your sins, all you have to do is ask forgiveness for those sins. And then try to live a life that's pleasing to God."

"Ma took me to church when I was a young'un. I do believe that Jesus is God's Son. I just never thought much about it."

Rachel smiled. "That's wonderful. Now all you have to do is ask God to forgive you of your sins."

The young woman scowled. "It sounds too easy. Shouldn't I have to do some kind of penance?"

"No, Carly. Just tell Him you're sorry and that you want Him to come into your heart and forgive your sins."

A myriad of expressions crossed Carly's face, and then she slowly nodded. "Will you help me?"

Rachel smiled. "Of course I will."

They bowed their heads, and in a matter of seconds, the angels were rejoicing in heaven over another lost lamb that had been returned to the fold.

Jack stood at the crossroads and looked back toward town. She was too far away to see Lookout, but she knew it was only about a mile over the last hill she crossed. She'd never been this far out of town alone, and though it was an adventure of sorts, hesitation nagged at her like a pesky gnat.

Ma had always lectured her on the dangers of wandering too far from town. Besides wild animals like coyote or even a wolf, there were outlaws, and the possibility of a renegade Comanche slipping across the Red River from their reservation in Indian Territory. Jack brushed her hair from her face. Did Comanches scalp people? She swallowed hard and looked at the road to town again. If she turned and walked back that way, the road would eventually turn into Bluebonnet Lane and lead right to her front door.

But what if her ma was out there somewhere, waiting. . . praying for someone to save her? She looked across the open prairie. Both Ricky and Jonesy lived out that way, though she'd never been to either's home.

She was dying for a drink of water. Why hadn't she thought to take some?

If she kept walking straight, she'd eventually come to the river, but if she turned and went to one of her friend's homes, she could get a drink and maybe discover news about her ma.

One thing was for certain: She wasn't stupid enough to venture any farther from town unarmed. She tugged the gun from the bib of her overalls and removed the tin from her pocket. She opened the can and found eight bullets. Though she'd never loaded a gun before, she'd watched Luke do it several times.

She slid open the cylinder, and with a shaky hand, dropped one of the bullets into the empty hole. One by one, she filled each slot and then snapped the cylinder in place. With the tin back in her pocket, she lifted her chin and walked away from town. The gun weighed heavy in her hand, but with it loaded, she was afraid to put it back in her overalls. Besides, if she needed the weapon, she wanted it to be handy.

Her feet ate up the dry ground, and the heat from the sun

made the top of her head hot. Ma would berate her for not wearing a bonnet, but she could hardly do that when she was wearing overalls. What she needed was a decent felt hat like her friends wore.

As she topped the next rise, a small, white house rested in the distance. Two people walked her way, both carrying fishing poles. Jack's heart jumped. Ricky and Jonesy. She jogged toward them, but as she drew close, both boys' eyes widened and stared at the gun.

"Who you gonna shoot?" Ricky asked.

"Not us, I hope." Jonesy laughed, but it sounded forced.

"Am I ever glad to see you." Relief washed through Jack, giving her energy that the sun had threatened to drive away. "My ma is missing. Nobody's seen her since last night."

"Whoa! What happened to her?" Ricky's blue eyes glistened with curiosity.

"Why are you way out here?" Jonesy asked.

"Luke found some tracks behind our house. I was following them, but I lost them somehow."

"The marshal let you come clear out here alone?"

Jack shrugged. "He don't know I'm here. He told me to stay at home with those two brides, but they were cooking up a storm in Ma's kitchen. I couldn't stay. I have to find her."

Jonesy took his pole off his shoulder and leaned on it. "What makes you thinks she's out here?"

"The tracks headed out of town in this direction, but before long, they got mixed with the other prints on the road. I just kept walking, hoping I'd find her."

Ricky looked around then refocused on Jack. "Why would she be out here?"

Jack stomped her foot, and tears stung her eyes. "Aren't you listening? I told you someone took her. I saw a man last night in Miss Blackstone's room, and I told Ma, but she didn't believe me. When I got up this morning, I noticed Ma had never been to bed. And Miss Blackstone was missing, too."

"Maybe that bride took her." Jonesy offered.

"But why?"

"Well, you said Luke liked your ma's pie best. Maybe she decided to get rid of the competition."

Jack hadn't considered that angle. "But how would she know Ma was the anonymous bride?" She narrowed her gaze and scowled at her friends. "You didn't tell anyone, did you?"

Both boys shook their heads and eyed the gun again as if they thought she might shoot them if they had. Jack nearly laughed at their comical expressions, but she wasn't in a laughing mood.

"Is that thing loaded?" Ricky lifted his hat and raked lines with his fingers in his white-blond hair.

"What good would it do me if it wasn't?" Jack wasn't about to tell them that she'd just loaded the gun.

"You even know how to shoot it?"

Jack shrugged. "Just point and pull the trigger. How hard can it be?"

Her friends glanced at each other, and their brows lifted. Ricky turned back to her and held out his hand. "Maybe you'd better give that to me. I wouldn't want you to get hurt—or uh, shoot one of us by accident."

Jack backed up two steps and held the gun against her chest. "But I need it to find Ma."

Ricky shook his head and handed his fishing pole to Jonesy. "No, you don't. Give it to me, and we'll help you search for your ma."

Tears sprouted in her eyes. "You will? Truly?"

Both of her friends nodded. Ricky stepped forward, hand held out in front of him. "C'mon. Gimme that gun. You're too young to be messing with it."

Jack glanced down at the heavy black weapon. Truth be told, the gun made her nervous. She handed it over to her friend. "But I gotta get that back and hide it before Ma finds out I took it."

Ricky quickly unloaded the gun and put the bullets in his pocket. He shoved the revolver into the waistband of his pants and crossed his arms. "Now, start at the beginning. When did you last see your ma?"

Jack related the story to them. "I think Ma must have gone upstairs to check Miss Blackstone's room, and the man must've taken her prisoner."

"Why would he do that?" Jonesy asked.

Jack flung her arms up. "I don't know." She told them about the key and unlocked door and Luke finding the trail. "So I followed the prints."

"Hey!" Jonesy shoved Ricky in the arm, receiving a glare from the taller boy. "I just remembered something. The other evening I went out in the far pasture to bring in the cows for milking. You know that old shack we used to play in?"

Ricky nodded. "Yeah, so what?"

"I saw a stranger go into it, that's what. I meant to tell my pa but got busy milking and forgot until just now. And guess what else. He had two horses."

Ricky's eyes lit up at the same time hope sparked within Jack. "Maybe that's where he put Ma and that bride."

"Yeah, let's go check it out." Ricky spun around, his hand resting on the gun handle.

"Wait! Someone needs to go tell Luke about this," Jack said.

Ricky faced her again. "That's probably a good idea. You go."

Jack shoved her hands to her hips and glared at her friend. "I'm not going. It's my ma that's missing."

"I guess that makes sense," said Ricky. "But you'll have to be quiet and do what I tell you."

Jack nodded. Ricky was only a few years older than her, but he was bigger—and he was smart, for a boy.

"Then you need to go to town and fetch the marshal, Jonesy."

Their friend scowled. "I'm the one who saw the stranger. I should get to go."

"I'll let you have the pick of any of my commies if you'll do it." Ricky reached into his pocket and pulled out several clay marbles.

Jonesy's eyes widened. "You will?"

Ricky nodded, though his face looked pinched. His collection of marbles was his most treasured possession. Jack knew he was sacrificing one for her, and that meant a lot, considering how little money his family had.

"All right, I'll go to town and tell the marshal, but I'm coming right back, so wait on me before you do anything. And I'm not taking these fishin' poles." He dropped them to the ground and took off running toward town.

Ricky snatched up the rods. "C'mon. Let's run these back to my house, get some water, and go check out that cabin. Maybe we'll get lucky and find your ma."

Jack walked alongside her friend. Her ma had said both boys were too old for her to hang around with, but they'd always watched out for her and treated her like a sister. Maybe if the boys helped her find Ma, then her mother would allow her to spend more time with them. At least she could hope.

She followed Ricky back to his house, noting peeling paint and how it leaned to the right. A skinny brown and white hound dog lay with its nose hanging off the end of the rickety porch. She never knew Ricky had a dog. Ricky's pa was known to drink a lot and spend too much time at the saloon. Suddenly, she realized the sacrifice her friend was making for her by giving up one of his treasures. He didn't have many nice things in his life.

She hoped he wouldn't get hurt. Hoped they didn't have to use that gun. Her gaze darted upward at the pale blue sky.

Please, Lord, help us find my ma. Let her be all right. I'm sorry for not being a very good kid, and I promise to do better—if only You help us find her.

Chapter 32

Luke stared out over the town, itching to get back out there and look for Rachel. Mark had gone to Polly's to fetch them some dinner, and if it wasn't for the fact that Luke hadn't eaten since yesterday, he'd be out searching right now. Mark had talked him into taking a short break to see if any of the townsfolk had found Rachel.

They hadn't.

Luke's hand tightened around the porch railing. What was the point of being marshal if he couldn't protect the woman he loved? Where could she be? Was she injured?

He knew Rachel would be worried about Jack. His gaze flitted to the boardinghouse. Was the kid at home, or had she gone out somewhere with her friends? He was half afraid those two older boys were going to get her into serious trouble one day. Thankfully, he hadn't seen much of them since school had ended for the summer.

"You ready to eat?" Mark walked past the stage office and stopped in front of Luke, carrying two plates of steaming food.

Luke started to shake his head, thinking he couldn't eat while

Rachel was in danger, but then he caught a whiff of the beef stew and saw the golden corn bread Mark carried. His stomach let him know refusal wasn't an option. Besides, he needed to keep his strength up so he could keep searching.

Mark set the plates on Luke's desk. "What will you do if you don't find her by dark?"

Luke poured them both a cup of fresh coffee he'd just brewed. The inside of the jail was sweltering from the stove, but a man couldn't function without his coffee. "I'll keep looking."

Mark's blond brows lifted as he buttered his corn bread. "In the dark?"

Luke shrugged. "I don't know." He shoved a bite of stew in his mouth, but it tasted like paper. He shoveled in just enough food to keep him going.

"Look, you'd help Rachel better by getting some rest and being fresh in the morning. If you're overly tired, you might miss something."

Luke ran his hand across his bristly jaw and shoved the bowl toward the middle of the desk. "I know, but I can't stand the thought of her being out there, maybe hurt. Maybe alone."

"Yeah, I know."

Luke stared intently into his cousin's eyes. "No, you don't. I still love her. I want us to have a second chance."

Mark's brow rose nearly to his hairline. "Just when did you figure all that out?"

Luke fought a shy grin tugging at his mouth and lost the battle. "Last night. I realized I harbored an unforgiving spirit toward her when what happened was my own fault."

"How you figure that?" Mark shoved a corner of corn bread into his mouth.

Luke explained how he was responsible for James's attack on Rachel. Mark leaned back in his chair and shook his head. "You're not at fault for what James did."

"But I'm the one who sent him to meet her."

Mark frowned and shook his head. "Doesn't matter. Only James is responsible for what he did."

Luke slammed the desk. "No, it's my fault. I should have gone and met her myself. It would have only taken fifteen or twenty minutes. But no, I had work to do."

"You were trying to make money for a home so you and Rachel could get married."

Luke leaned his face into his hands. "None of that matters now. I need to get out and search while it's still daylight."

Quick footsteps sounded on the boardwalk, and one of Jack's friends skidded to a stop at Luke's door. He stood, and the boy leaned his hands on his thighs, head hanging down, and sucked in air like a suffocating man.

"What's going on? Did you find something?"

The boy held up his hand, chest heaving. "Water."

Luke glanced around the office then handed the boy his coffee. The kid took a big gulp and then spewed it out, all over Luke's floor. "That's hot! I said water."

Mark jumped up, rushed outside to the hitching post where his horse was tied, and yanked the canteen off his saddle. He leaped up the stairs and shoved it at the boy. The kid gulped down several swigs then drew his sleeve across his mouth. Several of the townsfolk who must have seen him running were gathering outside Luke's office.

Luke took hold of the boy's shoulders. "Take several deep breaths."

He did as ordered. "I saw a stranger. . .at an old shed. . .on our property. . .two days ago."

"So?"

"Jack told me and Ricky. . .about some man taking her ma, and they've gone. . .to see if she's there."

Luke tensed. If the man who kidnapped Rachel and Miss Blackstone was at that shack with them, Jack and her friend could be in danger. He tightened his grasp. "Where is this shed?"

"A mile or so past my house. Southwest of town. I can show you."

Luke glanced at Mark. "C'mon, this might be the break we've been waiting for."

Both men grabbed their rifles and followed the boy out the door. The crowd parted and let them pass. Luke touched the kid's shoulder. "You're that Jones boy, aren't you?"

"Clarence Jones, sir. But most folks just call me Jonesy."

Luke nodded and mounted Alamo. "Put your foot in the stirrup, and I'll pull you up."

Jonesy attempted to do as Luke ordered, but the boy was too exhausted to get his foot up high enough. Mark dismounted and boosted Jonesy up behind Luke.

"You got some news, Marshal?" Dan Howard, the broad-shouldered livery owner asked.

"Maybe. This boy thinks he knows where a stranger's been holing up."

"You want some of us to come?"

Luke shook his head. "No, I need y'all to keep searching closer to town. This might be a dead end, and I don't want all our eggs in one basket."

Dan nodded.

Luke reined Alamo around. "Hold on tight."

He kicked his horse, and in seconds, they were on a dead run down Main Street. The boy nearly swerved off as Luke turned Alamo down Bluebonnet Lane and headed out of town, his hope building for the first time that day.

Please, Lord. Let me find Rachel at that shed. And let her be safe.

Rachel felt as if she were falling down a deep well, and she jumped. The tiny cabin came into focus as she awakened. Her mouth was as dry as if she'd been sucking cotton, and her head ached. If only she could have a drink.

Carly had also fallen asleep. The heat from the cabin had wilted them both like summer flowers in a drought. Occasionally a hot breeze blew through the holes where the window panes once rested, but that did nothing to cool the room. At least the sun was no longer overhead and was making its western plunge toward sunset. Nighttime would bring cooler temperatures, but she dreaded it. How long could they survive without water?

She tried to work up enough saliva to dampen her mouth and started sawing again. "Carly. Miss Payton. Wake up." She kicked the table leg, and it screeched across the floor, making the young woman stir.

"Did I fall asleep? Oh, ow. My shoulders are killing me."

Rachel didn't voice that hers were, too. "We need to keep working. I don't know where your brother went or why he's been gone so long, but we've got to get free before he returns."

"Maybe he just left us here to die."

Rachel shook her head. "Don't think that—and even if he did, that's not going to happen."

The dullness in Carly's eyes disappeared all of a sudden, and then she winced. "I've nearly sawed through the rope. But I keep cutting my fingers and dropping the glass."

"I'm sorry. Just do your best. I'm not having much luck here. I broke off the point on the chair leg, so now there's nothing sharp to cut my bindings."

Carly looked to be sawing with renewed vigor. She worked hard for a few minutes; then she turned her head to face Rachel. Something she'd said earlier was grating on Rachel.

"Did you tell me that there was a fourth shirt entered in the bride contest?"

Carly blinked and stared at her. "You mean you didn't enter it?"

Rachel shook her head. "No. I decided that if Luke wasn't willing to forgive me for how I wronged him in the past, there was no chance he'd want me for a wife, so I didn't enter the second contest."

Carly rocked back and forth. "That's strange. There was four entries. If you didn't enter, then who else could've? I'm certain that blue shirt was the same one you kept in your drawer."

Rachel pursed her lips as the truth dawned. "It was Jacqueline. She argued up one side of the wall and down the other, wanting me to enter that contest. I told her I wouldn't, so she must have taken the shirt and entered it without anyone knowing." Rachel shook her head at her wily daughter.

Carly smiled a sad smile. "The mayor said that's the one the marshal liked best. I bet you don't get it back—oh!"

The young woman's shoulders heaved violently, and Rachel's heart jumped. Was the heat getting to her?

Suddenly, she pulled her hands in front of her and started rubbing her shoulders. "Look, my hands are free!"

After some finagling, Carly managed to untie her ankles and staggered to her feet. Rachel noticed that both of Carly's hands and wrists were covered in blood. "Oh, your poor hands."

Carly held them up and grinned as if they were a badge of honor. She turned and looked around on the floor, stooped, then plodded toward Rachel. "Now we just gotta get you untied."

"Maybe we should just get out of here and worry about that later."

"You cain't run with your ankles bound together." Carly shook her head, shoved the battered chair away, and squatted behind Rachel.

"I'm worried about your hands."

"They'll heal."

Carly worked for several minutes, and then Rachel felt the ropes loosen, and the tension in her shoulders released just a smidgeon. Suddenly, the ropes broke. Carefully, she swung her arms forward and rolled her shoulders. "My, but that feels good."

Rachel made quick work of freeing her feet and stood on wobbly legs. "We'd best get out of here while we can. Did your brother leave any water?" She searched the small room as Carly headed for the door.

Suddenly, Carly froze. "I hear voices. Quick. Lie back down on the cot and pretend you're still tied up."

Her frantic gaze made Rachel's heart ricochet in her chest. Had they worked so hard only to have Ty Payton return now?

Rachel didn't take time to question her but did as ordered. The putrid scents of the thin mattress almost made her retch, but with no food or water for a full day, Rachel managed to keep from gagging. Reluctantly, she forced her hands behind her still aching shoulders and lay down. Carly seemed to be searching the room for something. She snatched up a leg that had come off the chair and squeezed in the small space behind the door with the weapon over her head.

Rachel held her breath, praying that Ty Payton hadn't returned. Tears threatened, but she blinked them back. She wanted to be ready if Carly needed her help.

A shadow passed by the window, and then a face appeared. Jacqueline?

Were her eyes playing tricks?

And there was Ricky's blessed face.

Rachel bolted up off the cot so fast, her head swam. Carly spun toward her, looking at her as if she were having a conniption.

"Ma?" Jacqueline squealed.

Carly lowered her club, and Rachel yanked the door open. Jacqueline charged in, nearly bowling her over. She grabbed her daughter and clung to her.

"Ma, I prayed we'd find you. I thought I'd never see you again."

Jacqueline's tears wet the front of Rachel's dress, and tears of her own streamed down her face. Suddenly, her relief was overpowered by the reality that her daughter was far from home. "Just what in the world are you doing out here?"

"You smell awful." Jacqueline pulled away, hurt darkening her eyes. "We were looking for you. Jonesy remembered seeing a stranger at this cabin two days ago and thought we should investigate it."

"Oh! I could just blister your backside, but I'm so happy to see you."

Ricky entered the cabin, looking shy. He held up a canteen. "Anybody need some water?"

Rachel held Jacqueline close again while Carly drank. Then the woman passed the canteen, and Rachel savored the lukewarm water, gulping it down.

"I don't wanna spoil this family reunion, but it won't be so happy if my brother returns before we get away." Carly pressed her lips together, looking like a no-nonsense schoolmarm.

"She's right. We need to leave. Now."

"Maybe it'd be better if we all went to my house," Ricky said. "There's not much cover along the road, and if'n that stranger returns, we could be in big trouble, even though I do have a gun." He pulled out James's old pistol, and Rachel gasped. She turned a stern glare on her daughter.

Jacqueline ducked her head and then smiled. "Well, you did say a woman should never go far from town unarmed. I was just obeyin' you, Ma."

Rachel grinned at her incorrigible daughter and looped her arm around her. "I'm sure that's not exactly what I said, but we'll talk about it when we get home."

Ricky led the way, keeping them in the tree line as much as possible. They passed what he said was the Jones farm and continued across a field to a farmhouse in the distance. All of a sudden, they heard horses' hooves pounding down the lane. With no trees for cover, they bunched together. Rachel shoved Jacqueline behind her, and tried to put on a brave front. It had been one thing to face an outlaw knowing her daughter was safe in her bed, but another thing altogether when her child was in danger.

"Give me that gun, boy." Carly faced Ricky, but the kid stepped back.

Ricky shook his head. "I'll protect us."

Carly stomped toward him and yanked the gun free of his grasp. She winced but held the weapon in spite of her injured hands.

"You'd shoot your own brother?" Rachel asked.

"I don't wanna, but I will if it means saving you and the kids. Get down." They squatted in the thigh-high grass.

"She's gonna have to load it if she hopes to shoot anyone." Ricky reached into his pocket and yanked out the bullets.

Carly quickly loaded the weapon and ducked down, turned toward the road, and held the gun outward.

Rachel hoped in the waning light of dusk that the riders might pass on by and not see them in the field. She held her breath and kept an arm around her daughter. "Please, Lord, make us invisible."

Two horses rounded the wide bend in the road at full-gallop. Rachel studied their silhouettes as the setting sun illuminated them. She couldn't make out their faces, but she recognized the lead rider and bolted up.

"Get down." Carly waved her hand behind her.

Rachel cupped her hand around her mouth and yelled, "Luke!"

Jacqueline jumped up and took off running, waving her hand. "Luke, over here."

Rachel jogged past Carly, half worried that she'd accidentally shoot Jacqueline. Her heart soared with relief to see Luke. He would protect them from the outlaw. *Thank You, Lord!*

Luke reined his horse to a stop so fast that it nearly sat down. Someone riding behind Luke flailed his arms and rolled off onto the ground. The second rider's horse jumped him and skidded to a halt. Luke vaulted to the ground and ran to Jacqueline.

"What are you doing out here? I told you to stay home."

Rachel could see the white of her daughter's teeth as she smiled. "I found Ma."

"Yeah, and you could have gotten hurt." Luke hugged Jacqueline and then stooped down and kissed her cheek.

Rachel slowed her steps. She was thrilled to see Luke, but he might not feel the same way. Oh, he'd be happy to find her safe—

Luke's gaze captured hers, and all thoughts ceased. He set Jacqueline aside, tweaked her nose, and strode toward Rachel, his eyes smoldering. Her heart leapt at the intensity of his gaze. He stopped and placed his hands on her shoulders, looking both sorry and relieved. "Are you hurt?"

She shook her head, barely able to breathe. Afraid to allow hope to take wing.

"I'm so sorry, Rach. Sorry for not forgiving you. It was all my fault."

"This wasn't your fault. Carly's brother is the one who kidnapped us."

"That's not what I meant." Luke's brow wrinkled. "Who's Carly?"

Rachel peered over her shoulder. Mark stood next to Carly, relieving her of the gun. Rachel heaved a sigh. "It's a long story, and we're starving and exhausted. Can it wait until we get back home?"

Luke pressed his lips together and nodded. "Rachel, there's so much I need to say. I—"

Fast approaching hoofbeats silenced whatever he'd been about to tell her. He shoved Rachel behind him. "Jack, hit the dirt!"

Rachel tried to see past Luke to find her daughter in the twilight, but all that caught her eye was a lightning bug. Her heart choked. Jacqueline was between Luke and the road.

Luke shoved Rachel down. "Stay here." He strode forward, gun in hand.

Had they been rescued, only to be caught again? Rachel shook her head and prayed hard.

A rider rounded the bend, and Luke shouted out. "Stop where you are, or I'll shoot."

The horse pulled up, snorted at the quick stop, and pranced in circles. "Luke? That you?"

Relief surrounded Rachel like the growing darkness as she recognized Garrett's voice.

"Yeah, I'm sure glad it's you, cuz," Luke said.

"Well you won't be glad when you hear my news. The bank's been robbed."

Chapter 33

Though anxious to get back to town and check things out, Luke rode back into Lookout at a slower pace than when he'd been searching for Rachel. He wouldn't risk injuring his horse by galloping in the dark. Besides, Garrett had explained that the outlaw was secure in Luke's jail with Dan Howard keeping watch.

He hated leaving Rachel, but his cousins would see her, Miss Blackstone, and Jack home safely. The two boys were close enough to their homes to walk, so all Luke needed to concentrate on was the robbery.

But his rebellious mind kept wandering back to Rachel. She was filthy and exhausted, but was that hope he'd seen in her eyes? Did he dare think she felt something more than friendship toward him after the way he'd treated her?

He'd been such a fool.

There was so much more he wanted to say to her, but that would have to wait.

The lights of town glimmered in the black night. He rode into Lookout a few minutes later and headed straight for the bank. The lights were on. Was Ray Castleby still there, or had he decided to go home and left a lantern burning to discourage others tempted to relieve the bank of its funds?

Luke dismounted, secured his horse, and then knocked on the bank door. "Ray, it's me, Luke. You in there?"

He heard the jingle of keys; then the lock clicked and the door opened. Ray Castleby looked more haggard than Luke had ever seen him. Luke studied the serene bank. The wood shone even in the flickering light of the lanterns, and the room smelled of beeswax with the faint hint of gunpowder. One of the floor planks contained a splintered hole where a bullet had been fired into it.

"I'm sure glad to see you, Marshal. Though all the excitement's over now, I still can't quit shaking." Ray motioned him to come in. The thin man's clothing was rumpled, and one sleeve had blood on it. Ray pushed his wire-rimmed glasses up his pointy nose.

"Did you get hurt?" Luke pointed at the banker's sleeve.

Ray glanced down and stared at the spot that blemished his snow white shirt. His hand trembled as he reached toward the stain. "Uh. . .not my blood. Belongs to that thief."

Ray was a high-strung man who looked to be on his last leg. The robbery attempt must have really shaken him up. "Let's have a seat, and then tell me what happened."

Nodding, Ray moseyed back to his office, and Luke followed. Ray owned the biggest desk in town, even larger than Mayor Burke's. The dark wood gleamed under the fancy lamp. Papers were stacked in neat piles. A picture of an English foxhunt covered a large portion of the wall behind the banker. Luke couldn't help staring. He'd never had reason to visit Ray's office and now stared at the largest painting he'd ever seen, with the exception of one he'd glimpsed in a saloon in Wyoming.

"I was closed, and Gerald, my clerk, had gone home."

Luke forced his attention away from the picture to what Ray was saying.

"I wanted to finish up some paperwork for a local rancher, so

I was working late." He rambled on about the robber knocking then shoving his way in when Ray answered.

Luke's mind drifted back to Rachel. He wanted to see her again. To make certain she was all right and unharmed.

The banker chuckled and shook his head, and Luke realized he'd missed something.

"Uh. . .would you repeat that?" he asked

"I wouldn't have believed it myself if I hadn't witnessed it. Bertha Boyd came in the door right on the heels of that thief. At first, I thought she was another gang member. The robber swung around to face her, and she smacked him on the arm with that new cane she's been using, causing him to drop his gun. He picked it up, and Bertha plumb knocked him on the temple with another swipe of her walking stick. The gun fired, and I guess either the bullet or a wood splinter cut the thief's arm. The man collapsed at Bertha's feet, but she didn't pay him any mind. She just looked at me and said my clerk had short-changed her when she took out some cash earlier."

Ray leaned back in his chair, hands on his belly. "I've never been so happy to see that gabby woman in my whole life. I didn't even question her about the error but took the money right out of my own pocket and paid her. She might well have saved my life."

Luke grinned at the thought of the large woman foiling a bank robbery. Jenny Evans would sure have some news to post in her paper this week. "So you didn't lose any money?"

"No, we never got more than five feet from the door. It's nothing short of a miracle."

Luke stood, anxious to check on his prisoner. "God works in mysterious ways."

Ray let out a belly laugh. "That he does."

As he entered the jailhouse moments later, Luke nodded at Dan Howard sitting behind the desk, reading an old Dallas newspaper. Max lay on his blanket in the corner and didn't even lift his head. Luke walked past the livery owner to the two cells at the back of the jailhouse and stood eye-to-eye with the prisoner. Something seemed vaguely familiar about the man leaning against the cell wall. His dark hair was greasy, and several days' whiskers covered his square jaw. Piercing blue eyes studied Luke, as if taking his measure. Cleaned up, Luke suspected most women would find him handsome. He glanced at the man's bandaged arm. "Guess the doc took care of that, huh?"

The prisoner shrugged one shoulder. Luke spun around and marched back to his desk. Dan stood and stepped away, as if he felt guilty for sitting in Luke's chair.

"Thanks for jailing the robber and watching him for me."

Luke bent and tugged on the middle drawer as a thought raced through his mind. He yanked out his stack of wanted posters and thumbed through them. He looked at a half dozen before he found the one he wanted. A slow grin tugged at his mouth as he stared at the likeness of his prisoner. Ty Payton, leader of the Payton Gang that had terrorized southwestern Missouri. He handed the poster to Dan.

He took it and then let out a low whistle. "That's him all right. Imagine, a real wanted outlaw in our little town." He shook his head. "What's this world comin' to?"

Luke peeked at the man he suspected was Ty Payton again. The prisoner had slumped down on the small cot and placed one arm over his eyes. Luke stared at him. What had brought the man from his normal hunting grounds in Missouri to Texas? And where was the rest of his gang? "Payton?"

The man lifted his arm and glanced at Luke.

"You Tyson Payton?"

"Maybe." He lowered his head and turned to face the wall, but not before Luke saw a smirk tug at the corner of his mouth.

He was Payton, all right. Luke read the information about the gang on the poster. Payton normally traveled with two other men and sometimes a woman. It was suspected that the woman was Carly Payton, Tyson's sister.

The hairs on the back of Luke's neck stood on end, and his gut swirled with uneasiness. Where had he heard that name before?

Dan stood beside Luke's desk with his hat in his hand. "Marshal, there's a woman at the boardinghouse who came in on the evening stage while you were gone. You're gonna wanna talk to her."

Exhaustion made Luke's brain foggy. He needed to head to bed, but instead, he had a long night ahead sleeping in his jail and keeping watch on his prisoner. Part of the man's gang might still be around and plan to break him out of jail. "Can't it wait?"

Shaking his head, Dan rolled up the edge of his felt hat. "I don't think so. You probably should head on down there while I'm still here."

Luke sighed and strode out the door. He couldn't imagine what could be so important that it couldn't wait until morning. But at least he'd get to see Rachel again.

He thought about the outlaw's sister—Carly Payton. Suddenly, he stopped in the middle of the road. Rachel had said something about someone named Carly. As unusual as that name was, she had to be Payton's sister.

Luke broke into a run and charged toward the boardinghouse. His heart thundered. Was Rachel in danger again?

Rachel thanked the Corbett brothers for helping them to get home and entered the house. She glanced around as if seeing everything for the first time. It looked so wonderful. Miss Bennett and Miss O'Neil both sat in the parlor and jumped up as they entered.

" 'Tis wonderful to have you all home again." Miss O'Neil hugged Rachel, then Carly and Jacqueline.

"Yes, we were so worried about you." Miss Bennett cast an odd look at Carly. "We. . .uh. . .kept some food warm for you, if you're hungry, that is."

"We're starving!" Jacqueline squeezed past them and made a beeline for the kitchen.

"Don't forget to wash up first." Rachel said.

Jacqueline tossed a scowl over her shoulder, but suddenly her expression changed. "Yes Ma."

Rachel looked into the surprised eyes of the other women. Maybe her being kidnapped had made her daughter thankful enough for her return that she'd be more obedient. She could hope so, at least.

"I'm so happy that you're all right." Miss Bennett hurried forward and hugged Rachel. She released her and looked at the floor, her hands wringing in front of her. "I owe you and the other ladies an apology. I've been so worried about what would happen to me if I lost the competition that I haven't been very nice." She looked up at Rachel and then glanced at Shannon and Carly. "I'm sorry. I would like for us to be friends, no matter how the contest ends."

Shannon's green eyes lit up. "Aye, I would like that. I have felt the same way, and I, too, want to apologize."

"I'm sorry, too, if I was mean to ya." Carly pressed her lips together.

Rachel stepped forward and embraced all three women. "Everything's forgiven, and maybe we could drop the formalities and call each other by our given names."

The women nodded and wiped their damp eyes. Everyone smiled, and the tension that had been there earlier left the room. Rachel muttered a silent prayer of thanks to the Lord.

A door opened upstairs, setting Rachel's heart pounding. Garrett had said they'd captured the bank robber, but she didn't know if he was the same man who'd kidnapped her. A young woman with her arm in a sling appeared at the top of the stairs, followed by a man. Rachel saw the woman's gaze move past her and her expression change to a scowl. Turning slightly to look behind her, Rachel realized the woman was staring at Carly.

"Um. . .I hope you don't mind that I gave these folks two of your rooms. They came in on the late stage today. I didn't want to turn them away since there's no other decent place for them to stay in this town." Leah Bennett wrung her hands as if fearing Rachel would be upset. "I didn't take any money, but I told them they could square things with you when you returned."

Rachel smiled to ease the young woman's discomfort. "Thank you. I appreciate that."

Leah smiled and nodded, looking relieved. "If you don't mind, I think I'll head on to bed."

"Good night, then, and thank you for saving us some food."

"I shall go also. We did feed the new guests." Shannon brushed past Rachel and stepped up the stairs.

After the two women ascended the stairs, the man helped the injured woman down. They looked enough alike to be siblings, with their dark hair and matching blue eyes. Carly shuffled beside Rachel, seeming restless. Did she know the new boarders?

Stepping forward, she smiled. "I'm Rachel Hamilton, owner of Hamilton House. Welcome, and I hope you will forgive my appearance. We've just been through a trying ordeal."

The man nodded. "I'm John Blackstone, and this is my sister, Ellie Blackstone."

Rachel felt her eyes widen and turned to face Carly. She stood with her head down, but she saw Rachel looking at her and gave a slight nod.

So this was the woman Carly had impersonated. "I'm glad to see you're doing so well, Miss Blackstone."

The man's eyes narrowed. "What do you know of her troubles?"

"Not much, I can assure you, and what I do know, I just learned about today. I'm sure the two women who just went upstairs told you what happened to us."

When he shook his head, Rachel sighed. "Could we all sit down in the parlor, please? We've had an extraordinary day."

"Does this have something to do with that blond woman asking me if we had family staying here already?"

Rachel offered him a smile. "It's complicated."

Miss Blackstone shook her head. "I'm not getting any closer to *her*." She pointed at Carly. "What's she doing here anyway? And why is she wearing *my* dress?"

Carly stepped forward, looking twice her age. Her shoulders were slumped and her head hung down. "I came here pretending to be you."

The real Miss Blackstone gasped and moved back. "See, John, I bet she's the one who stole my satchel."

"I'm sorry for that. I thought you were dead."

The front door flew open, banging against the wall, and everybody in the entryway jumped. Rachel's heart stampeded as Luke charged inside. His gaze pinned on Carly, and he pulled his gun. Carly shrank back.

Jacqueline raced in from the kitchen, her napkin tucked into the neck of her shirt. "What's goin' on?"

"Carly Payton, you're under arrest."

Rachel gasped, as did the Blackstones. Carly's eyes looked like a trapped mustang's. "Luke, surely this isn't necessary."

His gaze darted to her and back to Carly. "Did you know you were harboring a criminal?"

Rachel shook her head. "Not until today. Carly told me everything while we were. . ." She glanced at the Blackstones. "While we were tied up. And she gave her heart to God."

"She's still a wanted outlaw. I can't ignore that, Rachel."

She stepped forward and laid her hand on his arm, pushing slightly, until he lowered the gun. "She's not going anywhere. Let us get cleaned up and eat something. Neither of us has eaten since last night's supper."

Carly stepped forward, twisting her hands. "I'll go with you peacefully, Marshal. But I would appreciate the chance to clean up and eat first."

A myriad of expressions crossed Luke's face before he finally relaxed. "All right. But you're not leaving my sight."

Rachel sucked in a breath. "That's hardly appropriate, Luke.

I'll stay with her while she cleans up, and you can wait for us in the kitchen."

A muscle in Luke's jaw ticked. "I don't want you or anyone else getting hurt, Rach."

"Carly is a believer now. She's not going to hurt anyone."

John Blackstone stepped forward. "This woman has been impersonating my sister. She stole from her and left her for dead after a stage robbery. I demand justice."

"I thought she *was* dead. If I'd known she was still alive, I'd have done different." Carly ducked her head again under John Blackstone's glare. "Her belongings are upstairs."

Luke studied the group then turned to the Blackstones. "I can assure you that Miss Payton is under arrest. She and Mrs. Hamilton have been through an ordeal today, and I'm going to let them do as they requested. Then Miss Payton will be taken to jail."

Mr. Blackstone observed them for a moment then nodded his head. He turned and motioned for his sister to go back upstairs.

"I'll need to get a statement from you both tomorrow. I can come here if you'd rather not come to the jail."

Mr. Blackstone nodded. "Here would be good. As you can see, my sister is still convalescing."

"I'll come by tomorrow morning, then, after breakfast." Luke turned to face Rachel. "Do your cleaning and eating quickly. Dan Howard's watching the jail for me, and I need to get back."

Jacqueline stepped forward and grabbed Luke's hand. "C'mon in the kitchen with me. There's food and hot coffee."

Rachel marveled at how Luke allowed her daughter to boss him around. He followed Jacqueline into the kitchen, and chairs scraped across the floor. She escorted Carly to the washroom downstairs, her heart aching for the young woman. "I'm sorry about all this."

"It ain't your fault. I only pretended to be Miss Blackstone 'cause I truly thought she was dead. I thought if'n I got away from my brother, I might could start a new life."

Rachel cringed at the thought of Luke marrying an outlaw, even though she didn't think Carly was hardened like her brother. She feared what would become of Carly and her fledgling faith. The young woman had admitted taking part in several bank and train robberies. Rachel hated the thought of the young woman locked up in jail, but she would have to pay for her crimes. Though that was the right thing, Rachel wanted mercy for her. Hadn't Carly repented of her sins? She was a new person now and needed to grow in the Lord and put her old life behind her, but how would she do that in prison? *I'll do whatever I can to help her, Lord. Protect Carly, and help her through the difficult days ahead. And help me to be a better mother to Jacqueline.*

One thing she'd decided while being held captive, if Jacqueline didn't have better guidance and more consequences for her bad behavior, she could well turn out like Carly had. As much as she disliked disciplining her child, Rachel knew it was God's will.

Give me the strength I need, Lord, to be a good mother.

Chapter 34

Saturday afternoon, Luke paced from the parlor of his small house to the foot of his bed. Was he doing the right thing?

If everything went as he hoped, he would be making the most creative marriage proposal he could imagine; but if things went the other way…

A hard knock sounded on his front door. He crossed the small room and yanked the door open.

"It's time," said Mayor Burke. "You ready?"

Luke shrugged, making the mayor scowl.

"Half the county has come to town. Women are selling food, baked goods, and lemonade, coffee, and tea to make money for the church. You're not thinking of backing out, are you?" The mayor shoved his hand to his hips and glared at Luke. "Why, this bride contest has been the biggest thing to hit this town in months. Everyone's speculating on which of the remaining two boardinghouse brides you'll pick." Mayor Burke chuckled. "There's even a few folks holding out for you to marry that outlaw bride you hauled off to Dallas."

Luke sighed and shook his head. "I can assure you that won't happen."

Why had he ever agreed to marry like he had? He didn't normally allow people to ramrod him into doing things. Romancing and wedding proposals were supposed to be done in private between two people in love and not made some public spectacle. But he'd given his word. And he'd prayed and prayed and still felt his plan was God's will. He only hoped Jack followed through on her end, or he'd be in big trouble.

He grabbed his hat from the peg near the door. "All right. I'm ready."

"Good. I'm glad to see you've come to your senses."

Luke shook his head and closed the door. If anything, he'd taken total leave of his senses.

"I'm not going." Rachel sat on the end of her bed, wringing the edge of her apron in one hand.

Jacqueline tugged on her arm. "But you hav'ta go, Ma."

She shook her head, trying hard to fight the tears threatening at the thought of Luke marrying Leah or Shannon. Yes, things seemed better between her and Luke, but she hadn't seen him for three days, not since the evening he arrested Carly. She didn't even get to tell the young woman good-bye.

No, she couldn't attend today's activities. She still had boarders to care for, although there might be one less by evening. Her chin wobbled. She had no idea which woman he'd choose, and she could not watch.

"But Ma, I think the brides need you to be there."

Rachel winced. One of her guests would be the loser today, and she would need comforting and encouragement. Both brides had everything riding on their hopes to marry Luke. The one not chosen would be devastated. Sighing, Rachel untied her apron and stood. Attending the bride announcement would be one of the hardest things she'd ever done, but she owed it to her guests. And she needed to be a good example to Jacqueline. She would congratulate Luke and his chosen bride and comfort the loser. But who would comfort her?

Jacqueline yanked on her arm. "Hurry, Ma. We don't want to miss the announcement."

Rachel grabbed her bonnet and tied it on her head. "Fine, I'm ready."

Jacqueline ran to the front door, flung it open, and started outside, then stopped and looked back as if to make sure Rachel was coming. She hurried out and closed the door, surprised to see Main Street filled with people. Buggies and horses lined Bluebonnet Lane in both directions as far as she could see.

Jacqueline bounced. "Hurry, Ma. Looks like we're the only ones in the whole state who aren't there."

Rachel couldn't understand why her daughter was so excited. Didn't Jacqueline realize things would be different between her and Luke once he married? She saw Luke mount the boardwalk and stride straight and tall toward his office, where he was to make the announcement. She watched him go, her heart in her throat. How did one quit loving someone?

Her eyes stung, but she lifted her head high. God orchestrated the path she was to walk. He would give her the strength to face the future without Luke.

She glanced at the bank as she walked down Main Street. On Monday morning, she'd meet with Mr. Castleby and the mayor to finalize the sale of the boardinghouse. She hated leaving the only town she'd ever lived in, but Kansas City offered more for her daughter and a fresh start for them both.

Pressing her lips tight, she walked on, fortifying herself for the next few minutes. She stopped at the back edge of the crowd and stood on tiptoes, trying to find Leah and Shannon, but the crowd was too thick.

Jacqueline jumped up and down. "I can't see."

"Well, go stand over there on the boardwalk in front of the mercantile."

Jacqueline eyed her suspiciously. "You won't leave?"

Rachel was tempted to roll her eyes, feeling as if she were the child. "Not until it's over."

"All right then." Jacqueline dashed around the back of the crowd and up the steps to the boardwalk, squeezing past people, making her way toward Luke.

With so many taller men in front of Rachel, almost all wearing hats, she decided to take her own advice and crossed the street to the boardwalk opposite Luke's side of the road. Though the area was jam-packed with people, she squeezed her way up to the top step in front of the newspaper office. The jail was directly across from her, and she could see that Shannon and Leah stood on the ground in front of Luke's office.

The noise of the crowd was deafening, and so many people in one place made the summer afternoon seem even hotter. Rachel fanned her face with her hand. If this thing lasted very long, some of the women would be swooning. From the higher viewpoint, she could see that tables lined either side of Main Street farther down where women were selling refreshments. She'd opted not to do that at this event. Everything was far too festive for her mood. All she wanted was to go home and mourn the loss of the only man she'd ever loved. *Oh God, why did You have to bring him back if You were going to give him to someone else?*

The mayor shoved his way through the crowd in front of Luke, and both men stopped in front of the jail. Mayor Burke raised his hands and mouthed something she couldn't hear. The crowd suddenly quieted.

"Thank y'all for coming out on such a warm day, but it's a day of celebration. Our marshal is going to pick his bride today."

The crowd cheered in unison, and Rachel watched three tossed hats drop back down. She was probably the only person in the whole crowd not excited. Well, maybe except for the two brides. They knew only one of them would come up the winner today. Rachel was determined to do all she could to help the loser, whether the woman wanted to move on to another town or stay in Lookout and try to find employment, hard as that was in such a small town.

The mayor lifted his hands again, and the crowd quieted. "After the bride announcement, we'll have square dancing in the street, and don't forget all the marvelous confections the ladies of Lookout have created for y'all to enjoy."

He waited for the cheers to die down again. "And now for what we've all been waiting for, I'll turn things over to our marshal, Luke Davis."

Rachel swallowed hard as Luke stepped up to the porch railing. He was nearly a head taller than the mayor, and he was so strong, so capable—until she peered at his face. She'd seen him look nervous only a handful of times, and this was one of them. Was he unsure of his decision?

She clutched the porch railing to her left, afraid that she might just swoon herself.

Luke straightened, though his gaze roamed the crowd. When it collided with hers, he smiled and started talking. "I threatened to throw my cousins in jail once I learned they'd ordered three brides for me."

The crowd chuckled, but Rachel's heart had tripped over itself. How could Luke look at her like that? Was he counting on her friendship to make things easier for him?

Irritation worked its way through her body like a bad case of influenza. But then she snuffed it out. He was her friend, her oldest friend, and it was her Christian duty to help him. She would swallow her pride and disappointment and do what she could. In another week, she'd be on her way to Kansas City, and she'd no longer have to look at Luke and his bride, anyway.

"But God has a way of using strange circumstances to get our attention," Luke continued. "I gave my heart to the Lord less than a year ago. Though I've read my Bible a lot, I know there's still a lot I need to learn about walking the straight and narrow path God has set before me. Through this whole bride contest, the thing I've discovered is that God doesn't want me to walk it alone."

Luke's gaze captured Rachel's again as he stared across the street over the heads of the townsfolk. Why did he keep looking at her?

Now that she knew where the brides were, she no longer needed to see so well and made her way off the steps to the ground. Luke disappeared among a mass of heads and hats.

"It's true that no matter what I face or what any of y'all face, God will be there to help us through, if we'll only turn to Him."

Rachel figured Mayor Burke was most likely scowling at Luke's preaching, but she was proud that he would stand before such a large group and proclaim his faith. He'd changed a lot from the determined youth she'd first fallen in love with.

"I need to make a big apology to Miss Bennett and Miss O'Neil. I'm sorry, but I can't marry either of you. My heart—"

Many in the crowd gasped, and Rachel missed the last part of what he said. Suddenly, heads were turning and people were looking at her. Though tempted to back away, she held her ground. The crowd parted in front of her like the line in the middle of Mayor Burke's hair.

Someone nudged her in the back. "Go on up there, Rachel. He's asking for you."

Rachel's head swam, and she held her ground. Just coming here at all had been hard enough, but to go up front? Suddenly, Luke's words soaked in. He couldn't marry either bride? But he gave his word.

"Rachel, will you please come up here?"

Hands all around her gently shoved her. She either had to move forward or fall down. Heaving a heavy sigh, she ambled toward Luke. Why did he need her up there? Wasn't she mortified enough with half the town knowing their history?

All too soon, she stood in front of the crowd next to Luke,

though she couldn't say how she'd arrived at that place. Jacqueline peered around behind him, grinning as if it were Christmas. What was going on?

Luke took her hands, drawing her gaze to his. "Rachel, I loved you when we were ignorant youths, unaware of the hardships life could throw our way. I promised to marry, but I never said that I'd marry one of the boardinghouse brides. How could I, when my heart has always belonged to you?" He cocked his head, love making his dark eyes shine.

Rachel gasped, unable to believe what she was hearing. "You still love me?"

Luke grinned, taking her breath away. "Yeah, but my love was hidden under a quagmire of bitterness and unwillingness to forgive. It took nearly losing you to realize that I still cared. I'm so sorry for not forgiving you sooner."

She stepped closer, placing her fingers on his lips. "Shh. . .none of that. We're both forgiven. Let's not go backward."

Luke pulled her into his arms and leaned his head against hers. "Could you find it in your heart to marry me?"

Rachel closed her eyes as the words she never expected to hear filled her whole being. The tears that had threatened all day broke forth like a flash flood. She nodded. "Oh yes. There's nothing I'd like more in this world."

"Hey, we can't hear. What'd you say to her, Marshal?" Bertha Boyd shouted and shook her cane at them.

Jacqueline squeezed in between Rachel and Luke. "Did you ask her? What did she say?" She yanked on Rachel's skirts. "Say yes, Ma. Please say yes."

Luke raised a hand in the air, and the crowd quieted. "It's no secret that Rachel and I have a long history. Most of y'all know that. Well, I've asked her to marry me, and she has agreed."

The whole town erupted in cheers, hoots, and hollers. Jacqueline squealed and jumped up and down, wrapping her arms around them both. Luke bent and whispered something in the girl's ear, and she nodded and stepped back, grinning wide.

Luke pulled Rachel into his arms. "When will you marry me? Today?"

Rachel smiled through her tears, knowing now she'd most likely never live in Kansas City. "Not today, but very soon. A gal needs time to prepare for a wedding."

"Two weeks. That's all you get." Luke tugged her closer and lowered his mouth to hers, wiping away any lingering doubts of his devotion. All too soon he pulled away.

"One week," she said. "That's all I can bear to wait."

Love for her illuminated his eyes. He no longer looked at her with hurt or bitterness. God had forgiven them both and given them a future neither one could have anticipated.

Oh, thank You, Lord.

"There's just one thing." Luke pulled back and gazed at her. "Earlier, I told both Misses Bennett and O'Neil that I couldn't marry them, but what do we do about them?"

"I suppose we'll help them however we can, but it's best we leave the boardinghouse brides to God. Maybe He brought them to Lookout for another purpose."

Luke nodded and pulled Jacqueline into their embrace. Rachel marveled at how God could take a relationship that was torn to shreds and patch it, repair it, and make it into something wonderful, something stronger than it had originally been. Never again would she doubt God's hand at work in her life.

Discussion Questions for *The Anonymous Bride*

1. Luke had a hard time forgiving Rachel for marrying James when she'd pledged to marry him instead. Have you ever found it difficult to forgive someone? How did you get past that?

2. Luke was a fairly new Christian. Did you struggle with faith issues when you first gave your heart to God? Are you struggling with any now?

3. After living with an abusive husband, Rachel found it difficult to discipline her daughter. How did this affect Jacqueline? Did you dislike Rachel because of this flaw? Do you think Rachel should have used a firmer hand in controlling her daughter?

4. The mail-order brides found themselves in a difficult situation. Have you ever found yourself in a situation where you had to totally trust in God even though there seemed no way out?

5. Do you think Garrett and Mark were playing a prank on Luke when they ordered the brides, or did they honestly hope to find him a wife?

6. Carly Payton, aka Ellie Blackstone, stole a shirt from Rachel after she'd been kind and opened her home to Carly. Have you ever had someone steal from you? How did you handle the situation? How could you have reacted better?

7. Luke agreed to marry to save his cousins from a possible lawsuit. Did he do the right thing? Keep in mind people often married more quickly back in the 1800s.

8. Rachel was placed in an awkward situation by having to host thc brides at her boardinghouse and help them with their contest entries. Do you think she responded in a Christian manner? How else could she have responded?

9. Rachel entered the bride contest because she didn't want to give Luke up without a fight. Was she right to enter? What else could she have done to win him back?

10. How would you have reacted if you were a mail-order bride with no husband in the 1800s? Where would you go and how would you make a living? Would you be tempted to blame someone else for the situation you found yourself in?

Second Chance **Brides**

Dedication/Acknowledgments

This book is dedicated to my good friend, Margaret Daley, award-winning author of over 70 books. The first time I met Margaret was at a local RWA chapter meeting. I'd read a number of her books—and loved them—but had no idea she lived in the same town as me. I literally stood there awestruck, shaking and thinking, "Oh my goodness! Margaret Daley lives in Tulsa?!"

I never could have dreamed back then that we'd become such good friends and travel across the U.S. together, promoting our books, attending writers conferences, and serving together as ACFW officers. Thanks so much, Margaret, for the encouragement you've been to me and for your patience when I vented and didn't believe in myself. We've laughed together and cried together and shared our joys and frustrations over many a meal and mile. I couldn't ask for a better friend, and I thank God for bringing you into my life.

Chapter 1

Lookout, Texas
August 1886

Any moment, the wedding would commence and signal an end to her dreams. Shannon O'Neil cast a longing glance back toward the safety of the boardinghouse. Whoever heard of a mail-order bride attending the wedding of the man she was to marry—especially when he was marrying someone else? "We should not be here." Her voice trembled almost as much as her legs.

Her gaze flitted over the huge crowd gathered in the open field next door to the church. Only because her friend Rachel had requested her presence had she agreed to come. "People are staring at us."

Leah Bennett sidled up beside her, mouth twisted to one side. "They've gawked at us ever since we came to town. Besides, we've got just as much right to be at this wedding as anyone else. Even more if you ask me. All things considered."

Shannon shored up her apprehension and forced her steps forward. She squeezed through the group of men clustered around an array of makeshift benches and hurried toward one of the few remaining spots on the back bench.

Several men gaped at them and whispered among themselves. That was nothing new, since she and Leah were mail-order brides without a groom. She'd been in Lookout more than a month but still hadn't gotten used to being the focus of attention. Shannon dropped her gaze to the ground, but that did nothing to silence the loud murmurs. Leah sat next on her left, her nose pointed in the air, not in the snooty way it sometimes was, but in a way that dared anybody to challenge her right to attend the wedding.

"I can't believe they had the nerve to show up," a man to their right slurred, his tone dripping sour like unsweetened lemonade.

"They'll ruin everything," another said.

"Of all the nerve. This is Luke and Rachel's special day, not theirs."

Crushing the handkerchief in her hand, Shannon willed her trembling to cease. But her efforts were futile. She leaned toward Leah. "Perhaps 'twould be better if we left."

"We're staying put. Rachel wants us here, and that's what matters. If those folks don't like it, *they* can leave." The sternness in Leah's voice made Shannon feel like a scolded child. If only she had Leah's boldness, perhaps her future wouldn't look so bleak.

Shannon peered up at the ash gray clouds—clouds that mirrored her future. Clouds that swirled in waves, taunting and threatening like a schoolyard bully.

Never had she seen clouds such as these, not in all of Ireland nor during the seven months she'd lived in America.

The oppressive heat sent streams of sweat trickling down her temples, back, and chest. A canvas canopy erected to protect the bride and groom in the event of rain lifted on the breeze and deflated as if it were a living, breathing being.

Let it rain. At least if showers fell, no one would notice her tears.

Men stood in a rough half-circle around the benches their womenfolk and children filled—benches they had constructed over the past few days. The pounding of their hammers had resembled a death knell to Shannon, with each whack bringing her closer to the end of another dream.

She looked around at the growing crowd. Nearly the whole town had turned out to see Lookout's marshal, Luke Davis, marry Rachel Hamilton, the owner of the boardinghouse—the very same boardinghouse where Shannon resided. The very same marshal she had expected to marry. Shannon's chin wobbled.

"Don't you dare cry, you hear me?"

Shannon blinked her moist eyes, stiffened her chin, and glanced at Leah. She, too, had come to town, expecting to marry the marshal, although she seemed less distraught than Shannon felt over losing him. She clenched her hands. What was she going to do now? Would she never have a home of her own?

Leah leaned closer, her lips puckered as if she'd eaten a persimmon. "If I can make it through this wedding without weeping, so can you. We're Texans now, and you're gonna have to find a backbone if you plan to survive here."

Leah was right. Crimping the handkerchief tighter, Shannon turned to face the front where the parson had taken his place. A fiddler off to the right zipped his bow across the strings, playing a lively tune she'd never heard before. The trees shimmied and swayed, dancing in the brisk breeze, cooling Shannon's damp neck.

Leah might be in the same boat as she, but the pretty blond had a family to return to—she just chose not to do so. Shannon would give anything to have her parents back, but no sooner had they stepped onto the shores of America than they'd come down with influenza and died. With her three siblings already dead and buried back in Ireland, she was completely alone in a foreign country.

Why hadn't God healed her parents when she'd begged Him to? Her throat stung as if she'd run a race in winter's chill. But the only thing cold in Texas was her future.

Sympathetic glances swept her way, along with the others. How was it possible to be so alone in such a large crowd?

Leah leaned toward her. "Here he comes."

The murmurs silenced as Luke Davis strode past the front row of townsfolk and took his place next to the parson. His two conniving, hooligan cousins, Garrett and Mark Corbett, followed, along with the old yellow dog that rarely let Luke out of his sight. The dog sniffed Luke's shoes, sending chuckles rippling through the crowd. Jacqueline, Rachel's ten-year-old daughter from her first marriage, sat on the front row. She smacked her lips, and

Max lumbered over to her and laid down at her feet. Jack, as the mischievous child preferred to be called, would benefit from having a kind man like the marshal for a father.

A sigh of longing slipped from Shannon's mouth as she pulled her gaze back to Luke. He looked so handsome in his new suit and hat. He was a comely man, in a rugged way. But her marriage to him had been doomed before she ever set foot in Lookout. Just imagine—three women coming to town to marry him when his heart already belonged to a woman who'd stolen it more than a decade before. Now, two of the marshal's mail-order brides were stuck in Lookout while the third was locked up in a jail in Dallas for bank robbery. Shannon shook her head and clutched her handkerchief to her chest. What a kettle of nettles.

And now that the marshal was marrying, she was stranded in one of the smallest towns she'd ever been in outside of Ireland. But this wasn't the first time, and if she had managed before, she could do it again. She dabbed at her eyes and stiffened her back. The music grew louder, and heads turned toward the rear of the crowd. Shannon stood along with the others, but her gaze didn't search out the bride. How could one feel happiness and sorrow at the same time?

Rachel passed Shannon's row and walked toward her groom, looking beautiful in the cream-colored dress her aunt had brought from Kansas City. The bride held her Bible in front of her, and on top lay a bouquet of daisies tied together with flowing rose and lavender ribbons that fluttered on the gusty breeze. Shannon sighed at the joyful smile on Rachel's face.

If Shannon ever doubted the marshal's love for his bride, she did so no more. His face all but glowed, as if he'd battled a hard-fought race, come out the victor, and won a coveted prize. Would a man ever look at her with such love in his eyes?

"I now pronounce you man and wife." A cheer rang throughout the crowd, and Shannon jumped. She blinked, realizing she'd been lost in thought and had missed the whole wedding.

"Well, that's the end of that." Leah stood and looked around. "There are plenty more unmarried men we can set our bonnets for."

Leah might be snippy and bossy at times, but Shannon

admired her determination. They'd once been competitors, but being the losers of the bride contest had put them in the same wagon, and they were becoming friends.

Shannon studied the townsfolk swarming the newly married couple, offering their congratulations. Men outnumbered women ten to one. "Aye, there's truth in what you say. There surely are many men in Texas."

"I suppose we should make our way over to the refreshment table and help serve. I know Rachel was hesitant to ask for our help, given the situation and all, but it seems the least we can do."

Shannon nodded and followed Leah over to the west side of the church, where a makeshift table had been erected with sawhorses and wooden planks. A lacy white tablecloth hid the ugliness and boasted the biggest cake Shannon had ever seen. "Miss Dykstra surely outdid herself makin' that lovely cake."

Leah nodded. "Don't know as I've seen one so big before. Why, it must measure three feet across."

"Aye, and 'tis so colorful." Lavender and yellow flowers dotted a green ivy vine that encircled the cake. Large letters saying, *Congratulations to Luke and Rachel*, along with the date, filled the center of the cake, which she hoped would serve the whole crowd. A haphazard collection of plates in various colors and designs were stacked on one end, as well as a collection of mismatched forks. It looked as if every family in town had donated their plates and forks to be used for the wedding.

A trio of ladies Shannon recognized from the church stood behind the table, awaiting the guests. All three cast apologetic glances at her and Leah. Shannon doubted a soul in attendance didn't know her odd circumstances. She glanced down at the ground and felt a warm heat on her cheeks. She despised being the center of attention and hoped that with the marshal now married, chatter about the boardinghouse brides—as she and Leah had been dubbed—would die down.

"You ladies need any help?" Leah offered.

Sylvia Taylor, the pastor's wife, smiled. "We just might at that. There's quite a crowd here today, and we need to hurry before the storm lets loose."

"Yes, that's true. I suppose everyone wanted to see for themselves that the marshal was truly marrying Rachel Hamilton and not one of you two," Margie Mann said.

Mrs. Taylor's brow dipped, while Agatha Linus's brow dashed upward.

"Now, Margie, I don't think that's a proper topic of conversation today. These young ladies are well aware of the importance of this event." Sylvia, always the peacemaker, Shannon had learned, tried to calm the turbulent waters Mrs. Mann had stirred up.

"Well"—Leah looked around the crowd—"I don't think we'll have much trouble finding another man to marry."

"It's true that there are many unmarried men in these parts," Mrs. Taylor said, "but don't jump into anything. Marriage is a lifetime commitment, and you want to be sure you marry the man God has set aside for you. You're both still young and have plenty of time to find a good man to marry."

Shannon pursed her lips. Plenty of time, aye, but an empty purse and no way to survive had driven many a woman into the arms of a less-than-acceptable man. That was why she had agreed to marry the marshal before meeting him. A man who enforced the law must be honorable and upright. Only she found out later that it wasn't Luke Davis who'd penned the letters asking her to come to Lookout to marry him but rather one of the Corbett brothers pretending to be Luke. Her gaze sought them out and found them plowing their way through the crowd, making a path so the bride and groom could get to the cake table.

The Corbett men were quite handsome, similar but different. They both had those sky blue eyes that made a woman's heart stumble just looking into them. Blond hair topped each brother's head, but Mark's was curly while Garrett's was straight. Mark's face was more finely etched than Garrett's squarer jaw. But they were pranksters, full of blarney, the both of them. Jokers who'd turned her life upside down. She clutched her hands together at the memory of that humiliating bride contest. Four women competing for one man's hand. Who'd ever heard of such shenanigans?

Mrs. Mann cleared her throat, pulling Shannon's gaze back.

"I don't mean to be rude, but it's probably best that you not help serve." She glanced at the bride and groom, halfway to the table, with Rachel's daughter holding on to the groom's right arm and grinning wide. "It might be distressing to the Davis family, what with all that's happened."

Leah scowled but nodded and turned away. Shannon realized what the woman meant. What bride wanted the women who'd competed for her husband's affection to help with her wedding? She slunk away and found a vacant spot under a tall oak tree, whose branches swung back and forth in the stiff breeze. Holding her skirts down, she searched for Leah and found her talking to a stranger.

A man cleared his throat beside Shannon, pulling her gaze away from Leah. A heavy beard covered the short man's smallish face, and dark beady eyes glimmered at her. "I was wonderin'." He scratched his chin and looked away for a moment. Shannon couldn't remember seeing him before. He captured her gaze again. "I ain't got a lot, but I do have a small farm west of town and a soddy. Since you ain't marryin' up with the marshal, I was hopin' we could get hitched."

Shannon sucked in a gasp. Was the man full of blarney? Why, he had to be twice her age. His worn overalls had ragged patches covering every inch of his pants' legs. He scratched under his arm and rubbed his beard again. She hated hurting people's feelings, but she could not marry this man, no matter how much she longed for a home. "Um. . .thank you for your generous offer, sir, but I don't plan to stay in Lookout. I'll be leaving by the end of the week."

His mouth twisted to one side. "I didn't figger you'd wanna marry up with me, but I had to ask. Guess I'll try that blond, though she's a might uppity for my taste."

With a mixture of relief for herself and pity for Leah, Shannon watched him approach her friend. Leah's eyes went wide, and then she shook her head. The poor farmer shuffled away and disappeared into the crowd.

As the last of the people wandered toward the refreshment table, a mixture of glances were tossed her way. She felt odd being at the marshal's wedding, and yet she'd wanted to support Rachel, who'd been so kind to allow the brides to stay at her boardinghouse. How difficult that must have been for Rachel when she was still in love with Luke.

Pushing her way through the people, Shannon drifted to the edge of the churchyard. She'd done what she felt was needed, and all she wanted to do now was to get away from the gawking townsfolk. She walked toward the street, feeling relieved to have made her getaway.

Mark shoveled cake into his mouth and watched Shannon O'Neil wander through the crowd, looking lost and alone. His gut tightened. With her auburn hair and pine green eyes, she reminded him too much of another pretty woman—of a time he'd just as soon forget. But he couldn't forget Annabelle any more than he could ignore his brother.

He tore his gaze away and handed his dirty plate and fork to the preacher's wife, knowing it would be quickly washed, dried, and returned to the cake table for someone else to use.

"Some wedding, huh? And pert near the best cake I've ever eaten," Garrett said. "Think maybe I'll get Polly to bake one up for your birthday."

Mark shot a glance sideways at his brother. "Just so you don't go orderin' me a bride like you did Luke."

Garrett grinned wide. "You ordered one, too, if I remember correctly."

Mark's lips twisted up on one side, and he ignored Garrett's comment. "It's good to see Luke and Rachel finally wed."

"I wondered if he'd ever get around to marrying. You suppose our ordering those brides had anything to do with it?"

Mark shrugged, wishing he'd never allowed himself to get caught up in his brother's scheme to marry off their cousin. If he hadn't, he never would have written to Miss O'Neil on his cousin's behalf, and she wouldn't be stranded in Lookout right now, stirring up rotten memories. "I reckon the Lord wanted Luke and Rachel together. Our messing with things just made them worse. Kind of like when Sarah in the Bible gave Abraham her maidservant."

"Oh, I don't know about that." Garrett rubbed his chin with his forefinger and thumb. "We've got two more pretty women of marrying age in Lookout than we had before. That can't be a bad thing."

Mark shook his head. From the tone of his voice, Garrett was scheming again, and this time Mark wanted nothing to do with it. They'd be out plenty of money before Miss O'Neil and Miss Bennett found a way to support themselves or got husbands, since the marshal had ordered him and Garrett to pay the ladies' room and board. Never again would he let his brother sway him into one of his schemes. Pranks were meant to be fun, but people kept getting upset at them.

The fiddler tuned up again. Men separated from their groups, seeking out their wives. Mark's gaze sought out Miss O'Neil again, and he found her standing at the edge of the crowd. She put him in mind of a frightened bird that desperately wanted to join the flock but was afraid of being pecked by the bigger birds. She looked as if she might flit away without a soul noticing.

But he noticed—and the fact irritated him.

"You gonna ask her to dance?"

"What?" Mark frowned at his brother. Had Garrett seen him watching the Irish girl and misinterpreted his stare?

Downing the last of his punch, Garrett seemed to be studying Miss O'Neil himself. "She's a fetching thing and free to marry now. Reckon we'll have to find her and that blond a husband soon, or we could be paying their room and board for a long while."

"Guess you should have thought of that before dreaming up that confounded plan to find Luke a bride. You'll remember that I warned you this could come back to bite you."

Garrett grinned. "Yeah, and I also remember you writing to one pretty Irish gal, pretending to be the marshal. If you were so opposed to my idea, why did you join in?"

Mark kicked a rock that skittered across the dirt. "Guess I just got caught up in your excitement. I wanted to see Luke settled and happy, too. He'd been through so much."

"Well, if you're not going to ask a certain redhead to dance, I reckon I will." Garrett set his punch glass on the church sign.

Mark grabbed for his brother's arm as he strode off, but he clutched air instead. Why couldn't Garrett let things be? He always had to meddle. But he had no way of knowing how Miss O'Neil set off all kinds of warning clangs in Mark's mind. He was wrong to compare the two women, but Shannon reminded him so much of Annabelle.

He clamped down his jaw. He wouldn't let another woman close like he had Annabelle. Not that Miss O'Neil was any threat. He just had to stay away from her. Not let his guard down around her. He'd fallen for a woman once, and it had been the worst mistake he'd ever made. If anyone found out, his reputation would be ruined.

The Irish girl shook her head at Garrett, and Mark smirked. So she was immune to his brother's charms. Good for her. A stiff breeze nearly stole his hat away, but he grabbed hold and pressed it down tighter. His gaze lifted to the sky. Shivers of alarm skittered down his spine. He didn't like the looks of those yellow-green clouds. Could be just a bad thunderstorm brewing, but they had an ominous look about them.

He searched for his brother and straightened when he found him waltzing with Miss O'Neil. His hand tightened into a ball. Why should he care? But knowing Garrett was just trying to raise his hackles—and doing a decent job of it—irritated Mark. He had half a mind to march over there and cut in, but that was probably exactly what his brother expected him to do.

The song ended. Garrett leaned toward Miss O'Neil and said something. She shook her head, then tilted it to the side. Mark read her lips. "Thank you."

She drifted through the crowd, looked over her shoulder, and then headed across the churchyard. She was trying to run away; he knew that. Things must be terribly awkward for her here. He watched her stop and talk with Leah Bennett for a moment until Homer Jones asked Miss Bennett to dance. Shannon watched the two walk toward the group of waltzing townsfolk.

If not for him and his brother, neither woman would be stuck in Lookout. He felt bad about that, but when he and Garrett had offered to pay their passage back home or somewhere else, both had refused. Maybe they liked it here.

He gazed at the town, trying to see it from their viewpoint. Lookout was small as towns went. The layout resembled a capital E, with Bluebonnet Lane the spine and Apple, Main, and Oak Streets the arms. Most of the buildings were well kept, but a few of them were weathered and unpainted and had seen better days. Yeah, they had a small bank, a store, marshal's office, livery, café, a church, and even a newspaper office, but that was about all. Why would a woman with no means of support want to stay here if she had family to return to?

Screams rose from the crowd, yanking Mark's attention toward the ruckus behind him.

"Tornado!" Frantic voices lifted in a chaotic chorus, joining with frightened wails.

Men grabbed their women and children and raced to find shelter. Mark shoved away from the tree he'd been leaning on. He looked back at Miss O'Neil. She stood on Bluebonnet Lane, her wide eyes captivated. Mouth open. Didn't she know the danger she was in?

Foolish woman. He quickened his steps. People scattered in all directions, yet she didn't move. He might not want to dance with her, but he sure didn't want her to come to any harm.

A flying tree branch snatched his hat off like a thief, almost knocking him in the head. He galloped faster, dodging men. Dodging women dragging their stunned children. "Run," he yelled.

But she couldn't hear him.

The menacing winds stirred up dust, flinging dishes and cups and forks like a naughty child throwing rocks at someone who'd angered him. Mark reached Miss O'Neil, but she stood immobile, her face as white as the wedding cake. He jerked on her hand, hoping she'd follow him.

Explosions, one after another, rent the air. Miss O'Neil squealed and flew toward him, clutching his arms. Mark's gaze swerved past her. The church bell clanged as if screaming with pain. His heart stampeded.

Fierce black clouds devoured the road at the far end of town. He scooped up Miss O'Neil and raced away from the encroaching whirlwind. She clung to his neck and buried her face in his shoulder.

The boardinghouse had a root cellar. If they could make it there, they should be safe. He didn't stop to look over his shoulder again, but he could feel the monster breathing down his neck.

Where was Garrett? Had he taken shelter? What had happened to Luke? To Rachel and Jacqueline? They were the only family he had.

Mark ran past the Dykstra and Castleby houses, knowing they could well be destroyed by the storm. The safest place for him and Miss O'Neil was underground. Flying debris pelted them. A frantic horse pulling a buggy with no driver raced ahead of him. The storm bellowed like a locomotive barreling down on him.

Miss O'Neil continued clinging to his neck, and her tears dampened his shirt. She was light as a child, but carrying her this far was stealing his breath. He dashed around the side of the Castleby house, glad to have a barrier between them and the storm.

Garrett galloped around the back of the house with Rachel's daughter under his arm. He reached the root cellar first, flung open the doors, and the girl ran down the stairs. "Hurry!" Garrett yelled.

Mark set Miss O'Neil on the ground and pulled her through the narrow opening onto the stairs, relief making his limbs weak.

Jacqueline lit the lantern, chasing most of the darkness from the small room. She glanced at them, then up at the door, her face pale.

"Did you see Luke and Rachel?" Garrett yelled.

Mark shook his head, his gaze dashing toward Jacqueline. "They were near the church. I'm sure they made it inside."

Jack huddled in the shadows against the corn crib, her eyes wide and her normal spunkiness subdued. She shrugged. "I—I couldn't find them once everybody started running around. And what about Max?"

Garrett stopped partway down the steps and wrestled the

doors shut. He held tight to the handles. With the drop-down bar on the outside, there was no way to lock them from the inside. The storm screamed in rage and fought to yank the doors off their hinges.

Still on the stairs, Mark looked past the Irishwoman and watched Garrett's struggle. He needed to get Miss O'Neil situated and then help his brother. Suddenly, she gasped and stumbled on the stairs. She fell into his arms, her momentum pushing him back. He flailed one arm, grasping for the handrail—for anything solid. His feet fumbled down the final half-dozen steps, and he fell, yanking Miss O'Neil down beside him on top of his arm. Something popped. His back and head collided with the packed dirt floor. Pain radiated through him.

Miss O'Neil cried out.

Mark squinted up at his brother. Garrett's form blurred, then darkened, and everything went black.

Chapter 2

Shannon lay on the hard, dirt floor, Mark's arm caught awkwardly under her back. Stabbing pain radiated through her foot and up her leg. She sat and grasped her leg, trying to catch her breath. Her ankle throbbed in unison with her pounding heart.

Jack crawled to her side. "Are you hurt?"

"Aye, my ankle." She scooted back against the dirt wall and huddled against the potato bin, trying to get comfortable and to catch her breath. She glanced up at Garrett, who still wrestled with the doors. The wind moaned and screeched, as if angered that it couldn't get in to devour them.

Garrett held tight to the handles, leaning back, using the full weight of his body to keep the doors shut. What had happened to all the other people? Surely there weren't enough cellars in town for everyone.

Why had she just stood there staring at the monstrous black cloud like some befuddled ninny? If that Mark Corbett hadn't grabbed her and hauled her off like she was a burlap bag of potatoes, surely she would have gotten hurt—or worse.

Had she thought if she allowed the storm to sweep her away her problems would finally end? That she would be reunited with Mum in heaven?

"Mark. Mark!" Jack's frantic cries drew her attention. She shook the man's shoulders. "Wake up!"

Shannon scooted over beside him and put her arm around the lass. Had she killed the very man who'd come to her rescue? *Please, Father, no. Let him be all right.*

Mark moaned and lifted his arm. Suddenly, he cried out, and his eyes shot open. He blinked and looked around, then reached for the arm Shannon had fallen on. "Oh, my arm. Feels like it's busted."

"You all right, brother?" Garrett held tight to the doors while gazing down over his shoulder at Mark.

"Do I look all right?"

Shannon's gaze leaped to Mark's right arm. Sure enough, his wrist had started swelling. At least the bone hadn't broken through the skin. Could be it was just a bad sprain. She prayed it was.

Mark attempted to sit up, and Shannon reached to help even though the effort made her ankle scream. "I don't need your help. You've done enough." She let go as if he'd been a rattlesnake, and he fell back to the ground with a sharp grunt.

Jack hurried to Mark's other side. "I'll help you."

"Take it slow, Jack. Besides my hand hurting like a horse kicked it, my head is buzzing." The girl pulled while Mark pushed off from the ground, and he managed to sit. He scowled at Shannon as if she were to blame.

She carefully moved away and leaned back against the potato bin. She hadn't meant to hurt him and felt awful that she had. Closing her eyes, she tried to remember being back in Ireland. The memories were fading, and it was getting harder to remember her mum's face.

She'd never wanted to come to this country, but she and Mum had followed along as Da chased his dreams. Would her parents still be alive if they'd stayed in Ireland? If her da hadn't been so insistent that they come to America?

At least she would be in a place where she had friends, friends who cared about her. But in America—in Texas—she had no one.

Her high-top shoe felt tighter than it had earlier. If her ankle swelled too much, her boot might have to be cut off, and these were the only shoes she owned. On top of everything else, she'd have to put her plans to leave Lookout on hold.

She scowled across the small cellar to the other side where Mark sat, rubbing the back of his head. His brother still clung to the doors, but they no longer rattled as if a bear were on the other side trying to get in.

Mark cradled his right arm with his other hand and winced when he shifted positions. His gaze shot fiery arrows at her. "Why did you just stand there gawking at the storm? Don't you know how dangerous a tornado is?"

A tornado. So the monster had a name.

She'd heard of them before, even in Ireland, but she'd never seen such a vengeful storm. Fear had melted her in the road like a spent candle stuck to a plate. Shivering, she clutched her arms around her. Had Mark just saved her life?

"Can you hear me, Miss O'Neil?" Mark leaned forward and grimaced from the movement. "Why didn't you run?"

Jack jumped to her feet. "I need to find my ma and Luke." She headed for the stairs, but Mark grabbed hold of her arm and pulled her back.

"You're not going anywhere until that twister passes."

"But they might be dead. And I gotta find Max."

Mark moved around, as if trying to get comfortable. "Your parents are safe; I'm sure."

Jack crossed her arms and leaned against a wooden bin. "How do you know?"

Mark grinned. "It took your ma eleven years to get Luke to the altar. She's not about to let a tornado steal him away on her wedding day."

Shannon watched the interplay between man and girl, amazed at how gentle Mark's voice was. She was also thankful that he seemed to be all right, except for his wrist.

"But what about Max? I saw him under the cake table just before that storm blew in." Jack flipped her long, auburn hair, almost the same color as Shannon's, over her shoulder, and she nibbled her lower lip. The pristine yellow dress she'd donned this morning was now covered in dirt and grime.

"Aw, you know that ol' yellow dog," Garrett said. "He's scared of his shadow. He's probably back hiding out in one of the jail cells, and not even a tornado could uproot one of those heavy iron cages."

"I guess so."

Shannon leaned her head back, glad that Mark had been diverted with the lass's questions and forgotten about interrogating her. She truly hoped nothing had happened to the newly married couple. Although not marrying Luke Davis had created a multitude of problems for her, she knew Luke was the love of Rachel's life, and Shannon couldn't begrudge them their happiness.

She glanced down, staring at her dirty hands. She brushed off the dust from her fall, but only soap and water would remove the rest. She allowed her injured foot to relax, but just the slight movement made her nearly scream out. Her boot felt unusually tight, and she was certain her foot was still swelling.

Mark glanced at Shannon. "You never answered my question."

She ducked her head again. "I don't know why I didn't run."

She hoped he would be satisfied and leave her alone. All her life, she had tried to make herself small. Tried to remain unseen. Tried to stay out of her da's way when he returned home from the pub. It had mostly worked—until she'd grown up and was too large to hide.

The chill of the cellar seeped into her bones, and no amount of rubbing her arms could drive it away. What was she going to do? How could she survive on her own?

A scrape and thud sounded on the stairs; then a shaft of sunlight illuminated the dimly lit room. Fresh air streamed in. Dust motes floated on the shaft of sunlight that fell through the open door. A mouse scurried under a set of shelves that held jars of green beans and jellies.

Shannon jumped up, instantly regretting her sudden movement. She held onto the potato bin, keeping her sore foot off the ground, and gazed up the stairs. How was she going to manage them?

Mark stood also, then fell back against a wooden bin that held onions. He hung his head, rubbing his brows with his thumb and forefingers.

"You all right?" Jack asked.

"Yeah, just stood up too fast. Got a tornado of my own swirling in my head."

Garrett clambered down the steps. "Most likely, it's from that blow you took to your head when you fell. We'd best have the doc take a look at it."

"I'll be fine." Mark swatted his hand in the air. "We need to get up there and see if any of the town is left. See if anyone is injured."

Shannon's pulse soared. Here she'd been worrying about herself when others may have lost their homes, livelihood, and even family members. She had to find out if Leah was all right. They may have been opponents at one time, but their similar loss had drawn them closer.

"What's wrong with your hand?" Garrett glanced at Mark's cradled arm. "Looks like it's swellin' up."

Mark wiggled his forefinger and grimaced. "Yeah. Broken wrist, I think."

Shannon lifted her hand to her mouth and sucked back a gasp. Mr. Corbett had been trying to help her, and she'd caused him injury. She longed to creep around the bin and hide in the shadows, but her wounded foot and shame held her immobile.

"You won't be able to help much until the doc sets your hand, so we might as well head over to his office first." Garrett hurried to Mark's side.

"I don't need any help, but I reckon Miss O'Neil does. Looks like she hurt her foot in the fall."

"Well, I'm goin' looking for my ma and my new pa." Jack dashed past Garrett.

He grabbed for her arm, but she slipped past. "No, wait!"

"You're too slow, brother." Mark grinned.

Garrett shook his head. "I wanted to keep her close—just in case." He swallowed hard.

Mark patted his brother's shoulder. "Yeah, I know. But Luke finally married the only woman he's ever loved. He's not gonna let a twister steal her away from him."

"I don't reckon he would, but that was one fierce storm."

"Yep, you're right there. Let's see what's left of the town." Mark undid the middle button of his shirt and stuck his injured hand inside, using it as a sling. He winced as he relaxed his arm; then he nodded at Shannon and walked up the stairs.

"What part of you is hurt, ma'am?" Garrett ambled closer to her.

She fought the urge to hide, knowing that Garrett Corbett was a prankster, but he was still a gentleman. What part of her hurt? *All of me. My heart. My dignity.* "Just my ankle."

"Might be easiest if I simply carried you up."

Shannon shook her head. "I can walk."

She lowered her foot and tried putting her weight on it. Pain ratcheted through it and up into her lower leg. She bit the inside of her cheek, and sucked in a breath. Had she broken her ankle?

Without so much as a warning, Garrett scooped her into his arms and carried her up the stairs. He was just like his brother, forcing a woman to do things she didn't want to do. If not for the Corbett brothers, she wouldn't even be in Texas. But she had to be honest, even if she didn't like it in this case. Without Garrett's help, she'd have had a difficult time climbing those stairs.

"Blessit be! The store is gone." Shannon's gaze roved around the town. Thank goodness, the boardinghouse was still standing, though it had sustained some damage. Shingles were missing, some windows broken, and debris littered the yard and porch, but the house itself had withstood the storm, as had the neighboring homes. The store was a different story.

Letting out a slow whistle, Garrett set her down. "I've never seen anything like this."

" 'Tis amazing so many buildings are still standin'." She held on to Garrett's arm, keeping her foot off the ground. People slowly crept out of every nook and cranny she could see, all looking first at the sky, where the sun had broken through the clouds, and then at their town. They crawled out from under wagons, out of buildings, and one man even crawled soaking wet out of the horse trough.

Mark was bent over a man lying in the street. He straightened and looked around. "Anyone seen the doc?"

People near him shook their heads, but several men turned in different directions as if looking for the doctor.

"Let's get you off that foot." Garrett picked Shannon up again and hurried toward the boardinghouse. "Get that boot off right away, raise up your leg, and stay off of it. That can help with the swelling, so I've heard."

"Garrett!"

Shannon locked her arms around Garrett's shoulders as he spun around. A wide grin lit his face. "Luke. Rachel."

"I found them in the church." Jack had an arm wrapped around both Luke's and Rachel's waists. She grinned like a kid at Christmas. "All the windows was blown out, but the church is still there."

"Glad to see you made it," Garrett responded.

Shannon knew his relief must be as huge as the ocean. Luke was his and Mark's cousin and their only living relative as far as she knew.

Rachel hurried toward Shannon, looking worried, her wedding dress damp and dirty, as was Shannon's garment. "What's wrong? Are you injured badly?"

"Not so much. 'Tis just my ankle that hurts."

Relief softened the worry lines on Rachel's face, and she smiled. "Well, thank the good Lord for that. Do you know where Leah is?"

Shannon shook her head. She was concerned for her new friend, but Leah was tough—Texas tough—and would surely be all right.

"That was some storm. We're fortunate that most of the buildings in town are still standing. Looks like the store's gone, though." Luke ran his fingers through his hair. "That's a shame. This town needs the mercantile."

Rachel nodded. "God was certainly watching over us. So far, there have only been minor injuries. Let's get Miss O'Neil into the house and then send for the doctor."

"I imagine the doc will have his hands full," Luke said.

"You're right," Rachel said. "I'll tend to Shannon, and you men see if you can help the others who might be trapped or injured."

Garrett followed Rachel back to the boardinghouse, shaking his head. "Not even married an hour, and she's already bossing you around."

Luke grinned wide. "Ain't it great! She's bossing you, too, in case you didn't notice."

Shannon felt Garrett's chuckle as it rumbled in his chest. She longed to have family—to feel the closeness these cousins felt for one another. But she was alone in this world—and she wasn't even sure if God was still on her side.

~

Using his left hand, Mark fumbled with his shirt button. "Ahh!" He flung his hand in the air. With this stiff cast keeping his right hand and wrist immobile, the pain was less, but even the simplest of jobs was nigh on impossible. The turkey egg bump on the back of his head ached, and his vision blurred if he turned his head too fast, but the wound had stopped bleeding. He looked down at his shirt and tried to fasten it again. He'd have thought someone had greased that little booger. He blew out a breath and flipped the irritating button with his finger. Who would notice his shirt partially undone with everything else that had happened?

He slapped on his hat, then realized it didn't fit right, what with his head bandaged and all. He adjusted the sling around his neck and marched out of the doctor's office, ready to help with the cleanup. The line at the doc's office had been long, but fortunately, most injuries were minor. In fact, his was one of the worst. And it wasn't the storm that had taken him down, but a bumbling Irish gal. Thank goodness nobody knew that except those who'd been in the cellar. He doubted Garrett or Jack would have reason to mention it to anyone.

Mark bent down and picked up a board lying in the street. When his vision cleared, he examined the plank but was unable to tell which building it had come from. At the end of the street sat a growing stack of debris, and he walked over and dropped the board on it.

Dan Howard dumped an armload of fragmented timbers, broken dishes, and unrecognizable things. "You oughta be takin' it easy, Mark. No one expects you to work with your injuries."

Mark shrugged. What had he done? Dumped one lousy board on the pile.

The mayor lumbered up beside them and tossed a broken chair on the growing stack. He patted Mark on the shoulder. "Yes sir, Mark Corbett's as good as they come. You won't find a finer citizen than him. Most men would go home and take it easy after being knocked out, but not Mark."

Shifting his feet, Mark winced from the compliment. He, least of all, deserved any praise. He was nothing but a scoundrel in sheep's wool. The problem was, nobody knew it but him. He longed to be a good citizen, a man people looked up to, and they did. But he was a phony, and there was nothing he could do about it. He craved the respect of the good, upstanding citizens of Lookout, but he didn't deserve it. One deed done years ago had been all it had taken to ruin his life.

The pastor had said confession was good for the soul, but Mark had never told a single person about what had happened in the small town of Abilene. He'd been a young man away from home for the first time, seeking adventure—and he'd certainly found it. The trouble was that adventure had almost destroyed him. He kicked at a piece of wood lying in the street. Maybe he should tell Garrett what happened.

His brother could be bossy and a tease, but he was a good man. Mark couldn't stand the thought of Garrett looking down on him because of what had happened. Or lowering his opinion of him.

Mark stuck part of the mercantile sign under his arm. *Sorry, Lord. I know You must be disappointed in what I did down in Abilene.* He shook his head and looked for something else to do. Hard work would pull him out of this foul mood.

He glanced around and felt his heart warm. The Lookout townsfolk might have their differences on occasion, but when disaster struck, they joined in and worked together to set things right.

"Mark!"

He swung around and found Rachel on the boardinghouse porch, waving at him.

Dodging the remaining debris—two shiny new coffeepots from the store, several articles of clothing, tree branches, and other items—he strode toward the porch. He slowed his steps as he reached his destination. "How's your building?"

Rachel shrugged. "Not so bad. Some broken windows. A tree limb went through one window upstairs, and the storm must have gotten the others. It's the weirdest thing, but there's a fork stuck in the wood just outside one of the upstairs bedroom windows."

Mark shook his head. "I've heard of strange things happening during tornados."

"Me, too." She lifted her chin. "How's your head?"

"Not bad. Better than my wrist, I reckon."

"So it was broken?"

Mark nodded.

"That will make it hard for you to do your bookwork and load freight."

He hadn't even had time to consider that yet. Garrett was the muscle man, did most of the loading of the freight, but he left the ledger and recording of information to Mark. It would be weeks before he'd be able to write again. What in the world would he do about that?

"Since Garrett's not so good with numbers and paperwork, I suppose you might need to hire some help." Rachel must have read his thoughts. Her eyes sparkled. "What about seeing if Miss Bennett or Miss O'Neil could assist you? That way you'd be getting some help back for the money you're out on their room and board."

Mark held up his hand, palm out. "Just hold your horses. The last thing we need is one of those women coming in and changing things all around."

Rachel shoved her hands to her hips and swung one side of her mouth up. "Nobody said anything about making changes, Mark."

"Well, isn't that what women do?"

She shook her head and crossed her arms. "You and your brother have been alone too long. It wouldn't hurt either one of you to marry."

Mark backed up several steps. "No thanks. I'm happy for you and Luke, but don't go playing matchmaker."

Rachel chuckled. "You're a fine one to be making that statement after you and Garrett ordered all those brides for Luke."

Mark backed up some more, taking care to avoid the debris. Time to get back to work. All this talk of matchmaking was making him antsy. "That was mostly Garrett's doing."

He tipped his hat and turned, but not before he heard Rachel's comment that he was as much responsible as Garrett. And she was right. He never should have allowed himself to get caught up in Garrett's scheme to find Luke a bride. But where his brother was concerned, good intentions never got him anywhere. Somehow, Garrett always managed to make Mark see his side of things. But no more. At twenty-seven years of age, he should be man enough to stand up to his brother.

He was tired of living in Garrett's shadow. Tired of working in the freight office, tired of hauling goods back and forth from Dallas to the ranches and smaller towns in the area. He had his own plans. His own dreams. And it was time he started reaching for them.

Chapter 3

Leah Bennett hoisted her skirts and attempted to climb out of the ditch again. Just like the previous four times, her foot slipped on the rain-soaked mud, but this time, she slid back and stumbled, falling to the bottom of the gully filled with cold runoff from the storm. Water dampened her backside and drenched the last dry spot on her dress. Having lost half of her pins, her hair threatened to fall in a pile around her shoulders. She shoved a handful out of her face and stared at the hill again. Somehow, she had to make it to the top.

The child who had wailed all during the storm, making Leah's eardrums ache, kicked his scream up another notch. Though frustrated to the core with his tantrum, part of her wanted to say, "I know just how you feel."

"Hurry up. The rest of us want out of here, too." The boy's father, one of the farmers who lived outside of town, wrinkled his brow and glared at Leah, as if all their problems were her fault.

A branch half the size of Texas had broken off a giant oak tree and blocked their exit from the far side of the culvert—a much easier climb, she noted. The section of the ditch where the man, his wife, and son had hidden sported moss-covered sides too steep to climb.

"Get a move on, lady. We need to get our boy into some dry clothes afore he catches his death."

His wife gasped. "Don't say such a thing, Herman."

Leah looked up at the steep incline again. She hadn't wanted to hide out from the storm in the grimy ditch, but when she'd tried to get into the church, it had been crammed full of people. A stranger had grabbed her arm and dragged her to this ditch, but he'd crawled out as soon as the tornado passed, saying he had family to search for. Now, she was stuck in the muck and mire of the ditch and couldn't get out. Could things get any worse?

A rope landed with a loud thud right beside Leah, and she jumped.

"Give me your hand, and I'll help you up, ma'am."

Leah looked past the thick hand that reached for her and found its owner. A huge, broad-shouldered man, probably six foot four at least, waited for her response. Past him, she could see the sky had brightened, and patches of blue peeked through the thinning cloud cover. None of the storm's ferociousness that had sent the whole town scurrying for cover remained. They had tornados in Missouri, but she'd never had one breathing down her neck, trying to devour her before.

"If you prefer, you can tie the rope around your waist, and I can haul you up."

Leah winced. That made her sound like a piece of freight. Standing, she shook out her skirt. She'd never get all the mud and stains from this garment, and she couldn't afford to lose one of her few dresses. Thin as they were, they were all she had.

Gathering her strength and fortitude for another attempt up the slippery slope, she stepped forward. The man above her looked well capable of lifting her weight. Wasn't he the town's blacksmith or something like that?

She wiped her muddy hand on her dress and held it up. He grabbed her around the wrist and pulled. Her body flew upward, but her feet felt as if they were anchored in quicksand, and for a second, she thought she'd be torn in two. But a sucking smack sounded, and her feet followed her body. Even her boots were still attached. Good thing, since they were her only pair.

She landed hard on solid ground and wavered, trying to regain her balance. The man kept a hand on her shoulder until she quit wobbling. She glanced up—way up into a pair of eyes so dark she couldn't distinguish the pupils from the irises. He nodded and released her, moving past her to help the family still in the ditch.

Watching him so effortlessly help the woman up and then gently reach down to receive the squalling baby quickened something deep inside of Leah. The man's wide shoulders had to be at least three feet across the back. If her father had matched her up with a man like this instead of that ancient curmudgeon, she'd have never run away.

The father of the baby shinnied up the slope, using the rope. He shook the big man's hand and smiled for the first time since the storm. "Thanks for coming to our rescue, Dan."

The big man—Dan—nodded and turned back to Leah as the family walked away. "You all right, ma'am?"

Leah snorted a laugh and looked down at her filthy dress. "Do I look all right to you?"

His gaze traveled down the length of her body, and a crooked smile tugged at one side of his mouth. "A little mud don't change a thing. You're mighty fine in my eyes."

Leah's heart skipped a beat, and she glanced up to see if he was serious. His eyes held no humor, no jesting. "Well. . .uh. . . thank you, Mr. . . ."

He yanked off his stained hat. "Howard, ma'am. I'm Dan Howard."

"Leah Bennett."

That quirky smile returned. "I know who you are, ma'am. I reckon the whole town does."

Leah's smile melted, and she pursed her lips. "I suppose you're right. Thank you for helping me out of that ditch."

"Happy to help, ma'am." He tipped his hat again and looked past her as if he wanted to be on his way. "Reckon I'll go help out at the store. Looks like it caught the worst of the storm."

Leah gasped as she noticed its remains. All that was left of Fosters' Mercantile were the floorboards, and debris of all kinds littered the boardwalk and street nearby. Even worse, the Foster home, which sat right behind the store, was lying in a crumpled mess across Bluebonnet Lane. Two dozen or more of the townsfolk were helping with the cleanup. How would the town get by without its only store? She allowed her gaze to roam over the small town. Thankfully, most buildings were still standing, though a number of them had minor damage and broken windows.

But what about the boardinghouse? Everything she owned in the world was in her room on the second floor. She stepped past Polly and Dolly Dykstra's garish pink house and gazed down Bluebonnet Lane. Relief flooded her to see the lovely Victorian home still standing. Painted a soft green with white trim, the house was always inviting.

At least it had been until the owner had agreed to marry the town marshal—the same man Leah had come to town to marry. Now things at the boardinghouse were uncomfortable, even though Rachel tried hard to make Leah and Shannon feel welcome.

Leah had hoped to find employment of some kind and to save enough money so she could find a small place to rent. If only she was a man and could do carpentry or window repair, she'd have it made. Instead, she could sew and clean, but who would pay her to do that? Most men would marry rather than hire a woman to do such menial chores.

Leah sighed and walked toward the boardinghouse. She needed to get changed and see what she could do to help with the cleanup, and she needed to get this dress soaking if she was to have any hopes of salvaging it.

Her life felt like that dress: muddy, torn, a mess. How was she going to get by?

Something shiny on the ground snagged her attention, and she bent and picked it up. How odd. How could a hand mirror get thrown so far from the store or the home it came from and not get broken?

It was like a message from God. Yes, she was wet and mangy as a stray dog after a thunderstorm, but God had brought her through the storm without a scratch. Yes, she was stuck in Lookout, but God had provided room and board for her through the Corbetts. But she couldn't live off of them forever and maintain her dignity.

What she needed was a husband. Her thoughts turned back to Dan Howard. Yes, he was strong and fairly comely, but was he a man she could spend the rest of her life with?

She shook her head, knowing the truth. She wanted a man with more standing in town than the livery owner. A man who didn't smell like horses when he came home each night. No, Dan Howard wasn't her idea of the perfect husband.

Rachel Davis added the final batch of potatoes to the stew and stirred it with the long, wooden spoon Luke had carved for her. She'd used her largest kettle and hoped it would be enough to feed the hungry mob cleaning up the town. Of course, once Jacqueline spread the word for folks to come and eat at the boardinghouse, other women would probably bring food here as well. Feeding folks at the boardinghouse just made sense with her having the biggest table in town, but even then, they'd have to eat in shifts or over at the café.

Footsteps sounded behind her, and she smiled. Luke ran his arms around her waist and tugged her back against his solid chest. He leaned down and nibbled on her earlobe and ran kisses down her neck. Finally, he sighed and rested his chin on her head. "Some wedding day, huh?"

Rachel turned in his arms and laid her head on his chest. "Certainly not the way I'd imagined our special day, but at least nobody will ever forget it."

Luke chuckled. "You're right about that. I'm just thankful nobody was hurt too bad."

"It amazing that there weren't any deaths, considering how fast that twister pulled together and attacked the town."

Luke brushed his knuckles along her cheek. "I'm sorry, Rachel. I wanted this to be the happiest day of your life."

"It is. Don't you know that? I married the man I've loved all my life. Nothing can ruin that." She smiled up at her handsome husband. "I still can't believe we're actually married."

"Oh, believe it." He leaned down and melded his lips to hers. At first, he was gentle, exploring, but then he became more urgent, staking his claim on her. And she didn't mind one bit. The back door slammed shut, and she and Luke jumped apart like a courting couple caught spooning instead of newlyweds.

Jacqueline's eyes widened, and she grinned. "Caught you smooching, didn't I?"

Rachel snickered as Luke's ears turned red. "You might as well get used to kissing in front of our daughter. You are her pa now."

Luke's mouth tilted up on one side, doing funny things to Rachel's insides. Oh, how she loved this man. A man she had thought would never be her husband. But God had worked a miracle and moved mountains of persistent regret and refusal to forgive.

"I like the sound of that—Pa."

"Me, too!" Jacqueline hurried over and wrapped her arms around both of them. "I wanted you for my pa almost since the first time I met you."

Luke pulled back from their embrace and cocked one eyebrow at Jacqueline. "From the first time? I seem to remember nearly getting drowned in the river the first time we met."

Jacqueline giggled. "Well, maybe it was when you adopted Max."

"Where is that ol' mutt, anyway?" Luke asked.

"Where do you think? Hiding in the jail. All that tornado ruckus scared him half to death."

Reluctantly, Rachel pulled away and stirred the stew again. The aroma of beef, onions, and other vegetables filled the air, blending with the scent of biscuits baking in the oven. "You two scoot on in to the dining room and set the table. I want things ready when folks start coming in to eat."

Luke shook his head, but his eyes glimmered. "Not even married three hours, and she's already bossing me around."

"Might as well get used to it," Jacqueline said. "She bosses me around all the time."

Rachel laughed with her daughter and husband. For far too long, this house had lacked joy and laughter. In spite of all that had happened today, she felt giddy. Tonight her dreams would come true, and she would be Luke's wife in all ways.

She walked to the back door and stared up at the clearing sky. The cool temperatures that followed on the coattails of the storm were giving way to the normal August heat. A bead of sweat trickled down from her right temple, and she swiped it away.

So many forces had worked to keep her and Luke apart, but the storm had come too late. She was Mrs. Luke Davis, and nothing could change that now. Rachel grinned up at the sky. "Thank You, Lord."

Leah stood in the hallway, wishing she could shrivel up and blow away like a piece of dust. She hadn't meant to eavesdrop—to see the marshal kissing Rachel or to overhear their private moments with Jacqueline. She'd only come to see if Rachel needed any help before venturing back outside to aid in the town's cleanup.

Though truly happy for Luke and Rachel, Leah couldn't help feeling disappointed that she wasn't the one married. She longed for a home of her own and a husband coming home each night, but after helping Ma tend ten younger brothers and sisters, she could well do without the child. She never wanted children. They were so much work, and a woman never had a moment to herself when she had a brood of young'uns. But what man would marry a woman who didn't want to bear him children?

Luke and Jack were in the dining room, rattling silverware and plates as they set the table. Leah backed up a few steps, hoping the floorboards didn't creak, then walked to the kitchen door, making her footsteps sound louder than normal. She cleared her throat. "Um. . .I was wondering if you needed some help."

Rachel spun around from the pot she was stirring and smiled. "That would be nice, Leah. I wouldn't normally accept your help, since you're a guest here, but with the wedding and then the storm. . .well, I hadn't planned to cook today, but it seemed the thing I could best do to help. People will need to eat after all their hard work cleaning up the aftermath." She blushed, as if she hadn't planned to make a speech.

"I don't mind helping. I thought I'd go back outside and work some more after changing clothes, but I'd prefer not to get all muddy again."

Rachel, still in her wedding dress, glanced around the near-spotless kitchen. "Hmm. . .the stew isn't ready, so we can't dish it up yet." She snapped her fingers. "Why don't you check on Shannon and see if she needs anything. She badly twisted her ankle running during the storm and is resting in the parlor. Then you can slice the pies. I made extra so I wouldn't have to bake for the next few days since. . .um, well, since I was getting married."

Leah smiled. "Congratulations. It was a very nice wedding."

Rachel chuckled. "Thanks, and wasn't that party afterward something?"

"I'm sorry your reception was ruined by the storm."

Rachel shrugged. "At least most everybody had eaten their cake."

Leah studied the ground a moment, curious about something but reluctant to ask. A table covered with a lacy cloth had been used to hold gifts from the townsfolk. The table had been piled high with handmade towels, table coverings, jars of food, baskets of fresh produce, and even a ham or two. She hated the thought of all those things being destroyed in the storm. "What happened to all your gifts?"

"Most things were spared. Folks grabbed an armful as they raced into the church. Only a few jars of beans were broken. It was awfully kind of folks to think of those gifts at a time like that."

Leah nodded. "People in Texas seem friendlier than where I'm from."

Rachel moved over to a bowl that held dough and started rolling it out. "Texas is a rough land, even in this modern time. People here stick together and help their neighbors. It's how we survive against the odds."

"Well, I'll just check on Shannon now." Leah slipped back into the dim hallway. Rachel hadn't said anything about her or Shannon moving out of the boardinghouse, but it must be uncomfortable for a newlywed to live with the two women who had been vying to marry her husband.

Glancing in the door to the dining room, she saw Jack race around the far side of the table and stop, grinning back at Luke, eyes gleaming. "I've got the last fork, and you can't have it." The girl's singsong voice sounded playful and teasing. One would never know she'd taken cover from a nasty storm less than an hour before.

Luke growled and lunged for the child. She squealed and ran back into the kitchen. "Save me, Ma!"

Leah shook her head. Such playful nonsense would never have been tolerated in her parents' home. With so many mouths to feed and her father a poor farmer, everyone was expected to work. Hard. There was little time for fun.

She stopped in the doorway to the parlor. Shannon lay on the sofa with one arm over her eyes. Her boot had been removed from her injured foot, which looked swollen even from across the room. How would she manage to get up stairs this evening when it was time to retire?

Leah tiptoed into the room, not wanting to wake her friend if she was sleeping. They'd been opponents, both competing for Luke Davis's affection. She hadn't treated Shannon very nicely in the past, mainly because she'd been so desperate to win the bride contest, but now they were in the same wagon.

A floorboard creaked, and Leah froze. Shannon lifted her arm and looked out from under it. She smiled, though pain creased the young woman's forehead and dulled her normally bright eyes.

"Rachel asked me to check on you. Do you need anything?"

"That's kind of you, but I'm fine."

Leah glanced at Shannon's ankle. It looked twice the size it should be. "Does your ankle hurt much?"

"Oh, 'tisn't too terrible."

Shannon attempted to sit up. She grimaced and stared at her ankle. " 'Tis a fine kettle of fish I'm in."

Leah rushed forward to help her. "I imagine in a couple of days your ankle will be almost back to normal."

"Aye, you're probably right, but I had decided to accept the Corbetts' offer for a ticket out of town."

Leah felt her own eyes widen at the woman's unexpected declaration. She dropped in a side chair. "But where would you go? I thought you had no relatives in America."

Shannon pressed her lips together until they turned white. "I don't, but 'tis so awkward here now that Rachel has married. Don't you think?"

Leah nodded. "Yes, but Luke and Rachel are good people, and she runs this boardinghouse. They will have others staying with them and sharing their table most of the time."

"Aye, 'tis true. But not the women who competed to marry her husband."

Leah wrung her hands together. Shannon was voicing the very same thoughts that she'd had ever since the day Luke announced that Rachel was the woman he loved. "What else can we do besides bide our time until we find someone else to marry or some kind of employment?"

Shannon shook her head. "You could return home to your family."

Leah stiffened her back. "That's not an alternative."

The pretty, auburn-haired woman's gaze flickered from Leah to across the room and back. "If I'm not stickin' my nose where it doesn't belong, might I ask why you can't?"

"It doesn't matter. I just can't." Leah stood. "If there's nothing you need, I'll go help Rachel." She spun around and scurried from the room like a rat caught raiding the pantry. She should have just told Shannon the truth—that her father had for all intents and purposes sold her to a creepy old man. If she returned home, she'd be expected to marry Mr. Abernathy. She shuddered, just thinking of his leering gaze and the white hair that grew from his ears and nostrils. No, she'd rather marry an Apache than that old curmudgeon.

Chapter 4

Mark snapped the pencil in half and tossed it across the room. The pieces clinked against the window, drawing a curious glance from a passerby. He exhaled a frustrated sigh. "How am I supposed to tally the ledgers and do bookwork if I can't write? Seems like the doc could have left more than just my fingertips free of this wretched cast."

"Patience, patience." Garrett propped his feet on his desk and sipped his coffee. "I've been saying it for a while: We need to hire some help."

"I thought you wanted to hire someone to lend a hand with deliveries, not the bookkeeping."

"Well. . .that changed when you busted your wrist. We could get someone to work in the office, and you can keep going with me on deliveries."

Mark harrumphed. "Fat lot of help I'd be. I can't lift freight until this heals." He held up his hand with the cast on it.

"You can drive the wagon while I sleep." Garrett grinned.

Mark tossed a paperweight at him. Garrett dodged it, flailing his arms like a young bird trying to fly, and fell out of his chair. Mark chuckled for the first time since the storm.

Garrett sat on the floor, his arms on his knees, and shook his head. "You're sure in a foul mood, brother."

"You would be, too, if you only had one hand to work with." Mark knew he was being a cantankerous grump, but he could use a little sympathy. The problem was, Garrett wasn't offering any. His brother had no idea how hard it was simply to do feats like getting dressed, shaving, or tending to his daily needs. Mark had just about decided to grow a beard. He'd nicked himself four times shaving today. Too bad Lookout didn't have a barber.

Garrett righted himself in his chair and sipped his coffee again. Mark strode over to the coffeepot, carrying his cup. He stood staring at the pot for a second before he realized he couldn't lift it and hold the cup at the same time. He smacked his cup on Garrett's desk, drawing a raised brow from his brother, and then poured his coffee. The fragrant aroma wafted up, calming him.

"I could have done that if you'd asked me to."

Mark scowled. "I'm not totally helpless."

Garrett grinned. "I noticed you managed to eat just fine with your left hand. Learning to write shouldn't be all that hard."

Mark ignored him and studied the map on the wall behind Garrett's messy desk. A pin was stuck in each of the surrounding towns where they delivered the freight they picked up in Dallas once a week. They'd been two kids from a poor family—two kids who'd pulled plenty of pranks and practical jokes—but they had realized Garrett's dream of starting a freight company and had built it into a successful business. In the beginning, the townsfolk had bets going on how quickly the Corbett Freight Company would fold up, but by the time he and Garrett had grown up and the business started taking off, the brothers had gained the respect of the town.

Respect was something Mark cherished. He'd had none growing up. Their father had drunk away what little money he made, and their mother took in laundry and cleaned the saloon just to get by. Mark liked having people look at him with respect in their eyes, but he knew he didn't deserve it.

And he was soon going to have to face facts. He no longer wanted to be in the freight business. He had dreams of his own. Dreams that had been squelched but refused to go away. He just had to figure out how—and when—to tell his brother.

Shannon closed her book and stared out the parlor window. The morning sun shone bright, and few traces of the storm still remained other than the damage to the buildings and trees. Boards covered most of the window openings she could see, and piles of broken wood and debris still littered the lot where the mercantile had been. Sweat trickled down her chest and back. Though only midmorning, the temperature was sweltering enough to sear bacon on an anvil.

After two days, her ankle was better, but she still had to stay off her feet a while longer per the doctor's orders. Walking was difficult, but she far preferred the pain to having Luke Davis carry her up and down the stairs, not that he wasn't capable of doing so.

"Silly lass." She heaved a sigh, reminding herself that he was no longer a free man. All her hopes and dreams had been placed on marrying him, but it wasn't to be.

She flipped open her book, and the wrinkled page of a letter stared up at her. Shaking her head, she knew it was foolish to write such a missive, but doing so had helped her in a small way. She glanced around the room, even though no one was there other than her. The wooden furniture gleamed with the fresh waxing it had received yesterday, and dust had not yet had a chance to settle and dull the shine. Two matching settees sat on opposite walls with a quartet of side chairs sitting at angles to the settees, and several small tables helped fill the room. A piano, not used since she arrived, sat looking as lonely as she along the far wall.

Smoothing open the letter, she stared at the words. What kind of person wrote a letter to a dead woman?

Dear Mum,

I miss you so much and wish you were here. I miss your smiles, your hugs, and kisses on my cheek.

You won't believe this, but I'm in Texas now. 'Tis such a grand, wild state, Texas is. Cowboys fill the streets, sometimes hooting like banshees and firing guns, but the marshal quickly confiscates their weapons and gives them some cooling-down time in his jail.

Shannon twisted her mouth up, disgusted with herself. The marshal, again. Shaking her head, she continued reading.

Lookout—'tis such an odd name for a town—is small compared to some of the Texas towns I traveled through on my way here from Louisiana. Things are so much drier than in our homeland. I miss the green of Ireland.

There's a high ridge across the river where outlaws and later soldiers used to watch for their enemies, so I've been told. That place is called Lookout Ridge and is where the town's name comes from. There's a river west of town that flows to the south. Then it makes a sharp turn at the ridge before traveling eastward. A pool formed there, and the townsfolk use it as a swimming hole when the water is deep enough. I have not been, though 'twould feel grand on a hot day like this one. Thankful for fall, I'll be.

I participated in a bride contest—have you ever heard of such a thing? Only in America. 'Twas quite an event. People for miles around came to town to see the competition and judging. Three women, me being one, traveled here to marry the same man, but one bride turned out to be an outlaw and is now in prison or jail somewhere. I've never been so close to an outlaw, unless one counted Da as one—forgive me, Mum. But Carly didn't seem like an outlaw. Lonely like me, she was, and I think she wanted to live a normal life. But 'twas not to be for her—nor for me.

Shannon's eyes stung, and she attempted to smooth out a place on the letter where several tears had dropped and crinkled the paper. Footsteps drew near, and she stuffed the missive into the book, slammed it closed, and held the novel against her chest.

Rachel stepped into the room and smiled. "How are you doin'? Anything you want?" Her gaze traveled around the room, as if searching for anything out of place.

Shannon shook her head. What she wanted was to live somewhere else, even though she loved her room upstairs. 'Twas the nicest place she'd ever stayed, yet she wanted to be free of the awkwardness that existed now that Rachel had married Luke. But the town had nowhere else a decent woman could stay. If only she hadn't injured her ankle, she would have been gone by now, on yesterday's stage. But to be fair, Rachel had been only kind and had tried hard to make the best of the situation. To act as if nothing had happened.

"It's a bit warm in here. Mind if I open a few windows?" Rachel smiled, the glow of being in love, of being a newlywed lingered about her. She pushed up a window, allowing in a gentle breeze that fluttered the curtains. She opened another, and a stronger gust cooled the room a small measure.

"You sure you don't need anything? Some tea or lemonade, maybe?"

"Nay, but I thank you. I would just like to be up and about, helpin' somehow."

"I'm sure you must be bored half to death." Rachel tapped her forefinger against her lips. "Perhaps there's some way you could help with the meals. I'll think about it and let you know."

Shannon nodded her thanks as Rachel started to leave.

The boardinghouse owner suddenly stopped and then came back into the room. She twisted her hands together, then lifted her pale blue eyes to gaze into Shannon's. "I know things seem difficult for you now. I can't imagine what you're going through, not knowing what the future holds, but I believe that God brought you to Lookout for a purpose."

She glanced toward the window, and when she looked back, her cheeks had a red tinge. "Though marrying Luke is no longer an option, there are a number of fine men in Lookout and others who live on surrounding ranches who would love to find a good woman to marry."

Shannon's cheeks warmed, and she turned to look out the window. A wagon drove by with a big man driving the team. Probably one of the town's fine specimen of a man.

"Don't give up, Shannon. Trust that God has a purpose for

bringing you here. He doesn't make mistakes. It took me a long time to learn that lesson." She flashed a smile and hurried from the room, as if she'd just uttered a speech she'd been building up to give.

Shannon laid her head back and stared up at the ornamental plaster design in the ceiling. Could Rachel be right? Had God merely used her supposed marriage to Luke to bring her to town for another purpose? It had been so long since she'd believed that God cared for her. Nothing but bad had happened since she came to America, and she'd spent the past few days since the storm dwelling on those things. Believing God had guided her steps and brought her to Lookout for some grand purpose was too mind-boggling to consider. Why would He care about her?

She shook her head and tried moving her foot. Her ankle didn't hurt as much as it had. Sitting up, she rearranged her skirts and tried putting some weight on her foot. A sharp stab made her suck in a breath. She grabbed the side pillow and smacked it against the settee. She'd do about anything to feel useful and to get her mind off her troubles. Leaning back down, she lifted her foot onto the pillows that had kept it elevated.

What she needed to do was figure out where she'd go when she left Lookout. There were a myriad of tiny towns like Lookout in Texas, but did she want to stay in the state? At least it was somewhat familiar now.

One thing she knew was that she had no desire to return to Louisiana. Only bad things had happened to her there. Maybe she'd go to Dallas. She'd heard it was a big city and would surely have opportunities for employment for a woman.

Her hand ran over the edge of the letter. It wasn't finished and probably never would be, for she'd lost the desire to complete it. Hasty footsteps sounded on the front porch, but where she lay, she couldn't see the visitor. A quick knock sounded, and the door opened.

"Rachel? Luke?"

'Twas one of the Corbett brothers, but she couldn't tell which from the sound of his voice. She scowled, not wanting to see Mark. What could she say to him? She felt a clod for being the cause of his broken wrist. If he hadn't come to her aid, he'd still be fine and not suffering, but she might well be dead.

"Hello?" Garrett stopped in the parlor doorway, and Shannon held her breath, hoping he wouldn't notice her. He looked down the hall, up the stairs, and turned his head. His eyes sparked when he saw her. He tipped his hat and grinned like a rogue. "Just the person I wanted to see."

Shannon sat up straighter, combed a loose strand of hair behind her ear, and peeked at her skirt to make sure it covered her ankles. Why would he be wantin' her? Would he expect her to pay the doctor's fee for setting Mark's arm? He'd be sorely disappointed, for she had not a penny in her handbag.

"Morning, Miss O'Neil." He approached, still grinning and his sky blue eyes twinkling.

" 'Tis a fine day, Mr. Corbett." She nodded, fearing the man was up to no good. Having been on the short end of his interfering with other people's lives, she was wary of him. 'Twouldn't happen again.

"Indeed, it is."

Rachel entered the room, wiping her hands on the bottom of her apron. "Garrett, what brings you here today? Luke's out somewhere doing his rounds."

"I don't need him anyhow. Came to talk to Miss O'Neil, here."

Rachel's brows lifted, and she made no effort to hide her surprise. "All right. Can I fetch something for you to drink?"

"No, thanks. I'm fine. Just had my last cup of coffee for the morning." He shifted from foot to foot and fiddled with the hat in his hand.

Rachel's gaze darted to Shannon. "Would you. . .uh. . .like me to stay?"

Garrett chuckled aloud. "No need. You know I'm a perfect gentleman."

Rachel's brows dashed clear up under the edge of the scarf that held her long, brown hair away from her face before they dropped back down. "I'm not so sure about that, Garrett. You're a rascal and a prankster."

Garrett's smile grew even wider, as if she'd offered him the greatest of compliments. "True, but I'm always nice to the ladies."

Shaking her head, a bemused smile wrinkled her lips. She looked at Shannon. "Would you like me to stay?"

Part of her wanted to say aye, but she didn't fear this man, in spite of all the trouble he'd caused her. "Nay, I'll be fine. If he bothers me, I'll conk him on the head with your lamp."

Rachel splayed her hand across her chest, her eyes dancing with mirth. "Oh, not my new lamp. Please. Use that footstool down there beside the settee. It's made of walnut and sturdy enough not to break against Garrett's hard head."

A wounded look crossed Garrett's face. "Ladies, please. I've simply come to do business with Miss O'Neil. I promise her virtue—and everything else—is safe."

"All right then. I suppose I'll go back to my kitchen. But if you need me, Shannon, just holler." Rachel left the room, casting a curious glance back over her shoulder at Garrett.

He grabbed a side chair and pulled it closer to Shannon. Even though she'd told Rachel not to stay, not knowing what Mr. Corbett wanted made her apprehensive. What business could he possibly have with her?

He placed his arms on his legs and leaned forward until his face was just three feet from hers. His startling blue eyes were the exact same shade as his brother's. His straight hair was a wee bit darker than Mark's curly blond hair, and though they looked similar, there was something about Mark that appealed to her. Something that wasn't affected by Garrett's presence.

"How's your leg? Better? Can you walk yet?" He fired questions like a shooter fired bullets.

" 'Tis somewhat better, but I cannot put much weight on it yet."

"Hmm. . .we can work around that." He stared into her eyes. "The reason I'm here is that I want to offer you a position of employment at Corbetts' Freight Office."

Chapter 5

Leah trotted downstairs to the lower floor of the boardinghouse. She simply had to find something to do or she'd go batty. As she reached the final step, she heard voices coming from the parlor. Slowing her steps, she glanced in as she reached the doorway. Shannon sat on one of the settees with her feet lying across the cushion. Her shoes were off, and one ankle had been wrapped in a bandage.

Garrett Corbett had moved one of the side chairs closer to the settee so that he could sit facing Shannon. What could he want with her? Maybe he was just checking up on her since his brother had been partially to blame for her injury. She longed to listen, but Garrett was speaking in such a low tone, and she knew eavesdropping was rude, so Leah forced her feet to keep moving.

She found Rachel in the kitchen, where the woman spent a large portion of her day. Leah knew what slaving over a hot stove for hours at a time felt like. Hadn't she cooked hundreds of meals for her family? At times she missed her parents and brothers and sisters, but she wouldn't return home for all the pecan pie in Missouri—and there was plenty, to be sure. She'd worked from before sunup to well after dark and never seemed to catch up. Her mother's health was poor from bearing so many children, and

Leah felt guilty at times for abandoning her, but her twin sisters were old enough to help out, and it would cause the girls to grow up.

Leah leaned on the door frame. Besides, if she'd stayed at home, by now she'd probably be married to old Mr. Abernathy and wouldn't be helping her ma anyway.

"Oh, Leah. I didn't see you standing there." Rachel rested her floured hand over her chest. "Do you need something?"

Leah straightened. "Sorry, I just got caught up thinking about home."

Rachel returned to braiding the lattice top of her apple pie. "Do you miss it?"

Leah pressed her lips together for a moment, fighting a smile. Rachel had an almost perfect handprint on her chest from the flour. Once she regained her composure, she nodded. "Sometimes I do."

"But not enough to return home?"

She shook her head. "No."

"Might I ask why?" Rachel paused, holding a strip of dough in the air.

What could she say that didn't make her sound selfish? That she didn't want to care for her siblings all the time but rather wanted a life of her own? That she couldn't marry the man who all but purchased her from her father? That she'd wanted an adventure before settling down to marry?

Leah fought back a snort. Well, she'd certainly gotten that, hadn't she?

She looked at Rachel, who still watched her. "I suppose it mostly comes down to the fact that I couldn't marry the man my father wanted me to."

Rachel's eyes widened. "You were betrothed?"

"No, not betrothed." She pressed her lips together and cocked her mouth up on one side. What did it matter if Rachel knew? She wasn't the kind of person to tell everyone. "There was an older man in town, one with a goodly amount of money, I'm told. He offered my father a sum of money to marry me, and my pa accepted."

Rachel's mouth opened and closed, reminding Leah of a fish.

"Your father sold you? I can't imagine how awful that must have felt."

Leah shrugged, not wanting to reveal the depth of her pain and betrayal. After working herself half to death, not socializing as young girls her age did because of her responsibilities, nearly raising her siblings because her ma had taken to her bed so often, her pa showed his gratitude by selling her. It sounded so much worse when someone said it out loud. "I might have gone along with it if the man hadn't been nearly as old as my pa and rather creepy. He gave me the shivers."

"I'm sure." Rachel wiped her hand on a towel and crossed the room. She laid her hand on Leah's shoulder. "I know it must be uncomfortable at times for you and Shannon to live here with Luke and me, but you're welcome for as long as you need to stay."

Leah offered a weak smile, grateful for Rachel's hospitality and compassion. "I'm much obliged for that. I'm not sure what I'll do. I just know I don't want to go back home."

Rachel nodded. "Would you like to sit down and have some tea?"

Leah glanced past her to scan the kitchen. Rachel tended to keep things tidy as she worked, so it didn't look as if there was much to do here to help her. Other than the area where she was making pies, the only thing out of place that Leah saw was a jar of what looked liked last night's stew. "I was actually hoping you might have some work I could help you with. I'm sick to death of doing nothing."

Rachel turned and looked around the room. "Um. . .well. . .I feel odd asking a guest to help me."

"You didn't ask; I volunteered."

Smiling, Rachel nodded. "I suppose that's true. Well, I was going to take a basket to Mrs. Howard, but you could do that if you wouldn't mind."

"Sure, I'd be happy to. It would give me a reason to go outside and take a walk."

"Clara's been ailing for a while. Her son takes good care of her, but he works hard, and I like to help them out with a meal now and then." Rachel opened her pantry door, rummaged around for a minute, and pulled out a basket and a bowl covered with a towel. "She's Dan Howard's mother. Do you know Dan? He runs the livery."

Leah felt her cheeks flush at the name of the man who'd rescued her from the ditch after the storm. She was grateful that Rachel didn't look up and was busy packing the basket.

"You'll like Clara. She's a real sweetheart, but she doesn't get out much anymore. I know caring for her is a weight on Dan's shoulders, but he's a good son and does what he can. Don't know that he's much of a cook, though." Rachel tossed a grin over her shoulder. "Clara is always so thankful when I bring food."

A few minutes later, with directions to the Howard home, Leah walked out the kitchen door and around the side of the boardinghouse. On her right was a house known around town as the Sunday house. It was a small structure with a roof that slanted down in the back like a lean-to. She'd gone there once to deliver a meal to the marshal and had seen the inside. One big room was used as a parlor, except it also had a table and chairs. In the back of the room where the roof slanted down was the bed. What would happen to the house now that the marshal was living at the boardinghouse with his new wife?

It would be the perfect place for her to set up a home, if only it had a kitchen and stove. But she had no means of making money to pay rent. She shook her head. No sense dreaming such foolish dreams as living on her own.

She crossed Bluebonnet Lane and stared at the pile of rubbish that had been the mercantile. People had been working to clean up the mess since the storm, but there was still a ways to go. How would the town survive without it? What a shame.

Two men she didn't recognize, who were working on the edge of the property closest to her, straightened and then tipped their hats. She nodded and smiled but continued walking. As she walked down Oak Street, she noticed that the Foster home, which had sat right behind the destroyed mercantile, was also severely damaged. A tent had been set up behind in the back yard behind where the house had sat. Were the Fosters living there? Or maybe they were keeping the stock they'd salvaged in it. Those poor people. How would they ever manage to rebuild after this devastating loss?

She shifted the basket to her other arm and counted houses until she found the Howards' home. The house looked well maintained, with a fresh coat of pale yellow paint and white trim on the woodwork. The lace curtains were closed, though. Could Mrs. Howard be resting, even though it was midmorning? What if she was asleep?

Leah hated bothering the woman if that was the case. She looked past the house to the livery and nibbled her lower lip. Perhaps she should ask Mr. Howard if it was all right to visit his mother. Besides, it would give her a chance to see him in his workplace.

She continued walking and stopped at the side entrance of the livery. Her eyes took a moment to adjust to the dim interior. The placed smelled of hay and horses and reminded her of her pa's barn. Six stalls ran down one side of the gray, weathered building, three of which contained horses.

She found Dan at the front of the building unloading a wagon filled with large burlap bags with another man's help. Dust motes drifted lazily on fingers of sunlight that stretched into the livery, attempting to drive back the shadows. Dan hoisted a heavy-looking bag over one shoulder and toted it to an empty stall, where he dropped it. The other man did the same but seemed to have a harder time lifting and carrying the large sacks. As Dan reached for another bag, the back of his shirt pulled tight across his shoulders, making Leah's mouth dry. Muscles flexed in his tanned forearms, made visible by his rolled-up sleeves. Dan was the tallest man in town, so far as she knew, and though he was wide-shouldered, he didn't look to have an ounce of fat on him. Perhaps she shouldn't be too hasty in ruling out Dan Howard as husband material. He had come to her rescue, after all.

She stepped farther into the livery, and when Dan's gaze landed on her, he stopped suddenly without acknowledging her. He stared for a moment, then turned and dropped the bag he'd been carrying. He strode across the livery to a bucket and tossed water on his face, arms, and hands, then dried off on a towel. He ran his hand through his brown hair and turned to face her as he rolled down one sleeve.

"What can I help you with, ma'am?" His gaze ran down her length, then back up, not in a leering way like Mr. Abernathy's but as if she was someone he cherished. She swallowed hard.

"I. . .uh. . .Mrs. Hamil—I mean Mrs. Davis sent over some soup and other things for you and your ma's dinner. I noticed her curtains were closed and wondered if I should knock on the door or just leave the food out on the porch. Of course, I'd hate for a stray dog to get into it, so I came over here to see if you thought your ma would be awake." Leah clamped her mouth shut. She was rambling more than the ivy running up the side of the town's only bank.

"It's near lunchtime. Give me a few minutes to tally up with Stephen, and I can walk over to the house with you."

Leah nodded. She wasn't sure if she wanted his company, but she'd best get used to the idea. At least she'd have a chance to get to know him better. But was that what she really wanted?

Yes, he'd been kind to her, but, no, he didn't fit her idea of the perfect husband. At least Dan should be a good protector, built like he was. She waited several minutes until he paid the man who'd brought the sacks, and then Dan Howard walked toward her, his near-black eyes capturing hers as he moved lithe and steady in her direction. "I'll carry that for you, ma'am."

She handed over the basket and tried to swallow, but it felt as if she had a biscuit stuck in her throat. Goodness.

She peeked at him as they fell into step together, walking toward his house. She liked how it felt to walk next to a man and could almost pretend he belonged to her. He stood a solid eight inches taller that she, and with his hat back on, even more. His long, brown hair was pulled back and tied with a leather strand. Though only near noontime, his beard had already started growing back in. She guessed his age to be somewhere around the midtwenties.

She stumbled on a rock, taking several quick steps to keep from falling, and his hand shot out, gently clutching her arm and stabilizing her. Heat stormed to her face. If she hadn't been gawking at him, she wouldn't have missed a step. "I, uh, thank you for assisting me."

His lips turned up on one side. "My pleasure."

At the porch steps, he handed her up, then followed. With him on the covered entryway with her, the area seemed to shrink in size. Dan opened the door, and stood back, allowing her to enter first. His steady gaze made her squirm, and she broke eye contact and stepped into the dim parlor. Heat slapped her in the face, and she wondered if a fire was burning in the stove.

Dan entered behind her leaving the door open. He went straight to the front window and lifted it open. The lacy curtains fluttered on the light breeze. "Sorry about it being so hot in here. When Ma has one of her spells, she keeps things closed up." He shook his head, walked through the dining room and into the kitchen, and opened the back door.

Dan set the basket on the kitchen worktable. "I'll check on Ma and be right back. Have a seat if you'd like."

"Don't make her get up on my account," Leah called as he disappeared around a corner. She looked around the Howard home. In the parlor, a sofa and two wingback chairs faced the fireplace. Though the furniture looked old, the room was tidy. Against one wall was a table covered in harnesses, bridles, and tools she didn't recognize. A dining table and hutch resided in the next room, which sported faded floral wallpaper. The house smelled musty, with the lingering scent of leather polish. Leah tugged at her collar as sweat trickled down her chest. How could Mrs. Howard stand this heat? And if she was so ill, how did she manage to keep her house clean?

A rustling sounded just before Mrs. Howard shuffled into the room with Dan close on her heels. A wide smile graced the woman's wrinkled cheeks. "Welcome, my dear. I'm so glad you could visit."

Leah pulled out a chair at the table, and Dan helped his mother to sit. "I'm happy to make your acquaintance, Mrs. Howard."

"Sit down, dear. Dan doesn't mind fixing the food, do you, sweetie."

Leah glanced up at Dan. She hadn't planned on staying to eat and preferred to leave the food and go, but she didn't want to disappoint this kind woman. Dan shook his head and turned to go in the kitchen.

She leaned toward Mrs. Howard. "Excuse me for a moment, if you would."

Leah followed Dan into the large kitchen, and he turned around, surprised to see her. "Let me do this, and you go sit down."

His thick brows lifted. "That wouldn't be proper. You're our guest."

Leah shook her head. "Nonsense. I came to help. Show me where the bowls are and then go visit with your ma."

He opened a cabinet and pointed at the bowls, as if she hadn't seen them. He rubbed the back of his neck, obviously uncomfortable with her serving him. She strode past him and reached for the bowls at the same time he did. His hand landed over hers. She lifted her gaze to his, and her heart stampeded. For a moment neither moved. His calloused hand warmed hers, and ever so slowly, he drew back, trailing his fingers over hers. All breath left her lungs until he stepped back. Her hand trembled as she took the bowls off the shelf.

Dan leaned back against the cabinet, his gaze watching her every move. What had just happened? She'd only ever been attracted to one other man—and Sam Braddock had been just a boy compared to Dan. Sam. How long had it been since she'd thought of her first love?

She busied herself so she could forget both Sam and Dan. "Do you have a ladle?"

Leah removed the jar of stew from the basket and unscrewed the lid, sending a savory fragrance into the air. Footsteps sounded behind her, and a ladle appeared over her shoulder. All she had to do was turn around, and she'd be in Dan's arms. She kept her feet from moving a speck and snared the ladle. "Thank you."

"Smells good," Dan's voice rumbled behind her, and her hand shook a little more.

"Do you...uh...have something to drink? For dinner, I mean?"

He stepped up next to her and grabbed a pitcher from the corner. "I'll fetch some water."

Leah finally caught a decent breath once he left the room. What was wrong with her? She was acting like a lovesick schoolgirl. She was acting like her twin sisters did over a cute boy.

Forcing her mind back on business, she ladled the stew into two bowls and carried them into the dining room. Mrs. Howard smiled again, and her faded eyes twinkled.

"Dan's a good son. He takes better care of me than most men would for their old mother."

Leah set a bowl in front of the woman and placed the second bowl on her right. "It's good that you have him then."

Mrs. Howard nodded. "Don't know what I'd do without him."

Leah returned to the kitchen and rummaged around until she found the silverware and some napkins. She folded the fabric and laid the silverware on top.

"But there's only two place settings. Where's yours, dear?" Mrs. Howard looked up with such a hopeful gaze that Leah hated hurting her feelings.

"Mrs. Davis is expecting me for dinner at the boardinghouse, but thank you for asking." She hurried back into the kitchen and placed the biscuits on a plate and then sliced some of the cheese that Rachel had sent.

Dan stepped back through the open door, his face and hair dripping wet, just like the tin pitcher. He held it up. "Got the water, and it's fairly cool."

Leah smiled at his exuberance. She couldn't imagine her own pa doing something so menial as fetching water. "That should taste good on a warm day like today."

He nodded and placed his fingertips in the top of three glasses and carried them into the dining room. In a half second, he stormed back to the kitchen. "Where's your bowl?"

Leah opened her mouth, prepared to explain again, but stopped. Rachel would probably figure out that she'd stayed and eaten with the Howards if she didn't return for the noon meal. Why not stay and learn more about the Howards and maybe even brighten an old woman's day? "I didn't get one, but I will now. Thank you for inviting me."

A few minutes later, they all settled down to eat. Mrs. Howard's eyes watched Leah and continued to sparkle as she nibbled her stew. Was the woman always so friendly?

"Tell us about yourself, dear."

Leah winced. She dreaded talking of her family. She dabbed her lips with the napkin and sipped some water before answering. "I lived on a farm in Missouri with my parents and brothers and sisters before coming here."

"We lived on a farm—before my Owen died. I'd always hoped for a big family, but Dan is my only child to survive. Do you have many siblings?" Mrs. Howard broke off a piece of biscuit and stuck it in her mouth.

Leah peeked at Dan. He shoveled his food in as if he hadn't eaten in weeks. He caught her watching and winked. Leah yanked her gaze back to Mrs. Howard and realized the woman had seen their exchange. "I come from a big family—eleven children at last count."

Dan dropped his spoon, but his mother's smile widened. "How wonderful. And where do you fit in that lineage?"

"I'm the oldest."

"Ahh. . .no wonder you came here."

Leah hastened eating her stew and stuffed the last bite into her mouth. She needed to leave before this woman had her married off to her son. Leah stood, and Dan hopped up. "Please, keep your seat. I'll just refill your bowl and then wash the dishes."

"Nonsense, Dan can do those."

Leah waved her hand at Mrs. Howard. "I don't mind. In fact, I'd like to help you, and that's the best thing I know to do."

Mrs. Howard leaned toward her son and mumbled something that Leah was certain sounded like, "She's a keeper, son."

Grabbing the bucket sitting by the back door, Leah charged outside. She pumped water as fast as she could. She couldn't help thinking about Dan. She liked him—a lot. He had a nice home, a healthy business—or so it seemed—and he was fine to look at. Yes, sir, she definitely needed to reconsider him as husband material.

Chapter 6

Mark slammed his book shut and muttered a frustrated sigh. Reading while riding in the wagon on a good day was difficult, but trying to hold the book steady with one hand just didn't work. His shoulder banged into his brother's as the creaking wagon dipped into a deep rut and then careened back out.

"Is that another one of those law books you're always reading?" Garrett glanced sideways. "Sure sounds like boring stuff to me."

"Yes, it's a law book, and no, I'm not reading. Can't hold it steady enough."

"What do you find in there that's so fascinating? I picked up one of those fat books and read a few paragraphs and found it more boring than looking at a wood wall all day." Garrett shook his head.

"It's just interesting to me. I can't explain it." Mark studied the rolling hills dotted with wildflowers. The tornado may have torn up the town some, but the heavy rains it brought had caused the grass to green up and wildflowers to bloom again. The sky was a brilliant blue with a few white, puffy clouds drifting by.

What would Garrett say if Mark told him that he was thinking about quitting the freight business and hanging out his shingle as a lawyer? He'd probably starve to death in Lookout. No, if he were to become a lawyer, he'd need to move to a bigger town like Dallas.

Mark rubbed his jaw. He'd left Lookout once before, and the situation couldn't have ended any worse.

"I've got a surprise for you."

Mark's gaze shot back toward his brother. The hair on his nape stood up. A surprise from Garrett could mean anything from sand burrs in your underwear to oiled front-porch steps. He nearly broke his neck the day he stepped on those and his foot flew out from under him. Then there was the time when they were still boys and Garrett hitched the wagon and handed the reins to Mark. When he slapped the reins on the horses' backs, instead of the wagon moving forward, Mark was yanked to the ground and dragged halfway across the county because Garrett hadn't hitched the harnesses up right. Narrowing his eyes, he glanced sideways at his brother. "What kind of surprise?"

Garrett grinned wide. "Guess you'll just have to wait till we get back home to find out."

His curiosity rising, he nudged his brother's arm with his elbow. "Go on, tell me what it is."

"Nope. Not gonna do it."

Great. Mark scowled. Now his imagination would run faster than a stampeding herd of cattle in a thunderstorm. What if his brother ordered *him* a bride, but no, he wouldn't do that again. Mark peeked sideways. Would he?

He adjusted the brim of his hat to keep the sun's glare from reaching his eyes. No, Garrett wouldn't order more brides when they were already supporting two. "You know, it's costing us a pretty penny to pay room and board for those two brides."

Garrett nodded. "Don't I know it. I guess we should be grateful things turned out like they did, and that third bride ended up going to jail."

He remembered how Carly Payton, a member of an outlaw gang, had pretended to be Ellie Blackstone, the third bride who came to Lookout to marry Luke. Carly was a pretty thing with her black hair and deep blue eyes, but she had a roughness to her. She was in prison now, and the real Ellie Blackstone had returned home with her brother. "I heard Rachel say she was writing to that outlaw bride."

"Yeah, that's what Luke said. If anyone can help her change her ways, it's Rachel."

"Yeah." Mark swatted at a mosquito on his hand. "Luke sure seems happy these days."

"Marriage agrees with him."

"You ever think of marrying up?"

Garrett grimaced but kept his gaze on the road ahead. "Yeah, sure. But I've never met a gal that interested me enough that I wanted to make a lifetime commitment to her. What about you?"

Mark thoughts raced straight to Annabelle. At one time he thought he'd die if she didn't become his wife. But he wasn't the one who had died. He gritted his teeth. What a disaster that whole situation had been. Since then, he hadn't trusted himself around women and had kept his distance. "No, I don't reckon I'll ever marry."

Garrett fired a surprised look in his direction. "Why not? Don't you want kids of your own? We've got a solid business, and you could support a family now—at least if we don't have to pay for those brides much longer."

Mark didn't answer. He couldn't tell his brother what had happened back in Abilene. All his life he'd wanted Garrett's approval, just like he'd want his father's, before their pa lost his business and became a drunk. But Mark never seemed to measure up to his pa's expectations. He liked to read, and his ma had encouraged it while she was alive, but Pa wanted him to work more, like a man, rather than spend his time with book learning. His pa couldn't read and didn't understand how a book could take you to a time and place you could never travel to yourself. In a book, Mark had explored the Alaskan wilderness, traveled on a ship to Europe, and fought pirates and rescued royalty and—damsels in distress. His thoughts returned to Miss Bennett and Miss O'Neil. Both were more or less stranded in Texas thanks to him and his brother. Who would rescue them?

"We've got to do something about those brides." Garrett

successfully yanked Mark right out of his musings.

"Such as?" Mark asked.

"We need to find them work or else someone to marry."

Mark held up his good hand. "Just hold on. You aren't concocting another one of your schemes, are you?"

Garrett held a hand to his chest. "You wound me."

"No, I just know you."

"I've been thinking on the situation, and what would it hurt to talk to some of our customers and see if any of them are looking to marry?"

"It could hurt a lot. We might lose all our customers."

"Stop being so cynical. We'll just ask around, and if we find someone wanting to marry, we can tell them about Miss Bennett and Miss O'Neil."

Mark leaned back in his seat and tugged his hat down farther. "No thanks. I'm not stepping in that pile of manure."

"You're making a mountain out of a molehill. I'll do the asking if you're not at ease doing it."

"Fine. You do that." Mark tried to get comfortable. He wasn't even sure why he'd come along since he couldn't load or unload anything unless it was something small. It wasn't likely they would get robbed since they were just hauling wood and building supplies for the new store and a few smaller crates for local ranchers, but you never knew when someone with a gun would show up. Even if he couldn't shoot, having two men together might steer away some thieves.

Mark listened to the jingle of the harnesses and the peaceful plodding of the horses' hooves. A light breeze stirred the hot air, cooling him a bit. He thought about the book he'd been reading. For years, he'd consumed law books. He felt ready to set up shop as an attorney, but somehow he had to find a way to tell his brother. And he had to consider leaving Lookout again. He could only hope and pray this time would turn out far better than the last.

A buzzing intruded into Mark's dreams, and he jumped, swatting a fly away from his ear. His blurry gaze sharpened, and he saw Garrett standing on Flip Anderson's porch.

"It's like I said, both those women thought they'd marry the marshal, but we all know that didn't happen."

Flip yanked off his hat and rolled the brim. The tall, thin rancher sported a moustache nearly as wide as his face. "Yeah, I kinda felt sorry for them gals. So ya think they're willing to marry someone else?"

Mark narrowed his eyes and glared at his brother. What was Garrett doing? He climbed off the wagon and stretched the kinks from his body, then ambled toward the porch. A dipper of cool water would taste good about now.

Flip nodded. "Mark, good to see ya."

"You, too. Mind if I grab a drink from your well?" Mark smiled at Flip, then cast a warning glance at Garrett.

"Help yerself. I just hauled up a fresh bucketful." He pointed across the yard to the well, as if Mark hadn't already spotted it.

The screen door creaked, and Flip's mother, Lucy Anderson, walked out carrying a tray covered in cookies, cups, and a coffeepot. Mark swung around and headed back to the porch.

"Mornin', boys. Come have a sit-down and take some refreshment." Mrs. Anderson set the tray on the porch table and started pouring coffee. After serving the men, she poured herself a cup and sat down. "I heard you talkin' about them gals. I sure wish that my Flip could marry one of 'em."

Flip turned beet red and seemed to be studying the porch floor as if something was wrong with it.

Garrett chuckled. "Well, maybe we need to figure out a way to get him together with them so they can meet face-to-face."

Lucy stared out toward the pasture, where several dozen head of short horn cattle grazed. "Hmm. . .I could invite them leftover brides out here for dinner. Maybe one of 'em would take a shinin' to my Flip."

"Ma, that don't hardly seem proper, inviting two unmarried women clear out here."

"And one of them has a twisted ankle. She hurt it during the storm." Mark wasn't sure why he'd come to the boardinghouse brides' defense, but it didn't seem right that everyone was talking about them.

"Yeah, it'd be better if you went to town, Flip. Maybe what you boys need is to have a shindig of some kind so's the local bachelors could meet them gals." Lucy helped herself to another sugar cookie. The older woman's faded blue eyes twinkled. "I'd sure like to see my Flip married before my foot's in the grave."

Flip's head jerked toward his mother. "Don't talk like that, Ma."

"I'd just like to know someone was taking care of you after I'm gone, that's all. And I'd sure like to see my grandkids."

Flip jumped up so fast the coffee cups rattled. "I reckon I ought to head back to the barn. Got a horse with the colic. Need to keep my eye on her."

Mark held back a chuckle. Seems like he wasn't the only man who didn't want folks matchmaking him.

They said their good-byes and returned to the wagon. Mark climbed up beside his brother, well aware that the wheels were churning in Garrett's mind. "What are you thinking?"

Garrett slapped the reins down on the horses' backs and yelled, "Heeyup!"

The wagon lurched forward, groaning and creaking. Once back on the main road, Garrett leaned his elbows on his knees, allowing the reins to dangle in his fingers. "I've been ruminating on some ideas."

Mark's stomach clenched. What was Garrett up to now? Whatever it was, he wanted no part of it.

"What do you think about starting up a social on Saturdays? Have some ladies fix food, have some music and dancing?"

"Why?" Mark's voice rose higher than intended.

Garrett's gaze darted in his direction. "So we can get those gals married off. That's why."

Mark leaned back and crossed his arms, shaking his head. It might sound like a half-decent plan, but something was sure to go wrong. "That's a bad idea, brother. You best leave well enough alone."

"Nope, I think it's a great idea. We'll get unmarried men to come, and sooner or later, someone's bound to catch the eyes of them gals."

"Have you considered that it will cost money to hire musicians?

And you can't expect the women to come and bring food for free all the time. If you did something like that, you'd need to hire Polly to cook, most likely. Besides, there are dozens of unmarried men, and just those two gals. Doesn't sound like much fun for either side."

"Hmm. . ." Garrett rubbed his chin with his thumb and forefinger. "You're probably right about the food. But the single men around here are desperate. They won't care if they only get one dance with a pretty gal, but maybe we could invite folks from other nearby towns and ranches. Maybe some of the ranchers will bring their older daughters. You're right. We'll need more than the two boardinghouse brides for the men to dance with."

"I'm warning you. This is a bad idea."

"Aw, stop your fretting." Garrett glanced at him and grinned wickedly. "Don't forget about your surprise."

Mark heaved a sigh, and his mind raced. He had forgotten, and from the look in his brother's eyes, he had a feeling he wouldn't like this surprise much.

Shannon practiced walking around the parlor using a crutch the marshal had borrowed from the doctor's office. The long branch had a nub halfway down where her hand rested, and though the V under her armpit had been wrapped with fabric, she still found it uncomfortable. But if she was going to work at the freight office, she had to get mobile.

Her skirt snagged against the long stick, making forward progress difficult and throwing her off balance. A chuckle sounded behind her, and she took several small steps in a half circle until she was facing the other direction.

Rachel smacked her husband on the arm. "Don't you dare laugh at her."

The marshal pressed his lips together for a moment. "Sorry, but I think that crutch is too long."

"Well, cut it down to fit her." Rachel glared at Luke playfully with her hands on her hips.

He shook his head. "I can't. It belongs to Doc Phillips."

"Well, I don't see how Shannon will manage that bumpy street when she can barely get around the parlor."

Shannon stared at the newlywed couple. Rachel looked pretty clothed in her brown work dress with tiny yellow sunflowers on it. A fresh apron covered the garment, and her long brown braid fell down over her shoulder, hanging clear past her waist. Dressed in black pants and a medium blue shirt, Luke stood next to her, staring down at the stick that held Shannon upright.

Truth be told, she didn't like the crutch, but the marshal had been so nice to fetch it for her that she hated to say so. She tried again and managed three steps before she lost her balance. She reached for a nearby table and missed.

"Oh!" Rachel squealed.

Shannon's hand brushed the arm of the settee, but she missed it, too, and landed on the floor. Pain clutched her ankle and hand, but it was nothing compared to when she first injured her leg. She tried to push up from the floor, but her long skirts had wrapped around her legs, and she was stuck between the settee and coffee table legs.

How humiliating!

Hurried footsteps sounded behind her, and she closed her eyes. Could things get any worse?

"Are you all right?" Rachel leaned toward Shannon's face.

"Aye, but I do feel quite foolish."

"Do you mind if Luke helps you up?"

Shannon shook her head. "I'm tangled in my skirts."

A quick knock sounded, and Shannon peeked through the table legs. Garrett Corbett strode in. "Mornin', folks."

Heat raced up Shannon's cheeks. What would her new boss think?

His eyes widened, and he hurried forward to help Luke assist her up. Back on the settee, she rearranged her skirts and avoided looking at anyone. Would they all think her a clumsy fool?

Rachel picked up the crutch. "Shannon was trying this out to see if she could walk with it."

Garrett grinned. "Uh, let me guess. It didn't work."

Luke stood beside him chuckling, and Rachel glared at her husband.

Garrett forced a straight face. "Have no fear, I brought the wagon."

Warmth flooded Shannon's cheeks again. He didn't even think she could walk a few hundred feet. She thought about the crutch again. Well, perhaps he was right. But if she couldn't walk that far and rode the wagon to work, she'd be stuck at the freight office, dependent on the Corbett brothers—and that was the last place she wanted to be. Wasn't that why she'd accepted the position of employment in the first place? So that she could support herself instead of relying on them?

"Maybe she should wait a few more days before starting work," Rachel said.

Three sets of eyes fell on Shannon, and she resisted the urge to squirm. She'd already lost almost two nights' sleep worrying over working with Mark Corbett. If she didn't start today, she'd only worry more. "Nay, I'll ride in the wagon."

"Are you sure?" The concerned look in Rachel's eyes warmed her. Made her feel as if someone cared about her.

"Aye."

"Great. Then let's go." Garrett strode toward her and swooped her up without asking permission.

Shannon wrapped her arm around his neck and sat up stiffly. These Americans were uncouth and did as they pleased without so much as a by-your-leave. She thought back to being in Mark's arms when they were running from the storm. She'd actually liked him carrying her. Liked being close to him. Then why was she so nervous about working in the same office?

Garrett helped her up to the wagon seat, and she climbed aboard and sat down. Rachel reached up her hand and laid it on Shannon's arm while Garrett walked around the front of the wagon. "I'll come down in an hour or so and make sure things are all right."

"That's not necessary, but I thank you. I'm sure I will be fine."

"It's no trouble at all." Rachel smiled, winked, and stepped back. "Don't let those yahoos boss you around too much."

Shannon finally smiled. "I won't."

"Hold on." Garrett lifted the reins and smacked them down on the horses' backs. "Heeyah!"

The wagon lurched forward and then settled. Shannon held tight to the side and gazed at the remains of the store. Boards that were long enough to be reused had been stacked along the property line. A half-dozen men and women were sorting through the last of the rubble. "'Tis a sad sight."

Garrett looked to his left and nodded. "Mark and I brought in a load of lumber from Dallas yesterday. Got another couple of trips to make, and then there will be a store raisin'."

"I've never heard of such a thing."

"It's just like a barn raisin' except we're building a store. Since it's the only one in town, we need it to survive, so everyone's chipping in to help."

They passed the remains of the Fosters' home, and Shannon wished there was something she could do to help the older couple. A man tossed a bucket of water into the dirt road, and one of Garrett's horses jerked his head up and snorted. The wagon creaked down Bluebonnet Lane, then veered left onto Oak Street. They passed a number of houses before reaching the end of the road, where they made two quick left turns and ended up on Main Street. The boardinghouse rose up in front of her at the far end of the street. It surely was a lovely building with its soft green color and white trim. The porch practically begged people to stop and sit in the matching white rockers. Perhaps later she could do that very thing, but now she had to concentrate on learning her new job.

"Whoaaa." Garrett pulled the wagon to a stop and set the brake. He hopped down, patted each horse on the forehead, and muttered something before coming around to help her down.

Shannon's stomach swirled. She'd never worked in an office before. Aye, she could keep it clean and tidy once her ankle healed, but Garrett had said something about helping Mark with the recordkeeping. How would she know what to do? Was Mark even agreeable to teaching her or letting her work with him?

Surely if he'd not been, Garrett wouldn't have hired her. Yet she had a hard time believing Mark would assent. Even though he'd come to her rescue during the storm, he didn't seem to favor her for some reason.

Garrett lifted her down and held her steady. "Guess I should haul you on inside."

Balancing her weight mostly on her good leg, she broke from his gaze and looked around. The marshal had left the boardinghouse and now stood outside his office, talking to several men. Two ladies exited Dolly's Dress Shop and walked toward them, talking and laughing.

"Perhaps you could walk on my weak side and offer support." She eyed the women, who'd suddenly taken note of her and Garrett.

"Mornin', Mrs. Mann. Mrs. Jenkins." Garrett tipped his hat to them. "Nice day, isn't it?"

Both women smiled at the handsome rogue, then turned suspicious glances in Shannon's direction. Fortunately, they continued on past the newspaper office and turned in to the bank.

"Curious ol' biddies. You know they're just fit to be tied wondering why you're here with me."

Shannon's mouth turned up in a grin. Aye, she could imagine. She knew the two ladies were quite the busybodies, from their visits with Rachel at the boardinghouse.

"Shall we?" Garrett's brow lifted.

Shannon gently put weight on her twisted ankle and grimaced, not so much from the pain but from the fear that it would hurt. Garrett wasted no time, and hauled her up in his arms. He grunted as he carried her up the stairs from the street to the boardwalk, and Shannon was sure she'd never regain her dignity.

Garrett fumbled with the door handle, then shoved it open, and stepped into the freight office. She glanced around and noticed right off that one desk was immaculate while the other was quite the mess. The tidy one had to be Mark's. He always took time to dress nicely and combed his hair, whereas Garrett seemed like a ragamuffin, with his mussed hair and his clothing often wrinkled.

Mark entered from a side room. His eyes went wide, and his

mouth dropped open. Shannon realized Garrett still held her.

Mark's gaze narrowed as he took in his brother holding her. "Please tell me you didn't run off and marry *her*."

Chapter 7

Jack baited her hook, tossed it into the water, then sat back against a tree and waited for a bite. She plucked a strand of grass and leaned to her left, where her good friend Jonesy had fallen asleep in the warmth of the August sun. Holding back a laugh, she stuck the stem under Jonesy's nose and tickled him. His loud snores shifted to a series of grunts and gurgles, and he reached up and rubbed his nose without even opening his eyes.

Jack giggled and sat back.

"Why do you continue to pester him? His pa probably worked him like a plow mule since sunup." Ricky, her other best friend, picked up a rock and tossed it to the far side of the river.

"How come he got to come fishin'?"

" 'Cause his pa had a hankering for fish for dinner."

"Well, his loud snores are scaring them all away." Jack stared out at her fishing line, wishing for a bite.

"Nah, it's probably just too hot for them to care about eating." Ricky yawned and stretched. The summer sun had darkened his skin and turned his blond hair white. "So how do you like having the marshal for a pa, *Jacqueline*?"

Jack shoved Ricky in the arm. "Don't you call me that."

"Your ma told me to."

She leaned back, keeping a hold on her pole. "I don't care. I hate that name."

"Why? I think it's kind of pretty, for a girl."

Jack swung her gaze back to meet Ricky's dark blue stare. Was he teasing her? His thick hair hung over his eyebrows and almost into his eyes. He was nice-looking, for a boy. "You really think so?"

He shrugged one shoulder. "Yeah, I guess."

Jack gazed up at the sky and considered that. She'd never once thought her given name was pretty, and she still preferred Jack, but it was nice to know someone liked her name.

The arms of the sun reached through the canopy of trees overhead, touching the river with its light. The quiet water rippled on the gentle breeze, but the heat still made her hot. She swiped at a river of sweat tickling her cheek. They ought to be swimming instead of fishing, but her ma would have a conniption fit if she swam with the boys.

A proper lady never swims with gentlemen, she'd said. But then, Jack knew she was far from a lady—or being proper for that matter. It seemed that women had so many rules they had to abide by while men got to do whatever they wanted. Why couldn't she have been born a boy?

Jonesy's snores grew louder, and she gave him a shove. "Hush up! I cain't hear myself think."

He murmured something in his sleep and rolled over with his back to her. Maybe now he'd be quieter.

She thought about her new pa and smiled. Things sure had changed since he'd married her ma.

"What's so funny?" Ricky asked.

"Aw, nothing. I was just thinking about all that has changed since my ma married Luke."

"Like what?"

She sat up straight and wrapped her arms around her knees. "I got my own room now. It's the yellow one upstairs, where that outlaw stayed."

"That must be nice. I share a room with my two little sisters. At least I got my own bed. Jonesy shares one with his two little brothers."

She leaned toward her friend. "I've got a double bed."

"All your own?"

"Uh-huh. I like it. Ma don't put her cold feet on my legs no more."

"That's no problem these days, as hot as its been. I get all sweaty at night, even with the window open. Half the time, I take my quilt and lay it on the porch or in the hay loft 'cause it's cooler to sleep there."

Jack nodded. "That's a good idea. I'd try it, but Ma wouldn't let me if she knew about it. She's such a worrywart."

Ricky stretched and rubbed his belly. "Maybe she won't feel so much that way once her and the marshal have some kids."

Jack bolted up. Thoughts of little brothers and sisters bounced around in her mind. "You think they will?"

He shrugged. "Couldn't say, but that's usually what happens not too long after a wedding."

Hugging her knees, she considered what it would be like to have a younger brother or sister. It would be fun while they were a baby, but she didn't think she'd like sharing her bed. "How long you reckon it would take?"

"For what?" Ricky yawned and rubbed the back of his neck.

"For them to. . .you know." She felt her cheeks grow warm. "To have a baby."

"At least nine months."

She leaned back and relaxed. That was a long while. Why, her whole life had changed in less than half that time, starting when Luke returned to Lookout after being away eleven years. And she'd met a real live outlaw, and her ma had even been kidnapped by one. Jack frowned, remembering how scared she'd been then. If her ma hadn't returned home, she'd have been an orphan. But now she not only had her ma, but a new pa, too. And maybe soon a new brother or sister. Yep, school was out, and life was about as good as it could get.

"You smell somethin'?" Ricky lifted his nose in the air and sniffed.

"Smells like a pigpen." Jack's gaze collided with Ricky's.

"Oh no." He looked past her just as she heard footsteps.

Jack turned and saw Butch Laird coming toward them, a fishing pole on his shoulder. As long as she could remember, he'd been their enemy. His pa was a hog farmer, and Butch always stank, just like he'd wallowed in the muck.

Jack stood. "Guess I'll head back home. We ain't catching nothin' anyhow."

"You don't have to go just 'cause of him."

"Ma don't want me around him. You know, since I got that black eye at the end of school."

Butch slowed his steps when he saw them. "Nice day for fishin', ain't it?"

"It was," Ricky said.

Jonesy sat up, rubbed his eyes, and sniffed the air, then looked up at Butch. "Thought I was dreamin' that I smelled hogs, but I really was."

"Go find your own place to fish, Laird." Ricky tossed a rock at Butch's bare feet, but the boy didn't move.

Jack reeled in her line, picked off the worm, and tossed it in the water.

"Hey, I coulda used that." Ricky shot her a glare.

"You can have the rest in my jar," Jack said. She wished she could go past Ricky to leave, but a downed tree blocked the way. She'd have to pass Butch. Holding her pole in one hand, she held her other hand over her nose.

Butch stared at her with his dark, solemn eyes. His skin had tanned even darker than Ricky's, reminding her of the rumor circulating that he was part Indian. His black hair hung thick and shaggy, where most mothers had sheared their boys' hair off for the summer. But Butch didn't have a ma and not much of a pa, so Luke had said. His clothes were torn and dirty. Though just thirteen or so, he was almost six foot tall, and half that wide. If he didn't smell so bad, she might feel halfway sorry for him.

He stood in the opening between the shrubs, so she had to squeeze close to him to get by. She held her breath and hoped she didn't retch from the stench.

Butch took a step, either to block her way or to get out of the way, she wasn't sure, but his foot flew out in front of him, shooting pebbles like bullets. His fishing pole flew one way, and he flailed his right arm, catching her right across the chest. Jack fell back onto the hard ground, hurting her hand on the rocks.

"Hey!" Ricky yelled and jumped up.

Before she could even check her sore hand, Ricky and Jonesy were on Butch. Though taller than both boys, Butch ducked his head and turned his back on them. When he wouldn't throw any punches, both Jonesy and Ricky stopped their assault.

"What's wrong?" Ricky's chest heaved. "You can hit girls but are a coward to face men?"

Jack's chest ached from the hard blow, and a few scratches marred her hand, but she didn't think Butch had hit her on purpose. He might be a bully, but she'd never seen him hit a girl. "Stop, y'all."

Ricky glanced down at her, anger filling his gaze. "A man don't hurt no woman."

"She ain't no woman. She ain't even hardly a girl." Butch mumbled as he straightened and cast a furtive glance her way. "Leastwise, she don't dress like one."

"But she's our friend." Jonesy ducked his head, growled loud, and struck Butch right in the belly. Butch backpedaled his arms, eyes wide, and fell backward into the river. He splashed and sputtered and then managed to stand.

Ricky hooted with laughter.

"At least he finally got a bath." Jonesy bent over, slapping his leg, and snorted. Jack just sat there watching them. She was grateful to her friends for their quick defense, but she kind of felt bad for Butch. She was sure he'd just slipped on the loose rocks.

Suddenly, Butch's face scrunched up, and he growled like a bear. Ricky and Jonesy both stood up straight and stared for a moment. Butch jolted into action, taking long-legged strides up the bank. Jack's two friends spun around and pedaled their legs but didn't hardly seem to be moving.

Jack jumped up, a scream ripping from her chest. She took off running toward town, not bothering to look behind her. Someone once said a person didn't have to outrun a bear—just outrun the slowest person in the group. She knew she couldn't beat Ricky in a race, but Jonesy was a cinch.

By the time she reached the edge of town, Jack's lungs were burning. She ran all the way to the marshal's office before stopping. Bending over, she sucked in air and tried to catch a breath.

Luke must have seen her, because his chair squeaked and he strode out of the office. "What's wrong, half bit?"

She gazed back in the direction she'd been running and saw Butch close on Ricky's tail. Jonesy was nowhere to be seen. She hoped her friend wasn't beat up or dead.

Luke pursed his mouth. "I'll take care of this. It's time that boy learned he can't pick on the good kids of this town. Maybe a few days in jail will make him think twice."

"But. . ." Jack didn't know what to say. If she told the truth, her friends might get in trouble, and she knew Jonesy's pa would take a tree branch to his backside. Ricky would be made to do extra work, and she wouldn't see either of them until school was back in session.

Luke glanced at her, then made fast strides to intercept Butch. Both boys stopped when they saw the marshal. She couldn't hear Luke's words but saw Butch talking with his hands up, as if defending himself. Luke took him by the arm and hauled him toward the jail.

Jack couldn't watch. Maybe Butch hadn't been the cause of this fight, but he'd started plenty of other brawls he'd never been punished for. Still, she didn't want to be there if Luke locked him up. She turned and started walking home.

"Hold up there, half bit."

Jack's heart jolted. She wanted to pretend that she hadn't heard Luke, but she knew he'd just follow her home. She turned around but didn't walk back toward him until he motioned for her to.

"Butch says he didn't do anything to start that fight with your friends. Is that true?"

Luke's piercing brown eyes gazed down at her, imploring her to tell the truth, but how could she rat on her friends when they were just protecting her? And Butch did say she wasn't even a girl. Maybe she should take his words as a compliment since she tried so hard to be a boy, but they just didn't sit right with her. She'd just tell as little of the truth as she had to. "He knocked me down, and Ricky and Jonesy were just defending me."

"That ain't true. I slipped." Butch's pleading eyes looked almost black compared to Luke's brown ones.

"Did you knock down my daughter?"

Jack's gaze darted toward Luke. She'd never heard him refer to her as his daughter. A warm feeling wrapped around her.

"I guess." Butch hung his head as if all the fight had gone out of him.

Luke's gaze swerved to Ricky. "Is that true?"

Ricky nodded his head, his blond hair shaking. "Yup, I saw him do it. Jonesy, too, but he. . .uh. . .he went on home."

"Hmm. . .well, I've had enough of you causing trouble in this town, boy. Maybe staying a few days in my jail will make you behave better."

Butch tried to pull his arm from Luke's grasp, his eyes wide. Almost crazy-looking.

Jack covered her nose. Now he didn't just smell like a hog, but like a wet, moldy one. "I cain't stay in yer jail. My pa expects me to tend to the hogs. He'll bust my hide if'n I don't."

"Maybe you should have thought of that before picking on a girl half your size." Luke hauled him toward the jail door.

Butch sent another frantic glance her way, but then he narrowed his gaze at her, sending caterpillars crawling up and down her spine. She could say he slipped, but her friends would get in trouble and be mad at her. Butch deserved being in jail, didn't he? Her chest still stung from where he'd whacked her.

She turned and trudged toward home, unable to look at him any longer. If he did deserve being in jail, why did she feel so bad?

Garrett kicked the door shut with his boot and carried Miss O'Neil farther into the office. A whiff of a soft floral scent whispered around Mark as she passed by, teasing his senses. He clenched his fist as thoughts of Annabelle surfaced.

To Miss O'Neil's credit, she didn't seem to enjoy being in Garrett's arms, but rather sat stiff. Prim and proper—at least as proper as could be in such a situation. For some reason he couldn't pinpoint, that made him happy. But why should he care?

Garrett set her down in Mark's chair, not his own, he noted. What was she doing here? He checked her ring finger and relaxed a smidgeon. Surely if Garrett had married the woman, she'd be wearing a ring. He tried to imagine his joke-playing brother and the shy Irish gal together, but the puzzle didn't fit.

An ornery grin revealed Garrett's straight teeth, and his eyes gleamed. Something in the pit of Mark's stomach curdled.

"Here's your surprise, brother."

Miss O'Neil's gaze jerked up to Garrett's face and then to Mark's. She looked as stupefied as he. Mark cleared his throat. "What are you talking about?"

Garrett crossed the room in three long steps and plopped down in his desk chair. "Did you forget I told you I had a surprise?"

"I don't understand." Miss O'Neil raised her hand and pinched the bridge of her nose.

"That makes two of us. What are you talking about, Garrett?"

Mark leaned against his desk and crossed his arms, keeping his back to Miss O'Neil. It was best he didn't look at the pretty woman. His expression would only trouble her, anyway.

Garrett leaned back and put his feet on his desk, looking smug. "You were complaining about breaking your wrist and not being able to keep up with the bookwork. Miss O'Neil needed to find work, so I offered her a job. Solved two problems at once."

"Well, she can't stay. I'll figure out something else." Mark crossed his arms and clamped his teeth together. He didn't need daily reminders of how he'd messed up his life.

Miss O'Neil gasped.

Garrett dropped his feet and rested his arms on his desk, all teasing now gone. "We need her, brother, and she needs us."

Mark closed his eyes, knowing the Irish gal couldn't see his face. How was he going to get out of this situation without hurting her feelings? But then it was probably already too late for that.

He pushed up from the desk and paced to the door, spun

around, and strode back to his desk. As much as he didn't like it, he could actually see the ingenuity of Garrett's plan. They were already paying Miss O'Neil's room and board, so if she worked for them, they might be out some additional money, but it wouldn't be nearly as much as if they hired someone else to keep the books and still had to support Miss O'Neil. And he didn't want just anybody knowing the state of their finances. The one favorable thing about Miss O'Neil was that she knew few people in town. He glanced at her, wincing at her troubled expression.

"There's been some mistake, I'm thinkin'. You'd best be helping me back to the boardinghouse, Mr. Corbett."

Garrett pursed his lips and stood. "Now see what you've done. You've ruffled her feathers."

Mark stopped right in front of his brother. "You could have at least discussed this with me first."

Garrett leaned closer. "There's nothing to discuss. We need her, and she needs a job. It's simple."

Mark didn't see anything simple about the situation. She reminded him of Annabelle, and that was the last person he wanted to think about. How could he work with her day in and day out? Maybe he could get her trained and then stay away from the office. Study his law books more. But they had a business to run. He shook his head and pressed his lips together.

"You don't have to look so disgusted, Mr. Corbett."

She stuck her cute little nose in the air and glared at him. Wisps of reddish-brown hair had escaped the net thing that held most of her luscious hair curled around her pretty face. Now that he'd taken time to look at her directly in the face, he realized she really didn't look all that much like Annabelle, other than her coloring. She was smaller, more petite, and younger—and dressed far more modestly.

Using the desk as support, Miss O'Neil pushed to her feet. "I shall leave."

She took a step, grimaced, and dropped back down in the chair. Mark had to admit that she looked pretty when she was riled. But could he work with her, day after day, when she reminded him so much of his past?

He ran his fingers through his hair and blew out a breath. His past wasn't her fault, and he wasn't being fair. "You can stay."

But he and his brother would be having a heated discussion tonight.

Chapter 8

Shannon sat stiff in the desk chair as Mark Corbett leaned over her shoulder, explaining the ledger books. With most of his right hand and half of his lower arm in a thick plaster casing, he couldn't write and keep the records.

Gathering her courage, she voiced a question. "Why does your brother not keep the books?"

Mark's lips pursed. "Garrett doesn't have an eye for figures and accounting."

She wasn't sure she did, either, but now that she was here, she would learn. She had to. Her independence and her very life depended on it. Having two unmarried men support her was humiliating and certainly not proper.

"So, does that make sense to you?"

Shannon's heart leapt. What had he just said? She'd been lost in her thoughts and not following along. "I. . .uh. . ."

Mark rubbed his hand across his cleanly shaven jaw and heaved a sigh. "Look, it's fairly simple when you've done it a while."

After his initial outburst, Mark seemed resolved to have her there, but she felt if he had his druthers, she wouldn't be. And if she could have walked out with dignity, she'd be gone. But Garrett hadn't taken her hint about leaving; in fact, *he* left without her, leaving her alone with his brother.

Shannon held her trembling hands in her lap. Every time the man came close, she shivered like she had in the frigid hull of that ship that had brought her family to America. To their deaths.

Mark opened a ledger book about two feet wide, sending up the scent of leather and old paper. He riffled through the large pages and stopped at the last page with entries. The date was two days before the tornado had hit.

"All right. In this book we keep track of each individual transaction, each thing someone orders. That's the file box over there where we file the order forms when we're done." He pointed to a rectangular metal holder sitting on a counter against the wall. The box had sheets of yellow paper standing upright in it, separated by metal dividers. "We record what each person has ordered on an ongoing basis."

She tried to wrap her mind around what he'd said, but she failed to see how the ledger and file box were different.

He moved around and sat on the edge of the desk, cradling his wounded hand with his other one. His cast looked awkward and uncomfortable. "Do you understand? If you don't, ask questions."

He stared at her. Oh, she had questions, but she hadn't learned enough to voice what they were yet. Maybe if he explained some more, she'd catch on.

He scratched his head and stared out the window. Shannon took a moment to study him. His jawline was more finely etched than his brother's, and his nose had a perfect slant. Both men had almost the same hair and the exact same eye color, though Mark's shorter dark blond hair had a curl that Garrett's didn't, tickling his collar in an enticing manner. He turned back to face her, and for a moment, she couldn't look away. Her breath caught at the intensity of his gaze. She loved the color of his eyes—a cross between the light blue Texas sky and a robin's egg—and they made her heart jump each time she looked into them. She might live a short life if that kept happening. Her heart could only take so much.

Breaking from his gaze, she looked down at the ledgers. How could she be thinking such thoughts about the man who didn't even want her here?

He cleared his throat. "Let's. . .uh, get back to work." He opened the middle desk drawer on the right side, pulled out a stack of papers, then shut it with his leg. "These are the orders for supplies. See how Mr. Foster's names is atop this one?"

Shannon nodded and noted the order for wood.

"This page shows Foster's order for a wagonload of lumber. This column shows the type of wood, this one the quantity, then the length, and the price. You record each of those in the appropriate columns on the ledger. Pretty simple."

Simple enough, if her mind wasn't befuddled by his nearness. His clean scent wafted around her every time he moved. She'd never known a man could smell so fresh. Even his clothing was spotless and wrinkle free.

"Miss O'Neil, do you need to take a break?"

"Nay, I'm. . .uh. . .beginning to understand. Perhaps if you'd permit me to record a few transactions, it would become clearer."

Mark nodded. He crossed the room, grabbed his brother's chair, and hauled it next to hers. Shannon's heart thudded like a dancer's feet pounding out a fast-paced jig. How could she concentrate when he was so near?

"All right. List Foster's name in the first column."

She dipped the pen in the ink bottle and did as asked, taking heed to make her printing neat.

"Now, see how he ordered different lengths and sizes of wood? Look across the top columns of the ledger and find the correct size of wood, then go across on Foster's line and record the amount ordered. There are columns for the other things people most often order, but if you can't find what you need, use the last column. There's room to write in the item description, if you write small. Try to be neat, because this is our permanent record."

She nodded, but his emphasis on neatness made her hand shake. She hadn't had call to write anything other than her name since coming to America. Pushing her fretful thoughts away, she recorded another entry. She dipped her pen into the bottle, and Mark heaved a boisterous sneeze. Shannon jumped. The bottle tipped sideways. Her hand shot toward it, but the ink spilled across the desk in a spreading pond.

Mark muttered something she couldn't make out and grabbed the ledger. "Bottom drawer. Ink blotters."

She tugged hard on the lowest drawer, pulled out a stack of blotting papers, and dabbed at the mess.

"Don't push on it." Mark snatched a stack of papers off the pile. "You have to dab it, or you'll press it into the wood."

Shannon sat back, feeling like the village *eejit*. She'd been here less than an hour and had already made a mess of things. Looking down to avoid Mark's glare, she sucked in a gasp. The ink on her hands had stained her dress. How would she ever get it out?

Mark threw the dirty blotters into the trash can. The pool of ink was gone, but a nasty stain marred his immaculate desk.

He shoved his hands to his hips and stared at it. Finally, he looked up at her. "I knew this wasn't a good idea."

He stormed out the back door, letting the screen slam. Shannon jumped. She wanted to flee back to her room at the boardinghouse, but she was stuck in Mark's chair. Tears blurred her eyes, but she forced them away. If she swiped at them, she'd probably end up with ink on her face. Oh, what a nightmare.

Leah had told her she needed to toughen up if she was going to survive living in Texas. But that possibility looked far slimmer now. Surely Mark would dismiss her, and if he didn't, how could she face him again?

A few minutes later, the bell over the door jangled. Shannon glanced up to see Rachel enter, carrying a teapot and two tin cups.

"How's it going so far?" Rachel's smile slipped from her face as she stared at Shannon. "What did those yahoos do?"

Shannon shook her head. "'Twasn't them. 'Twas me." She waved her ink-stained hand over the large blotch. "Not here one whole hour, and I've ruined Mr. Corbett's desk."

Rachel hurried over and set the teapot down on a clean corner of the desk. "Oh, dear. Is that why the men are gone?"

"Garrett left Mark and me alone right after dropping me off." She glanced down at her hands. "He hadn't even mentioned me to his brother. Mark was not happy at all about me being here. And then this happened."

Rachel sat in Garrett's chair and took Shannon's hand. "Things aren't as bad as they might seem. I've got a spare apron you can wear over your dress to hide the stain, and I would imagine the men can sand out the stain on the desk."

Shannon's heart flip-flopped. "You truly think it can be removed? I feel like an *eejit* for making such a mess."

Rachel smiled. "I'm afraid I have no idea what that is, but I'm sure you aren't one."

"I believe you say idiot or imbecile."

"Well, I know for certain you're not one of those. Let's have our tea before it's cold. Then I'll find Luke, and he can help you back home."

Home. Shannon liked the sound of that, but the boardinghouse wasn't her home. It was only a place she was staying until she could make it on her own or find a husband. In truth, she had no home.

Rachel held the lid to the pretty teapot covered with violets and ivy and poured tea into both cups. "I apologize for bringing tin cups, but I was afraid I'd break the china ones if I tried to lug them down here along with the pot."

" 'Tis fine. Thank you for thinking of me. I'm very glad you came when you did."

Rachel set a steaming cup of tea in front of her. Shannon sipped it, allowing the warmth to soothe her. "I don't know if I should be leavin' or stayin'. I need this job, but I don't think Mark Corbett wants me here."

"Maybe I could talk to him. I've known the Corbett brothers since I was a girl, and they're practically my relatives now. It's not like Mark to be unkind or inhospitable. He's a good man with a big heart. Far more patient and tolerant than most."

Shannon tried to get Rachel's description to match what she'd seen of Mark Corbett, but it didn't. Yes, he'd rescued her during the storm but had done so begrudgingly. And he'd been angry at her ever since, casting stormy looks her way whenever he saw her. For some reason, she brought out the worst of him. "I don't believe he wants me working here, but I so need the employment."

"Mark will come around. He doesn't like it when Garrett pulls something over on him." Rachel sipped her tea and gazed toward the window. "I don't know if you can tell, but Garrett is the oldest. Mark is the solid one, though, and Garrett is. . .well, let's just say he hasn't fully grown up yet."

Shannon smiled at that. "He does behave more like a lad."

"Yes." Rachel nodded. "Mark has always felt he followed in Garrett's shadow. Their pa didn't like that Mark could read and was studious, especially when he couldn't read and thought book learning was for womenfolk."

Swallowing hard, Shannon remembered how she had tried to please her da, but nothing she ever did made him happy. He'd wanted a son, not a wee lass. She ducked her head as the unpleasant memories of him repeating that every time she angered him made her tears burn her eyes. They were not so much different, she and Mark. Perhaps she'd misjudged him. All she'd done was cause him trouble, albeit not intentionally. She needed to prove to him that she had value. That she could ease his burden and do the work he needed her to do.

"I don't want to paint Garrett as a bad person. He has a good heart, but he just gets too carried away with his teasing and prank-pulling."

"Like when he ordered all of us brides for your husband."

Rachel's cheeks flamed. "Yes, like that. He wanted to help Luke get over me, but God had other plans." Rachel reached across the desk and laid her hand over Shannon's wrist. "I believe God used Garrett's scheming to get you and Miss Bennett to come to Lookout because He has plans for you here."

"Truly, you believe that?" A flame of hope flickered within Shannon's heart. Did she dare believe that her very steps had been orchestrated by the hand of God? She believed in God but felt He'd turned his face from her.

Rachel nodded and smiled, her pale blue eyes shining. "I believe it with all of my heart. If God can work the miracle He did to reunite Luke and me, it's a small thing for Him to bring you here—maybe to give you a husband, too."

Shannon so wanted to believe, but God had not answered many of her prayers since she'd come to America. Her parents had died in spite of the many pleas she'd sent heavenward. She'd lost the man she'd hoped to marry, and at the same time her only hope of support. And now she may well have lost her job.

Maybe if she could prove her worth, Mark might let her stay.

Rachel stood and stretched. "I'd better get back home and start on dinner. Noon will be here before we know it. I'll find Luke and have him come and get you."

"Nay, I'll stay, but if I'm not back by dinner, could you please send the marshal for me?"

Rachel nodded but stared at her with concerned eyes. "Are you certain?"

Shannon nodded. "If you could just hand me that ledger on Garrett's desk, perhaps I can show the Corbett brothers that I'm an asset and not a liability."

After having lunch at the café, Mark strode back into the office, and breathed a sigh of relief that Miss O'Neil was no longer there. But instead of enjoying that fact, guilt needled him. How had she gotten back to the boardinghouse? Had she hobbled home on her injured foot? Had his uncouth actions caused her more pain? More humiliation?

He crossed the office and stared down at the large stain on his desk. His mouth twisted up on one side. He'd worked hard to keep his desk looking nice, but Miss O'Neil had certainly made a mess of it. Thank goodness she hadn't spilled the ink on the ledger.

Speaking of the ledger, he looked around the room and found it on the shelf beside the file box. He snatched it up, determined to try and record the orders in spite of his cast. He'd just have to work slow—if he could even hold the pen.

He dropped down into his chair and opened the drawer that held the orders. At least half the pile was gone. His heart skittered. Surely Miss O'Neil hadn't opened the wrong drawer and used the orders to wipe up the spill. He tried to remember, but things had happened too fast. Trying to remember the details of all those orders would be a nightmare.

He yanked open the other drawers and searched them, then

he got up and rummaged around the stacks of catalogs and papers on Garrett's desk. He picked up the trash can and poked around the ink-stained papers but didn't see any of the completed order forms. He shoved his hands to his hips and looked around the office. Where could that frustrating woman have put them?

Seemed like every time he got near her, something unpleasant happened. She was like a bad luck charm. He lifted his nose and sniffed. Her flowery scent still lingered.

Heaving a sigh, he sat down and opened the ledger book. He found the page where the last entries had been recorded, and his hand halted. Several new pages of entries had been recorded in a slanted, feminine handwriting. He studied the entries, and each one looked accurate, based on his memory of those orders.

"Hmph! Would you look at that."

Maybe she was sharper than he'd given her credit for. But where were the order forms?

He carried the ledger back to the shelf and set it down. Then he thumbed through the file box until he found Foster's account card. Each of the items from Foster's last order had been recorded in the proper place, and the order form had been filed behind the account card as if he'd filed it himself.

Mark stared out the window, a slow appreciation for Shannon O'Neil growing within him. She'd stuck to her guns and finished her task, even though she'd been upset and hadn't been completely taught how to do the job. She hadn't tucked tail and hobbled back to the boardinghouse like he'd expected.

Evidently, she was quite capable of tending the books. But every time she got near him, something bad happened. Could he survive having her work here?

He thought about the worry in those big green eyes when she'd spilled the ink. She'd looked scared to death, as if he might strike her. He scowled, wondering what she'd endured in her young life that would make her so fearful when she'd just had an accident.

Yeah, she'd ruined the top of an expensive piece of furniture, but it could be repaired. He was certain he could sand out the stain and refinish the top of the desk. She didn't know how well he took care of his things and how it bothered him when other people didn't. Had his fierce reaction to the accidental ink spill wounded her?

He hung his head, ashamed that he'd lashed out and made her feel worse. Her feelings were far more important than a desk, and he was certain that he'd thoroughly stomped on them. A flicker of warmth welled up within him. A desire to protect Shannon O'Neil from further pain. As far as he knew, she had no one to take care of her. To watch over her.

He had no idea why and might well die trying, but the desire to protect her heated his chest.

Mark hung his head as another thought charged into his mind. Hadn't the very same reaction—the desire to protect Annabelle—been what had caused all his trouble in Abilene?

Chapter 9

Leah sat on the front porch of the boardinghouse, rocking her chair and staring out at the small town. She simply had to find some kind of work or she would go batty. But what kind of work could an unmarried woman do in such a small town?

When the Corbett brothers had offered to pay her way back home, she'd said no. Definitely, no. But maybe she should have allowed them to send her to Dallas or some other big town where there would be more opportunities for a woman.

At least here in Lookout, she knew a few folks, but in a big town, she would be alone.

The screen door creaked, and Shannon strolled out.

"Off to work, I see." Leah smiled. Now that they were no longer competing for the same man and were bound together by their similar situation, she and the Irish girl had become friends.

"Aye." She fanned herself with her hand. " 'Tis hot already. I will be happy when the weather cools some."

"Don't hold your breath. It may be awhile. I've heard it's sometimes November before cool weather decides to stick around."

"Blessit be, how will we ever make it that long?"

Leah shrugged. "We'll do what we have to do, just like we have been."

Shannon nodded. "Aye, you're right. We'll do as we must."

"Are things going better with the Corbett brothers, now that you've been there a few weeks?"

Shannon lifted one shoulder. "A wee bit. Garrett likes to play jokes on his brother and me, and Mark gets angry at him. I don't mind them so much, except that day he put a snake in Mark's desk drawer, and I was the one to find it. Ach! I nearly did an Irish jig. Good thing my ankle had healed."

"I'd like to have seen that." Leah chuckled and then shook her head, glad she didn't have to deal with the Corbett brothers on a daily basis. "That Garrett needs to grow up. Sounds like he's pulling schoolboy pranks."

"Aye, that's exactly what he's like. Maybe he just needs a good woman to settle him down." Shannon waggled her brows at Leah.

"Don't look at me. I've had my fill of those brothers. Mind yourself. You be careful around them."

"Well, I should be off. Have a grand mornin', and I shall see you at noontime."

Leah waved and watched Shannon walk away, her mulberry-colored skirt swaying. She'd purchased the new dress with the money she'd made working two weeks for the Corbetts, and well she needed one. Shannon had had only two old faded dresses when she came to Lookout, and one of them was stained with ink. Now the Irish girl wore an apron to work covering her new dress.

Leah leaned her head back and considered a new garment. Having one would be wonderful. Yeah, she had four, but like Shannon's, hers were old and faded.

She mentally calculated each item in her hope chest, wondering if there was something she could part with that might be worth some money. Sam—she smiled, remembering the man she'd hoped to marry—had made the small wooden trunk, which had served as her hope chest, for Christmas the year before they were to marry. But the trunk was all she had left, and her hopes and dreams had been buried more than two years ago, along with Sam.

She closed her eyes, trying hard to imagine his face. He always smiled, and his brown eyes had glimmered with orneriness and love for her. Tears moistened her eyes. Life would have been so much different if he had lived. Why, she'd probably be a mother with a child by now. At least she'd been spared that.

While most women longed to marry and have children, she was different. She wanted to marry—Dan Howard's tall form intruded into her thoughts—but she didn't want children. And what man would marry her, knowing that?

After changing hundreds, if not thousands, of diapers, wiping noses for her youngest siblings every winter, watching babies die. . .

No, she wouldn't put herself through that. If she couldn't find a man who didn't want children, she'd remain unmarried. She'd be a spinster.

But even a spinster needed a way to support herself. What could she do?

Teaching school was out of the question. Even if she had more than her sixth-grade education, there was still the issue of dealing with children day in and day out. She shuddered. No thank you.

She was an excellent cook, but she'd talked to Polly Dykstra, and the woman didn't need any help other than what she already had. Her sister was a seamstress and owned the dress shop across from Polly's Café, but with so few women in the town, she only worked part-time making dresses.

The screen screeched, and Rachel walked out. "My, it's cooler out here. The kitchen is always so hot. I halfway wish I had one that was separate from the house."

"That would help keep the rest of the house cooler, but you'd have to carry the food farther—and what would you do if we had rain?"

"True. I hadn't considered those issues." Rachel dropped into the rocker beside Leah's and fanned her face with her hand. "How are you doing today?"

"Bored. I wish you'd let me do more around the boardinghouse."

Rachel smiled and leaned her head back against the rocker. "I just can't let a boarder work. It doesn't seem proper."

"So? Who cares?"

"I suppose just me. I guess you've not had luck in finding employment since we last talked?"

Leah shook her head. "I was just sitting here, trying to think of something."

Rachel yawned and stretched her arms out in front of her. "Luke mentioned that his cousins are talking about having a get-together this Saturday and asked Polly to bake some cookies and pies. Maybe she could use help with that?"

She shrugged. "I asked her about working in the café, but she has all the help she needs." She glanced sideways at Rachel. "Just what kind of get-together are those conniving brothers planning?"

"A social, I think. It's a chance for unmarried men and women to meet."

Leah stiffened, and her hackles rose. "You mean they're trying to find husbands for Shannon and me?"

Rachel's brows darted up. She opened her mouth but then closed it. She stared down the street for a moment. "I hadn't thought about it that way."

"They are probably trying to marry us off so they can quit supporting us—or rather, me." Leah crossed her arms. "Well, it won't work, 'cause I'm not going. All those men can dance with each other."

Chuckling, Rachel shook her head. "It would serve those rascals right if only men showed up."

"I've had enough of the Corbett brothers matchmaking and interfering in my life."

A wagon drove by, and the driver lifted his hat to the two women. He stared until his wagon turned down Main Street.

Leah faked a shiver. "I sometimes feel as if I'm on exhibit."

"Men around here admire pretty women. There are so few of them to be had in Texas."

"Men everywhere admire women. Pretty or not. It's their nature."

"True. But if they know of one who is available, that piques their interest even more."

Leah crossed her arms over her chest and jiggled her foot. "Just who told them I was available?"

"I'll give you one guess."

"I guess it's no secret how that bride contest turned out." Leah shot to her feet, sorry for making Rachel squirm but irritated to the core. "I'm about ready to march over to the freight office and give those two scalawags a piece of my mind."

Rachel stood. "Try to see that they mean well. They messed things up by bringing you and Shannon to town, and now they're trying to fix that mistake."

"I can't believe you're defending them after the trouble they caused for you."

Rachel walked down the steps and plucked several dead leaves off a rosebush. "You know, if those two men hadn't sent for you brides, Luke might never have forgiven me and gotten up his courage to ask me to marry him. So in a strange, roundabout way, I'm beholden to Mark and Garrett."

Leah opened her mouth to comment, but Rachel held up her hand. She flipped her long braid over her shoulder.

"That doesn't mean I condone what they did. It was wrong to pretend to be Luke and to write to you. But now that you're here and neither of you want to leave, I guess they feel they owe it to you to find you a husband."

Leah shoved her hands to her hips and paced the porch. "I don't need their help in finding a mate. I've already got my eye on someone."

"Oh yeah?" Rachel's eyes lit up, and she cocked her head. "Who?"

Leah realized her mistake too late. "I. . .uh. . .am not ready to say. I don't even know if he's interested in me."

Leaning her arms on the porch rail, Rachel stared up at her. "Well then, going to the social could be a good thing."

Leah narrowed her eyes. "How so?"

"It would give you a place to get to know this man better. Other than outright courting, there aren't many opportunities for a man and woman to spend time together."

"Hmm. . ." Leah tapped her index finger against her lips. "You may be right. But it would mean talking to other men, too."

"True, but you might meet someone more interesting than the man you've got your eye on. Or you will confirm that he's the one for you."

What Rachel said made sense. But was getting to know Dan Howard worth having to dance with and talk to all those other men? Leah shuddered at the thought of being near some of the uncouth men. Still, she *would* be able to talk with Dan there and somehow let him see her interest. "I think you may be right."

Too bad she didn't have a new dress to wear to the social.

Shannon stared at the man standing in front of Mark's desk. "You want what?"

The lanky cowboy wore a faded, red plaid shirt, dingy denim pants, and worn boots. He twisted the brim of his hat in his shaking hands, and his ears turned the color of his shirt. "I asked if you'd like to get hitched to me, ma'am. Got me a ranch over toward Dennison a ways, and an ailing ma. I need a woman to help care for her and cook for my men."

"So you need a cook, not a wife?"

The man scratched his head, his hazel eyes darting around the office. "Uh. . .what's the difference, ma'am?"

Shannon's mouth quirked. She knew little of married life, but there had to be more than just cooking. She felt sorry for his mother, but she wouldn't marry unless she was in love. Her own mum had married the man her parents wanted—a man she didn't love—and she'd never been happy. "I'm sorry, Mr. Harkins, but I have a job already."

His brows dipped again. "I didn't offer you a job, ma'am. I asked you to marry me."

She felt sorry for the clueless cowboy, but she shook her head. A noise sounded from the right, and she saw Mark standing in the doorway to the side room, scowling. How long had he been there?

"I believe the woman said no, Abbot."

The cowboy frowned. "What am I gonna do, Mark? I need someone to help care for ma and feed my men."

Mark's gaze gentled, and he crossed the room and laid his hand on Abbot's shoulder. "I'm sorry to hear about your mother. If Garrett and I can do anything, be sure to let me know." Mark rubbed the back of his neck. "Maybe what you need is to hire a cook rather than take a wife. Or maybe a neighbor could help out for a while."

Abbot nodded and seemed to be studying the floorboards. "Maybe so, but ma has her heart set on seeing me married before she—" The man swallowed hard, and his Adam's apple bobbed.

"Marrying isn't something done in haste. You need time to develop a relationship and to fall in love."

Shannon watched Mark, admiring the gentleness in his voice and how he treated the man with respect in spite of his misguided mission. In the two weeks that she'd been working at the freight office, she'd come to admire Mark—on most occasions. There had been a few times when he'd dropped his guard and horseplayed too roughly with his brother for her taste or even argued with Garrett. She'd never had siblings who lived long, but she couldn't help thinking she'd fight less and love them more.

Abbot nodded. "I reckon you're right. You think that other bride would be interested?"

"In what? Marriage or being a cook?" Mark asked.

Abbot shrugged; then his eyes glinted with an ornery gleam. "Could be I'll just attend that Saturday social you and your brother are planning and see if I cain't win her heart."

Mark's gaze darted to Shannon's, and she didn't miss the apprehension there. What was Mr. Harkins talking about?

He patted the man's shoulder again. "You do that, Abbot. You've got as good a chance as anyone else."

The rancher nodded and tipped his hat to Shannon. "G'day, ma'am. Mark." His spurs jingled as he crossed the room and walked out the open door, carrying with him the scent of dust and cattle.

Shannon stood and crossed her arms. "What exactly is this Saturday social thing?"

An odd look crossed Mark's face, and the tips of his ears turned red. "Uh. . .just a gathering of folks and a dance."

Shannon narrowed her eyes. "Sounds like more than that. Why would the two of you be hosting a social? Could you be looking for a wife now?"

"No, we're not looking to marry." Mark crossed to the open door and stared outside. He heaved a heavy sigh. "It was Garrett's idea."

"Why does that not surprise me?" Shannon mumbled.

Mark leaned against the doorjamb and turned to face her. His blue eyes looked troubled, and his short hair twisted in enticing curls, giving him a softer look than his brother. "For the record, I told him that it was a bad idea and that I wanted nothin' to do with it."

"Why is it he felt the need to organize such an event?"

Mark's mouth twisted to one side, and he broke from her gaze.

"Do you not feel you owe me the truth?"

He captured her gaze again, and it set her heart thumping. She shifted her feet, not wanting to admit how attracted she was to him. Her pa had been rough, dirty, and hairy, but Mark was always clean and smelled fresh. Garrett's desk was always a mess, with things tossed haphazardly, but Mark's was always tidy, even while he was working. After he'd gotten used to working with her, he'd been only kind and patient in showing her how to do everything. But how could he stir her senses after all he and his brother had done? It made no sense to her.

"Garrett has. . .uh. . .been talking to some of our customers and discovered there are a number of them who'd like to marry. We also have found women in other towns who are looking for husbands."

Shannon's ire simmered to a boil, and she bolted to her feet as she realized the truth. "You mean your brother is hosting a social so that you can marry off Leah and me? Isn't that correct?"

Mark's silence was all the answer she needed.

Shannon lifted her chin and straightened her back. These men had meddled enough in her life. "I believe that I've finished working for today."

She marched to the door, but Mark didn't move. His fresh scent wafted over her. Looking up, she hated to see the pain she'd inflicted. Mark was somewhat a victim of his brother's shenanigans, but he was a grown man—a man who needed to stand up for what he believed and not be swayed by his conniving sibling.

"Shannon. . .Miss O'Neil."

"Pardon mc, Mr. Corbett."

His heavy sigh warmed her face, but he stepped back. Shannon strode out of the office, uncertain if she'd ever return.

Chapter 10

While Rachel was busy in the kitchen, fixing their noon meal, Leah tiptoed into the dining room and quietly set the table. Maybe Rachel wouldn't willingly ask for help, but Leah had decided to find small ways to help anyway. She completed her task without getting caught and left the room feeling good.

A shadow darkened the screen door, and Shannon strode in with a scowl on her face.

"What's wrong?"

"Oh, those. . .those. . ." She stomped her foot. "They fuel my ire like a match to lamp oil."

Leah's mouth twitched. She'd never seen Shannon so worked up before. Normally, the girl would turn quiet and withdraw when upset, but seeing her angry encouraged Leah that maybe Shannon had more of a backbone than she thought. "Those what? Or should I say who?"

Shannon's green eyes flickered with fury. "Do you know what those hooligans are plannin' now?"

"Ah, you've heard about the Saturday social."

"You know about it? Why didn't you say something?"

Leah held up her hand and leaned against the parlor doorjamb. "I just learned about it this morning."

"And are you goin'?"

Leah waved her hand toward the parlor. "Let's sit down."

Shannon followed her to the settee and turned to face Leah. Taking a moment to organize her thoughts, Leah straightened her skirt.

"Surely you are not actually considering goin'. 'Twould only encourage the Corbett brothers." Shannon eyed her with skepticism.

"Now hear me out. I've got my eye on a man."

"Aye?" Shannon leaned forward, brows lifted. "What man would that be?"

Leah pressed her lips together, not sure she was ready to share that information. "Uh. . .just someone I've met a time or two."

"How can you know a man when you've only just met him?"

Leah shifted on the seat. "That's the thing. I can't. Attending the social would give me the chance to talk with this man and learn more about him. He might even ask me to dance."

"If he attends it." Shannon seemed to be considering what Leah said as different expressions crossed her face. "Aye, I can see how 'twould be beneficial to you, but I won't be attending."

Leah gasped, suddenly not so sure of her plan. "Oh, but you have to. I don't want to go alone."

"Perhaps you can go with Luke and Rachel."

Leah shook her head. "They aren't invited. It's only for unmarried folks."

Shannon nibbled on the inside corner of her lip and stared across the room. "I don't know. 'Twould almost be as if I were advertising for a husband."

A warm breeze fluttered the curtains at the open window. A bird flitted on the bush just outside the window, chirping a lively tune. "I can see why you'd think that, but I'm pretty sure that it's just a social. Yes, men and women will meet, but what's wrong with that?"

Shannon shrugged and wrung her hands.

"I realize that you now have a job and are no longer dependent on the Corbett brothers for your support as I still am."

Shannon muttered something about quitting her job, then looked at Leah. "It's one and the same. I may be working and earning a wage, but I'm still dependent on those hooligan brothers since I work for them."

"I see your point, but it's different. You're earning your keep, I'm just a. . .dried-up old cow, no longer giving milk but too tough to eat."

Shannon sucked in a loud breath and whacked Leah on the arm. "Don't you say such a thing. You can't be much older than me."

Leah shrugged. "I know, but it just seems that way at times. I don't want those men supporting me, but what else can I do? There are no other jobs available."

"Perhaps I could help you. I have a wee bit of extra money."

Leah placed her hands over her friend's. "Thank you, but you know that isn't true. Maybe you have some money left after paying room and board, but it's precious little, I'd imagine. You need that to buy yourself some more dresses. You can't wear this one every day."

Shannon looked down and fingered her sleeve. "Aye, there's truth in what you say. Perhaps I could ask to work more hours."

Leah smiled, warmed by Shannon's desire to help, but she shook her head. "No, I very much appreciate your offer, but I need to make my own way. I need to find a man to marry or a job."

"So, you are serious, then, about attending the social?"

"Yes. It seems the thing to do. Hopefully, I'll be able to get to know the man I'm attracted to better, but at the same time, I can ask around about employment."

Shannon's grip tightened on Leah's. "Just be careful. Not all men are honorable. Don't be going off alone with any of them."

"Yes, Ma." Leah grinned, and Shannon chuckled. "Why are you back early from work, anyway?"

Shannon sighed. "I got irritated with Mark when I overheard him tell a cowboy about the social."

"Oh, it's Mark now, is it?" Leah couldn't resist teasing.

Shannon's face turned five shades of red, and she looked away. "I do work with two Corbett men, and 'twould be confusing to refer to them both as *Mr. Corbett*."

Leah couldn't help wondering if Shannon was attracted to Mark. She couldn't imagine having an infatuation with either man, but at least Mark seemed less ornery and more sensible than his brother. "Do you also call Garrett by his first name?"

Leah could hardly believe it possible, but Shannon's cheeks flamed more.

"I. . .uh, no. He isn't in the office very often, and it wouldn't seem proper."

Leah sat back, smiling. "I see the way of things."

"Nay!" Shannon held her palm toward Leah. "I. . .it just makes things easier since we work together so much."

"So, you're not attracted to him?"

Shannon ducked her head and fiddled with her apron, not answering at first. "It does seem hard to believe, but I am attracted to him, though he couldn't care less about me."

"Why would you say such a thing? You're a beautiful woman, and he has to be intrigued by your lovely accent."

Shannon lifted one shoulder and dropped it back down. "His brother hadn't told him that he'd hired me, and Mark was quite angry when he first found out. I was so embarrassed to witness their disagreement, especially with me being the topic of it. I wanted to run from their office, but I couldn't because of my ankle."

"Oh, Shannon, I never knew. What a horrible thing for him to do. I can understand why Mark would be upset."

"Aye, me, too, now that I've had time to step back and think about the situation. But Mark quickly adjusted and has been quite gracious and patient since then."

"Just give him some time. He's seems a levelheaded man, even if he does let his brother involve him in his high jinks." Leah squeezed Shannon's hand. "Let me tell you: That's often the case of a younger brother following his older one. I've lots of brothers, and it most always happens."

Shannon stood, as if uncomfortable with the topic of conversation. "I should go and clean up. I imagine dinner will be ready before too long."

Leah watched her scurry from the room. Had the girl already fallen for Mark Corbett? Leah shook her head, unable to envision such a union. She stood and walked out onto the front porch.

The heat of the day made her sweat, even though the August sun wasn't yet fully overhead.

A worm of jealousy inched its way into Leah's heart. If Shannon were to marry Mark Corbett, she'd have a home and a family—of sorts. Yeah, she'd be permanently supported by a Corbett, but that would be different since she'd be married to one.

Leah blew out a breath. She was getting the cart before the horse. Shannon seemed only mildly attracted to Mark. Besides, even if they did happen to get married, she should be happy for her friend, not jealous of her.

Shoving those thoughts aside, she studied the town. Several horses were tied in front of the bank and also the café. Their heads hung low, as if they, too, were bothered by the heat. Leah longed for the cooler temperatures of fall, but the uncertainty of her future nagged at her. There must be something she could do to make some money.

After lunch and an afternoon rest, Leah ventured down to the café. An idea had percolated in her mind, and she hoped that Polly would still be there. She passed the lot where the store had been, and the marshal's office, but she didn't look inside. It no longer mattered to her what Luke Davis did. He might have once been the target of her sights, but no more. He was a happily married man.

She opened the door to the café and stepped inside. Aromatic scents lingered even though all the customers were gone. The front windows were wide open, but the room was still overly warm. A fly buzzed near her head, and she swatted at it. Pots clanged together in the back room, so she made a beeline in that direction.

Polly was standing over a large pot with her arm clear down inside it. Leah hated to disturb her, but they needed to talk. "Ahem."

Polly jumped and turned. "Goodness, you nearly scared what little life I've got remaining out of me."

Leah smiled at the older woman's joking. Polly's chubby cheeks were bright red, and wisps of grayish-brown hair had escaped her bun and curled around her face.

"I'm sorry to bother you, but I wondered if I could talk to you about something."

"Sure thing. Just let me finish up this pot. Help yourself to some coffee, if you've a mind to."

Leah skipped the coffee and surveyed the large kitchen. Something simmered on the stove, and several pies cooled near the open window. Beside her was a large shelf that held dozens of blue tin plates, bowls, and coffee cups. Almost everything was in its place, ready for the next round of serving to begin.

"You picked a good time to come. The lunch rush is over, and supper won't start for a few hours yet." Polly lugged the big pot to the back door and tossed out the soapy water; then she poured in fresh water from a bucket, swished it around, and threw it out the door, too. She set the pot upside down on a table that had spaces between the wooden slats, which served as her drying table. Polly wiped her hands on her apron and set them on her ample hips. "Now, how can I help you—Miss Bennett, isn't it?"

"Care to sit down?" Leah asked. "I'm sure you must be exhausted. And please, call me Leah."

Polly nodded and limped into the dining room. She picked up a mortuary advertisement that was attached to a flat stick and started fanning herself. "I'm getting too old for all this work, but I've got to have some income."

"Have you never married?"

Polly lifted her hand to her chest. "Of course, but my Wilbur died young. So sad."

"How is it you have the same last name as your sister?"

Polly smiled. "Dolly and me married brothers, we did. They weren't twins like us, though. Walter was Dolly's husband. He lived two years longer than Wilbur. Farming is hard on men and can be dangerous."

Leah wanted to ask what had happened, but it wouldn't be proper. She might as well get to the point. "Mrs. Davis told me that you'd be baking cookies and pies for the social the Corbetts are hosting."

Polly swatted her fan at a fly but missed it. "Mercy sakes, I told them boys I don't have the time or energy for any more baking, but they insisted. They begged me and offered good money. It's hard to resist their handsome smiles and those charming blue eyes of theirs—and trust me—they use them to their advantage as much as they can."

"Well, that's what I wanted to ask you about."

Polly's brows darted up. "You interested in one of them boys? I think of them like sons, I do."

Leah's heart jolted, and she lifted her hand up. "No, that's not it at all. I was wondering if I might be able to help you with the baking. I need to earn some income, and I'm sure you understand that."

Polly leaned back in her chair. "Well, phooey. I'd sure like to see those boys marry you and that purdy Irish gal."

Leah choked back a gag. She would never marry a Corbett, no matter how desperate she was. "Sorry, but I don't think that will happen. Those two rascals are responsible for our being stranded here in town, as I'm sure you know."

Polly shrugged. "Maybe, but could just be God's means of getting you here. Time will tell."

Leah stared dumbfounded. Polly was the second person today to insinuate such a thing. Yes, she believed that God could work in miraculous ways, but why would He bring her to such a town as Lookout? And then leave her dependent on the ornery coots who had brought her here under false pretenses?

"How about this: What if I let you use my kitchen and supplies, you do the baking, and we split the money? You can bake, can't you? I remember them pies you gals made in that bride contest didn't turn out so well."

Leah nodded, feeling a tad bit offended that her cooking abilities were in doubt. "Of course I can cook. Even won some ribbons at the county fair for my pies."

"That's good to know. I wouldn't want to disappoint them boys. They're two of my best customers."

Leah considered the offer. In truth, it made perfect sense. How would she buy the supplies, even if she'd talked Polly into letting her cook the desserts for the social? And where would she have done the baking if the woman hadn't offered her kitchen?

She looked at the middle-aged widow, smiled, and held out her hand. "Polly, you've got a deal."

Rachel looked around her tidy kitchen, then pulled out a chair at her worktable. Too bad this room couldn't stay clean for more than a few hours at a time. She tugged a letter out of her pocket and smoothed it out, remembering Carly Payton. The black-haired, blue-eyed young woman had lived in the boardinghouse, posing as Ellie Blackstone. Rachel shook her head, thinking of how Carly had fooled them all, even Luke, though he'd been a bit suspicious of her. Carly had thought the real Ellie was dead, but she was, in truth, recovering from being shot and accidentally stabbed by a knitting needle during a stage robbery that took a bad turn.

She opened the letter and started reading:

Dear Rachel,

I'm still in Dallas, awaiting trial. There ain't much to do here. I'm locked up in a cell but kept apart from the men, thank the good Lord for that. When I was in a cell next to my brother, he pestered me the whole time, blaming me for his getting caught. How do you figure that? I wasn't even there when he robbed the Lookout bank.

Each day drags by so slowly. I'm bored half out of my mind, but I do have ample time to pray. I only wish I had a Bible and could read better. The marshal's kind wife, Iona, has taken me under her wing and is teaching me to read better. She's the one penning this letter for me. I can read some but hope to get better soon so I'll be able to read some books and God's Word to help the time go by faster.

They say my trial should happen by the end of the month. With all the trouble in this part of the state, the judge is backed up on holding trials. I don't know what's to become of me. Iona says most women who are jailed here are black women or Mexicans. They are often sent to the penitentiary. Sometimes the judge is lenient and will sentence a woman to work off her sentence for a local rancher. I'm praying for that but don't hold out much hope. I'm a Payton, and though I never shot no one, I did steal and pretend to be that other bride. I don't know what's to happen, and I'll admit I'm scared. Please keep me in your prayers. Have you married that marshal yet?

Truly your friend,
Carly Payton

Rachel bowed her head and spent the next few minutes thanking God that Carly had given her life to Him, just before her capture. How would the young woman have endured imprisonment without His help?

A noise sounded behind her, and she looked over her shoulder. "Leah, don't you look lovely?"

Leah's lightly tanned cheeks turned a rosy pink. "You really think so?"

She nodded. "I do. I'm glad you've decided to go to the social." She noted Leah's apron ties were hanging down her side. "Turn around, and I'll tie that for you."

Leah smiled. "Oh, would you? I appreciate your help. I've always had a hard time fixing my own bows."

Rachel motioned for her to turn around and then tied the bow to Leah's new apron and fluffed it up to make it look pretty. "I think this was a wonderful idea."

Leah spun around, glancing down and looking apprehensive. She smoothed the front of the apron. "You don't think it's too casual for a social?"

Rachel shook her head. "Not at all. If you'd made a white apron, then it wouldn't have looked as nice. The ruffles around the bib fancy it up, and the navy calico accents the lighter blue of your dress."

Leah chuckled. "Light blue—that's a such a nice way to say faded." She sighed. "I wish I had enough money to make a new dress."

"Stop worrying. You look beautiful, and those men will be stumbling over themselves to dance with you."

Leah's cheeks flamed. "I don't know about that."

"I do." Luke walked into the kitchen, staring at Leah. "There's more than a dozen cowpokes and other men down by the church already, and the social doesn't start for another hour yet."

"I certainly hope some other women attend. I don't think Shannon and I could dance with all the men who are likely to show up."

"I wouldn't worry about that. I've heard plenty of chatter all week. Everyone's excited about the social." Luke leaned back against the counter and shook his head. "I have to admit, though, I thought this was just another of my cousins' cockamamie ideas, but this one just might turn out well."

"From what Shannon said, it was mainly Garrett's idea," Leah said.

Luke nodded. "Most of them are. Mark's more levelheaded than his brother."

Rachel studied her husband, amazed again that God had given Luke to her. He caught her staring and winked. Butterflies danced in her stomach, and she felt her cheeks warm. How could he still move her as he had back when they were young?

Leah glanced from Luke to her and back. A playful smirk danced on her lips as if she'd understood Rachel's thoughts. "I suppose I should head on over to Polly's and start hauling the refreshments over to the social," Leah said.

"I'm available if you need help." Luke grabbed a coffee cup off Rachel's shelf and poured some coffee into it.

"That's probably not too warm, sweetheart. I let the stove burn down after fixing supper." Rachel touched the side of the pot. Lukewarm at its best.

"I'm obliged for the offer to help, but Shannon already said she would assist me, and Polly offered also. We'll be back before dark." Leah waved and turned down the hallway.

Luke set his cup down and growled. "Come here, wife. I'm hankerin' for some spoonin'."

Rachel glanced to the spot where Leah had been, then walked over and peeked down the hallway. She and Shannon were walking out the front door together, and Jacqueline was outside somewhere, which meant she and Luke were alone. She slowly turned back to face her husband. "If you want me"—she wiggled her brows—"come and get me."

Luke's brown eyes sparked, and a slow grin pulled at his lips. "You don't have to ask twice."

He pushed away from the cabinet, moving with unhurried but deliberate steps. When he got within three feet of her, Rachel squealed and spun down the hall. She darted into the dining room.

"Hey, darlin', you're not getting away." Luke chased after her, deep chuckles rattling in his chest.

Rachel gasped for a breath between laughs, and managed to keep the dining table between her and her husband. "You're getting slow in your old age. There was a time I'd have never gotten away."

"You're *not* getting away. Ever." His eyes gleamed with love and possession.

Suddenly, all teasing fled, and Rachel wanted nothing more than to be in his arms. She sauntered toward the end of the table, batting her eyelashes like she'd seen a saloon girl once do.

Luke held his position at the middle of the table as if he wasn't too sure that she wouldn't cut back the other way. But as she rounded his side of the table, a slow burn glimmered in his gaze, and he stepped forward. He lifted his hand and trailed it down her cheek; then he cupped her nape, tugging her up against him.

"You're so beautiful. You've no idea how many times I dreamed of holding you when I was gone." He crushed her against his chest. It was muscled. Solid. But his kiss was soft. Gentle.

Rachel stood on her tiptoes, kissing the only man she'd ever loved. Luke deepened the kiss, and their breath mingled together. Rachel felt lifted out of this world into a realm only a husband and wife madly in love could visit. Oh, if only they could go on like this forever.

The back door banged, and they jerked apart. Rachel grabbed the back of a chair for balance, and her chest heaved, and her pulse soared. Her lips felt puffy. Damp.

"Ma?"

Luke stepped back and acted as if he were straightening the chairs. Jacqueline's gaze swept back and forth between them. Her mouth swerved up to one side, and she crossed her arms. "Guess you two were kissing again. Is that all married folks do?"

Luke grinned wickedly, and his gaze sought Rachel's. "No, half bit, we do other things besides that."

Jacqueline scowled. "What kind of things?"

Rachel's heart stampeded. Surely Luke wouldn't mention things her daughter was too young to hear about.

Luke ambled toward Rachel, and her breathing picked up speed again. Just having the man near set her senses racing like a heard of mustangs. He put his arm around her shoulders.

"Oh, sometimes we hug, like this." He pulled her against his side.

Jacqueline's mouth curved up in disgust. "That's nothing. You hug me, too."

"Other times. . ." Luke gazed down at Rachel with an ornery glint to his eyes.

No, please don't tell her.

"Sometimes. . .we tickle!"

Luke's fingers dug into Rachel's side, and she jumped. "Don't! Stop!" Rachel giggled and tried to get free, but his other arm held her captive.

"Don't stop? Isn't that what your ma said, half bit?" Luke renewed his efforts.

Tears blurred Rachel's eyes. She wiggled and squirmed but couldn't get free. He held her tight, but not so much that it hurt. "Luke, please."

"Ah, now she's begging for more."

Jacqueline giggled and raced around the table. "I'll save you, Ma." She grabbed Luke's arm and tugged.

Luke released his hold as if the girl had overpowered him, but just that fast, he scooped her onto his shoulder. "Where do you want this sack of potatoes, Rach?"

Jacqueline screeched with delight. Rachel's heart warmed seeing her daughter and husband at play. This was what she'd longed for in a marriage.

"Help me, Ma."

Luke jogged around the table with Jacqueline hanging over his shoulder. Rachel smiled, knowing her interference was the last thing her daughter wanted just now.

Chapter 11

Butch Laird stood on the outskirts of the crowd, leaning against a tall oak, watching the dancing. Cowboys and ladies in pretty dresses sashayed around the circle, doing a complicated square dance he'd seen before. How did they remember what steps to do next?

His gaze drifted over to the table of food again. Several kinds of cookies sat in stacks next to a half-dozen pies. The two boardinghouse brides hustled about, setting out plates and forks. His mouth watered, and his stomach growled when the blond picked up a knife and began slicing one of the pies. Was the food just for the dancers? When was the last time he had pie?

He and his pa rarely ate anything except for pork, eggs, beans, and potatoes. Bacon, ham steaks, pork chops, ham, and beans. That was his lot in life as the son of a hog farmer. Some folks would envy him, but he was sick of pork—and sick of his own cooking.

Butch winced. The last time he'd had pie was when he'd stolen one off a windowsill. He closed his eyes at the memory of how good it had tasted. But he'd eaten the whole thing, and then gotten sick. Besides an upset belly, he'd been riddled with guilt. He'd found some work and earned a dollar, then returned the woman's clean pie plate to her windowsill with the dollar on it. He hadn't eaten pie since then.

He moseyed toward the food. At close to six foot tall, he had the look of a man—at least he would once he lost his pudge and muscled up more. People often thought he was older than just thirteen. But no matter how much he worked, he couldn't seem to lose his big belly. He was tired of the other kids making fun of him for being fat—for calling him Butch Lard instead of Laird. His stomach growled, reminding him that he'd skipped dinner. He just couldn't stand slicing another steak off the ham roast that sat on a plate in the kitchen. If he ever got away from Lookout, he'd never eat pork again.

A group of eight couples danced in and out to the lively music, and the women swirled around, their colorful skirts flying. Phil Muckley deftly swung his bow across his fiddle strings, while Nathan Spooner sawed his harmonica back and forth across his mouth. A man Butch didn't recognize played guitar and tapped his foot to the tune.

Butch's gaze swung back to the dancing ladies. He liked to watch them. Whenever they whipped past him, he got a whiff of their flowery scents. What would things have been like if his mother hadn't died when he was young? Would his pa have been different? Kinder? Not a drunk?

He shook his head to rid it of such glum thoughts. Movement on the other side of the dancers caught his attention. Jack—Jacqueline Hamilton—stood in the shadows of the church building, watching the dancing couples. She was probably too young to join in, as he was, but that didn't keep her from watching.

He scowled, thinking of how her lies had caused him to spend two days in jail for something he didn't do. And yet, he couldn't stay angry with her, even though his pa had beat him for not being home to care for the animals and to cook the meals. Even though he still hurt in places where his pa had taken a broken hay fork handle to him. He knew she had also endured a similar fate when her pa was alive, and for some odd reason, he wanted to protect her—if only she could tolerate him.

Jacqueline strolled over to the food table and started chatting with the two women. He couldn't hear what she was saying, but her lively facial expressions held him captive. He'd always wanted to be her friend. She reminded him of his little sister, Zoe, who'd had red hair and had been as feisty as a piglet. But Zoe had died before her first birthday, just before his ma gave in to the fever. He'd buried them together while his pa was away on a hunting trip. His pa returned without any meat and took out his grief and anger on him. But even a stiff beating didn't drive away the guilt. Somehow, he should have helped his ma and sister better.

One of the boardinghouse brides put a slice of pie on a plate and handed it to Jack, along with a fork. Butch shook his head. Why did such a cute girl want to wear overalls, go fishing with the boys, and be called by a boy's name?

He moved closer to the table, but lost his courage as he reached the back of the church. For some reason, Jack had it in for him. Yeah, sometimes he lost his temper when the kids ranted at him and blamed him for things he hadn't done, but he tried to get along. It just seemed that nobody wanted to get along with him.

He sniffed his shirt, hoping it didn't smell. The kids constantly berated him for carrying the hog stench, but he could never catch the odor on his own clothes. He hadn't taken a chance tonight, though. He'd scrubbed clean his nicest shirt and overalls, even though both were faded and frayed. The dance was for folks of marrying age—he knew that—but he had just hoped to be able to get a slice of the pies he'd heard they'd be serving. His mouth watered, and he forced his feet forward.

The bride whose hair was nearly the same color as Jack's saw him coming and smiled.

"Sure now, would you be caring for a slice of pie?" She smiled at him and held up the pie knife.

He sucked in a breath and nodded, unable to believe his good fortune. Jack eyed him suspiciously as she continued to finish her pie.

"Would you care for apple or peach?"

What a choice. "Um. . .apple, I guess." He was pretty sure he remembered his ma baking apple pies, but it had been so long that his memory had dulled.

The lady handed him a fork and a plate with a fat slice of pie. The dancers noticed the food being served and drifted toward the table while the music faded. Even the musicians were setting aside their instruments and heading for the feeding trough, as if they thought they'd miss out. Butch got out of the way and reverently carried his pie to where Jack stood eating hers.

She narrowed her eyes. "What are you doing here?"

Her spiteful tone grated on him. Why did she dislike him so much? "Same thing as you, I reckon."

"And what's that?"

"Eating pie."

She shook her head, tossing her long braid over her shoulder. "I can eat pie every day. I came to watch the shenanigans."

Her comment gored him to the core, but he doubted she meant to hurt him. Of course she ate pie every day; she had a ma to fix it and guests who probably expected dessert served with their meals. Even though he wanted to savor each bite, he shoved the pie into his mouth, and in seconds, it was gone. He licked his fork and then his plate, catching every little taste that was left.

"Eww. . .don't you got no manners?"

He halted mid-lick and glanced out the corner of his eye. His pa always licked his plate—said that was how he helped with the washing. Didn't other folks do the same?

Jack eyed him like he was a crude no-good. He lowered the plate and set it on the empty table behind the brides that held a bowl of soapy water. He shoved his hands into his pockets, not quite ready to leave. If there was any pie left after all the dancers got their share, maybe he could have another slice.

He moseyed back over by Jack. She took her last bite and frowned at him. She held up her nose and sniffed, then looked down at his boots. Butch ducked his head and gazed down. Rats, he'd forgotten to clean them, and he'd fed the hogs just before leaving. He sniffed, but didn't smell anything bad.

Jack walked around him and took her empty plate to the wash table. She cleaned her plate in the soapy water then dipped the plate into another bucket of fresh water, and dried it off. Then she did the same with his plate and their forks. Butch stood mesmerized by the action. Why would she wash his plate? Should he have done that?

He'd thought the brides would tend to the dirty dishes. He

wandered around the churchyard, waiting for the folks to finish eating and start dancing again. Soon enough, the music filled the night air again, and the ladies were quickly claimed while the men without partners stood around the dancers, awaiting the next song.

Jack washed more of the dirty dishes, with the brides helping once all the serving was done. Butch kept his eye on the half pie that was leftover. He couldn't tell if it was peach or apple, but that hardly mattered. He just had to get another slice. Maybe if he offered to help. . .

He meandered back to the food table. "I. . .uh. . .could fetch some clean water, if'n y'all need some."

"Why, 'tis a kind offer you make, young man." The Irish gal dumped the rinse bucket and handed it to him. "If you'd be so kind as to refill this, I'll have another slice of pie waitin' for you when you return."

His heart jumped, and he grabbed the pail. "Yes'm, that sounds fair to me."

He hurried around to the back of the church where a well had been dug, and in a matter of minutes, he'd filled the pail and returned to the washing table.

Jack leaned against one side of it, eating a cookie. She scowled at him. Butch grinned. Knowing he'd get to eat another piece of pie made his whole world look better, for the moment, at least.

He slowly ate his second slice, closing his eyes and savoring each bite.

"You're gonna have a bellyache, eating all that."

Butch eyed Jack, who held another cookie in her hand. "What about you? How many cookies have you eaten?"

She made a face at him, shoved her treat into her mouth, and then helped herself to another one. The rate she was eating those, there wouldn't be any left by the end of the next dance.

Dan Howard wandered back to the table, looking a bit green himself. He fiddled with the brim of his hat and stirred up dust with the toe of his boot. Miss Bennett kept casting glances his way, her cheeks turning red. Finally, Mr. Howard closed the distance between him and the woman. "Would you. . .ah. . .care to. . .ah. . . dance with me?"

Miss Bennett nodded, looking shy, but her eyes glimmered. She looped her arm through the livery owner's, and they strode off together. Butch finished his pie and got a sudden idea.

It wouldn't work.

But then, maybe it would.

He'd never know if he didn't try.

He set the plate on the table and walked back to Jack. She tilted her head to look up at him.

"What do you want?"

This was a stupid idea. He knew it, but he had to ask. "Would you care to dance?"

Jack's blue eyes widened, and he thought she would gag. She fanned her hand in front of her face and looked as if she couldn't catch her breath. Finally, she said, "Eww. . .you've got to be kidding."

Butch shook his head, not quite ready to give up.

"I don't know how to dance, and besides, I'm wearing pants. How weird would that be? Anyway, I wouldn't dance with you if you were the last person on earth." She crossed her arms, hiked up her little chin, and marched off.

Butch's insides ached as bad as when his pa had beaten him. He knew she wouldn't dance with the likes of him—and anyway, he didn't even know how to dance. She'd probably just kept him from making a fool of himself. Still, her rejection ached as bad as a gunshot wound would. Someone touched his forearm, and he jumped.

"Don't let the lass bother you." The pretty Irish gal—Miss O'Neil, he thought—smiled up at him. "She's at an age where she's not yet attracted to males. Give her a few years, and all that will change."

He offered the woman a half-smile and then sauntered away, tired of hearing the festive music. Jack wouldn't change, no matter how many years passed. Why did she have to hate him? What had he ever done to her?

One thing was certain: He would never ask her to dance again. Ever.

Jack stomped back home, her irritation burning, not so much

from Butch's offer to dance as from her reaction to his surprising question. Imagine, her dancing with Butch Laird. Why, her friends would never let her live that down. She shivered and turned around, walking backward. Her steps slowed, and her gaze scanned the crowd. He was gone.

His rank pig stink made her nearly retch, although she had to admit he didn't smell nearly as bad tonight. In fact, he looked as if he had on clean clothes. Had he been planning all day to ask her to dance? Had he gotten cleaned up just to look nicer for the social?

Something in Jack's gut twisted as she remember the hurt in his black eyes when she so adamantly refused to dance with him. She didn't like disappointing people, but why should it bother her to upset him?

He was her enemy.

But hadn't the preacher said something about loving your enemies? She shuddered as a sick feeling twisted her belly at the thought of loving Butch Laird. She'd rather eat a grub worm.

She picked up a stick and dragged it along the picket fence in front of Polly and Dolly's house, making a clicking sound with each picket it hit. Why did she feel guilty for being mean to Butch? The fact that she'd told a falsehood that caused him to spend two days in jail still bothered her. She heaved a sigh and flung the stick into the street.

Too late, she noticed the cowboy riding there. His horse squealed and kicked up his hooves when the stick hit its flanks. "Hey, kid!"

Jack took off running and dashed between the Dykstra house and Mr. Castleby's. She ran past her house and down the side of the Sunday house where Luke had lived before he married her ma. The house sat empty now, so she opened the door and darted inside. Her side ached, and her chest heaved. She peeked out the window, relieved when she didn't see the cowboy looking for her.

"It was an accident." She dropped the curtain and looked around the dim room. "I didn't mean to hit that horse."

Butch claimed he hadn't meant to hit her at the river that day, and she kinda sorta believed him. But hadn't he done other things to her and her friends?

She sat in the rocking chair across from the cold fireplace and rocked. Why did she struggle so much with her feelings for Butch? Was she being unfair to him?

He had been nice tonight. Hadn't done anything to upset her besides asking her to dance. And he'd politely offered to fetch that water for Shannon.

Jack squeezed her head with her palms. All this thinking about Butch was making her head hurt. Maybe he wasn't as bad as he seemed, but the thing was, if she befriended him, every other kid in school would turn against her. And how could she stand that stench all the time?

Nope, they just had to stay enemies. There was no way around that.

Chapter 12

Leah swayed to the rhythm of the lively music. Dan Howard wasn't a half-bad dancer, especially compared to the other men she'd sashayed around the grass with tonight. Working at the food table had kept her busy, but now that most everything was gone, she had no excuse not to dance with the men.

"That was some good-tastin' pie, Miss Bennett. As good as my own ma used to make. You ought to open up a bakery."

Leah felt her cheeks warm at Dan's compliment, and being so near to him made her pulse race. "Thank you. But what do you mean by 'used to make'? I know your ma was doing poorly that day I visited, but does she not bake at all anymore?"

Dan pursed his lips and stared over her head. "She hasn't been doin' too good the past few weeks."

"Oh, I'm sorry to hear that. Does she need some help with the house or the cooking?"

Dan's dark gaze pierced hers, sending delicious tingles throughout her body. Not since Sam had a man had such an effect on her.

"That's right nice of you to offer, ma'am. I don't like asking for favors, but Ma could use some help, and it would do her good to have another woman's company."

Leah smiled. "Then I shall go visit her under one condition."

Dan's eyes narrowed, as if he suspected she was going to ask for the world. "What would that be?"

"That you quit calling me ma'am. It makes me feel like a spinster."

Dan leaned his head back and laughed, warming her face and delighting her whole being. For a big man, he was quite comely. His dark hair and eyes blended well with his tanned face, sun-kissed from hours of working outside.

He pulled her a tiny bit closer and leaned down. "You've got a deal. . .ma'am."

"Oh, you." Leah smacked him lightly on the chest and felt it rumble as he chuckled. "Do you think your mother would be offended if I offered to do some cleaning or baking?"

Dan twisted his lips to one side, and he gazed up at the sky. "I don't know, but she needs more help than I can give. Maybe I should just hire you to clean house."

Leah stopped dancing and held up her hand.

Dan glanced around at the moving couples surrounding them and fidgeted. "Did I say somethin' wrong?"

"I offered my services freely. I will be offended if you try to pay me."

His lips twitched, and a gleam entered his gaze. He tipped his hat. "Yes, ma'am. I've been put in my place, well and good. But we should get back to dancing unless you'd prefer someone else for a partner."

Leah peered over her shoulder and saw several men staring at them, looking as if they'd like to cut in. She held out her hand to Dan and allowed him to pull her close. If it were proper, she'd only dance with him. She enjoyed how safe she felt in his thick arms. She loved his eyes, and how his deep voice sounded almost like a caress. He made her feel special with the looks he gave her and the gentleness of his touch. She never figured on falling for a livery owner, but she had.

Did she dare hope he might one day come to care for her?

The music ended, and several other men swarmed Leah. Dan stepped back, looking disappointed that their time together had ended. "Maybe you could save me another dance before things end tonight?"

Leah smiled and nodded. "I'd like that."

Dan tipped his hat and started to walk away, but he stopped. "When this shindig is over, I'll help you get all the dishes back to Polly's and see you home."

Leah curtsied, but another man claimed her hand as the music started. By the end of the social, she couldn't have said who all she'd danced with, but her feet ached, and her heart was full. Dan had stood at the outskirts of the dancers, watching her, almost as if keeping guard. The only other person he'd danced with had been Polly Dykstra. She and her sister came over to watch the dancing after finishing up at their businesses. But with all the lonely men at the social, the two older women were soon in the midst of it all. Leah smiled. Polly and Dolly had only lasted for three dances, but when they left, their cheeks were rosy, and both women were smiling. That was probably the best time they'd had in a long while.

Leah stacked the plates, surprised to find almost half a pie left when she lifted up a towel that had covered the dish. Had something been wrong with it? She swiped her finger through some juice on the empty side of the plate and stuck it in her mouth. The sweet taste of apples and cinnamon teased her senses.

"Ah ah, no sampling the wares." Dan Howard stood on the other side of the table, watching her with sparkling eyes.

"I just wondered if something was wrong with this pie since some of it was left."

"I think the men were more interested in dancing with you pretty women than eating."

Leah chuckled. "That's a first."

"You might be right about that." Dan shoved his hands in his pockets. "So what do you need me to do?"

Shannon hurried over. "I'm here. I'll start carrying the dirty dishes back to Polly's."

"I'll go with you." Leah glanced at Dan. "Just let me wipe down this table, and then you can return it to the back of the church."

"And the smaller table belongs in front of the pulpit. Perhaps one of the Corbetts will help carry it."

"No need. It's just a little table, ma'am. I can manage it myself."

Leah and Shannon exchanged a glance. Shannon collected the dirty pie and cookie plates, while Leah wiped off the table. Dan hoisted up the bigger of the two, and Leah hurried around him to open the church door. She followed him inside, but as the door closed, all went dark.

Dan banged into something. "Where'd you say to put the table?"

Leah struggled to see something in the blackness. "Against the back wall."

"Uh. . .where is the back wall?"

Leah couldn't help giggling. "I have no idea. Maybe I should get a lantern."

The table scraped against the floor as Dan moved it. Leah heard it clunk against something—the wall, she hoped. Dan's footsteps came in her direction, and he suddenly bumped her. Hard.

"Oompf." She flailed her arms and whacked his as he grabbed hold of her upper arm.

"Steady now. We don't want you gettin' hurt."

Her hand came to rest against his chest—his very solid chest. She felt the warmth of his skin through the chambray and the rise and fall as he breathed. Sam hadn't been much more than a boy when he'd first kissed her and asked her to marry him, but there was nothing boyish about Dan Howard. She just might swoon at being alone in the dark with him so near. His warm breath brushed her forehead, but he made no move to leave.

"Miss Bennett."

"Leah. Please call me Leah."

Could she hear a smile in the dark? Because she was sure he'd just smiled.

"Leah. . .I want you to know that you caught my eye when you first came to town."

Her heart turned a cartwheel. "I did?"

"Yep, but I thought for sure that Luke would pick you."

"Truly? Why did you think that?"

He was quiet for a moment, but his hand ran slowly up and down her arm, stirring her senses. She'd never considered he'd had his eye on her. Why would she when she was battling so hard for the marshal's affections? She'd never dreamed then that another man might be interested in her.

"Talking heart matters ain't easy for me. I'd. . .uh. . .like to take you for a buggy ride come Sunday."

Leah smiled. Since when was a buggy ride a heart matter? Maybe his feelings weren't as strong as hers. They hardly knew each other.

"I reckon we oughta go." He stepped forward, without warning, and nearly knocked her down again. His arms tightened around her and crushed her against his chest. She just stood there, and then slowly lifted her hands to his back and relaxed her head against his chest. His heart pounded a frantic rhythm that she was sure matched her own. Dan's hand caressed the side of her head.

"It's. . .uh. . .highly improper, since I hardly know you, but if I don't kiss you, Leah, I think I'll go loco."

Her breath caught in her throat, unable to believe him. Would it be wrong to let him kiss her? She was certain she was falling in love with him, but what if things didn't work out? It would make seeing him extremely awkward. Dan suddenly stepped back, but Leah grabbed the sides of his shirt to halt him.

"You sure you don't mind."

"No."

"No, you mind?"

"No! I don't mind."

"Oh." He chuckled and bent down, his breath mingling with hers. His full lips covered hers in a kiss so gentle, so tender, it stole all the energy from her. Her knees nearly buckled.

Something banged outside, and they jumped apart. "Come and get the door for me, brother."

Leave it to a Corbett to interrupt one of the sweetest moments of her life.

"I'll get it," Dan said.

The door opened, and the light of the full moon illuminated

the area. Mark Corbett jumped back and dropped the smaller table.

"Lord have mercy, Dan, you scared half my remaining years off me. What are you doing in there?"

Dan stepped out, and Mark's eyes widened as Leah stepped out from behind him. Mark's gaze darted back and forth between her and Dan and then to the dark room.

"Don't be getting no ideas, Corbett. We were just putting away the other table." Dan hiked his chin as if daring Mark to challenge him.

"Sure thing. I prefer putting tables away in the dark, too. It's much more fun than in a lighted room."

Leah was sure her cheeks were bright red, and she hurried back to where the tables had been set up. All the dishes were gone, as were Shannon and most of the people who'd attended the social. She and Dan couldn't have been in the church all that long. She glanced back and saw Dan holding the door as Mark wrestled the table through. Once he was in, Dan shut the door and hurried toward her.

His cheeks looked ruddy in the dim light of the two lanterns that were still lit. "I reckon we should head on over to the café before he comes back out. I don't care to listen to his teasing."

Leah nodded and started walking toward the café. Dan fell into step beside her. She longed to touch her lips, still tingling from his kiss, but she didn't. Tonight, her future had taken an interesting twist, and she couldn't wait to see what would happen.

Chapter 13

I don't know why them Corbett brothers had to go hire a gal to work for them. It ain't right that wimmen should work in a business. No, siree." Homer Sewell swiped at a streak of brown juice that ran down the side of his mouth. A lump of something in one cheek and his bristly beard reminded Shannon of a squirrel. He eyed her with his beady eyes.

"Well, they did, sir, so you can either give me your order or return when one of the Corbetts are here."

He scowled, and his cheeks puffed up. He gazed around the floor of the office.

Shannon's gut twisted. "If you intend on spitting, sir, I kindly ask you to step outside. There is no spittoon in here."

The man mumbled something under his breath and stomped out the door, leaving behind a foul odor. Shannon held her hand over her nose and hoped the man didn't return. Just that fast, she regretted the thought. The Corbetts could use the business, but she hated dealing with close-minded men who thought women should only be home, tending the house and babies. Not that there was anything wrong with that, but this was 1886, and things were changing. Women had more opportunities than in the past. She tapped her fingers on the desk, wishing that Leah could find a position of employment and not be dependent on the Corbetts for support.

She rested her cheek in her hand, remembering last Saturday's social. She'd danced with a number of men, but not the one she'd hope to. Mark had attended the social, but he didn't dance with any of the women. And she was surprised to see the social so well-attended. She had no idea there were so many women in the county who wanted to find a husband. Why had the Corbett brothers sent for mail-order brides when there were ladies already here wanting to marry? Had they not been aware of them at the time they were looking for someone to marry their cousin? Or maybe they just felt none of them were a good fit for the marshal.

Shannon sighed and watched the old codger stalk away. Evidently he'd had enough of her for now. She hated days like this where she was caught up with her work and there was little to occupy her time. Standing, she stretched and looked around. The office could use a good dusting and sweeping. Dirt from the road was always being tracked inside.

In the back room, she rummaged around until she found a halfway clean rag and set about dusting everything in sight. Evidently, the Corbetts didn't care whether five layers of dust coated the shelves and other sparse furniture. Afterward, she ran the broom over the floors of both rooms and even swept the boardwalk out front and the porch in the back. She leaned against the broom and stared out at the dry Texas landscape. Things here were so different than in Ireland. She missed the green—and the cooler temperatures—and the rain. With the arrival of September, the temperatures had cooled slightly, but it was still hot. The grass had dried, and most of it turned yellow from a lack of water. What she wouldn't give for a nice rain shower.

Sweat streaked down her cheek, and she wiped it with her sleeve. Such an unladylike action, but it seemed a common thing here. Where was the ever-present wind when she needed it?

The bell over the door jingled, and she sighed. Hopefully Mr. Sewell hadn't returned. The Corbett brothers had gone to Dallas, and she had no idea when they'd return. She set the broom in a corner and walked back to the office. A man she'd danced once with at the social stood shifting from foot to foot and repeatedly clearing his throat. He must have had important business in town since he was dressed in his Sunday-go-to-meeting clothes. He was a farmer, if she remembered correctly. His brown trousers and long, dark tan, frock coat looked too big for his lithe frame. A russet silk puff tie circled his neck and was tucked inside his fancy vest. He twirled a black coachman's hat in his hands.

"Good morning, Miss O'Neil."

Shannon nodded, her mind grasping for a name. She'd danced with a half-dozen men after serving the refreshments but couldn't for the life of her remember his. "Forgive me, but your name has slipped my mind."

"Terrence Brannon, ma'am."

The man had left the door open, and Leah walked up behind him. She waved at Shannon, held up a basket, and mouthed something Shannon couldn't understand.

She looked back at her customer. "How can I help you, Mr. Brannon?"

"Is Garrett or Mark here?" His hazel eyes flitted their gaze around the room like a hummingbird darting between flowers.

Shannon held back a smile. It seemed Texas men were either loud and overly bold or horribly shy around women. It was easy to see which Mr. Brannon was.

He tugged at the collar of his white shirt and suddenly dropped to the floor on one knee. Leah's eyes widened, and Shannon dashed forward. Had the man overheated, wearing that wool jacket?

"Mr. Brannon, are you all right?"

His face flushed twenty shades of red. "Um. . .yes, ma'am. I was just. . .um. . .wondering if, um. . ." He suddenly jumped up and grasped her hand. "Marry me, Miss O'Neil. I have a nice farm. A solid house—though it ain't too big. But I can add on when the young'uns start comin'." His words rushed out like a runaway train.

Shannon stepped back and tried to tug her hand away from his. He didn't release it. She glanced at Leah, whose lips were pressed inward as if to hold in a laugh. Her eyes glimmered, and her brows lifted in a teasing manner as if to say, "Answer the man."

"Don't say no, ma'am. I know you have plenty other men to choose from, but I'm hopin' you'll pick me. I'm young and hearty and would make a good father to our children, though I do hope they get your hair. What color is that anyhow?"

Leah snorted, and the man jumped and looked over his shoulder, eyes wide as a spooked cow's. Shannon struggled to hold a straight face. In spite of being tired of marriage offers, she knew this man was sincere and felt bad for his embarrassment. "Please come in, Miss Bennett. Mr. Brannon and I will step outside for a moment."

Leah walked in, not looking at all embarrassed by the odd situation. Once she passed the man, she grinned mischievously, leaned toward Shannon, and whispered, "Let him down easily."

Shannon sucked her lips inward and worked to keep a straight face. While the situation might be humorous to her and Leah, Mr. Brannon was dead serious and had his future riding on her decision. She was getting tired of disappointing suitors, especially when the one man she wished would pay her some attention remained distant.

Outside, she drew in a heavy breath and stiffened her back. Mr. Brannon had half worn out the brim of his hat and looked at her like she was a prize heifer. But she wanted more than someone's admiration. Was it too much to hope to marry someone for love?

"Mr. Brannon—"

"Call me Terrence—or Terry, ma'am."

"Mr. Brannon. Your sincere marriage offer warms my heart, but I'm afraid I can't accept it."

"But why? You need a man to care for you, and I need a woman to tend my home and to give me children."

Shannon resisted the urge to roll her eyes. He was steadfast, if nothing else. "Do you have feelings for me, sir?"

He blinked and stared at her as if she'd asked for his shirt measurements. "What's feelings got to do with anything?"

"A lot. When a marriage hits rough times, it's love and caring that pulls folks through. That and faith in God."

He scratched his head. "I reckon the feelings'll come after we marry. Won't they?"

Shannon shook her head. "A man and woman should care for one another before they marry."

"Well. . .I reckon I could court you a while so's you could get some feelings before we marry up together. Just so long as it didn't take too long."

Men! They were completely dense when it came to romance. "Mr. Brannon, I cannot marry you. Thank you for your offer, but I'm afraid my answer is no."

He stood staring down at his hat. "I reckon you made that clear enough." He glanced toward the freight office door. "You don't suppose that other boardinghouse bride would be interested, would she?"

Shannon shivered. What uncouth men these Americans were. They treated their woman no better than cattle. She hiked up her chin. "I can't speak for Miss Bennett on such a matter, but I don't think today is the proper day to ask her."

"Why not? She sick or something?"

Shannon shook her head, more happy each moment that passed that she hadn't considered this man a serious prospect. "If you'll excuse me, sir, I need to get back inside."

The man slapped his hat on his head and nodded. With a clenched jaw, he stalked down the boardwalk. Shannon slipped back into the office and found Leah had spread out a towel, teapot, saucers, and cookies on Mark's desk. Shannon dragged Garrett's chair toward Leah, whose eyes danced with mirth. Suddenly she doubled over and started laughing.

"Oh my, that was hilarious." Leah slapped her leg and dropped into the chair. "I thought that man had passed out, and the next thing I knew, he was asking you to marry him and have his kids."

Shannon's mouth twitched, and she broke into giggles. "Me, too. I thought the man had fallen in a faint because Mark and Garrett weren't here."

"And did you see his face when he heard me behind him?"

Shannon laughed. "Oh, the poor man was mortified."

Leah attempted to sober. "I tried to back away when I realized what was happening, but I was close to dropping the basket after carrying it from the boardinghouse. And then I. . .snorted."

Both women cackled again, and tears ran down Shannon's cheeks. After a few more attempts to be somber and more fits of laughter, the women finally settled down. Leah poured the tea while Shannon wiped her cheeks and eyes.

"How many offers is that now?" Leah handed her a teacup.

Shannon opened the middle drawer of the desk, pulled out a plain sheet of paper, and made a mark on it. "That makes six so far."

Leah shook her. "How come you're getting so many offers, and I haven't had a one?"

Shannon shook her head and sipped her tea. "Perhaps 'tis because you're at the boardinghouse all day, and men either have to go through the marshal or his wife to get to you. I'm here most mornings, and the Corbetts are often gone. I'm free game, you might say."

"Hmm. . .that does make sense when you put it that way. The marshal can be mighty intimidating, and so can Rachel. She's gotten tougher since they've married, don't you think?"

Shannon nodded. "Aye, there's truth in what you say. Ever since she was kidnapped and Luke Davis declared his love for her, she's been stronger, more confident."

"You think having a good man love you like he does her makes a woman better?"

Shannon shrugged. "I've seen little of happy marriages. My parents' was an arranged union. I don't believe my mum ever came to love my father." She stirred some sugar into her cup. "He was a hard man. But then perhaps he was that way because she didn't love him."

Leah stared into her cup. "My pa, too. All he did was work. My ma loves him, though."

"Do you think it's too much to hope to marry for love?"

Leah's eyes twinkled, and she reached across the desk, touching Shannon's arm. "No, and I'll tell you why." She looked into the back room and at the front door, as if making sure no one would overhear; then she leaned forward. "I've met someone."

Surprise washed through Shannon. Nobody had come calling on Leah at the boardinghouse, and she hadn't been seen around town with anyone in particular. When had she met someone?

During the social? "Who is it?"

Leah grinned and popped a half-eaten cookie into her mouth. "Dan Howard."

Shannon thought of the big man who ran the livery down the street. He was friends with the Corbetts and had been in the office a few times. He'd been kind and polite, not caring that a woman was working there. "I like Mr. Howard. He seems like a decent fellow."

"Oh, he is. And you should see how he cares for his ailing mother. I'm going over tomorrow to visit her."

Shannon ran her fingers around the edge of the tea saucer. "So does he return your affection?"

A soft smile lingered on Leah's cheeks, causing a slash of jealousy to rise up in Shannon. She was happy for Leah, but at the same time, she longed for Mark to notice her.

"I think he does." She leaned forward again, blue eyes dancing like a spring shower. "He kissed me."

Shannon's eyes widened. "Truly?"

Leah nodded.

"Blessit be. Are you thinking you could marry him? 'Twould solve your problem of having the Corbetts support you. I know you don't like that."

"No, I don't, but I wouldn't marry just to escape that. I have feelings for Dan."

"You've done a good job of hiding them."

Leah poured more tea into both cups, sending a spicy scent into the air. "I'll be honest; they come on fast and furious. I truly didn't know a woman could fall for a man so quickly."

Shannon stared out the window and saw the Corbetts riding by on their wagon. They'd probably go around and come down the alley and park in back. Her heart quickened at the thought of seeing Mark again. "I know just what you mean."

Leah's brows dashed upward. "You do?"

Her lips tugged up in a melancholy smile. "Aye."

Leah clutched Shannon's arm and leaned forward again. "Who is it? Tell me before I die of curiosity. I can't for the life of me imagine who he is."

Shannon glanced at the back door, knowing it was too soon for the brothers to have arrived. She looked at Leah, not sure if she should say anything, given Mark's lack of interest shown to her. She shrugged.

"Oh, come on. I told you."

Shannon sighed. "All right, but you can't tell a soul. I don't think he even knows of my attraction."

"Truly?"

She nodded. "Aye." She glanced at the back door again and nibbled her lip.

Leah shook her arm. "Tell me."

"'Tis Mark."

"Mark who?" Wrinkles plowed across Leah's forehead, then suddenly, her eyes widened, and her mouth and nose crinkled on one side. "Surely you don't mean Mark Corbett. Not after all he and his brother have done to us."

Shannon didn't respond, but sat staring into her nearly empty cup. How could she expect Leah to understand when she didn't herself?

The front-door bell jingled, and Homer Sewell strode in. Shannon resisted the urge to roll her eyes. She didn't want to deal with the man twice in one day. "How can I help you, Mr. Sewell?"

"Mark and Garrett back yet? Thought I saw their wagon." He eyed the teacups and empty plate with disdain. "Them brothers won't appreciate their business becomin' a ladies' tea parlor."

Shannon peeked at Leah, who battled a smile. Both ladies filled the basket quickly. Shannon folded the towel and handed it to her friend.

"Well, I shall be off. See you at noon."

Mr. Sewell stepped back and tipped his hat to Leah. Shannon noticed the back door open, and Mark walked in. Her heart skipped a beat.

"Well, if them brothers ain't here, I'm leavin'." Mr. Sewell backed toward the front door. Evidently he couldn't see Mark from where he stood. "Don't know why they let a gal tend to their business. Wimmen oughta be workin' in a kitchen, not an office. It's downright disturbin'."

Chapter 14

Mark stood in the back doorway, his gaze landing on Shannon. A fire in his gut quickened. He didn't like how his body reacted whenever she was near. His stomach swirled with queasiness. His mind worked as if it were trudging through a thick fog. His thoughts got confused, and his tongue seemed to quit working altogether. She was lovely, with her fair skin and auburn hair that his fingers ached to touch. She was young, but not so young that she wasn't all woman. Why did she fluster him so?

He recognized Homer Sewell's voice and cantankerous attitude before his eyes landed on the man. Mark stepped out of the back room, irritated at the man for lashing out at Shannon. "Good day, Homer."

Relief was written all over the man's wrinkled face. "'Bout time you got back here."

"You know my brother and I have deliveries to make and are frequently gone. That's why we hired Miss O'Neil to take orders and be here when we couldn't. I don't care for the way you treated her. She's an employee of Corbett Freight, and as such, deserves the same kindness you'd show us."

Mr. Sewell ducked his head and frowned. Mark's gaze latched onto Shannon's. Her wide green eyes stared back at him, and she sat up straighter. A tiny smile played at the corners of her enticing mouth. He broke his gaze and turned back to his customer. *I've no business noticing Shannon's mouth.*

"So, Homer, you can either place your orders with Shannon when Garrett and I aren't around or just keep coming back to town and try to meet up with us."

"I don't have time to do that. It's a good half-day's ride to Lookout."

"I guess you could try getting your deliveries by stage."

Homer shook his head. "Then I have to drive into town to get them. Costs me a whole day's work. That's why I pay y'all such extravagant prices."

Mark shrugged. "Miss O'Neil has been working here for several weeks, and she's learning fast. Next time you come in and we aren't here, give her your order. I'm sure you'll be satisfied."

"Wimmen ain't got no business working anywhere's but at home." He dug into his pocket and shoved a piece of paper and five silver dollars at Mark. The coins clinked in his hand. "Here's what I need. When can you get it to me?"

Mark noted that he wanted several rolls of barbed fence wire, some lumber, and a bag of nails. Nothing that Shannon would have had trouble ordering. "You still want the Glidden Square Strand wiring?"

Homer nodded. "Yep, and get me another dozen pairs of leather gloves. That wire eats right through them."

Mark did some mental calculations. "I'll probably need another two or three dollars to get all that."

Homer scowled but reached into his pocket and handed Mark a gold eagle coin. "Here, take this and give me those back."

They made the exchange, and Homer went on his way. Mark pocketed the ten-dollar coin and handed Homer's list to Shannon. "Why don't you fill out his order form?"

Shannon wrinkled her mouth, drawing Mark's gaze to it. "He wouldn't like that much."

Mark sat on the corner of his desk. "Try not to let men like him get to you. They're old-fashioned and think God created women to be slaves to men."

Her cheeks flushed a pretty pink. "Thank you for standing up for me. I tried to help him, but he didn't want anything to do with me."

"He's a fool."

Shannon's gaze darted to his, and for a moment, they stared into each other's eyes. His heart galloped, and he couldn't look away for the life of him.

The back door banged, and they both jumped. Mark shot up off the desk.

"You gonna lollygag all day or help me with this load?"

"I was tending to business."

Garrett waggled his brows. "Yeah, I can see that. How is business, Miss O'Neil?"

The pink on Shannon's cheek now flamed red as a Texas star flower.

Mark straightened. "Homer Sewell gave her some trouble."

The grin on Garrett's face changed into a scowl. "What kind of trouble?"

"Oh, you know his kind. Don't think women should ever step out of the house except to do laundry and go to the privy."

Shannon glanced down at the desk, her embarrassment obvious.

"Well, Homer's a good customer, but you don't have to take any guff off him."

"What should I do when a man refuses to deal with me?" she asked.

Garrett pushed his hat back off his forehead. "I hadn't really considered that would be a problem."

Mark knew his brother hadn't considered much when he'd decided to hire Shannon. He was just trying to figure out a way to get some work out of one of the boardinghouse brides in exchange for the money they were paying to support them. Garrett hadn't considered having Shannon work in the office might be difficult for her—or their customers—at times. That was one of the reasons he objected. Some men weren't trustworthy, and it bothered Mark when they had to leave Shannon alone for a long while when they were gone on deliveries.

"Well. . .I guess if you get any more hard-nosed fellows, just tell them they'll have to come back when we're here and talk with us."

Shannon nodded, then pulled a form out of the desk drawer and began recording Homer Sewell's order. She worked so diligently that he was having trouble keeping her busy. Too bad they couldn't hire her to clean their house. It sure needed it, but it didn't seem proper to ask an unmarried gal to clean for two old bachelors. Besides, having her scent teasing him at the office was bad enough. If she spent any time in his home, he was certain he would be awake all night thinking about her.

She nibbled on her lower lip as she concentrated on her work. How had she ever reminded him of Annabelle? There was nothing similar about the two women except maybe the color of their hair and their fair skin. Wisps of auburn hair hung down, curling in loose ringlets. They bounced each time she moved, and he longed to touch them and see if they were as soft as they looked. He swallowed hard. When had he grown to care for her?

Someone shoved him hard, and Mark stumbled sideways, bumping into the desk. "Gonna stand there enjoying the view all day?" Garrett grinned wide, showing all his teeth.

Mark ducked his head, embarrassed to be caught staring. Nothing could come of caring for Shannon O'Neil.

She was sweet.

Innocent.

Even if she did come to care for him one day, when she learned the truth about him, she'd hop the next stage out of town. No decent woman would want a man with a past like his.

Abilene, Texas

Annabelle Smith dodged the cowboy's groping hand and balanced the tray of drinks she held level with her face. Her ribs ached from the "lesson" Everett had given her after closing hours. Wincing, she placed the drinks in front of the man at the all-night gambling table and hurried away.

A young cowpoke called her name and grabbed as she passed, pulling her onto his lap. His warm, wet lips roamed across her bare shoulder. Annabelle cringed and smacked him atop the head with her tray. Raucous laughter erupted, and the young man rubbed his head, grinning.

What was it with these men? They knew all she did was serve drinks. She'd never been an upstairs gal, in spite of Everett's threats to toss her out on the street if she didn't soon change her ways. He'd been making those same threats for years, and he still kept her on, but she was getting older now, and Everett preferred younger girls who didn't yet reflect the hard lifestyle of working in a saloon and dodging men every night. What would she do if he kicked her out on the streets?

She sashayed in and out of trouble and back to the bar. The huge picture of the half-naked woman above the wall of bottles repulsed her. She still hated the odor of liquor and smelly cowboys, but most of the time she didn't notice. Why couldn't she have a decent job like being a seamstress or a cook? She snorted a laugh. What decent citizen would hire a saloon girl?

She might not be an upstairs gal, but to the good townsfolk of Abilene, she was one and the same. Her only chance for another life was to leave this town. But where could she go?

"Stop lollygagging, Annabelle, and get out there and sell drinks. You're costing me money," Everett snarled at her, then poured another round for the men at the bar.

She grabbed a fresh bottle and cups that Everett had wiped half-clean, then strolled around the saloon, stopping at a table with three businessmen. "Can I freshen your drinks, gentlemen?"

One man nodded, and another lifted his glass. The third man, a regular who always gave her trouble, eyed her as if he were a starving man and she a big, juicy steak. "I'm not thirsty, Annabelle. I'm hankering for some alone time with a purty gal."

She cringed but kept a smile pasted on her face. "I'm sure Trudy or Lotus would be happy to oblige you."

He stood, towering over her by a good six inches. "We've danced this dance for years now, and I'm tired of it. You're the one I want."

Annabelle backed up, as a scene from years ago rose in her memory. The same situation had occurred. A man thought he could have more than she was willing to give, but that man had ended up dead. This evening, however, no shining knight was around to rescue her from this vile man, only herself. She forced her voice to sound steady. "Sit down, Cal, and let me pour you a drink."

His eyes ignited, and he shoved his chair back. "Everett says I can take you upstairs whether you wanna go or not. I paid him good, too."

Annabelle's gaze shot over to her boss. A sickening smirk twisted his thick lips, and he lifted a cup to her as if in toast. Why, after all these years, was he forcing this on her?

She had to get out of there. She tossed her tray, bottle and all, at Cal and spun around. Deftly weaving in and out of the tables as she did daily, she headed for the swinging doors that opened onto the street. A growl roared behind her, and the crowd broke out in laughter and cheers, some egging Cal on, and others rooting for her.

Her heart pounded so hard she felt sure it would burst from her chest. A cowboy grabbed her flared skirt, slowing her down. The doors were just two tables away. She didn't dare look back. Plowing out the double doors, she breathed a fresh breath of air while her eyes struggled to adjust to the darkness.

Hide. Fast. Her brain repeated the mantra. *Hide.*

She rushed down the boardwalk steps and turned into the alley, just as she heard the doors fling open so hard they banged against the saloon's facade. A little farther, and she'd be free. At the back of the alley, something huge stepped from the shadows, and Annabelle plowed into the big, fleshy body. Thick hands latched onto her arms, pinning her against him.

"Not so fast, little lady."

Annabelle stiffened at Everett's deep voice. Footsteps charged behind her, drawing closer.

"You knew your days were numbered, but I guess our little talk didn't knock any sense into you. I've been losing money on you for some time now. But no more. Take her, Cal. She's all yours."

"No!" Annabelle kicked and jerked, trying to get free. "You can't make me do this."

Cal lifted her and slung her over one big shoulder and carried her through the saloon's back door. Hoots rose up from the crowd.

Upside down, she could see their leering faces and sickening grins. How many of them figured they'd be next?

She wanted to die. Maybe she could get to Cal's gun, shoot him, and get away. Maybe she'd just shoot herself, too.

One of the upstairs doors opened. Lotus stepped into the hall. "Well, well, it's about time someone brought Miss High and Mighty up here. Guess you won't be so snooty to us after tonight."

Bile burned Annabelle's throat. How could this be happening? Why hadn't she left her job sooner?

Cal kicked in a door, and Trudy squealed and grabbed for her cover-up. He cursed and opened another door. Annabelle was close to passing out from fear and being held upside down for so long, but she had to keep her wits about her.

Cal kicked the door shut with his boot and deposited her on the bed. She bounced twice, the old frame creaking and groaning.

"Just relax. You'll enjoy yourself, I promise."

What an arrogant imbecile!

Her mind raced. There had to be some way out of this situation. Maybe if she played coy, he'd drop his guard. Her gaze roved the room. There wasn't much to work with. Besides a bed, there was one ladder-back chair, and a small table holding a flowery ceramic pitcher and basin.

She crawled off the dirty bed, and stood in front of the table.

"What do you think you're doing?" Cal moved closer, unbuckling his holster.

She cast a coy glance over her shoulder. "A girl has to freshen up, doesn't she?"

Cal's gray eyes narrowed, gazing at her as if he didn't quite trust her. And well he shouldn't.

"You don't know how long I've dreamed of this, sweetheart." He stepped up behind her and ran his hands down her arms.

She turned, forcing a playful look. "Me, too. I was just playin' hard to get earlier."

His eyes sparked, and he pulled her into his arms. His lips roved her face, found her mouth, and she made herself play along. After a minute of impossible disgust, she pushed him back. "Don't you want to take off your shirt?"

He grinned and walked back to the door, locking it. He unfastened his buttons and turned to hang his shirt on a hook on the wall, then removed his belt. Repulsed, Annabelle swiped her mouth. She reached behind herself slowly, grabbed the near-empty pitcher, and crept forward. Cal turned slowly, and Annabelle slammed the pitcher upside his head. It cracked and broke, raining water and shards at their feet.

Cal stared at her, dumbfounded. Annabelle's heart raced. What would he do to her now?

He took a half-step forward; then his eyes rolled up in his head, and he fell toward her. She grabbed him, hoping no one would hear his fall, but his weight was too much, and he took her down with him. Stunned, she lay there a moment to catch her breath. But she couldn't rest long. She had to get away.

With some effort, she managed to slide out from under him. Blood ran down the side of his face and onto the carpet. She stared down at Cal, hoping she hadn't killed him, but she imagined that's what he'd do to her if he woke up.

She snatched up the belt and wrapped it around him, locking his arms to his side. The belt barely fit, but it should hold him for a while, giving her precious time to get away. She grabbed his shirt next, and rolled it up, fashioning a gag, using the sleeves to tie it on.

What about his feet? If he could get up, he could make it to the hallway where someone would see him. Her gaze raced around the room. His holster!

She removed his revolver, pulled his feet together, and wrapped the holster around it, hooking it as tight as she could.

Again, her heart stampeded. How could she get out of the saloon without being seen? How could she leave town when she had almost no money? The pittance Everett paid her was barely enough to live on.

She unlocked the door, wincing at its loud click, and opened it a hair. The other doors upstairs were closed. To her left were the rooms Trudy and Lotus were using and the stairs back down to the saloon. To her right was another door. Everett's room.

He'd sent her upstairs on occasion over the years when he'd

collected a pile of money. She'd always put it in the bottom drawer of his desk and locked it, returning the key to him when she got back downstairs. He never wanted to leave when customers were there, fearing they'd steal bottles of liquor or start a fight and tear things up.

She slipped into his room and allowed her eyes to adjust to the dark. The overpowering rank scent she recognized as Everett's nearly made her retch. Feeling her way, she found the desk and hurried around behind it. Opening the curtains allowed the light of the three-quarter moon to illuminate the room so she could see well enough. She tugged on the bottom drawer, knowing it would be locked. But to her surprise, it slid free. Way in the back, underneath a stack of papers, she pulled out the money box. The lock on it had long since broken, and Everett was too cheap to buy another one.

He'd be sorry.

Her heart thudded in her chest, as if it were a trapped bird frantically trying to get free. And wasn't that what she was?

She reached in the box. Everett would notice if she took all the money, but he owed her. She'd slaved for him and suffered at his hand, especially tonight. He would pay for her to start a new life.

She grabbed a handful of bills and several double eagle coins, then shoved the drawer closed. Annabelle stuffed the money in her corset and hurried to the back door. Everett's parents had died in a fire, and she'd be forever grateful that he'd had a rear stairway installed, leading from his bedroom.

She unlatched the door and hurried down the steps. Keeping to the shadows, she crept along. The only way to get away fast was to steal a horse, but that was a hanging offense—and she couldn't ride off in her saloon dress.

Untying the closest horse, she led him down the alley and several streets over to the room she rented.

"Hurry, hurry." She could feel Cal waking up and knew he'd make a ruckus until someone heard him.

In her room, she quickly changed into her one cotton calico, her decent dress. She removed the pillowcase and stuffed her hairbrush and undergarments in it. Taking a final look at the ratty place she'd called home for seven years, she knew she'd not mourn its loss.

Quickly, she mounted the horse and raced it out of town. She didn't look back. Nothing good had happened to her in Abilene.

But her luck was changing.

Now she had to decide where to go.

Only one thought came to mind. Find the one man who'd ever shown her true kindness.

She had to find Mark Corbett.

Chapter 15

Leah knocked on the door of the Howard house for the second time. She suspected Mrs. Howard was sleeping. Should she go ask Dan's permission before going inside? He had told her it was all right to go in if his mother didn't answer, but she still hated to do so.

She tested the handle and found the door opened easily. She peeked into the parlor and noted it could use a good straightening and dusting. "Mrs. Howard?"

She stepped into the entryway of the house. "It's Leah Bennett, ma'am. Your son said I could come in and visit with you."

Leah pursed her lips when no answer came. She set down her basket and looked around. On the right was an open door to a bedroom. From the manly clothing hanging on pegs on the wall, she knew that was Dan's room. She tiptoed through the parlor and into a short hall that separated the bedrooms. Mrs. Howard lay on her side, facing the wall. A light quilt covered her body. How could she stand the heat with that cover on and the windows shut? Leah crept back to the parlor and looked around.

She should probably leave. But wouldn't it surprise the older woman to awaken from her nap to a clean house with a meal already prepared? Looking around, she decided the kitchen would be her first chore. She opened the back and front doors, along with the kitchen and parlor windows, to let in some fresh air and cool things down.

The morning dishes had been washed, probably Dan's efforts. She found where they belonged and put the plates and coffee cups on the shelf with the other dishes. The silverware rested in a tin can that had long ago lost its label. Taking the cleaning supplies she'd borrowed from Rachel, she washed every surface from the windowsill to the shelves to the top of the canned goods that resided in a tiny pantry. She wiped down the table and chairs and found a broom and mop and tended to the floors. Lastly, she washed several small glass decorations that she suspected were Mrs. Howard's treasures. Standing back with her hands on her hips, she surveyed the spotless kitchen. Her heart warmed at having something to do and being able to help someone.

Rachel had given her a ham hock and some meat. As much as Leah hated lighting the stove and warming up the house even more, she found a large pot and started stewing the meat. She added a pinch of salt and a few other seasonings she found in the pantry and went to clean the parlor.

An hour later, she'd finished cleaning everything she could see, except for Mrs. Howard's room. She'd like to wash the woman's sheets like she had Dan's, but she didn't want to overstep her bounds and embarrass Dan's mother.

The only other thing she could think to do was the laundry. Dan's sheets and blanket were already nearly dry in the warm afternoon sun and brisk wind. The hardest task was heating more water, but Dan had made that duty less difficult with the device he'd made for his mother. An iron rack stood over a campfire in the backyard, and she just had to fill the pot with fresh water. She'd done the task once already when washing the sheets. With the water warming, she added a few chopped logs to the fire, and then stirred Dan's clothes into the water. While they simmered, she went back inside to cut up vegetables for the stew.

She halfway expected to find Mrs. Howard sitting in the kitchen or parlor, and when she didn't, she tiptoed back to the room. The woman was sleeping in the same position. "You must really be tired," Leah whispered. *Poor woman.*

She made quick work of cutting up the potatoes, carrots, and onions for the stew. Then she mixed up a batch of cornbread and put it in the oven. At the back door, she took a moment to rest. If she were to marry Dan, this would be her home, and these would be her daily tasks. She could easily see herself in the sturdy home. Rachel had told her that Dan's father had built the house when Dan was just a boy.

Turning back to look at the inside, she allowed her eyes to adjust. All the rooms could use a fresh coat of paint and maybe even some wallpaper in the parlor. She could do so many things to pretty up this house if she had the chance.

"Please, Lord. I ask that You'd give me that chance. Thank You for saving me from marrying Mr. Abernathy." A snakelike shiver coursed down her spine. "If it be Your will, please allow Dan to fall in love with me. I'd take good care of him and his mother. I promise You that."

After a few more moments of resting and praying for her family back home in Carthage, she washed and rinsed Dan's clothes and hung them on the line. Then she took the clean sheets inside and made Dan's bed. His quilt would need another hour on the line before it was dried. She straightened and rubbed her lower back. Doing the washing and cleaning the whole house in one day was a lot of work, especially since she'd been so inactive the past months with nothing much to occupy her time. She would sleep well tonight; that was certain.

She tiptoed back to Mrs. Howard's room, hoping to get her dirty clothing. The woman still hadn't moved. Leah wondered how Mrs. Howard kept her back from aching. If she'd slept in the same position for so long, hers surely would hurt. Leah studied the quilt for a moment, and she felt a sudden catch in her heart. She bent down and stepped closer. Surely the quilt was moving. Maybe she just couldn't see it in the dim light.

But moving closer didn't change a thing. The quilt didn't move in the least. With a trembling hand, Leah reached out to touch the woman's wrinkled cheek. It felt cool, but how could that be? Leah was sweating from the heat of the stuffy room.

Sucking in a steadying breath, she held her fingers in front of the woman's nose.

Nothing.

Not a single breath.

Leah gasped and jerked back her hand. *No!*

What to do? What to do?

She had to know for sure if Dan's ma had perished. Pressing her quivering fingers to the woman's neck, she hoped—she prayed—to feel a pulse.

She dropped onto the bed, knowing now that Dan's mother had gone to meet her Maker. She had to tell Dan, but how did one do such a thing? Maybe she should get Rachel?

But no, Dan was the man Leah loved. She was the one who had to tell him. She pulled the quilt up and covered Mrs. Howard's face, sad that she'd never get to know her.

Back in the kitchen, she removed the cornbread from the oven and stirred the stew. Dan would not likely have an appetite tonight.

She glanced out the back screen door at the light blue sky. "Lord, give me the words to say."

Ten minutes later, she stood in the back of the livery. Dan patted the rear of a black horse and told a man that he'd be happy with his purchase.

"Thank you. You came highly recommended." He handed Dan several double-eagle coins, mounted, and rode off.

Dan pocketed the money and smiled. She suspected he thought he'd had a good day. She hated disappointing him. Her heart ached for him. How had her feelings grown so swiftly? She hadn't even fallen for Sam this fast.

"Leah? Have you finished over at the house?" He walked toward her. "I was just heading over there to see if things were going all right."

"I—" Tears filled Leah's eyes and burned her throat.

Dan jogged toward her, a concerned expression marring his handsome face. "What's wrong? Did you hurt yourself?" He grabbed both her hands, turned them over and back, as if searching for an injury. "What's the matter, Leah?"

She tried to form the words but couldn't get them out. She reached forward and laid her hand on his chest. His brows crinkled.

"It's your ma."

He shot out of the livery like a cannonball. Leah picked up her skirts and hurried after him. She didn't want him to be alone at such a time. The front door was open when she arrived, and a wail rose up from the bedroom. Dan knelt on the far side of the bed, clutching his mother's body to his chest. He rocked back and forth, tears streaming down his face. Leah had never heard such a heartrending sound other than the one she'd made herself when she'd learned of Sam's death.

She hurried to Dan's side and laid her hand on his shoulder. His rocking ceased, and he laid his mother back on the bed, staring down at her. Finally he stood, covered her face, and turned to Leah.

"I should have stayed home today. I knew she was feeling poorly."

Leah shook her head and patted his chest. "No, I should have checked on her when I first arrived here, but I thought she was just sleeping."

Dan shook his head and wiped his eyes. "It's not your fault. Ma had been ailing for a while."

"But maybe if I'd done something—" Tears burned Leah's eyes again.

Dan cupped her cheeks with his calloused hands. "Leah, this isn't your fault. Ma was getting older. She had me when she was in her late twenties, and I'm no spring chicken."

In spite of her grief, Leah smiled.

"There's nothing either of us could have done. Ma has been missing Pa for a long while, and now they're together."

"What are you going to do?"

He stared up at the ceiling, and his chin quivered. Suddenly, he sobbed and pulled her against him, crushing her in his grief. She held him, caressing his back and cooing soft words of comfort. If he'd give her the chance, she'd always be there for him. She wasn't sure how long he held her, but finally his tears abated.

He pulled away and wiped his eyes again. "Sorry."

"Don't be. I'm happy I can be here so you don't have to be alone now." Leah rested her hand on his arm. She admired a man who wasn't afraid to allow his emotions to show, especially a big manly man like Dan. Her father rarely had, other than to express his displeasure.

His damp eyes warmed. His long, dark lashes stuck together in spiky clumps. He ran the back of his fingers down her cheek, and his gaze intensified. He leaned toward her, and she stretched up to meet him. If he found comfort in kissing her, so be it.

Their lips were just a hair's breadth away when someone pounded on the door.

"Dan, you here?" The marshal's voice intruded. "The livery's open, but no one's over there. Everything all right?"

Dan wiped his face on his sleeve, then patted Leah's cheek and walked to the parlor. "C'mon in, Luke." He dropped onto a chair and sat with his head hanging down, arms on his knees.

Luke's gaze shot over to Leah, his surprise at seeing her come out of the bedroom evident. He narrowed his gaze. "What's going on here?"

Leah waited for Dan to respond, but he just shook his head. Luke turned to her. "Dan's mother passed away."

Luke hurried to his friend's side and draped his hand over Dan's shoulder. "I'm right sorry to hear that. Tell me what I can do."

Dan cleared his throat and sat up. "I reckon you could fetch the pastor, if you don't mind."

Luke nodded and glanced at Leah again.

"I came over to help out Mrs. Howard. I did some cleaning, laundry, and made a ham stew, and didn't even know. . . ." Her lip quivered, and fresh tears stung her eyes. She sniffled, causing Dan to look up. He stood and hurried to her side, putting his arm around her shoulders.

Luke's surprise was evident, but her heart ached too much to be concerned about his reaction. She'd wanted to get to know Dan's mother, to become her friend, and to learn what Dan was like when he was young. She'd wanted Mrs. Howard to know that she'd fallen in love with her son.

Luke pushed his hat back and scratched his head. "I'll. . .uh. . .

go by the house and send Rachel over and then collect the pastor."

Dan nodded and Luke left. Another wave of grief hit Leah again, and she turned into Dan's arms, laying her face against his shirt. His arms embraced her tightly.

"It'll be all right, darlin'."

Leah stood beside Dan at his mother's funeral, longing to reach out—to touch him, but such an action wouldn't be appropriate for an unmarried couple in public. She wished Dan's sister and brother could have attended the funeral, but his sister was in the early stages of pregnancy and having trouble keeping food down. Travel was out of the question. Dan's brother couldn't come, either. His wife was away, caring for her best friend's children while her friend was down with a strange case of influenza, so Dan's brother was tending their five children. Surely having family present at this time of loss would have been a comfort.

The pastor's voice droned on about what a wonderful woman Clara Howard had been and how she was now in the Lord's arms. Leah wished again that she'd gotten to know the woman instead of wasting so much time doing a whole lot of nothing the past few months.

How would Dan get along living alone? He'd lived with his parents all his life and had worked side by side with his dad until the older man died. Dan had probably never done any cooking until his mother had taken to her bed. He would certainly be lonely and would have no one to comfort him during his grieving. She stepped closer to him, wanting him to know she was there for him.

He didn't look down, but the back of his hand brushed hers. He looped his little finger around hers and gave it a quick squeeze and let go. Leah's heart soared, but she hoped no one noticed Dan's finger hug.

After the service, she wandered over to stand by Shannon while the townsfolk offered their condolences to Dan.

" 'Tis hard to lose your mum."

"How long has it been since yours died?"

"Over a year now, it has. At first, I just wanted to crawl in a barrel and die, too. I didn't know how I would survive in a strange country without my parents, but God watched over me. I was angry for a long while, but I'm coming to see His hand in my life."

Leah hugged her friend's shoulders. "I'm so glad He kept you safe and brought you here."

Shannon chuckled. "Aye, me, too. I never dreamed I'd end up in Texas, though."

"Me, either. I just wanted to get away from that awful man my pa wanted me to marry. I'd have gone to California if I had to. At least Texas was closer."

Rachel hugged Dan and then walked up to the women. "People have been donating food for Dan. I thought I'd take it over to his house and set it up in the kitchen. He asked that we all join him."

She caught Leah's gaze, and her eyes gleamed as if she knew something. Had the marshal mentioned finding her alone with Dan?

"We'd be happy to help, right, Leah?"

She nodded her head, glad to have a reason to be with Dan for a while longer. "We can take an armload over there now, if you're ready to leave."

"Just let me find Jacqueline, and we'll both help." Rachel's gaze scanned the crowd. "Dan said it was all right for us to go on into his house, so go ahead if you want and get started. I'll be there as soon as I track down that rascally daughter of mine."

On the table at the back of the church, they found all manner of food. A small ham. Jars of canned beans, beets, and other vegetables and fruit. Several cooked dishes had been prepared and also three desserts. Leah needn't worry about Dan having food for the next few days. With their arms loaded, they made the trek across town to the Howard home. Leah's arms ached by the time they arrived. "Let's put all this on the kitchen table, and then we can arrange it once everything is here."

Shannon nodded and followed her into the kitchen. " 'Tis a lovely house the Howards have."

"Yes, it is." Leah surveyed the house. It looked much the same as it had yesterday, except that Dan's bed wasn't made. She hurried back to his room and made quick work of that task, lest he be embarrassed to have guests see it a mess.

"There's already enough food to feed every Texas Ranger in the state. I don't know how Mr. Howard will consume it all before it spoils." Shannon stood looking at the food with her hands on her waist, shaking her head when Leah reentered the dining room.

"I suspect that's why he invited us over. Let's put the canned items on that shelf next to the stove." Leah picked up two jars. "We'll serve the fresh food now, and Dan will have these for later on."

"Dan, is it? You sound right at home here." Shannon flashed her a teasing grin.

"Well, I'm not. I just spent half of yesterday here, so I guess I'm more familiar with things than you are." Leah's cheeks heated. "Besides, being the oldest of eleven children, I'm used to bossing others around."

"I would have liked having an older sister like you. All my siblings died before birth or passed shortly after."

"I'm sorry. Siblings can sure try your patience, but there's something nice about having a big family."

Shannon leaned against the counter. "Do you miss them?"

Leah ran her finger around the top of a jar lid. "Yes, sometimes, especially the younger ones, but I don't miss all the names they called me." She placed the jar on the shelf. "The older ones resented it when I was in charge and had to tell them what to do."

"Must have been difficult for you."

"It was, but it was the only life I knew."

"Will you go back someday?"

Leah opened the back door and stared out. "I don't know. I'd like to see my family, but I can't go back unless I'm married. Pa would give me to Mr. Abernathy faster than a magician could make a coin disappear."

Shannon crossed the room and laid a hand on Leah's shoulder. "I have no one, and you have no relatives here. Perhaps we can be family."

Leah turned, her heart warming at Shannon's offer. "I'd like that." She gave her friend a hug and saw Rachel and Luke come in the door.

Things turned hectic as the women set out the food and the

men gathered in the parlor, talking. Both Corbett brothers had come home with Dan. Leah set out plates and forks and filled a pitcher of water from the outside pump while Rachel sliced a small ham and Shannon mashed some boiled turnips a woman had dropped off at the house. Delicious scents filled the air and made Leah's stomach rumble.

"The food's ready," Rachel called to the men a short while later.

Dan glanced at the door. "The reverend's family was coming."

"Why don't you men go ahead and dish up and eat. We'll need to wash some of the plates in order to have enough." Rachel tapped her index finger against her mouth. "Or I could run home and get a few of my plates."

Leah reached up onto a shelf and took down several bowls. "No need. We can make sandwiches for the pastor's youngsters and send them out back and use these bowls for us womenfolk."

Dan smiled and nodded. "Sounds like a plan to me. Let's all gather around the table and pray over the food. Looks real good."

Dan led the way into the kitchen, now crowded with people. He walked around the table and stopped next to Leah. She kept her gaze ahead, not wanting people to know the depth of her feelings for the man next to her.

"Let's hold hands." Dan's deep voice rumbled next to her, and she felt his fingers searching for hers. He clutched her hand like a man grabbing the reins of a runaway wagon. "Dear Lord. Good friends and f–family. I ask that You receive my ma into Your arms and reunite her with my pa. They loved each other here on earth for a long while. Bless this food, and the friends gathered here today. Amen."

He squeezed Leah's hand before letting go. She stood back and allowed the men to dish up first; then she took a bowl and helped herself. If she let her mind go, she could pretend that she and Dan were married and living in this house. That they had invited their close friends over—well, all except the Corbett brothers.

She followed the other women outside to sit on the front porch. Dan's gaze followed her movement as she walked through the parlor, past the other men. Maybe her pretending wasn't that far off.

Chapter 16

Saturday evening arrived sunny with a north wind that brought slightly cooler temperatures. Shannon was ever so glad the stifling summer heat was gone, at least for the moment. But with this being Texas, heat was never gone for good, so she'd been told numerous times.

Lively music filled the air, and dancers promenaded, curtsied and bowed, and swung their partners in wide circles. The American square dance reminded her a bit of an Irish jig, though it seemed more organized.

She watched Mark, grinning wide, catch the hand of his pretty blond partner, and they danced forward and back, once, twice, three times. He looked happy. She sighed. He had no idea that her heart ached for him. Why couldn't he smile at her like that? All he ever did was stare at her, probing with those amazing eyes.

She'd never planned to fall for a Corbett, not after their shenanigans, but something about Mark called to her. He seemed happy enough on the outside, but there was a longing in his heart, something he yearned for or that pained him, something that he'd never expressed to her—and she doubted he'd ever spoken of it to his brother. Trying to talk seriously with Garrett was a waste of time, if you asked her. The man was full of blarney and had been born in the wrong century. He should have been a court jester. She grinned, thinking how silly he'd look jumping around in one of those jester outfits she'd seen in a book. Garrett danced his partner around Mark and bumped his brother, almost knocking him down. Garrett laughed, but Mark scowled.

"Those Corbett brothers must be happy with so many people showing up this evening." Leah wiped down the table that had held her baked goods. "It's hard to believe everything sold in less than ten minutes when it took hours to bake it all."

"You'll have to be making more next time. I'd be happy to help you."

"I might just take you up on that offer." Leah shoved her fist to her back. "I did so much baking that I don't think I can dance tonight."

"Not even with Dan?" She shot her friend a playful look.

"No, not even him. But he won't be here tonight. He's mourning his mother."

"Have you seen him since the funeral?"

Leah nodded, and her cheeks turned pink. "I walked over to the livery while you were at work yesterday morning and took him several of the muffins left over from our breakfast, but I haven't seen him today. I wonder how he's getting along."

" 'Twas nice how the Corbetts offered to cancel the social since the funeral was just two days past. But Mark said Dan told them to go ahead and hold it."

Leah nodded. "It would have been nearly impossible to get word out that fast, and he didn't want people coming all the way to town and finding out the social had been called off."

Shannon stacked the dirty pie pans into a crate and then added the soiled plates on top. "Do you think you made enough money to bake more next time and also get some fabric like you've been wanting?"

"Maybe, but I'll have to order the cloth, so I doubt if it would be here in time for the next social. I could have the Corbetts pick some up in Dallas, but the thought of having those two select fabric for me makes me cringe."

Shannon smiled, stopping beside her friend to watch the

dancers. "Have you heard the Fosters have decided not to rebuild the store?"

Leah spun to face her, surprise evident in her wide blue eyes. "But what will the town do without a mercantile? How can it survive?"

"Garrett told Mark that Mr. Foster's niece is moving here with her two children, and she will take it over."

"Is she not married?"

Shannon shrugged one shoulder. "He said something about her being a widow."

"I'm sorry for her loss. Maybe we should warn her that the Corbetts will try to find her another husband if she comes here."

Giggling, Shannon shoved Leah with her arm. "Nay, then she won't come, and we need the store."

"Too true."

"There's to be a store raisin' next Saturday. Mr. Foster wants to supervise the building project, and then he and his wife will move to Dallas to live with his mother, who's getting on in years."

"I know folks around here will miss them." Leah gathered the last of the silverware and set it in the crate, then wiped down the table. "I've heard they've been part of this town since its beginning."

A group of five cowboys who'd just arrived sauntered toward them. The hair on the back of Shannon's neck lifted. These fellows looked rough and right off the range. Most of the men who were looking for a wife had taken the time to bathe and, at the very least, put on clean clothes and slapped on some sweet-smelling stuff. These fellows looked like they were just out for a good time.

The tallest strode directly toward Shannon. He smelled of dust and cattle and had nearly a week's growth of beard. His jeans and boots were filthy.

"I'm not dancing tonight. I was just helping serve the food." She hiked up her chin to show him she meant business.

"Ah, a purdy little lady like her don't want to dance with the likes of you, Dom."

The tall man narrowed his eyes at the speaker. "Shut up, Chappy. She sure don't want an old man. She's young and pretty and needs a hearty man. Ain't that what this shindig is all about?"

Shannon backed closer to Leah. She didn't want to dance with any of these drovers. The tall man named Dom drew up near her and grabbed her wrist. "I rode two hours to get to this party, and I aim to dance."

"Leave her alone, you bully." Leah yanked at the man's hand and tried to pull it off Shannon's arm.

He elbowed her back and pulled Shannon toward the dance floor. Shannon dug in her heels, not making it easy.

A dark-haired man with an eye patch walked past her toward Leah. "C'mon, blondie. Guess you and me'll take a spin."

Shannon's heart pounded, and her legs trembled. The man swung her around and pulled her up close. She turned her face away to avoid smelling his foul breath, but not before she caught a whiff of liquor.

Suddenly, she was wrenched backward, and Mark and Garrett stood between her and the cowboy.

"Hey, that's my gal. Get out of my way." Dom glared at the brothers, his fists raised.

"This is a civilized gathering. Troublemakers aren't welcome," Mark said.

"That's right. You and your friends would be better served at the Wet Your Whistle."

"So says you." The man swung, but Garrett ducked.

Mark guided Shannon out of the way as the four other cowboys joined in to help their buddy. The dance stopped as most of the men set aside their ladies and came to Garrett's rescue. Mark hurried toward the crowd.

"No, Mark, your cast," Shannon yelled, but she doubted he heard through the roar.

Punches flew left and right. Upraised voices shouted from all directions. Men were knocked down, but most jumped right back up. Women screamed. Shannon lost sight of Mark. She wrung her hands and prayed, "Please, Father God, keep him safe."

A man stumbled toward her backward, arms flailing. She jumped out of his way, and dodged another man who fell at her feet.

Suddenly, the blast of a gun rent the air. Everyone froze. Marshal Davis sat atop his horse with his gun pointed at the sky.

The scent of gunpowder tinged the air. "That's enough of that. Garrett! Mark! What's goin' on here?"

Garrett shoved a man off of himself and stood, wiping the dirt from his clothes. "We were just having a friendly time here until these cowboys"—he looked around the crowd and pointed at the five men—"started some trouble."

The marshal waved his gun at the men. "All of you, get over here."

They begrudgingly did as told, mumbling and slapping dirt and examining bruised fists.

"Now, you can leave town, go down to the saloon, or get hauled off to jail, but the dance is over for you."

"Aww. . .we just wanted to take a spin with a purdy gal, Marshal." The shortest man of the five lifted his bushy face toward Luke. Blood ran down the corner of his mouth.

"This dance is for the purpose of people meeting with a mind to marry. I don't see how that applies to you cowpokes. These woman are ladies, not saloon girls, and as such, they deserve your respect and to be treated kindly. Get moving, and I don't want to see you at this social again. Not tonight. Not in the future."

Each of the men found their hats, which had been knocked off during the fight. They collected their horses, and the marshal escorted them down the street. A large man ran past them, and his steps slowed as he walked toward Leah. Shannon smiled. Had Dan heard the ruckus and been worried about Leah?

The music started up again, and Shannon looked for Mark. He stood next to the table, rummaging through the crate of dirty dishes. She hurried toward him. What could he be looking for?

"Can I help you find something?"

He turned, and she gasped. His lower lip had swollen, and blood ran down his chin. One eye was swelling shut, and the knuckles of his left hand were bleeding. He held his cast against his chest. Had he injured his arm again?

"Are you all right?"

"Fine. I just need a cloth or something to use to wipe this blood off my face."

The rag they'd wiped off the table with was still in the bucket.

She swished it around the water to clean it and then squeezed out the excess water. She tried to dab the blood, but Mark reached for the rag.

"I can do it."

"Just rest and let me tend to you."

He sighed but sat on the edge of the table and allowed her to clean his wound. He stared at the dancers and sat stiff as a fence post.

Shannon wilted a little inside. Did he despise her so much?

He had no idea how being this close to him made her feel. She tried to hold her hand steady. She'd touched him so few times and was rarely close enough to see the variations of blue in his eyes. Pressing lightly, she turned his chin toward her and dabbed at the blood. His left eye was ugly and swollen. If only she had a cold slab of meat to put on it. "Does it hurt you?"

Mark flexed his injured hand. "Not too bad."

Shannon took his large hand in hers and held it lightly, then laid the cloth over his knuckles and looked up. He'd been watching her. She longed to draw him close, to let him know how scared she'd been for him. No wonder he was so battered when he could use only his left hand to defend himself. He was too honorable to conk anyone with his cast, even if it meant he took the brunt of the fight.

Several stems of grass were stuck in his hair, and she boldly plucked them out. She longed to run her hands through his hair but instead dropped them to her side. He was staring at her, and she captured his gaze. Her breathing turned ragged, and she fought to control it. Her heart throbbed, and for a fleeting second, she thought he might kiss her. But he turned his head and stood, taking the cloth off his hand. He tossed it onto the table, muttered thanks, and strode off.

Shannon hung her head. What about her was so undesirable? Did he consider her nothing more than the hired help? Or was it the fact that she was Irish?

She'd read in the newspaper that in big cities like New York some employers had posted signs that said NINA—no Irish need apply.

Rinsing the cloth, she thought about that. He'd never treated her as if her heritage bothered him. Yes, he didn't want her working at the freight office at first, but he seemed to have gotten used to the idea. So. . .she could work for him, but she could never be anything more than an employee. Tears blurred her eyes.

How did she explain that to her heart?

Dan strode up to Leah and grasped her shoulders. His frantic gaze ran down her body. "Are you hurt? Did anyone bother you? What happened here?"

Leah offered a smile to calm him down. Why was he so agitated? It was just a brawl. Certainly not the first one in Lookout. "I'm perfectly fine. What are you doing here?"

He released her and paced to the end of the table and back, curling the edges of his hat. Various expressions crossed his face, but she didn't understand them. He stopped in front of her and looked around. "I need to talk to you. Alone."

"Shall we take a walk?"

He shoved his hat back on and nodded, offering his arm. A slow tune followed them as they meandered past the church and down the road leading out of town. The sun had not yet set and still cast enough light so that walking wasn't difficult. They crested a hill, and once they'd gone down the other side, blocking the town from their view, Dan stopped. He swiped his hat off again and resumed his pacing.

Leah almost smiled, but his anxiety seemed too real for jesting. She waited, twisting her hands behind her back, wondering what was on his mind. Maybe he was ready for her to clean out his mother's bedroom, as she'd offered.

A determined look crossed his face, and he strode right up to her, stopping only a few feet away. "I know the timing is rotten, and some folks will look down on us—because I'm still in mourning—but knowing you were near that fight and I wasn't around to protect you scared ten years off of me."

Confusion clouded Leah's mind. "It's not your job to protect me, Dan."

His mouth worked as if he were chewing something tough. "No, but I want it to be." He slapped his hat against his pants leg and walked off a few feet.

He wanted to protect her? Her heart quickened. Was it possible that he had fallen for her like she had him? She clutched her hands to her chest. *Please, God.*

He turned again. "It's lousy timing."

"What is?" She moved closer, daring to touch his arm.

His gaze lifted to the sky, and she studied his square jaw. Some women might say he was too rugged, too big to be handsome, but she liked him just how he was. He looked strong enough to protect her from anyone.

His gaze locked with hers. "Leah. . ." Her name sounded special on his lips. Cherished in the deep timbre of his voice. "I–I've never done this before."

"Done what?"

He studied her face, his dark eyes roving, caressing. "Asked a gal to marry me."

Leah felt her own eyes go wide. She struggled to swallow. To find her voice. "Are you?"

A soft smile tugged at his lips. "You wouldn't think me a cad to ask you to marry me when I just buried my ma?"

Leah smiled and tears blurred her vision. She shook her head.

Dan tugged at his pants leg, and knelt before her. A rainbow of emotions flooded her. Could this actually be happening?

He took her hands in his fingertips. "Leah, I know we haven't known each other long, but I've cared for you since I first saw you. I couldn't say nothin' when you were uh—" He looked away for a moment. "When you were competing for Luke's hand, but now you're free of that. Would you. . .uh. . .would you consider being my wife?"

Leah squealed, and Dan jumped up and looked behind him. She broke into a fit of giggles. He stared at her like she'd gone crazy. "What's so funny?"

Leah tried to sober but kept seeing him jump. "Nothing."

"Was my proposal so ridiculous?" Hurt laced his gaze.

All humor fled, and she touched his arm again. "Not at all. I'm sorry." She straightened and looked him in the eye, so he'd have no doubts to her seriousness. "I'd be delighted and honored to be your wife."

"You would? You're not joshin' me?"

Leah grinned. "No, Dan. My feelings for you have grown quickly, too." She longed to tell him that she loved him, but felt something so serious should come from the man first.

Dan grinned and shoved his hat back on. "When?"

"Whenever you're ready."

"How about tomorrow?" He chuckled, his eyes gleaming.

"A lady needs time to prepare." The thought of buying and making a wedding dress suddenly gave her cause for concern. Had she made enough selling pies and cookies to buy what she needed?

Dan took her hands. "What's wrong? I can see that something's bothering you. Is it the timing?"

Leah stared at the ground, not wanting Dan to know how little she possessed. He had a house, nice furnishings, food, even a business, but what did she have to offer? She didn't even want children, and that thought burned a hole in her heart. Would he still want to marry her if he knew?

She needed to tell him, but she couldn't do it now. She didn't want to ruin the sweetness of the moment.

He gently took hold of her upper arms again. "Leah, if it's money you need, I have some. Not a lot, but plenty enough to buy you a wedding dress and whatever other fripperies a bride needs."

"You shouldn't have to pay for everything. I just don't have much to offer, and it doesn't seem fair to you."

He pulled her to his chest, and she nuzzled in close. His head rested on hers, and she wrapped her arms around his waist. "Darlin', you're all I want. I don't care if you're wearing all you own. It's you that's important to me. Whenever I see you, my heart perks up and sings, like one of them songbirds outside my window each morning. Knowing you're near helps me to keep going even though ma is gone. If I have you, I'm not alone."

She hugged him hard. "Thank you. I feel the same way."

He released his grip on her slightly, caught her gaze, and

slowly bent toward her. His kiss was all—more—than she had dreamed about, and far too soon, he ended it.

"I'd love to stand here all night, spoonin' with you, darlin', but I reckon we oughta head back before someone misses you."

She sighed, not wanting the tender moment to end. "I suppose you're right. Besides, we need to get the table back in the church."

"Hmm. . .a dark church. No one there but us. Might be a good place to steal a kiss."

Chapter 17

Mark watched his brother walk back to the dance after helping the marshal escort the cowboys to the saloon. Garrett's eyes widened as he drew near. "Whoa, brother, looks like you've been in a fight."

"Yeah," Mark said. "And it looks like you all but missed it. There's not a mark on you. How is that possible when you were on the bottom of the pile?"

"There are some wounds, but you just can't see them." Garrett held his side. "I suspect getting out of bed tomorrow will be a chore. Why are you so beat up? You usually hold your own better in a fight."

Mark held up his dirty cast. He'd be getting it off soon—and good riddance. "It didn't seem right to crack people over the head with this thing. Besides, I didn't want to take a chance on breaking my wrist all over. And fighting left-handed isn't all that easy."

Garrett studied the dancers and then looked up at the sky. "I guess it's about time to call a halt to this party. Be dark soon."

"Yeah, next time you might want to start it an hour or two earlier since the sun is setting sooner these days."

Mark watched a young couple walk away from the dancing. About twenty minutes ago, Dan and Leah had walked down the road to Denison. He glanced in that direction and saw them returning with Leah holding onto Dan's arm.

Garrett watched, too. "Looks like our plan may be working. Soon, I hope, we won't have to pay room and board for Miss Bennett anymore."

"So, if both those boardinghouse brides get married, are you going to keep hosting the socials?"

Shrugging, his brother started toward the dancers. "Who knows? People seem to be enjoying it, and we've met new people who have become customers, so that's always a good thing."

"You do know folks are pokin' fun and calling us matchmakers."

Grinning, Garrett rummaged through the crate of dishes. "Yeah, I heard. Sure wish there was some of that pie left. That Miss Bennett is a good cook."

"Yep, she'll make some man a fine wife."

Garrett ran a finger over the juice left in a pie plate. "Yeah, it would be nice to have a wife who could cook so good."

"Why don't you ask her to dance? Maybe you'll like her."

"Nah, Dan has his eye on her."

Mark glanced at the couple as they drew near the dancers. Both faces were glowing, and the grins on their faces bested any among the dancers. *Hmm...*

"You could always dance with Shannon."

Garrett scratched behind his ear. "Don't think so. Someone else already has his eye on her. I predict two weddings before long."

"Who are you talking about?" Mark swung his head sideways and glanced at Garrett, then sought out Shannon and found her dancing with Tommy Baxter, the twenty-year-old son of a local rancher. Didn't she know he was just a wild colt who enjoyed wasting his father's hard-earned money? Mark clenched his jaw.

His brother slapped him on the shoulder so hard, Mark jumped. "What was that for?"

"Are you so blind that you can't see that you have feelings for Shannon?" Garrett waggled his brows.

"That's nonsense." Mark crossed his arms, knowing his response came too fast.

"Why? She's a lovely girl, and smart, too. Look how fast she's picked up the bookwork. In fact, I think we've gotten some new customers just because they come in to stare at her and all that pretty hair."

Mark glared askance. "What business of yours is her hair? I thought you didn't like her."

"Maybe not at first. She was awful shy, but she's coming around. It's not so much I didn't like her, as I didn't think she had what it takes to live in Texas. But she's proving tougher than I first gave her credit for."

"Come to think of it, she doesn't seem as shy and scared as when she first came here."

"Yeah, and if you noticed that, other men will, too. Better stake your claim if you want her. A young woman as pretty and enticing as her won't stay unmarried for long."

Mark leaned against a tree and scowled. He wasn't sure what he felt for Shannon. His admiration of her had risen as she quickly caught on at work. And there was no doubt about her being pretty. Maybe she wasn't gorgeous like a Dallas opera singer, but she had a sweet charm, and innocence about her. And she *was* a hard worker. He'd noticed how much cleaner and organized the office had been lately. He'd always tidied up but never had time to keep the place spotless as he would have preferred, but Shannon did. She'd even seen to it that his desk had been sanded and refinished and the ink stain gone.

He watched her smile and sashay around in a wide circle. She tended to keep her hair up in that thing she called a chignon, but tonight, it flowed long and free. His fingers twitched, and he ached to touch those long, wavy strands. Maybe he should dance with her. He pushed away from the tree. He'd kept his distance until now, but what could one little dance hurt?

After breakfast, Shannon headed toward the river for a quick stroll. She couldn't get Mark out of her thoughts after dancing with him the night before last. Her chest warmed as she remembered how he'd claimed her for the final dance—a waltz.

Knee-high grass swished around her skirts, and abundant sunshine brightened the morning. A rabbit zigzagged away from her. Everything looked beautiful. Thanks to recent rains, the grass had greened up again, and wildflowers were again turning their lovely faces toward the sky. She snapped off a tiny white daisy and sniffed. "For me? Why thank you, kind sir."

She held her hand to her chest. "You'd like to dance? I thought you would never ask." Curtsying, she fanned her face. "Why, I'd be delighted to waltz with you, Mr. Corbett." She spun around in a circle, round and round, until dizziness made her stop.

Giggling, she shook her head as she tried to regain her equilibrium. "Silly lass."

The truth of the matter was so much less thrilling as she'd been stunned into silence and had simply nodded to Mark. He'd taken her hand with his cast and placed his other hand on her waist, but discreetly kept his distance, even though she longed for him to draw her close. She imagined holding up the heavy cast for a complete dance had been tiring for him, and it had felt odd to her, clutching the hardened plaster. But they'd danced, and she'd loved every moment of it.

She couldn't say the same thing for him, though. He'd been stiff, didn't talk, and focused somewhere over her head. Her lack of finesse with American dances must have embarrassed him. Or perhaps something was simply bothering him. She sighed, halfway dreading going to work today. But work she must.

Making a wide arc around Lookout, she gathered a bouquet of yellow, white, and violet flowers, hoping to add a splash of color to the boring brown and grays of the office. As she strode up Main Street, she passed the livery and thought again how excited Leah had been Saturday night when she told the folks at the boardinghouse that she and Dan were getting married. Rachel had been so excited and offered to help her in any way.

She, too, offered to help Leah, but the fires of jealousy had burned within her—and still did. Oh, she was happy for her friend and glad Leah wouldn't have to depend on the Corbett brothers' support much longer, but she longed for the same for herself. She wished Mark would pay her some real attention.

At times she thought sure he liked her, but other times she was certain he didn't. 'Twas all so confusing. She heaved a frustrated sigh and looked up, noticing a crowd gathered outside the freight office, and for a moment, she considered heading back to the boardinghouse. The last thing she wanted was to get caught in the middle of a surly crowd. She heard the sound of a hammer; then she saw Luke remove his hat, tilt his head back, and laugh. He slapped his leg with his hat and leaned forward, still guffawing. Loud, masculine hoots and the roar of laughter filled the air.

What in the world?

Dan must have heard the noise, because he strode out of the livery and met her in the middle of the street. He was the biggest man in town, in height and breadth, but there wasn't an ounce of fat on him. Leah had roped herself a brawny man. The snake of jealousy raised its ugly head again, but Shannon whipped a prayer heavenward, lashing off the beast's head. She'd be happy for her friends and not think of her own future at the moment.

"What's goin' on?" he asked.

She shrugged. "I've no idea. The men are up to some shenanigans, I presume."

"Let's find out what kind." He offered his arm, and she accepted, grateful to have an escort through the dozen men.

"Congratulations."

He smiled down at her. "Ah, so Leah told you?"

"Aye, she's so excited."

Dan stopped at the edge of the crowd. Fine for him, but she couldn't see a thing over the tall men wearing hats. Worming her way to the front, she held a hand over her nose to avoid the putrid odor of the mob. Didn't Texas men believe in bathing? She reached the front, glanced up, and saw a new sign tacked to the outer wall of the Corbett Brother's Freight Office, right over the front window.

Mirth made her mouth twitch, and a chuckle worked its way out. She giggled and finally burst out laughing. CORBETT BROTHERS' MATCHMAKING SERVICE, the sign read. A large red heart encircled the lettering, and a cupid's arrow broke through the middle.

Shaking her head, she wondered how long the sign would stay

up. She climbed the steps to the boardwalk and entered the office. Neither Mark nor Garrett were there yet. She put the flowers in a tall glass, grabbed the bucket by the back door, and went outside to pump water. After filling the bucket, she added water to the flower glass and sipped a drink from the ladle.

Outside the front window, she noticed the crowd part and saw Garrett and Mark crossing the street from Polly's Café. Both brothers looked curious, but from her higher vantage point, she could see the moment they saw the sign. Mark reached up as if to tear the sign down, but Garrett grabbed his arm. Mark jerked away and took the steps two at a time. He yanked open the door, jingling the bell, and then slammed it shut. He noticed her standing by the window and scowled. His puffy, purplish-black eye looked angry and painful. "I suppose you find this funny, too?"

She tightened her lips, trying to keep a straight face. She needed this job. "Nay, sir."

A rebellious snort slipped out, and she grinned. "Oh, aye, I do. 'Tis a hoot, it is. Just some men havin' a wee bit of fun."

Mark's serious expression melted, and an embarrassed grin made his swollen lips twitch. He hung his hat on a peg near the door and ran his hands through his hair. "I suppose you're right. Garrett and I will once again be the laughingstock of the town."

"That's not so bad a thing. You've done good, too. You helped Rachel and Luke to realize they still loved one another, and now Dan Howard and Leah are gettin' married."

"Not just them." Mark opened a thick law book that he frequently carried and thrust a newspaper at her. "Read this."

She unfolded the small Lookout paper and read the headline. ONE FIGHT, TWO WEDDINGS. "I knew about Dan and Leah, but who else is getting married?"

"Keep reading." Mark dropped into Garrett's chair and laced his hands behind his neck.

"Two couples attending last Saturday's social have pledged to marry." She read about Dan and Leah and then about a young man from another town who was marrying a fifteen-year-old girl. She'd never liked the idea of a girl marrying so young, but life in Texas was hazardous at times, and folks didn't live as long here as they did back East. "Well. . .it looks as if your social was a success."

"Partly." He stared at the cover of his book and ran his hand over it.

What did he mean? It was only partly successful because she wasn't getting married? She turned her back on him and stalked to the back room, where she wouldn't have to look at him. Why would a man so bent on helping others find their life partner not want to find one for himself? He wasn't getting any younger. Why, he had to be nearly ten years her senior.

She busied herself dusting things that weren't dirty; then she swept the floor and the back porch, banging crates and even kicking the bucket so that it dumped over and spilled onto the porch. The water ran through the spaces between the boards, disappearing. What was she doing here?

She needed to focus on her work and forget about Mark Corbett. But every time she tried, those haunting blue eyes tormented her. What happened to him? Had a woman hurt him at some time?

She had some ledger work that needed to be done, and she couldn't avoid Mark all day. He hadn't even mentioned the flowers she'd set on his desk.

With the heavy ledger spread out on her desk—Mark's desk, she took a seat. He'd opened his law book and was busy reading. Half an hour went by before Garrett intruded on the quiet. He swung the door open and barged in, shaking his head.

"What do you think of our new sign?" He glanced from Mark to Shannon, eyes twinkling.

Mark closed his book, leaving his finger in it to mark his place. "I say take it down. It's just plain embarrassing."

Garrett turned to Shannon. "What do you think?"

She gulped down the lump suddenly in her throat. She peeked at Mark, who stared intensely at her. Why did Garrett have to ask for her opinion when it was opposed to Mark's? She shrugged. "It matters not what I think but what you two feel."

"I don't know why. . .but I kind of like it." He removed his hat and set it on a peg next to Mark's.

"We run a freight office, not a matrimonial society. We'll be the laughingstock of the town," Mark grumbled.

Garrett grinned. "I'm afraid we've been that ever since we sent for those mail-order brides."

"Well, if I recall, that was your idea, just like finding mates for—" He slammed his mouth shut and peered at Shannon.

She wanted to melt into one of the desk drawers and hide. They were talking as if she wasn't even there. She stared down at the ledger, but the numbers blurred together. If only there was some other job in town that she could do. Perhaps she ought to think more seriously about going to a bigger city like Dallas.

But she'd lose all the friends she'd just made. She'd be all alone again.

Who was she kidding? She was alone.

Rachel had Luke.

Leah now had Dan.

And even Jack had her friends and that old yellow dog.

Tears blurred her eyes, and she closed the ledger. She wouldn't sit here and listen to them talk about her like she was invisible. She stood and hoisted up the heavy ledger and turned toward the cabinet. The ledger banged the glass holding the flowers, and she turned in time to see it tip and fall.

"Yikes!" Garrett jumped back, but not before the glass broke at his feet, splashing water all over his shoes.

Shannon dropped the ledger back on the desk and strode into the back room and out the rear door, tears blurring her eyes. Couldn't she do anything right? As the door slammed, she heard Garrett shout.

"You'd better marry her or fire her, brother, before she kills us all."

Chapter 18

Jack pulled another weed and tossed it in the slowly growing pile. Max rested in the shade of several tall cornstalks, his head on his front legs.

"Why was it that vegetables die if they don't get enough water but weeds always grow? And how come birds and bugs never eat weeds?"

Max watched her, nothing moving but his eyes.

"I wish you could talk, you dumb ol' mutt."

She hated the hot chore that made her sweat. The only good thing was that her ma let her wear her overalls so she wouldn't get her dresses dirty. Tired of kneeling, she sat down and looked at the three rows she still had to weed before she'd be done. She picked up a clod of dirt and lobbed it at a blackbird that was fixing to land on a stalk of corn. "Git, you varmint. I ain't pullin' the darn weeds just so you can eat our corn."

"Mm-mm. If'n your ma heard you say *darn*, she'd wash your mouth out with soap."

"Ricky! What're you doin' here?" Jack jumped to her feet and waved at her two friends. "Howdy, Jonesy."

"Ma sent me to town to see if the Fosters had some thread left in their tent store."

She shook her head. "Don't think so, but we can go see. They been sellin' off stuff, because they're leaving town soon."

"Don'tcha need to finish your chores before leaving?" Jonesy scratched his belly and yawned.

Jack shrugged, knowing her friend spoke the truth. But she hadn't seen either boy in nearly three weeks, and she'd missed them. "Let's go before Ma sees me."

They took off at a run and didn't stop until they reached the Fosters' property.

"Wow, look at all that wood." Jonesy eyed the stack of lumber nearly as tall as he.

"There's to be a store raising come Saturday." Jack walked inside the large tent that served as the store for now. "Howdy, Mrs. Foster. Ricky here needs some thread for his ma. You got any?"

"Just a couple of skeins of red and one white left, though they smell of dust." The old woman got up from her chair, tottered across the room, and rummaged around some boxes.

"Thank ya kindly, ma'am, but Ma wanted black thread so's she could mend my pa's trousers. Don't guess he'd care much for red or white stitching on his pants."

"No, I guess not. Be a few more weeks before the new store is up and filled. Hope he can wait that long."

Ricky shrugged and hurried back outside. Jack followed, waving her hand in front of her nose. "Whoowee! All that stuff smells like sawdust and dirt. Don't know why anyone would want to buy it."

Jonesy grinned and nudged her in the arm. "Never guess who we just saw."

"Who?"

"Butch," both boys said in unison.

"Where?" Jack leaned in close, half-excited, half-scared to see the bully again. She hadn't seen him since that social when he'd asked her to dance.

"Over at that fat lady's house, choppin' wood."

"You mean Bertha Boyd?"

"Yeah." Ricky's eyes gleamed. "Wanna help us play a prank on him?"

Jack bit on the inside of her lip, thinking again of how she'd lied about Butch. Still, he was her enemy, and if Luke and her ma knew what she'd done, she'd be in big trouble—and that would be Butch's fault. "Sure, why not? What do you want me to do?"

She followed the boys, listening to their plan. Butch had done plenty to them over the years, so what harm could it do to play a little trick on him? "Why do I hav'ta be the one to talk to him? How come one of you can't do that?"

"We gotta move the wood he's chopped, and that's too hard of work for a girl."

Jack narrowed her eyes at the boys, not quite sure if she'd been insulted or not. Still, the thought of carrying wood sounded like a lot more work than just standing there and talking to Butch.

She sucked in a deep breath and strolled to the back of the faded white house where Bertha Boyd and her sister, Agatha Linus, lived, while the boys hunkered down and raced around the other side. Butch was in the back of the lot, chopping wood in the shade of a tall oak. It looked as if he'd chop a while and then stop and stack the wood up against the back of the house where the sisters had easy access to it.

She ambled toward him, trying to look casual, her hands crossed behind her back. "Hey there, Butch. Whatcha doin'?"

He narrowed his gaze and swung the ax down harder on this log than he had the previous one. The shirt he wore had no sleeves, just ragged threads where they once had been, and his arm muscles bulged as he brought the ax over his head and cut the half-log into quarters. Butch was taller than any other boy in their school, and she suddenly realized he was more man than boy. He'd thinned down since the last time she saw him at that Sunday social when he'd asked her to dance. He had also grown taller, if she wasn't mistaken, and looked more like a man. Jack backed away. Maybe she was making a mistake picking on someone so much bigger than herself.

"What do you want?" He spewed the words as he grabbed another log and put it on the chopping block.

Jack glanced over her shoulder to the side of the house and saw a hand reach up and snitch a piece of wood from the pile. The wind blew in her face, slapping her with the odor of sweaty male and hog. She angled behind Butch and around to the other side so he'd be upwind and wouldn't notice the boys. He watched her from the corner of his eye, as if he wasn't sure what she'd do next.

"Where's your friends?"

Jack shrugged. "Whatcha been doin' all summer?"

"Working. Sloppin' hogs. At least when I'm not in jail."

She winced at his backhanded accusation, but it hit its mark. She shouldn't have lied, but when it came down to Butch or her friends, it had been an easy choice. "Is that all you do?"

"Some folks don't have the luxury of having parents who give a hoot about them. People like you don't know what it's like to wake up each morning, not knowing if you get to eat or not that day."

She wondered what that would be like and felt bad he had to go without eating—even if he was her enemy. "Must be rough not having a ma."

He eyed her for a moment and then relaxed his stance. "Yeah, I miss her. She was real nice."

"Yeah, mothers are like that. I'd miss mine if something happened to her."

Butch leaned on the ax handle. "How do you like havin' the marshal for a pa?"

"He's all right. He tries to spend time with me each night, playin' checkers or doin' chores together." She leaned forward. "He even does dishes sometimes."

Butch eyes narrowed. "You're joshin' me now. I don't know no men that do dishes, besides me."

Surprise flittered through Jack, as she realized Butch and Luke had something in common. "You wash dishes?"

Color tinged his tanned cheeks. "Who else would if I didn't? I do all the cookin' too, or we don't eat. My pa don't do nothing but play cards and drink." He ducked his head as if the confession embarrassed him.

Jack had never considered how hard Butch's life was. No wonder he smelled all the time. She already knew he fished and hunted to eat. When would he find time to wash clothes and bathe? She didn't like feeling sorry for him.

She peeked at the woodpile and saw that it was lower than it had been a few minutes ago. She didn't know what the boys were doing with the wood quarters, but she hoped they weren't taking them far away. The old sisters who lived there would need the fuel come winter, and Butch would get in trouble. She kicked a rock. Why had she agreed to go along with Ricky and Jonesy?

Butch whacked another log in two. "I'm not like my pa. I'm going to make something of my life and be a man people can respect."

Jack resisted laughing. Pretty lofty dreams for the son of a hog farmer. "How you figure on doin' that?"

"Work hard and get an ed'jication. That's the key."

Remorse flooded through her. Had she been wrong about him? Maybe she'd made more of his being her enemy than she should have. She thought about him staying in jail because of her, and her stomach churned.

"Hey, boy!" Bertha Boyd—a woman as big as a stagecoach—stood on the back porch, shaking her cane at them. "I'm not paying you to converse with that girl."

Butch stiffened and brushed his hand at her. "Go on, before I lose this job."

Mrs. Boyd looked off the side of the porch at the woodpile. "Is that all you done? Why, anybody else could have chopped three times that much wood. She tossed some coins into the grass. "Here's your pay, boy. Just get on along. I'll hire someone who wants to do decent work for his pay."

Butch stared toward the woodpile, a confused expression on his face. He scratched his head, and just then, Jonesy peered over what was left of the stack of wood. Butch glared at Jack. "Y'all been stealing the wood I chopped? You're helping them by distractin' me?"

He raised the ax high, and Jack back-stepped. The ax slammed into the chopping block, and Butch shoved his hands to his hips and stepped right up to her, leaning in her face. "I'm tired of tryin' to be your friend. Folks say I'm bad, and I'm always gettin' in trouble, but it's because of *good* kids like you. I try hard to change my ways and walk the straight and narrow. I want to be a better man than my pa, and I'm sick of gettin' blamed for things I ain't done. I thought you were different than them boys, but I guess you're cut from the same mold. Git away from me and stay away, you hear?"

Jack's heart pounded like a rabbit's in a snare. She never should have agreed to help her friends.

Butch stalked toward the back of the house and searched the grass for his money. Then he strode back toward her, his black eyes narrowed into slits. She backed up, then raced past him in a wide arc, as fast as she could pump her legs. When she reached the front of the house, she slowed and glanced over her shoulder. Relief made her legs weak. He wasn't chasing her. He was stacking the wood he'd just cut.

Ricky and Jonesy raced toward her, both laughing. "Wasn't that a hoot?"

"Yeah, did you see that old bat yell at him?" Jonesy bent over and slapped his leg.

Jack looked back and saw Butch staring at them. Suddenly, he dropped the wood and charged. Jonesy let out a squeal that sounded more like a girl, took a hop, and sprinted down the street. Ricky ran toward home, and Jack sped toward Luke's office. Only the marshal could save her if Butch wanted revenge.

Shannon fingered the soft blue satin fabric. "What about this one? 'Twould make a lovely wedding gown."

Leah set aside the ivory muslin she'd been looking over and touched the satin. "Ooo, that is nice, but since I'll have to wear the dress on Sundays, I need something more practical—and cooler."

"Aye, that makes sense, but 'twould have looked lovely with your eyes."

"Thank you. Maybe we can find the blue in a more suitable cloth in another store."

They walked out of the Denison store and stood on the boardwalk, looking over the town. Denison was much larger than Lookout but was probably still considered a small town. At least it had a railroad. Shannon rubbed her back, still sore from the bumpy wagon ride. She'd taken off work for the day so she could serve as chaperone for Dan and Leah's trip.

"Do you suppose Dan has finished his business and will be looking for us?"

Leah shook her head and glanced at the sun. "No, he said it would take a few hours to locate everything he needed and get it loaded on the buckboard. We still have time, so let's get shopping. I simply must find some fabric for a dress."

'Twas nice of Dan to give Leah the funds to buy a dress and other things she would need as a newly married woman. Shannon shifted the large package that held Leah's new undergarments to her other arm. Thinking of her own ragged underwear that had been mended over and over, she tried hard not to be jealous. She was happy for her friend, but she longed for the same joy for herself.

"Let's try that dressmaker's shop down there. Maybe she'll have some fabric she'd be willing to sell us."

As they walked along, Shannon pretended she was on a shopping trip for her own wedding clothes. What color of dress did she want? Not blue, but perhaps a cream-colored gown. Or if she was going to be practical as Leah was, perhaps she'd pick a pale green to match her eyes, or a soft lavender.

They entered the dress shop, and the proprietor looked up from her stitching and smiled. "Welcome, ladies. How can I help you?"

"I'm Leah Bennett, and I'm to be married soon and am in need of a wedding dress. I was wondering if you sell fabric."

"Congratulations." The woman set aside the pink silk dress she was hemming and stood. "My name is Miss Bradshaw, and while I mostly keep fabric for my customers to have a wide selection to choose from, I do occasionally sell my cloth. What are you looking for?"

"Nothing too fancy. Maybe a sateen, but more likely a high quality cotton would do just fine. My friend Shannon here has graciously committed to make some Irish lace for the dress, which will fancy it up quite a bit."

Miss Bradshaw clapped her hands and looked at Shannon. "How very nice of you to offer to do such a thing. What type of lace do you make? Carrickmacross?"

"Nay, it's Kenmare. My mum learned it from the nuns who came to her village. Would you, by chance, have some linen thread I could purchase?"

Miss Bradshaw nodded her head. "I do. Come this way."

Shannon followed her to a crowded corner, and when the woman moved a navy calico dress, a thread cabinet was revealed. Miss Bradshaw opened a drawer filled with a rainbow of colors. "Oh, to have so many lovely choices. It must be a delight to come to work each day."

Miss Bradshaw nodded. "Ah, a kindred spirit, I perceive. Ever since I was a young girl, I've been fascinated with the magnitude of colors that fabric and thread come in. I can't imagine living without color in my life."

"Aye, me, too." Shannon ran her hand lovingly over the thread. If only she had the funds to buy several colors. She had some money saved from her work, but she dreaded spending it. What if she had to leave her job?

'Twas an odd feeling, this unreciprocated love for Mark. What if working for him became unbearable? 'Twould have been better if she hadn't fallen for him, but it certainly wasn't something she had planned to have happen.

While the other two women chatted about fabric, Shannon opened another drawer that revealed colors from a soft blue that almost looked white to dark indigo. Perhaps instead of stitching Leah a cream-colored or white collar, she could use a darker blue. But then there would be the problem of the darker color bleeding onto the lighter fabric if the dress got wet. Shannon sighed. Nay, better to stick with the plain shade. She picked up several ivory skeins and joined her friend.

Leah held up a bright periwinkle blue fabric under her chin. "What do you think of this shade?"

" 'Tis lovely. Very pretty with your eyes."

Leah smiled. "I like it, too, and won't it look beautiful with your lace on it?"

Shannon nodded. "Aye, and if there's enough time, I'll make cuffs for your sleeves, if that would please you."

Leah handed the cloth back to Miss Bradshaw. "That would

be wonderful, but I don't want you constantly working. The collar will be enough. I think I'll cover the buttons to make the dress fancier, too."

"An excellent idea," Miss Bradshaw said. She cut out the amount of fabric Leah requested, wrapped it up, and tied it with heavy twine, then took care of the thread for Shannon. "Thank you so much for stopping by my shop, and I do wish you the best with your wedding and your future husband."

Back outside, Leah shifted the heavy package in her arms. "Let's go back to the hotel and put these in our room. They're too heavy to lug around all day."

"What else do you need to purchase?"

"Dan told me to get whatever I needed and gave me plenty of money. I feel odd spending it, but he said I should stock up because he doesn't have time to come to Denison very often. Since he owns the only livery and is the only blacksmith in town, he doesn't like to be gone too often. I think the only thing left on my list is to get a new pair of shoes. These I've got on are past old age."

"I'm excited about eating in the hotel restaurant tonight. 'Twill be an adventure, for sure."

"Oh, me, too. I've never stayed in a real hotel." Leah's eyes danced with delight.

"What about when you traveled here? Surely it took more than one day."

"That's true, but I stayed in a boardinghouse, not a hotel."

Shannon thought of her own trip and how she'd slept one night in a barn on her journey to Texas. It had been the only place she could find off the street. Paying for a hotel had been out of the question.

But Dan had graciously paid for tonight's room, and she meant to enjoy every moment she was here. Excitement flittered through her, and she pretended she was a grand lady who owned a large estate, and she'd come to town to shop. She was grateful for a day away from Lookout.

Away from the pressures of working with the Corbett brothers.

Away from her pining over a man who didn't want her.

They entered their hotel, located near the Katy Depot. A

beautiful chandelier was the focal point of the tall-ceilinged lobby. Fancy brocade wallpaper decorated the walls in a pale gold, while red couches and chairs gave the room a splash of color. A man sitting in one of the chairs lowered his newspaper, and Shannon's heart squeezed.

What was Mark Corbett doing here?

Chapter 19

Jack raced to the marshal's office, praying Luke was there. She slowed her steps as she reached the office window and forced herself to walk past it. Her breathing came in ragged gulps, and as she rounded the door, she glanced behind her and gave a relieved sigh. Butch must have chased after the boys instead of her.

But Luke wasn't there. She hurried to the bucket and ladled out a drink and guzzled it down. Then she tiptoed back to the door and peeked out. A wagon was parked in front of the freight office, and several horses were hitched in front of the bank, but not a soul was on the street.

Where had her friends gone? Were they safe? Or had Butch gotten them?

She leaned against the jamb, keeping watch on the street. Now she wished she'd just gone home, but if she tried to make it, she might run into Butch.

What would he do if he caught her?

He said he didn't hit girls, but maybe he'd do something else like tie her up over an anthill. Or lock her in a hot, dark shed like that outlaw had done to her ma. Her knees shook as countless scenarios attacked her mind.

She'd halfway felt sorry for the big bloke when that old Mrs.

Boyd yelled at him and fired him. It wasn't his fault he'd gotten in trouble. Maybe she oughta go back and explain things to that old lady. But Bertha Boyd was as big as a draft horse and scared her more than Butch.

Jack threw her braid over her shoulder, trying to get her nerve up to make a mad dash for home. She saw Max toddling down the street. "Oh, wonderful. He'll give me away."

Heavy footsteps sounded behind her, and she turned, hoping to see Luke. But Butch crossed the street in front of the café, smacking his hand into his fist as if looking for a fight. She ducked back into the office and searched for a place to hide. Diving under Luke's desk, she held her breath and pulled the chair in close to her. *Please, God. Don't let him have seen me.*

The steps stopped just outside the door. Her heart pounded like Butch's ax, whacking that wood. Her heartbeat throbbed in her ears until she could barely hear. Was he still standing there?

She heard a noise nearby and tucked her knees up tighter. Something clicked on the floor, and a shadow darkened the wall. Max appeared and stuck his nose in her face and burped.

"Eww!" She waved her hand in front of her nose. "What in the world have you been eatin'?"

Footsteps hurried in her direction, and Butch yanked Luke's chair out from in front of her. "I thought I saw you."

Her whole body trembled, and she'd never been closer to crying. What would her ma say when she learned her daughter was dead?

"Git on up from there."

She hunkered back farther, keeping her eyes shut. Maybe he couldn't see her if she couldn't see him. Max whined and licked her hand.

Some guard dog he was.

A large hand latched onto her arm and pulled her out. Jack came kicking and flailing her arms. "You let me go! My pa's gonna lock you up until you're old and gray if you hurt me."

"I ain't scared of the marshal."

Butch held her by the scruff of her collar. She swung her arm and landed a hard hit in his midsection. His warm breath *oofed* out, and he bent over but didn't let go. "Stop it, you little beast. I ain't gonna hurt you."

Jack froze. "Then let me go."

"No. You need to be taught not to meddle in other people's affairs. You cost me a good job today, and I needed the work. If you was a boy, I'd pound the what-for into ya."

Jack went limp, her body exhausted. Fear battled anger. "W–what are you gonna do to me?"

He looked around and chuckled. "Just what you did to me."

He hauled her across the room, into a cell, and dropped her onto the cot. Then he hustled back out and shut the door. Stunned, Jack sat there, half-relieved and half-scared out of her wits. What if Luke didn't return soon or was out hunting down an outlaw?

And she needed to use the privy.

Butch grinned. "See how you like being locked up."

She bolted off the bed and clutched the bars. "You let me out of here right this instant."

"Cain't do it. I ain't got the key."

She swallowed hard. "Check the drawer. Maybe that's where Luke keeps them."

He pushed out his lips and shook his head. "Nope. I figure it's time you learned a lesson." He turned and sauntered toward the door, chuckling.

Fear washed over her like the time she'd jumped into the river and hadn't known which way was up. She hated being trapped in small places. Hated pleading with *him*. "Butch. Please. I promise not to do it again."

He stopped but didn't turn. "No, I'm tired of you and your friends going after me. All I wanted was to be your friend, but you and those boys have caused me trouble since the day I moved here. If I catch them, they'll be joining you in the next cell."

He walked out the door without looking back. Max trotted over to the front of the cell and laid his head on his paw.

"Butch!" she screamed. "Come back here, you hear me?"

She rattled the cell door, tears blurring her eyes. "I hate you. I'll hate you for the rest of my life!"

One look at Shannon's face, and Mark knew coming to Denison had been a mistake.

"What are you doing here?" Her cute brows dipped down, and her lips pursed into an enticing pout.

Had he mistaken the interest he'd seen in her gaze? He raised his chin. Maybe coming here had been the wrong thing to do, but he'd never let her know. "I had an urge to go riding and needed a few things, and I just ended up in Denison. You never mentioned you were coming here."

"So, you're headed back soon?"

He shrugged. "Maybe. I haven't yet concluded my business." And he might never finish it if she didn't thaw out a bit. She had no idea how hard it had been for him to seek her out. Half a dozen times he'd turned his horse around and started back to Lookout, only to turn around again. At least here, he could talk to her without the whole town listening in and making it tomorrow's headline. "So. . .you've been shopping, I see."

Shannon nodded and glanced over to where Leah and Dan were sitting on a sofa, holding hands and chatting. "Leah bought some fabric for her wedding dress."

Mark followed her gaze, still finding it hard to believe Dan Howard had asked a woman to marry him. As far as he could remember, Dan had never shown interest in a female. Maybe now that his mother had died, he realized he needed someone to tend the house, but no, as he watched his friend talk to Miss Bennett, he knew there was more to it. Dan had fallen in love.

Mark pulled his gaze to Shannon's, and their eyes locked gazes. He stared at her, unable to tell her the depth of his feelings. He wasn't even sure what they were himself, but one thing he knew: He'd never had such a strong desire to spend time with a woman before. Not even with Annabelle.

"I don't suppose that you'd allow me to escort you to dinner since we're both in town."

Surprise brightened her eyes before she narrowed them. "I thought you had to get back to Lookout. I'd hate to see you riding that far after dark."

"Are you worried about me?"

Her lips pursed again. "Not you. I'm concerned about your horse."

His heart lifted. "You're not a very good liar, Miss O'Neil."

She hiked her chin and glared up at him. "If anything happened to you, I'd be working solely for your brother." She shuddered as if the idea repulsed her.

Mark laughed aloud, drawing Dan and Leah's gaze. "We can't have that, can we?"

Shannon kept a straight face for a moment, then cracked a smile. "I do believe I'd have to resign."

He placed his hand on chest, acting as if the thought brought pain to it, and in fact, it did. Thinking of not seeing her each morning, not watching her nibble on her fingernails, brought an ache to his heart. When had he started looking forward to seeing her?

And what was he going to do about it?

Dan stood and helped Leah up, then both walked toward him. Dan slapped him on the shoulder. "What are you doing in Denison?"

"Had some things to purchase and needed to exercise my horse. He's getting fat and lazy since I hardly have time to ride him anymore."

"You could always let me keep him at the livery. I could feed him and rent him out in exchange."

Mark shook his head. "Thanks, but I don't think so. I may not ride him as much as I should, but I don't like the idea of a stranger maybe mistreating him."

"I hear ya. I do my best to make sure no greenhorns ride my horses, but even a seasoned rider can mistreat animals. Makes me so angry I'd like to punch them."

Leah grasped Dan's arm. "Let's not have any of that kind of talk, all right?"

"You're not even married yet, and the little lady is already bossing you around." Mark grinned.

Dan chuckled. "It's not so bad. You oughta try it yourself."

Both women's cheeks had turned red, Mark noted. But he

doubted it was for the same reason.

"Why don't you join us for supper?" Dan asked.

"I might just do that. What time are you eating?"

"The ladies need to make another trip to the store for a few more items and then get cleaned up." Dan glanced at the big clock on the wall behind the registration desk. "What about six? Will that give you enough time to finish your business?"

"Yeah, that should be fine. Meet you back in the lobby?" Mark's gaze darted to Shannon, who looked like she'd just eaten a sour pickle.

Was he making another mistake? Why were women so difficult to read?

"Sounds good. See you then." Dan took the packages the women held, and then the ladies exited the hotel while Dan ran up the stairs. As Shannon walked out the door, she cast an unreadable glance over her shoulder.

Mark slouched into a chair. Why had he thought it so important to come here today?

So what if he had feelings for Shannon. He couldn't act on them.

But the bottom line was, he wanted to be with her. To spend time with her without his brother teasing him—and this was about the only chance he'd get.

He leaned his head back and stared up at the decorative plaster ceiling. Was it wrong of him to dream of a life he couldn't have?

The preacher said that God forgave sins, but one of the Ten Commandments was "Thou shalt not kill."

And he was a killer.

Yeah, he'd only been defending a saloon girl's honor, such as it was, and he hadn't meant to kill that cowpoke. He'd just reacted when the man reached for his gun.

Mark ran his hand through his hair. Shannon deserved someone better than him, no matter how deep his feelings for her were. He wanted something he could never have—to be married. To be Shannon's husband. To be a father.

Yeah, coming here had been a mistake.

A big one.

Chapter 20

Shannon's stomach twisted into a knot as she walked down the stairs and saw Mark leaning against a pillar, watching her. His intense gaze never left her, and it made her feel cherished. Cared for.

But how could that be? He'd never once indicated having feelings for her. She glanced over her shoulder and realized he must be watching Leah. Her friend was wearing a new yellow dress that Dan had insisted she purchase when they went to look for material to make new curtains for the kitchen and parlor of their house.

Her hands trembled as much as her legs. How would she ever get through this meal? The supper she'd earlier looked forward to, she now just wished was over and done with.

Mark pushed away from the pillar and walked toward her. "You look lovely tonight."

Shannon ducked her head, certain her cheeks were bright red. She was wearing the same dress he'd seen earlier, but she'd washed and pinned up her hair. Not that it did much good. The stubborn wavy tresses came down almost as fast as she pinned them up, but Leah said men liked that look, so she'd left her chignon in their room.

"I'm so hungry I could eat a whole mule train." Dan rubbed his belly and chuckled.

Leah swatted his arm. "Oh, you. A big steak will taste much better."

He smiled and patted her hand. "You're right, my dear."

Mark looked at Shannon and rolled his eyes. She couldn't help smiling.

"Yes, dear. No, dear. You sound like an old married couple." Mark shook his head.

"Try it. You just might like it yourself," Dan challenged.

"What I'd like is some supper." Mark crooked his elbow and held it out to Shannon. "Care to join me?"

She nodded and took his arm. As they walked into the restaurant, her eyes took in everything at once. A dozen colorful, stained-glass lamps brightly illuminated the room. White tablecloths covered twenty or so tables, only half of which had customers dining at them. A small bouquet of flowers sat in the middle of each one. Somehow, she knew this would be a night she would dream about for a long time to come.

They placed their orders and dined. All too soon, the meal ended. Shannon and Mark followed their friends outside.

"Leah and I are of a mind to take a walk."

Shannon didn't miss the subtle hint that the engaged couple wanted to be alone. "I'll return to my room. It's been a long day."

"Nonsense." Mark waved at Dan and Leah. "You two be off, and we'll just head out the opposite direction. This town's plenty big enough for two couples to go walking without runnin' into each other."

Two couples? Shannon's heart leapt. Was he just saying that to keep Leah from worrying? Her friend gave her a questioning stare, and Shannon nodded. "Go on with ya. I'll be fine with Mark. 'Twill do me good to walk off that big meal before I retire for the night."

Leah stared at her as if she was unsure whether she should leave, but when Dan tugged on her arm, she followed. Shannon studied Mark as he watched the couple amble away. He had a handsome profile, with his straight nose and tanned skin. His blond hair curled over his collar in a boyish manner, but there was nothing childish about this man. He stirred her heart and made her wish for things that she didn't believe she'd ever have. A husband. A home. A family of her own.

He turned her way and smiled. Her heart somersaulted at the intensity in his eyes. "Shall we walk?"

She nodded and took his arm, feeling proud that she was the woman he was escorting. They strolled along, not talking, and she studied the town. Denison was much bigger than Lookout. Thousands of people lived here—had moved here after the railroad came through more than a decade ago. Denison had much more to offer than Lookout, but she missed the coziness of the smaller town.

"So, how do you like living in Texas?"

She wasn't exactly sure how to answer that, given all that had happened since she arrived. " 'Tis quite hot here."

Mark chuckled. "Yep, it's that."

"I like the people I've met here."

"All of them?" He glanced down, brows lifted.

She thought of that outlaw bride who'd tricked them all and Mark's rascally brother. "Most of them."

He led her down the boardwalk steps, holding her steady, and then up the next set of stairs. "Do you figure on stayin' in Lookout?"

"Where else would I be goin'? I've no family, nowhere at all." She thought how she'd so recently considered moving to Dallas. What would he say if she mentioned that?

"All that's left of my family is in Lookout. Garrett. Luke. I left once, you know."

She darted a look at him at that surprising news. "Where did you go?"

He shrugged and led her toward the edge of town. The sun had nearly set, casting brilliant hues of orange and pink on the underbellies of the clouds. The view took her breath away, made her believe anything was possible. *Bless You, heavenly Father, for creating such a masterpiece.*

"I traveled around some and then ended up in Abilene," he finally continued.

"Where is that?"

"A ways from here. Further west, more toward the middle of the state."

She leaned against a post, enjoying the timbre of his voice and their casual conversation. He'd never told her anything about himself before. "What was it that you did there?"

He remained silent for a while, and she wondered if he'd answer. He looked far away, lost in his thoughts. Finally, he cleared his throat. "I interned with a lawyer."

She had the uncanny feeling that more happened there than he was letting on. Now she understood a bit why he read so many law books. He must have been bitten by the lawyer bug while in Abilene.

He suddenly turned to face her. "Shannon, there's something I need to tell you."

She raised her hand to her chest, hoping, praying he was about to confess his affection for her. *Please, Lord.*

He reached out and tucked a strand of her hair behind her ear, stealing her breath away. The passion in his gaze made her reach for her dream.

"I want you to know you've been doing a fine job in the office. Much better than either Garrett or I expected."

As if a stiff wind had just blown through, she watched her dream slip from her grasp. He was happy with her work? That was all?

"I. . .you need to know something." He stared off at the sunset, a muscle ticking in his jaw. "I don't ever intend to marry."

Shannon sucked in a quick breath. Her hand relaxed as if she'd totally turned loose of any hopes of a life with Mark. Her body felt weighted down. Heavy.

He turned to her suddenly, his eyes pleading. "You have to know. You're just the kind of woman I'd want—if I were looking to marry."

She closed her eyes, not wanting him to see the pain his words brought. She wouldn't cry—not in front of him. "I. . .think we should be heading back." She turned without waiting for him, willing the sting out of her eyes.

"Shannon."

She ignored his call and hastened her steps. He grabbed her arm suddenly, pulling her to his chest. She fought his hold, knowing she had to get away or she'd lose all her composure. He held tight, refusing to let go until she stopped her struggle. Her breath came in short bursts.

"Shannon, this doesn't mean we can't be friends."

Friends. Ha! She wanted to laugh in his face. He was oblivious to the struggle she'd been having the past few weeks.

"Look at me."

She turned her face back toward the indigo twilight.

He cupped her chin, forcing her to look at him. His blue gaze captured hers, and he studied her face. "Why are you taking this so hard?"

She blinked her eyes, knowing she could never explain how he'd stolen her heart. But he didn't want it. Why couldn't he just let her go and be done with it?

His expression turned tender, and he cocked his head. "Oh, Shannon. Please tell me you haven't fallen in love with me. I'm nothing but a scoundrel."

His comment brought tears, and right on its tail, anger. How dare this Corbett meddle in her life one second more. She jerked, trying to get free of his grasp. "Let me go or I'll scream," she hissed.

"You don't want to do that."

"No?" She sucked in a breath, ready to call for help, and his lips crashed down on hers. She couldn't breathe. She didn't want to. She only enjoyed the moment, knowing it would never happen again.

After too short a moment, he jumped back, his own breath ragged. Running his hand through his hair, he stared at her in the growing darkness. "Sorry. I shouldn't have done that."

Irritation and loss soaked her like a downpour. She reached out and slapped him, then turned and stalked back toward the hotel. Not even when that college man at the Wakefield Estate she'd worked at in Shreveport had almost forced her into his room had she felt so horrible.

She held up her skirt to hasten her progress. She wouldn't cry. She couldn't. Not here.

Quick steps followed her, and she picked up her pace. Striding into the hotel, she nearly collided with another woman—a woman with almost the same coloring as herself. Shannon sidestepped her and made a beeline for the stairs. She had nothing more to say to that man.

"Well, well, if it isn't Mark Corbett. I thought I'd never find you again."

Shannon halted halfway up the stairs and turned. The woman, dressed in a purple sateen dress that would look more at place in a saloon than a classy hotel, blocked Mark's way. His face had gone almost white.

Who was that woman? How did Mark know her?

"What happened to your shooting hand? And what's this on your handsome face, darling?" She placed her hand on the red splotch where Shannon had slapped him and frowned. Mark's gaze lifted to Shannon, and the woman's followed.

"Who is she?" The words spewed out like snake venom.

Mark blinked and stared at the woman again. "Annabelle?"

❧

Jack rolled over in her bed and stretched. Sweat dampened her cheek, making her hair stick to it. She rubbed her eyes, then opened them. Was it morning?

No, it was dark outside, and she was still wearing her clothes. Why had she slept in her clothes?

Footsteps sounded across the room, and she bolted upright. The jail.

A match hissed and flickered; then someone lit the lantern. "There you are, Max. I was wondering where you'd gotten off to." Luke squatted and rubbed the old dog's head. "Why'd you come down here?"

Jack scooted back into the shadows, embarrassed for Luke to find her there. But if she didn't let him know, she'd be stuck for who knows how long.

"Get up, boy. I need you to help me find that ornery girl of ours. She missed supper, and her ma's worried."

Jack's stomach growled. She'd been there that long? All that yelling and being angry at Butch must have tuckered her clean out. Her eyes ached, and her throat stung.

Holding the lantern in his left hand, Luke headed for the door. She jumped off the bed. "Wait!"

He spun around, and yanked his gun out of his holster faster than she could sneeze.

She scrambled backward. "Don't shoot. It's just me, Luke."

He holstered his gun and hurried across the room, his boots thudding on the wood floor. He held up the lantern, and the light flickered against his skin, brightening the dark cell. His eyes were filled with concern. "How'd you get stuck in there, half bit?"

Ducking her head, she toed the brick floor. Keys rattled. The lock clicked, and the door creaked open.

Luke walked in, followed by Max, and the cot squeaked as the marshal lowered his large body onto it. He set the lantern on the floor. "Come sit by me, Jack."

That was something she'd always liked about him. Even though it angered her ma, he still called her Jack instead of Jacqueline—although she was growing partial to "half bit" as he sometimes called her. She did as he requested and leaned against his arm.

"Was it that Laird boy?"

After all that had happened, she hated to get Butch into more trouble, but it was his fault that she was trapped in the dark, stinky cell. She nodded. "Yeah, it was him."

"What happened?" He put his arm around her, tugging her close.

Here she went again. If she told him the truth, she and her friends would be in big trouble. But she didn't want to lie.

Luke turned and gently grasped both of her arms. His dark brows scrunched together, and his eyes looked worried. "Did he hurt you?"

She shook her head. "No. He just wanted to teach me a lesson."

A muscle in Luke's jaw twitched. "Somebody needs to teach that boy not to pick on smaller kids, especially not girls." Luke jumped up and paced the small cell. He smacked his fist into his palm, making such a loud smack that she jumped. "I'm going to chase him and that no good father of his clean out of Lookout."

Jack's eyes widened. She'd never seen Luke so mad. Not even when his cousins had ordered those three mail-order brides for him. She wanted to tell him that Butch hadn't started things this time, but her mouth wouldn't work. She scooted back against the wall. Her real pa had looked ferocious, just like that, before he started whacking on her or her ma. Her knees shook, and her heart pounded so hard she thought it might just break through her chest.

What if Luke started hitting when he got mad like her real pa? She shivered and glanced at the door. She sure didn't want to be stuck in a cell without her ma to protect her, if Luke started throwing punches. Taking a deep breath, she scooted to the end of the cot. Max had curled up on the floor next to the lantern so at least she wouldn't have to jump over him. She oughta take him with her, but surely Luke wouldn't punch his own dog.

When Luke paced to the back of the cell, she pushed off the cot like a cat with its tail on fire.

"Jack! What's wrong?"

She raced out the door, jumped off the boardwalk, and ran down the middle of the street as fast as she could. She had to find her ma.

Chapter 21

Mark stared at Annabelle, his mind grappling with the image in front of him. How had she found him? Had he ever told her where he lived?

He lifted his gaze to where Shannon stood halfway up the hotel stairs, looking down on him. Hurt, confusion laced her gaze. She obviously wondered about Annabelle, but she made no move to come back to the lobby. Suddenly, she turned, hiked up her skirt, and rushed up the stairs and out of sight.

He never should have kissed her, because it had awakened all his senses. Made him want something he could never have, especially now that Annabelle had turned up. He stared at her. "What are you doing here?"

She leaned up close, fingered his lapel, and purred, "I've missed you, and you never returned to Abilene."

He stepped back and glanced around the hotel to see if anyone had noticed her hanging on him. "You know why I couldn't do that."

She clutched his arm and rested her head on his shoulder. "I can't go back, either."

The clerk at the registration desk eyed them with curiosity. Mark grabbed her arm and led her outside into the darkness, where they'd have some privacy. The last thing he needed was someone from Lookout seeing him with her. His reputation would be in the trash heap.

He walked her down an alley and around to the back of the hotel, away from the lights of the open doors and windows. The tinny music of a saloon piano across the alley and several buildings away drifted toward them, along with the raucous noise and sometimes laughter or hollering of the patrons. At least this early in the evening, it wasn't too likely they'd be interrupted by a drunk.

The rear door to the hotel kitchen was open, and the clinking of pots could be heard, as well as the loud talk of the workers. The crickets and night creatures grew silent as Mark guided Annabelle to the edge of the light, back near the stable. Then he turned loose of her and started pacing. What was Shannon thinking right now? Had he hurt her terribly?

He knew she was developing feelings for him and thought that letting her know where he stood right up front was the decent and proper thing to do, but Annabelle's arrival had messed up everything. Her timing couldn't have been worse.

Annabelle smiled and moved in close again like a cat toying with its prey, walking her fingers up the buttons on his shirt. He didn't remember her being so. . .wanton before.

"Mark, aren't you happy to see me? It's been so long, darling." Her hand caressed his cheek; then her little finger brushed across his lower lip. His senses responded, in spite of trying to resist her.

Had she always played the temptress? As a man eager to be away from home for the first time, impatient to prove himself and to be out from under his older brother's shadow, had he unwittingly fallen under her spell?

"Stop it." He set her back from him. He was no longer impetuous and naive. Experience had made him cautious and wiser. "What are you doing here?"

She pouted, but finally stopped her vexing ways. "Everett decided to make me an upstairs gal, and I wouldn't put up with that, so I lit out of there. Fast and furious."

Truth be told, the only thing that surprised him was that she wasn't a lady of the night already. She certainly hadn't wasted any time getting *him* in her bed. He winced at the memory. *Forgive me, Lord.*

"I can't help you, if that's what you're wanting."

Annabelle flounced her head. "I have money. I just thought you might want to pick up where we left off. You ain't married to that redheaded tart, are you?" Her sultry smile twisted his gut. "Looks to me like you was tryin' to find a gal just like me. We look enough alike to be sisters."

He narrowed his gaze. "Shannon's nothing like you."

"I'm sure she isn't." Annabelle drew her index finger down Mark's cheek and under his chin.

He swatted it away and stepped back. "I was serious when I said to stop. You can either act civil, or I'll go back inside."

Her lips twisted up on one side. "You have changed, but I like it. You're no longer that sniveling whiner, complaining about his big brother all the time."

He jerked back as if she'd slapped him. Was that what she'd thought about him? He'd loved her—enough to fight another man who'd rough-handled her. Enough to shoot that man dead—in a fair fight, but he was dead just the same. He lifted his hat and raked his fingers through his hair. He'd been near his midtwenties—a grown man—when he'd met Annabelle, but he'd acted more like a runaway kid. It had taken him that time in Abilene to grow up. To make him see that his decisions affected others oft' times.

"You didn't answer me. I don't see no ring. Are you married to that gal?"

Mark shook his head. "She works for me and Garrett."

"And how is your big brother? Still making you do things you don't wanna?"

He clamped his back teeth together, knowing she'd hit the nail on the head. That was one thing that hadn't changed much. He was still hauling freight when he wanted to become a lawyer, but he wasn't about to admit that to her. "I'm going inside. It was. . . interesting seeing you again."

He strode past her, but she grabbed his arm. "Wait!"

Sighing, he turned to face her. With the light of the kitchen door shining bright, he could see how she'd aged. Yes, she was still young, probably only a few years older than Shannon, but working in a saloon all these years had taken its toll on her.

"What am I going to do? I was hoping you'd help me."

He shook his head, feeling sorry for her. "There's nothing I can do. It's time you stood on your own two feet."

"But I need you."

"No." He shook his head. "You don't. You never did."

He strode away, half-feeling he should do something for her and the other half wishing she hadn't come to town. One thing was for sure: Shannon would want nothing to do with him now.

~

Leah smiled up at Dan as he said good night. She longed for another of the kisses he'd stolen during their walk but knew the hotel lobby wasn't the place for a display of affection. "I suppose I should retire for the night."

Dan squeezed her hand, his dark eyes shining with love. "I wish we were already married, so I didn't have to let you go."

She touched her hand to her warm cheeks. "Be patient, my love. It won't be much longer."

He frowned. "One minute is too long. I've waited a lifetime to meet the woman I plan to marry. Maybe I should escort you to your room to make sure nothing happens to you."

"Da–an." She glanced around the lobby. "Do you want folks to think I'm a wanton woman?"

"Anybody who thinks that needs their attitude readjusted."

She grinned. She'd never again have to worry about being watched over and protected. Patting his solid upper arm, she leaned forward. "I will see you in the morning."

He nodded and released her other hand. Something behind him caught her eye, and she scowled. What in the world?

Mark Corbett walked in with another woman beside him. If she didn't know better, she'd think the woman was Shannon's sister. Their hair coloring and pale complexion certainly were strikingly similar, as was their height and size. Although, on closer inspection, this woman's build was a bit larger than Shannon's petite frame.

Dan noticed her staring and looked over his shoulder. "Who is that?"

"A better question is, where is Shannon?"

Mark's steps halted when he caught them gawking, and the color fled from his face. Leah stiffened her back and marched toward him. "Where is Shannon?"

Mark stared at them both, shifting his weight from side to side. "Uh. . .we finished our walk a short while ago, and she went up to her room."

"And who is this?" Leah nodded toward the woman. She was dressed in a purple sateen gown but had a hard look in her hazel eyes.

Mark tugged at his collar and cleared his throat. "This is. . . Annabelle. An old friend of mine."

Dan's brows lifted, and she knew that Mark had never mentioned this woman to him. "Annabelle who?"

Mark's brows dipped down, and he glanced at the woman. She cleared her throat and smiled, though it didn't reach her eyes. "Annabelle Smith."

"I'm Leah Bennett, and this is my fiancé, Dan Howard."

Dan tipped his hat and offered a tight-lipped smile. "Ma'am."

Annabelle took Mark's arm, as if he belonged to her. "So, how do you know Mark?"

Leah wanted to smack the woman off Mark, as if she were nothing but a pesky fly. His discomfort was obvious, but was it because he truly didn't want to be with the woman or because they'd caught him with her? "We all live in the same town."

"Oh?" Miss Smith cocked her head. "And where is that?"

Mark's eyes widened and he shook his head, at the same time Dan blurted out, "Lookout, ma'am."

"Lookout, huh?" She smiled up at Mark as if she'd won a prize. "Isn't that east of here?"

Dan shook his head. "No, ma'am, it's to the west."

Leah wanted to tromp on his foot or wallop his arm. Couldn't he see that Mark didn't want the woman knowing where he lived? Suddenly, she had an urge to check on Shannon. Did she know about the woman? What had happened during her walk with Mark?

"Well, if y'all will excuse me, I'll retire for the night. It was a pleasure meeting you, Miss Smith." Leah knew she'd have to repent from that white lie eventually. "Good night, Dan. Mr. Corbett."

"I'll walk you to the stairs." Dan took her elbow and led her away from the other couple. He leaned down next to her ear. "How do you suppose Mark knows her?"

She shrugged. "Beats me. You're the one who's friends with that lowlife Corbett."

Dan's expression turned scolding. "Now, Leah, we don't know what's going on. I don't know where Mark would have met her." He scratched his jawline with his thumb and forefinger, making a bristling sound against his chin that needed to be shaved again. "Mark did leave Lookout several years ago. Could be he met her back then. I know I've never seen her in Lookout."

"Well, I don't like her." She stood on her tiptoes. "What's he doing with her when he was just out walking with Shannon?"

Dan shook his head. "Makes no sense to me."

"I'm going to check on Shannon. I'll see you in the morning, dearest."

He smiled and pulled her to his chest, then quickly released her. "See you at breakfast. We need to get on the road right after that."

She nodded and hurried up the stairs, anxious to see her friend. When she stepped into the dark room, it took her eyes a moment to adjust. Had Shannon gone to sleep already?

Feeling her way to the dresser, she found the lamp and turned up the flame. The bed was still made, and Shannon wasn't in it. At first she thought her friend wasn't even in the room, but then she heard a sniffle, coming from the sitting area.

She crossed the room and found Shannon lying on the settee. Her eyes and nose were red, her face splotchy, and her lashes clumped together. Leah knelt on the floor beside her, rubbing her hand over Shannon's back. "What happened?"

Shannon sat up and wiped her nose. "Would you, perchance, have a handkerchief I could borrow? I've soiled both of the ones I brought with me."

"Of course." Leah pushed aside her curiosity and hurried to her satchel. She rummaged around and found two handkerchiefs and brought them to her friend. She sat down beside her. "Would you care to talk about what happened?"

Shannon's mouth puckered, and fresh tears ran down the side of her nose. She dabbed at them. "I was foolish."

"How so?"

Shannon stared at her lap and fiddled with the lace edge of the hankie. "I fell in love with a Corbett."

Leah knew that much already. In spite of her warnings, Shannon had dropped her guard and let Mark steal her heart. Though Leah would never fall for a Corbett, she had to understand what was upsetting Shannon so she could help her. "And why is that such a bad thing?"

Shannon's chin wobbled. "Because he said he never expects to marry."

Leah sat back as if she'd been slapped. He was willing to dally with a woman's affections but not to marry her? Or maybe he preferred a different type of woman than Shannon. Annabelle Smith intruded into her mind again.

"He knows I have feelings for him, and 'tis odd, but I believe he cares for me, though he claims he'll never marry." She stared at Leah with a confused expression on her face. "Why would a man not want to marry a woman he has feelings for? 'Tis because I'm Irish?"

Leah clutched her friend's hand. "No, I'm sure that has nothing to do with it. In fact, if he does truly have feelings for you, I'm sure it's partly because of your alluring accent and lovely auburn hair." She smiled, hoping to alleviate her friend's pain, but Shannon scowled.

"Perhaps he doesn't wish to marry me because he has another woman in his life already. A woman with hair the color of mine."

Leah gasped. "You saw him with her?"

She nodded. "We had just arrived at the hotel when she accosted him. I was on the stairs already, but I saw her."

Leah sat back in the seat. "How do you suppose he knows her?"

"I've no idea. But I've embarrassed myself and made a huge

error. I love a man who cares for another woman."

Shuddering, Leah stared at her friend. "How can you be in love with a Corbett? Just look at how they've messed with our lives."

Shannon lifted her chin. "You wouldn't be marrying Dan if not for the Corbetts bringing you to Lookout."

"I suppose you're right." She leaned her head back and stared up at the ceiling. How could she be so happy when her friend was so miserable? "I wish I knew what to say to make you feel better."

"There's nothing anyone can say. I must set aside my feelings and move on. It's not like I haven't had my choice of men to marry."

Leah chuckled. "How many proposals have you had so far?"

"Twelve. An even dozen. Just not the one I longed for." Shannon sniffled, and the tears flowed again.

Leah tugged her into her arms and rubbed her back. "Everything will turn out fine. You'll see."

Shannon pulled back. "But how can it? I can no longer work for the Corbetts. And if I don't, how will I get by?"

Leah thought a moment and then brightened. "I know! You can come to live with Dan and me. There's an extra bedroom."

Shaking her head, Shannon stood. "Thank you, but I'll not live with a newly married couple, and I'll not work with a man who's spurned me."

"Don't be hasty. Let's not make a decision in anger that you may live to regret."

Shannon ducked her head. "Aye, you're right. I should pray about these things, but I fail to see how I could ever work with Mark again."

Jack ran all the way home, threw open the front door, and ran straight to the kitchen. When she didn't see her ma, she panicked. Where was she? What if the outlaw that had kidnapped her had broken out of jail and come for her again?

Tears blurred her sight and burned her eyes and throat. She dashed into the bedroom, but she wasn't there. "Ma!" she screamed.

"Jacqueline?" Quick footsteps sounded overhead, and Jack raced for the stairs as her ma reached the top steps. "What's wrong? Where have you been?"

Footsteps sounded on the porch, and Jack froze. Would Luke be even more angry since she'd run away from him?

If she bolted for her ma, he'd catch her before she could get up the stairs. She turned and ran into the parlor, searching for a place to hide. She was much bigger now than when she'd hid from her other pa, but she dove behind the far side of the settee. Her heart beat like an Indian's drum she'd once heard.

"What is going on, Luke?" Her ma's voice sounded closer, as if she'd come down stairs—and it sounded angry.

"I have no idea. I found Jack locked up in my jail."

"What? Who would do such a thing?"

Jack took a deep breath and peered around the edge of the couch. Her ma looked madder than the chicken she'd dunked in the water barrel once.

Luke shoved his hand to his hips. "I'm pretty certain it was that Laird boy."

"Why would he do such a thing?"

"I don't know, but first thing in the morning, I'm riding over to find out."

Jack sucked in a breath. What if Butch told Luke what she and the boys did? Would he believe that bully?

Her ma held up her hand. "Hold on a minute. What does that have to do with Jacqueline's behavior just now? What is she afraid of?"

Luke shrugged. "I have no idea. One minute she was explaining what happened, and when I turned my back, she charged out of the jail like she was runnin' a race." He shook his head, looking perplexed, not at all mad.

Jack leaned back. Maybe she'd gotten things wrong.

Footsteps came her way, and she slinked back against the couch. "Come out of there, Jacqueline. You're perfectly safe now."

She swallowed hard. Luke was a big man, and if he decided to hurt her, her ma wouldn't be able to stop him. Why hadn't she considered that before?

"Let me talk to her, Rach."

Luke stooped down in front of her. She had nowhere to go. Her breath caught in her throat. "What's wrong, half bit?"

He reached out for her, but she turned her face away. She didn't like seeing the hurt in his eyes. "Did I do something that scared you?"

She nodded but didn't look at him.

"I'm sorry. Truly I am. Don't you know I'd never hurt you?"

She turned and looked at him with one eye. She'd never been afraid of him before, at least not after she'd gotten to know him. His kind, brown eyes looked pained.

"I'm not like your other pa, and I wasn't angry at you earlier. I was upset because of what that boy did to you. I love you, Jack. Don't you know that?"

She did, and now she felt foolish for her behavior. What had gotten into her? "I'm sorry, Luke. I just saw you punching your hand in your fist, and it reminded me of when my old pa would hit me. I just got scared."

"Come here, sweetie." He held out his open hand. She stared at it a minute and then took it, and he swung her up into his arms. He nearly squeezed her guts out. Then he set her back down and stared at her.

"I'm telling you here and now, I will never hit you or purposely do anything to hurt you. Ever. So help me, God. Do you believe that?"

She glanced at her ma and saw the gentle smile on her face. Her mother nodded, and so did she.

"Good. I will tell you that there are times I'll get angry"—he glanced up at her ma—"and maybe even at your mother, but I will never lose my temper to the point of hitting one of you. I don't hit women, and I never will. Do you understand?"

Jack nodded, and knew he spoke the truth. "Sorry, Luke. I guess I was still upset about bein' locked up."

He smiled and stood, lifting her clear off the floor. Then he pulled her ma into his arms, and they all hugged. "We're a family, half bit, and families stick together. I know that wasn't how it was before your other pa died, but that's the way of things now. Right, Rachel?"

"Yes, it is."

"And whenever you're ready, it would please me greatly if you'd called me pa."

Jack scowled. She didn't want to call him the same thing as her old pa.

"You don't have to if it bothers you." Luke's eyes took on that worried look again.

"It ain't that."

"Don't say *ain't*," her parents said in unison.

She grinned. "I just don't want to call you what I called *him*."

Luke smiled and nodded. "I understand that. It's perfectly fine if you just want to call me Luke."

She could tell by his expression that it wasn't really fine to him. "What about Dad? Or maybe Papa?"

"I'd like that. . .but only if you really want to."

She nodded. "I think you look like a papa."

Luke's smile warmed her insides. "That sounds fine. Just fine and dandy." He picked her up and swung her around in a circle. Laughter bubbled out of her, and she couldn't remember ever being so happy.

Chapter 22

A knock sounded on Shannon's open bedroom door, and she glanced up to see Rachel standing there. "How are you feeling this morning?"

"My head is throbbing in tune with that hammering." She offered a weak smile as she stared out the window and down the street where the men of town were erecting the new store.

"It is loud with so many men pounding, but having a store again will be wonderful."

"Aye, a town needs a store." Shannon fingered the edge of the curtain, wanting to talk to Rachel about what had happened, about her feelings for Mark.

The boardinghouse owner crossed the room and joined her at the window. The scent of fresh wood filled the air, and the street resembled a hive of worker bees hard at labor. Someone bellowed out a laugh, and others joined in. They looked to be having a grand time.

Rachel touched Shannon's shoulder. "I don't want to pry, but did something happen in Denison? You've been down in the dumps since you returned."

Shannon scowled, unsure what a dump had to do with what she was feeling. Now she felt the fool for having cared for Mark

Corbett, and yet her heart still betrayed her. Why didn't anyone tell her that falling in love could be so painful?

"Well, I just wanted you to know that I'm here for you if you want to talk. I need to get downstairs. I'm making a mess of sandwiches for when the workers break for the noon meal."

Shannon turned from the window. "Are you needin' some help?"

Rachel smiled. "I could use another pair of hands, but that's not why I'm here. I just want to be sure you're all right."

Shannon considered how years ago, Rachel had lost Luke, the man she loved, and married another. Perhaps 'twould help to talk to her. She stared at the older woman. Rachel was probably in her late twenties, a good ten years older than herself. But she had the look of a newlywed in love, not the harried boardinghouse owner and mother to a troubled child like she'd been when Shannon first arrived in town.

Shannon heaved a sigh and gazed at Rachel, wringing her hands. "I fear I have fallen in love with Mark Corbett, but he doesn't want me." Saying the words made her chin wobble and tears burn her eyes.

Rachel's eyes widened, and her mouth dropped open. "Oh dear."

"Aye, you can see my problem."

"Yes, but does this have anything to do with your trip to Denison? I thought you and Leah would have a good time shopping for her wedding supplies, but you looked miserable when you returned yesterday."

Shannon nodded and drifted back to the window. Her gaze immediately located Mark, carrying a long piece of lumber with his brother. Her heart squeezed at the sight of him, and then she remembered he didn't want her. She ducked her head. What had he found lacking in her?

Rachel took her hand and tugged her over to the bed. "Let's sit for a minute. Maybe things aren't as bleak as they seem."

"I work for the man I'm in love with, and he stated that he'd never marry, so how do I now face him and interact with him each day? If I quit my job, I shall be dependent on the Corbett brothers or destitute. Things seem awfully bleak to me." Shannon plopped onto the bed and sighed.

"I remember thinking the same thing. Luke had finally returned to town, but he wanted nothing to do with me. He refused to forgive me for past offenses, and then you and the other brides came to town. I was ready to sell out and leave."

"You were?"

Rachel nodded. "Yes. I came within a hair's width of selling this place." Her gaze lovingly roved around the room.

"I can't imagine anyone else owning this house. I'm glad you didn't have to do that."

"Me, too. But let me tell you that I firmly believe the good Lord has a plan for you in all of this. He brought you to Lookout for a reason."

Shannon was afraid to let hope take wing. "You truly believe that?"

Rachel grinned and shook her head. "What's hardest to swallow is that He used the Corbett brothers to get you and Leah to town."

"'Tis a difficult concept to fathom. Why do you suppose He would do such a thing?"

"Because God loves you. He has a plan for your life even if things seem their darkest."

"And you believe He brought me here to marry Mark?"

A loud cheer rose up outside the window, and the raised voices of happy men drew her attention for a moment. She longed to be part of the community, but so many people still looked at her as a mail-order bride who was found lacking.

Rachel shook her head. "I never said that. It's possible that God wants you to marry Mark, but He could have brought you here for another man—or another purpose altogether. You need to spend time in prayer and seek God. Try asking Him why you're here, and see what He says."

Shannon rose and walked to the window. It took her a moment to find Mark talking to Jack. The girl smiled up at him and nodded her head. Rachel joined her and peered out. "What's that girl up to now? I told her to stay out of the way."

"I fail to see how Mark can do much with his hand in that cast."

"You know, I just thought of something." Rachel tapped her finger against her mouth. "Mark left Lookout for a time. I don't know much of what happened because I had my own troubles back then, but I can tell you he was different when he returned. Quieter. More thoughtful and less reckless."

"Sounds as if 'twould do his brother good to get away, if he'd return the same as Mark."

Rachel chuckled. "I didn't say it was a good thing. Something bothers Mark deep down, but I have no idea what it is. He doesn't talk about it."

Shannon pondered all that Rachel had said. Could she have truly been brought here for some greater purpose? She remembered her mother saying something similar about their coming to America, but that had tragically ended in her parents' deaths. Couldn't they have just as well died back in Ireland? Where would that have left her, though?

There were many more opportunities for an unmarried woman in America, even though life was still difficult. Prayer was what she needed. For too long, she'd been angry at God for taking her parents, but perhaps it had been His will for her to come to this grand country. And if it was, He would provide for her and give her direction—if she only sought Him.

"Well. . ." Rachel pushed away from the window. "Those sandwiches won't get made by themselves."

"Thank you for your time. I'll be down in a few minutes to help you."

Rachel smiled over her shoulder and walked out into the hallway. "You really don't have to, but if you don't mind helping, I won't turn you down. A lot of men are out there, working up big appetites."

Shannon nodded and closed the door. She knelt beside the bed and folded her hands. "Father God, I beg that You forgive me my trespasses. Forgive me for being angry at You and not seeking You as I should. Show me why You brought me to Lookout. And show me, please, if Mark is part of my future."

❧

The rocking chairs had been moved and makeshift tables set up on the boardinghouse porch. The pounding of hammers and men's shouts across the street filled the air. Shannon set out a tray of sliced bread, while Leah rearranged the table to make room for the bowls of boiled turnips and buttered grits that the pastor's wife had brought. One of the local ranchers had delivered a smoked pig, which Rachel and Jack had partially sliced earlier.

Standing back, Shannon surveyed the tables. Every manner of food one could imagine was on one of the four tables. Jack burst out the front door, carrying a large bowl of buns Rachel had baked. The screen door slammed against the house, jarring the tables and making Leah jump.

"Good heavens, girl. You scared a dozen years off me."

Jack giggled and set the buns by the sliced bread. "You'd better not be wasting any years. You'll be a wife soon, and they work hard."

Leah smiled. "I will be married soon, won't I?"

Shannon nodded, enjoying the lightheartedness after the traumatic events in Denison. Her time of prayer this morning had helped her calm down and focus on the task at hand. Staying busy certainly helped keep her mind off her heartaches. She walked over to the porch rail, lifted her hand to shade her eyes, and looked for Mark. Men hustled here and there, carrying boards, hammering, sawing. There must be twenty men or more, yet they worked as a unified team. How did they each know just what to do?

She shook her head, impressed with their organization. The aroma of fresh-cut lumber scented the air, and the two-story skeleton of the new store was standing, straight and tall. The first story was framed in, and men were already attaching boards to the side walls. She supposed the new owner would be living up above the store.

Rachel strode out the door and walked past each table, surveying everything. The women of the town who had donated food stood in small groups on Bluebonnet Lane, watching the men work and talking. Rachel moved a plate to make room for a last-minute arrival, then clapped her hands. The ladies pivoted in unison and quieted.

"I do believe we are ready to eat. Shall we gather the men?"

"I'll get them, Ma." Jack shot off the end of the porch, not even bothering to use the steps. The girl had begged her mum to let her wear her overalls today so she could help Luke work on the store.

Rachel shook her head. "That girl should have been a boy."

The crowd chuckled. Shannon leaned on a porch post and watched Jack find her new da in the group. He smiled and patted her on the shoulder, then turned to the men and yelled, "Dinner is ready."

A masculine cheer rang out. Most men set aside their tools and headed for the women, but a couple finished their hammering first. Husbands found their wives and turned toward the packed tables. Shannon felt left out as she watched a man swoop down and steal a kiss from his beloved. Mark stood at the back of the line with several unmarried men. He said something to his brother, then slapped his shoulder, and the whole group laughed. She was glad they were having a good time.

Leah found Dan among the men and pulled him over to the food line. Shannon heaved a sigh. 'Twas such a melancholy thing to watch her good friend find love and prepare for her wedding while her own heart was breaking. She hung her head. How did one get over caring for someone who didn't care for them?

"Um. . .excuse me, ma'am. Could I slip past you so's I can get a couple of those fine dinner rolls?"

Shannon glanced up into the blue-gray eyes of a local rancher who'd attended the Saturday social. "Pardon me." She scooted back against the porch railing and allowed him to pass her.

He grabbed two buns and laid them atop the mountain of food on his plate. He turned and smiled, then touched the brim of his hat with his fingertips. "Rand Kessler, ma'am. I don't suppose you'd care to dine with me?"

His unexpected invitation stunned her, but she was in no mood for masculine company. "Well, uh, I need to refill the bread when it dwindles down."

His cheeks turned a ruddy red, and he ducked his head. "How about saving me a dance at the next social?"

Shannon forced a smile. He was a nice man, and she didn't want to hurt his feelings. Her heart wasn't in dancing at all, especially with someone other than Mark, but what did it matter now? "Aye, 'twould be my pleasure."

His wide grin made her glad she'd agreed. Mr. Kessler was a comely man, and she knew he owned a large ranch. He'd make a decent husband, she supposed, but not for her.

Garrett Corbett helped himself to a couple of buns and smiled. "Good day, Miss O'Neil."

She nodded, and realized this was just the chance she'd been waiting for. Mark was at the far end of the line, and she might not catch Garrett alone again. "Might I have a few moments of your time?"

His brows lifted, and he glanced over his shoulder. "Me?"

"Aye. You."

He took a bite of his bun. "Sure, as long as you don't mind if I eat. We'll be getting back to work soon."

"That's fine." She followed him off the porch to a shade tree next to the boardinghouse.

He leaned against the tree and stared at her. "What can I do for you?"

Now that she had his attention, she wasn't sure what to say. She couldn't tell him what had happened between her and his brother. He wouldn't understand why she wanted the change in her work hours, but what did that matter. "I think it's best if I only work in the office when you and your brother are out of town."

His expression remained passive, surprising her. He didn't seem the least bit taken off-guard. Had Mark told him what happened?

"That will mean fewer hours for you. Will that be a problem?"

She'd calculated how much money she'd lose, and aye, 'twould be a problem, but she had no choice. She wouldn't work with Mark in the office. She couldn't.

Garrett's lips twisted to the side. "My brother giving you trouble?"

Shannon shrugged. "I've had to clean and dust and rearrange things over and over to keep busy. You're wasting your money having me work so many hours when you don't need me."

"Shouldn't that be our choice? Maybe we want someone in the office more than just when we're out of town."

"Then you'll need to hire someone else."

He quirked a brow. "You're serious?"

"Aye."

He heaved a sigh and set his plate on a nearby fence post. "What did my brother do?"

Shannon's lips trembled. What could she say? " 'Tisn't important. Can we work it out that I'm in the office on the days you're gone, or not?"

Garrett ran his hand over his chin, obviously not wanting to comply, but finally he nodded his head. "I reckon it would work. I could let you know at the beginning of each week what our plans are, and you could come down after we leave. We can leave notes to each other, if need be."

"Thank you. I appreciate your flexibility."

He nodded and stared down at her, his eyes so much like his brother's that it made her heart ache. "I was hopin' things would work out between you two."

She turned away, not wanting him to see how much she wished the same.

"I'll have a talk with him."

"No!" Shannon turned back and touched his arm, then jerked her hand away. "He made his feelings clear. 'Tis best we both honor them."

He stared at her for a long moment, then nodded.

She turned away, hurrying toward the rear of the boardinghouse. She'd miss seeing Mark most days, but 'twas for the best. Her job was safe. She'd just have to pinch her pennies tighter.

Chapter 23

Leah finished sweeping the boardinghouse porch. She watched Dan lift up one of Rachel's heavy rocking chairs as if it were a five-pound bag of sugar and carry it to the middle of the porch, where he set it down.

"That the right spot?"

Leah smiled. "Perfect."

Dan nodded, a twinkle in his dark eyes, and fetched the other three rockers one at a time. Leah loved working on a project like this with him. Though they weren't yet married, she felt joined to him in a way she never had with another man. It was as if they were already partners. She leaned on the broom, imagining the days ahead when she would cook in the Howard home while Dan sipped coffee and read the town newspaper.

Dan brushed his hands together. "That's it. You done with your work now? Care to take a walk?"

She nodded, a teasing smile tugging at her lips. A walk with Dan meant stolen kisses. Her heart skipped like a schoolgirl's. "Just let me run this back inside."

She hurried to the kitchen and placed the broom in its spot. The whole room smelled of savory scents that made her mouth water. Rachel leaned over the dry sink with her arm halfway down in a large pot she was washing.

"Sure smells wonderful in here. What's for supper?"

Rachel glanced over her shoulder and smiled. "Ham and beans."

"Mmm. . .I can't wait. Dan asked me to take a walk with him, but if you need help, I can stay."

Rachel shook her head. "No, you two go on, but if you see my daughter, chase her home so she can get cleaned up."

"All right, I can do that."

Outside, Dan took her hand, and they passed the new store, heading down Bluebonnet Lane toward the river on the edge of town. "Too bad we didn't finish today."

Leah studied the new structure. "You probably would have if it wasn't for building that second story."

Dan nodded. "Yeah, we ran into a few problems that slowed us down. Several men have volunteered to work on it Monday, so maybe they'll finish up then."

"I can't wait to have the store open again."

Dan chuckled. "Ladies need to do their shopping."

"Oh no. It's not that." She feared he'd misconstrued her meaning and would think her a wastrel. "I don't shop all that much, but I do love walking through the store when I get bored and looking at all the lovely things. Not that I won't work hard once we're married."

Oh, now he'd think her lazy. He didn't realize she'd had hours on end with nothing to do since coming to town, and walking through the store occasionally had helped occupy her time.

Dan patted her hand. "I'm not worried. We won't be rich by any means, but you should be able to buy most things you need—or want—at the store."

"I don't need much. Being the oldest of eleven children, I never had a lot to call my own."

Dan wrapped his arm around her shoulders. "Well, I want you to get what you need. I have some money saved, and you don't need to do without anymore."

She leaned into him, enjoying having someone who cared about her. Someone to spoil her a little bit. She'd had so few treasures in her life—not that she needed many—that it would be delightful to buy some more soft, store-bought undergarments like the set she'd gotten in Denison and not have to use flour sacks any longer.

At the river's edge, they paused and watched the water. The gentle ripple of water splashing on the banks was calming after the busyness of the day. She'd helped Rachel and Shannon bake and fix a large portion of the food for the workers. Since Mrs. Foster had no kitchen, she'd hired Rachel to feed the men, although every woman whose husband was working had also brought food. The feast reminded Leah of the church potlucks back home, after Sunday service.

Thinking of home reminded her of Sue Anne. Had her good friend gone west as a mail-order bride and married her rancher as she'd planned? She'd received only one letter from her, telling of her engagement, but Sue Anne was an only child, and her father might have stopped her from leaving town if he'd found out about her plans. Knowing how happy she was having found her own love, Leah wished the same for her friend.

Dan turned to face her. "Just eight more days, and we'll be married."

Her insides swirled with giddiness. Had she ever been this happy before? "I can't wait."

"Me neither." He leaned down, capturing her lips, and pulled her close. He was so big, so powerful, but with her, he was gentle and loving. She'd never known such delight, and when he finally pulled away, both of them were breathing hard.

Her lips were damp and felt puffy, but her heart was racing. She would spend the rest of her life loving this man and enjoying every minute.

Dan lifted his hat and ran his hand through his hair. "I reckon I should get you back before I do something we'd both regret."

Leah knew just what he meant. She longed to love him more. To show him the depth of her love, but she wasn't free to do that as thoroughly as she wished until after their wedding ceremony. She sighed and nodded her head. Heading back was probably a wise idea.

He took her hand, and they walked to town again. "I reckon

we need to clean out Ma's room."

His voice cracked a bit at the mention of his mother. "I can do that after we're married, Dan. Don't worry about it now."

He squeezed her hand. "Thanks. I'd appreciate that. Don't know if I could do it."

"I know. I truly wished I'd gotten to know your mother better."

He wrapped his arm around her. "She liked you, you know."

She dashed a glance up at him. "Indeed?"

"Yep. She wanted me to ask to court you, but I didn't need her prompting, because I've had my eye on you since you first arrived in town. I figured Luke would pick you, what with you being so pretty and all."

She ducked her head, but was pleasantly delighted that he found her pretty. She wouldn't admit that he hadn't caught her eye back then, but she'd been focused only on winning the marshal's heart. She'd have willingly married a man she didn't love back then and would have missed out on the blessing God had for her in Dan.

But there was still one thing she needed to tell him. Something that might make him change his mind about marrying her. A fist of fear squeezed her heart. Could she marry Dan and then tell him she didn't want children? If she told him now, he might call off the wedding. And how could she survive without him?

She argued with herself all the way back to town. *Tell him. Don't tell him until after the wedding. Tell him.*

"Looks like someone has arrived in town."

She glanced up and saw a heavily loaded wagon stopped right in front of the boardinghouse. A woman stood on the porch, hands on her hips, starring at the town. Leah's heart hammered, and she grabbed hold of Dan's arm. "What is she doing here?"

"Who?"

"That woman we saw Mark Corbett with in Denison."

"I have no idea, but it can't be anything good."

Leah quickened her steps. "I have to get back. Shannon will need me."

As they neared the boardinghouse, she realized another woman and several children had also arrived. The wagon looked loaded down with furniture, household goods, and a great number of crates. The other woman stared toward the new store with her hand resting against her cheek.

"I had so hoped the building would be finished when we arrived."

Ah, so this must be the Fosters' niece. Leah strode up to her and held out her hand. "Welcome to Lookout."

The pretty woman with dark brown hair and blue eyes smiled. "Thank you. I'm Christine Morgan. I've come to run the store." She glanced behind her. "Come here, children."

A boy of medium height who looked to be twelve or thirteen came from around the back of the wagon. He eyed Leah with a steely blue gaze that made her want to scurry behind Dan. A girl of about nine shuffled along beside him, carrying a porcelain-faced doll dressed in a frilly blue dress.

Mrs. Morgan smiled. "These are my children, Billy and Tessa."

Leah nodded. "A pleasure to meet you. I'm Leah Bennett, and this is my fiancé, Dan Howard. Dan runs the livery, and I'm currently living at the boardinghouse."

"But not for long." Dan waggled his brows, then turned serious. "I can help you carry whatever you need into the boardinghouse and then store your wagon inside my livery. It will be safe there."

Mrs. Morgan splayed her hand across her chest. "Oh, I can't tell you how much of a relief that would be. Pretty much all I own is on that wagon." She glanced toward the building again. "I know I'm early, but I sure wish the store had been ready. I'm anxious to get settled."

"I imagine you are. Come on into the boardinghouse, and I'll introduce you to the proprietor, Mrs. Davis. You'll be quite comfortable here."

"And Rachel's a darn good cook," Dan offered.

"That's good news. I'm starved!" Billy rubbed his belly and headed toward the front door.

"Not so quick, young man. Grab your satchel and Tessa's." Mrs. Morgan stared at her son, as if not sure he'd obey.

The boy scowled but returned to the back of the wagon and fetched two bags. Leah hadn't seen Annabelle, but she now stepped out from behind the wagon, carrying two large handbags. She looked at Leah and frowned. Maybe the woman didn't recognize her. What could she be doing in a small town like Lookout? She had a feeling that nothing good would come of it, and that her being here would only bring Shannon more heartache. That Mark Corbett was a scoundrel to lead her friend on and then drop her once she'd fallen in love with him.

Leah strode toward the front door and opened it. She should introduce herself to the other woman, but her heart just wasn't in it. She left the door open and called for Rachel.

"In the kitchen," she cried out.

Leah stopped in the doorway of the kitchen, her stomach gurgling at the delicious scents. Rachel was placing cornbread onto a platter. "Some guests have arrived."

"This late? I hope I have enough food. How many are there?" Rachel dusted her hands and removed her apron. Smoothing down her hair, she hurried toward the front door.

"There are four of them. Two women and two children."

"It's good we're not filled up, then."

The quartet stood in the parlor with Dan behind them, holding several bags. He winked at Leah, sending delicious tingles radiating through her body. Her intended was a fine-looking man, and he was all hers.

"Welcome, everyone." Rachel smiled and relieved Mrs. Morgan of one of her bags. "I'm Rachel Davis, owner of this boarding-house. How can I help you?"

"I'm Christine Morgan, and these are my children." She glanced at the other new arrival. "Miss Smith caught a ride with us, but I believe she's staying here, too, if you have enough room."

"Yes, there's room for all of you." Rachel explained the rate and that meals were included, then headed for the stairs. "If y'all will just follow me, I'll show you to your rooms, where you can freshen up. Supper is ready to be served, so come on back down as soon as you can."

Leah watched them trounce up the stairs with Dan at the end of the line. He winked at her again, then followed the others. "I'll start setting out the meal, if that's all right, Rachel."

The boardinghouse owner looked down from the second floor and smiled. "Thank you. That would be wonderful."

Leah waited a moment, suspecting Rachel would show Miss Smith to the only available room on the second floor, and then the Morgan family up to the third floor. She started up the steps and waited until the others headed up the rear stairs, then made a mad dash for Shannon's door. Knocking hard, she didn't wait but opened the door and peered inside.

Shannon was halfway across the room, heading toward her. "What's wrong?

Leah waved for Shannon to hurry over to her. "Come downstairs with me. New guests have arrived, and Rachel is seeing them to their rooms. Supper is nearly ready and I told her I'd help, and there's something I've got to tell you."

Shannon followed her out the door, obviously curious. "And what would that be?"

Leah lifted her skirt and hurried down the stairs. "Wait till we get to the kitchen."

They hustled down the hall, skirts swishing, and entered the empty room. Shannon glanced at the stove.

"I told Rachel I'd dish up supper. Could you finish putting the cornbread on that platter?" Leah pulled one of the soup tureens from a cabinet and started ladling beans into it while Shannon attended to her job, casting curious glances her way.

They placed the food on the buffet in the dining room. Then Leah grabbed Shannon's hand, pulled her through the kitchen, and out the back door. Shannon's green eyes widened as Leah turned to face her. She leaned in close. "That woman is here."

Shannon blinked. "What woman?"

"The one Mark was talking to in Denison."

Gasping, Shannon clutched her chest. "Why?"

"I don't know. I just wanted you to be prepared and not surprised when you saw her."

Shannon straightened her back and hiked up her chin. "Why should I care if she's here? Mark wants nothing to do with me, so she can have him."

Leah's heart ached for her friend's pain. It made her own

happiness less enjoyable. She placed a hand on Shannon's shoulder. "It matters, and we both know it."

Shaking her head, Shannon stared off in the distance. "Nay, it doesn't. I must move past my feelings for him. It does me no good to hang on to them."

Leah clenched her fist. "Oh, those Corbetts. If I were a man, I'd knock them both for a loop."

Shannon's mouth turned up in a melancholy smile. "If you were a man, you wouldn't have an issue with them."

Leah blew out a frustrated breath. How could Shannon be so gracious? "Well, I suppose we should finish setting out the food."

Shannon nodded and followed her back inside. Leah opened a lid on a large pot and found a mess of greens with ham chunks. She dished them into another tureen while Shannon carried an assortment of jellies and a bowl of butter to the table.

Leah's mind raced. Why had that woman come to Lookout? Whatever the reason was, she had a feeling it would only mean trouble for her friend.

Chapter 24

Mark stared at the ledger, but his eyes couldn't seem to focus on the numbers. Nothing had seemed right since he'd told Shannon he'd never marry. The pain in her eyes that night haunted his dreams the few hours that he'd managed to fall asleep. He missed her. Missed seeing her in the office, sitting in his chair. Missed watching her whirl around, dusting cabinets and leaving her soft scent lingering in the air.

He rested his head on his hand and sighed. If only he'd never left Lookout. Then maybe he and Shannon could have had a chance.

Garrett walked in from the back room, still carrying his coffee cup. Generally, for the first hour or two each morning, his brother and the mug were attached to one another. He strolled over to the pot sitting on the stove and filled his cup, then turned and stared at Mark.

"You're looking rather glum these days, little brother." Garrett continued staring while he took a sip.

Mark shrugged, unable to deny the accusation. He was glum. And frustrated. And lonely.

"Care to talk about it?" Garrett pulled out his desk chair and sat down.

He'd wrestled with that very thought on a number of occasions, but telling his brother he couldn't marry Shannon would mean he'd have to tell him the whole story. And he wasn't prepared to do that.

His brother was all the family he had left, except for Luke, and he couldn't stand seeing the disappointment in Garrett's eyes if he ever learned the truth. He'd worked so hard to be an upstanding citizen ever since that calamity in Abilene, and he didn't want his reputation tarnished. If he ever was to become a lawyer, having an unblemished reputation was crucial. Who'd trust their future to a lawyer who'd killed a man?

Garrett swigged down the last of his coffee and stood. "Well, if you decide you want to get that burden you're lugging off your chest, I'll be tending the horses."

Mark sat with his head in his hands. Why couldn't he give this burden to God? He'd begged forgiveness—over and over again. He was sure God had forgiven him for killing that man, but how did he forgive himself?

That night in Abilene intruded into his mind again. He could hear the off-key piano, smell the smoke that filled the room until a hazy cloud hung in the air. Men gambled at different tables, while others drank away their hard-earned weekly pay. Saloon girls sashayed between tables, but Mark only had eyes for one of them.

Annabelle.

The first night he'd gone into the saloon, she'd offered to get him a drink. Their attraction was instant, and although he rarely frequented saloons, visiting the Lucky Star where she worked became a nightly obsession. Even remembering the Bible verses about avoiding wanton women that his mother had quoted to him and Garrett when they were becoming young men didn't stop him.

Annabelle had been his first love. She'd managed to squeeze out short moments to sit with him or stand and talk between serving drinks to the other patrons. He'd never drank before, but he kept buying liquor to keep her coming around. And that drinking made his head fuzzy. Made him do things he'd not normally do.

He hung his head in shame as he remembered the first night he'd waited until Annabelle was off work and had walked her to the small room she rented. One kiss led to two. Two led to three. His whiskey-befuddled mind assented to her request to come inside, and the rest was history. He'd not had the power to refuse her pleas to stay the night.

Mark clutched his hair in his fists. It had all happened so fast, and his need had been so strong that he couldn't resist her charms. Afterward, he'd felt so dirty and ashamed that he'd taken advantage of her that he hadn't returned to the saloon for a full week. But the siren's call had been too strong to resist.

And he'd forever pay the price.

If only he could go back and do things differently.

"Forgive me, Lord."

The bell on the door jingled, pulling him out of his reverie. He blinked, sure what he was seeing was an apparition.

Annabelle stood in the doorway, giving him that saucy smile that had made him weak years before. He stood, still unable to believe she was standing in his office. In his town.

"Hello there, handsome."

"What are you doing in Lookout?"

She strutted toward him, looking deceptively sweet in that dark blue calico dress, but he knew inside lay a vixen who could make the strongest of men sway from his beliefs. Warnings clanged in his mind. He was a stronger man than he'd been back then. He was a man who'd tasted her spoils and by God's grace would never fall in that quagmire again.

She pressed her hands on his desk and leaned forward, her gaze never leaving his. Mark's heart pounded like a creature caught in a trap. He stepped back until he met the wall to distance himself from her.

He cleared his throat. "I asked what you are doing here. I thought I made it clear in Denison that anything between us was over. Way over."

She smiled and waved her hand in the air. "I knew you'd change your mind if you could see how different I am. I'm going to find a respectable job and start my life over. There's always room for a good man in it."

Mark crossed his arms. "I'm not that man."

Annabelle shrugged and stared out the front window. "Things got bad recently in Abilene. I couldn't stay there anymore, and besides, I was sick of men pawing at me. I want to know what it's like to be a lady whom men respect."

Something in Mark's heart cracked, but he quickly shored up the breach. Annabelle might fuss about working in the saloon, but he felt certain she liked the attention she'd received. And while he couldn't blame her in the least for not wanting to be an upstairs gal, she hadn't had any qualms about taking him to her bed. A shiver charged down his back at the memory.

He'd been stupid.

Thought she had eyes for only him.

But he was older and wiser now.

"There are plenty of towns you could live in. Why come here?"

She spun around, her head cocked. "Because you're here. We can finally have the life together that we talked about."

Mark ran his hand through his hair. "That was a long time ago. I don't mean to be unkind, but let me put it clearly—I'm no longer interested in a relationship with you."

Her lips pushed out into a pout. "It's that Irish gal, isn't it?"

A vision of Shannon entered his mind. If she learned about his past rapport with Annabelle, it would crush any hopes that he might have of restoring his relationship with her. Yeah, he'd told her he would never marry, but deep inside, he still held out hope that something could work out between them. A horrible thought rushed into his mind. "Where are you staying?"

A sly grin tilted her mouth. "At the boardinghouse, of course. Where else would a decent woman stay in this dumpy, little town?"

Mark's fingers tightened on the back of the chair, and he ground his back teeth together.

"I'm so looking forward to getting to know Shannon better. I think she and I could be good friends."

"What do you want, Annabelle? Why are you really here?"

Her mouth twisted, and she shrugged. "I didn't know where to go. You're the only man who ever defended me, and I truly wanted to see if there was any chance for us to be together again."

He strode around the desk and leaned into her face. She swallowed hard, showing the first sign of vulnerability he'd seen since she'd entered his office. "Let me tell you again. I made the biggest mistake of my life in Abilene. There is no chance this side of heaven of us being together. I'm sorry you've had a rough life, but part of it was your own choosing. You could have left the Lucky Star years ago, but you didn't. I sincerely hope you can turn your life around, but I won't be a part of it. The best thing you can do for me is to leave town."

She flounced her head and scowled. "That was rather harsh, don'tcha think?"

"No, it's simply the truth."

"I was hopin' you'd give me a job."

Mark shook his head. "Shannon already works here."

"Then why isn't she here? It's already midmornin'."

"We. . .ah. . .don't have enough work for her to be here all the time. She mostly works when we're gone now."

"I can see that you need time to get used to my being here. I'll give you a few days, and then we'll talk again." She swung around, hurried for the door, and yanked it open.

"Annabelle. I meant what I said."

She slammed the door without looking back. Mark slumped against his desk. "Dear Lord, help me."

Shannon sat in the parlor, staring out the front window. She needed to finish the lace she was making for Leah's wedding dress, but her heart wasn't in it. She might have lost Mark, but she never expected to have another woman come to town vying for him.

Perhaps she was making a mountain out of a molehill, but that Annabelle Smith had gone on and on at breakfast about knowing Mark in Abilene. Why, she'd all but insinuated there was something between them. Had that woman hurt Mark so deeply that he never wanted to marry?

'Twould explain a lot.

But Mark didn't seem jaded toward women. He'd always been friendly to her, except when Garrett first hired her to work for them. She sighed heavily. This was her first day to not go in to work, and she sorely missed being there. Missed seeing Mark.

But she'd made her decision, and 'twas for the best. Her heart couldn't heal if she had to work with Mark, and listen to his baritone voice, smell his fresh scent, or watch him work. She longed to see those brilliant blue eyes gazing at her as she'd caught them on more than one occasion.

"You silly lass." She shook her head to rid it of thoughts of Mark and focused back on her stitching.

Leah walked in and sat down on the settee beside her. "Oh, that is so lovely. You do such fine work. I bet you could easily sell your lace."

"Thank you. Perhaps I will talk to Mrs. Morgan about that very thing. If I could sell some that would help offset the money I'll lose by not working at the freight office so much."

Leah puffed up. "I wish you didn't have to work there at all."

"Aye, 'twould be for the best, but I'll not have the Corbetts supporting me again, so I must work there until I find something else."

"That Miss Smith is looking for employment also."

"Would that I could give her my job at the freight office, then she and her beloved Mark would be together."

Leah's brows lifted. "Is that cynicism I hear?"

Shannon shrugged. "I just got so ill listening to her go on about Mark at breakfast. If they were such good friends, why have we never heard of her before seeing her in Denison?"

"Maybe she's not someone Mark wants to remember. She seems awfully. . .shall we say, rough around the edges?"

"Aye, I sensed that, too. What do you suppose it means?"

"I have my suspicions, but it's best I not voice them, in case I'm wrong."

Shannon laid down her stitching again. If she sewed while angry, she had a tendency to pull the thread so tight that it bunched up. "She can have him, for all I care."

Leah laid her hand on Shannon's arm. "I'm so sorry things

didn't work out between you two. It's hard to be happy with Dan knowing all you're going through."

Shannon turned toward her friend. "The last thing I want to do is steal your joy. The good Lord is helping me. I still care for Mark, but I need to look elsewhere for a husband. If I can marry, I will no longer have to work at the freight office."

Leah closed her eyes for a moment. "Just don't rush into something. I know you've had at least a dozen marriage proposals in the past weeks, but take your time and pick a man who will be good to you. A man you might one day be able to love."

She considered the wisdom of her friend's advice and nodded. Quick, heavy footsteps on the front porch drew their attention. Someone pounded on the door, and then it opened.

"Leah?" Dan's frantic deep voice boomed through the house.

Leah jumped up and hurried from the room. "I'm right here. What's wrong?"

"Come outside, I've got to talk to you."

The front door shut, then opened again, and Annabelle walked into the parlor. "Looks like the lovebirds might be having a spat."

Gathering up her lace, Shannon stood and crossed to the window. Dan looked very upset. What could have happened?

"I was just over talking to Mark."

The woman said his name as if it were sweet candy. "So. . . there's no law against talkin' to the man."

Annabelle smirked. "I don't know what's going on with you and him, but Mark and I have a past. I just need a little time to win him back."

"Good luck with that, I say."

Annabelle blinked and looked taken off-guard. If the woman expected her to fight for Mark, she'd be disappointed. Shannon headed out of the room. She might have to be cordial to Annabelle, but she didn't have to socialize with her.

"I must have been wrong. I thought for sure you and Mark had something going on."

Had was the key word. "I don't believe Mark is interested in any woman. He told me himself that he'd never marry. If you ask me, you're wastin' your time with that one."

Annabelle's eyes widened, and her mouth opened, but nothing came out. Shannon hurried up the stairs, closed her door, and locked it. At least in the privacy of her own room she could be free of that woman. She laid the lace on top of the dresser and sat in the chair, worried about Leah.

What was going on?

Chapter 25

Why can't we get married right away?" Dan stared at her with hurt in his eyes. "Then you can travel to Dallas with me to see to my brother's estate."

"I'm so sorry to hear about your brother's death, but I'm not ready to marry. My dress isn't finished yet, and there are a hundred other details to take care of."

Dan paced to the end of the porch and stared off in the distance. Leah's heart ached for him. He hadn't gotten over his mother's death yet, and now a telegram informed him of his brother and sister-in-law's deaths. "Couldn't I just go with you, and we could get married when we return? We're both adults and able to handle the situation respectfully."

He shook his head. "I won't take a chance on ruining your reputation. There are some folks in this town who'd look down on two unmarried people traveling together."

She closed the distance between them and laid her hand on his shoulder. "I'm so sorry about your family. Can you tell me what happened?"

He turned and wrapped his arms around her. "I don't know much. The telegram was from my sister, Louise, and just said that Aaron and Irene had died and for me to come to Dallas as soon as possible."

"Did they have any children?"

He nodded and swallowed so hard that Leah saw his Adam's apple move. "Five, and they're all fairly young."

Tears stung Leah's eyes. "Oh, those poor children. What will happen to them?"

"I'm sure my sister will take them in. She's known them all since birth and is very close to them since they only lived a half-mile away."

Leah hugged Dan hard, not caring if anyone saw. He rested his chin on top of her head. She wanted to go along with him, but he was right. People would think it inappropriate. "When are you leaving?"

"I thought to wait until morning to take the stage, but if you aren't coming, I'll leave as soon as I can get packed and ride to Dallas."

She leaned back and stared up into his damp eyes. His thick lashes clung together in spikes, and she knew he'd be embarrassed if he became aware that she knew he'd been crying. He was a big, tough man, but he cared deeply for his only brother. "Will it be dangerous for you to ride alone?"

"No. I'll be riding fast, only stopping to rest my horse. In fact, I may take two and trade off riding them. I should be there in a few days if I do that."

She lifted her hand and touched his face. "Please be careful, and come back to me. I couldn't bear losing you."

He smiled through his sadness. "I love you, sweetheart."

Right there in broad daylight on the boardinghouse front porch, he pulled her back into his arms and kissed her thoroughly. When he stopped, she swayed, nearly dizzy with love for this man. She almost wavered and decided to go with him.

"I'd better get going."

"Once you're packed, stop back by here. I'm sure Rachel won't mind if I make you a lunch to take with you."

He nodded and strode away. Leah's heart thumped hard. What if something happened to him, and he didn't return? How would she find the strength to go on?

She muttered a prayer as she walked through the house to the kitchen. Just like when her pa had sold her to that horrible Mr. Abernathy and she'd found the strength to run away and become a mail-order bride, God would help her to go on without Dan. But she prayed hard that such a day never would come.

Annabelle sat on the edge of the bed and stared at the wall of her room in the boardinghouse. It was the nicest place she'd ever stayed, except maybe for the hotel in Denison. She picked at some lint on her serviceable dress, so plain compared to her saloon garb and yet it made her feel respectable. How odd that a simple dress could change a person's perspective of her. If the folks in the boardinghouse knew the truth about her, they'd boot her out the front door and send her packing.

She blew out a heavy breath. Her plans had not turned out as she'd hoped. Instead of being happy to see her, Mark acted like he couldn't stand to be around her. At least he would keep silent about her past, since he had more to lose than her if he spilled the beans. Maybe that's why he was so nervous around her. Maybe he was afraid his friends would find out that he had socialized with a saloon girl.

He sure had changed from the fun-loving man she'd known several years ago. She lay down on the bed and pulled the spare pillow against her stomach, remembering how she'd once shared her bed with him. He'd liked her back then. Maybe even loved her.

He certainly had come to her defense in the saloon when that randy cowboy had mauled her and forced her to kiss him. She shivered at the thought of her mouth pressed to the man's, his hands freely roving her body. Who knew what might have happened if Mark hadn't called a halt? When the cowboy pulled his gun, she'd screamed, sure that Mark would be killed. But the cowboy died that night when Mark shot him.

She'd thought Mark a soft, intellectual type and had been attracted to him at first only because of his unusual, robin's-egg blue eyes and curly blond hair. She'd been drawn to the gentle innocence of his gaze, but she soon discovered she liked him. Then it became a quest to see if she could get him to marry her.

He was her best chance to ever get free of the saloon. To live a life she'd only dreamed about.

Now what was she going to do? She'd wandered through the few businesses in Lookout, and nobody had a job opening of any kind. She thought about stopping in the Wet Your Whistle, but that would be going right back to where she'd been before. How was she going to get by?

Everett's money wouldn't last forever.

The night of the next Saturday social was perfect. A cool north wind had blown in, making the temperature bearable. The sun hanging low in the sky showed the beginnings of a beautiful sunset with its brilliant orange glow. But Shannon's heart wasn't in dancing or enjoying the sunset. Why had she allowed Leah to drag her along?

Dancers kicked up their heels to the lively music, stirring up a low-hanging cloud of dust. A couple of the men let out whoops as they twirled their dance partners in a circle. The size of the crowd was more than triple that of the first social. Since news of Dan and Leah's engagement and that of another couple's, unmarried folks had flocked here from miles away to meet new people and have a good time.

Both Shannon and Leah had remained behind the table, much to the disappointment of the men who'd asked them to dance. The only man Shannon wanted to dance with wasn't in attendance. Annabelle, on the other hand, had yet to say no to a single man, Shannon was sure. She watched the flirtatious woman laughing and twirling with a handsome cowboy. If she had designs on Mark, no one would know it tonight.

Someone to Shannon's right cleared his throat, and she glanced sideways.

The comely rancher smiled. "I do believe you promised me a dance tonight, Miss O'Neil."

Inwardly, Shannon sighed. Why had she agreed to dance with this man last weekend? She forced a smile, knowing she couldn't go back on her word. "Aye, that I did."

Relief widened his smile, and he took her hand, leading her to the lot beside the church where the dancers were. She placed her free hand on his shoulder, finding that she could barely reach it. Why did men grow so tall in Texas?

"In case you didn't remember, my name is Rand Kessler."

She remembered. She also knew he was the man who had once hoped to marry Rachel, before Luke returned to Lookout. He seemed a nice enough man, and he must be for Rachel to have agreed to see him.

"I own a ranch outside of town a ways. We raise shorthorn cattle and horses."

Mr. Kessler spun her around in time with the music and held her gently, not possessively, like so many of the men did. She liked that about him. "Have you always lived in Texas, Mr. Kessler?"

"Call me Rand, ma'am. And no, I haven't. My daddy came here after our Georgia plantation was destroyed in the war. I was just a young boy when we first arrived here. But I've lived most of my life here, and Texas will always be my home."

That explained the slight Southern twang to his speech. She thought about his traveling here from Georgia and realized they had something in common—they were both immigrants to this land.

"How did you happen to come here?" Rand's ears suddenly turned red, and his gaze shot everywhere but at her. "I mean, I know how you came to be in Lookout since you were one of the... uh...mail-order brides the Corbetts ordered, but how did you get here from Ireland?"

She scowled at his mention of the Corbetts. For a whole two minutes, Mark hadn't entered her mind. But Rand wasn't aware of how the name affected her, and she chose to forget about it. "My da had the grand idea of coming to America, the land whose streets are paved in gold. Imagine his surprise when we arrived in New Orleans."

"Where are your parents now? If I may ask?" He cleared his throat and again looked uncomfortable. "I mean, why would they allow you to travel to Texas alone as a mail-order bride?"

She broke eye contact and stared off in the distance. He was just being cordial and had no idea how his questions stirred up hurts. They danced around another couple and in and out of the crowd. Finally she worked up her nerve and looked at him again. "My parents died shortly after we arrived in New Orleans."

His eyes widened. He danced her over to the edge of the crowd, and then stopped and rubbed the back of his neck. "I'm sorry, ma'am. I had no idea. Have you no brothers or sisters?"

She shook her head.

"Me neither. I'm an only child. Well, I am now, but I did have a little sister. She died from a snakebite." His lips pursed as if mentioning the old accident still pained him.

Shannon laid her hand on his arm. "I'm sorry, Rand. I, too, have lost all my siblings, but 'twas a long time ago, back in Ireland."

He nodded. "Care to take a walk?"

"Aye, 'twould be nice."

He offered his arm and guided her around the dancers and back toward the refreshment table. As they passed Leah, she lifted her brows and smiled in a teasing manner. Shannon hoped her friend didn't make too much of her walk with Rand. He was a nice, lonely man, and she was a lonely woman. "Tell me about your ranch."

"It's small compared to some ranches in Texas, around ten thousand acres."

Shannon gasped, and he stopped and stared at her. "That's small?"

He shrugged, but pride pulled at his lips. "For Texas. There's so much land here, it can take a month to cross it all."

"Surely it must take a long while to cross ten thousand acres."

"Well, we don't normally ride the whole thing at one time. The ranch is kind of in the middle of it all."

They walked down the street, talking, and by the time he saw her back to the boardinghouse, she'd made a decision.

If Rand Kessler ever asked her to marry him, she'd accept his offer.

Her heart might belong to Mark, but since he didn't want her, she needed to look elsewhere. And Rand seemed as good as they came.

Chapter 26

Silverware clinked around the table as the boarders enjoyed breakfast. Leah looked around the group and realized how close she was becoming to the Davis family and to Shannon. She'd been desperate last spring when she wrote to Luke Davis about becoming his mail-order bride, but things certainly hadn't turned out as she'd expected. Soon she would marry. This coming Sunday after church, if Dan returned on time, but not to the man she originally thought she would wed.

Christine Morgan carried on a lively conversation with Rachel and Annabelle, while Shannon stared into her coffee cup. There ought to be something Leah could do to encourage her friend, but then she was pining away, too.

She moved the last of her eggs around on her plate. She missed Dan terribly. Had he settled his brother's estate and gotten the children situated at his sister's house? Was he already on his way home?

"Have you had any news from Dan?" The marshal stared at Leah while adding a spoon of sugar to his coffee.

She shook her head. "No, I didn't really expect to hear from him. I figure he could be home in less time than it would take to send a letter. Besides, I don't see Dan as the letter-writing type."

Luke grinned. "You might be right about that. He's far better suited to a hammer and anvil."

Rachel buttered her biscuit and slathered apricot jam on it. "That's such a shame for Dan to lose his brother and sister-in-law right on the heels of his mother's death."

"Yes, it is. My heart aches for him. I don't know how he holds up." Leah laid her napkin next to her plate.

" 'Tis difficult to lose two family members at once."

Heads nodded around the table. Everyone knew about Shannon's loss.

Leah patted her friend's shoulder and offered a smile, then looked at Rachel. "Thank you for another wonderful breakfast. It was delicious as always. Can I help with the cleanup?"

Rachel waved her hand as usual. "No, thank you. Just go off and finish that dress. Sunday will be here before you know it."

Shannon stood, too. "I almost have the lace completed. I just need a few more hours' work."

"I love the lace you gave me for a wedding gift. It will always be special to me." Rachel smiled at Shannon and then turned to her daughter. "You'd better finish up and head to school. You don't want to be late on the first day."

Jack shoved a piece of biscuit into her mouth and winked at Billy Morgan. "We wouldn't want to be late, would we?"

"I love school." Tessa pushed away from the table, her eyes sparkling. "Do you have a nice teacher?"

Jack stood and gulped down her milk. "Yeah, she's all right, but let me tell you about Butch Laird. He's the class bully, and you'll want to stay away from him."

"I don't think you'll have to worry about that boy. I had a good talk with him and scared him straight." Luke stretched and downed the last of his coffee.

A knock sounded on the front door, and Leah moved toward it. "I'll grab that, so you just enjoy your biscuit, Rachel."

As she entered the hall, she realized how brash that sounded. Here she was, a guest at the boardinghouse, and she was answering the door and telling the owner what to do. She smiled to herself. At least Rachel was kind enough not to mind her guests bossing her around.

She pulled the heavy door open, and her heart did a somersault. Dan stood on the other side of the screen door, devouring her with his eyes. He looked so handsome. So wonderful. He yanked the screen open, and she squealed and jumped into his arms. He turned a circle, taking her with him.

"Welcome back, Dan." Shannon smiled softly and hurried up the stairs.

Dan watched her, and when she opened her door and disappeared into her room, his lips came down on Leah's, hard but gentle. After a moment, he pulled away and stared into her eyes. "I don't ever want to have to leave you again."

Tears dripped down Leah's cheeks, and she knew exactly what he meant. He'd been gone just shy of a week, but she'd missed him so much that she'd lain awake at nights. Now that she had a good glance at him, she realized he looked exhausted, haggard. Her cheeks were chafed from his unshaven face. "I'm so glad you're back. I didn't expect you so soon. What happened?"

He took her hand and pulled her outside. "Walk with me to the house. I brought a surprise back with me."

What could he have brought her? Something for the wedding? A treasured family heirloom that he'd retrieved from his brother's house? "How did you manage to finish everything so quickly?"

"I didn't. Stanley is going to see to the selling of Aaron's farm, then pay off the debts and split whatever income there may be between us and him and Louise."

"So you had the funeral?"

He nodded as they walked down Bluebonnet Lane and turned onto Oak Street. "Louise had it all planned. I'd have missed it if I'd waited and taken the stage. People are buried quickly in these parts since it tends to be so hot here much of the year."

Leah hugged his brawny arm. "I'm so glad you got to be there. I know that was important to you."

Dan sobered. "Yeah, it was. Louise missed it, though."

"She did? Why?"

"She's been awful sick. She's carrying, and the doctor suspects it may be twins. He's making her stay off her feet until the babies are born."

"Oh, that poor woman. I know all about twins. My ma had two sets of them."

Dan patted her arm and then waved at Martha Phillips, who was sweeping off her front porch.

"Good to see you back. How'd your trip go?" The doctor's wife tucked a wisp of hair back under her scarf.

" 'Bout as I expected, all except for one thing."

"Well, I suppose that's good then." Martha smiled and resumed her sweeping.

Dan leaned in close to Leah. "I reckon you and Martha will get to know each other better, being as she and the doc are our closest neighbors."

"If we ever need the doctor in the middle of the night, at least we won't have far to go."

Dan chuckled. "That's right, darlin'."

A large wagon with two stock horses still hitched to it was parked in front of Dan's house. It looked loaded to the top and more, but a well-secured canvas tarp prevented her from seeing inside. Maybe Dan had brought some of his brother's furniture back with him. Leah almost rubbed her hands together in anticipation. The current furniture was frayed and scratched from years of use and could stand to be replaced. She redecorated the room in her mind. Would he let her repaint it or maybe even apply some wallpaper?

A loud crash sounded from inside the house, followed by a squeal. Leah jumped and her gaze dashed to Dan's. "Sounds like someone left a pig in the house. You didn't bring one back, did you?"

Dan chuckled again. "Not quite."

The front door flew open as they walked up the porch steps. A young boy ran out the door and right into Dan's legs. A dark-haired girl not much older, maybe eight or nine, chased after him.

"I told Ben to stay on the couch, Uncle Dan, but he didn't mind. I'm gonna find a switch and tan his hide." The girl stood with her hand on her hips, looking like a little mother.

Leah's breakfast swirled in her stomach, and she watched in disbelief as two smaller children hurried out onto the porch. The youngest two huddled around their big sister, holding on to her skirt. Leah stepped back down the stairs, not wanting to accept what she was seeing. Her head suddenly started throbbing, and her heart sank into a deep, dark pit. This could not be happening to her. Wasn't Dan's sister supposed to keep the children?

"Where's the baby?" Dan asked.

"I put her down on one of the beds since she was sleepin'," the oldest girl answered.

Five children. Almost half as many as her mother had, and Leah wasn't even married yet. How could Dan do this to her?

"Children, this is Leah. She's the woman I told you about." Dan smiled at her, but then his gaze faltered as he studied her face. "She's. . .uh. . .the woman I'm marrying on Sunday."

Leah gasped for breath. She could not—would not faint. Not in front of these children. It wasn't their fault she didn't want to be their mother—or anyone else's. She took another step back.

Dan's questioning gaze darted between her and the children. He lovingly caressed the oldest girl's head. "This is Caroline, but we all call her Callie. She's eight, and quite the little mother. Ben is next. He's seven and loves horses. Then comes Ruthie, who is five." The little girl leaned her head against her sister and gave Leah a shy wave. Dan picked up the towheaded toddler whose near-black eyes were as dark as his. The child laid his head on his uncle's shoulder. "And this little fellow is Davy."

Leah's heart took another hit. Davy, just like her youngest sibling. Her Davy had barely been crawling when she left home in late spring, but he was probably close to walking by now.

"Maggie is the baby," Callie said. "She'll be one next month. Mama was gonna have a party." The girl stared up at her uncle, her chin quivering. "We can have a party, can't we?"

Dan nodded. "Of course we can, darlin'. I bet Leah would be happy to bake a cake for Maggie, wouldn't you, sweetheart?"

All five of them stared at Leah. She swallowed hard. Dan's gaze begged her to say yes, but nothing could move past the lump in her throat. Tears stung her eyes. She stared at Dan and pleaded him to understand. "I–I'm sorry, but I c–can't."

Dan's shocked gaze turned angry. "Callie, please take the children inside. I'll be there in just a minute. There's some crackers in a jar in the kitchen if you want a snack."

Leah turned and fled back toward the boardinghouse. Thank goodness Martha Phillips had gone inside. Her shame covered her like a cloak, and she was grateful no one was there to see it. Keeping her head down, she walked as quickly as her skirts would allow. Fast footsteps pounded behind her, and Dan grabbed her arm, jerking her to a halt.

"Just hold on. What's gotten into you? How could you be so cruel to those young'uns who just lost their parents?" Dan breathed out his nose, his nostrils flaring like an enraged horse. "It wouldn't hurt you to bake them a cake. You're a great cook."

"You don't understand."

He forked his hand through his hair. "You're darn right, I don't. Care to explain?"

Leah broke from his gaze and stared between two houses at the river in the distance. She should have told him before now. She shook her head and gazed up, begging him with her eyes to understand. "I was the oldest of eleven children, Dan."

"So? Lots of folks have big families." He shoved his hands to his hips.

"I washed more laundry than I've made biscuits, and that's got to be in the hundreds of thousands. I never got to do things with friends because I always had to hurry home after school or church to help Ma. I never had a room or even a bed to myself. I've never had a life of my own. I left home so that I could."

"So? What's that got to do with these kids?"

Leah closed her burning eyes. *Help him to understand, Lord.*

She reached out and caressed his cheek. His eyes closed, and he leaned into her touch. "I love you, Dan, and I desperately want to marry you, but I don't want children."

His mouth dropped open, and he stared with disbelief. He blinked his eyes several times as if trying to grasp what she said. "How can that be? All women want children. It's what God made them for."

"Well, I don't."

"Well, it's too late for regrets. We have five of them."

Leah shook her head. "Not me. *You* have five of them. I'm sorry, Dan. I just can't raise another passel of children. You should have left them with your sister." She turned to walk away, but he grabbed her arm again.

Fire smoldered in his gaze. "I told you that Louise has been sick in bed most of her pregnancy. Friends have been caring for her child. She was in no shape to take the children, and there ain't nobody else."

Leah wrung her hands together, not ready to give up on her dream of marrying him. Her gaze tore up and down the street, and she hoped no one was eavesdropping on their private disagreement. "Surely someone would take them in."

Dan released her and backed up a step. His stunned expression made Leah regret voicing her thoughts.

"If you think that, you ain't the woman I thought you were."

"I want to be a wife, Dan. I'm not ready to be the mother of five children."

"And I'm not ready to be the father of them, either, but I'll not turn my own flesh and blood out on the streets."

Leah pursed her lips. "That's not what I said, and you know it."

Dan leaned in close and glared at her. "It's the same thing. You want me to give them away to strangers who'd most likely mistreat them and use them for child labor."

"I'm sorry. I just can't do this, Dan."

His anger fled, replaced by desperation. "Leah, I need your help. How can I make a living with five young children to watch? The oldest two can go to school, but I can't expect a five-year-old to tend a toddler and a baby—and I can't take them to work. It's too dangerous. I need you now more than ever."

Tears coursed down Leah's face. She wanted to help him, but to do so went against everything she'd dreamed of. How could she give in? How could she face herself in the mirror each morning if she did? How could she stand to lose him?

She shook her head and backed away. "I'm sorry, Dan. I can't do it. I can't marry you now."

She turned and fled up the street.

"Leah, wait. Don't do this!"

Everything had been so perfect. Why did his brother have to die? "Why did You let this happen, Lord?"

Mrs. Foster shook out a blanket and stared at her from the entrance to her tent. Leah turned away, refusing to meet the woman's gaze.

She needed time alone.

She couldn't return to the boardinghouse.

The Sunday house, which sat next to the boardinghouse, was always open, and nobody was currently staying there. Leah dashed into the small house and collapsed on the bed in the far end of the room.

Her sobs filled the air. How could this happen, just when she was ready to get married? Her heart broke as her tears soaked the pillow. She missed Dan already.

She hated disappointing him and leaving him in a lurch.

And she hated herself for doing it.

Chapter 27

Jack walked down Bluebonnet Lane toward home with Tessa Morgan beside her. The girl had worn a blue dress with ruffles on the bodice and hem to school, and her blond hair hung in loose ringlets, not nearly as tight as they'd been this morning. Jack shook her head and stared down at her own serviceable calico. The dark blue pinafore kept her dress cleaner, so her ma said, but it made Jack hot. If her ma had her druthers, she would put her in something as fancy as Tessa's dress, probably a pink one. She shuddered at the thought. Too bad girls couldn't wear overalls to school like some of the boys did.

"I really like Mrs. Fairland. She's real nice." Tessa flounced a ringlet over her shoulder. "But there sure aren't many girls in your school."

"Yeah, they're mostly younger than me. That's why I hang around with Ricky and Jonesy."

Tessa turned up her nose. "I don't understand why you like those boys. They're just a couple of rabble-rousers, and their clothes are all worn out."

Jack shoved Tessa's shoulder, receiving a glare from the girl. "Huh-uh, you take that back."

Tessa hiked her nose in the air. "I can think what I like, and I don't have to like them just because you do."

Jack clenched her fist, ready to smack that smirk off of Tessa's face, but she didn't. She'd get in trouble, and besides, hitting others wasn't a good thing, unless the other person was Butch Laird.

And where had he been, anyway? Had he decided not to attend his last year of schooling? Most of the children in Lookout went to school up to the eighth grade, but sometimes the boys were needed at home for work and didn't attend when they got older.

They moved to the side of the road as a wagon drove down the street. Surely she wasn't missing Butch. He did add some excitement to her mostly boring life. Although Billy Morgan was doing a good job of taking Butch's place. Jack grinned, remembering how Mrs. Fairland had done a jig when she'd opened her desk drawer and found the tarantula Billy had put in it.

Pounding footsteps sounded behind them, and she whirled around. Billy ran toward them. He slid to a stop and grinned, blue eyes twinkling. His blond hair hung over his forehead, much like Ricky's did when it was long. "Wanna do something fun?"

Jack studied the tall boy. She had yet to decide if she liked him or not.

"Mama said to come straight home from school."

"What kind of fun?" Jack couldn't resist asking.

Billy grabbed her arm and pulled her into the alley that ran behind the bank. "Over here."

They stopped beside a big bush that sat behind the mayor's house. "Look on that porch. You see that pie on the table?"

Jack stood on her tiptoes and peered over the bush. Sure enough, there was a pie cooling on the porch table. "So."

"I can't see, Billy," Tessa whined.

"Shut up before someone hears you." Billy glared at his sister.

She crossed her arms and scowled, her lunch bucket swaying at her side.

"You go knock on the front door," Billy said to Jack, "and I'll sneak up there and get the pie."

"That's stealing, Billy, and you know you'll get in trouble." Tessa stomped her foot, covering her new shoe in a cloud of dust.

Billy leaned into his sister's face. "Not if you don't tell, and if you do, I'll find that dumb doll of yours and break her head."

Tessa gasped and turned white. The porcelain doll was her dearest possession. Jack had never played with dolls and couldn't understand Tessa's fascination with it, but she didn't want to see the pretty doll destroyed. "Leave her alone."

Billy shoved his hands on his hips. "If you don't help me get that pie, you don't get to eat none of it."

"I get all the pie I want at home, and besides, my ma's cooking is far better than Mrs. Burkes's. I'm leavin'." Jack knew better than to steal a pie. Stealing was breaking one of the Ten Commandments, and she was already in enough of a stew pot with her lying. She peeked up at the sky, knowing she was lucky God didn't strike her down dead for all the things she'd done. She still wanted to tell Luke that she'd lied about Butch, but she was afraid of what would happen to her. Would he quit loving her if he knew she'd lied and that Butch had spent two days in jail and lost his job working for Mrs. Boyd because of something he didn't do?

She jogged across the street with Tessa on her heels, her mouth watering for the snack her ma always had waiting.

"Wait up. Mama said ladies shouldn't run." Tessa hurried across the street, walking as fast as she could without actually running.

"I ain't no lady."

"Mama says we shouldn't say *ain't*."

Jack halted and stared at the girl. "Well, she ain't my ma, so I don't have ta mind her."

Tessa's mouth worked like a fish, opening and closing. "Don't get all tetchy. I didn't mean nothing by it." She looked over her shoulder where her brother had been and then leaned in close to Jack's ear. "Billy's always doing bad things. Mama says it's because he don't have a pa, but I don't have one, and I don't do the things Billy does. That's one of the reasons Mama wanted to move here. Folks back home are fed up with Billy's shenanigans, and the sheriff was threatening to lock him up."

Jack opened the front door of her home, not the least bit surprised by Tessa's confession. Billy had a cantankerous gleam in his eye that set her on edge. Not even Butch had that look.

Butch mostly got picked on because he was so much bigger than the other kids and he always stunk like pig slop. But she'd finally realized that he had a big heart. She needed to work up her nerve to go see him and apologize. She couldn't forget how he'd said he just wanted to be her friend and how he thought she was different from the other kids. What made him think that?

She set her books on the bench of the hall tree and walked down the hall while Tessa ran up the stairs to her room. The pastor had preached about hell last Sunday and told folks they needed to repent of their sins and make *resti*—what was that big word? Make amends, that's what he said. She didn't want to apologize to Butch, knowing it would taste worse than eating a grub worm, but it was better than burning in the Lake of Fire and not going to heaven when she died. Her first pa was surely in the Lake of Fire, and that alone made her not want to be there.

Ma wasn't in the kitchen, but Max lumbered to his feet and wagged his tail. "Hey, ol' boy. How was your day?"

The dog whined a greeting and followed Jack upstairs to her bedroom, where she shucked off her dress and put on her overalls. She'd spend ten minutes in the garden so her ma wouldn't make her put her dress back on.

She helped herself to one of the three small plates of cookies her mother had set out for her and the Morgan kids, then downed some water and headed outside. Max opted to return to his position near the stove. If her ma was out visiting, she'd be returning soon to start supper, so Jack quickened her pace, wanting her ma to see her hard at work in the garden without even being told to do so. Plopping down next to the bean patch, she started pulling weeds. Thankfully, not too many had grown since she'd last cleared them.

Someone ran toward her, and she peeked through the climbing vines of beans. Billy jogged in her direction, carrying the pie plate. The scent of apples and cinnamon teased her nose as he passed close to her. He looked her way, and she ducked down.

"I see you. Too bad you didn't help with this pie. It's apple. My favorite."

He walked down the dirt row, not even taking care to avoid the plants.

"Hey! Watch out. You're crushing the spinach."

He flopped down right beside her, holding the half-eaten pie on his lap. "So, I don't like that green stuff." He faked a shiver. "But I do like pie."

Jack plucked another weed and tossed it at Billy's shoe. "You'll get sick eating that whole thing."

He shrugged. "Nah, I won't. I've done it before."

Jack's mouth watered at the fragrant scent, but she wouldn't dare ask for a bite. That was stolen food, and he'd be lucky if it didn't give him the hives.

Two hours later, Jack sat at the supper table, watching Billy shovel in his chicken and dumplings like he was starving. How could he eat so much and not get sick?

Luke finished his meal and pushed his plate back as he glanced around the table. Jack could tell he had something on his mind. The table was nearly filled with her family, the Morgans, that Miss Smith, and the two boardinghouse brides. Shannon looked fairly well for the first time in weeks, but Leah's eyes were red, as if she'd been crying. What had happened to her?

Luke cleared his throat. "The mayor's wife came to my office today and told me somebody stole a pie from her back porch. You kids know anything about that?"

Jack glanced at Billy and then Tessa. She'd gone white, but Billy kept forking food in his mouth.

"Mrs. Burke said she thought she saw a boy running away." Luke tapped the table with the end of his fork.

Billy took a drink. "I bet it was that Laird kid. I've heard he causes lots of trouble in this town."

Jack blinked and stared at the boy. How could he lie through his teeth like that and still look so innocent? She almost wanted to learn to do it herself, but lying put a bad taste in her mouth. She'd done it to protect her friends, but no more. She didn't like how she felt afterward.

"Hmm..." Luke stared at Billy, who suddenly smiled.

"That schoolteacher sure is pretty," the boy said.

Luke finally cracked a smile and nodded. "She is at that."

Jack stared at her plate. She ought to tell Luke that Billy was lying about Butch, but then she'd have to admit to being in the alley with him. Maybe that wasn't so bad. She'd had a chance to do something wrong and had walked away from it. Wouldn't Luke be proud that she'd done that?

On second thought, she oughta just keep quiet. What would Billy do to her if he knew she'd tattled on him?

She took a bite of buttery biscuit. Maybe Butch would be at school tomorrow. If so, she'd find a way to talk to him and tell him she was sorry.

Luke pushed away from the table. "I reckon I oughta go talk to that Laird boy. Somehow I've got to make him see that he can't steal from decent folk. I thought I'd gotten through to him last time I talked to him, but I guess I was wrong."

Her ma stood and hugged him. "Be careful, sugar. I just got me a new husband, and I aim to keep him a while."

Luke stared into her ma's eyes, and Jack knew if they'd been alone, he would have kissed her. Yuck! Why did grownups do that so often? Seemed a good way to get sick, if you asked her.

Maybe when she talked to Butch, she'd warn him about Billy. It hadn't taken the Morgan boy long to figure out exactly whom to pin blame on for his own misdeeds. As much as it surprised her, she actually felt sorry for Butch.

Shannon stared at the ledger book, but the numbers all blurred together. The Corbetts had left three days ago and were due back tomorrow. She'd seen Mark just before they left, and the longing gaze he'd given her had made her toes tingle. But she couldn't dwell on that.

She finished recording the last of the orders and blew the ink dry. She left the ledger open while she filed away the order forms. There wasn't much left to do here, so she might as well go back to the boardinghouse—or maybe she'd go check on Dan and see how he and the children were doing.

She stared out the window at the livery. How in the world was he managing to run a business and tend to five children? How could Leah just up and leave him like she had?

The bell jingled over the door, and Rand walked in, looking tall and a bit apprehensive.

"Good afternoon." Shannon smiled. "What brings you to town midweek?"

He tipped his hat and then removed it, twisting the brim with his big hands. "I met a man here who wanted to buy a couple of horses. He lives on the other side of town, so Lookout was about halfway for both of us."

She nodded. "That makes good sense." She forced herself to stand still and not fidget. Rand was a kind man, but she couldn't help wondering what he wanted.

"You're working late."

"I had some orders I wanted to get recorded before the Corbett brothers return tomorrow."

He glanced out the front window and then back at her. "I was. . .uh. . .wondering if you would. . .uh. . .have supper with me."

"Today?" As soon as she'd spoken, she realized what a dumb question it was. Of course, he meant today.

He nodded, his ears turning red. "Yep, I thought we'd eat at Polly's."

Excitement battled with hesitation. Would she be leading him on by dining with him? But then again, she'd decided to marry the next man who asked her, and she couldn't do much better than Rand. He was well respected in the town and known for his ethical dealings as a businessman. Besides, if she were to marry him, she'd live on his ranch and only get to town a few times a month, if that much. Mark Corbett would be out of sight, and hopefully out of mind. She nodded.

Rand grinned and blew out a breath. "You took so long to answer I was certain you'd say no."

"Well, I've nearly finished all the work there is to do here, but I should let Mrs. Davis know I won't be taking supper with her."

"If you need to finish up here, I can run over and tell her." His blue-gray eyes looked eager to please.

Shannon nodded and closed the ledger.

"Be right back." Rand scurried out the door and down the boardwalk.

She tried to imagine life with him, but Mark's smiling blue eyes intruded into her mind. She grabbed the broom from the corner and swept the dust from the floor as she brushed Mark from her mind.

Rand soon returned and escorted her to Polly's Café, where they took a seat and ordered the house special, pot roast. He spun tales of his ranch that made her long to see it. "Rolling hills as far as the eyes can see, and when we get a good rain, the grass greens up and wildflowers pop up all over the place. My ma loved all those flowers and used to put vases of them around the house. I never did figure out how she had time to gather them when she had so much other work to do."

"What type of work?" Shannon ventured to ask.

"Well, she cooked for all the workers, maintained our home, and sewed many of our clothes. There was even a time when we first came here that she would make her own fabric, but once the ranch started turning a profit, Pa insisted she work less and buy her fabric in town."

Shannon toyed with the edge of her napkin. She could never cook for a crew of hungry cowboys. She barely knew how to cook at all. Maybe this wasn't such a grand idea.

"Of course, now we have a cook who fixes meals for our workers. I generally eat down there now that my folks are gone."

She wondered if he was lonely in his big house all alone. But then he saw his workers every day and probably was glad to get away from them for a time.

"I heard that Dan Howard came back from Dallas with a whole wagon filled with kids. That right?"

Shannon nodded. "Aye, five of them."

"Whew! That's quite a lot when you're not used to any of them. I bet he's sure glad he's getting married soon."

Shannon pressed her lips together. Evidently Rand had only heard part of the town's gossip, but she wasn't about to mention Leah's decision to call off the wedding. She still didn't understand how her friend could leave the man she loved in such a lurch. Leah had hardly left her room, and when she did, it was obvious she'd been crying.

They talked about menial things as they ate their food, and then Rand escorted Shannon back to the boardinghouse. "Do you like working at the freight office?"

She bristled. He had no idea what a loaded question that was.

"I mean, I just wondered. I know some women enjoy working a job, but most I know prefer tending their home."

"I work because I must support myself." Working for the Corbetts was no longer her ideal job, but it paid her room and board and gave her a wee bit extra. "I like doing the book work. I find it quite rewarding."

Rand nodded. "My ma used to help my pa with our book-keeping. She always said she was better at calculating than he." A soft smile tugged at his lips, and he seemed lost in his memories.

Someone was playing the piano in the boardinghouse parlor, and the lively jig switched to a slow tune. The soft music set Shannon in a mood for romance. Her thoughts shifted to Mark, but just as fast, she tugged them back to the man beside her. She could make a life with Rand; she felt sure of it. He was kind, thoughtful, and, she suspected, a good provider. His clothing was always nice, albeit a bit dust-coated, and his boots looked well worn but cared for. If he treated his wife as well, she could live a decent life. She sighed. Maybe not the one she'd dreamed of, but she'd finally have a home. If he asked her to marry him, she would say yes.

"You mind watching the sunset with me?"

Shannon swallowed hard and shook her head. Rand turned left on Bluebonnet Lane, and they walked to the edge of town and stood, watching the sunset. Pink and orange hues turned deep purple as the light left the sky. A near-full moon took up where the sun left off. Crickets sang in the tall grass along the side of the road, and in the distance, a coyote howled.

"I reckon we oughta get back. Thank you for walking with me, Shannon."

"My pleasure." She smiled, captured by the intensity of Rand's expression. Her heart thumped.

He looked as if he was trying to say something but couldn't quite figure out how to do it. Suddenly, he yanked off his hat and held it in front of him, as if guarding his heart. "I know we haven't known each other long, but I wondered if you would consent to marry me. I've got a nice ranch house, and you'd be comfortable there. We're close enough that you could come to town once in a while to visit with your friends, and there's all the beef you could ever want to eat."

Shannon's stomach clenched, and her heart nearly leapt from her chest. A rather unconventional marriage proposal, but 'twas what she wanted, was it not?

She had to be practical. Rand wasn't the man she loved, but she needed a home, and his was as good as any. Her head nodded, but her heart still argued. Was she making the biggest mistake of her life?

Chapter 28

You kids had better hurry, or you'll be late for school." Luke eyed Jack, even though she knew he was talking to the Morgans, too.

She swigged down the last of her milk and stood. "All right. I'm goin'."

Billy and Tessa followed her into the kitchen, where they all retrieved their lunch pails. They clomped down the hall toward the front door. Jack hated this part of the day, with a full morning of lessons ahead. She longed to run over to the newspaper office and see if Jenny Evans had any work she could do. Ever since Jack had helped the newspaper lady at the bride contest, Jenny occasionally let her assist her or sell papers.

"Jack, hold up a minute."

She turned to see her papa had followed them to the door.

"You kids go on; I want to talk to my daughter a moment."

Billy eyed them with curiosity but shrugged his shoulders and walked outside with his sister.

"I wanted you to know that I was finally able to get over to see that Laird boy yesterday evening. He claims he didn't steal that pie—that he wasn't even in town."

Jack's mouth went dry. Should she tell him it was Billy? What would he do to her if he found out she'd told? She had a feeling he wasn't the kind of person to go easy on someone who'd gotten him in trouble.

Luke shook his head. "I don't know as I believe Butch, but he did look sincere. If he was lying, he sure fooled me. Well, anyhow, I wanted you to know I talked with him. Don't think he'll be causing any more trouble, since they're leaving town."

"What do you mean?"

"Mr. Laird sold all his hog stock, and he and his boy were packing a wagon. Guess they figured the boy had caused enough trouble in town that they'd best move on. Wise decision, if you ask me."

Butch was leaving? The thought partly made her want to cheer, but it also made her feel bad, for some odd reason. Was it her fault they were leaving their home? How could she ever apologize to Butch if he was gone? She'd have to find a way to go over and see him before he left. If she didn't repent of her sins and apologize to him, would she go to hell when she died? She swallowed hard, her breakfast churning in her belly.

"You all right, half bit? I thought you'd be thrilled at the news."

She forced a smile. "Oh, I am. But I need to get to school. Wouldn't want to be late, would I?"

Luke eyed her as if he didn't quite believe her, and at times like this, she so wished her new papa wasn't a lawman. He was too perceptive. She scurried out the door and shut it behind her. How was she going to talk to Butch?

"Wait till you see this, *Jacqueline*."

She hated the snide way Billy said her name, but curiosity pushed her feet in his direction. He pointed to the bank wall, and what she saw on the side of it froze her to the road. Her heart pounded like the hooves of a runaway horse.

Billy hee-hawed. "Ain't that a hoot?"

"I don't think that's very nice thing to do," Tessa said.

Jack wanted to close her eyes, but the giant, barn red letters stared back at her: JACK IS A LIAR.

Tessa gasped and pointed across the street. "Look, it's not just on the bank. It's also on our new store. Mama isn't gonna like that."

Dread gripped Jack as she turned and saw the big letters painted on the fresh, raw wood of the store's walls. JACK IS A LIAR.

She should have repented sooner. Should have told her papa what she'd done. Now the whole town would know. Nobody would believe a word she said. Ever.

Billy's laughter echoed behind her. She wanted to punch him quiet, but she'd done enough already. With dread in her heart, she stared down Main Street. Almost every other building had the hated words painted on them.

JACK IS A LIAR.

JACK IS A LIAR.

The words bounced around in her mind until she thought her head would explode. Jenny was out front of her office, already scrubbing the letters. She saw Jack, dropped her rag in a bucket, and walked toward her. Jack wanted to run. To hide. But she couldn't move.

"Jack, do you have any idea who did this?"

"I don't know." She shook her head. But she did know, and now she was telling another lie. "I might."

A sudden thought raced across her mind. She felt her eyes widen. "You're not going to print anything in the paper about this, are you?"

Jenny's eyes turned compassionate. "I'm sorry, honey, but this is news, and I'm in the news business. Who would be angry enough to do such a thing? Did you upset one of your friends?"

Jack closed her eyes. Everyone in the county would soon know that she was a liar. How could she face anybody again?

"Jacqueline, I need to see the marshal, right away." Dolly Dykstra waddled down the dirt road, her rose-colored skirts swaying from side to side. The near gray-headed woman had to be almost as wide as she was tall. "Do you know who defaced my building? Do you know how difficult it is to find paint the color of a thistle?"

Why was the lady angry at her? She was innocent, and it was her reputation that had been ruined.

Just like she'd help ruin Butch's.

"Do you know where the marshal is or not?" Miss Dykstra crossed her arms over her big bosom and tapped one finger against her shoulder.

Her papa was the last person she wanted to see right now. She had to get away. Billy's laughter rang through her mind. How many other schoolchildren had seen the paint on their way to school? It hardly mattered that many of them were too young to figure out the words, because the older kids would gladly tell them what they said.

A sob escaped, and she tore down the street, tears streaming from her eyes and making it hard to see. She had to get away from town. Away from those awful words.

She had to find Butch and beat him to a pulp.

She'd never apologize to him.

How had she even considered it?

As long as she lived, she'd hate Butch Laird.

Leah sat at the table even though everyone else had gone. Shannon had hurried to her room to work on some project she'd started the day before. Dishes clinked in the kitchen where Rachel was cleaning up, and the low hum of voices from her and the marshal drifted Leah's way.

Her heart felt battered, as if a herd of cattle had stampeded it into the ground. She rested her cheek on her hand, unable to find the energy to move. What was she going to do now that she couldn't marry Dan? How was he managing with all those little children?

In spite of everything, she longed to see him. To be held safely within the confines of his strong arms. To kiss his warm, eager lips. But she never would again. Tears blurred her eyes, and someone pounded on the door. Luke hurried down the hall to answer it. Leah heard raised voices, and the door shut. Some emergency must have pulled the marshal away from home again.

Maybe it was time for her to return home. Would her parents accept her back? She was pretty certain her ma willingly would, but her father was another issue. She'd wounded his pride and made him look bad in Mr. Abernathy's eyes. It didn't matter that the old man wanted to buy her. No, her pa would only see that she'd made him a laughingstock by running off. The only thing that had surprised her was that he hadn't come and found her and hauled her back. Just the thought sent a shiver down her spine.

Rachel entered the dining room, holding a cup of steaming coffee in her hand. She set it on the table and sat in the chair next to Leah. "It might help to talk about things. You've been moping around ever since Dan returned with the children. I haven't even seen you working on your wedding dress."

Leah's chin wobbled. "I'm not working on it anymore."

Rachel blinked, looking confused. "Why ever not? The wedding is the day after tomorrow. We need to plan the menu for your wedding dinner."

Leah stared at the tablecloth and flicked her finger at a crumb. "There isn't going to be a wedding."

"What?"

Leah shook her head and pursed her lips, trying to keep additional tears at bay. "I called it off."

Shock engulfed Rachel's face, and her pale blue eyes opened wide. "Why? I know you two love each other. It's evident to all who see you together."

Leah shrugged one shoulder, ashamed to confess why she canceled the wedding. It sounded cruel and petty to say she didn't want to mother those poor orphans. Her heart ached for them, but she couldn't be their new ma.

"Is it the children?" Rachel patted Leah's arm. "I know that was quite a surprise. Dan should have telegraphed you and told you about them before he brought them back, so you'd have time to get used to the idea."

She shook her head. "I doubt that would have helped. After practically raising my siblings, I've decided I don't want any children, much less five that aren't even my own."

Rachel looked taken aback, but she continued on. "I realize that it's not an ideal situation, but those poor children are orphans. They need two loving adults to raise them now that their parents are gone. It's a noble thing Dan is doing, and it's that big heart of his that you fell in love with."

"I know, and I feel awful. I've hurt him something horrible, but I don't know what else to do. I can't go against what I believe.

I'd just make everybody miserable."

Rachel stared at the window and tapped her index finger on the table. "Hmm. . . have you prayed about this? Asked God what He wants you to do?"

Guilt washed over Leah as if someone had dumped a bucket of cold water on her. She'd been so upset that she hadn't prayed. What kind of a Christian was she?

"In Psalm 127, the Bible tells us that 'children are an heritage of the LORD.' It also says, 'As arrows are in the hand of a mighty man, so are the children of the youth. Happy is the man that hath his quiver full of them.'"

Yeah, happy is the man, but what about the woman? Leah shifted in her seat. Was her thought blasphemous to the scriptures?

"If you don't mind," Rachel said, "I'd like to pray now. It's never too late to seek God's guidance. He's in the business of changing hearts. Just look at me and Luke. When Luke first returned to Lookout, he wanted nothing to do with me, but God changed his heart and made me a very happy woman. He can change your heart, too, Leah, if you let Him."

Well, therein lay the problem. She didn't want to change. She wanted Dan but not a houseful of children. Still, praying couldn't hurt, so she bowed her head.

Rachel grasped Leah's hand. "Heavenly Father, I know Leah didn't count on being a mother right from the start of her wedding day, but You know all things. You knew these children were going to lose their parents, sad as that is, and that they'd need new ones. Open Leah's heart. She is a kind woman with lots of love to give. Let her see that children are a blessing sent from You, and You will not give her more than she can bear."

Rachel sat silent for a few moments, then raised her head. "I know life wasn't easy for you, helping your mother with all your siblings, but things are much different when you're the mother. God puts so much love in your heart for each child, and like I prayed, He'll never send more your way than you're able to handle."

Leah considered her friend's words. She'd been so upset the past few days that she hadn't prayed. Hadn't wanted to talk to God. Couldn't He have prevented Dan's brother and wife from dying or his other sister from being pregnant just at the time the children would need her?

She winced, realizing again how selfish her thoughts were. But Rachel didn't understand. She only had one child.

"What's going through that head of yours?" Rachel smiled. "I can see the wheels turning."

"I just don't think I can do it."

"What? Marry Dan? Raise his nieces and nephews?"

"Yes, I mean, I still want to marry Dan, with all of my heart, but I don't want to be a mother, especially not so soon." She wrung the edge of the tablecloth in her hands. Would Rachel be disgusted for her lack of compassion?

"It's a big shock, I know. But we do what we must. I think if you will spend some time in prayer that God will speak to you."

Leah nodded. She believed in her heavenly Father, and He seemed more approachable here than back in Missouri. Perhaps His help was needed more here in Texas with the harsher living conditions and the dangers surrounding them. Part of her longed to cry out to God, but the other part was afraid. What if it was God's will for her to marry Dan and mother the children? How could she bear it?

Footsteps sounded on the porch, and the door burst open. "Rachel!"

The boardinghouse owner bolted to her feet at her husband's frantic voice. "In here, Luke."

He hurried through the doorway and grabbed her hand. "C'mon. Something's happened."

Leah jumped up and followed them, curious as to what had gotten the mild-mannered marshal so agitated. Rachel stopped as she walked down the porch steps, and her hand covered her mouth as she stared across the street. "Who would do such an awful thing?"

"I have my suspicions," Luke said. "But the important thing is that Jack saw it and got upset and ran off somewhere. We've got to find her."

Leah glanced across the street and saw the harsh red letters: JACK IS A LIAR.

Jack was an ornery child and definitely a tomboy, but she wasn't mean and didn't deserve this shame heaped on her. Leah's heart ached for the girl. "I can help search."

Jack ran all the way to Butch's land. Her lungs screamed for her to stop, and a pain grabbed her side. Finally, she smelled the hog pens, and she slowed her steps. Gasping for breath, she pressed her hand to her aching side and studied the old place. The house was set at an odd angle and looked smaller than the parlor in her own home.

She lifted her hand to her nose. Where were all the hogs? They might be gone, but the stench sure wasn't. The only sounds she heard were the thudding of her heartbeat, her ragged breathing, and birds chirping in a nearby tree.

The place was empty. Butch was gone, and she was too late. Too late to apologize for lying. Too late to knock Butch to the ground for doing such an awful thing to her.

Slowly, she walked toward the house. What would it have been like to live in such a dirty place and to smell the stomach-churning odor every day? To get up first thing in the morning and face the reeking stench?

Dropping onto the chopping block, she hung her head in her hands and stared at a beetle crawling on a stem of grass. Butch was gone, and that was that.

But how could she face the people in town? They'd all wonder what she'd lied about and if she was lying whenever she talked to them. Nobody would trust her, ever again.

She picked up a rock and flung it at the house.

Butch had ruined her life.

And she hated him for it.

Maybe the best thing for her to do was leave town, too. Just run away. But she'd miss her ma—and her new papa. The worst thing of all would be staying and seeing the disappointment in their eyes.

Her vision blurred as tears formed.

"What do I do now?"

Quick hoofbeats approached, and the horse slid to a halt.

Someone dismounted and walked toward her, but she was too embarrassed to lift her head.

Luke.

She recognized his boots.

Would he hate her now?

"Half bit, what are you doing here?"

She shrugged. How could she explain her reason for coming here when she didn't understand it herself?

Luke squatted on his boot heels in front of her. "I'm sorry about those words in town. I'll make sure they're all gone today."

Love for him flooded her. She sucked in a loud sob and leaped into his arms. He grabbed her with one arm and struggled not to fall backward. Then he stood, taking her with him. She cried on his strong shoulders, and he just held her, patting her back. "Shh. . .everything will be all right. You'll see."

She shoved back and wiggled her legs, so he let her down. "It won't never be right again."

He reached out and ran his hand down the side of her head. "It seems that way now, but you'll see."

She crossed her arms and paced toward the hog pen, then reconsidered and walked over to Luke's horse and patted his neck. "Everybody will think I'm a liar."

"Once those letters are painted over, folks will quickly forget about them."

She shook her head. "No, they won't. Jenny's gonna print them in her newspaper, and the whole world will know."

"I'll talk to Jenny and see if she'll mention what happened but keep you out of her article as much as possible. Most folks won't even know which 'Jack' the words are referring to, and besides, what happened isn't your fault."

Luke strode over and stood behind her, his hands resting on her shoulders. "Don't make too much of this, half bit. Butch was just lashing out, trying to hurt you. He wasn't even man enough to stay and face the consequences of his behavior."

Jack's insides swirled, and she knew she had to come clean or forever be in misery. "What he said was. . .true."

Luke gently turned her to face him. "What do you mean?"

She couldn't stand seeing disgust in Luke's eyes when she finally confessed the truth, so she stared at his boots. "I lied about Butch. Several times."

Luke lifted her chin with his forefinger. A muscle in his jaw flexed. "About what?"

She pulled away and stalked down the road several feet. "About when he pushed me down at the river. And I didn't correct you when you thought he'd stolen that pie from Mrs. Burke, even though I knew Billy had done it."

Luke uttered a heavy sigh, but he didn't say anything for a while. Finally, she couldn't stand waiting for his wrath and turned around. He stood with his head hanging, hands on his hips. "I'm disappointed, half bit."

Her lips wobbled and tears filled her eyes. Would he not want to be her papa now?

"When you lied and I believed you, I had a talk with Butch. I accused him of things he didn't do, and that made me look bad and made him angry and not trust me. Do you understand?"

She hadn't thought about how her lying would affect Luke. She'd made things difficult for him. He always believed her and acted accordingly. She was pond scum.

"It's important for people to trust me as marshal. I wrongly accused that boy and even made him stay in jail for several days. Maybe there was more to him than I gave him credit for."

"I'm sorry, Luke."

"Me, too." He looped Alamo's reins over his head. "C'mon, your ma is worried. I need to get you back to town."

He climbed on, then held his hand out to her. She looked up, despising the sad look she'd put on his face. "Do you hate me?"

His expression immediately changed. He pulled her up behind him. "Of course not. I'll always love you, no matter what. But I am disappointed you didn't trust me enough to tell me the truth."

She wrapped her arms around his waist and leaned against his back as he guided his horse back to town. "I didn't know you so well back then."

Luke patted her hands. "I guess that's true, but you know me now and didn't tell me the truth about the pie."

She winced. "I was afraid Billy would do something mean if I snitched on him."

"I see. When we return home, we'll have a talk with your mother, and if she agrees, I'll expect you to help me repaint the buildings that were defaced."

She nodded against his back. If she helped him, the dreaded words would be gone all the sooner—and she'd miss a day of school.

At least she knew Luke still loved her. And she wouldn't lie anymore. It hurt too many people.

But she still hated Butch for painting those words.

Chapter 29

Mark tossed the ropes into the back of the empty wagon. He walked around, checking the horses' harnesses, even though he knew Garrett had already done that. He glanced over at the new store. It looked fresh and bright with its new coat of paint. It would soon open. That would enable him to be in town more since they wouldn't be going to Dallas so often for supplies. Then maybe he could get back to reading his law books.

The door to the boardinghouse opened, and Shannon walked out and closed it behind her. She glanced down the street, then strode toward him with purpose evident in her steps. He longed to pull her into his arms and show her the depths of his heart, but she deserved so much better than him. If only he'd never gone to Abilene.

But he couldn't change what had happened there, and he'd never ask Shannon to marry a murderer.

Yeah, it was a fair fight. The other man drew first—even fired first, but he'd missed. Mark had pulled his gun in self-defense, fearing for his and Annabelle's lives, and he'd accidentally killed that man. It didn't matter that the marshal had said it wasn't a crime. He'd taken a life. Shame twisted his insides and made him refuse to grasp hold of what he wanted most in life—to marry Shannon.

She glanced at the office, then back at him, and stopped near the door. He walked up the boardwalk steps and stared at her. Did she still have affections for him?

He thought so by the look in her eyes. Her lips pursed, and she looked away.

"Is Garrett here?"

Mark winced. What did she want with his brother that she couldn't tell him? "He's over at Polly's, gettin' a lunch packed for us. We're heading out to Dallas as soon as he returns."

Shannon nodded but nibbled on her lower lip. "I suppose I can tell you. Could we go inside?"

He opened the door and held it as she glided inside, her skirts touching his pants and her flowery scent wrapping around him. He missed her. Missed working with her. Missed staring across the room at her while she was putting numbers into the ledger. He sighed hard. "What do you need? I left all the new orders on the desk under the paperweight. I imagine this will be the last big pile you'll have to work through since the store is reopening soon and our workload is likely to go down."

She nodded and paced the room, looking everywhere but at him. She glanced over her shoulder but kept her back to him. " 'Tis a good thing, then."

"What is?"

"That the workload is lessening."

"And why is that? It's been great business for us."

"Because I need to inform you that next week will be my last one."

His heart took another stab. Shannon was quitting? He'd never see her if that happened. "But why? I thought you liked working here."

"I do, but my circumstances are changing."

Had she decided to leave town? Found another job? "Changing? How?"

She was quiet so long that he thought she hadn't heard him—or maybe she wasn't going to answer. "I'm getting married a week from Sunday."

Mark grasped Garrett's desk to keep from falling to his knees at her declaration. How? Who? "You can't be getting married."

She whirled around, her eyes no longer compassionate but filled with fire. "Who are you to tell me I can't marry?"

"I. . .but. . ." She was right. He had no claim on her even though his heart belonged only to her. *Why, God? Why couldn't I have stayed in Lookout and kept myself pure for this woman? Why did You place her in this town when You knew I couldn't have her?*

His chest hurt so bad he wondered if he was having heart failure. She stepped forward, a concerned look replacing the anger. "Are you all right?"

He straightened and forced a smile. "Of course. I just can't believe you found someone to marry so fast."

Her nostrils flared and eyes sparked. "Just because you find me lacking doesn't mean other men do." She yanked open the desk drawer and pulled out a sheet of paper. It was the one with tic marks on it. He'd wondered what it meant. She marched over, holding the paper in front of his face. "You see this? Each mark represents a marriage proposal—ones I got in this office, no less. There are plenty of men who want to marry me, even though you don't."

"I never said I didn't want to marry you." The words fled his mouth before he could yank them back.

"What?" She blinked and stared at him, the paper zigzagging as it floated to the floor.

It was his turn to break from her gaze. He hadn't wanted her to know the depth of his feelings. It wasn't fair to her. "Nothing. That was a slip of the tongue."

"I see. Well, you now know that I'll be quitting. It's possible that Leah may want this job, though I've not talked to her about it."

Mark frowned. Hiring Leah Bennett was the last thing he wanted to do after the way she'd dumped his good friend. "We'll manage. The doc says he'll take my cast off on Tuesday, so I can do the bookwork from now on." He rubbed the back of his neck. "Just who are you marrying, if I may ask?"

Her mouth worked, pulling his gaze to her beautiful lips. She did the most intriguing things with them. She frowned as if she didn't want to tell him. He swiped his hand through the air. "Fine. Don't tell me, but word will be around town soon enough. I'm just surprised I hadn't heard about it already."

"I haven't told anyone yet. A marriage is a private affair between a man and a woman."

Mark snorted a laugh. "Maybe in Ireland, but not in America. Here, a wedding is generally a celebration of family and friends. I just don't see how you found someone so fast to marry. Are you sure you're not jumping into this too quickly? Maybe you shouldn't be in such a hurry."

Shannon gasped. "Ach, who are you to be tellin' me what to do? Do you or do you not wish to be a lawyer?"

Mark shifted his feet and crossed his arms. "What's that got to do with anything?"

"You stand there judging me. You, who didn't want me, now thinks you can give me advice on when to marry? You don't even have the nerve to face your own brother. To tell him that you want to be a lawyer and not in this business with him. I have changed my mind. I quit as of this moment."

Her quick steps clicked on the floor as she made a beeline for the door. She was right, of course. "Wait! Please."

She paused with her hand on the door. "What is it?"

He ran his hand through his hair, but what he needed to say couldn't be said to her back. "Shannon, would you look at me? Please?"

She sighed and turned, arms crossed over her chest.

"I. . .did something. Several years ago. I'd give anything to undo it, but I can't."

"What sort of thing?"

He shook his head. "I can't tell you. I've never told a soul, not even Garrett, but suffice it to say, that's what's standing in the way of our relationship. If I could marry you, I'd do it in a heartbeat."

Surprise engulfed her face, but her expression quickly changed. "How could you say such a thing to a woman you know is getting married? You had your chance at winning my heart, but I remember clearly you saying you'd never marry. And now because I am, you think you can waltz in and say you would marry me if you could? I don't see a thing to stop you."

"You don't understand."

"You're right. I don't. I'm sorry, Mark. I think we could have had a wonderful life together if you would quit living in the past. God forgives us for our wrongdoings. Maybe we can never marry, but you need to find His forgiveness for whatever happened in the past and move on. Don't let it keep you from living a happy life and becoming a lawyer. You'd make a fine one, you would."

She yanked the door open, strode out, and slammed it shut. He sat there numb—even more so than that night in Denison. He felt gutted. Empty. The only woman he'd ever truly loved was marrying someone else. She would, in fact, be married before he returned to Lookout. How could he ever be whole without her in his life?

"Well, well, well. She sure gave you a piece of her mind, didn't she?"

Mark jumped and turned to find Annabelle standing in the back room. "What are you doing here? And just how much did you hear?"

"All of it." She grinned. "I looked for you out back, and when I didn't find you, I came in the rear door and was going to walk through the office, but then I heard you two come in and hid."

"A decent woman would have left out the back door or else let us know you were present."

A saucy smile pulled at her lips. "And just what do you think dear, sweet Shannon would have said if she found me in here?"

Mark swatted the air. "Does it really matter? She's getting married."

"I know. I heard." She sashayed toward him. Her clothes might be different, but they didn't disguise her flirtatious, saloon-girl ways. "You actually love her, don't you?"

He shrugged. "So what if I do? She's marrying some other yahoo. She must not have cared for me much if she could agree to marry someone else so soon."

Annabelle shook her head and leaned back against his desk. "You men can be awfully dense at times."

"What does that mean?"

"Just what do you expect Shannon to do? Do you have any idea how hard it must be for her to come here several days a week and work for you when she's in love with you, but you've all but told her you don't want her?"

"That's not what I said."

"But it's what she heard. She's all alone in this world, from what I understand. You can't expect her to keep working here with things as they are. And where does that leave her? With no job, she has no other alternative except to marry—or work in a saloon." Her teasing smile turned his stomach.

Mark strode across the room and leaned into Annabelle's face. "Don't you talk about her in such a manner. Shannon would starve to death before working in a saloon."

"Ah, so you do love her." She sighed heavily. "Guess that leaves me out on the streets again."

"What do you mean?"

"Why do you think I came here, Mark? I was hoping we could pick up where we were before you shot that cowboy."

Mark's stomach turned at the verbal mention of his misdeed. Had she told anyone about that? If so, he'd probably want to run away like Jack had after that bully painted those words on half the buildings in town. What if Annabelle had done that?

Mark is a killer.

He shuddered at the thought.

"Are you just going to let her marry Rand Kessler?"

"Kessler?" The fact that Shannon was marrying an honorable, well-to-do rancher didn't soothe him at all.

She smirked. "Shannon didn't tell you? I hear he's a fine catch."

"I thought you heard everything she said."

She shrugged. "I might have missed a few words."

"What is it you want, Annabelle? I need to get on the road."

"I came here to woo you myself, but I can see that your heart belongs to another. So, you gonna let her get away, or are you gonna be the man I know you are, put your past behind you, once and for all, and marry the gal you love?"

"You make it sound so simple."

"It is." She laid her hand on his arm. "What you did back in Abilene was an honorable thing."

Mark harrumphed. "Since when is killing a man honorable?"

"You were protecting me from being mauled by that cowboy. All you did was tell him to stop. He's the one who got mad and pulled the gun. You were just defending me and yourself. Why is that so hard to understand?"

"When you've been raised in church, you're taught that killing someone is a sin."

"So, isn't your God supposed to be the forgiving type?"

Mark nodded. How odd to have an ex-saloon girl preaching to him.

"Well, if He forgives you, then it's time you forgave yourself."

He pondered her words for a while, and then suddenly, Annabelle stood up and shook her skirts.

"Well, I suppose I should get back to the boardinghouse and pack."

"Pack?" Mark pulled himself from his stupor. "You're going somewhere?"

"This town's way too small for me. I think I'll head up to Dallas."

He could see past her fake bravado. She'd hoped he'd fall for her and marry her. Make a decent woman out of her. "It was good seeing you again."

She narrowed her gaze. "You mean that?"

He nodded his head. "I hope you can find a job—not in a saloon—and do something good with your life."

She laid her hand against his cheek. "You, too, Mark Corbett. Don't you think it's high time you started your lawyering business?"

Mark barked a laugh. "You're the second person today to say that." He reached into his pocket and handed her a wad of dollars.

"Don't." She pushed his hand away. "I have enough money to start over, courtesy of Everett." Her eyes twinkled with mischievousness. "Have a good life, and if you ever happen to think of me, say a prayer to that God of yours."

"He's your God, too."

"What would He want with the likes of me?"

"You'd be surprised. Promise me that you'll attend church wherever you settle and give God a chance."

"We'll see." She flashed him another saucy smile. "Farewell."

The bell on the door jingled, and just that fast, a second woman walked out of his life.

Leah wrapped the last loaf of bread in a clean towel that Rachel had loaned her and put it into the basket, also borrowed.

"This is a kind thing you're doing." Rachel smiled at her from the other side of the worktable.

"I feel like I ought to be doing more, but I don't want to give Dan false hopes. I've spent a lot of time in prayer the past few days and feel that God wants me to help them by providing bread and some cookies or maybe a pie, now and then."

"I'd be happy to send some things along from time to time. I can't imagine how Dan is cooking for five small children."

Leah winced again at being reminded of Dan's hardship, but she was doing as much as she could. "I'll just run these over, and then I want to get back and help Shannon finish up her dress."

Rachel leaned against the door frame. "I still can't believe she's getting married to Rand. I thought for sure that she was in love with Mark."

"I think she is, but since he made it clear he doesn't want her, she's moved on. I think she's doing the wise thing. I can't imagine her married to a Corbett."

Rachel pressed her lips together. "They aren't as bad as they may seem. They may be teasers, but both are actually honorable men."

Leah snorted a laugh. "Tell that to someone who didn't have her whole life changed by them."

"It hasn't all been bad, has it?"

She stared up at the decorative ceiling and realized Rachel spoke the truth. "No, it hasn't. I've made a number of friends here and fallen in love with a wonderful man."

Rachel pushed away from the door and crossed the room. "Won't you reconsider? Dan needs you now more than ever before. I truly believe you'd be happy with him and the children."

Shaking her head, Leah grabbed the basket off the table and placed the handle on her arm. "I can't. I promised myself I'd never get in that situation again."

"Well, you'll bless them with your kindness and this food. I'll see you later."

Leah nodded and hurried down the hall before Rachel decided to give her another talk about marrying Dan. If only she could do that. Her heart ached. She missed him dearly. Maybe she'd catch a glimpse of him working at the livery when she delivered the food.

Her feet quickly ate up the short distance to Dan's home, and she noticed the differences immediately. Clothing of all sizes was laid out on the porch railings to dry in the September sun. A wagon, ball, and discarded doll littered the yard. She almost dreaded seeing the inside, but she climbed the steps and knocked on the door.

The middle girl—Ruthie, wasn't it?—opened the door. She stared up at Leah with big brown eyes. "I know you."

Leah smiled. "I met you the day you arrived. I'm Leah, and I've brought you some snacks and bread."

"What kind of snacks?"

"Oh, sugar cookies and some apple bread."

The girl straightened and licked her lips. "Can I have some now?"

"Well, maybe we should ask Callie first. Or your uncle. Is he here?"

Ruthie shook her head, her untidy braids flying back and forth. Dirt smudged one side of her face and around her mouth, and her hands were filthy. "Uncle Dan isn't here. Him and Ben's working."

Little Davy toddled to the door and stared up at her. Tears still dampened his lashes and clung to his eyes. He reached up his hands to her. "Hold'ju."

Leah felt a crack form in the wall she'd erected around herself. She cleared her throat. "How about a cookie. Would you like that?"

"Tookie!" The boy clapped his hands and disappeared into the house. Leah longed to shove the basket into Ruthie's hands and flee back to the safety of the boardinghouse, but the load was too heavy for the child, and she needed to return Rachel's towels and basket. She swallowed hard. "May I come inside for a moment?"

"Shut that door, Ruthie. You're lettin' in flies." Leah couldn't see Callie but recognized her voice. "And don't you dare let Davy out again, you hear?"

Leah cringed. Callie was just a small version of what she'd been like. She'd had to take care of her siblings as far back as she could remember. Her heart ached for the little girl who'd have to grow up far too soon and would probably never get to be a playful, young girl again. Why, if she had to care for her siblings all the time, she wouldn't even be able to attend school.

Footsteps pounded on the floor, and Callie appeared in the doorway. "What are you doing here?"

Leah winced inwardly at the animosity in the girl's voice. "I brought some fresh bread for you and some cookies."

She longingly eyed the basket, but her glare quickly refocused on Leah. "We don't need your handouts. I can make bread."

"So you already have all you need?"

"Nuh-uh. We don't got no bread. You told a lie. I'm gonna tell Ma." Ruthie's scolding expression suddenly changed, and she frowned, her lips quivering. "I'm. . .uh. . .gonna tell Uncle Dan."

Callie glared at her sister. "I didn't say we had any, just that I could make it."

Leah wasn't taken in by her false bravado. "Well, since I have all this bread, I'd hate to see it go to waste." She strode in and her heart nearly broke. Clara Howard's tidy home was a complete mess. Crates of clothes, toys, and other items were stacked along the empty spaces of the parlor. Two small chests of drawers lined the wall of the crowded dining room. Everything from sticks and rocks the boys must have dragged in to clothing and diapers covered the furniture and made walking difficult. Davy picked up a stick and whacked the door frame. Leah smiled, hoping to distract him. "Come, time for a cookie."

When he toddled past her, she took the stick from him and laid it out of his reach on top of one of the dressers and carefully made her way to the kitchen, where dirty dishes covered the table and countertops. She stacked several soiled plates to make room for the basket.

A woman was definitely needed here. The workload was far

too much for an eight-year-old. Leah tried to ignore the guilt assaulting her. Was she being completely unreasonable? Dan needed her, and so did these children.

But how could she jump right back into the situation she'd so recently fled?

Ruthie climbed up on a chair, and Davy attempted to do the same. Leah picked him up and sat him in the chair next to his sister. "Before you eat, we need to clean those hands. Callie, could I please borrow a washcloth?"

"Suit yourself, but I'm not washing any dishes they dirty."

"Why not?" Leah asked as she searched for a clean cloth.

Callie shrugged. "I got too much to do watching these young'uns to do dishes. Uncle Dan does them at night."

Leah's heart took another blow. Poor Dan. Working all day, tending these orphans, and then most likely having to fix dinner and wash dishes afterward. At least she could help with this one chore. After washing off the children's hands, she rolled up her sleeves and filled the bucket. The children were done with their snack and playing in the parlor when she finished. She tidied up the kitchen, putting containers back on shelves, and then she swept the floor. Her heart felt good knowing Dan wouldn't come home to such a mess.

She rummaged around for something to cook, but when she didn't find any meat, she decided to make a pot of potato soup. It would taste good with the bread she'd baked. She checked on the children and found Davy asleep on the floor. Poor little thing. Callie sat on the settee looking at a picture book with Ruthie, whose eyes were nearly closed. Leah picked up Davy, receiving a scowl from Callie, then took the boy into Dan's room and laid him in the middle of the bed. She brushed his hair from his forehead and smiled. He was a comely child.

Not having heard a peep from the baby the whole time she was there, she tiptoed into the bedroom that had been Clara's. Her heart jumped. Not a thing had been done in here. Clara's clothes still hung from the pegs, and her brush and comb rested on a small vanity. Her shoes stuck out from under the bed, where Maggie slept with her thumb hanging just out of her mouth. Her lashes were spiked as if she'd been crying, and the girl's tongue moved as if she were nursing. For the first time, Leah realized that the baby probably still had been nursing when her mother died. "Oh, you poor thing."

What was Dan going through trying to comfort five young children who missed their parents and had their whole world yanked out from under them? She hung her head. How selfish she'd been. Tears coursed down her cheeks, and she broke into sobs. "Forgive me, Lord," she whispered. "I've been so selfish."

She stared up at the ceiling, fortifying herself for the tasks at hand. God would give her the strength to do His will; she understood that now.

Quietly, she gathered up Clara's dresses and shoes and carried them into the parlor, where she placed them in an empty crate.

"What are you doing?" Callie stared, her mouth twisted to one side and her brown eyes sparking. Ruthie had slumped over and was asleep. "We don't need your help."

Leah realized she needed to mend some bridges, so she sat beside the girl. "I need to apologize to you. I. . .uh. . .wasn't prepared for Dan to bring you kids home with him. It was a surprise. A very big surprise."

"It was a surprise to us, too. I wanted to live with my aunt." Callie crossed her arms and stared across the room.

"I'm so sorry, Callie." Leah cupped the girl's cheek. "I can't imagine how hard it must be to lose your parents."

The child teared up, and she swiped her hand across her eyes. "I miss them."

Leah pulled Callie into her arms, surprised she didn't try to get away. Instead, she curled against Leah and sobbed. Tears pooled in Leah's eyes as she realized how much this tough little girl needed her, and she cried with her for the pain she'd caused the children. And for Dan. She'd let her own pain get in the way of helping others who desperately needed her.

Leah sat for a long while, praying and caressing Callie. Finally, the child quieted and pulled away. Her face was splotchy, her nose ran, and she looked a tad embarrassed.

"Sorry."

Shaking her head, Leah ran her hand down the side of Callie's face. "Don't be, sweetie. I'm the one who needs to apologize."

"You just did." Callie offered the tiniest of smiles.

"I guess I did, but now comes the hard part. I need to go have a talk with Dan."

"Are you going to marry him?"

She nodded. "If he'll have me."

Callie grinned wide. "He will. I think he misses you."

"Well"—Leah stood—"we shall see."

A few minutes later, she paused outside the rear door of the livery, shaking like a wood shack in the midst of a tornado. But her storm had passed, and she truly believed good things lay ahead—if only Dan would forgive her.

Dust motes floated through shafts of sunlight, almost looking like snow. She couldn't see Dan but heard a clanging coming from the front of the building. A tall, brown horse in a stall nickered at her as she passed by. Leah's heart pounded as if she'd just run a long race. In a way she had, but it had been a mental marathon—a test of the mind and heart. She couldn't help grinning as her love for Dan overflowed.

But then she stopped as doubts attacked. What if he couldn't forgive her shamelessness? What if his feelings had changed?

For a second, she wavered. Almost tucked tail and ran.

But then she heard the deep rumble of Dan's voice—and it pulled her toward him. She stepped out of the shadows in the back of the livery and walked to the front, where the open doors allowed the sun to shine in and illuminate the area. Dan pounded on a loose board and said something to Ben, who stood beside him. The boy noticed her first and stared with wide eyes. Dan straightened and slowly turned. His lips parted when her saw her, and his eyes sparked before he schooled his expression.

She could hardly blame him after the way she'd left him in a lurch. Her hands wouldn't be still, so she tucked them behind her. "I brought some cookies over to the house. Do you suppose Ben could take a break and go have a snack?"

"Can I, Uncle Dan?"

He nodded, and the boy shot for home like his feet were on

fire. Dan laid his hammer down and closed the distance between them. His beard was growing in, giving him a more rugged look than normal. Had he not had the time to even shave the past few days?

He shifted his feet and seemed to have as hard a time being still as she. "What do you need, Leah?"

She closed her eyes, loving the timbre of his voice. So manly. So strong. Just like him. "I'm sorry, Dan."

When she gazed back up, she saw the confusion in his eyes, and maybe even a spark of hope.

"Sorry about what?" He wasn't going to make this easy.

"You know. For being pigheaded and selfish as a goat."

His lips twitched, and he cocked his head.

"What?"

"You're the prettiest goat I've even seen."

Tears filled her eyes. "I'm really sorry. I let my fears keep me from the man I love and from helping those poor children." She ducked her head. "I was so selfish."

His forefinger lifted her chin, and he thumbed the tears away. "I'm sorry, too. For not giving you more warning. I should have telegraphed you and prepared you." He broke from her gaze and sighed. "I figured you wouldn't want me with all those kids as part of the deal."

"Oh, Dan. I do. I want you with all of my heart. The children, too."

His dark eyes came alive with passion, and he tugged her to him. "Are you sure? It won't be easy for you."

She placed her hand on his chest, feeling the fervent pounding of his heart. "I'm positive. I want to be your wife and the mother—or aunt—to the children. I'm already falling in love with them."

"And what about me?"

She thought to tease him, but he'd been through enough already, and she chose to be merciful. "I have loved you for a while now."

"Is that so?" He grinned wide, setting her heart soaring.

"Yes, it is, Mr. Howard."

"Then I reckon we need to get married. Could you be ready by a week from this Sunday?"

She toyed with a loose button on his shirt. "No."

His eyes dimmed a bit. "How long, then? I want to be with you, Leah."

"I was hoping for tomorrow, after Rand and Shannon's wedding Sunday afternoon."

He let out a whoop that made one of the horses whinny and grabbed her up, spinning her in a circle. His lips collided with hers, melding their breath and sending her senses in a tizzy. Her arms wrapped around his neck, and she felt loved.

Safe.

Home.

This was where she belonged. Right here in Dan's arms.

Chapter 30

Mark leaned forward on the wagon seat, his head in his hands. The harnesses jingled, and the wagon creaked and groaned and rocked on the rutted road. Though this one had only been a day trip, it seemed to have taken forever. He wanted to be home, yet he dreaded returning to Lookout. He wished he didn't have to return until after Shannon was married. He would definitely skip church tomorrow because he couldn't stand watching the wedding ceremony scheduled for right after the service. It would gut him to the core.

Why was he so miserable? He was the one who'd told Shannon he couldn't marry her. Was he making the wrong decision?

Garrett shoved his arm. "All right, out with it. You've been miserable this whole trip, so what is it that's got you more frazzled than a steer tangled in barbed wire?"

Where did he begin? Everything in his life was jumbled up. "There's too much to talk about it."

Garrett guided the horses around a sharp curve that signaled only a few miles left before they'd be home. "Just pick a spot and start there."

Mark breathed in a strengthening breath through his nose and sat up. "I've decided to become a lawyer, so I'll be quitting the freight business."

His brother's blond brows lifted. "I wondered if you'd ever get around to doing that."

"You mean you're not surprised? Not upset with me?"

"You've been reading those law books for years. What's the point of that if you don't plan on becoming a lawyer one day—and then you apprenticed with that lawyer in Abilene, but things didn't seem to go well there, so I've never brought it up."

Mark winced, but he realized the time had come to tell his brother the truth. "Things didn't go well there, but that had nothing to do with working for Mr. Conrad."

"No?" Garrett stared at him, curiosity etched on his face.

He shook his head. "Nope. It centered around a pretty saloon gal."

"I don't believe that for an instant. I've never seen you go into the saloon."

"What can I say?" He shrugged. "I got curious, and it was the biggest mistake of my life."

Garrett slung his arm around Mark's shoulders. Mark fought back the tears that stung his eyes. He loved his brother and knew Garrett loved him, but they rarely showed their affection other than teasing one another. He cleared his throat, dreading to see his brother's face. "I killed a man."

Garrett stiffened for a moment but quickly relaxed. "I'm sure you had a good reason for doing such a thing."

"I didn't mean to kill that cowboy. He was roughhousing the woman I thought I was in love with. I told him to stop, and he just shoved Annabelle away and pulled his gun." Mark lifted his hat and ran a shaky hand through his hair. "I just reacted. I pulled my gun and fired back. I didn't even think I'd hit him, much less killed him. It was just a gut reaction."

"Why were you wearing a gun? You don't normally."

"I don't know. Pretty much everyone in Abilene wore one, so I guess I had to. Just to fit in."

"Did Mr. Conrad?"

He nodded. "Actually, he did. He had a shoulder holster and wore it under his suit coat. You couldn't see it, but he had his weapon in case he needed it."

"It must have been a fair fight since you weren't thrown in jail and didn't stand trial." Garrett stared at him. "You didn't, did you?"

Mark shook his head. "Plenty of folks in the saloon spoke up for me, and that cowboy had a reputation for causing trouble. The marshal actually told me he was glad not to have to deal with the man anymore. But that didn't make me feel any better. I took a life." He hung his head in his hands and stared at the dirty wagon floorboards.

"Have you asked God to forgive you for killing that man? Knowing how tenderhearted you are, that must have been eating away at you all these years."

"Yeah, I've asked the good Lord to forgive me a thousand times, but the ache never goes away. I took a man's life, and there's no way to make restitution for that."

"No, but God has forgiven you. It sounds like you haven't accepted that."

Mark stared out at the rolling hills. In the distance, three deer munched on the tender grass just outside of a clump of oaks. All he had to do was raise his rifle, and they'd have venison for dinner. But he'd had enough killing to last him forever.

"I think the problem is that you need to forgive yourself. Whoa. . ." Garrett pulled the wagon to a stop. The horses snorted and shook their heads as if they knew home was close by and they wanted to keep going. His brother turned in the seat to face him. "It was an accident, Mark. You've got to let go of this and believe that God has forgiven you. If He has, don't you think it displeases Him for you to keep hanging on to your misery? Let it go."

Mark leaned his elbows on his knees. "How?"

"Just do it. Repent, once and for all, and believe God loves you and forgives you. You're God's child. If you were a father, and say your child accidentally killed a squirrel or even a dog, would you hate that little one?"

"No, of course not."

"Well, you're God's child, and He doesn't hate you, either. He wants you to get past this. Turn loose of it, brother."

Mark nodded. It was time. No amount of feeling sorry could

change a thing. He bowed his head. "Father God, I'm so sorry for killing that man. You alone know how much, but please forgive me. And help me to forgive myself and put this behind me. Help me to move forward from this day on."

"Amen, Lord. Show Mark how much You love him—how much I do, too." Garrett cleared his throat and swiped at his eyes.

Mark sat up and blew out a breath that puffed up his cheeks. "I do feel better."

Garrett slapped him on the shoulder and grinned. "That's great. Now let's talk about the other thing that's bothering you."

"You mean about me quitting the business and leaving you in the lurch?"

"No, I've been expecting you to change careers for a long time. I'll manage just fine—not that I won't miss working with you. I mean Shannon."

"What about her?" He'd just confessed the worst thing he'd ever done to his brother, but he wasn't sure he wanted to talk about the woman he loved.

He blinked, as reality set in.

He did love her.

"Are you just going to let her marry that Kessler guy without a fight?"

Mark looked off to the right, avoiding his brother's stare. "It's too late to do anything about that."

"It's not too late until she's married the guy. I've seen how you look at her. Don't tell me you don't love her."

Mark shook his head. "It took me a while to figure that out, but I couldn't ask her to marry me after what I did."

Garrett looked at him with a blank expression. "What did you do?"

He gazed at his brother as if he'd gone crazy. "I just told you. I killed a man."

"Really? You killed a man?"

Mark crossed his arms and leaned back against the seat. "Not funny."

"I'm serious. God not only forgives our sins, but He forgets about them—at least that's what the reverend says. God makes us pure, white as snow, after we confess and ask His forgiveness. It's as if we'd never committed the sin."

"If I didn't know better, I'd think you were studying to be a minister."

"Ha, ha, now who's joking? I'm serious. Guess I've just been paying more attention in church. I see no reason at all that you can't marry Shannon if you love her, other than your own stubborn pride."

Hope swirled through Mark like a flash flood. Was it actually possible?

He did love her with all his heart. But would it be fair to steal her back from Rand, even if she agreed, at this late moment?

"Would it be better for her to marry a man she doesn't love, when the one she does wants her so badly?"

He stared up at the blue sky. Had that thought come from God or from his own desires?

"I made her for you."

Mark sat up straight. God had made Shannon for him? Was it really possible?

His chest warmed. Suddenly, he grabbed the reins and slapped them down hard on the horses' backs. "Heyah!"

"Hey, what's going on?" Garrett stared at him wide-eyed and grabbed hold of the bench as the wagon lurched forward.

"I've got to get to town and stop a wedding."

Shannon walked around the kitchen in Rand's home. The big room boasted a large stove, plenty of work area and cabinets for storage, and even a huge pantry. Tall windows allowed in plenty of light and a cooling breeze during hot weather. A table that seated six was shoved against the far wall. "'Tis far grander than I expected."

"There's a door to the cellar under this rug." Rand kicked the braided mat out of the way and lifted a door.

"Why, I've never seen the likes of it. How grand 'tis to have the entry inside the house. 'Twill be very handy, especially in cold weather."

"Yeah, my ma liked that a lot, too." Rand looked proudly around the room as if seeing his mum working there. "I'd like you to make a list of whatever you need. Food, sewing stuff, cloth, anything, and I'll have Mrs. Morgan order it for us."

"That's very kind of you, Rand."

He shook his head. "No, it isn't. I want you to be happy here."

Did he think buying her things would make her happy? In fact, coming to his ranch did the opposite and made her question if she was making the right decision. The Kessler ranch was much farther from town than she'd expected. They'd left at first light and hadn't arrived until noon. After she toured the house, they'd be heading back. She ran her hand down the doorjamb. She loved this house, but the problem was, she didn't love Rand. Could she truly be happy here? Would he be happy?

"The parlor's this way." She followed him into another large room with logs and chinking on the walls. A dark blue settee faced a large window revealing a beautiful view of rolling hills dotted with cattle. 'Twas a serene scene that did nothing to calm the stormy sea roiling within. What was wrong with her?

"The other room at the front of the house has a number of uses." Rand opened double doors and stepped inside. "As you can see, that wall serves as a library of sorts. 'Course we don't have anywhere near the books that the boardinghouse has. That old Mrs. Hamilton—James's ma—collected them like most folks do children. I reckon Mrs. Davis would loan you some of hers if you don't find what you need here."

"I'm sure this will do just fine." She studied the rest of the room. A desk rested on one side as well as several comfortable wingback chairs for reading, she supposed.

Rand grinned and pointed up. She lifted her gaze, contemplating the fact that his smile, friendly as it was, did nothing to excite her. A large, wooden frame hung from hooks affixed to the ceiling. Ropes were attached that she assumed would lower the rack down. "What is that?"

"Ma's quilting rack. She refused to have it down and in the way all the time, so my pa rigged up this system so she could lower it when she wanted to quilt and raise it up when she wanted it out of the way."

Shannon had never seen such a device. " 'Tis very practical."

Rand chuckled. "I guess, but the problem Ma had was that she had to go round up three other people each time she wanted to raise or lower it."

She nodded. "Aye, I can see 'twould be a problem, for sure."

"If you prefer to leave it down, doesn't bother me. 'Course, you might not want to once we have children running around and messin' with things." Rand's ears grew bright red at the mention of children.

Shannon hurried to the window, not wanting him to see her flaming cheeks. How could she maintain this facade? Living with a man she didn't love was one thing, but being intimate was something she hadn't considered. *I can't do it.*

"There's one bedroom downstairs, but it's small, so I use the large one upstairs at the front of the house. You can go up and look at it and the other two if you want. I'll. . .uh, stay down here, for propriety's sake."

Shannon's cheeks warmed again. "That's all right. I don't need to see them. I suppose we should start back soon so we'll be in town well before dark."

He nodded. "I just need to run upstairs and get some things. Look around some more or have a seat if you'd like. I won't be long."

He took the stairs two at a time, like an eager schoolboy on the last day of class. Shannon dropped into one of the chairs and looked out the window. She would love living in this house. Never had she resided in one so fine, except for places she'd worked or the boardinghouse. But she was fooling herself. She might be delighted with the house, but marrying Rand was a mistake she would quickly regret.

She once promised herself that she'd never wed unless she married a man she dearly loved. Maybe she couldn't have Mark, but she realized now that she couldn't marry Rand. It simply wasn't fair to him. He was a good, kindhearted man who deserved to marry a woman who loved him deeply. A woman who'd be happy to bear his children.

How could she tell him, though? He'd be so disappointed, and she dreadfully hated disappointing him.

He didn't love her, but he thought her pretty and liked her accent, so he said. He probably could have fallen in love with her, but alas, her heart belonged to another.

Chapter 31

Shannon leaned against the boardinghouse post, watching Rand drive the buggy out of town. With the wedding called off, he'd decided to return to his ranch instead of spending the night in town. Her heart ached. He was such a good man—a lonely man. "Father, send him a woman who will love and cherish him."

Not quite ready to go inside and tell everyone her news, she sat down in a rocker and stared down Main Street. What could she do now?

She didn't want to work for the Corbetts and had pretty much nailed that coffin shut. She had enough money to travel to another town and maybe stay a week. Would that be enough time to find a job?

And what if she didn't, and her money ran out?

She blinked back the tears stinging her eyes and stared up at the sky. "What do I do now, Lord? I feel like I'm right back where I was when I first came to Lookout, only I no longer have a prospective husband."

She sat there for a long while, rocking. Numb. What was to become of her?

A couple walking arm-in-arm rounded the corner by the Fosters' vacant lot. With the arrival of their niece to tend the store,

Mr. and Mrs. Foster had left town. Shannon suddenly realized the couple was Dan and Leah. She smiled, so happy to see they'd come to their senses and were back together, and yet the reunion only made her own circumstances more bitter to swallow.

She rose as they approached, but lost in each other's eyes, they didn't notice her at first. "Shall I be going inside so you two can be saying your good nights?"

"Oh, Shannon."

Leah's cheeks were bright red from embarrassment, or the heat of passion—Shannon wasn't sure.

"Uh, no, that's all right. We need to talk to Rachel. Dan and I are getting married tomorrow, right after you and Rand." Leah beamed.

Shannon couldn't toss water on her friend's delight, so she kept her news to herself for now. At least the food Rachel had already prepared for Shannon's wedding wouldn't be wasted. That would ease her guilt. "I'm so happy for you both."

She hugged Leah and smiled up at Dan. "You'll both be very happy together. I'm sure of it."

Leah all but bounced on her toes. "Thank you. We're going inside to tell Luke and Rachel now. See you in a bit."

Dan nodded, his eyes burning bright. He opened the door for Leah, and they both went inside. Shannon wandered to the end of the porch, her heart heavy. How could she endure tomorrow? Instead of getting married, she'd have to watch her friend's ceremony. The ache of her loss was almost too much to bear.

Footsteps sounded behind her, but she didn't turn around. She couldn't face anyone just now. Suddenly, she realized she hadn't heard the front door open, so who could be behind her? She started to turn, and a sack flew over her face, blocking out the light. She flailed her arms, hitting someone hard. The *oof* she heard was decidedly masculine, and then the man hauled her up in his arms.

She opened her mouth to scream and sucked in dust. A round of coughing kept her from calling for help. And then she was tossed up and landed on top of a horse. The man climbed on behind her and kicked the horse into a run.

Save me, Lord. Protect me.

All manner of thoughts attacked her mind. Why would someone make off with her? Had the outlaw who'd kidnapped Rachel that summer returned? Why did he want her? Could he be one of the men who'd proposed to her?

She shivered, and the man tightened his arms around her, not in a cruel manner but as if he were trying to protect her.

But a man who wanted to keep her safe wouldn't kidnap her. "Let me go."

She broke her arm free and elbowed the man in the stomach. Getting away from him while they were still close to town was imperative. If he took her miles from town, she'd never find her way back, and she'd be completely at his mercy. She leaned forward, prepared to rear back and butt him in the head, but something poked her in the side. A gun?

Her breath grew ragged, but she forced herself to relax. Maybe he didn't have nefarious purposes. Maybe he was a widower and just needed a woman to care for his children. But then why would he put a gun to her side?

Long before she expected, the horse's steps slowed, and then stopped. Over the pounding in her ears, she could hear water. Had he just taken her to the river?

He slid down, and she felt him gently lift her off the horse and set her on the ground, keeping his hands lightly on her sides until she gained her balance. The sack flew off, and Mark stood in front of her.

She blinked hard and sneezed, then socked him in the gut.

He doubled over, grabbing his stomach. "What was that for?"

She stomped her foot and glared at him. What kind of shenanigans was he up to? " 'Twas for scaring half my life off of me. And you shoved a gun in my side? Just what do you think you're doing?"

He looked chagrined and toed the dirt. "I wanted to talk to you. And that wasn't a gun, it was just my finger."

"Ach!" She threw her hands in the air and stormed toward the edge of the river. "Why didn't you just ask to speak with me?"

He was silent for a moment, then finally spoke. "Because I didn't think you would."

He was probably right. In her state of mind, she hadn't wanted to talk to anyone, least of all him.

"Shannon, please listen to me. You can't marry Rand Kessler."

She spun around, her curiosity and ire stirred. "I can marry anyone I want to."

He yanked off his hat and forked his fingers through his hair. She watched, longing to do the same. She swallowed hard and returned to watching the water bubble over the rocks. The sound soothed her inner turmoil. "What is it you're wanting?"

"I. . .uh. . .want you to marry me instead."

She whirled around again. "Don't you be teasin' me, Mark Corbett."

His blue eyes held the truth. Her heart felt as if it were a bird on the edge of a steep precipice, ready to take wing and soar. "Why would you want that? You, who doesn't want to marry anyone?"

"Because you stole my heart, you little Irish thief." He grinned, almost apologetically. "You whisked into my life and made me want things I didn't think I deserved, and when you were gone, I was nothing but a miserable wretch."

"Me thinks you still are one."

He grinned wide. "You're probably right. But do you think you could forgive this wretch and at least put him out of his misery?"

She held her trembling hands in front of her and cocked her head. How could this be happening? Fifteen minutes ago she'd been a huddled ball of misery, but now. . .

Mark closed the distance between them. "I was stupid, Shannon. I allowed my past to interfere with my future. Everything is changing. I told Garrett that I'm quitting and setting up a law business. The only thing is, I can't do it here. There aren't enough people who need the services I'll offer. I'll probably move to Dallas." His gaze intensified, and his blue eyes sparked like fire. "I know I don't deserve you after all I put you through, but will you give me a second chance? Will you marry me?"

She stared at the man she loved, barely able to comprehend that he'd proposed. Her heart soared, and she laid her hand against his cheek. "Are you certain?"

He cupped his hand over hers, his wonderful blue eyes ablaze with love. "More than I've been about any other thing in my life."

Shannon's heart overflowed with love and happiness. Could this actually be happening? "Aye. I'll marry you, Mark Corbett."

He snatched her up, and their lips collided in an explosive kiss that ended far too soon. He pulled away, touching his forehead to hers. "Will you marry me tonight?"

She smiled at his eagerness and shook her head. "A girl needs time to plan these things."

"When, then? I don't want to take a chance on your changing your mind."

She caressed his cheek. "There's not a chance this side of heaven that would happen."

Suddenly he set her back from him, his expression solemn. "What about Rand?"

"I told him tonight that I couldn't marry him. 'Twas a difficult thing to do, but I'm so glad I did now."

"Me, too, but I do feel sorry for him. He's a decent sort." Mark stared down at her. "Just why did you do that?"

"My heart broke for him. He was terribly disappointed, but he deserves to marry a woman who'll love him as I love you."

Mark's wide smile lit up the darkening twilight. "I love you so much. I thought I'd go crazy wanting you."

She stepped into his embrace, and this time his kiss was light, almost teasing. She leaned in for more, but he gently pushed her back. "Careful, now. Let's save some for the wedding night. And speaking of that, just how much time do you need to get ready?"

She tapped her lips and stared up at the dark trees above her. Light from the sunset still illuminated the western sky with gorgeous hues of pink and orange. "Hmm. . .I'm thinking a day."

Mark blinked and stared as if he didn't comprehend what she said. "Just one day?"

She shook her head. "Not even a whole day. What about a half a day?"

He smiled and caressed her hand. "Tomorrow? After the service."

She nodded, hoping the depth of her love shone from her eyes. "Right after Dan and Leah's wedding."

"What? How did I miss hearing about that?"

"I saw them just before you kidnapped me." She walloped him again.

"Ow! You gonna do that every time you mention that?"

She cocked her head and batted her lashes. "Perhaps."

Mark reached up and rubbed the back of his neck. "I just thought of a problem."

"What?" She couldn't for the life of her think of anything standing in the way of them marrying.

"Where will we live?"

Suddenly she realized the dilemma. Mark shared a house with his brother. "Aye, 'tis a problem. What if we asked to use the little house next to the boardinghouse?"

Mark stood with his hands loosely anchored to his hips and shook his head. "I don't see how that will work since there isn't a stove for you to cook on."

She swallowed hard. "Perhaps 'twould be best if we kept a room at the boardinghouse until we're ready to leave for Dallas. And to be honest, I'm not too great a cook. We didn't have much to fix back home, mostly porridge or soup."

Mark snapped his fingers. "Aw, shucks. I was hoping not to have to cook anymore." He kept a smile on his face, so she knew he was teasing.

"If we stayed at the boardinghouse, I imagine Rachel would be willing to teach me to cook better."

He pulled her close and nuzzled her neck. "That idea is sounding better and better."

She wrapped her arms around his waist and rested her head on his shoulder. How this day had changed. She'd started out intending to marry one man, but ended up with the man of her heart. An hour ago, her life looked dismal. Hopeless. But now her hope knew no bounds. God sure was in the miracle-working business.

Mark kissed her forehead. "It's getting dark, sweetheart. I'd better get you back home before Luke starts rounding up a search party."

"I'm so happy, Mark. I thank the good Lord you finally came to your senses."

He placed a quick peck on her lips. "Me, too, darlin'. Me, too."

Chapter 32

Excitement coursed through Shannon's limbs. In the next half hour, she would become a married woman. She would no longer be alone, but instead, she would be married to the man who'd stolen her heart.

Soon she'd be Shannon Corbett.

Mrs. Mark Corbett.

If only her mum was here with her.

She shook her head and stared at herself in the tall oval mirror in her new room on the third floor. Rachel and Leah had helped her move her things up last night once all the cheers had died down after she and Mark had told everyone they were getting married. The bedroom was a bit larger than her last one, and it had a door leading into a small parlor. The place would be perfect for them until they moved to Dallas.

She couldn't quit smiling. During this morning's service, every nerve had been on edge. She hadn't been able to quit bouncing her knees, and several times, Mark had actually held them down with his hand for a brief moment.

Her heart was so full that she was afraid it might burst. Crossing the room, she stared out the window and up at the sky. "I thank You, Father, for pulling me out of the misery I was in yesterday and changing my world. Thank You for stopping me from marrying Rand, and give him a wonderful woman to love. He's a very good man and deserves a good woman.

"And thank You so much for opening Mark's heart. For giving him the courage to put his past behind him and pursue his dream. Thank You for everything, even bringing me to this tiny Texas town. I see now that You had Your hand on me even when I wasn't aware of it."

She returned to the mirror and repinned a stubborn curl that didn't want to be held captive by the hairpin. Smoothing down her new, light green dress, she studied her image. Would Mark like what he saw? Would he be disappointed that she'd opted for a more practical dress rather than wearing white like many new brides were starting to do?

A knock sounded, pulling her away from her concerns. It was time!

She opened the door, and Rachel stood smiling at her. "Oh, you look beautiful." Her hand lifted to the Irish lace collar. "And this is perfect. You do such fine work. I bet you could make this beautiful lace and sell it in Dallas, if you need to make some extra income while Mark is building his business."

"Thank you. 'Tis a grand idea." Shannon dreaded the day she'd have to say good-bye to Rachel and Leah, but she would. Supporting her husband and keeping him happy would be her biggest goal from now on.

Rachel looked past her into the room. "Will this suite work for you? I know it's not as big as Mark's house."

"Aye, 'tis perfect, and we don't have to share it with Garrett."

"Indeed. There is that." Rachel smiled and clutched her arm. "We'd better get going before Mark thinks you've changed your mind."

"That will never happen." She bounced on her tiptoes. "Were you this excited when you married Luke?"

"Even more, I believe. I'd waited so many years for him to forgive me, and then to become his wife. . ." She shook her head. "It was a dream come true."

Holding up her skirt, Shannon followed Rachel down the

back stairs. "I'm so happy for you that it all worked out."

"And now it's working out for you and Leah. Isn't God good?"

"Aye, He is at that."

Rachel shook her head at the bottom of the stairs. "We're friends now, but when y'all first came to Lookout, all vying for Luke's hand, I didn't have hope the size of a pea that I'd end up with him. And having to house y'all here and provide meals, well, it certainly was a test of my faith. But now I see God's plan in all of it."

"Aye, me, too. At first 'twas such a mess, and I thought those Corbett brothers were full of nothing but foolery and blarney."

Rachel lifted her face to the sky. "Our God is amazing. He orders our steps, and we fuss and fight Him all the way, at times, but He sees the whole picture."

"Aye, and now I'm to marry."

Rachel grabbed her arm. "So true. Luke has a buggy waiting out front."

"But 'tis only a short walk."

"Pish posh." Rachel swiped her hand through the air. "A bride can't walk to her wedding."

They arrived at the front of the house and found Leah already in the buggy—a fringed-topped surrey. She looked charming in her light blue dress, complete with the lace Shannon had made for her. "And don't you look lovely?"

Leah pushed her skirt out of the way as Shannon sat beside her in the backseat. "Did you look in the mirror? You're stunning."

"Thank you, and isn't this buggy grand?"

Leah nodded. "It is. Dan borrowed it from a man he knows in Denison. I think it's a bit extravagant since we could walk to the church faster, but he wanted our wedding to be memorable."

"He's a thoughtful man."

Luke handed Rachel up into the front seat. "Where's Jacqueline?" she asked.

He hurried around the front of the surrey. "She's helping Jenny Evans with her camera. Miss Evans is taking pictures. She thinks the double wedding is the biggest news since we got married." He chuckled and climbed into the buggy. "I'm glad

Jack's friendship with Miss Evans wasn't hurt long-term after Miss Evans published that article about the words painted on the buildings."

"Me, too. When Jacqueline's helping Jenny, she's kept busy doing something productive and maybe even learning a trade." Rachel leaned against her husband's arm.

Shannon couldn't wait until she was married and was free to show her husband affection in public. She glanced at Leah. "Are you certain you and Dan don't mind having a double wedding? Mark and I are perfectly content to let you two marry first, if you wish."

Leah grabbed her hand. Her blue eyes sparkled like only a bride-to-be's could. "No, we love the idea. It's perfect. You and I came to town to marry, but neither of us are marrying the man we thought we would."

Shannon nodded and wrung her hands together. Now that the time was here, her nerves were all a twitter. Her happiness knew no bounds, but she was a simple woman. Could she make Mark happy?

The lot next to the church looked almost the same as it had when she'd left it an hour ago. With the sun shining bright and the cooler, early October temperatures, they'd decided to hold the Sunday service and wedding ceremony outside to accommodate the large crowd expected. Fortunately, no storms brewed on the horizon this day. And it looked like nearly everyone in the county, save Rand, had showed up.

"Look!" Leah pointed to where the pastor stood with Dan and Mark on either side of him. "Someone's erected an arbor."

"Aye, and attached flowers to it. How lovely!"

The buggy stopped, and Luke hopped out and helped each of them down. Shannon's stomach swirled. The chicken leg and roll she'd had for dinner weren't sitting too well, just now. Her gaze sought out Mark, and even across the distance, she could see his wide smile and twinkling eyes. Oh, how she loved him.

Rachel stood in front of her and Leah. "Let me make sure everything is perfect." She straightened collars, checked bows, and then tapped her lips. "Something is missing. Luke?"

Luke stepped out from behind them and handed each of them a beautiful bouquet of colorful wildflowers. White, purple, yellow, and red blooms had been gathered up and tied with long, flowing ribbons that matched their ivory lace collars.

"Oh, they're lovely." Shannon thanked Rachel with her gaze.

Leah hugged Rachel's neck. "Everything is perfect now."

The fiddler and guitar player from the Saturday socials started up something that sounded like a minuet. All heads turned toward them.

"It's time." Rachel smiled. "Leah, you go first and join Dan, and then Shannon will follow."

Leah stole a quick glance at Shannon. "I know we started out as adversaries, but I'm so grateful to God that we became friends." She gave Shannon a quick hug and started up the aisle.

Dan's nieces and nephews turned in the seats on the front row, and the oldest boy yelled, "Hurry."

A chuckle reverberated through the crowd. When Leah was halfway up the row between the benches, Rachel gave Shannon a gentle nudge. "Your turn. Go meet your beloved."

Shannon's heart took wing and sailed high. She peeked at Luke as she passed by, and he winked at her. Then her gaze found Mark's. He stood tall, so handsomely dressed in a new black suit. His curly blond hair gleamed in the afternoon sun, and his eyes drew her like a butterfly to a flower's nectar.

He held out his hand as she drew near, then pulled her to his side and leaned close to her ear. "You're the most beautiful thing I've ever seen. Looks like Corbetts' Matrimony Service has another success story."

Shannon giggled.

The pastor cleared his throat and eyed Mark over his glasses. "Shall we begin?"

Shannon listened to his opening words, and then the pastor moved to his right and let Dan and Leah recite their vows first. She listened, but her thoughts were elsewhere. She was awed at the steps God had taken to bring her to this point in life. First she left Ireland because of her da's restlessness and desire to live in America. But her parents died, and a series of events left her so desperate that she'd agreed to become a mail-order bride and marry a stranger. Then she was one of the leftover brides—the boardinghouse brides—when Luke chose Rachel, but God brought Mark into her life.

She gazed up at him as the pastor made his way toward them again. As she recited her vows, her gaze never left Mark's. She pledged her loyalty and devotion, as he did. His grip on her hand tightened, and then he lifted it and slid a shiny gold band on her ring finger. Her heart overflowed with love for this man.

The pastor returned to his place up front and offered up a blessing on both new households. The he smiled and looked at each couple. "Gentlemen, you may kiss your bride."

And Mark did. He pulled Shannon up against him, and her lips met his. How could her love have blossomed and grown so quickly? Only God could have done such a thing.

When Mark pulled away, his eyes twinkled, promising more to come.

The pastor lifted his face to the crowd. "Ladies and gentlemen, I present to you Mr. and Mrs. Daniel Howard and Mr. and Mrs. Mark Corbett."

As she and Mark and Dan and Leah turned to face the crowd, an earsplitting roar erupted. People cheered, whistled, and clapped, all sharing their joy. Dan guided Leah down the aisle, and Mark offered his arm to Shannon.

"Ready to begin our life together, Mrs. Corbett?"

"Aye, I am, sir."

Garrett stopped them at the first row of benches. "Congratulations, brother." He hugged Mark and slapped him on the back, then turned to Shannon. "Welcome to the family, sis."

She smiled and hugged her rascally brother-in-law. Having a family member like him would surely keep things interesting.

As they continued down the aisle, she saw the smiling faces of the townsfolk she'd grown to care for. She might not live in Lookout much longer, but it would always hold a special place in her heart.

God had taken an orphan, an alien to this country, and given her a man to love and a family to cherish. Never again would she doubt His hand in her life.

Discussion Questions for *Second Chance Brides*

1. Shannon and Leah were basically stranded in Texas after the man they came to town to marry married someone else. Have you ever been in a situation where you felt you were stuck or there was no way out?

2. Leah traveled to Lookout to escape marriage to an older man she couldn't abide, but things just seemed to get worse. Have you ever done something you thought was God's will for you, but it turned out different than you expected?

3. Later on, Leah thought marriage to Dan was the answer to her problems, but then he took in his brother's orphaned children and she called off the wedding. How do you think she could have handled this situation better?

4. Do you think God was trying to stretch Leah? Has He ever stretched you? How did you handle the situation?

5. Shannon felt completely alone. Her parents were dead, and she was living in a foreign land. Was there ever a time in your life that you felt all alone?

6. Mark wanted to become a lawyer rather than working in the freight business with his brother for the rest of his life, but he was afraid to step out and make the change because of past failures. What's holding you back from stepping out and making a change God may want in your life?

7. Mark loved his brother but always felt he was living in Garrett's shadow. He believed his father loved his brother

more than him. Have you experienced issues with siblings and feelings of inadequacy? How did you handle the situation?

8. Jack disliked Butch because he smelled like hogs all the time and seemed to cause trouble. Do you think she was right in her feelings toward him? Was Butch the town bully?

9. Jack hated Butch for painting "Jack is a liar" on the buildings before he left town. Has anyone ever purposely harmed you or attacked your good name? How did you handle things?

10. Each of the main characters grew closer to the Lord through the story. Did *Second Chance Brides* inspire you to trust God more? How did it encourage you in your own walk with God?

Finally a Bride

To preach deliverance to the captives,
and recovering of sight to the blind,
to set at liberty them that are bruised.
LUKE 4:18

Chapter 1

Lookout, Texas
August 1896

Jacqueline Davis had done a lot of daring things in her life, but this deed had to be the most foolhardy. She held up her skirt with one hand, holding her free arm out for balance, and slid her foot across the roof's wooden shakes. The mayor's chimney was only a dozen more steps away. She peered down at the ground far below, then yanked her gaze upward when a wave of dizziness made her sway. She sucked in a steadying breath. If she fell the two stories to the packed dirt below, *she'd* become tomorrow's news instead of the story she intended to write about the mayor's latest scheme.

She just had to find out what he had up his sleeve. Weeks had passed since she'd landed an exciting story for Lookout's newspaper. She had to get the scoop—whatever the cost. Maybe then she'd have enough clippings in her portfolio to land a job in Dallas as a reporter and finally leave Lookout.

The sweat trickling down her back had nothing to do with the bright April sun warming her shoulders. A moderate breeze whooshed past, lifting her skirts and almost throwing her off balance. Her petticoat flapped like a white flag, but she was far from surrendering. She swatted down her skirts and glanced around the streets, thankful no one was out yet. "Oh, why didn't I don my trousers before trying this stunt?"

"Because you reacted without thinking again, that's why." She scolded herself just like her mother had done on too many occasions to count. Would she never learn? Sighing, she carefully bent down, reached between her legs, pulled the hem of her skirt through, and tucked it in her waistband. Holding her arms out for balance, she righted herself again.

The hour was still early, but with the mayor's house resting right on the busy corner of Bluebonnet Lane and Apple Street, she couldn't exactly stand outside his parlor window, listening to the meeting he was holding inside. If the two well-dressed strangers hadn't ridden right past the boardinghouse while she'd been sweeping the porch, she'd have never known of their arrival.

Her knock on the mayor's door for permission to listen in and to take notes had resulted in a scowl and the door being slammed in her face. Scuttlebutt was running rampant around town that Mayor Burke had some great plan to bring new businesses to Lookout. He was up to something, and she meant to be the first to find out what it was.

She slid her left foot forward. Listening through the chimney opening was her only alternative. She just hoped the men's voices would carry up that far. Sliding her right foot forward, she held her breath. Her task must be completed quickly before anyone saw her.

"Jacqueline Hamilton Davis, you come down from that roof right this minute—or I'm calling off our wedding."

Jack jumped at Billy Morgan's roar. She twisted sideways, swung her arms in the air, wobbled, and regained her balance on the peak of the house. Heart galloping, she glared down at the blond man standing in the street beside the mayor's house and swiped her hand in the air. "Go away!" she hollered in a loud whisper. If she'd told him once, she'd told him a dozen times she had no intention of marrying him.

Her foot slid toward the chimney. She had to get there right now or Billy's ruckus would surely draw a crowd, and she'd have to climb down without her story.

A high-pitched scream rent the air. "Don't fall, Sissy!"

Jack lurched the final step to the chimney and hugged the bricks. She peered down at her five-year-old sister and swatted her hand, indicating Abby needed to leave, but the stubborn girl just hiked her chin in the air. Abby was so dramatic. She'd even practiced her screams until she could blast the shrillest and loudest screeches of all her friends. Parents no longer came running when the young girls practiced their hollering. Jack shook her head. It would be a shame if any of them ever truly needed help one day and Abby screamed, because not a soul in Lookout would come to her aid.

She peered down to see if Billy was still there, and sure enough, the rascal stood in the middle of the dirt road with his hat pushed back off his forehead and his hands on his hips.

Uh-oh. Across the street, her ma carefully made her way down the front porch steps of the boardinghouse—the bulge of her pregnant belly obvious even from this distance. She shaded her eyes with her hand as she looked around, probably checking on Abby.

Jack ducked down behind the chimney. With her ma so close to her time of birthing another baby, she didn't want to cause her distress—and finding her twenty-year-old daughter on a rooftop would certainly set Ma's pulse pounding.

Movement on Main Street drew Jack's attention. She peered over the bank's roof to the boardwalk on the far side of the street. Oh, horse feathers! Now her pa was heading out of the marshal's office and hurrying toward her mother. He probably thought she'd drop that baby right there in the street. Their last child, two-and-a-half-year-old Emma, had been born in a wagon on the way back from Denison, almost a month early.

She glanced down at Billy, who stood with his hands on his hips, shaking his head. Her ma was looking down Main Street now. With precious few moments before the jig was up, Jack stood on her tiptoes, concentrating on her task. She listened hard, trying to decipher the muted words drifting up the chimney. The strong scent of soot stung her nose, but all she could hear was the faint rumble of men's voices.

She glanced back at the far edge of the roof, trying to decide whether to return to the tree and shinny back down or wait until her mother and stepfather went back inside. Would Billy give her away?

Jack heaved a frustrated sigh. Even if he didn't, Abby would surely tattle. She peeked at her sister. Abby ran toward their mother, her finger pointing up at the mayor's roof. Oh fiddlesticks.

Why did they have to come outside before she concluded her sleuthing? And now, thanks to Billy's caterwauling, a crowd was gathering on Bluebonnet Lane.

She quickly studied the town from her vantage point. This was the perfect spot to view any events taking place in Lookout and garner the news, but it was also dangerous. How could she manage to take notes and still keep her balance? Perhaps she could talk Jenny into building a platform with a fence around it atop her newspaper office so they could view the city whenever community events were happening.

"Jacqueline! Oh, my heavens. What are you doing up there?" Her ma splayed her hand across her chest. Abby stood beside her, looking proud that she'd gotten her big sister in trouble.

Jack held tight to the edge of the chimney and laid her forehead against the bricks. She was as caught as a robber in a bank vault on Monday morning. She turned to head back, but her skirt snagged on the chimney bricks and pulled loose from her waistband, causing her to lose her footing. Her boot slipped, shooting her leg forward and raining wooden shakes on the people below. They squealed and scattered then gawked up at her once they were a safe distance away. Jack tightened her lips to keep from giggling. She shouldn't, she knew, but she'd never seen Bertha Boyd move so fast. That woman had to be as wide as a buckboard.

Jack's fingertips ached from clinging to the bricks, and a streak of blood pooled on her index finger from a scrape. She supposed she should admit defeat, even though the thought of it left a nasty taste in her mouth. She stared across the roof and swallowed hard. Going back wouldn't be as easy as moving forward, not with so many people watching.

The warm spring breeze blew across the rolling green hills, and she tried to hold her skirts down lest the folks below see something they shouldn't. Oh, why hadn't she worn bloomers? Or better yet, trousers?

Her foot slipped again, and she reached behind her, grasping hold of a brick jutting out of the chimney. Maybe going sideways would be easier. Facing the crowd, she balanced on the peak of the roof. She slid one foot to the left and then the other. *Just concentrate. Don't think how many people are down there. Don't think how disappointed Ma is.*

"Take it slow," Ma yelled.

Loosening her death grip on the brick, Jack slid her foot sideways. The wind lifted her skirts again, and she dropped one hand, hoping to contain them. She swayed forward and swung her free arm for balance and regained it. Had the wind been this gusty when she'd first crossed the roof?

She dared to peer down at the crowd again and saw Billy Morgan staring up with a big grin on his face.

Wonderful.

Just wonderful.

"Want me to come get you?" Without waiting for an answer, Billy strode forward until she could no longer see him.

She didn't need his help, and if he gave it, she'd never hear the end of it.

As it was, she'd never live this down. And right now, her plan didn't sound half as good as it had when she'd concocted it after the mayor slammed the door in her face. She heard a scratching noise off to her left and slowly glanced that way.

"Stay where you are, Half Bit. I'm coming out to help you."

Jack rolled her eyes, then realized the action made her dizzy. Relief that Luke had beaten Billy to the rescue made her legs weak—and that was the last thing she needed just now. "I can get down by myself, Papa. Although I sure would like it if you'd make that crowd go away."

She heard him snort and then chuckle. "Your mother is spitting mad. What in the world were you thinking?"

She slid another foot toward her stepfather. "You'll be upset if I tell you. It's probably best if you just tell her that I wasn't thinking. She'll believe that."

Luke coughed, but she thought it was more to hide another laugh than because he had something caught in his throat. "Slide on over here—carefully. No young lady in a dress belongs on a rooftop."

"Are you saying it would have been all right if I'd worn my bloomers?" She scooted her foot another three inches and looked up to see how much farther it was to the tree. The wind tugged at her skirt as if purposely trying to make her fall.

"You know that's not what I meant. Just be careful. On second thought, I'm coming out there."

"No, I got up here, and I can get back down. Besides, these shakes are half-rotten, and I doubt they'd hold your weight."

"Take it slow and easy then. I don't want you getting hurt."

Abby let out another bloodcurdling scream as Jack glided her left foot along the peak. The sole of her shoe slipped on another loose shake and shot out from under her, the right foot following. Like a child on a sled, she slid down the roof on her shame and mortification. Luke lunged for her, stretching out his arm, but he missed. The last thing she saw before going over the side was his frantic brown eyes.

A sudden jerk jarred her whole body, and she stopped sliding. Her hips dangled over the edge of the house. She heard a tear, felt a jolt, and then she hurled toward the ground.

She flapped her arms like a winged bird but gained no altitude. Abby's scream rent the air. The ground rose up to meet her like an oncoming locomotive. Billy lunged sideways, reaching for her. They collided—her head against his chest—and landed in a pile in the street. Searing pain radiated through her leg and head.

Jack lay there for half a second before she realized she was on top of Billy. She let out a screech that surpassed Abby's and rolled sideways, ignoring the pain in her leg, fighting fabric to gain her freedom. Struggling to catch her breath, she stared up. Her mother's anxious pale blue eyes blurred from two to four. "I'm all right, Ma."

Laying her aching head back against the dirt, she closed her eyes. If she wasn't dead in the morning, she could just imagine the headlines in tomorrow's newspaper: MARSHAL'S DAUGHTER ATTEMPTS TO FLY.

Finally a Bride

Noah Jeffers slowed his horse at the creek bank and lowered the reins so Rebel could get a drink. He stretched, then dismounted and walked around, working out the kinks from his long ride. He'd experienced many blessings during his month-long circuit of preaching to the small towns of northeastern Texas, but he'd be glad to be back home.

After a few moments, he led Rebel away from the water and hobbled him in a patch of shin-high grass. He removed the horse's bridle and hung it on a tree stem where a branch had broken off. He rummaged around in his saddlebags and pulled out the apple, cheese, and slice of roast beef that Mrs. Hadley had sent with him this morning when he'd left for home.

Settling under a tree, he bit off a hunk of apple and watched the creek water burble over the rocks. Shadows from the trees danced with the sunlight gleaming on the water in a soothing serenade. A rustling caught his attention across the creek, and he tensed, but then a mallard with seven ducklings waddled into view. Noah smiled, enjoying the tranquil scene. The mother led her tiny crew into the water and drifted downstream.

Peace settled over him. He finished his lunch then leaned his head against the trunk and thought about all the folks he'd met during the past month. Most had been more than friendly, offering him a bed if they had a spare and three meals a day whenever he was in a town. Yes sir, he'd eaten well—for the most part. But he missed his bed—and Pete. A yawn pulled at his mouth. He'd take a short rest then head on home—

A scream yanked him from a sweet dream, and he sat up, listening. He rubbed the sleep from his eyes. Had he just dreamed that he heard someone yell?

"Help! Somebody help me!"

Noah bolted to his feet at the child's cry and searched the trees to his left. "Where are you?"

"Over here. Help!"

He plunged through the brush alongside the creek and ducked under a tree branch. The undergrowth thinned out, and he noticed a girl no more than six or seven hopping beside the creek a short distance away. A half-dozen men's shirts and lady's blouses lay drying on bushes.

The girl saw him and ran in his direction, her untidy braids flopping against her chest. "Please, mister, my brother—" She pointed toward the creek. "I cain't swim."

Noah's heart tumbled. He saw no sign of anyone in the quiet water. Dropping to the ground, he yanked off his boots. "Where'd he go in?"

The girl's face crumpled. Tears ran down her freckled cheeks, and red ringed her blue eyes. "I don't know. He was sitting on the blanket while I was doing the wash. He must have crawled in when my back was turned."

Crawled? That means a tiny child—one who can't swim a lick. Noah plunged into the creek. It was deeper than he'd expected. The warm water hit him waist level. He bent down, running his arms back and forth as he turned in a circle. Nothing.

"Ma will turn me out for sure," the girl wailed from the edge of the creek. "Oh, Benny. Where are you?"

Noah ducked his head below the surface, hoping to search underwater, but his thrashing had stirred up too much mud. He moved forward several steps and hunted some more, swiping his hands through the water. His heart pounded as his dread mounted. "Help me, Lord. Where's the boy?"

He stilled for a moment and gazed over at the tattered blanket where the child had been. If he'd crawled in from that point, he'd most likely be upstream a bit. Noah quickly pulled his legs through the water then ducked down. Stretching. Reaching.

His left hand brushed something.

Fabric?

He lunged forward, snagged the cloth, and tugged. A frighteningly light-weight bundle rose up to the surface. Noah turned the limp baby over, grimacing at his blue lips.

"No!" The girl collapsed on the bank, her face in her hands. Her sobs tore at his heart.

Noah lifted the tiny boy by his feet as he once saw a father do at a church social when his young daughter had fallen into a lake. He waded toward the bank, whacking gently on the baby's small back.

On shore, Noah laid the child over his forearm and continued smacking him. "Please, Lord. Don't take this young boy. He has his whole life ahead of him."

Water gushed from the boy's mouth; then he lurched. He gagged and then retched. He clutched Noah's arm and coughed up more water. When the worst had passed, Noah turned him over. Benny's eyelids moved. He jerked, then gasped and uttered a strangled cry.

The girl jumped up and hurried to him, hope brimming from her damp eyes. "He ain't dead?"

Goosebumps charged up Noah's arm as tears moistened his eyes. The boy, no more than six months old, quieted and stared up at him with blue eyes that matched his sister's. His wet brown hair clung to his head.

"C'mere, Benny."

The boy heard his sister's voice and lunged for her, wailing again to beat all.

Noah smiled, then lifted his gaze heavenward. This was as close to a miracle as he'd ever witnessed. "Thank You, Father. Blessed be Your name."

Stirred up from the day's events, Noah rode all night. The next morning, he put Rebel out to pasture then headed inside the house he shared with his mentor, Pete. He set his saddlebags across the back of a kitchen chair and glanced around the tidy room. It was good to be home again.

Pete shuffled in from the parlor. "Noah! Thought I heard someone in here, but I weren't expectin' it'd be you."

Noah hugged the older man. "I rode all night so I could get home sooner."

Pete pulled out a chair and dropped into it. "Howd'ya like being a circuit rider?"

Needing time to think on his response, Noah walked over to the stove and felt the side of the coffeepot. He pulled two mugs from a shelf, poured the dark brew, then placed one cup in front of Pete and sat down, holding the other one. "It was all right. Met a lot of nice folks."

Pete stared at him with an intense gaze. From the first day they'd met, Noah had never been able to pull the wool over the old man's eyes. "What're you not tellin' me?"

Noah's stomach clenched at the memory of the baby in the creek, but he told the story. "Mrs. Freedman is a widow. She'd been sick and was slow to recover, which was why the girl was doing the wash and caring for the baby. She offered to let me stay the night in her barn, but I was anxious to get home." He rubbed his bristly jaw and eyed Pete, knowing his mentor would find this next piece of information humorous. "Just as I was fixin' to head out, she told her girl to give me a piglet as a thank-you for saving Benny."

The old man's lips twitched, and his eyes danced. A chuckle rose up from deep within, making Pete's shoulders bounce. "Wish I'da been there to see your face when they gave you that critter."

Noah scowled. "It's not funny. You know I can't abide pork of any kind—dead *or* alive."

"What'd'ya do with it? Turn it loose?"

He shook his head. "I might despise pigs, but I couldn't turn the thing loose and let a wolf or coyote get it." He looked into his mug and swirled the coffee. "I gave it to the next family I came across. They were mighty glad to have it."

"How many of them folks that you stayed with fixed bacon or sausage for breakfast?"

"I don't want to talk about that." But there was something he needed to discuss. "I'm not sure that I'm cut out to be a traveling preacher."

Pete sipped his coffee. "How come?"

He shrugged. "I think I'd rather be a minister in a small town where I could shepherd folks instead of just dropping a sermon and riding on, not knowing how folks are until I come around again the next month." He'd traveled from one place to another as a kid and didn't cotton to doing that again. He hadn't lived in the same place more than a couple of years until he moved in with Pete. One thing was certain: With the exception of the pork he was often offered, he had eaten plenty of good home cooking on the circuit—something he and Pete often lacked.

"Well. . .that's more'n you knew last month."

Noah nodded. The older man had a way of putting things in perspective. "Yeah, I guess you're right."

Pete stared at him for a few moments, and Noah wondered what he was thinking. "Got me a letter whilst you was gone."

"Who from?"

"Thomas Taylor."

Noah stiffened, tightening his hold on his cup, remembering the man from the town he wanted only to forget. "Why would Reverend Taylor write to you?"

"So you know him, huh?"

Noah nodded. Was Thomas Taylor still the minister in Lookout, or had he moved on? Was *she* still there?

"We've writ to each other for years. Thomas used to be a student of mine."

Noah stood so fast that the chair fell back and banged against the floor. He picked it up and pushed it under the table. "How come you never told me about that?"

Pete shrugged one shoulder. "Didn't see how it mattered."

He gripped the back of the chair until his knuckles turned white. "It matters."

His mentor shook his head. "What happened in Lookout is over and done with. You've gotta let go of the past, son. It'll eat a hole in your belly and ruin your future."

"I've tried. Nothing I do washes that town from my mind."

"Just what was it that the town did to you?" Pete scratched his temple. "I don't recollect you ever sayin' much about it."

Noah stared out the window. Of all the places he had lived, Lookout was the one that had left the worst taste in his mouth. It was the one place he'd never talk about much to Pete. He didn't understand himself why the memories of that town bothered him so much, so how could he explain it to his friend?

"Well, anyhow. Thomas is takin' a leave of absence. His wife's ma is doin' poorly, and they're traveling over to Fort Worth to tend her. He didn't know how long he'd be gone, so he asked me to take his place."

Watching Rebel roll on his back in the grass of the pasture, Noah thought how lonely this place would be without Pete. And he'd have to eat his own cooking again. "You gonna do it?"

Pete didn't respond, and when Noah heard the chair creak, he turned from the window. His friend stood with his hands on the back of the chair, staring at the table. Generally, that meant Pete was sorting something out in his head. Noah waited.

"Actually. . ." The old man looked up, his expression unreadable. "I prayed 'bout it and feel you're the one who's s'posed to go."

"Me! You can't be serious." Noah thought up a hundred reasons why he couldn't go. At twenty-three, he was far too young and inexperienced to pastor a church, as much as he might desire to. And he wasn't married. Nor had he been to seminary. The only credentials he had was the knowledge he'd gained from Pete's years of teaching him the Bible, a mail-order certificate he'd received after completing a series of lessons on the scriptures, and years of hard living before he came to Christ.

"Serious as a prairie wildfire durin' a drought."

Noah ran his hand through his hair, remembering all the things that had happened in Lookout. "I can't do it."

He couldn't go back there. Not when so many memories of the place still haunted his dreams. "I won't."

Pete harrumphed. "You just said you'd prefer to shepherd a flock in a town rather than ridin' a circuit. Well, here's your chance to do that."

"No fair using my own words against me."

"All I'm asking you t'do is pray about it. Will you do that?"

Noah stared at the scratched wooden floor and heaved a sigh. The old man didn't know the meaning of playing fair.

Chapter 2

Jack lay on her side, squinting out the window—directly at the mayor's house. The bright light caused an ache deep in her head, but it wasn't as bad now as it had been when she'd first fallen. Closing her eyes, she willed her blurry vision away. She'd been in bed for three days now, and neither the doctor nor her mother would let her get up. Sweat dampened her cheek where it lay against her arm. If she didn't get out of this room soon, she'd go plumb loco.

Yesterday, between headaches, she'd spent the afternoon trying to think of a story angle, even though she hadn't heard a peep up on the mayor's roof. What could he be planning? Mayor Burke wanted Lookout to grow, despite the fact many of the town's residents preferred to keep it small. She exhaled a sigh. She needed to get out of this bed.

Looking around the bedroom she shared with her two sisters, she pretended it was all hers. The pale floral wallpaper that the bedroom had been decorated in when she first moved in after Shannon O'Neil had married ten years ago had been stripped off and painted a soft green. Floral curtains had replaced the spring green ones, reminding her of a flower garden. But that had been many years ago, and now the room needed to be redone. Perhaps she'd talk to her ma about painting it lavender, even though the room had always been called "the green room."

"Ugh!" She smacked the mattress. How could she be so bored that she was actually redoing her room?

She heard a noise, and then the bed creaked and the mattress tilted. A small body crashed into her back, sending sharp pain spiraling down her leg. Jack sucked in a breath. Her younger sister's giggles softened the throbbing ache. Jack rolled over on her back, wincing at the stabbing in her head. "What are you doing in here, Emmie?"

The sweet urchin patted Jack's stomach. "No no, sleep. The sun camed up."

Jack stroked Emma's wispy blond hair. "I'm sick—sort of."

Emma scowled, her little brows dipping. She turned and reached toward Jack's injured knee, which the doctor had wrapped in a bandage. Emma patted it. "Sissy gots a owee."

Jack's mother rushed in the door—as much as she rushed these days—relief evident when she spotted Emma. "What are you doing upstairs, young lady?"

Emma fell back against Jack's arm. "Me sick."

Her ma bit back a smile and crossed the room. She felt Emma's head. "Oh my, if you're so sick, I guess I should put you in your own bed."

Emma elbowed Jack's chest and shot upward to sit. "Me all better now."

Jack grinned at her ma. "Me better now, too."

Her mother shook her head and smiled, her light blue eyes twinkling. "What am I going to do with you two?"

Emma stood and bounced on the bed. Gritting her teeth, Jack turned her head so her mother wouldn't see her pain.

"That's enough, Miss Emma." Ma picked up her youngest daughter and set her on the floor. "Let's go back downstairs." She patted Jack's hip. "Do you need anything?"

"I'd like to go downstairs. I'm going batty being unable to move or see anyone."

Her mother pressed her hand against her rounded stomach. "You know I can't help you down, and Luke's not home right now. Besides, the doctor said to stay abed for a week."

Emma grabbed Abby's doll off her bed and hugged it.

Jack placed her arms behind her head and sighed. "I know, but I'm bored to death up here. I need something to do."

"Oh, that reminds me. I brought you something." A smile twittered on Ma's lips. She reached into her apron, pulled out a newspaper, then crossed her arms. "Now that you're feeling better, would you mind explaining why you haven't told me you were getting married?"

"What?" Confusion clouded her thoughts as she grasped for a memory of a wedding proposal. "I'm not getting married. What are you talking about?"

"Hmm. . .must be that head wound causing you to forget." Ma tossed the paper on the bed. "By the way, the new minister is arriving sometime today. I've got to get the pies out of the oven and then see to his room."

"Me get pie!" Emma shot out of the room, leaving the forgotten doll on the floor.

"Oh, no you don't, little missy. Don't you touch that stove." With a fist pressed into the small of her back, Ma trudged out the door, leaving Jack in silence again.

She scooted up in the bed, trying to ignore the pain in every part of her body, and unfolded the newspaper. Her heart jolted, just as it had when she'd slid off the mayor's roof. The skin on her face tightened, and the blood drained from her face as she read the headline: Billy Morgan Saves Fiancée's Life.

Jack's mouth went dry, and the words on the paper blurred as her hands started trembling. "No!"

The whole town would think she was marrying Billy Morgan.

Not in a thousand years.

Not if he were the only man in Texas.

She laid her head back and closed her eyes. This was the worst thing to happen to her since Butch Laird painted *Jack is a liar* all over the town's buildings, ten years ago.

"How will I ever live this down?"

She heard Abby giggle and clomp up the stairs just before she entered the room with Tessa Morgan and Penny Dempsey. Abby leaned against the doorframe. "You got guests, Sissy."

Tessa trounced in, a smile twittering on her lips. "You're marrying my brother? When were you planning on telling me? You know that means we'll be sisters, Jacqueline."

Tessa twisted back and forth, obviously proud of herself. For years she had tried to get Jack to see Billy's virtues, but as far as Jack was concerned, he didn't have a single one. The only reason he turned her head at all was because of his handsome looks, with that white blond hair and those deep blue eyes. But good looks alone weren't nearly enough to persuade her to marry him. She knew too much about him. Had seen his ornery side too many times.

Penny glanced at Tessa, then sent a sympathetic look at Jack. "Congratulations. . .I guess."

"Penny!" Tessa whacked her friend on the arm. "You sound as if you're sad. I think it's perfectly wonderful that Jacqueline is marrying Billy."

Jack groaned and bounced her head against the wall, stopping when a fist of pain clutched her head. She gazed at her sister, still lingering at the door, then lifted her finger. "Out, Abby."

The child swung back and forth, her blue skirts swaying like a bell. "It's my room, too."

"Yes, but I have friends visiting, and I'm stuck in bed, so we have to stay in here. Please go downstairs."

Abby stared at her for a moment, then noticed her doll on the floor. "Oh, Nellie. Did you fall out of bed like Sissy fell off that roof?" She rushed over, picked up Nellie, and hugged her.

"I didn't fall." Jack realized the ridiculousness of that statement the moment it left her mouth. "I just. . .uh. . .slipped."

Abby's eyes glimmered, and Jack knew she hadn't fooled her five-year-old sister. Abby stuck out her tongue at Jack and flounced out the door.

Tessa shuddered and dropped onto Abby's bed. "For heaven's sake. I'm so glad I don't have any little brothers or sisters. They can be such a pain in the neck."

Jack twisted her lips to one side, knowing that's probably exactly what Billy thought of Tessa. Her own siblings irritated her at times, but she loved them fiercely and would protect them for all she was worth. Tessa also annoyed her on many occasions, but she and Penny were her best friends, the only women her age in town. Tessa would be disappointed, but Jack had to set the record straight. "I am *not* marrying Billy."

Tessa's surprised gaze darted to her. "But—but, the paper says you are."

It was Jack's turn to smirk. "You can't believe everything you read in the newspaper." While she tried hard to be accurate in the stories she wrote, she knew the paper's editor, Jenny Evans, sometimes stretched the truth to make the news more interesting and to sell more papers.

"Billy will be heartbroken. You know he's in love with you." Tessa's bottom lip pushed out in a pout that didn't look good on a grown woman. She tossed her curls over her shoulder. "I don't know why you don't like him. He's comely, isn't he, Penny?"

Penny was wise enough not to step in that quagmire, Jack was certain. Her friend's eyes lit up unexpectedly. "I'll tell you who's truly handsome."

"Who?" Jack hated that she leaned forward the same as Tessa.

"The new reverend."

Tessa gasped. "You haven't seen him. Why, he isn't even in town yet. Besides, what's so interesting about an old minister?"

"Did too. I saw him get off the stage and walk over to the Taylors' house just before you came out of the store. He's so tall." Her dreamy gaze sparkled, and she touched Jack's arm. "He's even taller than your stepfather. And he certainly isn't old."

Luke was a good six feet two and the tallest man in town with the exception of Dan Howard. "What color is his hair?" Jack asked.

Penny shrugged. "I don't know. He was wearing a hat. Dark brown. Maybe black. But I can tell you one thing: he's young—and he was alone."

Tessa perked up. "Just because he was alone doesn't mean he's not married. Was he wearing a ring?"

Penny shook her head. "No." Her cheeks turned as pink as the tiny flowers on her gray dress. "At least I didn't notice one."

Tessa leaned forward, blue eyes blazing. "You looked, didn't you?"

Her words were an accusation, not a question, Jack noticed.

"So what if I did?" Penny hiked her chin. "It's not like there are many marriageable men our age in this dumpy town." Penny leaned against the wall and studied her fingernails. "If it weren't for you two, I'd go crazy. Half the time I wish we'd never moved here."

"Well, if Jacqueline doesn't want Billy, you can have him. One of you has to marry him. I don't want anyone else for a sister-in-law."

Jack glanced at Penny and noticed her friend's shudder. Penny wanted to marry Billy as little as she. Billy rarely helped his ma at the mercantile. He merely wanted to have fun. Only Tessa was blind to her brother's lack of motivation where work was concerned, probably because she hated laboring just as much.

"I'm telling you both right now: I claim first rights on the reverend. I think I'd make the perfect minister's wife." Tessa fluffed her skirt and twirled back and forth, then lifted her brows when neither woman commented.

Jack worked hard to keep a straight face. Tessa was the most spoiled person she knew. She couldn't imagine her lowering herself to tend the sick or take food to the poor like a minister's wife would surely do. She just about had her amusement under control when a completely unladylike noise erupted from Penny. Tessa glared at her, and Jack's giggle worked its way out.

"Really, Penny, you sound like a retching donkey." Tessa tossed her curls over her shoulder again and scowled as she looked at Jack. "You're laughing, too? Just what's so funny?"

After being cooped up for days with nothing to amuse her, Jack couldn't help letting her laughter break forth. Her head ached, but it was worth it. "Oh, Tessa, you'd be miserable as a pastor's wife. You know they don't make much money and have to serve the whole community. How would you get by without all your fripperies?"

"Well! I can see what you two think of me. I'm not nearly as shallow as you think." Tessa spun around and stalked out the door, stopping in the hall to glare at them. "Some friends you two turned out to be." She stomped off down the stairs.

Penny shook her head and wiped her eyes. "I didn't mean to hurt Tessa's feelings, but I couldn't keep from laughing. She's the last person I could ever see as a minister's wife."

Jack felt bad, even though she couldn't rid her mind of the humorous picture of pampered Tessa serving beside the pastor. "I know. The thought is beyond absurd, but I do feel bad for hurting her feelings."

A loud knock sounded downstairs. With her bed next to the window at the front of the house, Jack knew whenever a visitor arrived. She recognized the squeak of the front door that her ma had been hounding Luke to grease, and the word *reverend* drifted up.

He was here!

She hadn't thought about it earlier, but why wouldn't he be staying at the parsonage? And until Penny had mentioned him being young, she hadn't thought much about the man's arrival.

A sharp screech echoed from the hall, footsteps pounded up the stairs, and Tessa flew back into the room. "He's here! Right in your entryway."

"How do you know it's him?" Penny asked, her eyes dancing.

"Because he's the tallest man I've ever seen, and he's young, and he has black hair."

Penny nodded. "That does sound like him." She tiptoed to the door and looked out. "Did he see you galloping up the stairs?"

"I did not gallop, and no, he didn't see me. At least I don't think he did." Tessa skirted Penny, standing just outside the door. Jack wished she could get up and sneak a peek.

"Why do you suppose he stopped at the boardinghouse?" Penny asked.

Tessa glanced over her shoulder and lifted her index finger to her lips. "Shh! I can't hear," she whispered loudly.

Jack crossed her arms and scowled at Tessa's back. Penny suddenly sucked in a breath and backed up. Tessa let out an "eek!" and scurried back to Jack's bedside.

"They're coming upstairs." Penny pinched her cheeks, turning them a rosy red. "Maybe your ma asked him to pray for you."

"Actually, he's staying here." Jack's insides twisted as she glanced down at the pale blue bed jacket covering her nightgown. She pushed herself up straighter. "He can't see me like this. Quick, close the door."

Tessa scorched her with a narrow-eyed glare. "He's staying *here*?" She frowned and ambled across the room, seemingly in no hurry. Jack flipped the sheet over her legs and pulled it all the way up to her neck.

She heard her mother's voice as she came up the stairs. Three heads jerked toward the doorway.

"Hurry, Tessa!" Jack's heart pounded, as if something monumental was about to happen, but what was so special about meeting a new pastor? She didn't want a new one. She liked Reverend Taylor's thought-provoking messages, and his wife was one of the kindest women she knew.

"This is our second story." Her ma's voice drifted into the bedroom. "Our children have rooms on this floor, and if we have any women boarding with us, they reside here. There's a third story where you'll be staying, as well as any other men who arrive."

Tessa gave the door a half-hearted push, then spun around, walking back to the bed. "You're such a lucky dog. I'd be jealous if you hadn't said you don't plan to marry."

Ever so slowly, the door drifted open. Jack saw the back of her mother's dress. The door drifted back toward the wall and made a soft thud. Jack's heart pummeled her chest. All three women seemed to hold their breath in unison.

A surprisingly tall man with black hair glanced in as he passed the entrance to the room. He held his hat in one hand and a satchel in the other. His dark brows lifted as he noticed the trio of females staring at him. His eyes widened for a second, then he yanked his gaze away. Suddenly, it flew back to Jack, setting her heart pounding as if she'd run a long race. His steps slowed, and for the briefest of moments, she felt as if they alone were connected. She swallowed hard.

A tiny smile lifted the corners of his lips; then he jerked his head forward again and strode out of sight.

Penny glided over to Abby's bed and dropped down. "Oh my. He's so handsome."

Tessa flopped down and bumped Penny's shoulder. "Heavens to Betsy, I think I'm in love."

"Get in line." Penny stared at the door as if she could conjure up the man again.

Shaking her head, Tessa frowned. "I already claimed him for myself."

Penny gazed at Jack with a knowing look. Heat raced to Jack's cheeks, and she broke her friend's gaze. Had Penny noticed the way the man stared at her? Downright scandalous behavior for a minister, if someone asked for her opinion.

Jack laid her head back, feeling exhausted but also exhilarated. Irritated but intrigued. Why should one look from a handsome man set her heart to throbbing? Perhaps she'd simply had too much excitement today.

On second thought, the investigator in her went on alert. She had the oddest feeling that she'd seen the man before.

Tessa preened again. "Did you see how he had to take a second glance at me?"

Penny's gaze shot across the room to Jack's. "Yes, he couldn't take his eyes off of you."

Heat scorched Jack's cheeks, irritating her even more. She never blushed.

"I don't suppose you'll be able to attend the social this Saturday, what with your leg hurt and all," Tessa said. "I'll make sure to greet the new minister and welcome him to Lookout. Who would have thought he'd be our age?"

"I don't think he's our age. He looks a bit older—in his mid-twenties maybe, and I'm not going if you aren't, Jack." Penny smiled at her. "In fact, I'll come and keep you company since you'll probably be all alone if your family goes."

"Ma will stay home, and Papa will stay with her unless there's some kind of problem in town. Besides, I should be able to leave my bed by then."

"But you won't be able to leave the house yet." Tessa stood, straightened her skirt, and flounced to the door. "I'm going to the dressmaker's shop. I'll need something extra special to attract that man."

After Tessa left, Penny shook her head and giggled. "I declare, that girl and her high ideas. If she was the parson's wife—well, I can't even imagine that."

Jack grinned. "Tessa is one of a kind, that's for certain. But she's a good friend."

Penny lifted her brows. "Hmm. . .I saw the way that man looked at you. He didn't even notice Tessa and me. He must like redheads."

Jack squealed and tossed a pillow at her friend. Penny dodged it, giggling. "I do not have red hair. It's auburn."

"Don't matter what color it is—that minister couldn't take his eyes off you."

Jack fingered the edge of the sheet, remembering how she used to cower in the corner whenever her first father went on a drunken rampage. She never wanted to feel afraid like that again. "It doesn't matter. I'm not interested in gaining a man's attention. I don't ever plan to marry."

Penny gasped and hugged the pillow. "Stop saying that. One of these days, you'll meet some man who'll sweep you off your feet, and you'll regret those words. I don't know why you feel that way, anyhow."

"Nope, I won't." Jack shook her head. "You don't know how things were when I was little and my first pa was alive. He was just plain mean and a liar to boot."

Penny crossed the room and placed the pillow behind Jack. She rested her hand on Jack's shoulder. "I'm sorry you had to live through that, but my pa was the kindest man on earth, just like Luke is. You've lived with a good man for a pa for a long while. You need to bury your past, so that it doesn't affect your future."

Jack crossed her arms and stared at the dust motes floating on a ray of sunshine that had crept into her room. How could anyone who hadn't lived through what she had empathize with her deep-set fear? Not even having a kindhearted stepfather had driven it totally away. She was afraid to believe it was possible to have a marriage like her ma and Luke had. What if the dream never came true? "You don't understand."

Penny smiled gently. "I know, but I'm praying that God will help you. I'd better head home. Mama will be wanting my help with the chores."

Jack watched her friend leave. Penny was sweet, but she didn't understand the scars an abusive father could leave on a child.

She laid her head back, thinking of the handsome pastor. He was young. And why had he stared at her? Had her ma told him about her injury, making him curious?

The investigator in her sensed there was more to him than one glance could take in. But one thing was for certain: If Tessa wanted him, she could have him.

Jack had no desire to chase after a man. As long as she never married, a man couldn't hurt her.

Chapter 3

Noah followed Mrs. Davis into the tidy room.

"I hope you'll be. . .comfortable here, Reverend. . .Jeffers." Her chest rose and fell as she struggled to catch her breath. Leaning against the door, she supported her large stomach with one hand while the other was splayed across her chest. She looked as if she could give birth any moment.

Noah felt a warm flush creep up his neck at the thought. "Would you care to sit down for a moment?"

"No, but thank you. Those stairs get steeper every day." She smiled and glanced away as if embarrassed to hint at her condition. "My eldest daughter has been tending these rooms lately, but her injury has her in bed all week. My husband and I are delighted to have you staying with us."

"This is far more than I expected, Mrs. Davis." His gaze scanned the two-room suite. The walls were painted a light blue, and white curtains with small navy flowers fluttered at the open window. A dark blue sofa rested along one wall, with a nice-sized walnut desk against another, and a table with two chairs beside the third wall. He could see one corner of a bed covered with a colorful quilt through the doorway of the other room. "I'm not sure I've ever stayed anywhere this fine, ma'am."

Mrs. Davis beamed. She'd aged some in the years he'd been gone from town, but she was still a pretty woman. "I'm glad you like it. I serve breakfast at seven, dinner at noon, and supper at six. Be sure to let me know if you have an aversion to any particular foods and if you get hungry and would like a snack. I like to satisfy my guests."

He smiled and set his satchel on the sofa. "Do you need help getting downstairs, ma'am?"

She swiveled her hand in the air, then laid it on her chest again. "Thank you, but I hobble up and down these steps all day. I do need to get back downstairs, though. I don't dare leave my son, Alan, watching his sisters for long. That's a recipe for disaster."

She ambled out the door, and he followed. "Might I ask a question before you go?"

She stopped and nodded, her pale blue eyes kind but assessing.

He needed to think how to word things without letting her know just how much he knew about her family. His heart hammered in his chest. He hated deception, but he wasn't yet ready to reveal his true identity. He'd recognized Jacqueline the moment his eyes had connected with hers. She was no longer the ornery child he remembered, but a beautiful young lady who'd sent his pulse soaring. He prayed nothing was seriously wrong with her. "I. . .uh. . .happened to notice a woman in her bed on the second floor when the door blew open as I was passing." He warmed his face to admit he'd looked in the room, but he hadn't expected anyone to be in there, much less three young women. "I'm assuming that was your. . .uh. . .daughter. Could I inquire if her injury was serious?"

"Yes, you may." Mrs. Davis nodded, but her gaze held a gentle scolding. "That's my oldest daughter, Jacqueline. She fell off—" A rosy hue colored her cheeks, and she looked away for a moment. "I suppose I should just tell you, because you're sure to hear from someone else—or read about it in the newspaper. My eldest daughter is. . .umm. . .rather. . .lively. She's a reporter for our town newspaper, and for some reason, she was on a rooftop, trying to get a story, when she fell off." She rushed out the words as if they were difficult for her to admit.

Noah's stomach tightened. Jack could have easily broken her neck. "Is she all right?"

"She will be. She has a concussion, a twisted ankle, and she wrenched her knee. I dare say it won't slow her down for long. I fear my Abby is going to be just like her."

"I'll pray for her swift recovery." And to gain some common sense—although the Jack he knew rarely exercised that particular character trait. She was ruled by her heart, by impulse, more than her head.

"Thank you." She moseyed toward the stairs, then turned back. "I forgot to tell you, but the washroom is that door at the end of the hall. We recently installed indoor plumbing." She smiled, as if proud of that fact. "Please let me know if you need anything."

He nodded, relieved that she hadn't recognized him. "I will. Thanks." He watched her carefully make her way downstairs; then he strode back into his room and shut the door. The grin he'd been holding back broke loose. Jack had been on a roof. It sounded as if she hadn't changed all that much. He shook his head, but inside, he was delighted that she hadn't lost her spunk.

Noah crossed to the bedroom and looked around. This place was nice. Even better than Pete's cabin. He dropped onto the bed and laid back with his hands behind his head, remembering how Jack had stared into his eyes earlier. Had she recognized him as one of her old schoolmates?

No. There'd been curiosity in her gaze but not recognition. Besides, he was no longer the chubby youth he'd been when he lived in Lookout. He heaved a sigh. How was he going to face her every day at every meal? Pastor Taylor had offered him the use of the parsonage while they were gone, and that's where he had expected to stay, but the mayor thought he'd be more comfortable at the boardinghouse with his meals prepared each day.

Mayor Burke had no idea how difficult it would be. If Noah had known he'd be staying here, he just might not have come.

He stared up at the ceiling. No, that wasn't true. God had made it clear that Lookout was where He wanted him.

He rolled onto his side and heaved a heavy breath. Lookout, Texas, was the last place he'd ever expected to be again. Nothing good had ever happened to him here.

Jack hobbled around her room, testing out the crutches Luke had borrowed from the doctor. They pinched her underarms, even through the fabric of her dress, but they meant mobility and a chance to leave her room. Luke leaned against the doorframe, watching her. A hammering resonated in her head like Dan Howard pounding a horseshoe on his anvil, but she shoved away the pain. If Luke knew about it, she'd be back in bed before she could bat an eyelash.

She forced a smile. "Well, what do you think?"

Luke grunted and watched her. "I think you should still be in bed, but I doubt you want to hear that."

She grinned at his candidness. "Oh, c'mon, Papa. I'm going loco stuck in this room."

"I kind of thought you might like hiding up here."

She frowned. "Why?"

"Oh, I don't know. Maybe because you and Billy Morgan are headlining the newspaper this week."

Her mouth suddenly went dry. "It's all a horrible mistake."

"You're saying you're not marrying him?"

She gasped. "Eww! No! You should know I'd never marry that hooligan. He reminds me too much of Butch Laird, and well, you know how I feel about him."

"You don't know how glad I am to hear that, Half Bit. I was worried you'd taken leave of your senses." Luke forked his fingers through his hair and blew out a loud breath. "Morgan isn't the kind of man I want you associating with, much less marrying, even if his sister is one of your good friends."

"Have no fear. Jenny took advantage of something Billy said when I was on that roof, but there's no backbone to it. He never actually asked me to marry him, and I would never agree if he did. I don't care what Tessa says about him."

Luke relaxed. "Good. God has a special man out there for you. It's worth waiting until he comes along."

Jack snorted a laugh. "I'll probably be an old spinster by then."

"I didn't realize you were in a hurry to wed."

"I'm not, really. I just see how happy you and Ma are, and part of me hopes I can find that for myself. But the other part fears getting close to a man. What if he turns out like my first father?"

Luke pursed his lips and glanced at the ceiling. "There are good men and bad in this world; you know that. Trust God to bring you the man He has for you when the time is right. And pray about it."

"I will, but don't think this talk of marriage is going to make me forget what I really want to know. Will you talk Ma into letting me come down for supper?"

He narrowed his eyes. "Are you sure you're not just wanting to eat downstairs because the new minister will be there?"

All manner of thoughts dashed through her mind. The memory of that brief connection she felt when their gazes had locked buzzed in her mind. He was so tall and good looking. So young. She'd expected an older man to replace Reverend Taylor, not someone just a few years older than she. How could he have enough life experience to be a decent pastor?

Luke's brows lifted when she didn't respond to his questions. A knowing smirk twisted his lips.

She leaned heavily on her crutches, her knee ranting at her for being on her feet, and lifted a hand. "It's not what you're thinking. Tessa has already claimed him, and Penny is besotted, although I don't see how they both can have the same man. We might have to have another bride contest." She grinned, hoping the reminder of Luke's mail-order bride fiasco before he married her mother would lighten him up.

"Now who's changing the subject?" Luke's penetrating brown eyes stared into hers. He pushed away from the door and crossed his arms over his chest. "I was a soldier for a decade, and I've been a marshal and your stepfather for another ten years. You can't pull the wool over my eyes. What are you up to, Half Bit?"

She resisted the urge to squirm and instead focused her attention on backing up and sitting down. Her leg was beginning to throb. There was no point in trying to fool her perceptive pa. She exhaled loudly. "Jenny Evans came to visit this afternoon. She knows I'm chafing at the bit to get back to work and suggested that I do a story on the new minister, being as how he's staying here and all."

Luke lifted his chin, and she knew then he believed her. "That's not a half-bad idea, just so long as you don't push yourself too hard. A concussion is something to take seriously, not to mention your knee injury. With all the antics you've pulled over the years, I can't believe you've never broken a bone." He shook his head. "And I hope you learned your lesson." His chin went down again as he stared at her. "No more rooftops."

"I've already decided that. I know what I did was stupid, but I was desperate, and it was the only way I could think to listen in on the mayor's meeting."

"And why was that so important? All he and the town leaders ever talk about from what I hear is town stuff."

Jack shrugged. "Jenny seemed to think Mayor Burke is up to something. Besides, he was talking to two well-dressed strangers, not the town board."

Luke leaned back against the wall. "I saw those men and wondered why they weren't staying at the boardinghouse. I know Burke's been trying to bring more businesses to town, but that's no secret."

"Jenny said something about a gambling hall."

"Has she got evidence?" Luke straightened. "That's not anything we want in Lookout. It's bad enough having the saloon. Maybe I need to have a talk with Mayor Burke."

Jack toyed with the crutch's wooden hand rest. "No evidence that I know of, but there is something else. Jenny's received unofficial word that the railroad may be adding a spur out this way."

Luke's countenance brightened. "That's great news. Sure would cut down on my being away when I have a prisoner to take to Dallas. I'm surprised I haven't heard anything about that."

"It's in the very early stages of development—if it's true at all. I was hoping the mayor would mention something about that in his meeting."

"Ah, now I understand why you'd risk your neck. That would be some story if you could get proof and be the first to write about it."

Jack nodded. "Yeah, but I don't guess that's going to happen with me laid up like I am."

Luke crossed the room and took the crutches from her. "Well, don't be so down in the dumps. This week of bed rest will be over before you know it. And I'll talk to your ma and see if she'll let you come to dinner tonight, since it's our first family meal with the new minister. If she agrees, I can carry you downstairs."

"I'd appreciate that, Papa." She nibbled her lower lip, not wanting to voice her other thought. Still, if Luke hadn't thought of it yet, he soon would. "What will happen to Garrett's business if the railroad comes here? I mean, he can still deliver freight from the depot out to area ranches, but it seems it would cut his business sharply since he would no longer be needed to pick up deliveries in Dallas. It would be much quicker for them to come by train."

"Hmm, I hadn't thought of that. I'll talk to him about that. He's been thinking of making some changes anyway. Might be a good time."

Jack leaned forward. "What kind of changes?"

"Ah, no you don't." Luke grinned and tweaked the end of her nose. "I'm not one of those ogling, loose-lipped sources you can bat your long lashes at and get to spill the beans. If and when Garrett decides to make a change, you'll find out like everyone else."

She lifted her wrapped leg onto the bed, scooted up against her pillows, and faked a glare. "No fair. Why'd you say anything if you weren't going to tell all? You know how curious I am."

"That I do." He placed the crutches in the corner behind the door. "Maybe hiding those there will keep your sisters from messing with them."

"I doubt it."

Luke chuckled. "Me too. I'd better get back to work. See you later."

"Don't forget to talk to Ma about supper."

Luke waved. "I won't."

She leaned her head back and closed her eyes. Having Luke become her papa was one of the best things that had ever happened to her. He was easier to talk to at times than her ma, who worried too much.

Shifting her thoughts to the minister, she wondered what his name was. A man that large had to have a strong name like Sam or Duke, but then Duke hardly sounded like a pastor's name. Max would have been perfect, but that had been the name of her and Luke's dog. The old mutt had been dead more than two years, and she still missed him.

On second thought, she hoped that wasn't the preacher's name. He'd have to be very special to deserve the same name as her beloved dog.

Fragrant aromas emanating from the kitchen two stories below his room pulled Noah away from his studies. His stomach growled, reminding him that he hadn't eaten since breakfast. He stood and stretched then strode to the bedroom window that gave him a bird's-eye view of Main Street.

Lookout had certainly grown since he was last here. The town had been shaped like a capital E before, but now it spread out almost clear to the Addams River. If he had to guess, his best estimate was that it had tripled in size. Pretty unusual for a town so far away from the nearest train depot. But folks in Texas tended to congregate wherever the water was, and Lookout had the river on two sides.

Feminine squeals burst into his thoughts, and he glanced down, his gaze landing on the porch roof. Jack's room was directly below his. He could hear high-pitched laughter emanating from her open window and wondered what she and her friends found so amusing. He didn't like the thought of her hobbled to a bed. She was like a butterfly that needed to be free—free to flit from flower to flower, brightening the world with her beauty.

"Mercy!" He sounded like a poet or something. He'd best stay focused and remember that Jack had done her fair share to get him in trouble more than once. He'd tried to be her friend, but as a young girl, she'd lied, connived, and partnered with those two male friends of hers to pull tricks on him. He ran his hand through his hair and paced into the parlor. Hadn't he given all those bad memories to God? Hadn't he forgiven Jack?

If just the briefest glance had him warring with his thoughts again, what would happen if he ever talked to her? How could he minister to the townsfolk when half his thoughts centered on Jack?

He'd never been clear about what he felt when she was near. He'd longed to be her friend more than once, but he'd hated her, too. Her lies had gotten him in trouble, both with the marshal and with his own pa.

But maybe she'd changed.

He certainly hoped so. Back in the bedroom, he knelt down and rested his head against the quilt. It smelled clean and fresh—of sunshine. Had Jack made the bed with her own hands?

"Ugh! Help me, Father. My job is to minister to this town. To make up for my past offenses here by making retribution for what I did before I knew You. Help me, Lord, to stay focused and to treat Jacqueline Hamil—uh—Davis like any other woman I encounter."

But she wasn't like any other he'd ever known—and that was the problem.

She intrigued him. Riled him. Made him want to throttle her—kiss her.

He bolted to his feet and ran his hand through his hair. "I can't do this."

Bending, he yanked his satchel out from under the bed and opened it. He hurried to the dresser and snatched up his undergarments and tossed them at the bag. Then he caught his reflection in the mirror above the chest of drawers.

He stared at himself. No longer was he the beaten-down son of a cruel drunkard. He was the son of a King. The King.

What kind of man was he if he couldn't handle one feisty redhead?

Heaving a sigh from deep within, he gathered his things and shoved them back in the drawer. Pete was counting on him. So was Pastor Taylor and the town of Lookout. Maybe even Jack needed him.

No—he couldn't think that. He'd focus on the town. Not everyone here knew God. Folks needed to hear the Bible—needed to hear about God's love. He closed his eyes, determination overcoming his doubts. He'd studied years for this moment, and Pete thought he was ready. He *was* ready.

He tucked in his shirt, then combed his hair and headed downstairs. He wouldn't let his eyes stray as he passed her room. Hadn't Mrs. Davis said Jack would be in bed a week? At least he'd have several days more than he'd first expected to get used to seeing her regularly. By the end of the week, he'd be ready to face her.

He had to be.

Chapter 4

Dallas

Carly Payton dabbed her eyes with her handkerchief, then blew her nose and shoved the fabric square back into her pocket. She washed her hands and returned to her task. Her heart ached today as much as it had that first day she'd been locked up in the Lookout jail for bank robbery. She missed Tillie. She thought back to the funeral Reverend Barker had spoken at only an hour ago. Shaking her head, she placed cookies one by one onto Tillie's favorite platter. A man shouldn't have to preach his wife's funeral, especially a man who'd been married to that woman for fifty-two years.

Now it would be her job to care for the elderly pastor and to offer words of comfort to him as he and Tillie had when she'd first come to live with the Barkers. Carly walked down the hall, carrying the platter in Tillie's stead and trying to keep it from shaking. A number of people from the church had come to offer their condolences to Reverend Barker, but she never knew how they'd treat her. Few had accepted her like the Barkers. Not even the "good" church people. Tillie had said to give them time, but she'd waited four years and still didn't feel a part of the small community church. At the sound of raised voices coming from the parlor, she quickened her steps. Why would anyone be arguing with the pastor today?

She forced a smile as she strode into the room. Every head

swiveled toward her, but instead of finding a welcoming smile, she encountered six pairs of glaring eyes. An uncomfortable silence reigned. All that remained of the earlier crowd was the church's three elders and their wives. Mrs. Harding, wife of the head elder, stared down her long, pointed nose at her. Swallowing hard, Carly ducked her head, skirted around the two men standing in the parlor's entrance, and set the platter on the coffee table. She checked the coffeepot and hurried out of the room, finally exhaling the breath she'd been holding.

"It's not proper for that woman to live here, I tell you," a female voice spat.

Carly halted just outside the parlor door. Were they talking about *her*?

"I have to agree with Gertie, Bennett." Carly recognized Mr. Harding's voice. "I tolerated you letting that ex-convict live in your home when your wife was alive, just because Tillie needed the help, but with her gone now, you need to get rid of that jailbird."

Carly clutched the doorframe to the kitchen. They wanted Reverend Barker to turn her out? How could they broach such a topic on the day Reverend Barker buried his wife? Who would take care of him? Who would fix his coffee just how he liked it with a spoonful of sugar and two mere droplets of milk?

Tears stung her eyes, and her throat clogged. "Please, Lord. No."

She slipped back into the kitchen, where she and Tillie had spent so many wonderful hours together, baking and talking about God and the scriptures. For four years she'd lived in the Barkers' home, after finally leaving the prison she'd been locked away in for six long years. Carly pulled out a chair and slumped into it. Her heart felt as if it had been dragged behind a runaway horse. Foolishly, somewhere along the line, she'd come to think of this place as home. After all, she'd lived here longer than she had any other place—except prison—and she could hardly call that horrid place home.

How could she have let her guard down? Other than coming to know God and living with the Barkers, nothing good had ever happened in her life. She was stupid to have hoped life would continue on as it had when she knew Tillie was so ill. Lifting her head off her arm, she looked around the cheery kitchen. She should have been better prepared for this day.

Perhaps if she proved herself indispensible, Reverend Barker would let her stay and not bend to the will of his elders. She pushed up from the chair and hurried outside to pump a bucket of water. Then she dumped it in the stove's reservoir to heat. The beef stew was already simmering for their supper, and all she had left to do was mix up a batch of biscuits.

A short while later, the front door banged, and Carly jumped. Had those busybodies finally left?

She dusted off her hands and shoved the biscuits into the oven. Recognizing the pastor's shuffling, she turned, her heartbeat running like a chicken chased by a fox. Reverend Barker stopped just inside the kitchen door, his gaze searching the room as if he expected to find Tillie there. His eyes downcast, he stood silently, his shoulders bearing more of a burden than they should have.

Carly pulled out his chair. "Come sit down, sir. It's been a long day."

He nodded and ambled forward, dropping hard into his chair. She'd rarely seen him so listless. He'd loved his wife dearly and had to be missing her. Why didn't the church elders realize this and let him be, at least for today? Quickly she fixed him a cup of coffee, adding just the right amount of sugar and milk, then set it before him. His wrinkled hands wrapped around the cup, and he sighed. "Have a seat, if you will."

Carly lowered herself to the edge of her chair. Her chair—had she ever actually had one to call her own before living here?

Her legs quivered, and she pressed her hands into her lap, hoping to make them stop.

"I reckon you heard them. They didn't make any effort to soften their voices."

Carly nodded and swallowed hard. How could she think of herself when he had lost so much today? She reached out and laid a hand on his arm. "We don't have to talk about those things today. You've had enough stress for the day already. Why don't you take a nap until supper's ready?"

He rested his hand over hers, and she studied the differences.

Hers was smooth and lightly tanned from working in the garden, while his skin was thin, creased, spotted, and showed his blue veins. They were so different, yet she loved him as if he were her own grandfather.

He glanced up with tears in his eyes. Her lower lip wobbled at seeing him so distressed. "You know I care for you like you were my own daughter?"

She nodded but couldn't swallow the lump in her throat.

"The elders don't think it's proper for you to stay here now that T–Tillie is gone." He looked away and brushed his damp cheek with his shoulder. "I don't want you to go, but being the minister here, I have to maintain a presence that is above reproach. I can't be a stumbling block to others by having an unmarried woman living in my home."

Carly blinked, trying hard to keep her tears at bay. She was a stumbling block?

He squeezed her arm. "I don't want you to go. You understand that, don't you?"

She nodded. "B–But. . .who will take care of you?"

"I've always relied on the Lord, and He won't fail me now."

"But you also had Tillie. Who will cook your meals and clean your clothes?"

He gave her a teary-eyed, tight-lipped smile. "I think it's best if I go live with Maudie."

Carly jumped up, no longer able to keep from moving. She paced to the open back door and stared out at the garden she and Tillie had spent so many hours cultivating. She'd never see its harvest now, but her thoughts were more for him than herself. He'd spent the past thirty years living in this house and ministering to this town. He was too old to be forced into such a change. Didn't the elders give a fig about him after all he'd sacrificed for them? "You'd have to give up your ministry if you moved to San Antonio to live with your daughter."

He took a sip of coffee and shook his head. "I can minister anywhere for the Good Lord, and to be honest, I just don't think I can live in this house without my Tillie." He swiped his eyes again. "But I'm more concerned with what will happen to you. I told the board they would need to provide you with a train ticket to wherever you'd want to go and a month's wages. And Mrs. Wilcox said you could stay with them until Thursday, when the train comes." He fell back against the chair, his arms dangling beside him as if spent.

Carly's thoughts turned to Mrs. Wilcox's son. The man had made it clear that he wanted her for his own, but she couldn't stand him. Just the way he looked at her made her want to go jump in the nearest horse trough and wash off. Hugh Wilcox couldn't hold down a job and preferred drinking and hanging out in the saloon to attending church and doing the Lord's work. She'd had her fill of such men during the days she was forced to live with her brother and his outlaw gang. Never again would she put herself in such a position. She shook her head. "I have a little money saved. I'll pack my things and get a room at the hotel."

He pushed to his feet, looking far older than she'd ever seen. "But that will use up some of your funds. You should take up the Wilcoxes on their offer."

She shook her head. "I can't abide living under the same roof as Hugh Wilcox."

"Ah, now I understand." He trundled to the kitchen doorway and looked back at her. "I'm sorry, Carly. You have to know this isn't what I wanted."

She pressed her lips together and nodded. "I know. I'll pack while supper is cooking and then leave right after we eat and I clean up in here."

He nodded, then disappeared down the hall.

Carly leaned her head against the back-door jamb and closed her eyes. "What do I do now, Lord? Show me where to go."

She had lived in many places, but she had no desire to see any of them again except one. Lookout. Rachel still ran the boardinghouse there, and the woman's letters had been the only thing besides God's fortitude that had helped her make it through those horrible years of prison.

Could she return there? Would the townsfolk welcome her back or take the first opportunity they could to get rid of her like the elders had?

"Where do I go, Lord?"

Lookout. You'll find what you seek there.

Carly stared out the door. Was that God speaking to her? Or was that only her own wishful thinking?

And just what was it she desired?

A permanent home.

People who cared about her.

Someone to love.

Dare she hope she could fulfill all her dreams in Lookout, Texas?

~

At the bottom of the steps, Noah stopped in the entryway and glanced into the parlor, finding it empty. The front door suddenly burst open, and a young boy ran in, colliding with him. The dirty child bounced off Noah's leg, stumbled, then righted himself.

"Sorry, mister."

Noah smiled and shook his head, then closed the door. "That's all right."

The boy turned into the kitchen without so much as a second glance. Noah wasn't certain if he should follow him, go on into the dining room, or wait in the parlor. He hadn't stayed in many boardinghouses before.

A high-pitched scream reverberated down the hall, and Noah took a step toward the kitchen.

"Alan Michael Davis, don't you touch those biscuits until you wash up! Abby, stop screaming in the house."

Even though he couldn't see the boardinghouse owner, Noah recognized Mrs. Davis's voice coming from the kitchen's open doorway. So the boy was one of hers. He'd seen the woman's two little girls when he'd arrived, but not her son. He must have been at school.

"But I'm starvin', Ma."

"You get yourself outside and wash up, young man. Dinner is ready."

Mrs. Davis had her hands full, from the sound of it. Too bad Jack was laid up.

Noah's mouth watered at the scent of fresh-baked biscuits, something he and Pete didn't often have. A man could only eat so many pancakes and cornbread. He walked to the parlor and looked around, his stomach complaining at his turning away from the kitchen.

He studied the tidy room. The walls were papered in a blue and white floral pattern. Two dark blue sofas lined the east and west walls with a pair of deep red wingback chairs facing one of them and a low table in front of the other. A piano sat in the far corner, and ivory-colored curtains fluttered on the afternoon breeze. He'd stayed in a half-dozen or more homes while riding his circuit, but he'd never gotten comfortable. Moving from house to house reminded him too much of his childhood—of never staying in one place for much more than a year or so.

He shook off the unwanted memories. Could he get comfortable in this house? He peered over his shoulders at the stairs that led up to Jack's room. Not likely. Not with *her* living here.

He checked his pocket watch and ambled to the dining room, standing in the doorway. The toddler Mrs. Davis had been holding on her hip when he first arrived was seated in a child's chair, munching on half a biscuit. The cute, blond little girl with pale blue eyes like her mother's studied him for a moment, then grinned and held up her biscuit.

"Bicket."

"Is it good?" he asked.

She nodded and grinned, revealing tiny teeth. The child was obviously used to having strangers in her home. "Bite?"

"No, thanks. I'll wait for the rest of the folks."

Mrs. Davis entered, carrying a huge platter covered with a towel. The fragrant odor of meat teased his senses. She set the heavy load on the buffet lining the wall to his right. She smiled and used her wrist to move the hair from her eyes. "Afternoon, Reverend. Dinner will be served in a few minutes. How's your room?"

"It's far more than I expected." Heat rushed up his neck when she lifted her brows. "It's nice. Very nice. I didn't know I'd be getting two rooms."

"I'm glad you like it. Be sure you let me know if there's anything you need. Did I mention the fresh towels in the washroom?" She fanned her flushed face and continued when he nodded. "Why don't you go ahead and take a seat?"

He glanced at the twelve empty chairs and felt odd sitting before anyone else.

"Mama, me thirsty." The little girl pounded on the table with her spoon.

Mrs. Davis hurried over, picked up a cup that had been wisely set out of the child's reach, and gave her a drink. "We have one other boarder—a businessman who's in town to meet with Mr. Castleby—but I'm not certain if Mr. Cameron will be taking dinner with us or if he's dining with our bank president."

"Ow! Mama! Alan pinched me." The young blond girl Noah had seen earlier trotted into the dining room with her brother right behind her.

"I did not. I just squished a bug on her arm."

The girl glanced down, licked her finger, and wiped it across her arm. "Nuh-uh, you pinched me."

"Not on purpose." The boy glanced up at his ma with brown eyes that resembled the marshal's.

Noah studied the three children. They were an interesting combination of their parents. The boy more resembled his father with his dark hair and eyes, while the youngest girl was the spitting image of her mother, and the middle child seemed to have received traits of both parents. He'd never before considered being a father, and his thoughts immediately shifted to the auburn-haired beauty upstairs.

Noah shook his head, trying to rid his mind of the vision of Jack sitting in her bed. The boy peered up at him with an odd look on his face.

Mrs. Davis sighed. "Reverend, I don't believe I introduced my younger children to you." She patted the boy's head. "This is Alan. He's seven. The older girl is Abby, who is five, and this is Emma, who's two and a half."

"We call her Emmie." Abby reached out and snatched a piece of biscuit from in front of Emmie. The toddler squealed, then threw the hunk of biscuit she'd been munching at her sister.

"Children! Enough."

Emmie's lower lip puckered at her mother's scolding, but the other two children didn't react at all. "Abby, fetch the bowl of biscuits I made. Alan, go fill the glasses with water."

Noah watched the children do their mother's bidding, but the second she turned her back, Abby stuck her tongue out at her brother. Noah bit back a grin. So this is what he'd missed by not having siblings. He wasn't quite sure if he was relieved or not.

"I'm sorry, Reverend. I sincerely love my children, but they are a handful. They know I'm not at my best with this baby on the way, and they take full advantage."

Noah swatted his hand in the air. "It doesn't bother me, ma'am. In fact, I've never been around small children much and"—he stared at her, wondering if he would offend her—"well, I find it entertaining and informative."

She lifted her light brown brows again and gave Emmie another piece of biscuit. "Informative?"

"Yes, ma'am. As a pastor, I need to know a little bit about everything. I counsel people who are having problems sometimes, and seeing the, uh. . .natural side of children's behavior is eye-opening."

"How so?" She cocked her head.

"Um. . .well, I didn't expect them to be so devious, even when they're young—and I hope that doesn't offend you. I saw the same thing at the home of a family I stayed with that had seven children."

"No, it doesn't offend me at all. As much as I wish my children were perfect, I haven't had one that is. All of them have been lively. Emmie is probably my mildest-mannered child." She stroked the toddler's wispy blond hair. "So, have a seat. I need to fetch the rest of the food so we can eat. Luke should be home any minute."

"Is there anything I can help you with?" His gaze shot to the large container of biscuits Abby carried into the room. Her mother took the bowl and set it on the buffet.

"Thank you, but no. Everything is dished up and just needs to be brought in here." She turned and shuffled back to her kitchen.

Noah wondered how long she had before her baby was due. Surely it must be soon. He looked around the table, trying to figure out where he should sit. Did the children have their favorite spots? He finally settled opposite Emma and watched her munch on her food. She caught him staring and gazed back. Suddenly she lobbed her biscuit across the table, and the wet, gooey substance hit his cheek, clung there for a moment, then dropped into his lap.

Emma giggled, then searched the empty space in front of her. Her lower lip came out again. Noah didn't know what to do with the goo in his lap. He glanced in the kitchen, then grabbed it and tossed it back. Emma's eyes lit up, and she snatched back her treat and shoved it into her mouth.

Good thing he'd changed out of his travel clothes earlier and was wearing clean pants.

The front door opened and shut, and Noah expected to see the marshal. Instead, he heard quick footsteps hustle up the stairs, a knock, and then the creak of a door. Mrs. Davis returned with a large steaming bowl, which she placed beside the platter. His mind was running rampant, trying to guess what she'd cooked. He suspected she must be an excellent cook since she ran a boardinghouse and her family looked well-fed.

Abby followed with two small bowls filled with butter. She placed one at each end of the table then took a seat next to Emma. The five-year-old grinned at him. "We're eatin' pot roast. Don'tcha just love that?"

He nodded, and Mrs. Davis returned to her kitchen. A loud thump pulled Noah's gaze to the hall door. His pulse took off like a race horse at the sound of a starter's gun, and he shot to his feet.

There stood the marshal with Jack in his arms. Her eyes widened when her gaze collided with his. The air left Noah's lungs, and he pressed one hand against the table to steady himself. He couldn't look away for the life of him. Her medium green dress looked lovely with her reddish-brown hair. And—he took a second quick glance—bare toes peeked out from under the hem of her dress.

"Could you pull out a chair for me, Reverend?"

Noah jumped into motion at the marshal's request. He yanked out the chair beside him.

"I usually sit on the other side of Emmie so I can help feed her if she needs it," Jack offered.

"Oh." He hurried around the table, pulled out that chair, and stepped back.

Jack's gaze connected with his again, but for the first time close up. He could see the deep blue coloring and her curious stare. He forced himself to look away and hurried back to his seat. Feigning interest in the floral design of his empty plate, he kept his head down, afraid to look up now that Jack sat almost directly across from him.

His hands shook as badly as they had the first time he ever preached a sermon on a street corner. Why did she affect him like she did? Why couldn't he treat her like any other woman of marrying age? How would he eat with her right there?

Come to think of it, his appetite had fled.

Chapter 5

Jack peered over her shoulder at her stepfather as he entered the kitchen. How could he leave her alone with their guest?

Rearranging her skirts, she swallowed the lump in her throat, wondering why it bothered her so much. She'd never had a problem chatting with their visitors before, but remembering how she couldn't take her eyes from the new minister's the first time she saw him, she felt her cheeks warm. How could she have shamelessly gawked at him like that?

She peeked up, glad to see he was watching Emmie as she reached for Abby's spoon. Abby scowled at her little sister, snatched the spoon from the youngster's hand, and put it on the far side of her plate. The pastor's lip pressed tight, but the corners of his mouth turned up. His black eyes glimmered with humor—eyes that were more intriguing than those of any man she'd ever met. His thick, dark hair refused to lay in place, instead falling forward onto his tanned forehead. And he was so tall. His gaze flicked to hers, then darted away.

Alan set a glass of water beside her, and she picked it up and took a sip. Had the reverend noticed her staring? What was wrong with her?

"Alan says you're the new preacher." Abby tossed out a glare like it was a challenge. Alan set a glass next to Reverend Jeffers and glanced up with a worried look. He scowled at Abby and went back to the kitchen.

"I don't like going to church," Abby said.

Jack choked on her water and erupted into a fit of coughing. Her gaze whizzed across the table at him, and his concerned look didn't help any. She cleared her throat several times and focused on her sister. "Abby, that's a dreadful thing to say, especially to our new pastor. You apologize right now."

"No, it's all right. I appreciate Abby's honesty." He lifted a hand, palm facing outward. "I realize sitting through a church service can be difficult for youngsters." He smiled, but it did little to put her at ease.

"Have you been a minister long?" she asked.

"A little over a year."

"Mary's ma says you're too young to be a preacher." Abby tossed a sideways glance at Jack then smirked. "And you ain't got no wife, neither. Preachers gotta have wives."

He looked at Jack as if asking who Mary was. She reached across Emmie's lap and squeezed Abby's arm. "We don't repeat gossip." She gave her sister a gentle shake. "You just sit there and be quiet. You're being very rude to our guest."

Jack cast him an apologetic glance, relieved that he looked more amused than upset. "I'm sorry. Abby can be rather. . .um. . . outspoken." His lips quirked up in a smile. Then his gaze moved past her, and she heard footsteps. Her parents took their places at the table, as did Alan, who brought the last two glasses of water.

Luke looked over at Reverend Jeffers. "Would you care to ask the Lord to bless our food, Reverend?"

He gave a brief nod. "I'd be happy to." He bowed his head, and the others around the table followed. "Heavenly Father, we thank You for this delicious-smelling meal and for the hands that prepared it. We ask that You bless this food to the nourishment of our bodies, and I ask Your blessing on this household and this town. Amen."

"Good. He don't pray them long-winded prayers like Pastor Taylor did." Alan jumped out of his chair and snagged a biscuit off the buffet.

"Son, don't talk poorly of Pastor Taylor," Luke said. "He's a good man. And set that biscuit down. You know we allow our guests to go first."

Alan flopped back in his chair. "Sorry, Pa, but I'm starvin'."

"Please, Reverend, help yourself." Jack's ma held her hand toward the buffet.

The minister looked down at his plate. "Thank you, but it doesn't seem proper for me to go before you ladies and the children."

"I knew I was gonna like him." Alan grabbed his plate and jumped up, but her papa snagged her brother's arm and pressed him back onto his chair.

"Since the pastor has expressed his wishes, we'll let the ladies go first, Son."

Alan scowled into his plate, while Abby grinned. Jack could almost hear her sister's taunting, "Na–na–na–na–na! I get to go before you."

"That's kind of you, Reverend." Her mother stood, took her dish and Jack's, then soon returned with both plates filled with food.

Jack wondered how she'd manage to eat so much pork roast, green beans, and potatoes with *him* sitting across the table. And just why did that bother her so much?

She'd already decided she wasn't going to chase after him like some schoolgirl with her first crush. Tessa had made it clear that she meant to lasso the poor, unsuspecting man.

With her head lowered, she watched him through her lashes. He waved and smiled at Emmie while he waited on her siblings to fill their plates. Finally, he followed Luke to the buffet. While his back was turned, she took the opportunity to study him. Luke was a solid six feet two, so Reverend Jeffers had to be at least six feet four. His shoulders were even broader than Luke's, but he wasn't husky for a large man, nor was he a string bean. In fact, he looked well-muscled—a man more used to physical labor than studious pursuits. As far as she could tell, Noah Jeffers was close to perfect. She exhaled a heavy sigh then noticed her mother watching her. A smirk danced on her ma's lips, and a knowing gleam lit her eyes.

Appalled that her ma must think she was attracted to the

man, Jack shook her head and stabbed a bite of meat.

The minister returned with a full plate and a contented smile and sat down. She imagined a man his size had a big appetite.

"This sure looks delicious, Mrs. Davis." He poked some green beans with his fork and took a bite.

"Thank you," her ma said. "Pastor Taylor didn't tell us much about you when he mentioned you'd be taking his place. So, where do you hail from?"

"Emporia, ma'am."

"Isn't there a sawmill in Emporia?" Luke set his plate down and reached across the table for the butter.

"Yes, there is. They cut a lot of wood there, but most of the lumber is shipped by train to Houston." Using his fork, the minister lifted one corner of his meat, which he'd covered with the red-eye gravy her ma had made.

Intrigued, Jack watched him. His brow crinkled, and he leaned down, as if to sniff his food, then glanced up and caught her watching. Quickly he cut a bite of meat and shoved it in his mouth. He chewed it a few times, and she'd have sworn—if she swore—that he turned three shades of white before he all but turned green. His cheeks puffed out as if he'd belched. A panicked look engulfed his handsome face as he glanced one direction and then the other. Suddenly he leapt from his chair and rushed out of the room.

"My heavens." Her mother looked at Luke. "What do you suppose that was about?"

Luke shook his head and glanced at his plate. He blew out a sigh. "Don't know, but I'll go check on 'im."

"If'n he's done eatin', can I have his food?" Alan reached over to take the pastor's biscuit.

Her ma snapped her fingers. "Don't touch that. I'm sure he'll be right back." Then she glanced over and met Jack's eyes. Her brows lifted.

Jack shrugged. "That was the strangest thing I think I've ever seen."

Noah's stomach swirled and cramped, and he bent over the porch railing and heaved. Once he retched, his belly settled. With his hands spread apart, he leaned on the railing, his head hanging. What a fool he'd made of himself. How could he go back in there?

"You all right, Reverend?" Mr. Davis stopped a few feet behind him.

"I'm sorry, sir." He straightened, pressing a hand to his stomach, and turned. "I guess I should have told your wife that I can't eat pork. It's just that I thought your daughter—the middle one—said it was pot roast."

Luke smiled. "Abby sometimes gets confused on the meat we're having. If it looks like a roast, it's a pot roast to her."

Noah rubbed his hand across his mouth, making a mental note to look the meat over better before taking any in the future. "I hate to think I hurt your wife's feelings. I feel bad about that."

"Think nothing of it. Rachel's run this place for close to fifteen years. She's used to people having particular tastes or not being able to tolerate certain foods."

"I just don't want her going to any extra effort on my behalf."

Luke clapped him on the shoulder. "Don't worry about her. She's a good-natured woman and wants to please her guests." He stared at Noah; then his brows dipped. "Have we met before? There's something familiar about you."

Noah's heart jolted. He wasn't ready to tell people his true identity. What would the marshal say if he knew who he actually was? Would he kick him out of his home? Out of town?

A wagon rolled to a stop in the street, and the marshal turned his attention to it. He smiled. "When'd you get back home, Garrett?"

Noah studied the man in the wagon, grateful for the reprieve. He fully intended to answer the marshal's question, but he needed more time first. He had things to do in this town—to make recompense for injuries he'd caused in his youth.

"Afternoon, Luke. I just rolled into town. I suppose you've already had your lunch."

Luke shook his head. "We've just started eating. C'mon in and join us."

Noah recognized Garrett Corbett, the older of the marshal's

two cousins. The man glanced down at the mess Noah had made in the grass,then back up. His brows lifted. "Is Rachel trying out a new recipe? Or did Jack cook?"

Luke chuckled and shook his head. "Neither. This here's our new parson, Reverend Jeffers." Noah extended his hand toward Garrett.

"I'd appreciate it if y'all would call me Noah."

"Nice to meet you, Reverend." Garrett nodded."Just let me take the wagon around to the freight office and tend to my horses; then I'll wash up and come back." He clucked to the horses, and they plodded forward.

Luke waved and turned to face Noah. "Are you ready to go inside now?"

Noah hung his head. How could he face Mrs. Davis after his uncouth flight from her table? How could he face Jack?

"Don't be worrying so much, Noah. You're not the first in this house to air their paunch."

"I hope I didn't make your wife feel bad. The beans I ate were delicious."

Luke crossed the porch and opened the front door. "C'mon. Rachel will be fine. I'll explain to her."

"If you could show me where a bucket and the water is, I'll take care of"—he motioned toward the porch rail—"uh. . .that."

Luke shook his head. "No need. I'll tend to it. Just come on back inside."

Noah nodded and trudged across the porch. He hadn't been here a full day yet, and he'd already made a fool of himself. If only Abby hadn't said the meat was pot roast, then he wouldn't have taken any. He hated wasting food, but there was no way he could eat two bites of that pork—much less that large slice he'd taken. He could only hope Mrs. Davis would forgive him.

Jack watched Noah Jeffers wolf down his food—everything, that is, except his meat. Whatever had bothered him earlier no longer affected him. Perhaps he didn't like the flavor of the meat, or maybe something had gotten stuck in his throat.

"When is your next trip to Denison, Garrett?" Her mother pulled a biscuit in half and buttered both sides then handed one to Abby and the other to Emma.

"I was thinking about headin' that way in a day or two." Garrett stabbed a bite of meat and shoved it in his mouth. "Why?"

The parson turned his head away, looking pale again. Jack glanced down at her slice of pork. Was something wrong with it? She hadn't noticed that it tasted odd. She cut a bite and lifted it to her nose and took a quick sniff. Fine. No, not fine, it smelled downright tasty. She put the bite in her mouth, relishing its delicious flavor.

"I have a package that needs to be picked up at the train depot in Denison, and I wondered if you could get it for me."

Garrett nodded and forked some green beans into his mouth. "Sure thing. Do you know when it's supposed to arrive?"

Jack thought of Garrett Corbett as more of an uncle than her stepfather's cousin. Even though he was close to forty, he was still a handsome man with blond hair and eyes that often gleamed with mischief. She loved his blue eyes. If only hers were that vivid hue that put her in mind of a robin's egg instead of being so dark a blue.

"Yes, it should be there in two days."

Luke stared at Ma then lifted his brows. Jack glanced at her mother in time to catch her smothering a grin. What was that about?

She couldn't think of anything her ma had ordered. They had just celebrated Luke's birthday, and nobody else had one for a few months, so it couldn't be a present. She spent the rest of the meal contemplating that mystery. The reporter in her just couldn't let it go.

Alan stood up first. "Can I be excused?"

"*May* I," Abby stated like a little teacher.

"I asked first," Alan whined and curled up his lip at Abby.

"You may both take your dishes to the kitchen," her papa said. "Alan, fetch a bucket of water and set it on the front porch. Abby, you can help your ma clear the table and clean up."

Abby scowled and glanced at Jack. "What about Sissy?"

Her mother wiped Emmie's face with the towel tied around the girl's neck. "You know Jacqueline can't be on her feet yet. She needs to rest her knee. In fact, she shouldn't even be downstairs so soon after her accident." She cast her husband a mock glare.

Luke shrugged. "She's all right, Rachel. I'll make sure she takes things easy."

Jack's mother sighed. "Fine. I suppose it won't hurt her to rest on the sofa or even sit in a rocker on the porch for a bit."

Luke grinned and winked at Jack. She couldn't help smiling back at him. They were shameful to gang up on her ma, especially when she was going to birth a baby in the next few weeks, but Jack had to get out of that bedroom. How else was she going to get a story about the parson?

She peeked over at him. He was listening to Garrett tell a story about a duck that hitched a ride on his freight wagon. She smiled at Garrett's animated expression and his arms, which flapped like wings. Emmie giggled at him and lifted her arms up and down.

"Well, I need to get the wagon unloaded."

All three men stood at once. Luke picked up his plate, as well as Garrett's and Mr. Jeffers. "Have you heard anything from Mark lately?"

Garrett swigged back the last of his water and set the glass down. "Yep. He and Shannon are talking about maybe moving back here."

"Truly!" Jack's ma hurried back into the dining room. "It would be so nice to see them more often."

"I don't know if they will, but they're considering it since Lookout is growing so much. Dallas is gettin' really big now, and Shannon wants to raise the children in a smaller town." Garrett lifted his hat off the corner of his chair and set it on his head. "I just don't know if we have enough call for a lawyer here, though."

"The closest one I know about is in Denison, and you know that's several hours' ride away. Some of the folks who live in the small towns around Lookout may need one on an occasion." Luke wrapped his arm around Rachel's shoulders.

Garrett stretched and scratched his belly. "The food was great, as usual, Rachel. Thanks for letting me invite myself to dinner."

"Anytime." She smiled.

Garrett held his hand out to the minister. "Nice to meet you, Reverend."

"It's Noah, and a pleasure to meet you, too."

"I guess I'd better carry Half Bit back to her room, although I don't know if I can manage after eating all that good food." Luke kissed Ma's head and winked at Jack. "Maybe you could sit in the parlor for a spell until my food has time to settle."

Jack bit back a grin. "I could manage that for a while."

"Oh! You two." Ma gently swatted Luke's stomach. "You're not fooling anyone with that act of yours." She pushed away from him and grabbed the bowl of beans off the buffet.

"Ma, Alan spilled water on the floor and got my shoe wet."

Ma rolled her eyes. "I'm coming."

Luke reached down and hoisted Emmie into his arms. He nibbled her neck, eliciting a giggle from the toddler.

A melancholy smile lifted the parson's lips. He pushed away from the chair's back he'd been holding on to. "I reckon I'll go back upstairs and study my sermon some more."

Jack jumped up, immediately regretting her quick action as a sharp pain clutched her knee. She tried not to grimace but must have failed because Luke set Emma down and hurried to her side. She gazed back at Noah Jeffers, who stared at her with compassion in his obsidian eyes. "Actually, I was wondering if I could interview you for the town newspaper—the *Lookout Ledger*."

Chapter 6

Noah followed the marshal as he helped Jack make her way into the parlor. Things would have been a whole lot quicker if Noah had scooped her up in his arms and carried her, but that would hardly seem proper. He paused at the stairway that held his escape and glanced up to the second floor. The last thing he wanted was a newspaper article about him.

"You're not thinking of running out on me, are you, Reverend?" Jack's expressive tone alerted him that she'd had her eye on him and wasn't about to take no for an answer.

He resisted tugging at his collar, which suddenly seemed too tight against his throat. Sighing, he strode into the parlor as the marshal slid a chair toward the couch.

Jack discreetly lifted her injured leg onto the seat and rearranged her skirts. "Would you mind bringing me some paper and a pencil, Papa?"

"I don't mind, but be nice to him, Half Bit." The marshal flashed Noah a teasing grin. "We don't want the parson leaving town before we get to hear him preach."

Noah thought they all might just be better off if he did leave, but he kept his thoughts to himself. Doubt was something he frequently battled. Pete had told him often to not belittle his efforts, because Noah prayed hard and studied God's Word before preaching a sermon, and if his message was God-inspired, then disparaging himself was also demeaning the Lord. He perched on the end of a chair across the room from the couch where Jack sat, bouncing one leg.

His gaze ran around the large parlor, but it kept stopping at Jack, no matter how hard he tried to not look at her. She'd matured from a rowdy tomboy who preferred overalls to dresses into a lovely young woman, but the ornery gleam still sparked in her pretty eyes—eyes the color of blueberries. She flipped her waist-long hair, which was tied with a yellow ribbon, over her shoulder. He couldn't be certain until he saw her in the sunlight, but he thought that it had darkened over the years, looking more brown than red. His fingers moved, as if to reach out and touch her creamy skin, which held the faint hint of the sun. He sighed again and looked out a nearby window. Coming to Lookout had been a bad idea. If only he could convince the Lord of that—then maybe he could hightail it back to Emporia.

Jack's gaze flitted to his then back to the doorway. She fidgeted with her skirts and tugged at the cuff of each sleeve. "I wonder what's keeping Luke."

His brows lifted. "You refer to your father by his first name?"

Jack's cheeks actually pinked up. "Luke's been my stepfather for ten years now, but he's the only father I've ever cared for. I guess I sometimes call him Luke because that's how I referred to him before he married my ma."

Noah leaned back, his hands holding on to the arms of the chair. He knew that, but she didn't know he did. Maybe he could get some answers to his own questions. "So, I'm guessing that you didn't care much for your real father."

Jack's eyes flashed, and he recognized the spunk that had often gotten her in trouble in past years. She lifted her nose in the air. "I hardly see what that has to do with anything."

He offered her a placating smile. "We are who we are because of our past, Miss Ha—uh. . .Davis." Sweat beaded on Noah's forehead at his near-miss. He'd almost called her Miss Hamilton—the name he'd known her by previously. He'd have to watch himself and be extra careful around her.

Jack's narrowed gaze pierced him, but he forced himself to sit still and return her stare. The marshal strode back into the room, paper in hand. "Here you go."

Jack took the items without breaking Noah's gaze. His heart thumped harder. The marshal glanced from her to Noah and back. He scratched his hand, then rested his thumbs in his waistband. "You want me to stay, Half Bit?"

Finally she looked up at her stepfather and offered a cordial smile. "No, thank you. That's not necessary—that is, unless the parson is afraid to be alone with me." She wielded her smile like a weapon.

A bead of sweat trickled down Noah's spine, but he forced himself not to move. He was not without the means of affecting an unabashed female when the occasion warranted. He planted a smile on his face—his best feature next to his dark eyes, so he'd been told—and when the marshal glanced at Jack again, Noah winked at her.

Her mouth opened wide, and the marshal spun back toward him, obviously wondering what he'd missed. Noah resisted chuckling and affected a straight face then rubbed his eye. "Your daughter is safe with me, I promise, Marshal."

The man stared at him for a long moment then gave a quick nod and spun on his heel, leaving the room.

Jack leaned forward, her lids lowered halfway, her blue eyes cold as ice. "Are you in the habit of winking at single females, Reverend?" Her snide tone left no doubt that she'd taken offense.

"I beg your pardon." He rubbed his eye again, and she blinked. Confusion wrinkled her brow, and she stared at her blank paper.

"Um. . .never mind. I must have misconstrued your actions." She scribbled something on the paper. "So tell me, Reverend, where do you hail from?"

"Emporia, like I said at the table."

"And have you always lived there?"

He swallowed hard and stared at the top of her head while she wrote some more. Too soon she glanced up and lifted her brows. His heart flip-flopped at her direct perusal. "Uh. . .no, not always."

"Where else have you lived?"

He straightened, knowing he'd have to divert her train of

thought if he was going to stay truthful—and he fully intended to as much as possible. "I fail to see what that has to do with anything."

Her mouth quirked to one side in an enticing manner, and he focused on the bottom of her bare foot, which faced him where it lay on the chair. How could her feet be so small?

"Where did you receive your ministerial training?"

"From the man who took me in after my father died. His name is Pete Jeffers."

Her gaze darted up from her notes. "You changed your last name?"

He nodded.

"Isn't that a bit drastic? I mean, was your original last name so awful you couldn't abide it?"

He lifted his brow at her question and turned the cards on her. They were more alike than she realized. "Was your original surname so awful *you* couldn't abide it?"

"What?" Her expression blanked out, and he knew the moment she realized what she'd asked. "Oh dear. I suppose that did sound rather crass." Her pinks grew rosy, and she chuckled. "My birth name was Hamilton, but after Luke married my ma, I chose to use his surname. It wasn't my name that was awful, Reverend Jeffers, but rather my father."

He'd remembered hearing scuttlebutt about James Hamilton, but the man had died before Noah first came to Lookout. His fist tightened to think that Jack's father could have hurt her so badly that she'd still be bitter today. "Have you found it within yourself to forgive your father, Miss Davis?"

She straightened rigid as a newly cut piece of lumber. "I hardly see how that's any of your concern."

"I'm your pastor now. It's my duty to minister to you, and if I notice an area that you need help in, I feel I should do my best to assist you in overcoming it. An unwillingness to forgive eats away at a person, Miss Davis. It does more damage to the one who carries the weight of not forgiving than it does the person who originally committed the deed."

Her face wrinkled up. "Nevertheless, I'm the one asking

questions today." She scanned her paper then tapped a line with her pencil. "You said you received your training from this Pete Jeffers. Has he had any formal training as a minister?"

Noah shrugged. "You know, I don't think I ever asked him. Pete lives his life as a witness to those around him. I never doubted that he loved God with all his heart and had dedicated his life to serving others and helping them find peace in the Lord. He knew his Bible from end to end. He taught me as much as I could learn in the years I lived with him. I felt God calling me to minister to His flock. What other training is required?"

Jack heaved a sigh. Was the man being purposefully vague? He had deftly deflected most of her queries like a skilled outlaw evading a judge's questioning.

"Let me ask you this," he said. "What college did you graduate from to become a reporter?"

Her mouth opened, but she didn't know how to respond. Did he know she hadn't been to college? But how could he? Were her interviewing skills so lacking that he picked up on it?

He smiled. "Ahh. . .so you didn't. What gives you the right to drill me on my credentials?"

Jack narrowed her eyes. This man was unlike Reverend Taylor in just about every way. "You have effectively avoided answering most of my questions. Do you have something to hide, Reverend?"

For the briefest of seconds, Jack was certain he blanched, but then he smiled.

"What an imagination you have, Miss Davis. Perhaps you should be writing novels instead of newspaper articles."

Indeed. She'd worked at the newspaper off and on longer than her ma had been married to Luke. Jenny Evans had taught her well how to interview and to read people and catch deception. But what could a minister have to hide? Maybe she was too suspicious. Or maybe she was imagining things that weren't there because she wanted so badly to score a big story to offer a Dallas paper.

Jack scanned her list of questions again. She had precious

little information for an article. "You never mentioned where you grew up."

He shrugged again. "Here and there. My folks never stayed in one place for long, and after my ma died, it only got worse."

Jack wanted to grit her teeth and scream at the evasive answer. She studied the man. His eyes were so dark that she couldn't tell if they were deep brown or black. Shouldn't a minister have caring, blue eyes instead of ones so dark and mysterious they threatened to suck you in like a whirlpool?

Yet they weren't unkind eyes. There was something compelling about them. Compelling her to believe in him. Compelling her to trust him.

Her mind flashed back to another time. Another place. Another set of dark eyes begging her to believe. But just that fast, the memory was gone.

She shook her head. What was that? Who was that?

Reverend Jeffers leaned forward. "Are you all right, Miss Davis? Your mother said you'd recently had an accident. Maybe you are pushing yourself too hard." He reached his hand out as if to touch her then pulled it back into his lap. "We can continue this interview some other time if you need to rest."

Her mind swirled as it had right after she first fell off the roof. Maybe she wasn't ready to be working again. She closed her eyes and leaned back against the sofa, trying with all her might to grasp hold of the memory that had assaulted her. It was too late.

"Do you need a drink, Miss Davis? Should I fetch your mother?" At his concerned voice, she opened her eyes again. His worry seemed real. Maybe she was searching for a story where there wasn't one. She glanced down at her questions a final time, then a new one popped into her mind. "Have you ever been to Lookout before?"

There it was again. That brief, frantic look before he schooled his expression. He leaned back and crossed his arms, a smile on his lips—a smile that looked decidedly forced. "That would be rather ironic, wouldn't it? Can't you just see the headlines? Town Delinquent Returns as New Pastor."

He shook his head and chuckled, as if he'd cracked the funniest joke in years.

Jack studied him until he sobered and glanced into the hallway at the stairs again.

The new minister was hiding something.

She was certain.

Chapter 7

Denison, Texas

Carly once again checked the engraved pocket watch that had belonged to Tillie. She snapped the cover closed and ran her thumb over the swan figure etched into the silver, encircled by two curved branches, thick with leaves. Reverend Barker had said he wanted her to have something by which to remember Tillie. The watch would always be her most cherished possession, but she didn't need it to remember. Tillie Barker would always hold a special place in Carly's heart.

She placed the watch in its velvet drawstring bag and put it in her handbag. Lifting her hand to shade her eyes, she scanned the rolling hills to the west. The telegram she'd received from Rachel said that Garrett Corbett would pick her up. She placed a hand against her jittery stomach. Would the man remember her?

She hoped that Mr. Corbett and the town had forgotten all about her association with the Payton Gang. She hadn't thought of her brother in a long while but allowed a moment to reflect on how her life had changed. Ty was long dead now. He hadn't been a good brother, but he had protected her from his gang members, and for that she was grateful. If only they'd had parents to love and nourish them like the Barkers had cared for her, then surely things would have turned out different.

She searched the green hills again, then sat back down on the depot's bench in the shade. Though only late April, the sun shone down with a vengeance, heating the still air. But then, even if it had been winter, she'd probably still be sweating just because of her nervousness. Her foot jiggled relentlessly as she wondered what she'd face in Lookout.

Rachel had written her that the town had grown a lot in the past ten years. That meant there would be many newcomers who wouldn't know her story and how she'd pretended to be one of the mail-order brides who'd come to town, hoping to marry the marshal, although in truth, she'd had more sinister plans. None of the mail-order brides the Corbett brothers had brought to town ever had a chance, least of all her. The marshal had long ago lost his heart to Rachel, but he had a quagmire of bitterness to work through before he realized that.

Carly sighed, leaning her head against the wall. She yawned and closed her eyes. She'd worried so much last night that she hadn't slept much. Would she be welcomed in the town? Would she be able to find work to support herself? Would people remember that her brother had attempted to rob the Lookout bank? She heaved another sigh. The Bible said to not worry about tomorrow because today had enough cares of its own—and wasn't that the truth?

"All right, Lord, I'll try to not be concerned about my future, and will place it in Your hands."

God had brought her so far—out of the life of crime her brother had forced her into, out of prison, out of sin. She would give her future to Him, and at least for today, she'd try not to worry.

Garrett crested the hill, and the outlying buildings of Denison came into view. The horses must have sensed an end to their journey, because they picked up their pace. The wagon creaked as it hit another rut in the road and bounced out.

How many times had he made this drive from Lookout to Denison? Garrett shook his head. Too many to count. But with news of a railroad spur coming to Lookout, he might be facing the end of such trips.

He stretched, trying to work the kinks out of his back, and

chuckled to himself. His horses could probably make this trip alone, if only someone on the other end could load the freight and head the animals back toward Lookout.

Rubbing his hand along his jaw, he considered his future. If the spur did come through as the mayor said it would, he'd be out of business, for the most part. Yeah, he could pick up deliveries at the depot and take them to surrounding ranches, but his profit would be cut way down. He'd been trying to decide what else he'd like to do, but so far nothing came to mind.

Duke flicked his long tail, gaining Garrett's attention. He loved both of his stock horses. He hated the thought of putting them out to pasture, especially when there was a need for good work horses in the county, but he doubted he could part with the two animals, which had been so faithful. Sitting up straighter, he allowed a thought to take wing. Maybe he could raise stock horses. Farmers and ranchers always needed quality animals. He rubbed his jaw, getting excited for the first time in a long while.

He drew the horses alongside the depot and pulled back on the reins. "Whoa there."

Smiling, he hopped down and jogged up the steps and into the depot.

The clerk glanced up and nodded. "Howdy, Garrett. H'aint seen you in a while."

"Virgil." Garrett nodded. "Ain't been here in a while. Been back and forth to Dallas, hauling wood and freight for a rancher who's building a new house."

"Guess you won't be doin' that much longer, what with the new rail spur going in over to Lookout." Virgil's prominent Adam's apple bounced up and down over the man's black string tie. The cuffs to his white shirt were faded a dingy gray, matching the clerk's eyes.

Garrett shrugged. "Haven't exactly decided what I'll do yet. Got some ideas I'm kickin' around, though. I'm supposed to pick up a package for Rachel Davis. You know where it is?"

Virgil scowled and riffled though a pile of papers. He turned and studied a stack of crates behind him then spun back around, smiling. "Ah. . .you had me goin' there fer a minute." He squealed out a laugh that resembled a cat choking, and his bald head bobbed up and down as he fought to regain his composure.

What in the world? Garrett couldn't think of a thing he'd said that the man would find humorous.

The clerk swiped his eyes on his sleeve and pointed out the window to the waiting area. "You'll find yer package out there on the bench."

"Thanks." Garrett glanced back at the man a final time before exiting. It was far too early for the man to be drinking, but Virgil's behavior sure seemed odd. And why would the clerk leave a package out where just anyone could pick it up—unless it was so big Virgil couldn't carry it himself. Garrett flexed his arm muscle as he opened the door. He'd manhandle the load alone, just to show Virgil what he was made of.

The door banged shut, and a woman on the bench jumped. Garrett glanced around the platform for the package, then swung back for a look at the woman. Her gold-colored dress was wrinkled, and her hair was pulled up tight in a stark bun at the back of her head and covered with a straw hat tied down with a sash. She stretched and yawned. His gaze immediately landed on her chest, where the fabric of her dress pulled tight as she locked her hands together and stretched again. She rubbed her eyes, then stared at him.

Embarrassed and feeling guilty to be caught watching her, he spun around and walked to the other end of the deck but found no crates of any kind. He lifted his hat and scratched his head. What was Virgil up to?

"Mr. Corbett?"

Garrett pivoted again and studied the woman's face. She looked to be in her late twenties and was fairly pretty with her black hair and unusual light brown eyes. She had all the right curves for a woman, even if she was on the thin side. But how did she know his name? The woman's eyes narrowed, but she didn't look away. There was something oddly familiar about her. Had he stumbled across her path before?

"You are Garrett Corbett, correct? Or are you Mark, perchance?"

Now she really had his attention. How did she know his

brother? "Who are you, lady?"

She flinched as if he'd slapped her, making him regret his harsh tone. "I received a telegram from Rachel Hamilton saying you would be by to give me a ride to Lookout. Did she neglect to inform you?"

"*You're* Rachel's package?"

She blinked, confusion marring her features. "What?"

Garrett lowered his head and stared at the floorboards. Now that odd look Rachel and Luke had exchanged at the dinner table made sense. They'd set him up. But why? Who was this woman? And why would Rachel not just tell him he was supposed to pick her up?

The woman turned back toward the bench and snatched up a worn satchel. "Never mind. I'll find another way to get to Lookout. Sorry to have imposed on you."

Garrett opened his mouth to reply, but nothing came out. He was still trying to figure out what Rachel was up to when the lady opened the depot door and scurried inside. She walked up to the counter and said something to Virgil, who glanced through the glass at him and pointed. The woman shook her head. Virgil shrugged, and the lady stood still for a minute, then spun toward the front door and walked outside.

Why wouldn't Rachel tell him he was to pick up a woman passenger? He could think of only one reason—she had something up her sleeve.

The window in the depot door rattled when Virgil yanked it open. "What did you say to that lady? H'ain't you gonna give her a ride? Makes no sense for you not to when yer goin' right back to Lookout. You are, h'ain'tcha?"

Garrett nodded.

"Then why you standin' here? That lady waited for you nigh on two hours. Git on out there and give her a ride."

Garrett bristled at Virgil's scolding. "What's it to you?"

The clerk shook his head. "What's wrong with you? Did she say something that set you off?"

Rubbing the back of his neck, Garrett shook his head. What *was* wrong with him?

He didn't like people getting his goat or pulling the wool over his eyes—and yet he couldn't quite decide if Rachel had. His feet moved forward before his mind clicked into gear. He had been rude to the lady—not intentionally—but rude all the same. And he was returning to Lookout, so he had no excuse for not giving her a ride.

He didn't waste time responding to Virgil but charged out the door and searched the road that ran past the depot. Skirts swinging like a church bell, she marched down the road that led out of town. Was the fool woman going to walk all the way to Lookout?

Garrett climbed back into the wagon, released the brake, and slapped the reins against the horses' backs. "Giddyap, there!"

The wagon jolted forward, nearly tossing him into the back. Guiding it in a wide circle, he finally sat and focused on his target. The gal had stopped and looked one way and then the other. She set her satchel down, untied her bonnet strings, and then retied them and picked up her bag again. As he drew near her, she turned and gawked at him, then spun around and started walking faster.

He pulled up beside her and tugged on the reins to slow his team. "I'll give you a lift to Lookout."

"No thanks," she tossed over her shoulder. "I can find my own way. I don't need your help."

"Whoa there, Duke. Daisy." He wrestled with the horses, which weren't ready to stop, seeing as how they'd just started their trip home, but they finally came to a halt. He jumped down and hurried after the confounded woman. Couldn't she see he was trying to help her?

Garrett caught up and reached for her bag. She spun around, yanking it from his grasp, and glared at him. He held up his palms. "Whoa, lady, I'm just trying to help."

"So, now you want to help. Well, you're too late. I told you I'd find another way to Lookout."

Garrett shoved his hands to his hips and couldn't hold back a grin. "Like walking?"

"What?" She swirled around and looked down the road. Only a few dilapidated buildings littered the lane. "Uh. . .that train man said the livery was this way and that I could rent a buggy there."

"Ah. . .I see." Good thing he came to her rescue or she might have been wolf bait come nightfall. "The livery is the other direction, ma'am."

Surprised flickered in her eyes, and she looked back toward town. She spun around again and marched back in the direction she'd just come. All this swirling was making him dizzier than doing do-si-dos at a square dance. But no female, no matter how irritating she might be, was going to get him into trouble with Rachel. His cousin's wife just might get it into her mind not to allow him to eat at the boardinghouse any more, and a near-forty-year-old bachelor could only eat so much of his own cooking. He hurried after her again.

This time, he wasn't taking any chances. Garrett caught up with her. "Stop! Right now."

The woman scowled at him and kept on walking.

"I aim to give you a ride to Lookout whether you want one or not, so stop walkin', you hear?"

If she did, she sure didn't obey well. Garrett ran past her, turned, and halted right in her path. She had no choice but to stop, go around, or knock him to the ground, and given that he was a good half-foot taller than she and twice her breadth, he doubted the last choice was much of an option. Then he noticed the satchel flying toward his face.

Carly gasped as her travel bag collided with Mr. Corbett's head. The man staggered backward then fell flat on his rump. She couldn't help the giggle that rose up in spite of her irritation. The man was more of a pest than a wasp nest in a privy.

He hopped right back up and glared at her, his lovely robin's egg blue eyes flashing. "What was that for?"

"I don't like to be pushed around by men."

He stepped closer. "I didn't push you."

She leaned toward him. "You know what I mean. I don't like to be bossed around. I've had enough men telling me what to do to last me a lifetime."

He flung his arms out to the side. "Well, I'm sorry, lady, but there are no women here to assist me."

She gasped. No women indeed. "Then what am I?"

He blinked. "What?"

"You said there were no women around, so I just wondered what you considered me?"

His gaze traveled from her eyes downward. She hiked her chin. His stance relaxed a smidgen as a cocky smile tugged on one side of his mouth. "I never said you weren't a woman. You've just got me all—all—discombobulated."

Carly sighed at his confused expression. He was like a little boy in a man's clothing—only he was all man. In the ten years since she'd last seen him, his shoulders had gotten broader, but his blond hair hadn't grayed at all. She knew he must be pushing forty, but he looked as if he could take on a man half his age. Maybe she'd been unwise stirring his ire. "Did Rachel send you to get me or not?"

He leaned in again but this time didn't look so menacing. His warm breath touched her cheeks, sending tingles up and down her spine. "She asked me to pick up a *package* at the depot. A *package*, not a *woman*."

"Oh." No wonder he'd been so confused. Why would Rachel say such a thing? Had she gotten mixed up on the date she was arriving and actually meant for Mr. Corbett to pick up something she'd ordered? "Maybe she also had a package that needed picking up."

He shook his head. "Virgil said she didn't. He just motioned me outside and said my *package* was out there. No wonder he was about to bust his gut laughing."

"I don't see anything funny about the situation." Carly rubbed her hand across her face. Making him feel guilty about the situation wasn't very Christlike. "I'm sorry. I just assumed that when you saw me, you decided you no longer wanted to give me a ride—and that made me mad."

"Why would I care about who you are? I've never met you before."

Taken aback by his lack of recognition, she moved away from

him. Was it really possible that he didn't know who she was? Obviously, Rachel hadn't informed him. If he didn't know, then maybe the rest of the town wouldn't remember her, either. But they would once they heard her name. And so would he.

She strode over to the wagon, tossed her satchel in the back, and climbed up. It was best he didn't learn the truth until he was too far along to turn back.

Chapter 8

Noah glanced down at the note again. Was he doing the right thing? Would his apology be as effective done anonymously rather than in person?

Well it would have to be, because that was the only apology he could offer at the moment. He shoved the paper in his pants pocket and entered the mercantile. All manner of aromas tickled his senses, from coffee to spices to pickles to leather. Pushing his hat back on his forehead so he could see better, he gazed at the crowded shelves and colorful displays.

A pretty woman with dark hair tucked up in a neat bun smiled at him as he glanced around the store. "Good morning. I'm Christine Morgan, and this is my store. Can I help you find something?"

Noah lifted his hat. "A pleasure to meet you, ma'am. My name's Noah Jeffers."

"Oh!" The woman's hand flew to her chest. "You must be the new minister."

"Yes, ma'am. I am that." At least for the time being. Once people learned his true identity, he might be tarred and feathered and sent away on foot—barefoot. "I don't need much and thought I might just look around to see what all you have."

She nodded. "Take your time. I'm not going anywhere."

Noah meandered down one aisle and up another until he

found the pie tins. He peeked over his shoulder at Mrs. Morgan. How could an unmarried minister living in a boardinghouse explain purchasing pie pans?

He blew out a deep breath. Well, there was no getting around it. There were two styles of pans: one a blue granite with white specks and the other a plain silver pan with wavy edges. He looked around the store, glad that no other customers had come in, and tucked two of the silver pans under his arms. Heat warmed his neck, and he shook his head. A grown man buying pie plates. Paying retribution was going to hurt more than his money pouch.

He picked out a new comb and then stopped at the ready-made shirts. He needed a new white shirt for preaching in, but that would have to wait until he'd earned his first wages. Mrs. Morgan watched him approach, and her brows lifted when she caught sight of the pans.

"What do you plan to do with those?"

Noah shrugged. He didn't want to tell a lie, but neither could her tell her the truth.

"I guess they might make good collection plates for the church," she said.

He turned them over and knocked on one. "They might at that."

She tallied up the items and wrote something in a small ledger book. Noah paid her the required sum and picked up his purchase. "Will I see you and Mr. Morgan in church this Sunday?"

She glanced out the open door for a moment then faced him again. "There is no Mr. Morgan. My Jarrod died years ago, Reverend."

Noah winced. He'd have to be more careful addressing people he didn't know in the future. "I'm sorry for your loss, ma'am."

She swatted her hand in the air. "It was a long time ago. I will be at church Sunday, along with my daughter, Tessa, and my son, Billy, if I can get him to come. It's getting harder and harder these days."

"I'll pray for Billy, ma'am. That God would get a hold of him like He did me. Don't give up hope."

Her sweet smile warmed Noah's insides. "If there's ever

anything I can do for you, Mrs. Morgan, please let me know. I'm staying at the boardinghouse."

She nodded. "Thank you for your generous offer. You may have already met my daughter, I believe. She's a good friend of Jacqueline Davis."

Noah's heart quickened just hearing Jack's full name. It was a beautiful name, and he'd never understood why she preferred being called by a boy's name. "I don't think I have met your daughter yet, ma'am, but I look forward to it."

Mrs. Morgan leaned back against the counter, a gleam sparking in her blue eyes. "Tessa is close to your age, and she's quite a pretty girl. She has my blue eyes and her father's blond hair."

A warning bell clanged in Noah's mind. This wasn't the first time a young woman's mama had tried to get him to notice her daughter. He smiled and stepped toward the door. "If she looks anything like you, ma'am, I'm sure she is." He tipped his hat and hurried outside, certain he'd seen a blush rising to Mrs. Morgan's cheeks.

Maybe he shouldn't have made that last comment. When was he going to learn to think before he spoke? The Morgans hadn't lived in Lookout when he was last here, so he'd never made their acquaintance. Was Billy older or younger than his sister? Either way, he must be a grown man. Suddenly, the vision of the young ladies he'd seen in Jack's bedroom that day he'd first arrived entered his mind. Had one of those visitors been Tessa Morgan?

Noah ventured away from the boardinghouse and down the street. He passed the marshal's office but didn't stop. Luke Davis hadn't asked him again if he'd ever been in Lookout before, and for that he was grateful.

He passed the stage depot and then the café, where his steps slowed. After living much of his life without decent food to eat, the scent of something baking always gave him pause. He inhaled deeply, wondering if Polly Dykstra still managed the café that held her name. The older woman had been kind to him, allowing him to chop wood for her in exchange for a meal or occasionally a pie. His mouth watered, even though his belly was still filled with Mrs. Davis's delicious cooking.

Pushing on, he noticed that the saloon had been moved to the far end of Main Street and several new businesses had been erected. A dentist office sat where the old saloon had been, and Noah noticed a sign on the door. He crossed the street, dodging a wagon, and loped up the steps. Squinting, he read the sign. CHECK AT THE SALOON IF I'M NOT HERE. Staring down the street, Noah couldn't help wondering if the dentist also worked at the saloon or spent his time drinking. Either way, he wasn't too sure he'd contact the man if he ever needed a tooth pulled.

He continued his tour of the town, making note of the other new buildings and businesses. At some point, he ought to stop in each one, introduce himself, and invite those working there to church. Pastor Taylor had told Noah in a letter he'd written about the church that only about one-half of the town attended services at his church, which was the only one in town. Noah sent a prayer heavenward. "Lord, help me to make a difference in this town while I'm here. Give me a chance to redeem my early years before I knew You."

He paused at the end of Apple Street and stared past the houses lining the lane. A half-mile northeast of town was the site of his old home, a shack really—if it was still standing. Part of him longed to go see if anything remained, but another part didn't want to have anything to do with his past. He kicked a rock and sent it skittering across the dirt road. Most of his memories were bad ones, anyway.

The pie plates under his arm slipped, and he pressed his arm tight against his body to keep them from falling. They'd reminded him of the task he still had to complete. His heart pounded harder the closer he got to the mayor's house. What if someone saw him and asked what he was doing? How could he respond without telling a falsehood?

Lord, I believe in my heart that You want me to make restitution for my past deeds, so give me the courage to complete this task.

Jack moseyed into the store and searched the building, disappointed to find it empty except for Mrs. Morgan. She was certain she'd seen the parson enter when she'd glanced out her bedroom window a few minutes ago. There was nothing particularly odd about a minister going into a mercantile, but her reporter instincts sensed Noah Jeffers was up to something.

"Morning, Jacqueline." Mrs. Morgan smiled. "It's good to see you up again. I hope you're feeling better after your fall."

Jack grimaced at the mention of her plummet off the mayor's roof. She'd been halfway surprised he hadn't marched over to her house to lecture her about respecting people's property. The fact that he hadn't confirmed in her mind that he was working on some big plan for the city. She just had to discover what it was. She leaned against the counter and took the weight off her injured leg. "I'm still a bit sore, but I'm getting better. Thanks for asking."

"If you're looking for Tessa, she isn't here. She ran out the door, mumbling something about needing to go to Penny's for a while."

"No. Actually, I was wondering. . . . Didn't Noah Jeffers come in a little while ago?"

Mrs. Morgan nodded, picked up a feather duster, and started swiping the cans of vegetables on the shelf behind the counter. "Yes, he was here about ten minutes ago. Bought a few things and left. He's a nice young man, and quite handsome with that dark hair and eyes, don't you think? Tessa can't quit talking about him."

Jack wasn't about to admit that she did indeed find Reverend Jeffers attractive, much to her consternation. Shouldn't a minister be plain looking so a woman wouldn't waste time dwelling on his features instead of his message? Why, the man had even invaded her dreams. How was she to fight something like that? Forcing her frustrations aside, she smiled at Tessa's mother. "Yes, she made it clear to Penny and me that she intends to marry him."

Mrs. Morgan's blue eyes widened. "She never said a thing about that to me. Isn't it ironic that I just gushed about her attributes to the parson?"

Jack pursed her lips. The poor man hadn't been in town two days, and the Morgans already had him in their sights. At least she hoped she was no longer in Billy's. A shudder wormed its way down her back.

Mrs. Morgan paused. "Tessa told me that you don't plan to marry Billy." She nibbled her lower lip and stared out the door. Finally she met Jack's gaze again. "I can't say as I blame you, although I was hoping to welcome you into the family. Billy has always been a handful, and now that he's far bigger than me, I don't know how to handle him."

Jack shifted her feet, uncomfortable talking about Billy with his mother. From the day the Morgans first moved to town, she'd known Billy was a wild child. He seemed to pick up where Butch Laird left off when he left town. She hadn't been very kind to the lonely youth. She'd thought Butch a big bully but had had second thoughts after she'd talked to him once. It seemed the boy who stank like pigs wanted to make something more of his life than his father had. What had happened to him?

She shook Butch from her mind and refocused on Billy's mother. The poor woman looked to be at her wit's end. "Maybe you could get Reverend Jeffers to talk to Billy. There's not all that much difference in their ages, I imagine."

Mrs. Morgan's expression brightened, and she stood taller. "Why, that's a wonderful idea. Do you think he'd do it?"

Jack shrugged. "I don't know why not. He seems nice enough." Secretive, but nice.

"I may come over and talk to him this evening, if you're sure he won't mind."

"It's part of a minister's job to counsel folks who need help, isn't it?"

Mrs. Morgan nodded. "Yes, I do believe it is."

A shadow darkened the doorway, and Christine Morgan glanced past Jack, her face erupting into a brilliant smile. The woman—who had to be in her late thirties—reached up and tucked a loose strand of hair behind her ear, then licked her lips. She dropped the duster on the floor and quickly shed her apron.

Interesting.

Jack slowly turned to see who had so effectively snagged the woman's interest that she'd primp and grin like a school girl. A tall cowboy stood in the doorway, his gaze equally riveted to the store clerk's. Jack smelled a romance in the making.

Mrs. Morgan hurried toward the door. "How can I help you, Mr. Kessler?"

Jack ambled down an aisle and paused in front of the ready-made dresses. She picked up the hem of a dark rose calico and pretended to be studying it. A person with better manners would leave and give the lovebirds some privacy, but she wouldn't become a full-time reporter if she didn't do a little snooping. Besides, neither Mrs. Morgan nor Mr. Kessler seemed to notice she was still there.

Something tickled the back of her mind, and she struggled to grasp hold of the thought. Suddenly, as if someone had turned on one of those electric lights she'd read about, the memory was revealed: Rand Kessler had once asked her ma to marry him—so she'd heard. Then she remembered that he used to come around for a while but had stopped after Luke returned to town.

Jack eyed him over the skirt of the dress. She'd heard Garrett talk about him over dinner before. The man owned a large ranch a few hours' ride from Lookout, if she was remembering correctly. She dropped hold of the dress and fingered the trim on a dark green one that she actually liked. Pants were still her preference, but she rarely got to wear them now that she was grown up. Her ma nearly had apoplexy the last time she'd donned them, and that wasn't a good state for a woman carrying a baby to be in.

Mr. Kessler must have suddenly remembered his hat, because he yanked it off. His tanned cheeks and ears had a reddish cast to them. He was nice looking for such an older man. Jack guessed him to be in his mid-forties—far too old to come courting.

"It's a pleasure to see you in town mid-week, Mr. Kessler." Mrs. Morgan leaned back against the counter, flashing a wide smile at him.

"I. . .uh. . .had some business to tend to at the freight office, but Garrett wasn't there."

"I saw him ride out earlier this morning, just as I was opening the store. Must have gone to pick up something, because his wagon was empty."

Mr. Kessler shrugged. "Don't matter none. I just left him a note."

"Oh well, good thing your trip wasn't wasted."

A smile tugged at one corner of the man's mouth. "It's never a waste when I get to see you, Christine."

"Oh!" Mrs. Morgan fanned her face with her hand. "What a nice thing to say."

"It's just the truth, ma'am." He curled the rim of his hat and glanced down.

Jack grimaced. If things got any more syrupy, she just might retch. Why did perfectly normal people become fools when romance came calling? Even big, tough ranchers who would never back down from a fight or could break the wildest bronc became sweet like honey when they fell for a woman. Would a man ever act like that toward her? Did she even want one to?

A movement out the window and across the street snagged her attention. She strained her eyes to see who was walking toward her, past the mayor's house. Her pulse picked up its pace. Noah Jeffers! What reason would he have to walk between houses? Most normal folks stuck to the boardwalks. The sun reflected off something under his arm. He ducked down—or did he bend to pick up something? Then he turned onto the alley and disappeared behind the bank. Intrigued, Jack started to follow but held her ground, hating to miss out on whatever happened in the store.

"I was wondering. Would you. . .ah. . .consider going with. . . ah. . .me to the social this Saturday? That is if you're not going with someone else already."

Sucked right back into the blossoming romance, Jack abandoned all thought of following the minister. How much trouble could a man of God get into, anyway? She lowered the skirt of the green dress, wishing she had something to write notes on. If Mrs. Morgan didn't answer the man fast, Jack feared he'd be buying a new hat before he left.

Mrs. Morgan's hand flew up and rested on her chest. "Why, I'd be delighted, Rand."

The grins on their faces reminded Jack of when her ma and Luke had first gotten married.

Mr. Kessler slapped his crumpled hat back on his head. "That's great. I'll pick you up a little before six, and I'd like to purchase a bag of that horehound candy and another of the lemon drops."

With his difficult chore over, Mr. Kessler seemed business-minded once again. Mrs. Morgan bagged the candy and set it on the counter, quoting the price. He dropped several coins into her hand and pocketed one bag of candy and handed her the other. "This is for you. I recall how you mentioned that you loved lemon drops."

Mrs. Morgan clutched the surprise gift to her chest. "Why, Rand, that's so nice of you. I'm much obliged."

He nodded, spun on his heels, then stopped just outside the door and glanced back. "See you on Saturday."

Mrs. Morgan watched the door for a long while then lifted the bag of candy with both hands and held it to her nose. She closed her eyes, and Jack imagined she must be inhaling the tangy scent of the hard candy. After a moment, the store owner hurried to the back room, and Jack took that opportunity to dash out the door. When a pain charged up her leg, she slowed her steps and carefully made her way across the dirt road, dodging the horse flops.

The newspaper was due out tomorrow, but if Jenny hadn't filled up all the space, just maybe she could post a brief vignette about shopping for love in the mercantile.

Noah hurried down the street, thankful that nobody was out and about, then skulked past the east side of the mayor's house. As he passed under a window, he could hear a woman humming. His heart quickened again. He ducked down, scurried past the window, then slowed his steps as he came to the back of the house. The Burkes had a large back porch, and Mrs. Burke had often left her pies on a table there to cool. They'd been much too conveniently located within easy reach for a poor boy who never got to eat home-baked goods. Noah winced, remembering the two pies he'd stolen from that same porch.

Pulling the note and a dollar from his pocket, he glanced around again, then tiptoed across the grass and onto the porch.

He all but dropped the pie plates on the table with the note and dollar, then hightailed it back across the yard and onto Bluebonnet Lane. He quickly headed for the church. His heart thrummed, matching the thumping in his ears, and he licked his dry lips. His legs wobbled like jelly. Peering over his shoulder, he was relieved not to see anyone following him.

Never had doing a good deed felt so. . .devious.

One down, about a dozen more to go.

Chapter 9

After picking up a load of supplies for Dan Howard, the livery owner, Garrett drove the wagon back toward home. His passenger hadn't uttered a single word for the past hour. At least she wasn't one of those gabby gals who yakked a man's ear off.

He'd never admit it to anyone, but he rather liked having a pretty female by his side. At some time or another, he had started thinking more about settling down and starting a family, and at nearly forty, he couldn't afford to wait much longer. He actually envied Luke and Mark. Both were married and had children, while he'd been content to work and have fun in life. But living alone wasn't fun anymore.

And did he want to leave this world one day and not leave behind children—his legacy?

He let the idea simmer in his mind. Yeah, he was ready to marry. The problem was there was no woman in Lookout who snagged his attention enough that he'd want to spend the rest of his life with her.

The woman beside him gasped, and he reached for his rifle. Her hand shot out and grabbed his arm. "What is that?"

Pulling the rifle into his lap, he scanned the prairie but saw nothing except grasses and colorful wildflowers waving in the light breeze. "I don't see nothin'."

She tugged on his sleeve, sending tingles up his arm. He

shook them off as if they were pesky flies and followed the way her finger pointed. "Over there. I've never seen a bird so blue. What is it?"

Garrett relaxed, hearing the trill of the bird that sat twenty feet away atop a bush. He'd half expected she'd seen an outlaw. He'd encountered few of them during the years he'd been hauling freight, but you never knew what to expect, so he had to stay alert. "That's an indigo bunting."

She turned to him, gazing at him with curiosity, not anger. He'd never seen light brown eyes like hers before, yet they seemed oddly familiar. Had he known someone else with similar ones?

Her teeth brushed over her lower lip in an enticing manner, stirring Garrett's senses. He forced himself to look away. How could a woman who'd efficiently fueled his temper an hour ago—a woman whose name he didn't know—stir him in a way no other woman had in a long while?

"Um. . .why is it called an indigo bunting when it's so blue? Isn't indigo a purple color?"

Garrett shrugged, frustrated with himself for noticing so much about the woman. "I don't know. Maybe the guy who named it was colorblind or something."

Her brows dipped, and she turned away. "You knew the name of the bird. I just thought you might know more about it."

"Well, you're wrong. I just happen to know the name because I got bored one night and thumbed through one of the books my brother left behind. There were gray and white pictures of the bird, and the book said it was a dark blue, so I guess indigo is a dark blue."

"The lady I lived with used a deep purple fabric in a quilt she was making and always called it indigo. That's why I thought that."

Garrett grunted. He was a man. What did he care about colors? Other than to notice a woman in a pretty dress. "I'm sorry your brother moved away." She caught his gaze again and narrowed her eyes. "He was always the nicer of you two."

Garrett scowled at the intended slur. Here he was offering this nameless woman a ride, and she had the gall to insult him! "How do you know my brother? And how do you know my name?"

Her bold gaze melted, and she returned to watching the prairie. The wind picked up a strand of her hair and tossed it about. "I lived in Lookout for a short while, but it was a long time ago."

He searched his mind but still came up empty. "How do you know Rachel Davis?"

"I stayed at Hamilton House."

Garrett let that thought stew. Rachel's home and boardinghouse hadn't been called Hamilton House for almost ten years, not since shortly after she married Luke. Rachel didn't want the name to constantly remind Luke of her first husband, so she asked the townsfolk to quit calling it that. It had taken awhile for folks to get out of the habit, but most people now just referred to it as "the boardinghouse" or "Rachel's place."

Garrett wasn't one to play games unless he was the instigator, and the woman's evasiveness was starting to wear thin on his nerves. "Why don't you just tell me your name and get it over with?"

She sucked her lips inward, as if that could keep her from talking, but she finally heaved a sigh of resignation. "It's Carly. Carly Payton."

Garrett stared at the landscape, rolling the name over in his mind. Carly was an unusual name—a pretty one at that. "Well, Miss Payton, nice to meet you."

She looked at him as if he'd gone loco. "We've met before."

"When? The name does sound a bit familiar."

She uttered a very unladylike snort and shook her head.

Garrett didn't like her mocking him. Was she telling the truth about her name or just stringing him along? Suddenly, like the headlight of a locomotive coming ever closer in the dark, his mind grasped hold of the name, and realization hit him upside the head. She was that outlaw bride! The gal who'd pretended to be one of the mail-order brides that he and Mark had ordered for Luke years ago before he married Rachel. The sister of the man who'd kidnapped Rachel and tried to rob the Lookout bank. That was her—the criminal who'd been sent to prison for her unlawful deeds.

He pulled back on the reins, set the brake, and jumped down.

The horses snorted. One pawed the ground, but he ignored them. Pacing through the knee-high grass, he tried to wrap his mind around something else. That look Rachel and Luke had exchanged at the dinner table suddenly took on meaning. He stared at Miss Payton, and it made complete sense. Rachel was aiming to match him up with that outlaw lady.

Not today.

Not tomorrow.

Not ever.

He wouldn't fall for Rachel and Luke's scheming, and if he wasn't already closer to Lookout than Denison, he'd turn the wagon around and take the jailbird back.

She watched him but said nothing. Yeah, she was pretty, and yeah she'd stirred up his senses, but he would never lower himself to marry an ex-convict—a woman who'd robbed banks and ridden with an outlaw gang. What kind of mother would she be to his kids?

"I'm sorry. If I'd known it would upset you so much to ride with me, I would have found another way to get to Lookout." She swiped her eyes and turned her body so that her back was to him.

Great. Just great. He flung his arms out to the side, then hauled them back down and slapped his thighs. Now she was trying to use tears to weaken him.

Well, it wouldn't work.

He climbed back onto the buckboard. Suddenly a shot rang out, and a fire like Hades itself seared his shoulder. The surprise and the force of the blow knocked him back, and he fell to the ground. The sky blackened before turning blue again. He could hear riders galloping closer and tried to sit, but the pain nailed him to the ground.

"Are you all right?" Miss Payton stood. Her frantic gaze leapt from him to the riders and back.

"Go!" He swatted his good arm in the air. "Get out of here."

"I can't leave you. Get on up here and hurry!"

"No time." He might not like the woman, but neither did he want to see her suffer at the hands of robbers. 'Course, she might just know the men and be in no danger at all. Maybe those fellows were a welcome-home party. He huffed a cynical laugh, then peered under the wagon to see how far off the riders were. Not far at all.

Two more bullets pinged off the side of the wagon. Miss Payton ducked. She seemed to be wrestling with indecision. Then she steeled her expression and snatched up his rifle. She spun around and shot both men out of the saddle with just two shots.

Garrett's mouth hung open, and he struggled to make sense of what he'd seen. Not even Luke could shoot like that, and he'd been in the army for a decade. He lowered his head back against the ground. Grass tickled his ear and cheek, making his face itch. How could a woman shoot so well?

Maybe it was God's protection. He stared up at the sky and thanked his Maker. He believed in God, but he wasn't as faithful to pray or even attend church as he should be. Realizing how he could just as easily be lying there dead instead of wounded made him conscious of things he rarely thought about.

Miss Payton climbed down and hurried toward him. "Are you hurt bad, Mr. Corbett?"

"Where'd you learn to shoot like that?"

She shrugged and leaned over him, checking his wound. "If I bind it, do you think you could make it to Lookout? It's closer than Denison, right?"

"Yeah." He nodded, still impressed with her coolness under fire and the fact that she refused to leave him. He couldn't help thinking if the situation had been reversed, he might well be racing toward home, with her lying alone on the prairie. "Who taught you to shoot?"

She nibbled that lip again, making his belly turn somersaults. "My brother, Tyson. I picked it up real fast. He said I was a natural."

"I'm duly impressed."

A shy smile tilted her lips, and she hurried back to the wagon and started yanking garments from her satchel. When she came to what looked like a nightgown, she used her teeth and ripped off the six-inch-wide ruffle along the bottom. Rushing back to his side, she tore off a smaller square and folded it in quarters. She knelt beside him and dabbed the square against his wound.

Garrett hissed at the burning pain but sat still, letting her tend him. With her head bent, he could smell the floral scent of her hair. She must have washed it recently. It was black as a raven's wing. The wisp that had pulled loose fell across his cheek, taunting him.

He didn't want to like her.

Didn't want to be drawn to her.

When he thought of marrying, he wanted a woman people respected. He had worked hard to gain the town's esteem after his wild years as a rowdy youth, and that was important to him. He wanted to wed a gal who could cook, sew, keep house, and raise children. Thinking back to the bride contest a decade ago that had been held to determine which mail-order bride would make Luke the best wife, he remembered that Miss Payton—or Miss Blackstone as she'd been called then—couldn't cook or sew. What good was she to a man? Other than to shoot bandits out of their saddles.

She pulled tight on the two sections of fabric, and Garrett gasped at the stinging it caused.

"Oh, stop being a baby. He just grazed your arm."

"Try getting shot and see how you like it, lady." He grunted when she tightened it again.

She stood and walked back to the wagon. "I have been. Twice. And I can tell you, it's not the worst thing I've endured."

He shook his head. Surely she didn't say she'd been shot before. The bullet wound must be affecting his head somehow. Carefully he stood, taking a moment to shake off the dizziness. He needed to check on the two men she'd shot and get them tied up before they came to—if they were even alive.

By the time he made it to the wagon, he felt as if he'd been breaking mustangs all day. How could one shot that only winged him affect him this much? Maybe the blow his head took when it collided with the packed dirt was making him woozy—that and thoughts of marriage and Miss Payton all in the same sentence. This was all Rachel's fault.

Miss Payton headed toward their attackers, frayed nightgown and rifle in hand. He shook his head and followed after her. She'd never be able to overpower even one of those men if he came to.

By the time he finally got to where the men had fallen off their horses, she had one unconscious man tied up and was working on the other. He bent down and tugged at the man's bindings, not a little impressed with the good job she'd done. A grin teased his mouth when he noticed she'd tied the man up with pink fabric that was covered in tiny red roses and had wrapped his head wound with the same. Suddenly his smile slackened, and he glanced at his own wound. A groan erupted that drew her attention.

"You all right?"

He nodded and strode across the grass toward the closest horse. He'd have to get these bandages off before he got back to Lookout, or he'd be the laughingstock of the town.

Chapter 10

Noah's stomach still churned, and his legs hadn't fully quit wobbling, but the pie plates had been delivered, and he felt better for having completed that task. He walked around the church, praying for his congregation and making mental notes of things that needed repair. The outside of the white building was in decent condition but could use a new coat of paint, and a cracked window needed replacing.

He still found it hard to believe that God had entrusted this church and its people into his care. Who was he? Nothing but a rowdy kid who'd met God and changed his ways. He'd grown up some, too, but he felt inadequate in so many ways to shepherd a flock of believers.

Pete had told him numerous times not to dwell on his doubts but to shove them away and trust God. Mentally, Noah packed his insecurities back in a box and refocused on the church. The shin-high grass needed cutting before Sunday services. He walked around back, hoping to find a lawn mower, but he didn't. He'd have to ask Marshal Davis about that.

He strode back to the front of the church, eager to see inside. This building had also served as the schoolhouse when he lived in town, not that he had fond memories of those years. The other children had made fun of him because he'd been fat and smelled bad. His pa had been of the opinion that a man only needed a bath once a month, and with his ma dying when he was young, nobody had taught Noah otherwise—until he met Pete. He certainly hoped Mrs. Davis didn't mind him taking several baths a week. He shivered at the thought of how filthy he used to be and promised himself to never be that way again.

Slowing his steps near the front door, he noticed a large man waddling toward the church. Something about him was vaguely familiar. Noah crossed the churchyard and met him under a tall oak that had only been a little more than a sapling when he was last here. "Morning."

The man slowed, his chest heaving from his exertion. He leaned one hand against the tree trunk and struggled to catch his breath. "I'm Titus—Burke. Lookout's mayor. You the new preacher?"

Noah nodded. "Yes, sir. I'm Noah Jeffers." The mayor had always been a heavyset man, but now he was as wide as an ox. His dark hair, which used to be parted in the middle and stuck down, had thinned, and what was left had been brushed forward in an ineffective attempt to cover his bald spot.

"Sorry I haven't come to the boardinghouse sooner to meet you, but I've had some pressing business to attend to." The mayor pushed his wireframe glasses up on his nose with one thumb. "Aren't you rather young to be a preacher?"

Noah shrugged. "I don't reckon age has much to do with sharing God's Word with folks."

Mayor Burke harrumphed. "You're wrong. How are you going to counsel people with problems when you haven't had time to experience things yourself? You married?"

"No, I'm not. And you might be surprised to know of the trials I've endured. You don't have to be old to have experienced the bad things in life."

The light breeze taunted the mayor's hair, lifting it up and setting it down in a different place. The long, thin hairs looked odd, but Mayor Burke smashed his hand down on top of his head and pressed them back into submission. Noah suspected the strong-willed mayor browbeat some of the people in town the same way, but he wasn't going to become one of them.

"Look, Mayor, I had a wonderful mentor—a godly man who dearly loved the Lord, who personally instructed me in the ways of God for a number of years. We studied the Word for hours a day. I'm not perfect by any means, and I may be younger than most ministers, but I feel God called me here to fill in for Pastor Taylor, and I plan to do the best job I can. All I ask is that you give me a chance to prove myself."

The mayor studied him as if taking his measure, then finally nodded. "Fair enough. Ray Mann, our church board director, told me about you and gave his recommendation. My missus and I'll be sittin' in the pews come Sunday."

Noah nodded, and the mayor turned and made his way back across the street. Noah had talked with Mr. Mann when he first arrived in Lookout and was relieved to know the man had given him his approval. Releasing a huge sigh, he glanced up at the sky. "I sure need Your help here, Lord. Equip me to do the task You've set before me."

Hot, musty air met him as he stepped inside the church building, so he left the door ajar. Walking the center aisle, he remembered his school days and noticed all the changes. Gone were the chalkboard, desks, maps, and schoolbooks, replaced by a podium and skillfully constructed pews. He'd never attended church when he lived here previously, but the building was still familiar. A colorful array of lights danced on the floor just past the podium from the sun shining in the large stained-glass window. That was new. The window depicted several scenes of Christ's life, and he rather liked the idea of it being behind him when he preached, almost as if God was looking over his shoulder.

His stomach swirled at the thought of standing before the town that he'd once despised and telling its inhabitants about God's love. Memories of fights he'd been in flooded his mind. Yeah, he'd started some, but he'd been blamed for many more that he'd never participated in. He became the scapegoat, and the teacher never believed him when he proclaimed his innocence. He dropped onto the first pew, head in his hands.

Did those former students still live in town? Would they be the very people he'd minister to in a few days? In spite of believing

God had sent him to Lookout, he felt so inadequate.

He knelt on the hard floor and placed his elbows on the pew. "Help me to forgive those who wronged me in the past, Lord, even as I ask that the people I wronged will forgive me. Give me strength and guidance. Don't abandon me, Father. I need You now more than ever."

He clenched his hands together. Everyone he'd ever loved had abandoned him. His mother had died when he was a young boy, but even before that, his tiny little sister had passed on. Then his father had died when he was fifteen, not that he shed many tears over him. Even Jack had turned on him—although they'd never been friends. It ate at his gut to think she might have been afraid of him, and she'd have been justified. Like his father, when his temper reached its limit, he spewed on whoever was nearest, and the flame of his anger had scorched Jack more than once. At one time, he'd fancied himself in love with her, but she'd made it clear that she couldn't stand him. If she knew his real identity now, would she give him half a chance to prove he was a different person?

Noah muttered a groan. He wasn't here to think about her. He had a purpose. He was no longer the lonely boy who craved a friend and wanted to prove he could be a better man than his drunken father.

If he could just keep his thoughts off of Jack, he'd be all right.

But the question remained: How could he do that?

"So, what do you think about my story idea?" Jack watched Jenny Evans. She'd told the newspaper editor about what she'd overseen at the mercantile and couldn't wait to set pen to paper.

Jenny squeezed her lower lip together with her thumb and index finger, as she often did when deep in thought. "Hmm. . .it's interesting, but I'd hate to do anything that might scare Rand Kessler away. Catherine Morgan could use a husband, and Rand has wanted to marry for years."

Disappointed, Jack leaned back against the counter. She hadn't considered that her story might scare Rand away or otherwise affect the budding relationship. "What if we did the story but kept it anonymous? What if we said something like, 'A certain town widow was seen cavorting with a local rancher'?"

Jenny slowly nodded. "I like it. But be careful how you word the story so it's not too obvious who you're talking about, and *cavorting* is a word that could be taken the wrong way, so try to think up a better one." She tapped her pencil against the desktop. "And maybe you should say *cowboy* instead of *rancher*—or just say *man*."

Staring at the ceiling, Jack contemplated Jenny's wise suggestions. "I can do that."

"Good. Then write it up, and get it back to me as soon as possible. I planned to start printing the papers this evening."

Jack nodded. "I'd hoped to have something about the new minister for you, but he's not very talkative."

Chuckling, Jenny grinned. "Well, that's something different—a preacher who doesn't have the gift of gab. Now that's a rarity. I just might have to come and hear him preach, given his messages are likely to be short."

Jenny had misconstrued what she'd tried to say, but Jack kept that thought to herself. She wasn't quite ready to admit to others that she suspected the preacher of harboring secrets.

"I'm glad to see you're healing quickly and that you didn't get hurt too bad trying to get that story on the mayor."

"Thanks. I'm still sore in places, especially my knee, but it could have been a lot worse. I don't know what I was thinking going up on that roof in my dress." Suddenly she straightened. "And just where did you get the idea that I was engaged to Billy Morgan?"

Jenny grinned again and leaned back in her chair with her hands clasped behind her head, elbows sticking up. "Billy told me, and others repeated what he'd said about not marrying you if you didn't come down."

"Well, you should have checked with me first." Jack crossed her arms and pinned a stern glare on Jenny. "I am not now nor ever have been engaged to Billy Morgan. That's just an odd fancy he's got."

Jenny shrugged. "You might change your mind in a few years. He's a nice-looking young man."

"Yeah, but he's a sponger. He only helps his mother when he has to and then gallivants around town, getting in trouble. It's like he doesn't want to grow up. I don't want to marry that kind of man."

"Guess I'll have to print a retraction, but it did make interesting news." Jenny's shameless grin proved she wasn't sorry about what she'd done. "So just what kind of man would you want?"

An image of Noah Jeffers shoved aside all other pictures of the men she knew. Jack shook her head to rid him from her thoughts. She just found the man attractive, that was all. "I don't know that I'll ever get married. I've told you how I want to move to Dallas and be a big-city reporter."

Jenny straightened and leaned forward, her arms resting on her desk. "Don't forget I used to live in Dallas."

"Why would you leave there to come to a small town like Lookout?"

Jenny seemed to be pondering her response. "For one, I had a broken heart and needed to get away from the man who canceled our engagement. And two, men run the bigger towns, and women often have a harder time breaking into their world. I'd worked for some Dallas editors—all men. A few were nice, but most resented a woman working in their realm. I longed to start my own paper, but it would have been nearly impossible for me to do so in Dallas and to have to compete with the other already-established publishers."

Jenny had always encouraged her to seek her way in a man's world, so it took Jack off-guard to know her friend left Dallas rather than stay and compete for what she wanted. "Well, I don't see that there's much for me here. Besides, I don't plan to start my own newspaper, I just want to get a job where I can report the news and support myself."

"Have you talked this over with your mother?"

Jack nibbled on the inside of her cheek. Her mother would never want her to go. Luke wouldn't either, but he'd probably be more understanding. And how could she even begin to discuss such a topic when her ma was fixing to have another baby?

Jenny smiled. "I can see that you haven't." She stood, walked around her desk, and gently took hold of Jack's shoulders. "Big towns seem exciting and glamorous, but if you have no family or friends there, they can be frightening and lonely. I don't want to lose you here, but whatever you decide, you know I'll support you and help however I can." Jenny pulled her into a light hug then released her quickly. "Well, I'd best get the typesetting done if we're going to have a newspaper any time soon."

"I'll go find a quiet place to work on my story." Jack grabbed a pad of paper and pencil and hurried out of the office, probably just as embarrassed as Jenny at her rare show of affection. Jenny was a tough lady and rarely needed anyone, so it seemed. Maybe she'd just gotten her heart broken and no longer trusted men.

Hobbling down the boardwalk past the bank, she glanced across Bluebonnet Lane at the boardinghouse. If she went home, the kids would pester her, and she wouldn't finish her story in time. Her gaze traveled down the lane to the church. She loved sitting there when the place was empty, watching the sun shine through the lovely stained-glass window, but her knee was already aching.

With a sigh, she started across the road toward home. A sudden screech coming from her bedroom window halted her steps.

"Maaa! Alan hit—"

Jack turned toward the church. If Alan and Abby were fighting again, home was the last place she'd find any quiet. Taking it slow, she made her way down the street. She paused when she noticed the church door open, but this wasn't the first time someone had forgotten to close it. She stepped inside and shut the door. Instantly peace filled her. She dropped onto the nearest bench and blew out a breath. The ankle she'd twisted ached, and her knee throbbed. Doc Phillips had said that knee injuries could be slow to heal, but she'd hoped he was wrong. Hobbling along like someone's great-grandmother wasn't her normal speed.

She turned sideways on the bench and lifted her injured leg to the seat. After pulling up her skirt and petticoat, she rubbed her kneecap for a few minutes. When the pain lessened, she finally pulled out her paper and stared at it.

How could she slant the story without people guessing who she was referring to? Several ideas popped into her mind, but nothing was exactly what she was looking for.

"Hmm. . .maybe I should concentrate on the title first." She tapped her pencil against her mouth and stared at the colorful glass panes. She'd been so excited when the town decided to install the stained-glass windows after a tornado had blown through town and broken many of the clear panes in the church.

Shaking her head, she closed her eyes and tried to concentrate. Maybe "Shopping for Love" would work. But no, that might make people think of Mrs. Morgan since she ran the only mercantile in town.

Hmm, maybe "Lassoing Romance." There were many ranchers and cowboys in the county, so people wouldn't likely figure out who the man was. Or what about "Be on the Lookout for Cupid"?

She couldn't help giggling at the clever way she incorporated the town name. She scribbled it down before she forgot it.

A loud sound—as if someone were sawing wood—echoed through the church, and Jack froze. Her gaze darted to the front, then the sides and back of the building. Her heart pounded so hard she thought it might break through her skin. What in the world?

She concentrated on listening, but also remembered the open door. What if some wild animal had wandered inside? But she'd never heard a creature that made such a sound.

For several minutes she sat frozen, listening to her heart pound in her ears, then finally shook her head. Maybe she'd imagined the noise or it had come from outside. She glanced down at her paper, determined to get her story written.

Spring is in the air. New creatures are being birthed on ranches across the rolling green hills of the countryside, and romance has come to town. A certain lonely widow has been seen in the company of an equally forlorn rancher.

Remembering what Jenny had said, she scratched out *rancher* and changed it to *cowboy.*

She closed her eyes again and willed the words to come. Writing articles was generally difficult at first—until her creative juices started flowing.

A loud snort ricocheted through the building. Jack jumped, and her pencil flew out of her hand and rolled under the pew in front of her. Her frantic gaze traveled the room. The only thing she knew that made a sound like that was a pig—and if it was in the church, it must be a wild one. She pulled up her legs and stood on the bench seat, her whole body shaking. Luke had warned her about wild pigs. They were mean and could tear a person apart.

She glanced at the door. Could she make it outside before the creature got to her?

Would her knee hold up if she tried to run?

Could wild pigs leap up onto pews?

A deep moan made her jump again.

If the creature was wounded, it would be even meaner. Her heart raced like a runaway horse, and she found it hard to breathe. Her gaze flew to the stained-glass window and the image of Jesus standing in the boat, calming the seas. "Could You calm a wild pig, Lord? Please?"

She lifted her skirts and side-stepped along the bench, keeping careful watch on all the aisles. She'd never been one to scare easily and hated feeling helpless. If she could just get close enough to the door. . .

A huge figure rose up at the front of the church, and Jack couldn't squelch the scream that would have made Abby proud. A man spun around, wide-eyed, and stared at her. He frowned, then rubbed his eyes. "Ja—uh. . .Miss Davis?"

Jack's knees bent, weak with relief. She giggled, mortified to have squealed like a pig and to be caught standing on the pew by the minister, no less. What would he think of her?

What did it matter?

Like a flame to kindling, her embarrassment sparked her irritation. "Why were you hiding up there like some child and making those weird noises? You scared me half to death."

He ran a hand through his messed-up hair, causing it to stand up in an enticing manner. Creases lined one cheek. His neck and ears turned beet red, and his shy grin did odd things to her stomach, which still hadn't settled from her fright. "I was praying. Guess I fell asleep."

"Those were snores I heard? Well, I pity your wife."

He walked toward her, hanging his head, a saucy grin on his lips. "I don't have a wife, remember?"

She did, but he would soon acquire a spouse if Tessa had anything to say about it. "Yes, well, you won't have one long if you do marry and you snore like that every night."

He stopped at the end of her aisle and gazed up at her with his ink-black eyes. They were so dark she couldn't even see his pupils. She swallowed hard, not wanting to admit how attractive she found them.

"Allow me to help you down, Miss Davis, since I obviously scared you half to death."

"I wasn't scared," she blurted out before she could stop the words.

His brows lifted. "Ah, so let me guess. . . ." He glanced upward. "You're standing on the pew because you were just about to dust the ceiling."

She scowled. "Don't be ridiculous."

His hands found his hips, but his impudent grin seemed glued to his face. His eyes sparkled. "Then why are you standing on the pew?"

"I, uh. . .dropped my pencil." *Oh, horse feathers.* He had her, and he knew it.

His gaze lowered as he searched the floor. He stepped to the row in front of hers, bent down, and held up her pencil. "Imagine that, it was on the floor, not the ceiling."

"Ha ha, our minister is a jokester. That should certainly liven up the services." She snatched her pencil from his hand and stuck it in her hair over her ear. Obviously she wouldn't find any peace and quiet here with this joking preacher present. She reached down to take hold of the back of the pew in front of her. Before she could touch it, his hand snaked out and grabbed hers. "Let me assist you, Miss Davis."

Her eyes collided with his. Her rebellious heart pummeled her chest again. With him so close, she found it hard to breathe, but judging by his warm breath touching her face, he sure didn't. Slowly, she straightened. He laid her hand on one wide shoulder, claimed her other one and did the same. Then his hands wrapped around her waist. As if she weighed no more than Emmie, he lifted her down, his gaze never leaving hers.

Her legs had decided to pretend they were made of noodles, and her knees refused to lock. She sank down, but his hands tightened their grip, holding her steady.

"Are you all right?"

She shrugged. That was a highly debatable topic. How could any woman be completely composed with the handsome preacher so close—and he smelled so clean. "I. . .uh. . .think I may have overdone things, walking this far on my injured knee."

He frowned, but in the next instant, he scooped her into his arms. Jack gasped, yet she was amazed at how easily he held her and how good it felt. She lifted her gaze to his—so close, she could barely breathe. His lashes were long and thick, his eyes almost pleading. Many emotions crossed his face, but she couldn't read them. Up this close, she could see the slightest beginnings of his beard starting to grow in, even though she was certain he'd shaved this morning. Would his cheek feel smooth or rough?

He glanced down at her lips. Then he blinked several times, and an icy reserve replaced the warm look in his eyes, splashing onto her like a cold bucket of self-control.

"I'll carry you home, Miss Davis."

"No, just put me down."

"But you're hurt. I don't want you to injure your leg any more than it is."

"Why do you care?"

Although he didn't respond for a moment, his eyes revealed an inner struggle. Could he possibly have feelings for her?

No, it wasn't possible.

They'd only met.

Yet she couldn't help thinking she could spend the rest of her life in his arms. Tessa would be so mad if she found out.

"I'm your pastor. It's my job to care."

"I'm a reporter, and it's my job to get my story, but you refuse to answer my questions. What do you have to hide?"

"Most men in Texas are hiding something."

She wiggled her legs, and he loosened his hold but didn't set her down. "Most men in Texas aren't the only preacher in town, either."

He released her so suddenly she had to grab the back of the pew to keep from falling. "My past is my own. I've changed and am not the man I used to be, Miss Davis. God forgave me of my sins and set me on a new path. If you have a problem with me being the minister here, take it up with Him—or the church board."

He spun on his heel and marched out, slamming the door.

Jack lowered herself onto the bench. She shouldn't have pushed him, but she hadn't been prepared for her strong attraction to him. His arms felt so strong that he could shoulder any burden, yet she sensed she'd hurt him somehow. Would it have been so bad to let him carry her home?

Yes! It would. The whole town would be talking, and he just might lose his job, and she'd lose Tessa's friendship, such as it was. She found her paper and held it to her chest. How could she face him again?

But even more important, how could she discover what it was in his past that he wanted to keep secret?

Chapter 11

Carly twisted her hands as Lookout came into view. If things went as bad this time as on her last visit, she didn't know what she'd do. Jobs for unmarried women were hard enough to find, but for her, it was much more difficult. Few people wanted to hire an ex-convict.

She studied the buildings as thcy drew closer to Lookout. The town had grown quite a lot over the past decade. They drove past a schoolhouse that hadn't been there before and then the church. Would the members of this congregation be more accepting of her than the last?

Shaking off her worry, she glanced at Mr. Corbett. "How is your arm? I truly didn't mind driving."

"It's nothing." He gnawed on a stem of dried grass he'd plucked after he'd tied the thieves' horses to the back of the wagon. "Those fellows still passed out back there?"

Carly twisted around on the seat and studied the two robbers that they'd thrown over the horses and bound. One man's head was lifted, but thankfully it was turned away from her. The other man didn't look as if he'd moved a muscle. She sincerely hoped she hadn't killed him, even though they'd probably planned to rob them. She knew well how individuals with a tainted upbringing could change when God got ahold of them, and she muttered a brief prayer for their souls.

The wagon slowed, and she turned to see the boardinghouse. The light green, three-story home with white trim looked exactly the same. The porch railing, with its white spindles, still encircled the house, and even the rocking chairs survived, awaiting someone with a few minutes to relax. She swallowed hard. Rachel would welcome her with open arms, but what about the marshal? He'd been the one to arrest her and take her to Dallas all those years ago, once he learned she was a wanted outlaw, pretending to be one of the mail-order brides who had come to marry him.

What if he *had* picked her and they'd married? Would she have actually gone that far? All she'd wanted was the chance to get away from her brother and stop living an outlaw's life. Her plans to find out about gold shipments had failed, but she'd made some good friends—one in particular. She was counting on that friend to allow her to live in her home for the time being.

Shoring up her nerves, Carly thought about the past. She knew in her heart that back then, she *would* have married the marshal if given the chance, even with the constant threat of him figuring out she was a member of the Payton gang—albeit a reluctant member. Nothing was more important to her than having a home and people who cared about her. Even her own brother had wanted her around only so he could use her to his advantage. A sharp pain stabbed her heart. At least he could never hurt her again.

The wagon stopped, and she heaved a sigh. Time to find out how things would be. If the marshal was uncomfortable around her, she couldn't stay. Rachel had saved her life by leading her to Christ, and Carly wasn't about to cause her strife in her own home.

"What are you so antsy about?" Mr. Corbett set the brake, then looped the reins around the wooden handle.

Carly's heart leapt into her throat. "What makes you think I'm nervous?"

He grinned, revealing his straight white teeth. "Oh, maybe it was all the squirming you've done ever since Lookout came into view. Or maybe it was because you grabbed hold of my arm and wouldn't turn loose."

Carly gasped. "I did no such thing."

His head bobbed up and down. "You did. Wanna see the marks your fingernails made on my skin?" He winced as he moved his injured arm and started unbuttoning the cuff of his sleeve.

"That isn't necessary. I apologize for causing you so much trouble, Mr. Corbett. Thank you for the ride." She stood and reached over the seat to retrieve her satchel, but when she turned back, he tried to take it from her.

"I'll carry that."

"No, please let go. You're injured, and I'm quite capable of handling it myself." She gave it a sharp yank, but he didn't let go.

His interesting lips curved up in a grin that would probably melt the heart of a less-determined woman. This man had interfered in the lives of too many woman. She wasn't about to let him mess with hers. Such as it was.

"A gentleman always assists a lady."

Since when were the ornery Corbett brothers gentlemen? Carly tugged again on the handle, confused by his sudden desire to be her champion. Back on the prairie when he'd learned her name, he couldn't get away from her fast enough. She mulled over how to retrieve her satchel from his tight grasp. Surely she could out-tug a man weakened by a bullet wound in one arm. Maybe she just needed to distract him. "So, now I'm a lady? That ain't what you thought earlier."

His grin faded, and his gaze turned serious. "That was before you saved my life with your fancy shooting."

Dread churned in her belly like bad stew. "You ain't gonna tell no one, are ya?" Carly winced. Whenever she got upset, she tended to fall back into speaking how she used to—before Tillie taught her proper grammar.

His brows lifted up to the edge of his hat. "Why not? That's something to be proud of. Not many men can shoot that good, much less a woman."

Much less a woman. For some odd reason it hurt her to learn he was one of those men who thought women inferior. She wouldn't argue that men were stronger, but she had learned to be clever and resourceful just to survive. He watched her with those intriguing eyes. If he expected her to thank him for his off-handed compliment, he'd be waiting a long time.

She heard the front door to the boardinghouse open behind her, and Mr. Corbett's gaze darted past her shoulder. She took that moment to give another hard, two-handed jerk, and the bag not only fell free of his hand, but it sailed backward out of hers as well.

"Hey! Watch it."

Carly spun around from the momentum and nearly toppled across the nearest horse's rump. She swung her arms, struggling to regain her balance and not fall off the wagon. Mr. Corbett grabbed her arm, steadying her, and she saw Marshal Davis standing in front of the door, holding her bag against his chest, one brow lifted, an odd expression playing on his face. The sun glinted off the badge pinned to his shirt, and Carly dropped onto the bench seat. So much for making a good first impression.

Mr. Corbett chuckled and glanced up at the sky. "I've heard of it raining cats and dogs, but satchels? We'd better hurry up and get inside before any more fall from the sky. I've already conked my head once today, and that's enough." He held his hand toward Carly. "After you, Miss Payton."

The marshal set her bag in a rocker near the front door and strode forward. Carly's heart raced as if she'd just robbed a bank and was being pursued by a posse. She attempted to swallow the big lump in her throat, but her mouth was so dry she was about to spit cotton. Rachel's husband hadn't changed a whole lot except for looking a bit older. He was still a handsome man, but she'd hardly expected his welcoming smile or the lack of condemnation in his brown eyes.

He stopped next to the wagon and raised a hand. "Rachel's half beside herself from excitement to see you again. She's been baking all morning."

Steeling herself, Carly allowed him to help her out of the wagon. He released her hand, and she glanced up at him. She'd forgotten how tall he was. Mr. Corbett had to be close to six feet, and the marshal was at least two inches taller. He smiled at her then glanced at his cousin, still standing in the wagon. His smile dimmed as he looked at the two men tied to their horses. "What happened to you, Cuz, and who are they?"

Mr. Corbett hopped down and winced when his feet hit the ground. He grabbed his arm and gritted his teeth so hard that Carly could see his jaw tense. "They shot me."

"Shot? How bad is it?" The marshal glanced at Mr. Corbett's arm.

"I'll make it. I guess they'd planned to rob us, but they didn't count on—"

Carly cleared her throat, and both men's eyes swerved toward her. If she was going to be arrested because she used a weapon after the prison warden instructed her to never touch one again, she at least wanted to see Rachel first. "Would you mind if I go inside while y'all tend to those men? I'm anxious to see Rachel." *And to get away from you two.*

The marshal nodded. "Of course. My apologies, Miss Payton. I know you've had a long journey." He offered his arm, and she let him help her up the stairs. "Rachel's been holding lunch until you arrived."

"Lunch?" Mr. Corbett lifted his nose and sniffed. "Did someone mention food?"

"You're as bad as my kids." Marshal Davis shook his head and grinned. "And what's that on your arm? I didn't realize pink calico was the new style in arm bands."

Sticking out his elbow, Mr. Corbett flicked the loose fabric where Carly had tied a knot. His ears were red, but instead of acting embarrassed, he grinned. "Yeah, well, I'm not the only one wearing it. Them two probably need to have the doc look them over."

Carly resisted shaking her head. The man had been a joker when she'd been here before and never seemed to take anything seriously—except for when she'd told him her real name. He'd been more flustered than a rooster who had seen his last hen served up for someone's dinner. He hadn't cracked any jokes then. Still, she owed him a debt. "Thank you, Mr. Corbett, for giving me a ride here, in spite of the fact that you weren't expecting me."

The marshal grinned. "That was Rachel's idea. How'd you like her surprise?"

Mr. Corbett frowned at Carly, then mumbled something about seeing to his horses.

"You don't like it so much when the joke's on you, huh?" Chuckling, Marshal Davis grabbed her satchel, then opened the door. He paused and looked back at his cousin. "I'll take Miss Payton inside and send Alan over to fetch Doc Phillips. Then I'll help you with those fellows and the team. And I want the doc to check your arm." He opened the door and pushed it. "After you, ma'am."

Carly slipped past him, her stomach awhirl, and stepped into the boardinghouse. Fragrant aromas emanated from the kitchen, and she felt almost as if she'd stepped back ten years. The only difference she noticed right off was that the parlor walls had been painted light blue. Several toys littered the floor, as if a child had just hurriedly left the room. The marshal set her satchel on the hall tree bench, then strode toward the kitchen. He disappeared through the doorway, and Carly heard a high-pitched squeal.

Rachel bustled out of the kitchen and chugged down the hall like a locomotive building steam, her light blue eyes sparkling. "I'm so glad you're finally here." She pulled Carly into an awkward embrace. Then she stepped back and patted her belly. "Oscar, here, gets in the way of things at times."

Lifting one brow, Carly stared at her friend. "Oscar?"

Rachel laughed. "That's what Luke called our first baby before it was born, and it just stuck. They're Oscar while they're in my womb, but once they come out, they get a name of their own."

Carly had never heard of such a thing, but then she hadn't been around many women carrying babies other than the few who had visited Tillie. "It's so good to see you again."

Rachel nodded. "You, too. I'm glad you finally decided to come and stay with us."

The back kitchen door banged, and a boy charged out of the kitchen and down the hall, followed by the marshal. A girl of about five or six raced after him. Alan and Abby, Carly assumed. They were just as Rachel had described them in her letters.

"Gotta go, Ma. Papa needs the doctor."

Rachel's gaze jumped from her son to her husband. "Are you hurt?"

Marshal Davis shook his head. "Not me—Garrett and two men he shot."

Carly bit her lip to keep from correcting him. Maybe Mr. Corbett would keep her secret, but she doubted it.

"I'm goin' with Alan," Abby said.

The boy skidded to a halt. "Nuh-uh. Tell her to stay here, Papa. You said *I* could go."

Marshal Davis lifted a brow. "I'm the one who gives orders around here, Son, not you. Take your sister, but hurry back. Your ma has the food ready."

The boy's shoulders sagged, but his sister's grin illuminated the room. Carly smiled at the child. Alan's medium brown hair and blue eyes favored his ma, while Abby—if she was remembering right from Rachel's letters—had blond hair and her father's eyes.

"I'm gonna beat you." Abby lunged for the front door.

"Nuh-uh!" Alan charged after her, nearly knocking Carly down.

"Slow down and stay clear of the horses and wagons," Rachel hollered.

Carly watched the two children fight to get out the door first and shook her head. Rachel had written to her about the rambunctious children, but Carly hadn't believed they were so wild until she saw it with her own eyes. They reminded her of Jacqueline.

"Garrett's hurt?" Rachel asked. "How bad?"

The marshal glanced at Carly as if asking her to respond. "Not too bad. God must have been watching over him, because the bullet just grazed his upper arm. It's a deep gouge but should heal all right if Mr. Corbett doesn't overuse his arm for a while."

"Let's sit a minute while you tell me what happened." Rachel looped her hand around Carly's elbow and tugged her into the parlor as the marshal headed for the door, eating one of Rachel's biscuits.

Carly relayed the story, leaving out the part about her shooting their attackers and also the part about Mr. Corbett's reaction to finding a passenger at the depot instead of a package. If he wanted them to know of his shock, he could tell them.

Rachel shook her head. "I think that's only the second or third time a Corbett Freight wagon has been attacked before. At least you got the men, so they can't hurt anyone else. And Garrett truly seems to be all right?"

Carly nodded. "He's in some pain, but he wouldn't let me drive the wagon, and he was joking some."

"That sounds like him. Stubborn as Luke." Rachel shook her head and blew out an exasperated breath. Then she took Carly's hands. "I was so sorry to hear about Tillie and how you had to move out of the Barker home. I know you enjoyed living there."

Carly shrugged and pulled her hands back to her lap. "I do miss Tillie—and the reverend—but I can't say I miss that town much."

"Were the people unkind?"

She studied the braided rug at her feet, remembering how many of the church folks shunned her. "Some, but not all."

Rachel clutched Carly's hands again, drawing her gaze up. "I'm sure things will be different here. You can start over. I'm so excited to have you here."

Carly smiled, trying to stir up her enthusiasm to match Rachel's. "But I must find work, and who'll hire an ex-convict?"

Blinking, Rachel stared at her, looking confused. "Didn't you receive my last letter?"

Carly searched her mind, then shook her head. "The last one I got arrived about a month ago. Then your telegram that said, 'Come.'"

"I wrote you after you told me that it looked like Mrs. Barker was failing. Oh, Oscar is kicking me." She leaned back and rubbed her hand across the right side of her stomach.

Carly wondered if she'd ever get to experience being a mother—to feel her own child move and kick within. At twenty-eight, she was well into spinsterhood. She smiled as she held her hands tightly together to keep from fidgeting.

"Anyway, before Oscar interrupted, I was going to say that I wrote and asked you to come and help me."

"Of course I'll help. You know you don't have to ask after all you've done for me. I imagine you must get exhausted tending this big place and cooking and caring for your family, especially now with the baby so close to coming."

"Thank you. I'll admit it is harder when I'm this far along in my pregnancy." She turned and stared out the window, her cheeks pink, as if embarrassed to talk about such a delicate topic. "Jacqueline is a lot of help most of the time, but this week she's been in bed after. . .uh. . .taking a fall. She's getting up and around some now, but I don't want to have to depend on her all the time."

Carly's stomach growled at the delicious scents drifting through the house, and she placed her hand against it. "Is she still writing stories for the newspaper?"

"Yes." Rachel pursed her lips. "But that's not the worst of it. She wants to move to Dallas and write for a larger paper. She doesn't think I know, but I overheard her talking with her friends one day."

Carly knew how hard it would be on Rachel to have her eldest daughter move away, not just because Rachel wouldn't have help, but more so because of Jack's hankering after adventure and getting into trouble. "I'm sorry. That worries you, doesn't it?"

Rachel nodded and pushed up out of the chair. "Yes, it surely does. But she's a grown woman now, and I've got to trust God to take care of her." A smile flitted across her lips. "Don't tell her, but I've been praying the Lord would bring a nice young man to town who will steal her heart and make her forget about Dallas."

Carly stood and picked up her bag. "And has He?"

"Perhaps." With eyes dancing, she waggled her brows. "Let me show you to your room so you can freshen up before we eat."

Carly followed her friend up the stairs, remembering so many things from the past. Leah, the blond mail-order bride who'd come to marry Luke, had stayed in the first room on the left, while Shannon, the Irish bride, had the one to her right.

"My girls stay in the green room now, and we divided your old room in half. Alan stays in one side, and we use the other for stage drivers who occasionally overnight here, but with the expansion of the railroad, I don't expect stagecoaches will be around much longer." Rachel opened the second door on the left.

"Too bad there isn't a train that comes to Lookout." Then she could have avoided that uncomfortable ride with Mr. Corbett, and he wouldn't have gotten shot.

"I hope you'll be comfortable here." Rachel pulled back the blue and white gingham curtains and lifted a window. "Of course, in exchange for your help, your room and board is free. I know you'll need some extra for expenses, and if we have lots of customers, I'll gladly pay you a small salary."

"I never expected you to pay me." Carly set her satchel on the bed and glanced around the cozy room painted white. A lovely wedding quilt in various shades of blues and white covered the bed. "I offered to help you because you're my friend, and if it hadn't been for you, I probably would never have met the Lord."

Rachel wrapped an arm around Carly's shoulder. "The help I need goes beyond the bonds of friendship. I basically need someone who can take over and run the boardinghouse after I have the baby—at least for a few weeks."

Carly smiled. Maybe things were finally looking up for her. "You've got yourself a helper."

Chapter 12

Jack stared at her image in the long mirror at Dolly's Dress Shop. The bottom of the fitted bodice of the dark green dress angled down to form a V at her stomach, accentuating her narrow waist. The neckline also tapered to a V and was edged with wide lace, which lay across her shoulders. The short sleeves ended just above her elbows, but six-inch lace attached to the cuffs flounced across her lower arms. The full overskirt swirled when she twisted from side to side, but a stabbing pain in her knee made her grimace.

"What's wrong? The dress looks lovely with your coloring." Dolly Dykstra stared at her in the mirror, concern etching her features.

"Oh yes, I love it. But I twisted too far and made my knee hurt."

Tessa hiked her chin and fluffed her curls. "Your ma says you should still be abed."

Jack glanced at Penny, who rolled her eyes. Stifling a smile, she glanced back at the mirror. She actually looked pretty. She still loved donning britches, but she had to admit, if only to herself, that she was learning to enjoy dressing up.

"Don't you just love the shirred-up bottom of the green fabric and how it reveals the lace-trimmed underskirt?" Penny's eyes grew dreamy as if she imagined herself in the gown.

"I do love it, Mrs. Dykstra." Jack smiled at the older woman. "You outdid yourself."

Dolly puffed her chest and smiled, her chubby cheeks a bright red. Jack was glad she had ordered the dress, but she wasn't sure, as fancy as it was, if it would be suitable for a church dress. She'd hoped to be able to use it for more than special occasions.

She might look pretty at the Saturday social, but she sure wouldn't be dancing. An image of Noah Jeffers flashed across her mind. Would he be disappointed? Would he even be at the dance?

"I plan to wear a beautiful pale copper and soft sea green brocade tea dress that Mother ordered from Boston," Tessa announced. "It has pearl buttons. There was even a very similar dress on the cover of *Ladies' Home Journal*." Tessa hiked her chin and planted a smile on her face, obviously proud that her dress was much more elaborate than Jack's.

"I'm sure it will be lovely." Jack ignored Tessa's barb, as she did most times Tessa had to prove whatever she had was better than someone else's. She'd long ago decided if she wanted to be friends with her, she'd have to overlook Tessa's need to put herself above others. Jack didn't care. She despised hot, fancy dresses and much preferred the cooler calicos.

"That pine green color looks beautiful with your reddish brown hair." Penny stood off to the side, along with Tessa. Jack appreciated her friend's effort to make her feel better.

"I agree." Dolly pushed her large frame up from her chair and tucked a strand of gray hair behind her ear. "If you could stand on that crate for me, I'll measure the hem, and then you ladies can be off to tend to whatever it is you need to do."

Ever helpful and considerate, Penny hurried over and held out her hand, assisting Jack as she climbed onto the box. "Yes, you should finish here, so you can rest your leg. We want it well so you can go to the social tomorrow."

Tessa swirled sideways and back, her blue skirts swishing. "I thought you weren't going."

Jack shrugged. "I changed my mind." Or had Noah Jeffers changed it for her?

Tessa's blue eyes sparkled, and her face took on a dreamy

expression. "I can hardly wait to dance with the new minister. I'm sure he's an excellent dancer."

Penny scowled and glanced sideways, shaking her head. "How do you know he'll come? Reverend Taylor never did."

"Oh, I just know. Reverend Taylor was married, but a handsome man like our new parson has to be looking for a wife, and I plan to be there for him." Tessa picked up a fan from a nearby display and snapped it open. She held it across her face, leaving only her blue eyes showing. "I'll make myself irresistible."

Penny coughed and held her hand over her mouth, eyes dancing with mirth. Jack stared at her own image again. She was tall and lanky, where Tessa was shorter and had much fuller curves. Didn't men prefer women with curves? And blond hair?

She shuddered. What did it matter? She didn't want to attract a man. Then why was she going to the social?

"Hold still, Miss Jacqueline," Dolly said. "I know you like to be moving constantly, but if you want a straight hem, don't move."

Jack forced herself to stand quietly, even though her knee was screaming at her. She'd have to spend the rest of the day off of it. Maybe she could work some more on her story about the reverend. And maybe if he showed up, she could wheedle some more answers from him about his past.

She thought back to their encounter at the church several days ago. She'd never seen a man with such dark eyes who wasn't an Indian or Mexican. Noah's skin was nicely tanned but didn't have the coloring of those other races. And he was so tall. And strong. She heaved a sigh, drawing Penny's gaze. The young woman lifted her brow and grinned, as if she could read Jack's mind. She turned her face away, staring at Dolly's crowded store, and hoped her friend hadn't seen her blush.

Bolts of fabric lined the shelves of one whole wall, with all manner of sewing tools, thread, and buttons lining the drawers of a glass-topped credenza. The place was small but well-organized.

"All right, missy, you're done. Take care of the pins when you remove the gown."

Jack slid behind the dressing screen, undid the practical front buttons, and let the garment pool onto the floor. As she put on her navy skirt and shirtwaist, she couldn't help the envy that surged within her. Would Tessa turn the reverend's eye with her fancy dress and beguiling ways?

Something else bothered her even more.

Why did she care?

Jack stood on the boardwalk outside of Dolly's store, glad to have her final fitting complete. She'd return tomorrow morning to pick up her dress, just in time for the evening social. A whack sounded to her right, and she turned to see what it was.

Tessa tugged her arm, pulling her attention back. "Let's go over to Polly's Café and have some pie."

Jack shook her head. "I've got to head home. Emmie will be waking up from her nap soon, and I'm watching her and the other children so Ma can rest."

"Oh my. . ." Penny heaved an exaggerated sigh. She stood in the space between Dolly's Dress Shop and the freight office, looking down the alley.

Jack stepped off the boardwalk and stood beside her. Another whack echoed between the buildings. Past Dolly's purple dress shop, across the alley in Bertha Boyd's backyard, a bare-chested man was cutting wood—a very well-built man. She tried to swallow, but her mouth was so dry she couldn't even work up a good spit.

"What're you two gawking at?" Tessa shoved her way in front of Jack. "My goodness, what a fine-looking man."

"Why, isn't that the new pastor?" Penny glanced at Jack before resuming her staring.

"It is—and he's shirtless. Oh my. . ." Tessa fanned her face and started toward the alley. "I need a closer look."

Jack followed. She just might have to keep Tessa from getting into trouble. Penny trailed after them.

They stopped at the back corner of Dolly's building and lingered there. Noah Jeffers lifted the axe and brought it down hard, splitting the log in half. A memory flashed across Jack's mind of another time and another woodcutter. She winced, remembering the mean trick she and her two best friends had played on Butch Laird, the town bully. Yet Noah Jeffers was not a thing like Butch Laird, other than having the same color hair. And maybe eyes—or were Butch's brown?

Tessa leaned in close to Jack and Penny. "Have you ever seen anything so. . .so manly?"

He turned slightly toward them, picked up the half log he'd just cut, and set it back on the chopping block. Jack couldn't help noticing the dark hair that covered his chest and tapered down his flat stomach. The muscles in the minister's arms bulged as he lifted the axe again. His skin glistened with sweat across his broad shoulders when the axe hit its mark. Jack knew that watching him wasn't right, but she couldn't tear her gaze away.

"How do you suppose a preacher got so—uh—muscled?" Penny asked, without ever looking away. "And his back is so tanned. He must chop a lot of wood."

"We should go. If we startle him, he could slip and hurt himself." Jack pulled at her friends' arms. "It isn't proper for unmarried women to be watching a man without his shirt on.

"Oh, posh. Men remove their shirts around ladies all the time." Tessa tossed a glance back over her shoulder at Jack. "And are you saying it would be all right to observe him if we were all married?"

"I don't know." Penny's voice quivered. "I think we should go, like Jacqueline said."

Jack straightened, watching as the minister picked up an armload of the quartered sections and carried them to the woodpile that sat along the backside of the house. Butch would never have been able to carry such a hefty load. She shifted her feet, knowing she needed to get home. Her ma was constantly tired and needed every chance she could to rest. And the longer she stood there, the guiltier she felt.

"Back up, or he'll see us when he turns to go back to the chopping block." Tessa shoved backward, not even bothering to turn around. Penny pivoted, and her eyes went wide, just as Jack backed into a solid body.

"What are you ladies up to?"

Tessa squealed and turned, holding a hand against her heart, but she quickly pasted on her trademark smile. "Why, you scared us half to death, Marshal. Don't you know not to sneak up on a group of ladies?"

Ever so slowly, Jack glanced over her shoulder and lifted her eyes to her stepfather's. "We. . .uh. . .just left Dolly's shop and were. . .uh. . .heading home."

Luke quirked a brow and stared at her. Jack had to work hard not to squirm. "Taking the alley is longer than just walking down Main Street." The whacking resumed, and Luke's gaze moved past her. A grin twittered on his lips. "Ahh. . .now I see what has y'all so captivated. I was wondering if you were ever going to take an interest in a man."

Jack's heart somersaulted. "No, Papa, you've got it all wrong. I. . .um, I mean. . .we. . ." What could she say that wouldn't be a lie?

Tessa suddenly screamed. Luke's hand went straight to his gun, and Jack spun around to see what had happened. Had the minister injured himself?

Tessa danced from foot to foot then jumped behind Penny. "A snake!"

Luke chuckled and stepped past them. "It's nothing but a garden snake." He picked it up and dangled it in front of them.

Tessa gasped and back-stepped, pulling Penny with her, as if she were a shield.

Jack shook her head. "It's harmless."

Tessa wheeled around and charged past Jack, holding her skirts high. "You know I despise snakes!" She disappeared around the corner in a blur of blue dress.

Luke tossed the offending critter in the tall grass growing under the back porch of the freight office. "I think it's time you ladies moved along."

Jack nodded and took one last glance at Noah Jeffers. Her heart jumped clear up to her throat. He stood there, leaning on the axe handle, watching them just as they'd watched him.

∽

What were those gals up to? He'd heard the one woman scream and thought someone was in trouble, but then the marshal held a snake in the air. Noah chuckled. It sure wasn't Jack who'd let out that squeal. A little ol' snake wouldn't daunt her any.

But why had she and her friends been in the alley?

His mind flashed back to another day and time. He glanced at the stacked wood, relieved to see it was all still there. Old Mrs. Linus and her sister, Mrs. Boyd, had been delighted to meet him and duly impressed when he offered to chop some wood for them as a courtesy. The tea they'd offered him had been as tasty as the tiny cucumber sandwiches they'd fed him, but that delicious stuff they called fudge had been his favorite. He'd chop wood every day for another taste of that sweet treat.

He set another piece of wood onto the chopping block, but a motion in the corner of his eye caught his attention. The marshal ambled toward him, wearing his trademark denim pants and light blue cambric shirt. The sunlight glimmered off the badge on his chest, and Noah couldn't help noticing the gun that hung low on his hips. Noah's pulse sped up, and he worked hard to look casual. It made no sense that this man should cause him to be nervous, but he did.

"Afternoon." The marshal nodded his head.

"Marshal." Noah held his tongue, figuring the lawman would speak his mind without any prompting.

He pushed his hat back off his forehead. "Were you aware you had an audience?"

Noah's gaze darted toward the ugly purple building. They'd been watching him? He reached for his shirt.

Marshal Davis chuckled. "Too late for that."

Noah tossed it back across the tree branch since his job wasn't finished. "How long had they been there?"

"Not long. I saw them come out of Dolly's shop and then duck down the alley. I wondered what they were doing and followed." He shook his head and looked away for a moment. "You're new around here, so you probably haven't yet heard that my daughter can be a handful."

Though he knew just which daughter the man meant, he asked, "You have more than one daughter, sir."

Luke Davis grinned again. "Good point, Reverend. I was

referring to my eldest. She's actually my stepdaughter, but I think of her as my own. That feisty little Abby, though, sure is giving Jack a run for her money."

Noah nodded. He'd seen traits of Jack in her sister. "Do you think you could call me Noah or even Pastor, instead of Reverend? I'm uneasy with that title."

The marshal nodded. "I can do that." He hooked his thumbs in his pockets and stared at Noah.

Struggling hard not to squirm, he picked up his axe and leaned on the handle. He could see the marshal was working up to something. *Don't ask. Not yet.*

Luke's mouth twisted sideways. "I reckon I should warn you about those three gals. My Jack's never shown a great interest in men. I imagine that's the fault of her first father." Luke stared off in the distance, a muscle ticking in his jaw. "Let me just say he wasn't a kind man."

Noah had heard a few rumors about James Hamilton when he previously lived in town, but being just a kid, he hadn't thought on it much. Besides, the man hadn't sounded all that much different from his own pa. He was well aware of the issues that surfaced when a kid lived with a cruel father. Could that be why Jack had always acted so tough?

"Anyway, what I'm trying to say is that I don't think you have to worry about her or Penny, but I'd watch out for that Tessa Morgan. If she sets her hat for you, well. . .just consider yourself duly warned."

Noah had seen the blond gal looking at him more than once, and she always tried to weasel up next to him if she saw him alone. He swallowed hard, then looked Jack's stepfather in the eye. "I didn't come here looking for a wife, Marshal."

"Luke."

Noah nodded. "God sent me here to share His Word with the people of Lookout."

Luke pursed his lips. Then a wry smile tugged at his mouth. "I once thought God sent me back to Lookout for a certain reason, too, but things turned out far different from what I'd planned. Don't close any doors on God. He may have more for you here than you ever expected."

Noah's heart leapt before he lassoed it back under control. Maybe he could find a home here and the friends and respect he craved. But Pastor Taylor would eventually return to town, and then Noah would no longer be needed. Yeah, he could start another church, but he wouldn't do that. The parishioners would most likely stay with Pastor Taylor anyway.

"Well, guess I'll be moseying along. Have a good day. . .Noah."

Noah's grasp tightened on the wooden handle as he watched the marshal walk away. He exhaled a sigh of relief, knowing he'd dodged another bullet. He turned the log on the chopping block to get the best angle, then lifted the axe, just as the marshal spun back around. The man strode toward him with purpose. He eyed the axe and slowed his steps.

Noah lowered the tool and waited. Sweat ran down his temple, but he didn't swipe at it.

Luke shook his head. "I've been a marshal for ten years and was a soldier for another decade before then. One thing I've learned is to trust my gut, and it's screaming that we've met before." The marshal's gaze hardened, but he didn't look unkind. "Noah Jeffers isn't your real name, is it?"

Chapter 13

Jack and Penny's quick steps echoed along the boardwalk as they passed a moseying couple. Jack glanced over her shoulder just as the man and woman turned into the newspaper office. She blew out a heavy breath and allowed her steps to slow.

Penny copied her and peered back toward Dolly's shop. She patted her thin hand against her chest. "I don't know how you keep from having curly hair."

Jack stared at her friend. "What?"

Penny swatted her hand in the air. "The marshal is so stern. He scares me so badly my hair curls."

Shaking her head, Jack couldn't help grinning. "Luke may act tough, but he's just a big, lovable puppy."

"Nuh-uh." Penny stiffly shook her head, her eyes wide. "I'd better head back home before Mama comes looking for me."

Jack waved. "See you tomorrow."

Penny walked backwards down Bluebonnet Lane. "You gonna dance with the minister if Billy doesn't hog you?"

"No. I doubt I'll be dancing at all since my knee still hurts."

Penny shrugged and turned around, then continued down the lane at a quick clip.

"Well, now, that disappoints me."

Billy. Jack closed her eyes and took a calming breath. He was more annoying than a bad case of poison ivy. Forcing a cordial smile, she turned to face him. "H'lo, Billy."

His passionate gaze raked her from head to toe, a slow smile stealing across his mouth. "Sure am glad you didn't kill yourself when you fell off that roof."

"So is my ma." Jack resisted rolling her eyes at her dumb response.

Billy scowled and leaned against the boardwalk railing, crossing his arms. "What's that nonsense about you dancing with that new minister?"

"Nothing." Jack's ire simmered. It was none of his business who she danced with. "I won't be dancing with anyone because my knee is still tender."

"I've been looking forward to this social just so's me and you can kick up our heels a bit."

"Sorry to disappoint you. I need to go." She started across the street, but he intercepted her, blocking her way.

Irritation flickered in his blue eyes. He forked his fingers through his white blond hair. "Hold on now. Surely you could dance with me a little bit."

She glanced at the store and boardinghouse, half relieved no one was watching and half disappointed. Where was Luke when she needed him?

She'd told Billy over and over that she wasn't interested in him, but he failed to believe her. "I'm going to the social, but I won't be dancing. My knee is all right for walking, but I can't dance and risk twisting it and doing more damage. The doctor said it may take a long time to heal."

"Then why are you bothering to have that new dress made?"

She could hardly tell Billy she hadn't been all that interested in the dress her ma had ordered until Noah Jeffers came to town. Jack lifted her brows. "How do you know about that?"

"Tessa told me."

Ahh, Tessa. She'd probably bragged about how much nicer her own dress was and how it had come all the way from Boston.

He stood with his hands on his hips, staring down at her. She couldn't deny he was a handsome man, and that was part of the problem. He thought he could flash his dimpled smile and get every gal in town to swoon. Well, not her. She never swooned.

"Why don't you ask Velma Tate? She'd love to go with you."

He snorted and looked as if he might gag. "She's fat."

Jack crossed her arms. "She is not. Besides, she's really nice and likes you a lot."

"Well, I don't like her. You're my fiancée. It wouldn't look right for me to take some other gal."

Gritting her teeth, Jack leaned in close. "I—am—not—your—fiancée. And stop telling people that I am. You hear?"

His smile returned. "Oh, Jacqueline, are we having a lover's spat?"

"Oh!" Jack stomped her foot. The sharp pain that grabbed her knee like a bear claw instantly caused her to regret the action. She bent down, rubbing her knee through the fabric of her skirt and petticoat. "We're not lovers. And I thank you kindly not to ever say that again."

"You all right?" He had half enough sense to look repentant.

She straightened but kept the heel of her sore leg off the ground. "No, I'm not, thanks to you."

"I didn't make you stomp your foot."

Jack rolled her eyes. Men were so dense. A dog barked behind her, and she heard a harness jingle. She stepped to the side of the road and looked to see who was coming. A farmer she didn't recognize tipped his straw hat at her. His black-and-white dog sat on the seat beside him, wagging his tail. Jack smiled and waved at the man.

Billy scowled as the wagon passed them. "Who's that?"

"I don't know. I was just being friendly."

He stepped up close to her and brushed his fingers through the hair that hung into his eyes. "How come you ain't more friendly to me?"

She hated hurting people's feelings, but she was also getting tired of Billy's possessiveness. "Maybe because you won't take no for an answer. I'm not interested in marrying you, Billy. Or courting, either. I don't ever plan to marry, so you're wasting your time." As soon as the words left her mouth, an image of Noah Jeffers chopping wood invaded her mind.

"You're just too high and mighty, Miss I'm-the-marshal's-daughter." Billy's childish, singsong tone set her nerves on edge.

"Luke doesn't have anything to do with us."

The door on the boardinghouse flew open, and Alan stepped onto the porch. He shaded his eyes with his hand; then he saw her and waved. "Emmie's awake and wants out of bed. Ma said I should come find you, Sissy."

"I'm coming." She looked at Billy again. "I've gotta go."

A muscle in his jaw ticked, and he glared at her, his eyes as cold as ice. "Most girls in this county would be happy to dance with me. You just be ready come tomorrow night, or else."

Jack shoved her hands to her hips and leaned toward him. "Or else what?"

"You don't wanna find out." Billy spun on his heel and marched back toward the mercantile his mother owned.

Jack watched him go. She wasn't one to scare easily, but something in the tone of Billy's voice set her senses on alert. What would he do if she didn't dance with him? Hurt her? Or one of her siblings?

Besides her father, only one person had ever scared her like Billy just had, but he was long gone. Too bad Billy wasn't also.

~

Noah's hands sweated as he stared at the marshal. He found it hard to swallow, as if the man had his fingers around Noah's throat, but he couldn't lie—he wouldn't. All he could do was tell the marshal the truth and hope the man believed that he had changed. That he wasn't the troubled youth he'd once been. *Please, Lord, don't let him send me packing. I'm not done here yet.*

The marshal's eyes narrowed, and Noah broke his gaze and stared at the wood cuttings spread across the grass where he'd been working. If he had to leave Lookout now, his heart would resemble those chips—splintered and scattered.

"I am with you always."

Noah lifted his head, resolve coursing through him as God's words strengthened him. The Lord had sent him here on a mission, and Luke Davis couldn't keep him from it.

He caught the marshal's gaze again and nodded. "Yes, sir, we've met before."

Luke's jaw quivered, as if he was clenching his teeth. "When—and where?"

Noah glanced away again. "Here. Ten years ago."

The marshal's eyes lifted to the sky, and he seemed to be searching his memory. His brow dipped, and his mouth twisted to one side. His eyes suddenly widened. "You're not part of the Payton Gang, are you?"

Noah shook his head, surprised the marshal hadn't figured out the mystery yet.

"Nah, you're too young. How old are you, anyhow?"

"Twenty-four."

The marshal didn't seem in any big hurry to remember, so Noah waited, hoping he'd get distracted like the last time he asked. Finally, he shook his head. "I can't recollect who you are."

Noah kicked a chunk of wood, knowing his time was up. "Noah is what my ma named me. It's my real first name, but my pa hated it and refused to call me that. Said it wasn't a manly enough name for his son. I did change my surname, though."

He tightened his fist on the wooden handle as unwanted memories of his past assailed him. Of all the times he took a beating because he didn't do something fast enough for his pa or when he burnt the meal or came home late. "My pa was a lazy man and a mean drunk. We were living up near Emporia when he died. I was fifteen and old enough to be on my own, but a kind man named Pete Jeffers took me in anyway and taught me how to be a real man, and he taught me about God's love."

Noah leaned the axe against the chopping block. If the marshal got upset when he heard the truth and took a swing at him, he sure didn't want either of them to get hurt on the axe blade. "Pete was the only real father figure I ever had, and it just seemed the right thing to adopt his name."

The marshal nodded. "Sounds a whole lot like Jack's story and mine. She uses my last name now."

Hope spread through him. Maybe this man did understand. "Yeah, it does. Anyway, my real last name was. . .Laird." He attempted to swallow the lump in his throat. "And everyone knew me by Butch."

For a moment, the marshal's face remained passive. Then he scowled. "Butch Laird! You're Butch Laird? That bully who caused Jack so much trouble?"

Remorse weighted down his shoulders. "Yes, sir."

The marshal stepped closer, his gaze narrowed. "You don't aim to cause her any more problems, do you?"

Noah blinked, not the least bit surprised at the vehemence in the marshal's expression. The man had no idea how much trouble Jack had caused him by her lying and trickery, but he had no desire to be vindicated. The past was past. Why was it so easy to forgive her and not his own father? "No, sir. Nothing could be further from my mind. I came here to do the Lord's work—and to make restitution for the bad things I did in the past. I'm not like I used to be, sir. Let me prove to you—and the town—that I've changed."

Marshal Davis relaxed his stance and stepped back. After a few moments, a grin crept onto his face, both surprising and relieving Noah. "Would those two new pie plates Mrs. Burke said magically appeared on her back porch have anything to do with your making restitution?"

Noah shrugged and tried to keep a straight face, but he felt his lips quirk up on one side. "Maybe. The scriptures say that when you give, your right hand shouldn't know what the left hand is doing."

The marshal nodded. "All right. I hear you. But I do have to say that was the first time I responded to a complaint about intruders, only to discover they left something instead of taking stuff." He smiled then rested his hands on his hips and stared at the ground. "There's one thing I do need to ask—were you the one who painted *Jack is a liar* all over town that day you left?"

He'd all but forgotten that stupid deed and deeply regretted painting those words, but he'd been so angry. Jack had lied about something he no longer remembered, causing him to spend two days in jail, only to return home and take a beating from his pa for being gone so long and not being there to cook his meals. They even packed up and moved because his pa said he was getting into too much trouble, and they needed a fresh start. He stared at his fingers. It had taken days for that red paint to wear off his hands, a constant reminder of his stupid, impulsive deed. "Yeah, I did that, and I can tell you I've regretted it ever since."

Jack's father stared into his eyes, as if judging how truthful his words were. Finally, he nodded. "I believe you mean that."

"I do. If I could do it over, I'd do things differently."

The marshal placed his hand on Noah's shoulder, warming his skin and his heart. "You had a hard time of things, son, and I want you to know that Jack told me the truth about everything after you left."

Noah stared at the man, shocked all the way to his toes. "She did?"

"Yep. I'm sorry I was so hard on you back then, but I believed that little squirt. I never dreamed she'd tell me a falsehood."

"She could be convincing."

"And she had those two friends of hers always backing up whatever she said. It was your word against theirs. I'm sorry that I didn't take you more seriously." He yanked off his hat and smacked it against his leg. "I feel like I let you down, son. I'm sorry for not believing you."

Overhead, a robin chirped a cheerful tune, oblivious to the turmoil Noah was experiencing. He never expected the marshal to apologize and didn't quite know how to take it. He'd always been the one blamed whenever there was trouble, and no one had ever taken his side on things, even when he was the one who'd been wronged. "It's all right. I understand."

Luke Davis locked gazes with him. "I reckon you had more character back then than I gave you credit for."

A place deep within Noah sparked and glowed as he saw respect blossom in the marshal's eyes.

"I don't remember you ever tattling on Jack."

He shrugged. "It wouldn't have done any good. Nobody believed anything I said."

"Is that why you haven't told people who you are?"

Was that the real reason? Or could it have something to do

with Jack? He lifted one shoulder and dropped it again. "Maybe. Do you think anyone would come to church if they knew the old town bully, Butch Laird, was preaching?"

"You've got a point, but you might be surprised. Lots of new folks who never heard of Butch Laird have moved here and attend church, and plenty of others would come out of curiosity."

Noah watched a dog slink over to someone's trash pile a few houses down and snitch a piece of garbage. The mutt carried it over to a nearby tree and lay down in the shade, chewing on his find. He'd felt just like that unwanted creature when he'd previously lived in Lookout. "You honestly think if folks knew they'd give me a chance?"

The marshal set his hat back on his head, then rubbed his chin with his forefinger and thumb. "Some would, some wouldn't. But you'll never know for certain unless you come clean."

Noah wiped his sweaty brow with his forearm. "I plan to tell folks, but I'd hoped to wait a month or so and let them see me for who I am now. I'm a new creation in Christ, Marshal. I can assure you, I'm not like I used to be."

Marshal Davis nodded. "All right. I appreciate your being honest with me. But there's one thing I have to know: How does Jack figure in to all of this?"

At the mention of her name, his heart bucked, but she wasn't the reason he'd come back to Lookout. "When Pete first told me about the letter he'd received from Pastor Taylor, I closed my ears and wouldn't listen. Lookout was the last place I wanted to be."

The marshal grinned. "I reckon we've got more in common than we first realized. I felt the exact same way about returning here, but look what God did for me. He let me marry the only woman I ever loved, we've got four great—albeit ornery—kids with another on the way, and they're all healthy and smart. I'd have never dreamed all that could happen to me, but God has greater plans for us, son, than we can ever imagine."

Noah closed his eyes, accepting the man's encouragement into his heart. Growing up the way he had, not ever seeing anything good coming from his life, had been discouraging. Pa had beat him down both physically and verbally. Other kids had gotten him in trouble for things he'd never done. It was only by the grace of God that he was standing here. "Thank you, sir. I appreciate the encouragement."

He nodded; then an odd expression engulfed his face. "I just had a thought—that's why you won't eat pork, isn't it?"

"Yeah. Living on a hog farm, I ate pork three meals a day. Oft times it was all we ate. I just can't stomach it anymore."

"I noticed." The marshal grinned. "Well, I reckon I've kept you from your work long enough. All I ask is that when you feel the time is right that you tell Jack before you reveal your identity to the rest of the town. She'll probably need some time to work through that." He glanced down the alley for a moment. "She was real sorry after you left and told me that she had wanted to apologize for lying about you on more than one occasion."

"She actually told you that she lied?"

"Yeah." He nodded. "The deception ate at her until she couldn't hold it in any longer, and she had to come clean. Jack has a good heart, but she sometimes buries it deeply to protect it. Her other pa was cruel and had no problem hitting women. It's no big surprise that Jack has trouble trusting men. I've been trying for ten years now to fix the damage James did."

Noah wasn't sure if he should confess his current thoughts, but the marshal might as well know the whole story. "Though she did anger me at times, I always admired her spunk. I had a little sister for a few years who wasn't scared of anything, but she took sick and died. I suppose Jack reminds me a little of her. I just wanted to be Jack's friend, but she never gave me a chance." Bertha Boyd stuck her head out the back door and stared. She must have recognized the marshal, because she quickly ducked back inside.

The older man clapped his hand on Noah's shoulder again. "Jacqueline's changed—somewhat. Give her another chance, but just don't break her heart."

Noah snorted a sarcastic laugh. The marshal gave him far more credit than he deserved if he thought he'd have any influence over Jack's heart. "Hurting her is the last thing I want to do, but I seriously doubt you have anything to worry about on that account."

A strange look passed across the marshal's face. "Don't be too sure of that."

"What do you mean?"

"I've seen the way she looks at you."

Noah frowned. "What do you mean?"

"The Lord sure works in mysterious ways." The marshal grinned and shook his head. "Sorry, Noah, you're gonna have to figure that out on your own."

Chapter 14

Dressed in his Sunday preaching suit, Noah sat on the boardinghouse's front porch, trying to decide if he ought to go to the social or stay back and study his sermon some more. He tapped the edge of the chair in time with the lively music playing in the vacant lot next to the church.

Across the street at the mercantile, a buggy pulled to a stop, and a tall man climbed out and took the steps to the boardwalk two at a time. The door flew open, as if someone had been standing there waiting for him. Mrs. Morgan stepped out, looking pretty in a rose-colored gown, followed by her daughter in a fancy dress in a brown and light green fabric. Both women's hair had been piled onto the crown of their heads, although the daughter also had blond ringlets hanging down from her topknot. Dainty bonnets adorned their heads.

Noah shook his head, glad that he was a male and only had to comb his hair. How did they manage to keep all their tresses up with just a handful of hairpins?

The trio crowded into the buggy and drove down the street. Several groups of people wandered past the boardinghouse dressed in their finery. Men escorted their ladies, who were decked out in almost every color of the rainbow. They reminded Noah of a field of spring wildflowers. What color would Jack's dress be?

He gripped the end of the arm rest. Would she even come?

He'd seen her limping around the house this afternoon, but knowing she'd been watching him work without a shirt, he'd not been able to meet her gaze. He couldn't help wondering why she'd been staring and if she'd liked what she saw.

He sighed and shook his head. "Forgive me, Father. Keep my mind set on things above, not things on earth."

Closing his eyes, he prayed about Sunday. Prayed that he would preach a sermon that would touch hearts. Prayed that he wouldn't be so nervous that he'd mess up like he'd done the first few times he'd preached.

He kept his head back and eyes shut as he prayed for the Davis family. *Thank You, Lord, for Luke's support. Bless Mrs. Davis, and let her baby be delivered safely. And Jack. . .I don't even know what to say. Touch her heart, and draw her closer to You.*

He heard rustling and peeked out one eye. Alan and Abby Davis were hunkered down, tiptoeing around the side of the house. Quiet giggles filled the air like the sweet scent of pies cooking.

"He's asleep." Abby giggled again.

"No he ain't," Alan said. "He's just resting his eyes like Papa does when he's tired."

"Nuh-uh, he's sleeping."

Noah couldn't help letting out a fake snore as he peeked out one squinted eye.

"See! I told you." Abby shoved her brother's shoulder.

Curling his lips, Noah tried not to smile. Both of these children reminded him of Jack, even though he hadn't known her when she was so young.

He faked another snore then fluttered his lips as he blew out a breath. Childless laughter sounded to his right.

"Oh, dear."

That was no child's voice. His eyes flew open and landed on an emerald green skirt. Jack's skirt. He bolted out of the chair, and his hat flopped off his lap and rolled across the porch floor. Squeals of laughter echoed beside the porch.

"I wasn't sleeping. I was just playing with your brother and sister."

Jack lifted her brows as if questioning if he was being truthful.

Her dark blue eyes sparkled, and her auburn hair had been pinned up in a fashionable style that revealed her slender neck. His gaze traveled down her pretty dress, skimming past her bodice to her narrow waist and her flared skirt. Sometime in the past ten years, Jacqueline Hamilton Davis had blossomed from a coltish tomboy to a beautiful woman.

He lifted his gaze and smiled, receiving a shy grin back. A becoming rose red stained her cheeks. Her neck was lightly tanned, but the skin on her shoulders, which was normally covered by her shirtwaist, was a creamy white that just ached to be touched. He reached for the basket that hung on one of her arms to keep his hand busy and shoved the other one into his pocket. He shuffled his feet. He'd never known how to relate to Jack when she was a spunky young girl, but he felt even more discombobulated with this very pretty, feminine version. *Help me, Lord.*

Noah forced his gaze on the younger Davis girl. Instead of using the stairs four feet away, Abby climbed up the porch spindles and shinnied over the railing. "Yes, he was. I heard him snore'n."

"Me, too." Alan clambered up beside his sister, and both children dropped onto the porch floor with a light thud.

"You mean like this?" He snorted like a pig and bent down, gently poking Abby's belly, sending her into another fit of the giggles.

As he straightened, he picked up his hat and set it on his head. "Were you waiting on me?"

He shrugged, not sure if he was or wasn't. "Guess I just didn't want to go down there alone."

The disappointment on her face made him pause. Had she wanted him to escort her?

Jack turned away and pointed at her siblings. "Back inside, you two. Ma said it's time for your baths. There's church tomorrow."

"Ahh. . .do we have to go? Church is boring."

"Abby Louise Davis. I don't ever want to hear you say such a thing again." She wagged her finger in front of the child, as if she were Abby's mother. Noah cocked his head, realizing how nice an image that was.

Abby crossed her arms over her chest and frowned at her big

sister. "I don't want no bath."

"Me neither." Alan licked his finger, then swiped it across his shin below his short pants and held it up. "See, I ain't even dirty."

"Alan! That's horrid behavior—and don't say *ain't*. Both of you get into the house this instant, or I'm getting a switch to tan your hide."

Both kids glared at her with arms crossed but finally relented and stomped inside. Jack closed the door and swung back around to face him, bringing with her the fragrant scent of flowers. "I sure hope I was never half as bad as they are."

Noah couldn't help the gleam in his eye. The truth in his opinion was that Jack had been twice as bad as her siblings, but he could hardly say that.

"What?" She tilted her head, exposing her soft neck. The perfect spot to place a kiss.

Noah took a step back, stunned at his train of thought. He couldn't allow her to tempt him. "Uhh. . .nothing." He cleared his throat. "Are you the only one of your family going to the social?"

"Luke's helping Carly—uh, Miss Payton—bathe the kids and put them to bed, so Ma can stay off her feet. I imagine he'll mosey down to make sure things are going all right. He likes to keep a close eye on public events. You never know when some cowpoke will cause trouble."

He'd never before considered how the marshal was always on duty, much like a minister. Did that interfere with his family life?

"So, will you escort me to the social, Reverend?"

He tugged at his collar and stared down the street to where the crowd had gathered. Maybe some folks wouldn't think it proper for a minister to attend a square dance social. "Maybe I should just stay here and work on my sermon for tomorrow."

"Horse feathers." She pulled his arm down. "Don't be a stick-in-the-mud. This is a good time to get to know some of your parishioners before you preach to them."

Did she actually want him to go? Her eager expression and sparkling eyes hinted that she did. But in his heart, he knew that if she knew his real identity, she'd flee back to the house as fast as she could.

Jack held onto Noah's solid arm and tried to ignore how much her knee ached. She'd been on it far too much the past few days, but she'd had things to do to get ready for tonight, and she'd tried to help her ma as much as possible. With the baby due anytime, her ma tired much quicker and had less patience with the children. Having Carly here to help sure was a blessing.

"So, does the town have these get-togethers often?" Noah's deep voice rumbled beside her.

"This is the first one of the year. We have them the last Saturday of the month from April to September. These socials are the remnant of the Saturday Socials that the Corbett brothers started years ago."

"Corbett—as in your pa's cousin?"

"Yes, him and his brother, Mark." Jack smiled up at him. "You haven't been here long, so you probably haven't heard the story about the mail-order brides they ordered for my papa."

She felt him stiffen and glanced up. He smiled but had an odd look on his face. They passed a passel of buggies and horses lining both sides of the road. Up ahead, lively dancers were enjoying the do-si-do of the Virginia Reel to guitar and fiddle, while others stood around the refreshment tables and in small groups, talking with friends and neighbors. Jack scanned the busy area for Billy and allowed some of the tension in her shoulders to flee when she didn't see him.

She sure hoped he didn't show up. "Anyway, when Luke first returned to Lookout, he'd just become a Christian and felt God told him to come back and forgive my ma for marrying another man when she'd been engaged to Luke. His cousins thought if he had another woman in his life, he'd forget about Ma, so they ordered some mail-order brides. Even though they wrote to several, they thought only one would show up, but instead, three did. And so someone decided to have a contest to see which gal would make Papa the best wife." She glanced up to gauge his reaction and was surprised that his face remained passive. Maybe being a man, he didn't like to hear romantic stories. Why should that disappoint her?

She shrugged and continued her story. "Some things happened to make Papa realize he still loved my ma, and they got back together, which made me the happiest kid in the world."

He smiled down at her, his dark eyes intense, as if her happiness mattered to him. Her heart did a somersault, and she worked to keep her breathing under control so she could finish. "Needless to say, there were several brides left over after Papa chose Ma to marry. The Corbett brothers started hosting Saturday socials in order to find husbands for Miss Bennett and Miss O'Neil."

"And did they?"

Jack nodded and slowed her steps, not quite ready to share him with the rest of the crowd. "Sort of. Shannon O'Neil married Mark Corbett. Garrett hired her to work in the freight office, so she and Mark saw each other every day, and somewhere along the line, they fell in love."

A soft smile tugged at Noah's lips. "Good for them. Will they be here tonight?"

Jack shook her head and searched the crowd for Penny and Tessa. "No, they're living in Dallas right now. Mark is a lawyer."

"What happened to the other bride?" Noah held his hand out toward two empty chairs that rested against the wall of the church.

Jack sat, grateful to rest her leg. "Leah Bennett married Dan Howard, who owns the livery. I suspect they'll be here tonight."

He looked the crowd over, almost as if searching for the couple, but that was silly since he didn't even know what they looked like. She studied his strong profile. His nose was straight and not overly big. Most of the time, his sleek black hair was combed back, revealing his broad forehead, but when he'd been chopping wood, his hair had draped down across it. A vision of him working, his bare chest shiny with sweat, flashed across her mind. She touched her hand to her cheek. Was she actually blushing? What was it about this man that caused her to behave like a silly schoolgirl with her first infatuation with a boy?

"Something wrong?" He glanced down with concerned eyes. "Are you in pain?"

"I'm fine. Just wish I could dance, is all." Oh! Was that a lie?

No, but it wasn't the whole truth either. Whenever he was around, she was far from fine. Her heart beat faster, she couldn't catch her breath, and her legs turned into liquid like melted butter. The truth hit her as hard as if she'd been run down by a herd of stampeding cattle. She liked Noah Jeffers. No, more than liked him.

Wringing her hands, she wished someone would walk over and talk to her. She needed a diversion from her wayward thoughts. She couldn't like the minister. It wasn't part of the plans she'd made for her life.

"Uh, what do I do with this basket?"

"I'll take it to the refreshment table." Jack started to rise, but Noah's hand to her shoulder halted her. His warm, gentle touch set her rebellious heart thrumming, and she peered up at him. His gaze collided with hers, and she felt as if they were connected. Alone, though in a crowd. The music and conversation faded. His fingers moved ever so slightly, brushing across her skin and sending delicious chills scurrying down her spine. She swallowed the lump in her throat. Then he glanced toward her shoulder, scowled, and yanked his hand away.

"You. . .uh. . .sit. I'll um. . ." His words sounded hoarse—huskier than normal. Noah cleared his throat as he looked across the crowd.

"They're cookies. Just deliver the basket to one of the food tables, and the ladies there will take care of them."

He nodded but didn't look back at her. She watched him walk a few feet before Tessa intercepted him.

"There you are, Reverend." Tessa glided up to Noah and looped her arm possessively around his. "I hope you saved me a dance."

With his back to her, Jack couldn't hear his response, but if Tessa's fake pout was any sign, he must have turned her down. She knew that shouldn't make her happy, but she smiled anyway. Maybe the preacher was immune to Tessa's wiles.

Tessa clung to the preacher as though they were a couple, as they wove in and out of the crowd. Several more people stopped them before Noah made it to the table and relinquished Jack's basket to Polly Dykstra. He glanced back toward Jack, and she quickly looked to the side, not wanting him to catch her watching.

Two guitar players and a fiddler filled the air with their lively music, while a small group danced a quadrille. The women's dresses swirled around their partners' legs, and smiles lit up each face. Jack tapped her foot in time with the music. How ironic that she never really cared about dancing, but the one time she might have enjoyed it, she was unable to participate.

"There you are." Penny straightened her peach-colored skirt as she sat down. "I was beginning to think you weren't coming after going to so much effort to get that new dress. It's the perfect color for you."

Jack blew out a sigh, fluttering her lips. "Thank you, but I might as well not come. I can't dance with anyone."

Eyes glimmering, Penny leaned over close to her ear. "I noticed you had an escort—and a very handsome one at that."

Jack shook her head and chuckled. "He's not my escort. In fact, if I hadn't come out onto the porch just when I did, I fear he would have fallen asleep on the front porch or else scurried back up to his room."

"He didn't want to come?"

Jack shrugged. "I think he's just nervous about meeting so many folks."

Penny leaned back in her seat. "You'd better keep the parson close by, or Tessa will steal him from you."

"She can have him. I've no designs on him." Now why did those words leave a bad taste in her mouth?

Penny gasped. "Surely you don't mean that. I've seen how he looks at you."

Jack's pulse sped up. "What do you mean?"

Her friend's mouth puckered as if she knew a special secret, and she wiggled her brows. "Like you were the prettiest filly in the corral, that's what."

"Penny! You're comparing me to a horse?"

Her friend giggled as she watched the dancers. "No, of course not. But I just figured that's what a man might think."

Jack shook her head, but her gaze sought out Noah again.

"I'd make as good a pastor's wife as Tessa would." She couldn't help following that train of thought. Jacqueline Jeffers actually had a nice ring to it. If Noah's light touch on her shoulder sent butterflies swarming in her stomach, what would his kiss be like? She closed her eyes trying to imagine it. He'd lean down, his dark eyes burning with passion; their lips would touch lightly, then press harder as he pulled her to his chest. She fanned her warm face.

"Why, Jacqueline Davis, whatever are you thinking about? You have the oddest smile on your face."

Jack's eyes popped open at Tessa's question. Then her gaze darted to Noah, who stood a few feet away. She'd been so lost in her fantasy that she hadn't heard them return. She could hardly answer that question, could she? "I. . .uh. . ."

Noah held a mug out to her. "I thought you might be thirsty. We got a drink ourselves, but I wanted to bring you this—since you can't walk much, you know." He glanced at Penny. "Sorry, ma'am, I would have brought you a drink, too, if I'd known you were here."

"That's all right." Penny ducked her head, then glanced sideways at Jack, giving her a knowing grin.

"This is my friend, Penny Dempsey, and Penny, this is Reverend Jeffers." Jack waved her hand toward Penny and then Noah. "You already know he's staying at the boardinghouse."

Penny nodded. "A pleasure, Reverend."

"The pleasure's all mine, Miss Dempsey." Noah smiled at Penny.

"And you've already met Tessa Morgan, I see." Jack took a sip of her cider.

"Oh, yes. We're getting along famously." Tessa leaned against Noah's arm and batted her lashes at him.

Noah's gaze darted to the woman who all but hung on him then to Jack, as if pleading for her help.

"Why don't you sit with us, Tessa?" Jack patted the empty chair on her right. "I'm sure Reverend Jeffers would like to meet more people from the town."

Tessa scowled at her and shook her head. She twisted her

finger around a yellow curl hanging from her topknot and gazed adoringly at the bewildered minister. "I intend to dance with the reverend."

"I. . .um. . .don't plan to dance, Miss Morgan."

Tessa tucked her chin down, stuck out her lower lip, and batted her lashes. "Surely you don't want to disappoint one of your parishioners, do you? My mother owns the mercantile and gives quite generously to the church."

"Tessa!" Jack pushed up from the chair, knowing she needed the advantage of height to persuade her friend to leave the poor man alone. "I hardly think you'll convince Reverend Jeffers to dance with you by blackmailing him with your mother's tithes."

"Well, fine." Tessa shoved her nose in the air. "If he doesn't want to dance with me, plenty of other men will." She spun around, her skirts swishing in a mass of copper and sea green brocade, and marched over to the refreshment table. In a matter of seconds, she sidled up to a trio of young cowboys and started weaving her web.

"Uh, thanks for rescuing me." The parson's neck and ears were the color of a ripe strawberry.

"I'm sorry about Tessa." Her friend's behavior embarrassed Jack.

"She's not used to men turning her down." Penny shook her head. "I think I'll go see what there is to eat. See you later." She waved at Jack but ducked her head as she passed Noah.

"Penny seems nice." Noah's deep voice floated to her amid the harmony of the guitars and fiddle.

"She is, though she's shy around men."

Noah grinned. "I noticed. Your other friend doesn't have a timid bone in her body, does she?"

Jack shook her head. "No, she doesn't. Tessa sees what she wants and goes after it, no matter who is in the way or who gets hurt."

"I hope she doesn't end up being the one to get hurt one day."

"Me, too." Jack located Tessa and watched her dance with a handsome cowboy. Tessa's head was cocked, a brilliant smile on her face. She seemed to have already forgotten about her quest to win Noah's heart. Jack smiled up at him. "Why don't I introduce you to some folks? It will make things easier tomorrow if you meet some of them tonight."

Noah nodded and held his hand out to help her up. He mumbled something that wasn't clear over the ruckus of the crowd and the music, but it sounded as if he'd said, "Nothing will make tomorrow easier."

Chapter 15

Garrett stood off to the side of the crowd, sipping a glass of apple cider and watching the dancers. He wasn't even sure why he'd come. The social was more for younger folk than a man a few years shy of forty. How had life sped by so fast?

A picture of Carly Payton snatching up his rifle and taking down those two outlaws bounced around in his head. He'd been spitting mad to learn who she was, and it goaded him to be in debt to such a woman. Even worse was admiring her quick action, her calm in the face of danger, and her impressive shooting skills. He didn't want to like the woman and hated how she'd invaded his dreams ever since he'd delivered her to Rachel.

He forced his thoughts off the jailbird and watched Jack introduce Noah Jeffers to several couples who attended the church. She and the parson looked good together, but he couldn't imagine a rambunctious, adventure-loving girl like her ever being happy with a peace-loving minister.

"Didn't expect to see you down here, Cuz." Luke smacked him on the shoulder with his palm, scaring him right out of his thoughts.

Garrett held out his near empty cup and gave Luke a mock glare. "Hey, watch out. You nearly caused me to spill my drink on my clean shirt."

"Well, we can't have that, can we? Then you'd have to do

laundry twice this month." Luke chuckled and shook his head. "You need a wife."

Thoughts of marriage had been heavy on his mind of late, but he wouldn't tell Luke for fear of being teased to death. "Paying the Widow Schwartz to wash my clothes is a whole lot cheaper than a wife."

"Maybe so, but not nearly as much fun." Luke waggled his brows and shoved Garrett with his elbow.

He shook his head but was happy for his cousin. Luke had returned a somber man from his years as a soldier, even though he had become a Christian. The unforgiving spirit that ate at his heart almost stole his future, but God had intervened and brought Rachel and Luke back together. Garrett hated to admit he was jealous of the life his cousin had now. "If I could find a good woman like Rachel, I just might consider settling down."

Luke's eyes widened, and he pushed his hat back on his forehead. "I never thought I'd hear you say those words."

Garrett shrugged. "Don't go telling Jack, or next thing I know, it'll be in the newspaper."

"It would serve you right. Maybe you can get your own mail-order bride."

"No thanks." Garrett watched the dancers. Most of the men who weren't frowning from focusing on their dance steps had big grins on their faces. They actually seemed to be enjoying themselves.

Luke, too, surveyed the crowd, but Garrett knew he was searching for troublemakers. Though Luke was a family man with another child on the way, he took his job seriously and never seemed to be off-duty. Fortunately, Lookout was a peaceful town most of the time.

Leaning back against the church wall, Luke crossed his arms. "You know, there's a perfectly fine woman staying at the boardinghouse who'd be a good match for you."

The sip of cider he just took came spewing back out. A man dancing nearby cast a glare his way. Garrett coughed and waved an apology. "You can't be serious."

"What's wrong with Miss Payton?"

Garrett stared at his cousin as if he'd taken leave of his senses. "She's an ex-convict."

"So?" Luke's cool gaze needled him.

Pushing away his guilt, he formulated his argument. "If and when I marry, I want a decent woman, not one who was an outlaw and a jailbird."

"You disappoint me, Cuz."

Garrett straightened and crossed his arms. Why didn't Luke understand that he wanted a decent woman for a wife? "Why? Because I want to marry a good woman who can teach morals to my children?"

Luke pushed away from the wall. "Miss Payton *is* a good woman. She paid her debt to society, but even more important is that she's a new creation in Christ. She's given her heart to God. What more could you want in a wife?"

"Oh, I don't know. Maybe one that didn't spend six years in prison."

Luke glared at him. "You're a fine one to be talking."

"What does that mean? I've never been in jail."

"You look at life as one big joke. You and your brother ordered me not one but three mail-order brides, and almost caused me to lose my job and the woman I loved."

"But you didn't, did you?" Garrett forced a smile. He and Luke had rarely ever been at odds with one another, and he didn't want his cousin to know how much his lack of support hurt. "You still have both, and a passel of kids to boot."

"So could you if you weren't so stubborn." Luke stalked over to where Jack and the preacher were talking to Polly and Dolly at the refreshment table.

Garrett shook his head. Luke ought to know not to push him where women were concerned. He may be a joker and a tease, but he'd never felt truly comfortable with a woman. For some reason, they scared him. They seemed so delicate and sensitive that he feared he'd unwittingly hurt them.

He remembered all the times his own ma had watched his father leave home to spend the evening at the saloon. She carried her pain like a broken flower that refused to die. Had she known that his pa sometimes went upstairs with the saloon gals?

Garrett swigged down the last few drops of his cider. Not a soul, not even his brother, knew that he'd never been with a woman. Though in the eyes of God that was a good thing for an unmarried man, it was embarrassing for a man his age to admit.

He couldn't shake loose the image of the time he'd gone looking for his pa and found him laughing and chasing a scantily clad floozy up the saloon stairs. He caught her and jerked her into his arms, embracing and kissing her. Garrett's stomach churned. His mother had been home tending Mark, who was sick, and finishing the chores his pa should have done.

All that was in the past, but he never wanted to hurt a woman like his pa had, so he had steered clear of them for the most part. But loneliness was a powerful motivator. Garrett's foot kept pace with the lively guitar and fiddle music. He thought of his empty house and dreaded being alone for another night. Maybe it was time he seriously pursued finding a wife. Didn't the Bible say that "he who finds a wife finds a good thing"?

Carly Payton again intruded into his mind, but he cast her out. She might be pretty and able to shoot well, but she wasn't marrying quality.

Jack ate a slice of applesauce cake and watched Christine Morgan dance with Rand Kessler. When the couple had first arrived, they'd acted awkwardly toward one another, and their movements had been stiff. But now they both had relaxed and were talking and smiling. Romance was in the air.

Her gaze drifted to where Noah stood talking with Luke and the mayor. If her papa knew anything about the mayor's big plans, he wasn't sharing the information with her. Now that she was feeling better, she needed to resume her quest, but how could she find out what he was up to?

Her first thought was to sneak into his house or office, but after the roof fiasco, she knew she shouldn't press her luck. The mayor had been furious about her being on his roof, but he had backed down when Luke told him he'd repair the broken shakes for free.

"Well, it's good to see you're waitin' on me."

Jack stiffened as Billy drew up beside her and placed his arm around her waist. She swerved away from his grasp. "Stop it!"

"A man has a right to cuddle his fiancée." His stern glare dared her to disagree.

She glanced toward where Luke had been, but he was no longer there. Noah looked to be patiently listening to some kind of admonition from the mayor, nodding his head at the shorter man.

"Now don't you look pretty." He leaned close and tilted her face so she had to look at him. "And you smell as good as that fancy perfume Ma sells."

"Thank you, Billy, but you need to understand that I am not your fiancée, and calling me that over and over won't make it so." She tried to pull loose of his hold, but he only gripped her tighter. If she wasn't hindered by her sore knee, she might have just hauled off and kicked him.

"Got you a present." He dangled something shiny in front of her face. When she didn't react, he pulled her arm up and pressed it into her hand.

Her first thought was to ask him where he got the money for the shiny silver bracelet with floral engravings. It was beautiful, but how could Billy afford such a thing? She never saw him in the store, other than helping unload crates of freight whenever Garrett had a delivery and could cajole him into assisting him. She stared at the expensive jewelry, turning the silver band so that it reflected the evening sun. Nothing she owned equaled the gift, but she couldn't keep it. She held it out to him. "I can't accept this."

Billy yanked it from her hand. "Can and will. I want my gal to look better'n all the others in town." He flipped the jewelry over her wrist and quickly secured it closed, even though she tried to pull away.

"Billy, I said—"

"C'mon, we're having that dance." With his arm behind her back, he forced her forward.

A stabbing pain in her knee from fighting Billy made her stumble. He hauled her up and kept her close to his side. They moved toward the dozen couples who glided to a slow waltz.

Maybe she should just go along with him and get it over with, but it galled her to let him win. The only other choice she had was to pretend to faint, but she'd never swooned once in her life and didn't want folks thinking she was a weak woman. Nor did she want to get her new dress dirty. Her final option was to call for help. As they made their way into the dancers, she searched for Luke. *Horse feathers*. He was gone.

Christine Morgan and Rand Kessler glided past them. Tessa turned up her nose at Jack when she caught her eye. She'd get no help from her. Billy loosened his grip and turned to face her.

Jack glared up at him. "You'd better enjoy this dance, Mr. Morgan, because it will be the only one you'll ever get."

He yanked her against his chest. "Oh, I'll enjoy it, but it won't be our last."

Gritting her teeth, Jack tried not to wince whenever she had to move to the right. Billy held her improperly close. As he turned, she caught the minister's gaze and sent him a look that made him straighten. She lost sight of him on the next turn, then came around again and found he was gone.

Suddenly Billy halted and glanced over his shoulder. "You ain't cuttin' in, Preacher."

Noah stepped up beside Billy. "Miss Davis has an injured knee and has no business dancing."

Billy narrowed his eyes. "It ain't no concern of yours."

"I disagree. I'm the one who escorted her to the dance, so it's my responsibility to watch over her." Though his expression remained passive, the sternness in his gaze showed he wasn't intimidated.

Dancers whirled around them as the musicians played "The Blue Danube," but they were starting to stare. Jack tried to back away from Billy, but he only tightened his grip. He sliced a seething glance her way before bull's-eyeing in on Noah.

"I'm a man of peace, mister, but I haven't always been. I'm asking you to please turn loose of the lady." The tone of Noah's deep voice made the order more menacing, and his no-nonsense glare backed up his words.

"Just who are you, anyway?" Billy demanded.

"I'm Noah Jeffers, the new pastor."

A confused look passed over Billy's face, then he tilted his head back and laughed. His hand that rested on Jack's waist loosened, and he swiped it across his eyes. Noah slipped in between her and Billy, grabbing Billy's wrist. He yelped and let go of Jack's hand. She stepped to the side so she could see around Noah's tall body. If Billy was finally going to be put in his place, she wanted to watch. The dancers closest to them also slowed to a halt, as if not to miss the action.

"Hey, that hurts." Billy scowled at Noah and rubbed his wrist.

"Maybe you should have considered that it hurt Miss Davis when you forced her to dance."

Billy's face instantly changed from wounded indignation to fury. He hauled back and struck Noah's cheek with his fist, driving him backward. Noah regained his balance and dabbed at the cut below his eye. He stared at the blood, and his gaze darkened. He frowned. Jack held her breath, seeing the evident anger on the pastor's face.

"C'mon, *Reverend*. If you want her, fight for her." Billy held up his fists and danced on his feet like a boxer.

Christine Morgan stopped dancing and hurried to her son's side. Rand Kessler stood behind her, a silent support. The music squeaked to a stop as did the rest of the dancers. Mrs. Morgan reached out to touch her son, but he jerked away, his fists still in fight mode. "Billy, what's going on here?"

"Stay out of this, Ma. That new preacher wants to steal Jacqueline away from me, and if he wants her, he'll have to fight me for her."

Mrs. Morgan glanced at Noah, a shocked look on her face. "Is that true, Reverend?"

Jack watched Noah's angry expression soften as he regained control. Her heart ached for the position he'd been put in just because he tried to help her. Maybe she should explain things. "No, Mrs. Morgan, it isn't true. I told Billy I didn't want to dance tonight because my knee still hurts. Reverend Jeffers came to my aid because Billy wouldn't listen to reason and forced me to dance with him—and that's the honest truth."

Mrs. Morgan studied Jack's face, then the reverend's and her son's. She lowered her head and shook it. "Go home, Billy."

"No, I ain't letting him steal my fiancée."

"I don't belong to you, and I have no idea where you got that notion." Jack gritted her teeth to keep from saying something she'd regret. "I am not your fiancée." She looked around the curious crowd that encircled them. "Everybody, hear that? I have no intention of marrying Billy Morgan."

Billy lowered his fists, looking both hurt and angry. "I don't know why I give a hoot about you. Half the time you don't even dress like a lady, and you run around in pants like a man." He turned as if to leave, then ducked his head and charged Noah. Billy rammed his head into the preacher's belly, and both men went down.

Sitting on Noah's stomach, Billy pummeled his face with both fists. Noah held up his arms, protecting himself, but not fighting back.

"Billy!" Mrs. Morgan gasped, lifting her hand to her mouth. "Stop it."

"Wallop him, Preacher," a voice called out from the crowd. "Show him you ain't no coward."

Jack's heart pounded harder with each fist Billy planted. Why didn't Noah fight back? Surely it was all right for a preacher to defend himself.

Suddenly, Noah roared and shoved upward. Taken off guard, Billy was flung backward and rolled feet over head. Noah jumped up, far more agile than most men his size, and stood with his fists up. His chest heaved; blood trailed down his cheek from a cut over his eyebrow. He swiped his face with his white sleeve, leaving an ugly red stain on the once spotless fabric.

Billy lurched to his feet and charged, fury burning from his eyes like blue fire. The men in the crowd cheered the preacher on, but Jack heard women praying for him to stop. Noah drew back his right fist then brought it forward with a mighty force. It collided with Billy's cheek, knocking his head sideways. He staggered, then dropped to his knees and shook his head.

Noah, with fists still lifted, seemed to wake up from his stupor and glanced around. A frantic look crossed his face, and his arms fell to his side, as if suddenly boneless. Desperate remorse flooded his face, making Jack's heart ache. Was he sorry for defending her?

Rand Kessler, who stood half a foot taller than Billy, stepped away from Mrs. Morgan and took hold of Billy's upper arm. "That's enough fighting, young man."

"Let me go! You ain't my pa." Billy struggled but couldn't overpower the hardy rancher, who pulled him through the crowd and out of Jack's view.

Noah bent over, hands on his knees, head hanging down, breathing deeply. Dirt and grass covered his backside. Hadn't he told Jack that was his only suit and shirt? What would he preach in tomorrow?

"Are you all right, Reverend?" Mrs. Morgan asked. She pulled a handkerchief from her sleeve and handed it to him. "I'm so sorry. My son can be hotheaded at times."

Noah straightened, took the hanky, and held it against his cheek. He offered Billy's mother a pain-filled smile. "No, I'm the one who's sorry."

"You had to defend yerself, Parson," someone behind Jack yelled. Cheers of agreement battled those of condemnation.

"A preacher oughtn't to fight," came another voice off to Jack's left.

Noah lifted his hands, stilling the crowd. "I want to apologize to y'all." He pursed his lips and glanced at Jack. "Fighting is never the right choice, and I'm sorry that I was a bad example."

Murmurs sounded all around, both negative and positive.

"Let me pass, y'all here. Move out of the way."

Jack groaned inwardly as she recognized Bertha Boyd's voice. She was in no mood to tolerate the busybody tonight. What could she want?

Everyone knew Bertha only came to the socials to fill up on the latest gossip first and then the refreshments. Men and women backed up, clearing a wide path for the large woman.

Bertha stopped right beside Jack and Noah. "I want y'all to know what a good man our new reverend is. He spent two and a half hours yesterday chopping wood for me and Aggie. And he did it all out of the goodness of his heart." She nodded her head so vigorously, her three chins wobbled like a turkey's waddle.

Heads nodded and murmurs circled the crowd.

"I was happy to do it, Mrs. Boyd." Noah smiled, but Jack caught his grimace. He lightly touched his swollen cheek. The damaged skin around his right eye was puffing up so badly she could barely see his pupil.

Jack stepped forward, ready to be free of the crowd. "If y'all will excuse us, I need to get home and off my leg, and Reverend Jeffers needs his wounds treated."

"I'll go after the doc." Hiram Stone, a man who'd recently moved to Lookout, took off at a jog.

"I don't need a doctor," Noah called after the man, who either didn't hear him or ignored him.

With the action over, people drifted away, and the music started up again. Some of the men found their women and ambled back to the area in front of the musicians to dance, while others said their good-byes and headed for their buggies or horses.

Jack limped over to where Noah stood alone and looking crestfallen. "I disagree about the doctor. That cut on your brow may need to be stitched up. C'mon. Let's go home." Jack took hold of his elbow and led him across the field.

"I made a royal mess of things." Noah shook his head. "It wouldn't surprise me if nobody showed up at church tomorrow."

"Don't be so hard on yourself."

Noah stopped in front of Ray Castleby's home and stared down at her as if she'd gone loco. "I'm the town's minister, Jack. It's my duty to keep peace and lead by example, not fight with a hotheaded man upset over unrequited love."

"Oh and because you're a pastor, I guess you don't believe in defending a woman's honor. What if your wife were attacked by outlaws, like Garrett and Miss Payton were? Would you defend her and shoot the man who was about to attack her?" Jack shoved her hands to her hips.

"That's ridiculous. It's a theoretical situation that may never happen and has no bearing on this conversation."

"Fine, then. See your own self home, *Reverend* Jeffers." Jack stomped off, more livid than she could remember. She hadn't asked for his help. Yeah, she was grateful he had put Billy in his place, but she wouldn't be responsible for his being upset. He was the one who chose to fight.

Guilt nibbled at her heels as she left him standing in front of the bank president's house. It wasn't as if he couldn't find his way since the boardinghouse was within view, but the honest truth was he *had* come to her aid. And he had tried hard to not fight back and allowed Billy to pummel him far too long. Remorse battled her irritation. Tomorrow, battered and bruised, Noah would have to stand before the people who showed up and preach his first sermon. Many would support him, but others would oppose him.

She clenched her teeth as she climbed up one step to the front porch and then another, fighting the pain in her knee. Glancing back, she could barely make out Noah's tall form standing in the growing shadows at the edge of the glow cast from buildings along the street. She couldn't solve his problems. She could barely work through her own.

Her hand connected with the doorknob, and the bracelet on her wrist glimmered in the light from the parlor. *Horse feathers!* She'd forgotten about it in all the ruckus. She'd have to return it and dreaded seeing Billy again. But keeping it would give him the wrong idea.

She looked again to see if Noah was coming. Something niggled at the back of her mind. As if someone had turned up the flame of a lantern, the thought burst to light in her mind.

The preacher had called her Jack.

Chapter 16

After allowing the doctor to tend his wounds, Noah sat on the front steps to the boardinghouse, his face in his hands. Remorse weighed so heavily on him that he didn't have the strength to climb the stairs to his room.

He'd lost the respect of the townsfolk before he even won it in the first place.

He'd jumped out of the frying pan and into the fire.

This was a catastrophe. If only Pete were here to offer his sage advice.

But Pete wasn't, and Noah needed to take his burden to God instead of his mentor anyway. "I'm sorry, Lord. Sorry for not showing the love of Christ to Billy Morgan. Sorry for fighting instead of being a peacemaker."

He stared down Main Street, deserted now that everyone had gone home from the social. Some folks had waved as they drove past him, but the stern glare of others left him unsettled. Unable to find peace in his heart. He'd been right to stand up for Jack, hadn't he?

She'd sent him a panicked look when dancing with Billy Morgan that seemed a cry for help and stirred up within him a fierce desire to protect her. He hadn't wanted to fight—just to help Jack. But all he'd done was upset her and half the town. He'd be lucky if anyone showed up in the morning to hear his first sermon.

The quiet evening soothed his aching heart, and the stiff north breeze that had stirred up left a chill on his cheeks. The only sounds were insects buzzing around, crickets in the grass, and the distant revelry of the saloon. The noise of children inside the boardinghouse had fallen silent. Somewhere nearby, a dog barked.

Noah sighed. He generally felt closer to God outside. He bent his head in prayer, hoping to find peace and some direction for tomorrow.

"You're looking mighty down in the dumps."

Noah jumped at the sound of Luke's voice. The tension that was finally leaving his neck and shoulders returned in full force. He'd been wallowing so deep in doubt and despair and begging God's forgiveness that he hadn't heard the marshal's footsteps. "I thought you'd gone to bed."

"Naw. I tucked Rachel in earlier, then took a final tour of the town. I don't like to turn in until things quiet down." Luke let out a low whistle. "Looks like you'll have a shiner tomorrow. You want me to get you a slab of meat to put on it? Got some down in the root cellar. The cold might help with the swelling."

"Thanks, but no. It'll be all right, I reckon."

Luke nodded and hopped up the steps, opened the front door, and turned down the lamp in the parlor that threw some light on the porch. Then he took a seat on the steps next to Noah. "I don't know about you, but I sometimes find it easier to discuss things in the dark."

He could argue the point that the night wasn't fully dark with the half moon in the western sky, but he held his tongue. The truth was he could use someone to talk to.

"I heard all about what happened at the social. Sorry I wasn't there, but I'd come back to check on Rachel." Luke shook his head. "That Billy Morgan has been trouble since the day he arrived in town. It's time someone put him in his place."

"I shouldn't have hit him."

"Why did you?"

Because I lost control of my temper. "I didn't want to, but he had me down and wouldn't quit punching me. I finally got tired of it—no, the truth is, I went berserk. Something in me snapped, and I came up fighting."

"A man has a right to defend himself."

Noah shook his head. "This wasn't defending. This was revenge."

Luke was quiet for a moment. "You didn't know Billy when you lived here before, did you?"

"No, he must have come after I left."

Luke rubbed the stubble on his jaw, making a bristly sound. "Then how could it be revenge?"

Noah clasped his hands tightly together and wrapped them around his knees. He hated talking about his past—remembering how rotten his childhood had been—but the marshal already knew some of his story. "I'm sure you remember what my pa was like. He wasn't a nice man."

"Yeah. I had a few run-ins with him before you two left town. He'd drink too much, then start fights."

"Uh-huh. And he'd come home like that, and any little thing could set him off. I had more beatings as a child than I could count."

Luke rested his hand on Noah's shoulder. "I'm sorry about that, son. A man should love his children, teach them right from wrong, not be cruel to them."

"I think Pa blamed me for my ma's and sister's deaths."

"How so?"

Tears burned Noah's eyes, but he batted them away. The day his sister died was one of the worst in his life. "Pa had gone hunting when they took sick. I wanted to go for the doctor, but I couldn't leave them alone. Zoe wasn't even two years old yet, and Ma was too sick to care for her. When Pa came home and found them dead and me alive, something in him broke. He was never the same. The beatings started soon after that."

"I'm sorry, Noah. You did the best you could, I'm sure."

Noah crossed his arms. "I don't know. I can't help wondering what would have happened if I'd gone for the doctor when they first took sick."

"You can ask a million 'what ifs,' but it won't change anything."

"I know. I just wish I'd been the one who died instead of them."

Luke lifted his face toward the sky. "They're safe in the Father's arms now and will never know pain again."

"Yeah, I take comfort in knowing that. I told you all that because I want you to understand. When I was about fifteen, a year and a half after we left Lookout, my pa came home drunk and broke one night. He was spittin' mad that he'd lost what little money he had in a poker game, and he intended to take out his frustrations on me. Well, it had finally dawned on me that I was a whole lot bigger than him and stronger, too. I'd been working some, chopping wood for folks, and I decided then and there that I would never be beaten again."

"I see. So when Billy had you down on the ground, that fighting instinct kicked in."

Noah nodded, thankful the man understood. "Yeah. I know that as the town's shepherd, I'm supposed to be a good example to my flock, but I really bungled things tonight. Maybe it would be better for everyone if I pack up and head back to Emporia."

Luke draped his arm loosely over Noah's shoulders. "Don't hang up your fiddle yet. You told me God sent you here. Do you feel like you've fulfilled the work He wanted you to do already?"

Noah barked a laugh. "What work? I've been here less than a week."

"Well, there's your answer then."

"What is?"

Luke leaned forward and looked at him. "God sent you here for a purpose. You haven't completed the task, so leaving now isn't an option."

"Oh. I see what you mean." As much as he'd like to take the easy way out, Noah knew he wouldn't. "Guess I'll have to stand up there tomorrow and eat some crow."

"Like I said, there's nothing wrong with a man defending himself, and from what I heard, it all started when you stood up for Jack and made Billy stop forcing her to dance. Yeah, maybe you lost control in the fight, but you were defending yourself and an innocent woman. In many people's eyes, you'll be a hero."

"You didn't see the looks of disappointment I got from other folks."

Luke stood and stretched. "You'll never please everyone, Noah. I learned that long ago. So start with pleasing God and being obedient to your calling, and trust God to deal with the people."

Noah stood, feeling like an old man in his battered body.

"You need to get a good night's sleep." Luke opened the front door and held it for Noah to enter. "I, for one, am looking forward to hearing your sermon."

Noah allowed a small smile. "Yeah, well, don't set your standard too high."

They were finally done talking. Jack pulled her pillow out of the window and listened to the creak of the stairs outside her door as Noah climbed them. She hadn't heard much of what was said, since the men had talked mostly in low tones and Abby's loud snores filled the room, but she'd gotten the odd feeling that Luke knew far more about Noah than she did.

How was that possible?

Had they talked before?

Why would Noah open up to her papa and not to her?

One thing she *had* heard was a woman's name—Zoe. Who was she? Could the parson have a gal he left behind somewhere?

The cool breeze blowing in her window sent goose bumps racing up her arm, and she reached over and lowered the sash. Jack sat there, staring into the dark room, scowling and nibbling one corner of her lower lip. It shouldn't bother her that some woman might have already claimed his heart. In fact, it didn't.

What bothered her was that she hadn't been able to get her story. Being a lawman, Luke was fairly tight-lipped, but if she waited for just the right timing, maybe she could get him to tell her something more about Noah Jeffers. At any rate, tomorrow he'd preach his first sermon, and that alone should give her enough fodder for an article.

Lying back, she smiled. For a woman with skills and wiles, there was always a way to reach her goal.

Chapter 17

Carly dipped the last plate into the rinse water and laid it on the stack on the table. "Is there anything else that needs washing?"

Rachel set the dish she'd just dried on the stack of clean plates and leaned back in her chair, resting her arm across her large belly. "I don't think so, but the dining table may need to be washed off."

Ringing out the rag, Carly noticed Rachel lay her head back against the chair and close her eyes. "Is Oscar misbehaving this morning?"

Rachel's lips curved up in a soft smile. "Not so much. I just can't believe that breakfast is barely over, and I already feel the need for a nap."

Carly wiped down the kitchen counters, then rinsed the dishcloth and rung it out again. "Well, why don't you go lie down? I can finish drying the plates and silverware."

"I still need to dress for church and fix the girls' hair." With obvious effort, Rachel forced herself to sit up and dry another dish.

"Nobody will think bad of you if you were to miss church, considering you will be having a baby any day. I can fix your daughters' hair."

"It's not as easy as it sounds. Emmie isn't too hard since her hair is too short to braid. Just brush it, but trying to plait Abby's hair is about as easy as lassoing a cloud."

Chuckling, Carly found a dry towel and quickly started drying the silverware before Rachel could object. Her friend had offered her a job helping her, but that wasn't such an easy task. Rachel was so used to doing everything that instead of waiting for help, she just went ahead and did things. Carly was going to have to be on her toes and stay alert if she was to be any help around here.

Thinking of braiding Abby's hair reminded Carly of her last visit when Rachel would struggle to get Jacqueline to sit still long enough for her to fix the girl's tresses. "Is Abby much like Jacqueline?"

Rachel set the last dried plate on the pile and rolled her eyes. "Far more than I wish she was."

Remembering how young Jack had shed her dresses and donned her worn overalls every chance she got made Carly realize just how long she'd been away. Jacqueline had grown from a spunky ten-year-old who preferred fishing with her two male friends over school or housework, to a lovely young woman. She ambled into the dining room and washed off the table, chairs, and the buffet. She glanced around the clean room, a feeling of satisfaction rising within her.

A bird's cheerful song wafted in on the morning breeze, fluttering the white lacey curtains, reminding her of Tillie's house. She wondered how Pastor Barker was getting along without his wife or her to care for him. Had he moved in with his daughter yet?

Carly breathed a wistful sigh. She'd thought of the old couple as caring grandparents, even though she wasn't their kin. They'd treated her far better than she'd expected when she first arrived as a newly released convict. Her past hadn't mattered to them any more than it did to Rachel, but in truth, she wasn't family. She had no family.

And wasn't that just as well?

As she walked back into the kitchen, she thought about her brother. Tyson was dead now, God rest his soul, and she couldn't help feeling relieved. Yeah, he'd let her live with his outlaw gang and kept the men away from her with his vile threats, but he'd used her. Forced her into a life of bank robbery, stealing from hardworking people and being on the run. Thank the Lord those days were behind her.

She hung the dishcloth on the edge of the sink and looked at her friend. Rachel again sat back with her eyes shut. Carly reached down, taking her arm. "C'mon, it's back to bed for you."

"No, no. I wasn't sleeping. Just resting my eyes."

"I've heard that line before." Carly chuckled, helping Rachel to her feet. A streak of jealousy raised its head when she stared up close at the bulge the baby made beneath Rachel's apron. She squelched the snake of envy and guided Rachel to her bedroom. "When did you say your baby is due?"

"Not for another week or two." Rachel lay back on her quilt and released a sigh. "I think you're right about not attending church, although I hate missing Reverend Jeffers' first sermon and sitting with you."

Carly pulled a brown knitted coverlet off the back of a nearby chair and laid it over Rachel's legs. "I'll be fine, and so will the minister."

Rachel's pale blue eyes filled with concern. "I feel so bad that Noah has to preach his first sermon in town with that black eye. It looks atrocious."

Carly couldn't help comparing Noah Jeffers to Reverend Barker. Other than both being Christians, they were nothing alike, as far as she could tell in the short time she'd been at the boardinghouse. "Maybe it'll keep him from fighting again. I can't imagine Reverend Barker from my old church ever getting into a fight."

"Just remember, our reverend was trying to help Jacqueline. He never expected to get into a fight, from what Luke told me. I, for one, appreciate him standing up to Billy Morgan. I've known that young man since the first day he arrived in Lookout and stayed here with his mother and sister, and he's always been trouble."

"Now that he's been publicly put in his place, maybe he'll straighten up." Carly pushed away from the doorjamb she'd been leaning on. "Better round up your girls and make sure they're dressed,then finish getting ready for church myself. You have a nice rest, and don't worry. Jacqueline and I will handle things."

"Thank you, Carly. . . ." Rachel's words were already slurring together as sleep claimed her. "I 'ppreciate. . .you."

Carly left to take a final glance around the kitchen then hurried upstairs. Hopefully Jacqueline would have the younger girls dressed by now. At the top of the stairs, she tapped on the door. Childish squeals echoed from the other side.

"Come in."

Pushing the door ajar, she peered in. "I came to fix the girls' hair."

"I was just getting ready to do Abby's." Jacqueline cast a quick glance at Carly, then grabbed Abby, who attempted to chase after Emmie. "Oh, no you don't. Hold still and let me fix your hair. You don't want to look like a scarecrow, do you?"

"I do if it means I can stay home from church." Abby kicked at Emmie's ball as it rolled toward the bed. Emmie screeched and ran after it.

"Abigail Louise Davis! You don't mean that."

Abby nodded, pulling her hair free from her big sister's hand. "Uh-huh. I told that preacher I don't like church. It's boring."

Her deep blue eyes sparkling with humor, Jacqueline shook her head while braiding Abby's hair so fast, her hands almost blurred. She glanced up. "My sister is a heathen, Miss Payton."

Carly couldn't help the grin that pulled on her lips. "Won't you please call me Carly?"

Jacqueline lifted her brow and gave her a schoolmarm look. "Only if you'll call me Jack."

"Ma don't like that name," Abby said.

"Well, it's my name, and I can have folks call me what I want." Jack tugged gently on her sister's braid. "Hold still while I tie the ribbon."

Arms crossed, Carly leaned against the door and watched Jack patiently tie the ribbon on the wiggly girl. What would it be like to have a sister? She'd heard her ma had birthed another baby when Carly was two, but it hadn't lived. Glancing up at the ceiling, she offered a quick prayer that God would watch over Rachel and see that her baby was delivered safely.

"Is Papa back yet?" Jack asked.

"No. Your friend Tessa came to the door just after you came upstairs after breakfast. Said something about the mercantile being robbed."

Jack's eyes widened. "Truly? When did that happen?"

Carly shrugged. Emma toddled over to her and lifted her hands, and she picked up the child. "I don't know. Miss Morgan said the family came downstairs early and found the back window broken and a number of things missing."

"That's horrible." Jack tapped her sister's shoulder. "You're done. Now try to keep your dress clean."

Carly picked up a small brush off the chest of drawers and brushed Emma's hair then set the girl down. "It looks like you have things under control here, so I'd better change into my church dress."

Jack nodded and stood, smoothing out the skirt of her delft blue dress. Her pretty auburn hair wasn't piled up on her head like it had been last night but rather was tied with a blue ribbon and hung down her back to her waist. The gangly wild child had grown into a beautiful young woman.

In her room, Carly shed her apron and calico and donned her yellow gingham church dress. She stared at her hair in the tall oval mirror that hung on one wall. She had never gotten used to pinning it up as Tillie had shown her, but the ladies at her old church always wore theirs that way. Turning sideways, she looked at her long braid. Dare she try wearing it hanging down as Jack had?

Finally she shrugged. What did it matter? She wasn't trying to impress anyone—and yet the moment that thought fled her mind, a picture of Garrett Corbett in his Sunday best replaced it. From the parlor window, she'd seen him walking to the social the night before. He had probably been relieved to see that she hadn't shown up.

Snatching up her brush, she shook out her braid and brushed her hair. It wasn't as long as Jack's, having been kept short while in prison, but it had finally grown to the middle of her back. She tied a ribbon and looped it into a bow at her nape, then turned sideways to see how she looked. Some might actually think she was pretty. She pinched her checks, then found her Bible.

With onc hand on the doorknob, she considered the day's importance. Today she would either be received by folks in the town—or rejected. If they hated her, what would she do?

She breathed a prayer, "Please, Father, let them accept me."

Noah leaned over the hitching post at the back of the church property and retched. After a few moments of misery, he dabbed his mouth with his handkerchief. No amount of preparation ever eased his stomach before preaching a sermon, and this was by far the most nerve-wracking situation he'd ever encountered.

He glanced around, glad that no one had shown up early, then strode toward the water pump. The cool liquid tasted delicious but didn't sit well in his belly. He gazed up at the sky through the canopy of trees overhead. "Father, I ask that You settle my stomach. Help me to rectify the damage I did last night, and enable me to share the message that You've laid on my heart."

A wide yawn slipped out, and he covered his mouth. He'd slept little last night. The fight with Billy and then the disagreement with Jack weighed heavily on him. Doubts swirled through his thoughts like debris in a tornado. Would anyone recognize him as the former town bully? Would the church people be angry that he'd gotten in a fight? Would they be receptive to his message? Would they even show up?

Clutching his well-worn Bible against his heart, he opened the church door and stepped inside. Immediately the peace of God flooded him and calmed him. The morning sun peeked through the storm clouds overhead and glimmered through the stained-glass window, creating colorful patterns of light that danced on the floor and walls. Closing his eyes, he murmured a prayer of thanks to the Lord for His presence.

He opened all the windows, then sat down on the front row, read several psalms, and scanned his sermon again. By the time he was done, buggies were driving past the windows and parking in the lot next door.

Noah blew out a breath and went to greet his parishioners at the front door. A man he didn't recognize walked up to the entrance with his wife and two adolescent boys. The man smiled at him, but when the woman glanced up, her happy expression turned to shock. She halted so fast, one of her boys ran into her back.

"Hey, Ma, whatcha stoppin' for?" The boy backed up a few steps, nudging his brother with his elbows. Both youths glanced at him in unison, and their mouths dropped open.

Noah smiled. He'd seen his ugly purple eye in the mirror this morning, as well as his puffy cheek and eyebrow. He probably looked like some kind of monster that children conjured up in their creative minds. "Good morning, and welcome. I'm Noah Jeffers, the visiting minister."

"Uh. . .we'uns is the Cauldwells," the man said. "I'm Jethro, and this here's my wife, Maisy, and our boys Samuel and Josiah."

"Ah, good Bible names, I see. It's a pleasure to meet y'all." Noah held his hand out to the man.

Mr. Cauldwell glanced up, frowned, and then shook Noah's hand. "D'you have some kind of accident or somethin'?"

Noah winced. He'd hoped word had gotten around town, so all he'd have to do was repent to the crowd and not have to explain things. "No, sir. I mean, I suppose it was sort of an accident."

"Either it was or it weren't. Which is it?" Mrs. Cauldwell pushed her wire-rimmed glasses up her thin nose. Behind her boys, another couple waited to enter.

"Since I'm going to have to explain myself, if you wouldn't mind being patient for a short while, I'd prefer to give the details just once, rather than having to tell each person as they enter."

Mr. Cauldwell glanced at his wife, then nodded. "I reckon we can wait. C'mon boys."

Mrs. Cauldwell followed her husband, but the boys stopped in front of him. The older one leaned toward him, his brows wiggling. "That's a mighty fine looking shiner, Reverend. You oughta be proud of it. I hope you gave the other guy what for. Anybody who'd fight a preacher deserves a thrashing, right, Sammy?"

His brother nodded his agreement; then both sat on the third row with their parents. The next couple had similar expressions of surprise on their faces. He'd seen them around town but had yet to meet them.

"I'm Noah Jeffers. Welcome."

The man nodded a greeting, but his wife huddled close as if she feared Noah. Just the thought made him wonder again if he shouldn't pack up and leave. What was God thinking in giving him a church to pastor?

"I'm Earl Hightower, and this here's Myrtle, my spinster sister."

Noah wasn't sure why the man felt the need to inform him his sister was unmarried since she had to be at least ten years his senior. He smiled. "A pleasure to meet you both. Come in and have a seat."

Agatha Linus hurried through the door. Her sister was still making her way across the street at a snail's pace. "Sorry I wasn't here earlier to practice the hymns, Reverend Jeffers. But I had to wait so I could help Bertha down the stairs. She doesn't handle them too good these days, what with her rheumatism being so bad and all. Should I play the two songs we decided on when we last talked?"

"That sounds perfect. Thank you, ma'am, and maybe I could come by your house this week and look over those stairs. Might be something I could do that would make things easier for your sister." Noah smiled at his organist, relieved that she had arrived.

"Wonderful! We'd love to have you visit again—and this time you won't need to chop wood." Agatha took her place on the organ bench and began to softly play a hymn.

Noah walked outside to the middle of the road, where Bertha Boyd rested on her cane, huffing hard. "Might I assist you into the church, Mrs. Boyd?"

"I'd be grateful. . .Reverend. This walk. . .seems longer. . .each time I. . .make it." She held one hand to her chest and struggled to catch her breath. The skin on her cheeks and throat jiggled with each breath she took.

Holding out his arm to her, he smiled. Bertha Boyd talked more than any woman he'd met and was the biggest woman he'd ever seen. Like Jack, the top of her head barely reached his shoulders, but Mrs. Boyd was a half-dozen times bigger around than the woman who refused to leave his mind. He'd learned a long time ago that Mrs. Boyd had the gift of gab and lived to gossip. Breathing hard, she leaned her weight on his arm and waddled into the church. She collapsed in the pew closest to the door and waved a thank-you.

"I say any Texan has a right to defend himself, pastor or not."

"A minister shouldn't oughta be fightin'."

Noah's attention was pulled back to the door by the raised voices. Two men he recognized as the bank tellers wrestled each other to get in the door first.

"Good morning, gentlemen." He considered asking them to lower their voices as they entered God's house but chose to take another route.

Both ceased the shoving and gazed up at Noah. One man smiled, and the other scowled. Behind them, a family with a large number of children waited quietly.

"Jess Jermaine, Reverend." He slipped in the door. "A pleasure to meet you."

The other man hurried in, head down, and slunk to a nearby pew.

"Don't pay him no never-mind. He's a passa— uh, passa—"

"Pacifist?"

Mr. Jermaine shook his head and removed his hat. "Yeah, that's it. He thinks nobody should ever fight." Mr. Jermaine leaned closer. "But he's from Boston. Them city folks don't know that a man who doesn't defend himself in Texas just might'n live to see the sunset. You did the right thang last night, Pastor."

Remorse again gutted Noah. If he hadn't fought Billy Morgan, people's minds would be on God this morning and not whether the pastor should or shouldn't have defended himself.

A familiar-looking man almost as tall as he held out his hand for his wife to enter. Noah recognized the blond woman as one of the boardinghouse brides the Corbett brothers had brought to town a decade ago. She'd lost the marshal's hand, but it looked as if she'd been highly successful in attracting another man and raising a large brood of children.

The woman smiled, her blue eyes shining. "It's a pleasure to meet you, Reverend. I'm Leah Howard."

Noah shook her fingertips. Then she motioned for her children to come in. They were like stair steps, from a young woman about Jack's age to a baby she held in her arms, an even combination of boys and girls. The man watched them scurry past, a proud smile on his face.

"That's quite a family you have there."

"Yes sir, we've been blessed by the Lord, for sure." He held out his hand. "I'm Dan Howard. I own the livery."

"Of course. The day I arrived, you were receiving a load of hay, so your assistant helped me. Isn't that him?" Noah nudged his chin toward the tallest boy, still standing in the aisle.

"Yep, that's our oldest son, Ben. He's a good help."

"How's my horse doing?"

Mr. Howard smiled. "Good. We feed him ever' day, give him fresh water, and put him in the pasture each morning."

"I wasn't questioning your care, Mr. Howard. I've neglected to exercise him like I should and feel bad about that."

"Davy, my thirteen-year-old, is real good with horses. He'd be right pleased to ride yours around town if'n you'd like him to."

Noah smiled. "I'd be obliged."

Mr. Howard nodded and took his seat beside his wife. His family took up two whole pews.

For the next ten minutes, people filed in, greeted Noah, and took their seats. As his pocket watch hit the top of the hour, Noah headed for the front, trying to shake his disappointment that Jack and her family had failed to come this morning. Was she still angry with him?

On second thought, maybe her not being present was a blessing. He cared deeply that his parishioners would receive him as their pastor and friend. But it mattered immensely more what Jack thought—and that idea threatened to shatter his tenuous peace. Grasping hold of the podium, he stared at the crowd and determined to shut Jack from his mind—at least for the next hour.

He glanced at Agatha Linus and nodded. The woman began a flowery introduction of "At the Cross." He smiled. "Would you please stand and join me in worship to our God?"

Most of the crowd rose to their feet, leaving Bertha Boyd and a few old folks and youngsters still seated. Noah closed his eyes, offered a final, quick prayer that God would speak through him and that the congregation would forgive his actions of the previous night, and then joined in the singing:

"At the cross, at the cross where I first saw the light,
And the burden of my heart rolled away,
It was there by faith I received my sight,
And now I am happy all the day!"

Chapter 18

Carly quickened her steps as voices lifted in song emanating from the church filled the muggy air with a beautiful serenade of praise to God. Time had gotten away from them, and the last thing she wanted was to go in after the service had started and receive the scolding stares of those already seated—the very people she hoped would accept her.

"Horse feathers. We're late." Jacqueline hoisted Emma into her arms and hurriedly shooed her siblings along like a mother hen.

"Horses ain't got no feathers." Alan shook his head, his short legs pumping fast to keep up.

"Goodness, Alan. Where'd you ever learn to talk like that?" Jack grabbed Abby's hand to keep her from dashing back home to her ma. "C'mon."

"Yeah, don'tcha know *ain't* ain't a word?" Abby stuck her tongue out and made a face.

"Abby! Stop that. You two better behave, or you'll get no pie today." Both kids frowned but settled down at Jack's warning.

Carly wondered how Rachel would manage having another child when the ones she already had were so rambunctious. Hopefully the new baby would take after Emma, who seemed to have the most docile character of the bunch.

The open doors of the church looked more like a monster's mouth ready to swallow rather than welcome her. Now that they had arrived, a part of Carly wanted to rush back to the security of the boardinghouse to stay with Rachel. But if she were there, Rachel would feel obligated to stay up and talk, and the poor woman needed her rest. And Carly desperately needed to hear an encouraging message this morning.

Thunder sounded to the west, and she glanced up at the gray sky. Even the heavens looked unsettled today. The air hung heavy with moisture, and sweat already dampened the back of her dress.

At least she'd met the new minister and had shared several meals with him and the Davis family. He seemed kind and accepting of her; then again, he didn't know about her past. But with him being new, wouldn't most of the church folk be focused on him and whether his sermon passed muster and not concerned about a new woman in town?

They entered the doorway and shuffled down the aisle to the closest empty row. Emmie squealed when she saw the reverend and waved. "Howdy, Pas'er."

Most folks nearby chuckled, but a few cast stern glares their way. Reverend Jeffers grinned, even though singing, and waved his fingers at the toddler. Carly sat down and bit back her own smile. Jack had her hand wrapped securely over the girl's mouth and had leaned over to whisper something in her sister's ear.

Carly joined in the third verse of the song, which she'd learned at Reverend Barker's church:

"Was it for crimes that I had done;
He groaned upon the tree?
Amazing pity! grace unknown!
And love beyond degree!"

Carly's heart clenched, and she closed her eyes. Jesus had suffered on the cross partly because of her own sins. *Forgive me, Lord.* She knew in her heart that He had pardoned her, but remembering the price Jesus had paid for her salvation kept her humble. She had much to be thankful for. God had freed her from prison and given her peace—at least most of the time. And He'd blessed her by making it possible for her to live in Lookout again with her dear friend who had told her about salvation. God's faithfulness was truly great. She prayed again that He would open the townsfolk's hearts toward her and that He'd give her the home she'd never had before.

She rearranged her skirt and smiled at Alan, who sat next to her. From behind, she heard the loud whispers, "Outlaw. Convict."

Her heart clenched, and her hope wilted like a daisy in a drought. She closed her eyes as the pastor prayed. *Help me, Lord.*

She simply had to make a stand here in Lookout, because she had nowhere else to go. Either people would accept her, or they wouldn't. If their scorn was the worst she had to face, then she could endure. *But please, Lord, don't let things get any worse.*

Footsteps shuffled down the aisle, and someone squeezed into the small space between her and the edge of the pew. She scooted closer to Alan then glanced over to see who had just arrived. Garrett Corbett stared down at her with those intriguing blue eyes. Her hands started sweating, and she yanked her gaze away. *Oh, Lord, why'd he have to sit here?*

Jack scooted to the end of the pew so that Carly could move over and not have Garrett crowding her. She probably should have mentioned that he often sat with her family and then came over for Sunday dinner.

Agatha Linus started playing the chorus of "What a Friend We Have in Jesus," and the pastor started singing, his deep voice clear and surprisingly on-key. She pulled Emma back against her, hoping the warmth of the room would put the toddler to sleep, and continued listening. Who would have thought Noah could sing so well?

His handsome face looked dreadful. His black eye had all but swollen shut, and his other cuts were puffy and red. She wondered why he hadn't worn the bandages the doctor had put on his wounds last night. Maybe he wanted folks to know he had nothing to hide.

If that was the case, why wouldn't he talk about his past with her? The fact that he refused to stirred up her investigative senses and made her want to discover his secrets. But what if he was hiding something that could hurt the town? Didn't people have a right to know that?

What if he was a reformed train robber? Her gaze immediately shifted past the children to Carly. She'd been an outlaw, but God had changed her. So if He could change an outlaw into a kind, God-fearing person, He could change anybody.

But not Butch Laird.

Jack glanced to her right and gazed out the open window. Where had that thought come from? She hardly ever thought of her old nemesis these days. She had a hard time believing even God could change a fat, pig-stinking bully like him, but in her heart, she knew that He could.

She hadn't treated Butch kindly, either, but had ganged up on him with her two childhood friends. She'd even lied about him. But at least she'd come clean on that and had told Luke the truth. Jack remembered going to Butch's home to wallop him for the words he'd painted on the town's walls, but when she saw the shanty he lived in, her anger had fled, and she had the overwhelming urge to apologize. She'd never been certain which she'd actually have done, but he'd been gone. Had left town and never returned. Where was he today? Was he still alive?

Shaking thoughts of Butch from her mind, she concentrated on the words she was singing:

"Have we trials and temptations?
Is there trouble anywhere?
We should never be discouraged—
Take it to the Lord in prayer."

Jack ducked her head. She didn't pray half enough. She was always doing things she thought was right, but she needed to seek God more.

Emmie's eyes rolled back, and her lashes lowered. She'd open them wide for a moment, and they'd drift closed again. Leaning down, Jack placed a kiss on her sister's head. When was the last time she'd prayed for her siblings?

Abby shoved Alan, and he pinched her leg. "Ow!" Heads swerved in their direction.

Jack leaned over. "I'm warning you two. No pie."

Abby scowled at Alan and leaned on Jack's left arm. Her right arm was already going to sleep. Maybe she should talk to the reverend about starting some kind of Sunday school program for the young children to attend during the service.

"Thank you kindly, Mrs. Linus." Noah Jeffers nodded at the piano player as she left her bench and proceeded to the pew where her sister sat. The pastor cleared his throat and held on to the podium so tightly that Jack could see the white of his knuckles. He stared out at the congregation.

"I tried to introduce myself as each of you came in this morning, but I apologize if I missed anyone. I'm Noah Jeffers, and I'm filling in for Pastor Taylor while his family is out of town."

He lowered his head, pursed his lips, then looked back up with resolve. Jack wondered if he was as nervous as he looked. Preaching to a crowd for the first time would be difficult enough, but to be doing so battered and bruised. . .

"Last night, I had the misfortune to be in a fight."

Jess Jermaine leaped to his feet. "A man's got a right to defend himself, Preacher. Everyone saw that you tried hard to not fight that Morgan boy."

"Not when he's the pastor, he don't." A man Jack hadn't met before jumped up. "A pastor oughta be a man of peace."

"Gentlemen, please. Have a seat, and let me continue." He stood quietly while the two men stared each other down, then finally sat. "I want to apologize to y'all. I don't condone fighting."

Jack sucked in a breath. He was apologizing for defending her? She held Emmie so tightly the child began to fuss. She forced her arms to relax. Was he sorry for what he did?

"I can't deny that this is a rough land and men sometimes have to take actions to protect themselves and their families. But as your current pastor, I should have tried harder to resolve last night's situation without fighting. For that, I apologize. That's all

I want to say on the matter now, but if you feel it necessary to talk more, come and see me at the boardinghouse at your leisure."

He looked down and opened his Bible. Heat scalded Jack's cheeks. She stared down at Emmie's little fingers, feeling rejected and foolish. Everyone would have been better off if she'd just stayed home last night instead of attending the social when she had no intention of dancing. Then Billy wouldn't have created a commotion, and Noah Jeffers wouldn't have had to sully his reputation and suffer for her sake. The sooner she left town, the better it would be for everyone.

"I thought a fitting verse to start with this morning would be Matthew 5:46: 'For if ye love them which love you, what reward have ye? Do not even the publicans the same?' " Noah walked away from the podium and stood at the front of the pews. "Y'all know that a publican was a tax collector?"

Several heads nodded.

"Good. Well, we all know that nobody likes a tax collector."

Chuckles echoed across the room.

"Jesus is saying here that even men we might not like love their wives and children—people who love them. It's a simple thing to love people who care about you. But it's far harder to love a person who, say—pokes fun at you for something you did or said. And what about that man who cheated you last month? How easy is it to love him?"

"Downright impossible," Mr. Cauldwell shouted.

Reverend Jeffers looked at the man. "Maybe so, but it's what our Lord is instructing us to do. It's not easy. I'm proof of that. Last night I failed to show love to an angry man, and I'm the minister. But God doesn't always call us to do the easy thing."

Jack thought about that. In some ways, leaving Lookout would be very hard. Yeah, she might actually have a room to herself, but she would miss seeing her brother and sisters grow up, and the new baby wouldn't even know her. She stared out the window at the cloudy sky. Wind battered the trees, signaling a coming storm that mirrored the one going on inside her. Could she sacrifice all that for the opportunities and adventure she could have in Dallas? Would moving be worth the cost?

"Let's read a bit farther." Noah's words pulled her attention back to the front.

"Matthew 9, verses 10–13 says, 'And it came to pass, as Jesus sat at meat in the house, behold, many publicans and sinners came and sat down with him and his disciples. And when the Pharisees saw it, they said unto his disciples, Why eateth your Master with the pelicans and sinners?' "

Alan's head jerked up. He'd been sitting there quietly unraveling his sock. "What's a pelican?"

Jack shushed him and glanced at Carly, who shrugged, an embarrassed grin teasing her lips.

Old Mr. Carpenter, who always sat on the second row because he couldn't hear well, turned to his wife. "Did he say pelican?"

Poor Opal Carpenter held up her finger to quiet him, but the old man lifted his ear horn. "Eh?"

"Hesh up, Henry," the old woman said.

Chuckles rebounded around the room.

Noah cleared his throat, looking a bit confused. Jack couldn't help feeling sorry for him. Did he know about his faux pas?

He continued reading. " 'But when Jesus heard that, he said unto them, They that be whole need not a physician, but they that are sick. But go ye and learn what that meaneth, I will have mercy, and not sacrifice: for I am not come to call the righteous, but sinners to repentance.' Jesus chose to fellowship with the poor and lowly, but He was the son of a king—the King. Instead of demanding fine clothing, a feast, and jewels, He lived a life of poverty, so that He could be an example and reach those nobody else cared about."

Noah slowly paced back and forth across the front of the church. "Remember the parable of the two sons? The father told one son to go and work in the vineyard, but the son said no. Later he repented and went and did as the father asked. But the father went to his second son and told him to go to work. That son said he would but then failed to go."

He paused and looked over the congregation. Jack swallowed hard, knowing she was more like the second son than the first. Much of her life, she'd shirked her chores, preferring to be with her friends than help her ma. Remorse ran through her.

"So let me ask you a question. Which of the two sons did the will of his father?"

"The first," someone behind Jack shouted.

"Perhaps." Noah shrugged one shoulder. "Jesus said, 'Verily I say unto you, that the publicans and the harlots go into the kingdom of God before you.' It seems a harsh statement, doesn't it, folks? We strive all our lives to work hard, raise enough crops or make enough money to feed our families and provide for them, and all of this is good. But God looks at our hearts."

Noah remained silent for a moment and stared at the crowd. Jack ducked her head when he glanced her way. "What is your motivation, folks? Are you working hard to be the richest man in town? Or are you just trying to care for your family and serve God?"

Noah looked down at the floor and stood with his hands in his pockets. "I've never been a rich man, nor particularly care to be. But I can tell you that I've lived about as low as a man can go."

Jack perked up. Was he going to share something about his past? "My pa wasn't a kind person. Oh, he was all right until my ma and little sister died, but then he fell off the wagon. He was a mean drunk, and I was the one he took his anger out on."

Jack sucked in a breath.

"It's hard for me to believe that Jesus would have sought out my pa before. . .say, Pastor Taylor."

Jack's heart clinched at the pain etched on Noah's face. She'd once had a mean father and remembered hiding when he'd go into one of his rages. Remembered how it hurt the few times he hit her before her mother would distract him and take his brutality instead. She'd never have expected that she and Noah would have that in common.

"I doubt my pa ever heard about God. He never taught me about the Lord. And to be honest, it would be hard for me to accept that he might be in heaven." He huffed a fake laugh. "It's a good thing I'm not God. I'm imperfect. A sinner. Just like everyone else in this room. But there's good news, folks. Jesus came to save us sinners. If we turn from our wicked ways and humble ourselves,

God can make us new. Wash us clean as new-fallen snow."

He returned to the podium just as Abby slid off the bench and onto the floor. Jack motioned for her to get back on the seat, but she shook her head. Abby leaned her head against the pew in front of them and stuck her tongue out at Alan. Jack tried to shift Emmie to a different position to free up her arm, knowing an explosion was about to occur. Alan leaned forward, reaching for Abby's hair, but Carly snatched up the boy just in time to avoid a catastrophe. She hauled him onto her lap, but he shinnied off and climbed onto Garrett's, giving Carly an angry glare. Abby had already inhaled—ready to scream, Jack was certain—but instead, the girl slowly let out her breath, looking disappointed. Jack glanced at the ceiling. *Father, forgive me if I was anything like my siblings.*

Noah returned to his podium and ruffled the pages of his Bible. "Let me close with this. 'Two men went up into the temple to pray; the one a Pharisee, and the other a pelican.' "

"What is a pelican?" Alan whispered, far too loudly.

Garrett leaned down to his ear. "It's a kind of bird."

Alan nodded. "Thought so."

" 'The Pharisee stood and prayed thus with himself, God, I thank thee, that I am not as other men are, extortioners, unjust, adulterers, or even as this pelican. I fast twice in the week, I give tithes of all that I possess. And the pelican, standing afar off, would not lift up so much as his eyes unto heaven, but smote upon his breast, saying, God be merciful to me a sinner. I tell you, this man went down to his house justified rather than the other: for every one that exalteth himself shall be abased; and he that humbleth himself shall be exalted.' "

Noah closed his Bible, his gaze roving the crowd again. Jack didn't think he had any idea of the mistake he'd made. "I challenge you not to leave here today until you've made things right with the Lord. Don't be proud like the Pharisee, who boasted of his good deeds, but rather, see how you can help your neighbor or friend without expecting something in return. Shall we pray?"

Jack bowed her head, shame weighing heavy on her shoulders. She was so tied up in achieving her own dreams that she rarely thought of doing something nice for someone else, even her ma. *Forgive me, Lord.*

Thunder boomed outside, and though the prayer had yet to be completed, a number of heads swiveled toward the windows. The scent of rain filled the air, and Jack had a suspicion that many folks were going to get wet on their travels home. She couldn't help being thankful she didn't have far to go.

Alan squirmed on Garrett's lap, and the moment Noah said, "Amen," the child went slack and slid free of his captor. He crawled across the floor toward Abby. She spotted him, squealed, and scurried under the pew in front of Jack, with Alan chasing after. Jack bent and just missed snagging her brother's britches. Mrs. Abbott, sitting directly in front of Jack with her quiet trio of children, squealed and looked down. Then she turned and shot Jack a glare that could curdle milk. Jack shook her head and shrugged. *How did Ma get those two to behave?*

"Sorry," Garrett said. "I'll go after them."

Emmie sat up, her hair and the back of her dress damp with sweat. She rubbed her eyes and sniffled. "I tirsty."

"Why don't I take her back home and get the table set for dinner?" Carly smiled.

"Are you sure you don't mind? I probably should go rescue Garrett."

Carly held out her arms. "You wanna go home and get a drink?" Emmie stared at her for a moment, then fell forward. Carly stood and held the girl on her hip. "Let's go home before the rain starts." Thunder echoed through the room again, and Emmie buried her face against Carly's shoulder. They joined the crowd making its way outside.

Jack stood, stretching out the kinks in her shoulders and arms. She glanced down and gasped. The dress that had taken her nearly an hour to iron yesterday was a mass of damp wrinkles. She crossed her arms and slid out of the pew.

Mr. Abbott leaned toward his wife. "Oddest sermon I ever did hear. I don't remember reading nothing in the scriptures about pelicans."

"That's 'cause it's not there. Just a bad case of nerves, I reckon."

She flicked one finger, and her three children followed her quietly out of the church like ducklings behind a mama duck.

Her husband moseyed behind the group, scratching his head. "You know, Louise, come to think of it, I do believe pelicans are mentioned in the scriptures. Somewhere in Leviticus or Deuteronomy, but I sure don't recall any mentioned in the New Testament."

Jack glanced toward the front of the church. The mayor was forcing his way against the flow of people, up the aisle toward Noah. With such a crowd surging to the exit, she figured she wasn't leaving any time soon and started making her way to the front. If there was going to be some action, she wanted to be there.

She smiled and returned a wave from Callie Howard as she passed her friend's family. Sitting down in a pew several rows from the front, she tried not to look too obvious. Several small groups of friends and neighbors stood in clusters talking, but most of the people were leaving the building. The mayor squeezed his bulk past Agatha Linus and her sister, then strode toward the reverend with determined steps. The man sure didn't look very pleased.

During the sermon, she'd learned a bit more already about their mysterious pastor, but was the mayor going to fire him before she got a chance to write her story?

Chapter 19

Noah folded his sermon notes and stuck the papers in his Bible. He heaved a heavy sigh, glad to have his first sermon over and done with. Several people had come up front and thanked him for coming to Lookout. He glanced at the door, disappointed as most of the congregation made their way outside to their horses and buggies. He'd planned to stand at the door and send them on their way, but the threat of a thunderstorm had everyone hurrying home.

The mayor squeezed past Mrs. Linus and strode toward him. From the expression on his face, Noah was certain he wasn't happy. What could have upset him so much?

"Now see here, young man, what's all that talk about pelicans?"

Noah's heart lurched at the man's harsh attack. "What? I talked about publicans, not pelicans, Mayor."

The man wagged a beefy finger in Noah's face. "No, sir. I heard it with my own ears. You must have said *pelicans* a dozen times."

Noah's gaze darted over to where Jack sat several rows back. She watched them with obvious interest, but he didn't like the idea of her seeing him get wrung out by the mayor.

"I never heard the like of that message." The mayor's bellowing drew his attention back. Mayor Burke's eyes actually bulged. "If you want to keep your job here, you'd better not repeat today's fiasco. Do you understand me?"

Slowly, Noah nodded. He really had no idea what the man was ranting about. Had he just heard him wrong?

The mayor stormed down the aisle, mumbling. "I knew it was a bad idea to have such a young man. . . ."

Turning his back to Jack, Noah returned to the podium and pretended that he'd left something behind. The mayor should have waited and talked to him in private, not lambasting him while people were still in the church. Had he actually said *pelicans* instead of *publicans*? Surely not. He'd wanted to speak a message that would encourage folks to be nicer to their neighbors, but he'd evidently failed.

"Don't listen to Mayor Burke. He used to fuss at Pastor Taylor, too."

Noah faced Jack, grateful that she tried to soothe his rumpled composure. She was so pretty in her medium blue dress, which enhanced the color of her eyes. The bodice was all wrinkled, but he shouldn't be noticing that and pulled his gaze back up to her face. "Did he really do that? Fuss at Pastor Taylor?"

Jack nodded. "I saw him do it several times."

"Well, if he only complained a handful of times, I'll try not to be overly concerned."

"I don't usually stay later like today, though, so I can't really say how much he criticized the sermon." Jack smiled, setting his barely settled stomach to swirling again. She was so pretty—she always had been—even when dressed in overalls.

"So, what was all that talk about pelicans? It was a little confusing."

The blood rushed from Noah's face, and his heart pounded. "What do you mean?"

"You didn't hear Alan?"

Noah shook his head. "No, but I did hear several people call out things to me. I was concentrating, though, and didn't hear everything they were saying."

Jack leaned her hip against the podium and rested her elbow on the top of the wooden stand. "I'll admit I was a bit distracted by Alan and Abby, but was that just a slip of the tongue? Or did I completely miss the point of your sermon?"

He had hoped she'd come up to tell him how his sermon had enlightened her and encouraged her, but instead, she confused him. "I have no idea what you're talking about."

Her eyes sparkled, and she lifted a hand to cover a giggle. "Oh, dear. You really don't know, do you?"

"No, and I fail to see any humor in my message."

Jack's expression turned serious. "You did say *pelican* several times."

"Great. Just great." Noah closed his eyes. How had he made such a foolish error? "No wonder the mayor was so angry. That also explains the perplexed looks on so many people's faces."

Jack reached out her hand as if to touch him, then lowered it. "I'm sure it was a simple mistake because of nerves."

Thunder exploded overhead. Jack squealed and jumped, latching onto his arm so hard her fingernails bit into his flesh through the fabric of his shirt. Her reaction surprised him. He didn't think she was afraid of anything.

"Sorry." Her gaze was directed out the nearest window where the rain was coming down in torrents. "Thunder always makes me nervous, ever since the time a tornado hit the town on the day my folks were married."

"Yeah, I know." He patted her hand, hoping to reassure her, remembering that day well. Everyone had been excited about Luke Davis marrying Rachel Hamilton, Jack's ma, except maybe the boardinghouse brides who'd come to town to marry him. There had been cake afterward, but he hadn't gotten any. He'd watched from afar. Jack glanced down, her cheeks aflame, and tugged her hand out from under his.

"Huh? You know what?"

His heart quickened, and he scrambled to remember what he'd just said. "I. . .uh. . .don't like thunderstorms, either." He nearly smacked his forehead with his hand. That made him sound like a ninny. What man was scared of a storm? But he couldn't very well have said he remembered because he'd lived in Lookout and remembered the very same tornado, could he?

"Oh."

She walked over to the closest window and lowered it. "Rain

is coming in on this side."

He pushed his feet into action, chastising himself for thinking of her instead of the church. *Lord, help me to keep my focus on You and the church and not Jacqueline Davis.*

Jack closed another window and he managed to get two more shut. He searched for something to dry the floors but there was no cloth of any kind in the sparse building. He walked to the open front door to make sure the rain wasn't coming in there. Thankfully it was blowing from the opposite direction. Jack joined him, and they stood near the exit watching the rain cascading in torrents, as if it needed to water the whole world in a single day.

Noah stared down at the top of Jack's head and smiled. Her part was crooked and her long hair hung down her back in waves, tied back only with a wilted blue ribbon that sat catawampus. Along her pale neck, untouched by the sun's fingers, damp tendrils of curls clung to her skin. His fingers ached to reach out and touch her hair. They stood so close he could probably feel it without her even knowing. He balled his hand into a fist and sighed.

Jack glanced up over her shoulder, and he could see faint freckles smattered across her nose and cheeks. "It won't last long. These Texas storms blow as hard as a schoolyard bully, but they don't have any staying power."

Noah winced. He knew all about Texas storms, having spent his whole life here, but she had no idea how much her bully reference hit home. If she did, he had little doubt she'd race out in the storm rather than suffer his company any longer. He was fooling himself if he thought she'd ever be interested in him. No matter how much he'd changed.

Why had God sent him here? Was it so he could learn to control his emotions when tempted? Wasn't it so that he could make recompense for past misdeeds?

Jack leaned against the doorjamb and faced him, her arms crossed over her chest. "Was that true—what you said about your pa?"

His breath caught in his throat. Had he said too much? Jack was no common woman. She was smarter than most and, as a reporter, able to connect the dots. He swallowed and nodded.

"Unfortunately, my pa wasn't a nice man."

"I'm sorry, Pastor. My first pa wasn't either." She nibbled her lip and watched the rain. "He would drink and get really angry and he even hit my ma—and me."

"Sorry. As hard as it was to take Pa's beatings as a boy—and I wasn't a scrawny lad, either—I can't imagine how much more difficult it must be for women to endure such mistreatment." He wanted to clobber the man. No wonder Jack was such a tough kid when she was younger. She had to be just to survive. Her father was already dead when he and his pa moved to town. He was glad he'd never met the man.

"We managed. I mostly ran and hid whenever he went loco like that, and other times I was already in bed, so Ma had to face him alone." She looked up. "I wish I'd been big like you so I could have protected her."

He wanted to say he was glad she wasn't, but that would hardly be proper. He wanted to say he wished he'd been around back then to protect her, but he couldn't say that, either. So he said nothing.

Jack frowned. "You gonna tell me about your past, so I can write that article for the paper?" She grinned and wiggled her brows up and down, her eyes shining. "You're not hiding any deep, dark secrets you're ashamed of, are you?"

Noah worked hard to keep a straight face. She had no idea how close to home her teasing question hit. He shrugged, hoping it looked casual. "What Texan doesn't?"

He could see that sharp mind of hers at work. She suspected something, and he knew her tenacity. She was like a snapping turtle. Once she took hold of a notion, she wouldn't let go until her curiosity was satisfied. He needed to distract her—and fast.

"Do you think maybe you could call me Noah?"

Her blue eyes widened, and her mouth dropped open a bit. "Uh. . .do you think that's proper, I mean, with you being the pastor and all?"

He shrugged. "I don't see why not. I asked your pa the same thing. I've never cared for being called reverend. I looked it up one time in a dictionary, and it means 'worthy of being revered.' In my eyes, God alone deserves that honor."

Jack nodded. "That makes sense. I reckon I could call you Noah when it's just you and me around, but it's probably not a good idea in public. At least not yet. Folks spread rumors faster than wildflowers pop up in springtime around here."

"We don't want folks spreading rumors, do we?" He grinned.

She looked embarrassed but shook her head. "So, if I call you Noah, you'll have to call me Jack."

He quirked an eyebrow feigning surprise. "That's not a very ladylike name for such a pretty young woman. What would your ma say?"

Jack sighed and crossed her arms again. "She hates it, but that's what I prefer. Even Luke calls me Jack when he doesn't call me Half Bit."

Noah remembered hearing Luke call her Half Bit on several occasions, but he wasn't sure where the man had dug up such an odd nickname. "Why don't you go by Jackie if you don't like Jacqueline, which is a pretty name, if you ask me?" Noah knew he should rein in his bold tongue before it got him into trouble, but he didn't know if he'd ever have Jack all to himself like this again.

She shrugged. "Nobody's ever called me that. I guess I liked Jack when I was young because it made me sound tougher. I always wished God had made me a boy."

"I'm glad He didn't."

Her gaze jerked up to his, and he allowed himself the pleasure of gazing into her lovely, intelligent eyes. The dark blue was streaked with lighter blues and some gray. An inner ring of pale blue encircled her pupil, as if her ma had laid claim on a small section of her eye color. Jack's cheeks flamed, and she broke his gaze, a pleasant smile twittering on her lips.

"Oh, look. The rain's let up. We probably won't get too wet if we leave now. I need to get back and help get dinner on the table."

He set his Bible on a pew, not wanting to risk it getting wet. He'd come back for it later. Then he took hold of Jack's arm, and she stiffened. "It's wet out, and the mud will be slippery. I want to be sure you don't fall."

She nodded and allowed him to escort her outside. He stopped to close the doors, and she tugged away.

"I'll race you home!" With her skirts hiked up, she dashed into the drizzle and ran for all she was worth. He smiled. That was the girl he remembered. The daring one, full of heart and gumption. He longed to chase after Jack, grab her up in his arms, and kiss her. Walking out into the light rain, he glanced skyward. Above him, the sun broke through the gray clouds, casting its bright beams on the earth, as if the finger of God was reaching out to him.

Noah heaved a sigh and slowed his steps, allowing the warm rain to wash over him. What he truly needed was to go jump in a cold lake somewhere and cool his senses.

On second thought, maybe he'd already taken leave of his senses.

Chapter 20

Carly put Alan and Abby to work setting the silverware out on the table while she placed the plates in front of each chair. Garrett Corbett stood in the entryway, one arm still in a sling and the other holding Emma. He puffed up his cheeks and widened his eyes at the toddler. Emmie giggled and poked at his cheeks with her tiny fingers. Carly ducked her head, not wanting him to see her laughing at him.

She'd been more nervous than an inmate on parole day when he'd sat down beside her in church. The space had been so narrow that his leg had pressed against her skirts, and with Alan squished against her other side, she'd nearly panicked. Thank goodness Jack scooted over, making more room. Ever since being locked in prison, she hadn't liked confining spaces of any sort.

"You're such a good girl, Miss Emmie Poo." Garrett nibbled on the toddler's belly, eliciting squeals of delight.

Carly glanced at the wall as if she could see through it to Rachel's bedroom door. She must be especially tired since she hadn't gotten up when they returned home. She lifted a finger to her mouth. "Shh. . .we need to let Rachel rest as long as possible."

Garrett made a face, showing he hadn't thought of that. "Maybe I should take her out to the porch?"

She glanced around, unsure what to do. The food was ready, but Rachel wasn't up, Luke was still gone, and Jacqueline and the pastor hadn't returned from church. With all the rain, she figured they'd decided to wait it out. "I probably should help the girls change out of their church clothes."

He nodded and handed Emma to her. Their hands brushed during the exchange, sending her heart skipping. He gazed down at her with a perplexed look on his face. She didn't want to like him, but she loved his eyes—almost the color of a robin's egg, but bluer.

"What should I do?" he asked.

She glanced around and spied Alan standing in front of the buffet and eyeing the pie. He reached up real quick-like, pinched off a piece of crust, and stuck it in his mouth. "Uh. . .Alan, do you need help changing?"

The boy rolled his eyes. "I'm seven, for Pete's sake." He stomped past them shaking his head.

Garrett grinned and leaned toward her. "Yeah, he's seven—an old man already."

"He ain't old." Abby shoved her hands to her hips. "You're old, Uncle Garrett."

Carly couldn't help laughing. "Yeah, you're ancient, Mr. Corbett."

His smile was conspiring, but his gaze serious. "Call me Garrett. Everyone does."

She swallowed hard.

"Or"—he wiggled his brows—"if you prefer, you can call me Uncle Garrett." He grinned wide, as if cracking the funniest joke in town. If the man had a serious bone in his body, it must be his little toe.

Keeping a straight face so as not to encourage him, she shook her head and gave him a schoolmarm look. She still didn't quite trust him and wasn't sure she wanted to get first-name familiar with him, but rather than disappoint him, she avoided his comment altogether. "If you could maybe stir the beans for me, I'll hurry up and get the girls changed."

"I'm a big girl. I don't need help." Abby marched out of the kitchen just like her brother had done.

Garrett shook his head. "I don't know what Luke and Rachel

are going to do with another young'un. Before long, they'll have to close the boardinghouse because they'll need all the rooms for their own family." He chuckled and walked into the kitchen.

"Stay out of that extra cornbread." She wagged her finger at him then hurried upstairs. If he was anything like Reverend Barker, he'd already be wolfing down a square.

She made quick work of getting the girls changed. Abby skipped into Alan's room, and Carly carried Emma back downstairs. Garrett stood at the stove, stirring the beans, and she wondered if he had been the whole time she'd been gone.

He peered over his shoulder at her. "Looks like the rain is letting up."

"Good. That means Jacqueline and the preacher should be here soon."

She set Emma down on the floor and hoisted the heavy platter of cornbread. "You can stop stirring now."

He laid the spoon down, then took the platter from her, holding it in one hand. "Where do you want this? On the buffet?"

She couldn't help noticing the crumbs on his lips. He licked them, probably realizing she'd caught him, and then grinned, turning her insides to the consistency of hot grits. "Uh. . .yes, put that on the buffet." She followed him into the dining room, as if he couldn't do such a simple chore on his own.

"How come there's a big pot of beans and a smaller one?" He leaned against the buffet, looking as comfortable as if in his own home.

His broad shoulders, wide from lifting crates of freight for years, filled out his white shirt. He'd already removed his black string tie and had stuffed it into his pocket, leaving a tail hanging out. His skin was tanned from years of driving wagons across the rolling hills of northeast Texas. Though she couldn't quit looking at the man, she knew him to be a rogue and a joker. She'd never truly been attracted to a man before. The men she'd known had never been the trustworthy sort. They tended to have three things on their minds most of the time—food, drinking, and women.

So, why did he weigh so heavily on her mind? Why had she dreamed about him last night?

When she didn't respond to his question, his blond brows lifted. "Oh. . .the extra pot. It seems the reverend can't tolerate pork, so I made a smaller batch for him without the meat."

"Oh, yeah. I saw what happens when he eats it. Not a pretty sight." He feigned a mock shudder. "Poor man. I can't imagine not eating bacon, or ham, or gravy with sausage." Suddenly he paused and stared at her. "Wait a minute. You cooked the beans?"

"Yes, and the cornbread, too."

His gaze dashed to the platter on the buffet and back to her. "But I thought you couldn't cook."

She shoved her hands to her hips. "Whatever gave you that idea?"

"Uh. . .well, that pie you made for Luke's bride contest wasn't worth feeding to the hogs."

It took great effort, but she resisted stomping her foot on his narrow-mindedness. "That was more than ten years ago, *Mr.* Corbett."

He shrugged. "So?"

She narrowed her gaze. How in the world could she have been attracted to this. . .this. . . "A person can learn a lot in a decade."

The bedroom door rattled, and Carly jumped. She hurried into the hall. Rachel leaned on the doorjamb, holding her lower belly and breathing hard. Carly felt Garrett standing right behind her. "Are you all right?"

Rachel shook her head. "Where's Luke?"

"I don't think he ever came back from investigating the mercantile theft. He wasn't in church."

Rachel closed her eyes and groaned. "Find him. The baby is coming."

As the rain stopped, Jack slowed her frantic pace and climbed the steps of her home. Catching her breath, she looked back down the street, halfway disappointed Noah hadn't chased after her. That would hardly be proper. He was already on the mayor's bad side, and chasing after a woman would get him fired, for sure.

And she would regret if that were to happen.

A glimmer drew her attention, and she stared down muddy Main Street where puddles of water glistened in the brilliant sunlight that had chased away the storm clouds. Looking upward, she gasped. A rainbow stretched over the town, almost as if God had sent her a prism of promise that things would work out. But just what things, she wasn't sure.

Would she get that Dallas job she wanted? Would she figure out what the mayor was up to? Would Noah kiss her?

She dropped into a rocker, stunned at her train of thought. Where had that idea come from? She didn't want to like Noah, but there was an odd connection with him that she'd never experienced with another man—almost as if they'd known each other for years. And they had similar pasts. Only someone who'd suffered such ill treatment from a parent could understand how she used to feel. In fact, she suspected, his life had been far worse than hers.

She undid the laces on her mucky high tops and started loosening them. Her ma would have a fit if she tracked mud on her clean floors. She set them beside the rocker nearest the door then reached for the knob. The door flew open in her face, and a startled squeak slipped out. Garrett nearly collided with her, his eyes wide. "What's wrong?"

"Your ma! Gotta find Luke." He ran his hand through his short blond hair, looking more flustered than she'd ever seen him. "The doctor. Gotta get him, too."

"What happened?" Her heart pounded. Had her ma burnt herself or gotten cut?

Garrett's face blanked for a moment, and then he said, "The baby's comin'."

"Oh!" Her heart leapt. "Move out of the way, and let me by." He turned sideways in the doorway, and she slipped past him. She swatted a hand in his direction. "Go! Get Doc Phillips, and find Papa."

"I'll go for the doctor." Noah stood in the doorway, his hair flattened with dampness.

She nodded. "Go! Both of you."

Garrett grinned. "Have you found the women in this house

to be uncommonly bossy?"

Noah grinned, but Jack didn't have time to analyze what that did to her insides. She had to get to her ma. Her stockinged feet padded down the hall to her parents' room, and she peeked in. Her ma sat on the side of the bed, eyes closed and breathing hard. Sweat ran down her cheek. Emma played quietly with her dolly on the far side of the bed, oblivious to her mother's toiling. Carly bent and wiped Rachel's face with a cloth.

Jack nibbled her lower lip, hating to see her mother in pain. "Ma, are you all right?"

"Ha!" Rachel rubbed her hand across the front of her stomach. "Ohh, sure." The *oh* sounded more like a moan than normal speech. "I'm perfectly fine. In fact, I just love being in pain like this."

Jack lifted a brow. It wasn't like her ma to be sarcastic. Maybe her pain was worse than with previous childbirths.

Sitting down beside her, Jack took her ma's hand and held on to it. "What can I do to help?"

"Make sure the kids eat dinner. Then put Emma—oh—" Rachel gritted her teeth, and her whole body seemed to tense. She clenched Jack's hand so tight Jack thought some bones might break. Carly backed up against the wall looking frightened half out of her wits. Evidently she'd never attended a birthing, either. "Here comes another one."

"Another what, Ma?"

"Birth. . .pangs. Ahh!" She leaned her head back and moaned. "I don't know. . .if I can. . .do this again."

Jack couldn't help smiling. "You don't have much choice at this point."

Emmie patted her mother's back. "It be all wight."

Rachel tucked in her chin and growled a long grunt. "I'm too old. . .for thi–sss."

Jack sat there, allowing her ma to hold her hand and wondering what it would be like to carry a baby. What if it were Noah's child? Heat flooded her face, and she was glad her ma was so busy or she surely would have noticed. Jack glanced at Carly to see if she'd noticed the blush, but she was focused on Ma. Jack mentally berated herself. *A decent young woman doesn't think of such things.*

Carly handed the cloth to Jack. "I'll see to the youngsters' meal and get Emmie down for her nap so you can tend your ma."

"Oh, that was a big one." Rachel leaned back on her hands, her face more relaxed, the birth pain evidently over. "Have you seen Luke? Anyone sent for the doctor?"

"Garrett is looking for Papa, and Noah went for Doc Phillips."

Carly walked to the other side of the bed and clapped her hands. "Are you ready to eat?"

Emmie glanced at her ma and Jack, then stood and fell into Carly's arms. Jack was happy that her little sister had bonded so easily with Carly. Knowing that Miss Payton was here to help her ma would make leaving and going to Dallas much easier. She wouldn't worry about her ma overdoing it as much.

Loud footsteps sounded in the hall, and Jack stood. "I'll be right back, Ma."

She nodded. "Be sure there's plenty of hot water boiling."

"I will." Jack strode out the door.

Noah stood near the parlor door as if afraid to enter any farther. He rubbed the back of his neck, his brow crinkled.

"What's wrong?"

"The doctor wasn't there. He's gone out to a ranch where a cowhand got hurt and isn't expected back until this evening. His wife was home and said she'd come over as soon as she found somebody to watch her young'uns."

Panic shot through Jack like a bullet. She knew nothing about birthing babies. What if she did something wrong and hurt the baby or her ma? The baby could die. Her ma could die. Her knees trembled. She steepled her fingers and held them against her mouth. Her mind seemed like a quagmire of quicksand, and her thoughts sank so fast she couldn't grab hold of a single one.

What should she do? She could ask Carly to watch the doctor's children to free his wife to come and assist in the birth, but who'd watch her siblings?

Noah gently clutched her hands and pulled them away from her face, a sympathetic expression enveloping his face. "Tell me what's going on in that mind of yours. How can I help?"

His calm demeanor soothed her frenzied nerves. "I don't know what to do. I've never witnessed a birthing and have no idea what I should do."

"Has the doctor's wife delivered any babies?"

Jack nodded. "I think so. I'm sure she's assisted her husband before. She has to know more than I do."

Noah pulled out his pocket watch. "How much time do you think we have before the baby comes?"

Flinging up her arms, Jack blew out an exaggerated breath at the ridiculous question. "How should I know?"

Noah shoved his watch back in his pocket. A deep red glow crept up his neck. "Maybe you could ask your ma."

Jack rolled her eyes. "Every birth is different. She won't know."

He placed his hands on her shoulders. "Calm down, Jackie."

His use of the unexpected nickname grabbed her attention.

"Let's pray and ask God for direction."

She started to open her mouth to tell him they didn't have time to pray, when his hands slid down her arms, sending chills cascading across her skin and firmly locking her lips together. He took hold of her hands and bowed his head. "Father, we ask that You give us wisdom to know what to do. Help Mrs. Davis with the delivery of this child. We ask that You protect both mother and baby and show Garrett where Luke is so he can return home. Calm Jackie, and give us direction. In Jesus' name, amen."

He glanced up as if expecting she'd already have an answer to her dilemma, but she didn't. God hadn't seen fit to reveal His plan to her. She probably wasn't worthy enough. She hung her head, but the clopping of shoes on the stairs gave her an idea. "We could ask Carly to watch the doctor's children, and you can watch Alan and the girls."

Noah's eyes went wide, and he took a half-step back. "Me? I don't know anything about children."

"Well, there's no one else to do it. You for sure can't stay with Ma, nor would I ask you to care for children you don't even know. It just makes sense. We'll ask Carly to watch the doc's kids, and you can watch ours—I mean my. . .uh. . .siblings." Jack touched her hands to her cheeks, sure they must be bright red. Had he caught her reference to "our children"?

He tugged on his earlobe, then rubbed the back of his neck. "I reckon I could watch them for a while. What would I have to do?" Carly and the children reached the bottom of the stairs and clumped down the hall into the dining room. Carly glanced at her and Noah but didn't stop or question them.

Emmie waved as Carly carried her past Jack and Noah. "I eat p'cakes."

"No, sweetie, we're having beans and cornbread."

Emmie bounced in Carly's arm. "Me like cor'bread."

A gentle smile pulled at Noah's lip as he watched her sister. Jack wondered what he was thinking. Did he wish he was a father?

Rachel groaned, and Jack jumped. "I need to get back to Ma. Why don't you sit down with the kids and eat?" She didn't wait for his answer but proceeded into the kitchen. Carly stood at the buffet, dishing up the children's plates. She glanced at Jack, and Jack explained her plan. Carly contemplated it for a moment then nodded her head. "I'd be happy to watch the Phillips' young'uns, if that's how I can be the most help." Jack paused. "Have you ever delivered a baby before?"

Carly shook her head with vigor. "No. I've never even seen one delivered."

"Then I think the best help would be for you to watch the Phillips' children."

She placed a square of cornbread on each plate and then spooned on the beans. "I can do that. Just let me eat a few bites of beans. Then I'll run down there."

"Thanks. I'll be close by in case Noah has need of me."

Carly's brow lifted, and Jack wondered if it was because she used the pastor's Christian name. "All right."

Jack glanced up at Noah as he entered the room. "Go ahead and eat with the children. Afterward, take them back upstairs to Alan's room to play. Emmie may take a nap—or not, since she had one in church."

Noah nodded, picked up a plate, and held it out to her. "You need to eat, too."

"Just let me check on Ma first." She spun around and hurried to the bedroom that she used to share with her ma—before Luke married her and moved in. Ma was still seated, wearing her day dress, but her face was creased with pain. Jack fished a cloth out of the bucket and wrung out the water then dabbed her mother's face. "Are you all right?"

"Will be." She rubbed her hand back and forth across her stomach. "After Oscar comes."

"We should probably get you into your gown before Mrs. Phillips arrives."

Ma's pale blue eyes lifted, looking right at her. Sweat dampened her face, and fatigue lines crinkled around her eyes. "Hank's not comin'?"

"Not for a while." Jack offered a sympathetic smile. "But Carly's going to go watch their children after she gets ours fed so Martha can tend you."

Rachel nodded. "She's a good midwife." She slowly stood, hunched over like a hundred-year-old woman. She kept one hand on her stomach as if holding the baby in. Jack fetched a clean gown and held it out, noticing the back of her ma's dress was sopping wet. "Do you want me to get you a chamber pot, or is it too late?"

Rachel shook the gown down around her legs and sat again. Jack picked up the dress and carried it to a peg.

"No. That's not what you're thinking. My water broke while y'all were at church."

Jack dropped the calico dress as if it was covered in ticks and kicked it against the wall. She wiped her hand on her skirt. "Ma–aa! What does that mean? Are you all right? Is the baby?"

"Calm down. We're fine." Rachel giggled and brushed her tousled hair with her fingers. "You should have seen how fast you dropped my dress. You've never been squeamish."

"I'm not. It was just. . .unexpected. That's all."

"Have no worries. The dress will wash clean." Rachel's smile faded. She pressed her lips together and moaned, low and long. She spent several minutes in deep concentration, never screaming like Jack had heard men say their wives had, but just maintaining that eerie keening like when the wind blew beneath a closed door in winter.

"Oh!" Ma tucked her chin to her chest. The muscles in her face tensed, and all color fled from her skin.

Jack's heart jolted. She dropped to her knees. "What's wrong?"

"Got. . .push–ing. . .urge."

"Push what?"

"The baby. It's coming."

"Tell me what to do, Ma." She couldn't do this. Jack ran to the door, glanced down the empty hall, then hurried back to her ma's side. She needed help. "You wanna lie down? Want some water?"

"Wait!" Rachel grabbed hold of Jack's arm, nearly crushing it. Her mother's eyes squeezed shut, and her teeth clenched, lips parted. Ma strained so hard her whole body shimmied.

What's wrong? Help her, Lord. Show me what to do.

Never had she felt so helpless. So powerless. She was used to fighting for what she believed in, but how could she fight this? If she did something wrong, her mother or the baby could die. She glanced around the room. There must be something she could do. Her gaze landed on the tall stack of newspapers beside the ladder-back desk chair. Hadn't her ma mentioned needing those when the baby came?

Stretching out her free arm, she could just reach the pile without breaking her ma's connection on her other one. She pulled an inch-high stack over to her, shook them open, and began lining them over the wooden floor at her mother's feet. She kept stacking them until her ma breathed out a more relaxed breath and loosened her grip.

"Whew! Oscar is anxious—to be born." Her ma panted and rubbed her stomach. She leaned back on her hands. After a few moments, she finally looked up. "Good. Stack all but a few of those on the floor." Rachel slowly pushed up from the bed and stood. "Lay the rest so they are half on and half off the bed, then cover them with those towels." She took a deep breath and blew it out, as if preparing for the next battle. "This quilt is old, but I'd like to protect it if we can."

Jack snatched the faded towels from the chair seat and spread several on the bed. Her mother sat back down.

"You want a drink?" Jack patted the damp skin on her ma's face.

"Can't. It makes me sick to my stomach." She rubbed her hand across the top of her stomach. "I didn't want you to have to witness this." She grimaced and ducked her head again, holding tight to the bed frame with one hand. "Hurry! Get hot water. Knife."

"I don't want to leave you."

"Go!" One brisk swat of her ma's hand in the air set her in motion.

Jack jumped up and ran into the kitchen, peeking through the door into the dining room. No one was at the table, although the dirty dishes remained. She prayed that Martha Phillips would hurry. Jack grabbed a bowl and ladled boiling water out of the pot on the stove. She found a clean knife and hurried back to the bedroom. What in the world was the knife for?

"It's coming." Her ma had slid off the bed and was squatting beside it, grunting. "Ohh. . . . Knife in water."

Jack obeyed. "What else?"

Her mother glanced down.

Jack's eyes went wide.

"Catch Oscar."

Chapter 21

Noah looked around Alan's room. What would it have been like to have had such a nice room all to himself and a bed, instead of sleeping on the dirty floor?

He cradled Emma's head against his shoulder, reluctant to put her on the bed. Sweat curled the waif's wispy hair, and her soft breaths touched his cheek like a feather. The bed sat against one wall, but with all the noise Alan and Abby were making, he was sure Emma would awaken if he stopped rocking her.

He needed to put Emma in her own bed, but everything within him shouted that it was wrong for him to enter the girls' bedroom. Ambling through the upstairs hall, he walked to the stair railing and glanced down. Why hadn't the doctor's wife arrived? Or Miss Payton returned? What could be keeping them?

He stared at the girls' closed door—Jackie's door. He snorted a soft laugh. When had he started calling her that? It fit her better now than Jack did. There was something softer about it, like she was soft.

Abby squealed, and Emma jerked in his arms. The poor toddler would never sleep unless he put her someplace quiet. He looked at the door again, remembering Jackie sitting in her bed. He couldn't have told a soul what color the room was, because he'd only been able to focus on her that day. "Forgive me, Father."

He twisted the knob and pushed on the door. A garden of

beauty opened up before him. The walls had been painted a soft green, and colorful curtains covered in a multitude of flowers flapped in the afternoon breeze. His gaze landed on Jackie's bed, which sat under the front window, covered in a vivid quilt. He yanked his gaze away, feeling guilty for even looking at it.

A smaller bed sat on the wall opposite the big one, and to his right was another small bed with rails along the side. He laid Emma down on that bed. Should he cover her up? The room was warm, even with two windows open. He glanced down at Emma's chubby legs sticking out from under her dress, and he bent and touched the back of her calf. She felt plenty warm to him.

He backed away, watching to make sure she didn't awaken, and then closed the door. His heart pummeled his chest, whether from being in Jackie's room or just succeeding in getting the little girl to sleep, he wasn't sure.

Now what? He peered downstairs again but couldn't tell if anyone had come in. He moseyed back to the other children, unable to keep his mind from wondering how things were going downstairs. He had no doubt that Jackie could handle just about any situation, but would she know how to deliver a baby if need be?

Help them, Lord. Protect mother and child. Help Jackie to not be afraid.

He leaned against the doorframe and watched Alan and Abby playing checkers. The girl glanced over at him and smiled. While her face was turned, her brother snatched one of her kings off the board. Alan glanced over at him, his guilt obvious. Noah lifted his brow, and the boy scowled and looked away.

"Hey! Where'd my other king go?" Abby glanced around the floor, and when she was turned away from the table, Alan set the checkers back on the board. He frowned.

Abby turned back to the table, and her mouth dropped open. She rubbed her eyes and stared again. "I must be gettin' old, like Papa."

"Yep." Alan nodded his head, a sheepish grin pulling at his mouth.

Noah tucked under his upper lip in his effort not to laugh at the precocious child. The only children he'd spent any time around were those of his congregation whom he'd eaten meals with during his circuit-riding days.

The simple room called to him. Besides Alan's bed, there was a small table with a chair and a crate the boy used for a second seat. A half-dozen pegs lined the wall about three-and-a-half feet up from the floor and held the boy's clothing. Some mismatched pieces of wood filled another crate, and a blue and gray rag rug covered the center of the floor.

He wanted a home of his own. He was tired of traveling—of never putting down roots. All his life, until he'd moved in with Pete, he'd traveled from one shack to another.

Before he came to Lookout, he'd never thought much of marrying and starting a family. But how could he when he didn't own a home or land? He wasn't even sure how long he'd be in Lookout or what he'd do once Pastor Taylor and his family returned.

But the biggest issue was Jack—Jackie. He'd held a fondness for her even as a troubled youth. It made no sense to him when she caused him no end of problems. She'd lied about him, even causing him to spend two days in jail for something he hadn't done. 'Course, he'd settled up with her on that account the day he locked *her* in her pa's jail.

He shook his head. Walking away with her begging and pleading to set her free had been one of the hardest things he'd ever done, but he felt she needed to learn a lesson. Whether she did or not, he never knew. They'd moved once again shortly after that.

Noah stretched. He could use a Sabbath rest himself. He hadn't slept much at all last night, worrying over his sermon and Jackie. He yawned and toyed with the idea of scrunching up on Alan's bed.

"I won!" Abby held up two black checkers.

"Nuh-uh, you cheated." Alan leaned back against the wall and crossed his arms so hard he made a clapping sound.

"Why don't you play another game. I bet you'll win this time." Noah hoped they would agree. He had no idea how to entertain two such strong-willed children. He eyed the bed again, then crossed the room and eased down. The metal frame creaked and groaned under his weight. Slowly testing its strength, he relaxed and leaned back against the wall. Maybe he could grab a little catnap when the children played another game. He yawned and closed his eyes.

He claimed Jackie's hand, and together they strolled along the Addams River. Adolescents splashed in the pool where water collected in the spot where the river made a sharp turn and traveled on. A gangly youth swung out on a rope and dropped down into the pool, screaming a yell that would make a Comanche proud.

He led Jackie down a path to a quieter spot. Overhead, birds battled in song. Sunlight played peek-a-boo, first hiding behind a tree branch and then sprinkling its rays across the water. He turned Jackie to him and ran the back of his finger down her cheek. His breath hitched. She was so lovely. His hand trailed down the unbound auburn tresses. She smiled, love for him glowing in her blue eyes.

Contentment made every muscle, every bone in his body relax. He dug his hand into the hair behind her nape, then cupped her neck and drew her to him. Suddenly, her expression turned to horror, and she screamed his name.

Noah jerked up. Where was he? He saw the empty table and lurched to his feet. Where were the children?

He spun around, and his heart loosened. Abby lay on the end of the bed, curled up on Alan's pillow, fast asleep. But where was the boy?

"Noah!"

He jerked toward the door at Jack's frantic cry. His feet pushed forward, and he charged down the stairs. His gaze searched each room as he raced by, but there was no sign of Alan. Had something happened to him?

He skidded to a halt outside Mr. and Mrs. Davis's bedroom, his heart racing. "Jackie?"

"In here. Hurry!"

At Jack's hysterical cry, Noah rushed through the bedroom doorway, pushing aside his reservations. She held a lifeless newborn in her arms. Tears ran down her cheeks. Her plaintive gaze begged for his help. "He's not breathing! I don't know what to do!"

"Give him to me." He didn't know what to do, either, but he had to do something. Jack gazed into his eyes, obviously reluctant to let go of her brother. "Jackie, let me have him. Hurry!"

She carefully passed the damp baby, and Noah swallowed hard when he saw the boy's blue lips. Making sure to keep his eyes averted from where Mrs. Davis sat on the floor, he cradled the child's face in his palm with the limp body resting on his arm. *Show me what to do, Lord.*

He held the baby so that his head was down and gently patted the soft skin on his back. Nothing happened. Visions of the young boy who'd fallen into the creek flashed in his mind. Jackie would never forgive him if he didn't help her brother. "Noah!" Jack's near hysterical plea touched a place deep within him. He could not fail her. He couldn't fail this child. He whacked the baby harder.

"Don't! You'll hurt him." Jack pulled at his sleeve.

Rachel fell back onto the bed, her eyes wide, face pale. "Lord, save my son."

Noah turned his body away and gave the child a downward shake, then whacked him a bit harder. The baby jumped, arms outstretched. He gagged, then uttered a strangled cry. Easing up, Noah continued to tap and hold the baby's head down. Jack grabbed a cloth and swiped the boy's mouth. After several more fervent coughs, a pitiful squeal that resembled a lamb's bleating filled the room and sent spears of relief straight through Noah.

Jack dropped down on the side of the bed and peered at the infant's face, tears making her eyes glimmer. "Oh, thank God!"

Noah shifted the child to his other arm, relishing the sounds of ever-strengthening wails. Dark, damp hair was matted to the baby's head. A thick cord protruded from where his navel should be, and someone had tied twine around it. Noah had never seen a brand-new baby before and sure hoped that was normal. The boy's cries magnified, and his face pinked up, then turned red. "I think he wants his mama."

He passed Jack her newest brother. His heart warmed, watching her kiss the newborn's forehead and pass him to Rachel. Noah turned and hurried out of the room, knowing he was no longer needed. He made it as far as the kitchen before he sagged against the doorframe. His whole body shook, and tears rolled down his face. "Thank You, Lord, for saving that baby."

A light touch on his back made him straighten. Jack stood there, her blue eyes glistening and tears of joy making rivers down her cheeks. "I was so scared. I th–thought he was. . .dead."

Suddenly she lunged into Noah's arms and hugged his waist. Surprise washed through him, but he shut his eyes and wrapped his arms around her. Jack's warm tears dampened his shirt. Fresh love for this woman flooded his heart. No, in truth, he'd loved her for years, even though she hadn't given a hoot about him. He was afraid to hope that God might change her heart—that she might ever come to care for him.

He couldn't fool himself. Gratitude was her motivation for this hug—and relief.

No matter, for this one moment, this single second, he savored having Jacqueline Davis in his arms.

Jack couldn't quit shaking. Her tears refused to stop. What if her ma hadn't made it through the birthing? What if she'd cut the cord wrong and the baby had died?

She'd feared he had.

And if not for Noah, he probably would have, but thank the Lord, the baby seemed fine now.

She never wanted to be in such a situation again.

Jack pressed her face against Noah's solid chest and hugged him tighter. *Thank You, God, for sending Noah to help. For saving the baby.*

Suddenly she stiffened. She was hugging Noah. The preacher. Her roiling emotions had caused her to momentarily take leave of her senses.

"H'looo, Jacqueline?" came a woman's voice from the front of the house.

"In here." Jack jumped back and swiped her cheeks. She couldn't look at Noah. His arms dangled at his side, and she deeply felt the loss of their comfort.

Mrs. Phillips scurried into the kitchen. "I'm so sorry to have taken so long, but I'd just started"—she glanced past Jack, at Noah, then leaned forward—"nursing my baby," she whispered. "I couldn't very well stop, not knowing how long I'd be away. Besides, I figured I had time since babies aren't generally in a rush to get here."

Noah chuckled.

The doctor's wife glanced back and forth between the two of them. "Is everything all right here?"

Jack nodded, feeling for sure that her mother's friend thought they'd been up to no good. "We're fine, but Ma could use your help. She's in her room."

"Of course, I'll just scurry on in there." She started to leave, then looked at Noah again. "Are you doing all right, Reverend? Your face isn't hurting overly much?"

"I'm fine, but thank you for asking, Mrs. Phillips. Your husband tended me last night and did an excellent job." Noah smiled but it looked more like a grimace, since one side of his mouth didn't lift as much as the other because of the cut on his upper lip.

Mrs. Phillips nodded. "I'm glad you're doing well." She spun out the kitchen doorway then suddenly halted and peered back over her shoulder. "Someone really ought to see to Alan before he makes himself sick."

The woman disappeared, and Jack wondered what she meant. Where was Alan? Where were all the children for that matter?

"You really should have told her," Noah's deep voice quivered.

Jack worked up the nerve to look him in the face. "About what?"

"Heavens to Betsy! The baby's here?" Mrs. Phillip's loud exclamation bounced off the walls and clattered down the hall.

"About that." Noah's lips were pressed together so hard they'd turned white around the edges, but his eyes danced with mirth. At least the one that wasn't swollen shut did.

"Oh. Surprise! Surprise!" A grin tugged at Jack's mouth. "I'd better check on Alan. Do you know where he is?"

The smile on Noah's face faded, and he shook his head.

Jack crossed into the dining room and glanced around the

empty table. All seats were vacant, but the dirty dishes remained and food still sat on the buffet. A loud belch pulled her gaze downward. She bent over and lifted the edge of the tablecloth. Her brother sat on the floor with a near empty pie tin on his lap, sugary juice and crumbs covering his mouth and chin. "Alan Davis, what do you think you're doing?"

She could hear Noah's chuckles behind her, and she scorched him with a glare. Obviously, he didn't realize that Alan would see that as support and it would just encourage the imp all the more. Her brother's blue eyes stared up at her from under the table. She saw the worry written there, but then they turned pleading.

"Come out from under there, and take care not to spill any more crumbs on the floor."

He slid the pie pan along the floor and crawled behind two chairs. He handed her the pan then glanced at Noah, as if looking for help.

Jack set what remained of the pie on the table and shoved her hands to her hip. "Well?"

"I was hungry, Sissy."

His whining tone was wasted on her. "Then why didn't you finish the food on your plate?"

His lip curled up, and his nose wrinkled. "You know I don't like them kind of beans."

"So you thought you'd eat a whole pie while everyone else was busy?"

His gaze dropped to the floor. "I didn't eat the *whole* thing." He pointed at Noah. "The preacher and Miss Carly both had a slice, and Abby had a *huge* one." He stuck his lower lip out.

"And you didn't?"

Alan shrugged.

Noah leaned close to her ear, and her stomach flip-flopped. "Miss Payton said he couldn't have any since he hadn't finished his beans," he whispered, tickling her ear and making it hard for her to think straight. She gave her head a little shake, hoping to recapture her thoughts. "But this is probably my fault. I—"

Jack cut a sharp glance at Noah. "No, it's not, and don't take up for him." She looked Alan in the eye again. "Since you disobeyed

Miss Carly, young man, and ate pie when you knew you shouldn't have, you can just march up to your room until I talk to Ma. It would serve you right if she doesn't let you have any dessert all week."

His eyes widened. "But that ain't fair."

"Not fair." Jack snatched a napkin off the table and wiped the mess off of Alan's face.

"That's what I said."

Noah uttered a little snort, and she elbowed him in the gut. "What I meant was that you shouldn't say *ain't*."

"Oh."

"Now, get on up to your room." She gave him a nudge on the shoulder.

"Aw. . ." Alan hung his head and trudged toward the door.

He was trying to make her feel bad, but it wouldn't work. Just as he reached the doorway, the baby let out a high-pitched shriek. Alan spun back toward her, eyes wide. "What was that?"

Jack contemplated not telling him, but she was too excited. "That was your little brother."

Alan's mouth dropped open. "The baby came?"

Jack nodded, pleased that she'd surprised him.

He gasped. "I have a brother!" He jumped up and punched his fist in the air, then turned and raced out of the room and up the stairs. "Wahooo!"

Jack grinned, and behind her, Noah chuckled. She spun around, and he seemed to struggle to contain his mirth.

"Should I not laugh at that?" He pressed his lips together, they quivered, and then he grinned.

"No, that was actually funny." Jack smiled, then forced a stern expression. "But never laugh at a child being scolded. Don't you know anything about children?"

His eyes dimmed, and he shook his head. "No, not really."

A jab of compassion pricked her heart, but then she remembered her sisters. "Hey, speaking of children, where are the girls? I just realized I haven't seen them for a long while, and that's not a good thing, especially where Abby is concerned."

He nudged his chin toward the ceiling. "Emma fell asleep not too long after dinner, so I, uh, put her in her bed." He swallowed so hard she noticed his Adam's apple move. "Then Abby fell asleep on Alan's bed."

"That was very gracious of you to watch them."

"It was an emergency. I was happy to help out."

"You helped out a lot today. You saved my brother's life."

He shook his head. "Not me. God did that."

"Well, you still helped." He was such a kind, humble man. How could he be so caring when he'd had such a rugged childhood and no example of a loving father, like she'd had in Luke? She hated seeing his handsome face marred and his eye nearly swollen shut. Her gaze landed on the damp spot on his white shirt where her tears had spilled over, and he looked down.

He lifted his hand and brushed it.

"Don't worry, it'll wash out." Jack winced when she saw the stains on his sleeves from where he held the baby. "You'd better change out of that and let me get it soaking."

One dark brow lifted.

"I'm serious. You don't want your shirt to stain, do you?"

He checked his sleeves, then shook his head. His dark hair, normally combed back, flopped onto his forehead, and Jack had a powerful urge to reach up and smooth it back in place.

"No. It's the only good shirt I've got to preach in."

"Well, go change, and I'll wash it."

"On Sunday?"

Jack heaved a sigh. "Sometimes you must do what you must. I just delivered a baby on Sunday." At the reminder of the baby's near death, her knees started shaking. Now that the danger had passed and she wasn't distracted by Noah or her brother, the realization of all that had happened made her weak. She reached out for Noah's arm.

"What's wrong?" He grabbed hold of her upper arms.

"I—I delivered my brother today." The wonder in her voice surprised even her. She started wobbling, and he yanked out a chair.

"Sit down."

She obeyed, then leaned over, resting her head in her hands.

Noah patted her back. "You're fine. Your ma's fine. And the baby's fine. You did a great job today, Jackie."

The momentary faintness passed at his encouragement, and she bolted upright. She craned her neck to see his face, so high from her seated position. "Why do you keep calling me that?"

He pulled out the chair beside hers and lowered himself. His gaze connected with hers, and she couldn't look away. "I used to know someone named Jack. Someone who caused all kinds of trouble." He shrugged and looked past her. "I just think Jackie fits you better."

A feeling as of warm honey glided through her. She'd never had a man call her by a special name, and she liked it. A lot. "I guess it won't hurt if you call me that, but you probably should be prepared to explain yourself."

His gaze snapped back to hers, and he smiled. "I can do that." His black eyes—even the one barely visible—shone bright with something that looked like affection. She licked her dry lips, wondering if he actually felt something for her or if he was just feeling emotional from all that had happened. How could he when he'd known her less than a week?

But surely he must, if he gave her a nickname.

His gaze dropped down to her mouth and lingered there a moment, sending her heart bucking around her chest like a crazed bronco.

He bolted out of the chair. "I. . .uh. . .should. . ." He cleared his raspy throat and walked toward the hall. "Better get changed. . .so you can set this shirt to soaking."

Nodding, she watched him stride away, surprised at her disappointment. Had she actually thought the preacher would kiss her? She shook her head at the foolish thought. He was just being kind, because that was his nature. She sighed and rested one arm on the table and leaned her head against it. What a crazy girl she was. She had no plans to be courted by a man or ever marry, and here she was getting starry-eyed over the new minister.

Surely it must just be from all the emotion swirling through her today.

Chapter 22

Jack pushed her shoe against the porch floor, moving the rocker in a gentle sway. Even though baby Andrew was only a few hours old, her mother had assured her it was fine to rock him on the porch as long as she stayed out of the sun, but she still worried. At least it was quiet out here. With the three children all excited about the new baby, sneaking outside was the only way she could have him to herself.

Andrew's head leaned back over her arm, and his tiny mouth formed an O. She lifted the flannel blanket her ma had made over his head and ears, leaving only his face peeking out. She ought to be inside, figuring out what to fix for supper, but she just had to hold her baby brother again while her ma rested up.

Jack ran the back of her finger along his soft cheek, and he smiled briefly. His chest rose and fell in quick cadence with each breath. She had a hard time imagining such a tiny thing could one day grow up to be a man like Luke or Noah. But then she highly doubted Noah had ever been so small.

She loved each of her siblings, but when the others had been born, she hadn't experienced the maternal desires that swelled through her like they did now. Maybe it was because she was older. Maybe it was due to helping deliver Andrew. Or his near death, which had drawn her and Noah closer. Butterflies fluttered in her stomach as she thought about Noah.

Her gaze lifted to the pale blue sky. Fluffy clouds created a wide shadow on Main Street. "Thank You, Lord, for saving my brother. For letting Noah be there to help. Watch over Ma, and help her heal quickly and regain her strength. And please send Papa home soon."

Her only regret of the day was that Luke hadn't been there to enjoy the excitement of his youngest son's birth. Mrs. Phillips had assured Jack she'd done just right in delivering her brother and explained that sometimes babies had trouble breathing right off. She said she'd have done the same thing Noah had to encourage the baby to take his first breath.

A dog barked across the street. Andrew threw out his arms, and his face scrunched up as if he prepared to cry. She lifted him to her shoulder and patted his back. Smiling, she remembered how she'd helped Mrs. Phillips give him his first bath, and now he was dressed in a gown her ma had stitched. She leaned her cheek against his fuzzy head, amazed at how much she already loved him.

How could she leave him and go to Dallas?

She felt as if her soul and his were stitched together. Was this anything like what it felt to be a mother?

A motion down Main Street caught her eye. She watched Bertha Boyd and her sister slowly make their way up the boardwalk. On the other side of the street, Leah Howard walked past Luke's office with several of her children following and went into the store. The mercantile was closed, so they must be paying a quick visit to Mrs. Morgan. Jack knew the names of each of Dan and Leah's children. Leah had called off her wedding with Dan when she found out he had brought his five nieces and nephews home to Lookout after his brother and sister-in-law died, but love won out. Jack knew all about most of the people in this town, like the Howards, but if she moved to Dallas, she wouldn't know a soul. She'd be all alone.

Jack leaned her head back. Why had she never really considered that before?

Ever since her fall off the mayor's roof, her life seemed to be changing. She hadn't finished a single article for the paper, and the fact that it didn't bother her like it would have in the past vexed her. What was happening to her?

Tessa strolled out the mercantile door, talking with Callie Howard. Soon Leah and her children left the store and headed down the boardwalk. Tessa ambled back inside, and Jack pursed her lips. Too bad her friend hadn't seen her and come over so she could show off her new brother. Not that Tessa would be impressed.

A wagon rounded the corner, momentarily blocking her view of the store's entrance, and when it passed on by, surprise gripped Jack. Tessa and Billy stepped off the boardwalk and walked toward her. What could Billy want? She hadn't seen him since the fight last night. That seemed years ago. She still needed to return that bracelet but had forgotten about it in all of the day's excitement.

Tessa stepped onto the porch, and her face scrunched up. "Are you holding Abby's dolly? I swear, Jacqueline, you do the oddest things."

Billy stood behind his sister, his nose swollen and black smudges resting below his eyes. He looked as bad as Noah. A smirk pulled at his lips, and he didn't look the least bit repentant. Maybe ignoring him was her best option.

Jack pulled the blanket back, and Tessa gasped. "It's real? Wherever did you get it?"

Jack rolled her eyes. Given the condition her ma had been in the last few months, Tessa's question bordered on ridiculous. "Where do you think? He's my new brother."

"But I thought it wasn't due for several more weeks." Tessa's reaction fell flat.

"Babies have their own time schedule, don'tcha know?" Billy poked his sister with his elbow.

Tessa swatted him, then leaned over and stared at the precious baby. One side of her face curled up. "He's awful red, and his head has a funny shape. What's wrong with it?"

Jack sucked in a breath, flipped up the blanket, and held Andrew to her chest so they could no longer look at him. Why couldn't Tessa say anything nice? "He looks like any newborn. His head will take its normal shape in another day or two. Mrs. Phillips and Ma both said so. I think he's perfect."

Billy snorted. "A baby's a baby. Why you makin' such a fuss?"

Jack tossed him a hooded glance. "Babies are precious. You were one once, remember."

He snorted a laugh and booted the rocker rung nearest her, setting it in motion. Tessa halted it with a hand to the arm of the chair, then plopped down and straightened her dress. She huffed out a breath, crossed her arms over her chest, and laid her head back against the chair. "My life is over."

Jack sidled a glance her way. "What do you mean?"

"That robbery was the straw that broke the camel's back," Billy said.

Tessa shot him a glare. "I'm telling her, not you."

Billy narrowed his gaze in a menacing stare that didn't in the least faze Tessa. She tossed her blond curls over her shoulder. "Ma is getting married."

"Truly?" Jack's mind raced. Maybe she could write up the story before word passed around the whole county, if Tessa hadn't told many people. "To Rand Kessler?"

Nodding, Tessa set the rocker in action. Billy casually leaned against the porch railing, watching Jack. His close presence gave her the creeps. He was a nice-looking man, but his character left something to be desired.

"Please give your mother my congratulations," Jack said.

"No, no, no!" Tessa shook her head with vigor. "I don't want to live clear out on that man's ranch. I'll never see my friends or have any fun. What will I do? It will be so boring."

Tessa's whine mirrored Abby's when she wasn't getting her way—kind of like when Butch Laird would run his fingernails across his slate in school and make all the girls squeal. Jack couldn't help wondering why Butch had been on her mind so much lately. She gave her head a little shake and tried to think of something to make her friend feel better. "I think it would be nice living on a ranch. You could ride all you wanted and have lots of peace and quiet, unlike living in a town. No music or ruckus from the saloon to bother you when you're trying to go to sleep."

Billy made a grunting sound. "That's one reason I ain't goin'."

"You have to go, Billy. You don't have a choice, and neither do I."

Tessa all but stuck her tongue out at him.

Billy straightened, then bent down, placing each hand on the arms of Tessa's chair. "I'm a grown man. I don't have to go nowhere I don't wanna go."

Tessa leaned back, obviously stunned at his spiteful tone. She blinked several times. "But what would you do? You don't have a job. Ma's gonna sell the store, so where would you live?"

Billy's blue gaze darted to Jack, then away. "I have ways of gettin' money."

This wasn't the first time Jack had wondered just where he got his cash. How could he have afforded that bracelet he gave her, even with the discount he probably got from his mother? He claimed to want to marry her, but he still lived with his ma and sister. A thought came to her. "Why couldn't you two stay in town and run the store? You're certainly old enough and have plenty of experience."

Tessa tucked a loose tendril of hair behind her ear and curled her lip. "I'm sick of the store. The work is dirty—opening all those crates, dusting everyday, and people can be downright snippety."

Jack ducked her head and placed a kiss on Andrew's head in her effort not to laugh. That was the pot calling the kettle black.

"What am I going to do?"

Jack considered a different tactic. "Doesn't that cute cowboy you danced with last night work on the Kessler ranch?"

"He does." Tessa uttered a heartfelt sigh and fanned her face with her hand.

"Ma said she cain't see him no more." Billy lifted his chin, looking proud to have revealed that piece of information.

"Why not?" Jack thought the man seemed nice enough, and he was always decently dressed and polite.

"Because he's just a cowhand, that's why."

Tessa jumped up from her chair. "Stay out of this, Billy. You'll be just as miserable out at that ranch as I will." She spun toward Jack. "I'm parched. I think I'll go get something cold to drink." She waved her fingers at Jack and glided toward the steps. Suddenly she stopped and stamped her foot. "Oh, drat. I'll probably never have another cold drink if I have to move to that dreadful ranch."

Jack watched Tessa march across the dirt road and shook her head. "She sure isn't happy."

"No, but Ma seems to be."

Jack snapped her gaze back to his, surprised to actually hear Billy say something halfway nice. "You really think so?"

"Yeah, but this move sure will cause me and Tessa problems."

"What will you do?" Andrew started squirming, so Jack patted his back. Almost instantly, he belched.

Billy cocked his head and stared at her with a contented smile that made ants crawl up her spine. With Tessa gone, she should probably go back inside, but first she needed some information about the robbery. "Did the thief steal much from your store?"

"I guess so." He shrugged and looked away. "Left a big mess, too. Dumped over the cracker barrel, then walked all over them. The marshal said there'd been some strangers coming into town of an evening lately, and he rode off to see if he could find them."

"I'm sorry. So how did the thief get in? Did he break down the door? It doesn't look damaged from here."

He shook his head. "No. Came in that storeroom window under the stairs out back. You know, the stairs that lead up to our rooms."

"Yeah. Do you know if the robbery happened last night or this morning?"

Billy shrugged. "Your pa still out hunting for the thieves?"

Jack nodded, and Billy smirked. He pushed away from the railing, pulled the rocker Tessa had sat in around to face Jack's, and sat. He fingered the cut on his upper lip, which Noah's fist had made. "Why don't you take that scrawny thing back inside and let's you and me take a walk?"

"Billy! That *thing* you're referring to is my brother." Jack stood and shot knives at him with her eyes. How could he be so rude and then expect her to follow him around like a stray pup?

His gaze hardened. "Don't you think you owe it to me after last night?"

"Of all the. . ." *Pigheaded nincompoops.*

He flipped up his thumb, pointing it at his nose. "Look at me, Jacqueline."

She stared closely at his battered face. His nose was swollen and bent like a letter *C*, marring his near perfect features. She shoved aside a wave of sympathy. "You shouldn't have hit the minister."

"He shouldn't have butted in. I just wanted to dance with you."

Jack hugged Andrew close to her heart. She needed to get him away from Billy before he did something stupid. "I need to take Andrew inside and fix some supper."

"I just want to spend time with you." The whine in his voice mirrored Tessa's and did nothing to endear him to her.

"I'm sorry, but that's the problem. I'm not interested in spending time with you. I've tried to tell you nicely, but you refuse to listen."

His countenance darkened, and he grabbed her elbow. "You'd better—"

A man strode down Main Street, and Jack's heart leapt. Billy must have noticed, because he glanced over his shoulder. A muscle in his jaw ticked, and he stepped back, relaxing his stance and pasting a smile on his face. "Evening, Marshal."

Luke's gaze narrowed, and he looked between Billy and her. His gaze dropped. His brown eyes widened. "Do we have company?" He glanced down at his clothes and brushed a dusty patch off his knee. "Whose baby is that?"

Jack tried hard to hold back her smile, but it insisted on bursting forth. "It's your new son, Papa. Ma said his name is Andrew."

The cavalry yell that poured forth from Luke's mouth made both Andrew and Billy jump. The baby screeched, and Billy bolted off the porch. She couldn't help giggling at the picture Billy made —like a stray dog with his tail between his legs—as she gently soothed the frightened baby. "You want to hold him?"

"Of course I do." He held out his arms, then looked down at his hands.

"Um. . .maybe you should wash up first," she offered.

"I reckon that's a good idea. How's your ma? She all right?"

Jack nodded. "She's fine. Tired and missing you, but fine." She smiled again. "Guess what?"

He shrugged and peered at his son. "Looks a bit like Abby, don'tcha think?"

"Papa, I'm trying to tell you something life altering."

His gaze bounced up to hers. "What? Did something happen while I was gone besides the baby comin'?"

"That's it. I delivered Andrew."

Luke shoved his hat up his forehead, revealing the lighter skin near his hairline, and grinned. "You're joshin' me, Half Bit."

"I'm not. Honestly."

He placed his hands on his hips. "Well. . .I'll be. Ain't that somethin'?"

"Papa!" Jack scolded.

His hand dropped to his pistol, and he glanced over his shoulder, then back at her. "What?"

Jack shook her head. "I wondered where Alan learned to say *ain't*."

Luke shook his head and started unbuttoning his shirt as he walked across the porch. "We're not havin' that conversation. I need to clean up and see my wife and hold my new son."

Just before he stepped off the far side of the porch, Jack called, "Did you catch the thieves?"

He shook his head and broke into a jog.

Chapter 23

The bell above the freight office door jingled, and Garrett glanced up from the *Horseman* magazine he'd been scouring. Luke moseyed in, hat down low on his forehead. Garrett leaned back in his chair, lacing his hands behind his head, and grinned. "Well, there's the proud papa. How you doin'?"

"Still proud but exhausted." Luke shuffled across the room like an old man, pulled out the chair that used to belong to Mark, then fell into it with a heavy sigh.

Garrett dropped all ideas of jesting and leaned forward, arms on his desk. He rarely ever saw his cousin looking so haggard. "Is Andrew all right? I know he had a rough start, with nearly dying and all."

"Oh, *he's* doing great—at least during the day—sleeps like a baby." Luke chuckled and ran his hand over his eyes, then down his unshaven face. "Emmie was such a good baby. She slept through the night almost from the start. I'd forgotten about how Abby and Alan stayed awake like Andrew does, until Rachel reminded me." He groaned and rested his face in his hands. "I'm getting too old for this."

Shaking his head, Garrett rose and poured his cousin a cup of coffee. In spite of Luke's fatigue, he couldn't help being a bit jealous. At forty, Luke was the father of five, albeit Jack was his adopted daughter. Garrett set the cup in front of Luke, then walked to the window. He'd concentrated on building his business all these years and let time slip by. He rubbed the back of his neck. Was thirty-nine too late to get married and start a family?

"What's eating you, Cuz?" Luke slurped his coffee and smacked his lips. "Mmm. . .just what I needed."

Garrett watched the busyness on the streets as people shopped or visited. Two cowboys moseyed by on their horses. Garrett shrugged. "I don't know."

"You wouldn't happen to be thinking of a pretty, black-haired gal, would you?"

Maybe he shouldn't have been so quick to share his coffee and revive Luke. If he'd known his cousin was going to meddle, he wouldn't have. He turned and leaned back against the window frame, feigning a confused look. "What brunette are you talkin' about?"

Luke grinned, but his lips quickly transformed into a yawn. Not the least bit tired, Garrett copy-catted with a yawn of his own. His cousin scratched his chest and leaned back. "I think you know."

Ambling back to the coffeepot, Garrett took his time answering. It wouldn't do to let his cousin know he'd been attracted to Miss Payton. He took a sip of the hot brew and peered over the edge of his cup. He needed some kind of response, but what could he say when he didn't understand his own feelings toward the woman? "She's too young for me."

Luke grunted. "No, she's not. Lots of men marry younger women. It's a good idea if you want to start a family."

Watching his coffee swirl, he thought about that fact. His cousin was right, but he wasn't about to let him know. Marrying younger did make a lot of sense.

"What's your hesitation? I saw how you looked at her that day she first arrived." Luke stretched then crossed his arms over his chest and propped his boots up on Mark's old desk.

Garrett's thoughts flashed to his brother. He knew Mark was very happily married and enjoying fatherhood. He couldn't believe that his brother had been married almost a decade. Where had the years gone?

"You gonna answer me, Cuz?"

Garrett shrugged. "Marrying an ex-convict wasn't ever on my chore list. I want a respectable woman. How'd you like your kids being raised by a gal who'd spent six years in prison?"

Luke jumped to his feet so fast Garrett jumped and sloshed coffee on his sleeve. Stomping across the room, Luke's eyes fired bullets. "Miss Carly *is* a respectable woman. She had a rough life when she was young. Her ma died when she was fourteen, and she had to go live with that no-account outlaw brother and his gang—or be forced into being a saloon gal." He took a breath and continued, "She served her time for the crimes she committed and became a Christian. All is forgiven in God's eyes. So, if He can overlook her past, why can't you?"

Garrett's eyes widened, and his brows hiked up all on their own. He'd never seen his cousin this agitated, not even when he and Mark had written off to a trio of mail-order brides and they all came to town, hoping to marry Luke. "I don't reckon God has any inclinations to marry her."

"And you do?" Luke's hackles were still lifted, and his bloodshot eyes reminded Garrett of a crazed bull that he and Mark had tormented until it had charged them.

He lifted up one shoulder and dropped it. "I don't know. Could be."

Luke blinked, his expression softening. "Really?"

He ran his hand through his hair. "Good thoughts or bad, I can't seem to quit thinking of her."

"Well. . .good." Luke loosely held his hands on his hips. "You're a good man, Garrett. You'd make a great father, and you deserve to know the joys of being married." Luke grinned wide. "And trust me, there are some excellent benefits."

"I can imagine."

"Nope, I don't think you can." Luke's eyes took on a faraway stare, and one corner of his mouth curved up. "There's something real special about coming home to a woman who thinks you set the moon up in the sky. To be able to cuddle up with her soft body on a cold winter's night, and to share your dreams or just hear about how the children got in trouble."

Garrett rolled his eyes, not because he was disgusted with his cousin's soliloquy, but because Luke's sincerity embarrassed him and made him jealous. "All right, I hear you. But even if. . .say. . . I had some inclinations toward Miss Payton, I have no idea what to do about it."

Seeming pacified, Luke returned to Mark's desk and sipped his coffee. "Women want to be noticed and to feel they're special to a man. They like to receive flowers."

"Aw, Luke, I can't go walkin' down Main Street carrying a wad of flowers. Every man in town'd be laughin' at me." He didn't mind them heehawing at his jokes, but laughing *at* him was altogether something else.

"You can if you want to catch a woman. Don't forget how I stood in front of the whole town and told Rachel she was the only gal for me. Always has been."

"Yeah, well, I haven't exactly been pining my heart away after Carly Payton all these years. In fact, I'm not sure I even thought of her once the whole time she was gone."

Luke rubbed the back of his hand across his cheek. "Well, you haven't known her all your life like I knew Rach—" He yawned, his eyelids drooping. "Why don't you try prayin' about it?"

Luke folded his arms, laid them on the desk, and rested his head on top of them. Garrett stared out the window across the street to where a couple stood in front of the café. The man glanced around then leaned down and gave the woman a little peck on the cheek. She ducked her head, but Garrett could tell she was pleased. Would Carly be agreeable if he tried to kiss her?

He snorted a laugh. Probably not. She'd most likely yank a derringer from her skirt pocket and shoot him.

"Sure is nice and quiet in here. No kids running around like Indians, whooping it up and making the baby cry."

Garrett strode across the room and tugged on Luke's arm. "C'mon, ol' man. You can't sleep here. I've got a business to run."

Luke, limp as an old rope, stood and weaved a bit. "Where we goin'?"

"I have an empty house. No women. No children. All quiet."

"Mmm. . .sounds perfect."

Luke managed to stumble across the room and out the door, leaving it wide open. Garrett wondered if he should walk him across the street, but he didn't want to embarrass the marshal in front of the townsfolk. They might think he'd taken to the bottle, but Luke would never do that.

Garrett thought about his house. All empty. No one to greet him when he came home—unless Luke was still there. It had never bothered him all that much before, but now it sounded lonely.

He stared out the door window and down the street to the boardinghouse. Would Carly give him a chance if he approached her?

There was only one way to find out.

Noah swiped his sleeve against his damp forehead. Just a few more boards and he'd be done painting the mercantile. The memory of the angry youth who'd smeared ugly red letters all over the town resurfaced. *Jack is a liar.*

It had been a dumb thing to do, and he now regretted it, but he'd taken all he could back then and had lashed out. His pa finally sold all their hogs and forced him to leave town because he feared Marshal Davis had it in for Noah—or rather Butch. Swallowing hard, Noah dipped the brush into the paint and resumed his work.

He hadn't wanted to leave back then and had been young enough to hope that things might change. Their home hadn't been much more than a shack, but it was home. Or at least it had been for a while.

He still didn't have a permanent place to call home. Glancing to his right, he stared at the boardinghouse. It was nice—and the food was certainly some of the best he'd had in years—but having Jackie living there, avoiding him for over a week, made things awkward. He kicked at a rock on the boardwalk, sending it flying. The stone hit the marshal's office next door and made a loud clunk then dropped to the ground. Paint dribbled onto his boot top.

Noah ground his back teeth together. Why couldn't he quit thinking about Jackie?

He yanked his handkerchief out of his pocket and swiped his boot, leaving an ugly white smear on the brown leather. Sighing, he dipped the brush then stroked the building again.

Mrs. Morgan strolled out of the shop, broom in hand. "Oh! I suppose I should wait to sweep until the paint dries."

Noah nodded. "Probably a wise idea, ma'am."

The pretty woman smiled, her blue eyes beaming. "That looks so nice, Reverend. I just don't know why you felt you had to go to so much trouble for us."

"No trouble, Mrs. Morgan. I'm glad to help out." He lifted his hat and set it back on his head. "And congratulations."

The near-forty-year-old woman swung back and forth in her purple calico dress, grinning like a schoolgirl with her first crush. Her dark brown hair, which was pulled up into a neat bun, didn't hold a hint of gray. "I guess Rand came to see you then."

"He did." Noah nodded, remembering the shy rancher who couldn't quit grinning when he'd tracked Noah down at the church Tuesday afternoon. "The wedding is set for two weeks from this coming Sunday."

She glanced down, her cheeks crimson. "I know. I'm so thankful to the good Lord for bringing Rand into my life. I can hardly believe I'm marrying again after all these years." Nibbling her lip, she glanced down the street. "Rand almost married Rachel Davis, you know?"

Noah remembered seeing Mr. Kessler sitting on the porch with Mrs. Davis years ago—back when she'd been the Widow Hamilton, but the man quit coming around once Luke came back to town. "I don't think you have to worry. Mr. Kessler is smitten—with you, ma'am. I probably shouldn't tell you, but he couldn't quit talking about you and how happy he is to finally be getting married."

Her eyelids blinked quickly, and she dabbed one corner with her fingertip. "I haven't been this happy in years." She glanced over her shoulder into the store, then leaned the broom against the wall and walked over to him. "I'm concerned about Billy and Tessa though," she said, her voice lowered. "Neither one seems keen on my marrying Rand. Nor do they want to move out to the ranch."

He hadn't counseled many women, much less a woman alone. He glanced around the street and boardwalks. Dolly Dykstra stood outside of her dress shop, hands flapping in the air as she chatted to a woman he hadn't met. There was no one else on the street this evening.

Mrs. Morgan wrung her hands together. "I don't know what to do."

Noah glanced down at the drying paint and decided helping the storekeeper was more important than painting her building. He set the brush across the open tin can. "I reckon you've talked to them."

"I have, but they get angry whenever I bring up the subject. They've both always been so stubborn. I admit I may have spoiled them, but raising them without a man to help wasn't easy."

Noah wasn't all that much older than Billy, he imagined. Three or four years at the most. What did he know about dealing with grown children—or any children for that matter? *Give me wisdom, Lord.*

"If they have no interest in living at the ranch, why not let them run the mercantile?"

She shook her head. "They don't want to do that, either. I don't like to talk bad about my own children, but the truth is they're both lazy. I found out a long time ago that it was easier to do things myself rather than fight Billy or Tessa to do them." She kept her head down. "You must think me a terrible mother."

"Not at all. It's not my place to judge you, ma'am." He started to lay his hand on her shoulder, but the mayor turned the corner just then with two other men and walked in their direction. "It just might do both of your children some good to live on the ranch and have Rand Kessler as a stepfather. He's used to dealing with hired help and probably could control them."

She glanced over her shoulder, then nodded. "I think you may be right. I just don't know if I can force them to go, especially Billy." She grabbed her broom and stepped back to let the men pass.

The mayor smiled at the men who accompanied him. "Ah, good. Gentlemen, let me introduce you to our storeowner and our minister." He waved his hand toward the only woman present. "This is Christine Morgan, who runs our only mercantile, and this is our temporary minister, Noah Jeffers. This is Mr. Humphrey and Mr. Brown. They are here in town on business."

Noah didn't miss the intended emphasis on *temporary*. He studied the men while Mrs. Morgan greeted them. Mr. Humphrey was close to six feet but almost as thin as Mrs. Morgan's broom handle. His dark hair and handlebar mustache were in stark contrast to the shorter Mr. Brown, with his white hair and neatly cropped beard. Their clothing looked storebought and expensive. Rich city folk. When the men turned their eyes on him, he held out his hand. "A pleasure to meet you both. If you're staying in town, I hope you'll attend Sunday services."

Mr. Brown grunted, but Mr. Humphrey's eyes went wide. Then he turned to the mayor, whose head jerked back at the man's glare. "We must be on our way," the mayor hastily said. "If you'll excuse us."

Noah nodded and stepped back to make more room for the trio to pass. The boardwalk shimmied as the men's footsteps thudded across the wooden planks. When they were in front of Polly's Café, Mrs. Morgan scurried to his side.

"I wonder what kind of business they're in," she said, her hands holding tight to her broom handle. "Scuttlebutt says it's the railroad."

"I thought talk of the railroad coming here was just rumors." He glanced down at his paint can, hoping it wasn't getting too dried out.

She shrugged. "I don't think so.

"That would be good for the town."

She nodded then glanced at the can. "I suppose I should let you finish your work so you can go home."

"I'll pray for you and your children and that God will give Rand wisdom as you all become a family."

A shy smile lit her face. "Thank you, Reverend. I appreciate that." She slipped back into the store, closed the door, and he heard the bolt slide to lock it.

He bent and resumed his work, sending up prayers to God for

the Morgan family and for Rand Kessler.

Awhile later, Noah slapped paint on the last board and stood back to admire his handiwork. Mrs. Morgan may not have owned the store when he'd committed his wicked deed, but at least he felt he'd done all he could to make recompense for it. He pressed the lid on the paint can. He turned toward the boardinghouse but noticed Jackie, skirts held high, hurrying down the opposite side of the street, away from her home.

He stooped down again, pretending interest in the can. Jackie slowed her pace as she approached the saloon. She glanced in all directions, but if she noticed him, she didn't act like it. Besides her, he was the only person on the street. All the businesses were closed up as tight as a spinster's coin purse, and most decent folks had gone home for the night. That was one reason he'd waited to paint—fewer people on the road meant less stirred-up dust to soil his wet paint.

Jackie tiptoed to the saloon windows and pressed her nose against the glass. It wasn't likely she could see through the dingy, smoke-covered panes that he'd noticed once or twice as he'd passed by. She tiptoed to the swinging doors, pushed one open a little, and peered inside. Noah stood. After a few moments, she darted to her right and around the far corner of the building, waving her hand in front of her nose.

What in the world?

He scratched the back of his head. He never paid much attention to the Wet Your Whistle, but he couldn't imagine what would cause Jack to slink down the street like a wolf on the prey and peek inside such a place. A man stumbled out and tottered to his horse, which was tied to the hitching post in front of the saloon. After four tries, he managed to mount the poor critter. Noah shook his head. Not even dusk yet, and the cowboy was already drunk. After the man rode out, barely staying in his saddle, Jack reappeared and hurried to the double doors again.

Noah lifted the brush up and down, close to the wall but not touching it, so she would think he wasn't watching—but he was. His curiosity had definitely been piqued.

Jack jumped back, then darted around the left side of the

building. The saloon owner burst through the doors, sending them flying against the wall. He shoved his hands to his hips, looking back toward town. Noah set the paint and brush just under the porch steps, so they'd be out of the way, and broke into a jog.

He didn't know what that ornery gal was up to, but he intended to find out.

Chapter 24

Jack's heart pounded as she raced around the side of the saloon. Holding her hand over her mouth, she tried to quiet her cough. How could those men stand being in that smoky, smelly place for hours?

She leaned against the rough wood, willing her heart to slow down. This was just another of her harebrained ideas that was probably nothing but an effort in futility. She ought to run back home before she was missed, but she knew she wouldn't. There was a story here, she could smell it.

If she hadn't been outside hanging Andrew's diapers on the line to dry, she wouldn't have noticed the mayor and his two companions strolling down Bluebonnet Lane. Her heart had pounded as she followed to see where they were headed. She hadn't even known that those men—the same ones who'd been at the mayor's home the day she climbed on the roof—had returned to Lookout. They had stopped at the end of Bluebonnet Lane, past Elm Street, where there was nothing but a few houses, then open prairie all the way to the Addams River. The mayor had waved his hand, almost as if offering the land to the men.

They must be going to build something, but what? The town could use many types of new businesses, but the way the mayor was keeping this project such a secret made her suspicious.

Something banged hard against the wall she leaned on, and

she jumped. Night was falling. She needed to finish her task and get away from this vile place before Luke saw her or something bad happened. Her papa had warned her to stay clear of the Wet Your Whistle, even during the daytime. He didn't need to warn her about being here at night.

Pushing her feet into action, she tiptoed to the end of the building and peered in both directions. No people were out, but crickets and lightning bugs already heralded the coming darkness. She'd seen the mayor and his friends at the bar; then they'd headed upstairs. She surmised that there must be a private meeting or maybe gambling room the men planned to use. She swallowed hard as she worked her way around to the back stairs. She sure hoped the men hadn't come here with pleasure in mind.

The first weathered stair creaked from her weight. She winced and held her breath. Her fears were silly—who could hear a faint squeak over the ruckus coming from the saloon? The tinny piano music did little to mellow out the loud chatter, groans, and hollers from the men inside the building. And if the noise was bad, the stench was horrid. Unfortunately, she was downwind of the saloon's privies, and she suspected half the folks who ventured out of the building to use them never made it that far.

She hiked her skirt up farther and hurried quietly up the steps. She reached the landing, but she didn't dare go inside. The line had to be drawn somewhere. Her mother would be proud that she was finally learning to set some boundaries for her behavior.

To her left, the two windows on the rear of the saloon were dark, but light flowed from the ones to her right. She reached up toward one of the open windows, but it was too high and too far to her right to grasp. Jack glanced around, making sure no one was about, then lifted her skirt and climbed onto the landing's railing. Too bad she hadn't had time to don her bloomers.

Deep voices echoed from the window. "It's good in theory, but if the railroad fails to come here, we'll have wasted a small fortune."

"That's true, and we will also lose the faith of our investors."

Jack didn't recognize either voice. She held onto the railing support that ran up the side of building. She glanced down, barely able to make out the ground below in the growing darkness. If she fell that far, she could well injure her knee again, and the pain had just barely stopped biting her with its sharp teeth.

She shook off her apprehension like a winter cloak. This was nothing compared to walking on the mayor's roof.

"I understand, gentlemen, but I just received a certified document stating that the Katy Railroad will definitely be building a spur track from Denison to Lookout and on farther west. Construction of the rails is set to commence in a few weeks."

Jack's heart soared at the mayor's declaration. She'd gotten her scoop! The railroad was coming to Lookout, and she was the only one who knew except for these men. She needed more details and to find out what they planned to build. Maybe it was the depot. But no, wouldn't the railroad company take care of that?

She held her breath and leaned sideways to reach the window frame three feet away. Her right foot slipped, flailing, unable to find a place to land. Her fingertips latched onto the window casing, keeping her from falling. She managed to get her foot back on the railing, but now she leaned precariously to the right.

One man stood and walked toward the window. Jack sucked in a breath and leaned her head away from the light. If he looked out, he'd see her fingertips on the window's frame.

Sprawled out like she was, she felt like a newborn foal that had just stood up for the first time. Good thing night had come, or anyone below would have a clear view of her unmentionables.

"I'm not convinced this town has need of a hotel," Mr. Mustache, as she had dubbed the man, said.

Hotel?

They planned to build a hotel in Lookout?

Why. . .that would put the boardinghouse out of business. How could they compete with a brand-new hotel? Irritation at the mayor seared her belly and flared her nostrils—definitely not a good thing, given her closeness to the privies. She scrunched her nose shut on the inside, just like she did when she changed Andrew's messy diapers, but that did nothing to quell the fire burning in her gut.

No wonder the mayor had been so devious and wouldn't let

her listen in on his conversation with these men. Mayor Burke had once planned to buy the boardinghouse and make it his home back when her ma thought Luke would marry one of the boarding-house brides. But when Luke picked her, she canceled her plans to sell out and move away. The boardinghouse was far bigger and fancier than Mayor Burke's present house, and he'd always admired her home. Was that his purpose? To drive her family out of business so they'd have to move and sell the boardinghouse? Of all the. . .

"Our surveyor should arrive within the week."

"I'm not sure where we will put him," Mayor Burke said. "There's not another bedroom at my house."

"Perhaps he could stay at the boardinghouse and investigate our competition." Mr. Mustache chuckled.

The mayor snorted. "Mrs. Davis's place won't be much of a threat to your establishment. That minister is the only boarder she has now. At the rate she's birthing babies, it won't be long before she's filled the house with children and won't have any more rooms to let."

Jack sucked in another gasp, trying to keep quiet. Her fingers were starting to ache, as was her knee, bent in an unnatural manner as it was. She tightened her grasp on the window frame, halfway wondering how she was going to get back on the landing.

A drunk in the doorway mumbled something incoherent and fumbled with the screen door latch. Suddenly it flew open, banging into her hip and sending her flying.

For a fraction of a moment, she hung only by the fingertips of her right hand. Her body swung far to the right. Her fingers slipped. Her frantic heart tried desperately to escape her chest.

She would not fall.

Not again.

Help me, Lord.

She forced her trembling left hand up to the frame and grabbed on. Her boots slipped against the fabric of her petticoat as she tried to gain a foothold. If the men so much as glanced her way they'd see her hands. Her breath came in little gasps. The ache in her fingers intensified.

"Well now, what've we got here? Eh?" The man responsible for her precarious position leaned over the rail and grinned. The light shining out the window illuminated him. Several days' worth of sparse whiskers coated his cheek and chin, looking like mange on a dog. He belched, sending a putrid stench Jack's way.

She couldn't do a thing. *Go away!*

If she so much as whispered, the mayor would hear her. And what would he do if he found her spying on him a second time?

The drunk swatted at her arm. "Come over hear and give ol' Harvey a smooch. Yer a purty little thang."

"Git!" the mayor yelled.

Jack plastered her cheek against the building. Her fingers slipped. If that man didn't leave soon, she was in serious danger of falling. The drunk leaned over—and Jack hoped and prayed he didn't choose that moment to spew the contents of his belly all over her.

"C'mere." He snagged hold of her sleeve, then lost his balance and tilted over the rail. "Whoopsie-daisy."

She closed her eyes, expecting him to knock her off her perch. When no collision occurred she peered out of one eye. Relief made her weak—and she sure didn't need any more weakness—to see he had righted himself on the landing.

"I said get out of here. Can't decent men have a meeting in quiet?" the mayor yelled. Footsteps sounded in Jack's direction.

Yikes! Fall or get caught?

Neither option was favorable.

The drunk regrouped and took another swipe at her but missed. She hoped he'd attract the mayor's attention so he wouldn't notice her.

Falling was better than getting caught. Jack let go.

The mayor slammed the window shut.

Jack hurled downward, her skirts snapping like a flag in a wind storm.

"Tell us another story, Miss Carly." Abby sat on her bed in her nightgown, bouncing her legs.

"Not tonight, sweetie. Emmie is already asleep." She lifted the toddler off her lap and held her tight against her chest as she stood. She kicked out her skirts and carried Emma to her bed.

"Puh-leasse." Abby held out her doll and danced her across the quilt.

"Shh. . .I said no." She pulled a sheet over Emmie and placed a kiss on her head. Oh, how she'd grown to love these children. If she had to leave and move on one day, her heart would break.

"Miss Carr—llyy, I gotta go."

She turned toward Abby, putting her hands on her hips like she'd seen Jacqueline do. "Are you telling the truth?"

Abby nibbled her lip, then looked down at the floor.

"That's what I thought. Lie back now. It's time to sleep."

The girl did as told, but her frown proved she wasn't happy about bending her will. Suddenly her gaze turned apprehensive. "But Sissy's not home. I'm scared to go to sleep without her."

Carly laid the sheet over Abby's body. Was she really afraid, or was this another bedtime stalling tactic?

"Abby, you know that's not true." Luke walked into the room, making it seem smaller.

"But Papa. . ."

"No more talking. Time to go to sleep." He leaned over and kissed Abby's cheek. "I love you, punkin."

Carly left the room and started down the stairs. Luke turned off the bedroom lamp and followed behind her, chuckling. "That one is such a fireball. Reminds me of Jack when she was younger, although I didn't know her at Abby's age."

Carly didn't miss the regret in his voice. "I have to admit, I can't yet tell when she's pullin' my leg or bein' truthful."

Luke joined her in the entryway, shaking his head. "Neither can I, and I'm her father—and a lawman. And Alan's almost as bad."

"I never realized how difficult raising children can be." She'd probably never have any of her own. She ducked her head and studied the floor. A large ant crawled out from under the hall tree. Before she could even reach in her pocket for her handkerchief, Luke squashed the intruder.

"Raising children can be hard at times, but it's worth all the effort." A soft smile tugged at his lips.

Carly continued to be amazed at how he'd welcomed her into his home, given their past history. How he entrusted the care of his children to her. He didn't seem to hold any animosity toward her for her past.

He glanced down, his brown eyes anxious. The sun had ironed permanent creases in the tanned skin beside his eyes. His brown hair, the color of a pecan shell, had touches of gray at the temples and sideburns. "I wonder if I might ask a favor of you."

"Of course. Anything."

His smile turned him from a rugged lawman to handsome. "I'd like to get Rachel out of the house and take her for a short walk. Would you mind tending the baby and keeping an ear out for the children?"

"I'd be happy to." She loved holding the baby. It was her first time to be around one other than at church or when a young mother would visit Tillie.

"I'd be much obliged. We won't be gone long. I know Rachel is tired, but the fresh air will do her some good and maybe even help her sleep." He glanced at the window beside the front door. "Hmm. . .I wonder where Half Bit is. Do you know?"

Carly shook her head. "No, she was hanging up the diapers last time I saw her. Come to think of it, she didn't come in afterward."

He strode toward his bedroom. "Rachel and I can look for her. I'm sure she just got distracted chasing a rabid boar or trying to interview a cattle rustler for that paper." He shook his head and turned into the bedroom.

Rabid boar? Carly chuckled. She remembered all the stories about Jacqueline that Rachel had written to her while she was in prison. Those letters and Rachel's encouragement had kept her going when things seemed more than she could bear.

She walked into the dining room, turned up the lamp, and checked to make sure everything was in place. A light breeze blew in the window, but a flash of lightning pulled her across the room. If a storm blew in, she didn't want the floor to get wet. She shut the window and stared out, waiting for another flash.

Footsteps sounded behind her, and she turned. Luke strode in with Andrew on one arm. The baby's head rested in his father's hand, while the tiny body lay across Luke's forearm. Andrew looked so much smaller when Luke held him.

"Here you go. Rach' said he still needs to be patted since he just finished his supper." Luke handed her a clean diaper and waited while she draped it over her shoulder then passed his son to her. "Take care of him."

"I will." Cuddling the baby, she walked around the table, satisfying herself that all was in order and no food had been overlooked on the floor. Then she turned down the lamp. In the dimly lit parlor, she sat in the rocking chair and patted the baby's back. She liked sitting in the dark. It was a habit she'd developed in prison, not by choice but because the lights were turned off shortly after supper.

In the dark, she'd been able to pretend she was somewhere else—anywhere except the hot cell she'd been locked in. She closed her eyes and laid her head back. Andrew squirmed, pumping his legs, and uttered a squeak.

Footsteps echoed down the hall. Luke and Rachel stopped at the front door. He opened it, but she turned toward the parlor.

"Andy's fussing. Maybe I should stay." Rachel nibbled her lower lip and took a step in Carly's direction.

Luke snagged her arm. "Nope. C'mon, Mama, Andrew is fine, your other little chicks are in the coop, and now the rooster wants to take a walk with you."

Rachel laughed and took his arm. "Why, you have such a way with words, Marshal Davis."

"Yep."

The door closed, leaving Carly alone. She loved how Luke and Rachel teased one another and joked. Loved the affection brimming from their eyes whenever one stared in the other's direction. She loved it, but it only emphasized what she'd never have.

No man wanted a convict for a wife. The women in prison had told her as much, not that many of them seemed to care if they married. And neither had she until she'd come back to Lookout and observed how a couple in love lived.

Now she wanted it all. A husband. A home. Children.

She glanced up at the dark ceiling. "Help me to turn loose of those dreams, Lord. They only cause me anguish."

Andrew jerked and screeched. Carly stood and bounced him up and down. She glanced at the front door. How long would Luke and Rachel be gone? What should she do if the baby had a problem?

She walked down the hall, bouncing little Andrew and patting his back. The baby stiffened and wailed. If she didn't get him quiet, he might wake the other three, and she wasn't sure she was ready to handle all four children at once.

"Shhh, little fellow. You're all right." Her crooning helped but the moment she stopped, he kicked out his legs, and she nearly dropped him. "Hey now, settle down. Your mama will be back soon."

A knock sounded, startling Carly. She stared at the front door, knowing it wasn't locked. Who could be knocking at this hour?

Whoever it was pounded harder. Maybe there was a problem and someone wanted the marshal. She hurried to the door, baby crying, and peeked outside. Garrett Corbett's oh-so-beautiful blue eyes stared back, illuminated by dim light in the parlor. June bugs and moths flittered around the porch lantern. "Well, c'mon in before you let all the bugs inside."

He hurried through the door, shut it, and yanked off his western hat, revealing a sweat line that darkened his blond hair. "That wasn't exactly the greeting I was expecting." He flashed a teasing smirk. "What's wrong with Andy?"

"Sorry. And I don't know. He was fine until Rachel left. I'm supposed to pat him until he belches, but it's not working." Tears blurred her view of her guest. She wasn't qualified to care for a baby.

"Let me see him."

She tightened her grip on Andrew, raising her voice to be heard over his frantic wails. "What do you know about babies?"

"Watch and learn." He lifted Andrew out of her arms and carried him into the darkened parlor. He perched on the end of a chair, then set the baby on his lap. Holding the baby upright with his neck and head supported, Garrett patted circles on the baby's back. Andrew continued screeching.

"You're gonna wake the other children. Let me have him back." Carly reached for him.

Andrew stiffened suddenly, then a huge belch erupted from the tiny child, followed by a white arc of sputum.

"Ah!" Garrett spread his legs, but not fast enough. The milky white steam spread across his left leg.

Carly couldn't help the giggle that worked its way up. Garrett stared at his pants, unable to take his eyes off the stain. She covered her mouth and bent over, laughing harder than she had in years.

"It's not funny." He glared up at her.

"Yes it is. You should have seen your face." She yanked the diaper off her shoulder and handed it to him.

"Here, take this scoundrel. I try to make him feel better and he does *this* to me." He passed Andrew to her and attacked his pants with the diaper. "That's no way to say thanks, kid."

"At least he's quiet now."

Garrett grunted and held up the nasty wad of cloth. "Got another one of these?"

"Yes, just a minute." She turned up the lamp then hurried back to Rachel and Luke's room and laid Andrew in his cradle, hoping he'd be happy for a few minutes. In the kitchen, she grabbed a towel, dunked it in the water bucket, and took it to Garrett.

He scrubbed his pants like a man trying to wash away his sins. She noticed a spot on the floor and stooped down beside him to mop it up with a dry towel. His hand stilled, and she glanced up and found him watching her. She swallowed hard and stood. He copied her, which left them only a few feet apart.

Carly cleared her throat and backed away, wondering at the odd sensations surging through her body. "Did you. . .uh. . .need to see the marshal?"

Garrett shook his head and kept gawking at her. She glanced down to make sure she didn't have a button unfastened or some food on her bodice. She'd never been comfortable staring men in the eye. Generally, she saw things in their gaze that she didn't want to see, and that scared her.

"Um. . .well, did you need to talk to Rachel?" she asked.

"No."

Perplexed, she looked up. "If you came to see Jacqueline, she's not here."

"I didn't."

Carly shoved her hands to her hips. "All the children are in bed, so what are you doing here?"

The tiniest of smiles lifted his lips. "I came to see you."

"Me?" She blinked, trying to remember if there was something she was supposed to give him or tell him, but nothing came to mind. "Whatever for?"

His smiled faded. "I thought you might like to take a walk."

"A walk?"

He nodded.

"Why?"

He shrugged one shoulder.

"It's getting ready to storm."

"No, it's not."

"Yes, it is. I saw lightning."

He stepped closer, and she tried to back up, but her calves bumped the coffee table.

"The storm is moving away from town," he said.

"Oh. Well, how do you know?"

"I've lived in Texas my whole life. I know."

"Oh." Unable to hold his steady gaze, she glanced around the room. Why was he here again?

"So, do you wanna?" He held out his palms as if to hold her hand, begging her with his eyes to agree.

But those eyes made her mind go foggy, as if a cloud had taken up residence in her head. She placed her hands behind her back to avoid touching him. "Want what?"

"To go for a walk."

She shook her head. It would be completely inappropriate for her to walk with him in the dark. People would talk, and it could damage her reputation—such as it was. Besides, she couldn't leave the children unattended. "I can't."

"Oh." He shoved his hands inside his pockets. "All right. Guess I'll go then."

The light in his eyes dimmed. She watched him shuffle to the door, shoulders drooping, and a spear of regret stabbed her. Why would he want to walk with her? As far as she knew, he didn't even like her.

"Rachel and Luke aren't home, and neither is Jacqueline, so I can't go."

He spun back around. "You mean you would if you could?"

She shrugged. In truth, she would like to go, but she couldn't wrap her mind around why he'd want to. "I guess so. I just don't understand why you'd want to take a turn around town with *me*."

"Why wouldn't I?"

She stared at him. Had he been eating loco weed? "You know."

He shook his head. "Know what?"

Carly rolled her eyes and sighed. "You could hardly get off that wagon fast enough when you first learned who I was that day you brung me back here. Now you wanna walk with me in front of the whole town? I'm confused."

He scratched his blond hair and looked a bit perplexed himself. "I guess I've changed my mind."

"About what?"

"You."

"Why?"

His gaze flitted across her face, then her hair, and back down, as if he actually was attracted to her. She held her breath, not quite able to believe it might be true.

"You're different, and I—I kind of like it."

"Kind of?"

He flung his arms out sideways, making her jump. "Yes! No! Why are you making this so hard?"

"Making what so hard?"

He stared at her then suddenly spun away and stomped toward the door. "Never mind."

"Wait? Where are you going?"

"Leaving?" He yanked open the door.

"Why?" He had to be the most confounding man in the world.

He tossed a wounded glance over his shoulder. "I knew this was a bad idea."

Carly stomped her foot. "What is?" she all but yelled.

"Trying to court you."

"Court me?" Her voice rose to a high squeak. Could he actually be serious? Or maybe this was one of the pranks he was well known for pulling.

He must have noticed something change in her expression because he turned back toward her. "Didn't I make it clear that I want to court you?"

Carly laughed and shook her head. "No, you just asked me to take a walk."

"Isn't that the same thing?" The daft man looked honestly bewildered.

"Uh. . .no, it isn't." Carly shook her head, then felt her cheeks warm. She peeked at him, looked away, then glanced back. She'd learned to be wary of Garrett Corbett ten years ago, back when he and his brothers had ordered the mail-order brides for Luke. He had a reputation for being a prankster, but since she'd returned to Lookout, he seemed different—as if he'd finally matured. Did she dare risk trusting him, even though she was attracted to him now?

She'd watched him play with Rachel and Luke's children. He was always gentle with them, but fun, and he made them laugh. He made her laugh when she watched them play.

Maybe he'd changed as much as she.

Maybe God would actually make her dream of marriage come true. "Uh. . .yes, I would be interested in. . .um. . .courting."

Garrett's wide grin was worth all the frustration of the past few minutes. He reached out and nearly shook her arm off, as if they'd sealed the business deal of the century. "Good," he said, then looped his thumbs in his pants pockets. "Good."

Rachel pushed the door open, stepping inside alone. Her cheeks were rosy and her eyes dancing. "Who's courting?"

Chapter 25

Jack closed her eyes and braced for the hard landing, praying only that she didn't reinjure her knee or fall into a pile of broken liquor bottles.

"Oompf!"

The masculine grunt took her by surprise as rough hands flailed around her skirts. Her back smashed into a hard body. Strong arms fumbled around her waist then found purchase, crushing her back against a solid chest. Her feet dangled in mid-air. She didn't know whether to scream or be relieved or just enjoy the fact that she was still alive and uninjured.

Then the arms tossed her up and whirled her around. She squealed but then squelched the sound almost as soon as it left her mouth. She caught Noah's familiar scent as he once again stopped her fall. He lowered her gently to the ground.

"What—do—you—think—you're—doing?" Noah's warm breath bathed her face, and she allowed herself to relax in spite of his harsh tone.

"Let's go," she whispered and pointed up at the open window above them.

The drunk leaned over. "Hey, li'l darlin', don't leave. Uh-oh." He uttered a rolling belch then bent farther over and made a vile retching sound.

Noah didn't need a second warning. He scooped her into his

arms, raced past the back of Dolly's Dress Shop, and then stopped behind Corbett's Freight office and deposited her rather roughly on the porch.

He crossed his arms, and she could barely make out his features in the moonlight. "Explain."

She rearranged her skirts as she sat on the hard wood and hiked her chin. He may have rescued her and saved her from hurting herself again, but she didn't owe the preacher an explanation for her behavior. "No."

He leaned into her face. "Yes."

She swung her legs off the porch, then jumped up, forcing him to step back. "I don't have to explain my actions to you."

He heaved a heavy sigh, and she was certain he muttered something about patience. She needed to get home. She had a story to write, and her family had surely realized she was missing by now. Her papa would come looking, if he wasn't already. What would he think to find her alone in an alley in the dark with the minister?

The bigger question was what would he do to the minister?

She glanced back at the saloon. The screen door banged shut. The drunk must have finished his business and gone back inside. She and Noah were truly alone—and why did that thought excite her? She should be irate at his brutish bullying, but she was too thankful that he'd been there to catch her.

Wait a minute.

She crossed her arms. "Just what were you doing behind the saloon?" She thought of the spectacle he must have seen when she nearly fell the first time. Her cheeks flamed. Had it been light enough that he'd seen her unmentionables?

"Me? What were you doing hanging from the saloon window?"

Her mind raced for a logical explanation. Finally she shrugged. "You know me." Her voice rose at the end.

He barked a laugh. "Far better than you can imagine."

She crinkled her brow. "Just what does that mean?"

His humor fled as fast as it had come, and he stepped closer. "Why do you take such reckless chances, Jackie? Don't you know you're not invincible? You could have broken your leg or your pretty neck falling like that."

The sudden tenderness in his voice caused a lump in her throat, but her defenses weren't yet ready to surrender. "Why do you care?"

His sigh was a gentle caress on her cheek. "Because I do, that's all."

She wished she could read the expression in his eyes. How did he care? As a friend? Or as a man who maybe. . . "You're the minister. It's your job to care for your flock."

He grunted, stalked away, and leaned one hand against a nearby tree. Intrigued, Jack followed. He wasn't acting very preacherly, but rather like a man—dare she hope—in love. She held her breath. He would have to make the first move. Otherwise she'd never know for sure that his feelings hadn't come about because of her own for him.

She blinked in the dark. Maybe in the daytime she couldn't admit it, but here, alone with him in the moonlight, she knew the truth—she'd fallen hard for Noah Jeffers.

It made no sense.

It didn't fit into her plans.

But hadn't Pastor Taylor said on numerous occasions that God had far greater plans than man could ever imagine for himself—or herself?

Could it be God's plan that she be part of Noah's life?

Her stomach swirled with the possibilities of it all. Her knees—which hadn't shaken during her ordeal at the window—now trembled so hard she thought maybe she ought to sit back down.

Noah spun around so fast, she didn't have time to move. She must have surprised him because he jumped, then grabbed her upper arms. "Yes, I care about you because I'm the minister."

As if she'd licked her fingers and put out a candle flame, her hopes dimmed.

"But"—he gave her a gentle shake—"there's far more to it than that."

"Far more to what?" She hated how her voice warbled.

"I do care about you—and not just as a minister."

She licked her lips and swallowed. "You do?"

He didn't answer, but his head tilted downward. Her heartbeat skedaddled upward.

"I may be a preacher, but when it comes to you, I've never been able to express myself like I've wanted. I shouldn't do this, but will you allow me to show you how I feel?"

Her headed nodded as if she were a marionette controlled by strings and had no will of her own. She was too intrigued—too hopeful—to refuse.

His large hands cupped her cheeks, and she marveled that this big, strong man was trembling. He stood there a moment as if indecisive or possibly cherishing the moment, and then he bent down, his lips brushing hers as lightly as a wisp of Emmie's hair.

Jack's heart thundered in her chest and ears. She slid her hands up Noah's chest, and he deepened the kiss. Her senses popped to life, and she pressed her lips harder against his. He moaned and grabbed her up, clear off her feet, kissing her as if there were no tomorrow.

And then he all but dropped her and stepped away.

She swayed, still caught up in her roiling emotions and passion. She wanted to say, "Amazing!" but his stoic reaction held her silent. Did he regret kissing her? Had she not done it right?

What did she know about kissing? She'd never done it before—at least not with a man. Her one and only kiss had been when she kissed Ricky, her old friend, just to see what it felt like—and it was absolutely nothing like what she'd just experienced. She placed her hand over her heart.

"I'm sorry." Noah's deep voice sounded far huskier than normal. "I shouldn't have done that."

Jack narrowed her gaze, a different kind of fire simmering. How could he stir up all these feelings she never knew she had and then say he shouldn't have done that? Was she unworthy of his affections? She hauled back and clobbered him on the arm.

The moonlight illuminated his shocked expression. Then he started chuckling. "I probably deserved that."

"You did." But she wasn't sure if it was because he'd kissed her or because he hadn't kissed her again. She stomped her foot. Oh!

She was so confused—and she didn't like being confused.

He reached out and took her hand. "C'mon, I should get you home. Your folks are probably worried."

And she had a story to write and get to Jenny first thing in the morning. But she hated to go, leaving things as they were. Why had he kissed her? Should she tell him of her growing attraction to him?

Noah rubbed his thumb across the back of her hand, sending delicious chills racing up her arm.

"I didn't hurt you when I caught you, did I?"

"No, though you scared me half to death. Thank you for saving me from getting hurt, but you never said why you were behind the saloon."

"Neither did you." She could see his white teeth as he grinned. "Read the next edition of the paper, and you'll find out."

He stepped close and lifted a hand to her shoulder, still holding the other one. There went her knees a-wobblin' again.

"Jackie, please stop taking such chances. You're not a kid who can shinny up trees anymore; you're a grown woman—a very beautiful woman—in skirts and petticoats, not overalls." His grip tightened on her hand and she glanced up. "You could have hurt yourself in that fall, and I dread thinking what might have happened if that drunk had actually gotten 'hold of you."

He dropped her hand and took hold of her upper arms. "Please stop taking chances with your life. It's too precious to put in danger. Promise me you'll be more careful."

Tears blurred her eyes at the tenderness in his voice. No man had ever treated her with such care and sensitivity except for Luke. Not even her best friends growing up—Ricky and Jonesy. She nodded, but what came out of her mouth surprised even her. "I will if you'll kiss me again."

He stared down at her as if shocked. Then he glanced around and backed her up into the shadows of the building. "I shouldn't."

"That's what you said last time." She tugged on his shirt, pulling him closer. After having a father who spewed his anger like a snorting bull and battered his wife and daughter, she never thought to find a man she could fully trust. One so gentle that he'd never hurt her. A man like Luke. A man who went around town doing kind deeds for people—just because he had a good heart. Noah would never treat her cruelly or lie to her or hit her.

He shuffled his feet, as if he might bolt away any moment. "I can't. It isn't right. I'm the minister."

"Shhh. . .even ministers have a right to happiness and to find"—dare she say it—"love."

He sucked in a breath.

Yes, she loved him. She'd been fighting it for days. She had no clue how it had happened so fast, but she loved Noah Jeffers, and though she wanted to shout it to the world, she'd keep that secret to herself and savor it for a while.

The crickets seemed to cheer him on. Off in the distance an owl hooted. "Please, Noah, kiss me one more time before we go in."

He chuckled. "You're a wanton woman, Miss Davis."

"No, not wanton, just a woman on the edge of a cliff, who's about to jump off."

He exhaled another heavy breath. "Me, too, darling. Me, too." He lifted her up and set her back down on the bottom step to Garrett's office. "This way I don't get a crick in my neck—not that I minded all that much."

She couldn't help giggling and boldly reached up and placed her hands on his shoulders. They were far wider and more solid than she'd imagined. She continued exploring, letting her hands wander around his neck where she fingered the hair on his nape. He tilted his face up, eyes closed, as if enjoying the moment. She gently tugged him toward her.

Dallas was looking less and less appealing with each second that passed.

Carly stared at Rachel then glanced at Garrett, hoping he would explain the courting thing. He just stood there with his hands in his pockets, a silly grin on his face.

Rachel's pale blue eyes went wide as her hand flew to her chest. "Not you two?"

Garrett's smile slipped, and he crossed his arms. "What's wrong with that?"

"Nothing. It's just a shock." Rachel glanced between Carly and Garrett, then shrugged. "I mean, it's just that I've never even seen you talking to each other. Have you prayed about it?"

"Well, no, not yet." Garrett kicked at the leg of the nearest chair. "Can't a guy take a gal for a walk without everyone gettin' in an uproar?"

"Of course, I'm sorry. But you didn't say anything about a walk."

Garrett had that confused look again. He reached up and scratched his temple, and Carly's gaze wandered up to his blond hair. Would it be soft like hers or stiff and coarse? "What's the difference in walkin' and courtin'?"

Rachel nearly choked on a laugh. "You've got to be kidding, Garrett."

He shook his head. "I'm not. A man doesn't take a woman walkin' around town unless he's interested in her. Too many folks would start talkin'."

"Well, I can see your point, but you need to seek God on something so serious." Rachel didn't smile. Carly shifted from one foot to the other. Did her friend think it wrong for her and Garrett to be interested in one another? Rachel had everything, not that she hadn't struggled in years past, and now Carly wanted the same thing, with the exception of such a big house.

"Is Andrew asleep?" Rachel asked, seeming suddenly sober.

"I'm not sure. I laid him in his bed after he belched." Carly crossed her arms. Did Rachel think she wasn't good enough for her husband's cousin? She grimaced, rejecting that idea. Rachel was right that they should pray about courting, but was there anything wrong with getting to know a man first and then seeking God about their future?

"Where's Luke? I thought you two took a stroll." Garrett reached for his hat, rolling the brim on one side.

Rachel stopped in the parlor entrance. "Oh, Terrance Gruber ran up and told Luke there'd been another break-in, but I didn't hear where. Sometimes I wish the town had stayed small like it was years ago. With growth comes problems." She nodded at each of them. "I'd better go check on the baby."

A tight fist clenched Carly's chest. Would folks blame her for this newest robbery?

She stared at the floor. Left alone with Garrett, she suddenly felt awkward. She knew how to talk to this man when her ire burned, but what did she say now?

"Well. . ."

"I. . ."

They both talked at once. Garrett smiled, and she relaxed a bit. He really was a handsome man.

"You go first," he said.

She shook her head.

He gently touched her arm. "Go on. I won't bite."

She shrugged and stared down at his dusty boot tops. They needed to be cleaned and polished. The end of his trousers had frayed bits sticking where he must have torn them. The man sure needed a woman to care for him, but was she the right woman? Dare she believe God had sent him in answer to her prayer?

"Carly. . ."

She glanced up at his use of her Christian name, liking the mellow tone of his voice. "You'll probably think it's silly," she admitted, "but I'm afraid folks will think I caused the break-in."

His eyes went wide. "Why would they think that? You've been here all evening, haven't you?"

"Yes, but folks talk, especially when there's an ex-convict livin' among them."

Garrett winced as if she'd hauled back and punched him.

"Surely you realize the gossip you'll be facing if you and I court. Have you considered that it could affect your business?"

He lowered his head, and she could see that he hadn't. She feared the side of his hat would be as curled as Tessa Morgan's hair on Sunday morning if he didn't stop scrunching it. She tugged it from his hands then stretched up and set it on his head. "Go home, Garrett. Thank you for asking me to court. I am deeply honored, but before we consider such a thing, you need to think it through—completely. Reflect on how a relationship with me could hurt your business."

"I'm thinking about changing businesses."

Carly wondered about that, but now wasn't the time to discuss it. A moth flittered between them. Garrett reached out faster than she could blink and caught it. A shy grin tilted one side of his mouth—his very appealing mouth. He held up his closed fist. "Guess I'd better go so I can turn this critter loose."

She nodded and crossed to the door. "If you're serious about us courting, promise me you'll pray about it—and that you'll only ask me again if God gives His blessing."

He stared at her a long while then inhaled a deep breath through his nose. "I will. I should have done it before, but I just—just got it in my head that we'd be good together and headed on down here."

With a boldness she didn't know she possessed, she reached up and cupped his cheek. A day's worth of light stubble tickled her fingers. "Thank you. You have no idea how much your offer means to me."

He pressed his hand against hers, turned it, and kissed her palm. Then he scowled. "Shoowy! We smell like baby spit-up."

Carly giggled and gently pushed him outside. Jacqueline and the pastor walked across the street, and Garrett greeted them. She closed the door, then hustled up the stairs, not quite ready to face another inquiry about her and Garrett.

Standing with her hand on her doorknob, she listened for the children. Only the sound of heavy breaths—and one nasally snort—could be heard. She smiled and entered her room. Leaning back against the closed door she thought of how her life might have taken a new road this evening—and she prayed it might be God's plan for her.

Kissing Jackie was wrong, no matter how good it felt. Surely it couldn't be God's plan for him. Berating himself, Noah hurried upstairs while Jackie went to say good night to her folks.

But he had to admit, kissing her—holding her close—had been the fulfillment of a long-held dream, and far better than he'd ever dreamed. His steps slowed. Imagine Jacqueline Hamilton Davis kissing him. He shook his head. Maybe it had all been a dream.

That was it.

He must be sleepwalking.

But if that was the case, he wouldn't feel so guilty. He'd always admired Jackie's spunk and determination, even when it got her in trouble. He snorted a laugh—even when she got *him* in trouble. And she had. Plenty of times.

He closed the door to his room then dropped onto the desk chair. Bending over, he rested his elbows on his hands and forked his fingers through his hair. With the exception of a relationship with God, he'd never wanted anything as much as he desired a relationship with Jackie.

Was that wrong of him? Shouldn't a man of God be content to reach his whole flock and not be attracted to one pretty woman? One very beautiful woman who set his senses on fire and flamed his dreams. Dreams of a home—a loving wife—a family.

If only Pete were here, he'd tell Noah what to do.

The wind lifted a corner of the curtain, as if the Spirit of God drifted in. He needed to pray and find that comforting peace God always brought him, but part of his mind said he never should have come back to Lookout.

Yet in spite of all his initial objections, he realized now that a part of him had never left here.

He fell to his knees, head on the floor, and cried out to God. "Show me what to do, Lord. Help me to stay on the path that You want me to walk—and if Jackie isn't—" Just thinking the words gutted him. How could he say them out loud?

But to hold back anything from God was wrong. If he gathered Jackie up and held her close to his heart and refused to let her go, he'd be wrong. He had to give her to God—and if God chose to give her back, that would be the greatest day of his life.

Chapter 26

Jack strode into the *Lookout Ledger*'s office, relishing the familiar odors of ink and paper. She slapped her article down on top of the editor's desk.

Jenny jumped. She pushed her wire-framed glasses up her nose and scowled. "Can't you walk in all quiet and graceful, like most ladies?"

Ignoring her friend's intentional barb, Jack smiled. "I finally did it."

"Did what?"

"Got my scoop—the story I wanted that will land me a job in Dallas." As soon as she said the words, they tasted like curdled milk in her mouth. She'd stayed up half the night writing her article and the other half thinking about Noah's kisses and trying to decide what to do. Was she ready to give up her long-time dream for a man? Did she actually want to leave Lookout and go to a town where she knew no one?

Jenny glanced down and read the article. With an ink-stained finger, she followed the letters Jack had written. Jack looked around the familiar office. Papers littered the building, stacked in every nook and cranny, and the large black printer sat in one corner, looking alone and ignored for the moment.

Pulling off her glasses, Jenny eyed her, as if weighing the truth of the article. "You've actually confirmed that the railroad is coming? I've been trying to pin down that info for months, without a speck of luck. Who's your source?"

"I overheard the mayor talking with those two men he's been escorting all over town." Satisfaction welled up inside Jack, making her sit up straighter. She'd finally gotten her big story. There was a powerful feeling of success that she'd outsmarted the mayor, in spite of his avoiding her, and had learned what he'd tried so hard to keep quiet.

Yet writing this story, even though it was the biggest of her career, didn't excite her as she'd expected it would. What was wrong with her?

A vision of Noah illuminated by the moonlight drifted through her mind. She hadn't admitted it to Tessa or Penny, but she'd been attracted to him from the start. There was something about him that made her feel connected—as if they'd been friends for years instead of weeks. She couldn't believe she was in love.

"If that grin on your face means what I think, I'd say you've got a right to be proud. I've not heard hide nor hair about a hotel being built here. How does your ma feel about it?"

Jack sucked in her top lip. What would Jenny say if she knew that it was Noah on her mind and not the article? "I haven't told her yet. I don't know how."

Jenny lifted one brown brow. "You'd better tell her before the paper comes out."

"I will."

"Good job on this. It ought to stir up a lot of talk around town."

Jack nodded. "Probably so."

Jenny reached in a drawer and pulled out a letter, a tiny smile dancing on her lips. She held it as if it were something special, then handed it to Jack "I admit to having mixed feelings about giving you this, but I have a surprise."

Curiosity bolted through her as fast as a horse off a starting line. Her heart flip-flopped. The wrinkled envelope addressed to Jenny Evans had *Dallas Morning News* imprinted in the upper left corner. She ran her thumb over the embossed letters, her hand shaking. Could this actually be the realization of her dream? Her gaze lifted to Jenny, whose mouth stretched into a wide smile.

"Go ahead, open it."

She pulled the paper from the envelope and nearly dropped it. She lifted the top of the page and began reading:

Dear Jenny,

Thank you for your letter recommending Jacqueline Davis as a reporter for the Dallas Morning News. *I have read over the clippings you sent and am impressed with Miss Davis's writing skill and creative talent for recording details while keeping the story interesting. Coming from a small town, she would have a fresh perspective on life in Dallas.*

I've discussed Miss Davis with my superiors, and we are prepared to offer her a position in our Home Living Section. Should she accept the position, she will be responsible for posting a recipe each issue, researching and discussing new and innovative products that women could use in their homes, and covering fashion trends.

Jack's hopes sank. "What do I know of fashion? I'd never wear a dress if it was socially acceptable for a woman to wear pants."

"Just keep reading."

Not quite as enthused as a moment ago, she started reading again:

If Miss Davis proves herself, as I believe she will based on your recommendation, we can discuss moving her into a more challenging position in the future. Just one thing, I can hold this position only until the end of the month, so please inform Miss Davis to contact me at her earliest convenience should she desire it.

As always, if you're in Dallas, Jenny, be sure to stop in and allow me to take you to eat. We have some delightful cafés here.

Your friend,
Amanda Jones Bertram

Jack stared at the letter, trying to make sense of her roiling emotions.

Yes—she had a job offer from a Dallas newspaper.

No—it wasn't the job she wanted.

Yes—there was the potential to one day become a news reporter.

But did she truly want to leave her family? To leave Noah?

In less than three weeks?

Jenny leaned back in her chair, her mouth twisted to one side and brows lifted. Jack sincerely hoped her less-than-enthusiastic response didn't offend Jenny.

"Tell me what's going on in that creative mind of yours. I know the Home Living Section isn't what you had your heart set on, but I halfway expected you to be packing your bags by now."

She had no idea how to answer her friend. Stalling, she blew out a heavy breath and read the missive again.

"Humph. It's a man, isn't it?"

Jack glanced up as her pulse jumped. "What?"

A knowing smile softened Jenny's face. "You've met someone, and now you're not so sure you want to leave town."

"How do you know?"

"What else would stop a determined young woman like you from chasing her dream once it's finally within reach?"

"What should I do?"

Jenny shrugged. "Only you can decide that." She suddenly leaned forward, eyes narrowed. "But tell me who the man is. I may be the newspaper editor, but you really slipped the wool over my eyes on this story."

Jack tried hard to control the embarrassed smile that twittered on her lips, but she couldn't. "It all happened rather fast."

"Surely it's not that Billy Morgan."

She shuddered at the thought of it. "Certainly not. Though if he had his way, we'd be married tomorrow. I can't seem to get it through his head that I'm not interested."

"Then who is it?"

"I don't know if I should say. I'm not sure where things are headed."

"And yet it's serious enough for you to consider not following your dream to Dallas."

"I suppose."

Jenny lowered her head for a few moments, then looked at Jack again. "I know you're independent-minded and don't care for folks telling you what to do, but if you have some young man interested, one who can support you and cares about you, that's a far better choice than working your feet and fingers to the bone, trying to sniff out stories for a paper."

Jack's mouth fell open. "I never thought I'd hear you vote for marriage over work."

"I've lived alone for a long while and had time to reflect on things. I love my work, but as you get older, you think more about marriage and children. If I could do things over, I'm not certain I'd do them the same, but that's water under the bridge."

"You're not too old to get married."

Jenny snorted a laugh. "I'm too set in my ways. Besides, we're not talking about me. What are you going to do?"

"I don't know."

"Maybe you should talk to your folks and get some advice. 'Course, neither one will like the idea of you running off to Dallas. And mind me, I *will* find out who your beau is."

Jack knew she would. Jenny was good at her job. Hadn't Jenny taught her all that she knew about reporting?

"I'd better get back home. Ma will be needing my help." She held the letter to her chest. "I can't thank you enough for this, Jenny."

Her friend swatted her hand in the air. "Glad to help, although I don't know what I'll do without you."

Jack smiled and stepped outside. The May sun shone bright, promising another beautiful day. Wildflowers had popped up along the edges of the boardwalk, adding color to the barren dirt street.

She felt as if she were being pulled in two directions at once, both having tremendous possibilities. The job in Dallas would mean a whole new life. A big city. New friends. New adventures.

But how could she leave her family?

How could she not watch Andrew learn to crawl? To talk?

And what about Noah?

She hadn't known him long, but he sparked something inside her that she'd never felt before. He made her want to be a woman for the first time in her life. To try hard to be a better person.

As she crossed Bluebonnet Lane, she couldn't help wondering which side of the tug-of-war would win.

Chapter 27

Jack was glad Jenny was such an early riser and had been at her office before breakfast. Waiting any longer to turn in her story would have been difficult. She reached for the doorknob of her house. A shrill scream suddenly rent the quiet morning. She spun around, frantically searching Main Street. Nothing looked out of place. A wagon was parked in front of the livery, but no one was on the street or boardwalk. What had happened?

Jenny burst out of the newspaper office, as did several other shop owners, each one looking around. It was far too early to be a saloon girl's phony squeal when chased by an eager cowboy. Besides, the scream had sounded real—as if someone had been harmed or frightened out of their wits.

Agatha Linus stumbled from between Dolly's Dress Shop and the Corbett Freight office. Jack hurried down the steps of her home, stuffing the letter from the *Dallas Evening News* into her waistband. She hiked her skirts and ran down the street, hoping her ma didn't see her.

Aggie wobbled, then reached for the dress shop's porch railing and collapsed against it. One hand covered her eyes; her head hung down. Was she crying? Hurt?

"Please, help me." She shuddered and dropped onto the boardwalk steps.

Jack rushed to her side, as did Jenny and several others.

"What's wrong, Mrs. Linus? Are you ill?"

She swiped her eyes with her fingertips then reached out her hand, and Jack took hold of it. "Oh, Jacqueline, it's dreadful. I—I fear my sister is dead."

Jack's heart jolted. It had been a long while since someone in their community had died. "Bertha is dead? How? What happened?"

"I'll get the doctor to come and check her," said Mr. Mann, who had been eating at Polly's Café and still had his napkin tucked in his shirt like a bib. He took off at a quick clip down the street.

Aggie shook her head. "It's all my fault, you see. I was feeling poorly and slept late. I should have been up to fix Bertha's breakfast. She does like her biscuits and jam of a morning."

Jack glanced at Jenny, who gave a shrug and quick shake of her head, as if she couldn't make any sense out of the connection between breakfast and Bertha, either. There had to be more to the story.

Jack glanced over her shoulder and noticed Tessa standing just outside the mercantile door. "Tessa!" She waved her hand to catch her friend's attention. "Could you run over and see if Luke is still at home?"

Tessa glanced across the street at them as if she didn't want to miss anything, then nodded. She untied her apron, tossed it inside the store, and hurried to the boardinghouse.

Jack patted Aggie's wrinkled hand. She was as thin as her sister was wide.

Aggie, normally a shy, refined woman, sucked in a hiccupy sob. "Oh, what will I do without her?"

Shifting her feet to a more comfortable position, Jack couldn't help thinking Aggie would live a more peaceful life without her gossiping sister, who constantly ordered her around, but as soon as the thought breached her mind, she cast it off as not Christian. Her heart ached for Aggie, and her chest swelled with compassion. The woman had lost her husband years ago, and now she may have lost her sister.

The thud of quick footsteps drew her gaze up, and Jack's pulse soared. Right behind Luke, Noah followed, looking concerned.

His black eye had faded to a greenish-yellow tone, and the cuts from his fight with Billy had healed. His gaze collided with hers. She felt that connection—two separate beings that belonged together—soul mates.

"All right, move back, folks and let me through." Luke pushed his way into the crowd and squatted in front of Aggie. Noah stopped beside Jack, so close their arms touched when she moved. The back of his hand brushed against hers. Jack's throat clogged, making it harder to breathe.

"Tell me what happened, Miss Aggie." Luke pushed his hat back on his forehead, as if to see her better.

"I don't know. I came downstairs a bit later than normal and found Bertha lying on the kitchen floor." Her lower lip wobbled, and tears ran down her wrinkled cheeks. "Th–there was b–blood on the floor. My sister's blood." Aggie covered her eyes again, her shoulders shaking from her sobs.

Luke glanced up at Jack. "Take her back to our house, and let your ma tend her."

"No!" Aggie's hand snaked out and latched onto Luke's arm. "I need to be with Bertha."

Luke covered her hand with his. "Are you certain?"

Aggie nodded, and he helped her to stand. He caught Jack's eye, and she hurried to Aggie's other side.

"The rest of you folks go on back to whatever you were doing. You'll know soon enough what happened."

"I. . .I'd like the reverend to come along, Marshal."

Luke nodded at Noah, and he fell in step behind them. Jenny jogged up to Luke. "I want to come, too."

He shook his head. "Not right now, Jenny."

Scowling, Jenny caught Jack's eye, and she knew that her friend expected to hear every little detail later on. Jack gave her a brief nod, but for once, she had no desire to write a story. Shouldn't Aggie be allowed to grieve before the details were splattered across the paper for the whole county to see? Why had she never considered how covering the news might actually emotionally wound the people involved?

They cut between buildings and went in Aggie's back door.

Though Jack had visited Aggie and Bertha with her ma and had been in the parlor previously, she had never been in their kitchen. On the counter, several canisters were overturned with sugar and coffee spilling out. The pantry door lay open, revealing a mess with containers and jars sitting haphazard on the shelves, while others lay strewn all over the floor. Something definitely wasn't right here. Bertha may not be the tidiest person around, but Aggie most surely was.

Noah's hand gripped her shoulder, and she peeked up at him. He nudged his chin across the room where Luke and the doctor were kneeling on the floor. Jack's heart nearly lurched out of her chest at the large, unmoving body on the floor. She backed up against Noah, silently drawing his support. Aggie stood alone, staring down at her sister. Jack crossed the room and put her arm around the older woman's waist.

She winced at the blood pooling beneath Bertha's head. The woman's hair had been fashioned into the untidy bun that characterized her, and her colorful dress spread out around her like a spray of wildflowers.

Doc Phillips held his fingers against Bertha's neck. He looked up and shook his head. Aggie gasped and turned toward Jack, sobbing on her shoulder.

After a few moments, Noah gently took Aggie's arm. "Let's go in the parlor and let the doctor and marshal tend your sister."

Aggie allowed them to lead her from the room, but just as Jack stepped across the kitchen's threshold, she heard Doc Phillips whisper, "Murder."

Noah stood before a somber crowd of parishioners Sunday morning. He should be happy that more people had shown up this week, but he'd rather their motivation for coming to church be heartfelt rather than fear-driven. Three break-ins and a murder had folks quivering in their beds behind doors that had rarely been locked before.

"Agatha Linus asked me to personally thank those of you who attended her sister's funeral yesterday and for all the gracious condolences she has received. Let's remember to keep her in our prayers—as well as little Adam Howard, who fell and twisted his ankle yesterday. Lastly, congratulations to Luke and Rachel Davis on the birth of their second son, Andrew."

"And to you, too, Pastor," Dan Howard called out, "for saving the baby's life."

"Thank you, but that was the Lord's doing, not mine." He smiled. "Please join me in prayer." He directed a prayer heavenward, then opened his Bible. "In Jeremiah 29, we read, 'For I know the thoughts that I think toward you, saith the Lord, thoughts of peace, and not of evil, to give you an expected end. Then shall ye call upon me, and ye shall go and pray unto me, and I will hearken unto you. And ye shall seek me, and find me, when ye shall search for me with all your heart.'"

He stared at the faces in the crowd, hoping to touch some hearts today—to bring a lost soul to the Lord.

Jackie sat on the third row with most of her family, holding Andrew so that Rachel could sit with Mrs. Linus at her home. The peaceful scene of Jackie looking down at the baby, surrounded on both sides by wiggly children, created longings he shouldn't be having during a sermon. He caught Luke's stare, and the man lifted one brow as if asking what he was doing. Noah jerked his gaze away and focused on a scowling man in the back.

"God wants good things for us, folks. He truly does, but I know what some of you are thinking—what about Mrs. Boyd? How could God allow an innocent woman to be murdered?

"John 10:10 says, 'The thief cometh not, but for to steal, and to kill, and to destroy: I am come that they might have life, and that they might have it more abundantly.' God loves each of us, folks, and wants good things for us, but evil has entered this world. Evil lies in the heart of man. The scriptures say that 'all men have sinned,' but the good news is that we don't have to remain in sin. Jesus died to set us free—to forgive our sins."

Noah's heart pounded. He felt God's anointing on his message and believed it would bring change in someone's life. God had changed his life so much, and he longed to share the forgiveness and joy he'd received with others.

"We may never know why tragedies happen, but we have to believe in God and let Him strengthen us in hard times. Don't get angry at God when tragedy strikes, but rather run to His comforting arms. Know who your enemy is. And let me tell you, it's not your neighbor—or his goat that wanders into your garden, eating what doesn't belong to him." Titters circled the room, and heads nodded.

"Preach it, Brother!" Doc Phillips hollered.

"Don't be a casualty of war." Noah leaned across the pulpit, trying to get closer to his parishioners. Outside the open windows, birds flitted in the trees, chirping and singing as if cheering him on. "God is amazing, folks. Can you believe that the One who created the world cares about you—each one of you? He wants you to seek Him in all areas of your life, not just when tragedy strikes.

"Are you struggling with an important decision in your life? What line of cattle to purchase? Whether to plant wheat or corn next year? Whether to marry that pretty gal who's stolen your heart?" His gaze skittered to Jackie then dashed away. Luke straightened in his seat and crossed his arms, making Noah not a little anxious.

He cleared his throat. "The point I'm trying to make is that God cares. He cares about every little detail of your life. He wants you to draw nigh unto Him, confess your sins, and let Him wash you clean. Don't make important decisions without God's guidance. 'But seek ye first the kingdom of God, and His righteousness; and all these things shall be added unto you.' Shall we pray?"

Abby and Alan were on their feet and pushing past Jack the moment Noah bowed his head. She lifted one foot to block their escape during the prayer, then her papa snagged each wayward child by the collar and stuffed them back in their seat.

Noah's deep voice gently rumbled through the room. She loved the sound of his voice—so masculine and strong. His words—as if directed right for her—had pierced her heart. Most of her life she'd tried to control her circumstances. After living in a home so out-of-control when her first pa was alive, she'd sought to never be vulnerable again—and that meant being able to take care of herself. It meant making choices, even when it went against her ma, especially before Luke came into their lives. He brought stability and took care of them, but her independent spirit had already taken root. She'd done what had to be done—and never much considered if it was God's will for her life. Until now.

The tone of Noah's voice changed, drawing her from her reflections. "We'll be taking an hour-long break to enjoy the wonderful meal the ladies of our church have provided, and then the marriage of Rand Kessler and Christine Morgan will take place outside under the arbor." All eyes swung toward the engaged couple, and Mrs. Morgan blushed. Tessa sat beside her ma, dressed in a pink silk gown with enormously puffed leg-o-mutton sleeves and wearing a scowl. Jack hadn't seen Billy all week, but surely he'd attend his mother's wedding.

"If anyone cares to talk to me privately about today's message, just track me down. Y'all are dismissed."

Noah closed his Bible, and Jack couldn't help noticing that he glanced at her. She smiled. He gave her a brief nod then turned to shake Dan Howard's hand. Luke stepped into the aisle, carrying Emmie, and chased after Alan and Abby, who'd already made their escape and were no doubt headed for the food tables.

"Jacqueline, let me see that baby." Leah Howard pressed up the aisle against the flow of the crowd with seven-month-old Michael on her hip. The white-haired child grinned and reached for Andrew, his dark eyes dancing. Leah stood back, keeping her son from touching Andrew. Little Sarah held on tight to her mother's skirt and stared at the baby with wide blue eyes.

Jack couldn't help being a little jealous that the girl was so much better behaved than Abby. She held up her brother. "We're sure glad to get another boy."

"I bet your father and Alan are especially happy."

Jack chuckled. "You should have heard Alan's yell when he found out he had a brother."

Leah hadn't changed a lot in the decade she'd been married.

Her blond hair was fashioned into a bun and pinned on the back of her head. Jack tossed her loose hair over her shoulder and glanced at Noah. Would he like her hair better if she succumbed to womanly standards and wore it pinned up?

Leah smiled. "Our new minister is quite a handsome man, isn't he?"

Jack tried to mask her surprise at Leah's direct comment. "I. . . uh. . .suppose."

Baby Michael grabbed his ma's nose, and she pulled his hand away and kissed it then lifted her eyebrows at Jack. "You suppose?"

Jack couldn't help smiling. "All right, I noticed."

Leah laughed, her blue eyes sparkling. She nodded her chin toward the door. "I sure am surprised to see those two together. I'd never have thought it—not in a million years."

Jack turned and looked. Voices lifted in friendly chatter, and clusters of people stood near the door, including Garrett and Carly. "Me neither, but they seem happy, and I'm happy for them."

"Well, it will be good to see the last boardinghouse bride married—if things lead to that."

Leah's six-year-old son limped toward her. "Ma, I'm starvin'. Can we go eat? I wanna play with Alan."

"Ma, Adam disobeyed me." Naomi, half a head taller than her brother, pushed Adam out of the way and stood in front of her mother. "I told him to sit and wait for you and pa, but he didn't."

"You two may go outside, but don't get into the food yet." Leah stared at her son. "Mind your sister, and be careful. You don't want to hurt your ankle more. I'll be right out."

Jack watched the duo head for the door. "I imagine your house is busier than ours—and things get pretty hectic at ours."

"Yes, things are pretty busy. Remember when I broke off my engagement to Dan because I didn't want to be a mother?"

Jack nodded. "Yeah, I do."

"Let me be a testimony that God can change hearts. Nine children—I never could have imagined I'd be happy with so many."

"At least you don't have twins."

Leah lifted her hand to her forehead. "Oh my. I thank the

good Lord for that, but if He chooses to send a pair my way, I'll take them and be glad. Speaking of children, I should head outside and check on them all. The big ones keep good watch most of the time, but the little ones are fast and far too sneaky for my likin'."

"It's good talking to you."

Leah glanced over her shoulder as she made her way to the front. "You, too."

Andrew stretched and then muttered a squeak. Jack scooted out of the pew, just as Margie Mann strode toward her. Jack uttered a sigh and prepared herself for a lecture.

"Jacqueline Davis, what in the world are you doing with a newborn in church? What was your mother thinking?"

Jack lifted her chin a smidgen and tried to control her temper. "She was thinking of Mrs. Linus and how to best comfort her on her sister's loss. She didn't sleep well last night, and Ma didn't want the baby to disturb her rest this morning."

"Humph. I never took my young'uns out until they was a full month old." She turned and sashayed down the aisle.

Picking up the spare diaper she'd brought in case Andrew decided to relieve his belly, Jack moved toward the front. Noah was there alone, staring at her with a soft smile on his lips. Her thoughts immediately shifted to the memory of those same lips on hers, and her pulse sped up. "Your sermons are getting better each week."

Noah chuckled. "Wouldn't be too hard to improve on that first one."

"Yeah, well, it *was* entertaining." She grinned.

He sobered and shook his head. "I still can't believe I preached about pelicans. I don't remember saying that at all."

She wanted to reach out and rest her hand on his arm but resisted. Church wasn't the place to show affection, especially to the preacher.

"You going to eat?"

"Yes, but I need to run Andrew back to Ma first."

He stared down at her, affection shining in his eyes. "Will you forgive me if I don't sit with you? It might be a bit overwhelming for the townsfolk this soon."

Disappointment weighted her shoulders, but she forced a smile. "Sure. I'll have to help Pa with the children anyhow."

He glanced toward the door and stepped closer. "You know I'd like nothing more than to be with you, don't you?"

A lump formed in her throat, and she nodded. He smiled, then reached out and gently squeezed her upper arm.

Jack sighed and watched him go, affection for the kind, gentle man wearing down any remaining defenses she might have. She remembered Leah's words about how God had changed her heart and couldn't help wondering if He was changing hers, too.

Chapter 28

That was a fine sermon, young man." The mayor slapped Noah on the back, nearly dislodging the plate of food from his hand. Mayor Burke waved an ear of corn, dripping in butter, at him. "I'm certain you saved some sinners with that one. You might make a preacher yet."

Noah could barely abide the holier-than-thou man, but if he wanted to keep peace, he needed to hold his temper in check. And when the truth of his identity was revealed, Mayor Burke would most likely be one of his harshest opponents. "Thank you, sir, but I don't save sinners. Only God can do that."

"Yes, well. . ." The mayor glanced past him, then waved his corn again and strode off. "Perkins, hold up there."

Lord, save that man's soul. Noah couldn't help smiling at how Mr. Perkins side-stepped the mayor and hustled back to the food tables that lined the edge of the church's back lot.

Noah wandered through the crowd, mingling with the townsfolk, getting to know people he'd only met before, but his gaze kept drifting down Apple Street, where he'd last seen Jackie walking away from the crowd. She'd looked so pretty in her light green dress, which swayed like a bell when she walked.

"Parson Jeffers."

Noah turned back, and Dan Howard strode toward him, his sleeping baby balanced in one of the liveryman's big arms. Noah had remembered the livery owner was one of Luke's friends, and his wife was one of the women who'd originally come to town to marry the marshal.

"Mighty good message today, Parson."

Dan was the only man in town Noah could look eye-to-eye with, and he had a pretty wife and a whole passel of children. Noah hoped one day God would bless him as He had Dan. "How's my horse doin'?"

"Good! My boy spoils him with a carrot every now and then."

"I'm glad. I need to ride him more."

A young boy about Alan's size limped toward them and halted beside Dan. "Pa, Ma says to come 'cause it's time for d'sert."

"I'm coming." He ruffled the boy's brown hair, then glanced back at Noah. "This here's a good town, Parson. Don't let Mayor Burke put a burr under your saddle. You're doin' just fine. You'll hav'ta come to supper one night soon."

"I'd like that—and I appreciate the advice." Noah nodded, and Dan returned to his family.

Soon he'd perform the marriage ceremony of Rand Kessler and Mrs. Morgan—his first wedding. His stomach swirled at the thought, but not enough to make him set aside the plate of delicious food. He spooned in a bit of mashed turnips, almost yellow from the butter that had been added. He never would have thought that he would preside over his first funeral and wedding, one day apart.

Leaning against the side of the church, he finished his food as he watched friends and families joining together on old quilts to eat and converse. The sun shone bright overhead in a clear sky, but not so much to make the day too hot to enjoy. Children raced around the outskirts of the crowd, chasing one another, laughing, and having fun. A boy held up a garden snake, and Abby Davis let out a shrill scream that turned heads. Noah chuckled. He'd rarely felt so at home in a town.

A peace and contentment he'd never encountered, other than when he first gave his heart to God, wafted through him. An acceptance that filled a hollow place deep within. He wanted to stay in Lookout. To live here. To marry Jackie.

But he needed to tell folks the truth about his past before he could realize that dream.

He just needed a little more time.

Jack hurried down the street after passing a fussy Andrew back to her ma. She hadn't wanted to go in Mrs. Linus's house so soon after seeing Bertha Boyd's dead body, so she checked on her ma from the front porch and passed her brother through the doorway. Jack had covered a lot of stories for the paper, but rarely did they ever include a dead person. Mrs. Linus must be brave to stay in the house after all that had happened.

Jack's stomach growled, and she picked up her steps. She could see the townsfolk gathered in the lot next to the church and sure hoped there'd be some food left. If she'd been smart, she'd have asked someone to save her a plate.

She couldn't quit thinking about Noah's message. Having always been independent and resourceful, she had a tendency to act without thinking. As a child, thanks to her willful streak, she'd done pretty much what she wanted. No wonder her mother had been so frustrated with her back then. Under Luke's guidance, she learned to find joy in pleasing her mother, but she still fought stubbornness and the desire to do things on impulse.

She believed in God, but she hadn't prayed about her future, other than a few frantic pleas for help or guidance on occasion, like when Andrew almost died. She hadn't sought God first in her daily life, but Noah had helped her see the need to change that.

How could she make such an important decision like going to Dallas or staying here to see how things worked out with Noah without God's guidance?

A man suddenly jogged out from between two houses. Yanked from her musings, Jack jumped. A nut brown hat was pulled down low, blocking his face, and he strode purposely toward her. The only times she'd ever been truly frightened had been in her own home when her other pa was alive and when her ma had been kidnapped by an outlaw, but with all the robberies and now a murder, her nerves had a hair trigger. Jack glanced around for a rock or stick for defense, but then she recognized the man's walk—Billy.

Horse feathers.

She didn't want to argue with him again about getting married. That would never happen. She moved away from him, hurrying her steps, but he broke into a run, then skidded to a halt, blocking her way. Jack sighed, her doubts rising about there being any food left except for Margie Mann's baked beets, which everyone but newcomers knew not to touch. Since she couldn't get away from Billy, she might as well be cordial. "Where have you been? I haven't seen you all week."

He pushed his hat up his forehead and grinned. "Did you miss me?"

Well, she'd walked right into that quagmire. "I just noticed you weren't around. Why weren't you helping your ma in the store so she could get ready for her wedding?" Jack crossed her arms and tapped her toe. Her cordialness hadn't lasted long, but she had little patience with Billy, especially when he was standing between her and her dinner.

A frown replaced his smile. "I don't wanna be a storekeeper. It's boring."

"What do you want to do? If you don't run the store, how will you make a living?"

He shoved his hands in his pockets and lifted his chin. "I've got ways. And I got me a place to stay. I ain't goin' to that ranch."

Jack's stomach complained about its empty state. She stepped sideways, but Billy matched her efforts. "I want to eat, Billy, before the food's gone and the wedding starts."

"Come with me first. I got something to show you."

Jack flung out her arms, wishing he'd leave her alone. "There isn't time. I had to take Andrew back to Ma, and now I want to eat."

"Who's Andrew?"

Jack stared at him. "He's my new baby brother, remember?"

He shrugged, as if it were of no importance. She scowled and noticed his clothes. His tan shirt was wrinkled and stained, and his pants and boots dusty. "Is that what you're wearing to the wedding?"

He glanced down and swiped his hand across his thigh. "Ain't goin'."

"Billy! That's just plain mean. Your ma will be so hurt."

His steely blue eyes flashed. "She should have thought of that before she agreed to marry that man."

"What's wrong with him? He's got a nice ranch, and from what I hear, a big house. He can provide for your ma. She won't have to work so hard—and besides, they're happy together. I don't understand you and Tessa."

He yanked his hands out of his pockets and shoved them on his hips. "Tessa wants to live in town, not all alone on that ranch—even if she's taken a likin' to one of the cowboys out there. And I don't want that man bossing me around. I ain't a kid no more."

Jack pinched her lips together. She didn't know what to say to him. She just wanted to eat. "I'm leaving now. All the food's probably gone already." She picked up her skirts and dashed to the left. When he slid in that direction, she darted back to the right—and almost made it.

He grabbed hold of her arm, jerking her to a halt. "I've got us a place, Jack. I want you to come see it."

She almost groaned out loud. "I can't. I need to help Papa watch the young'uns, and I—want—to—eat." She emphasized each of the last four words. As she pulled away from him, her hands came down hard on her waist, and she felt something stiff in her pocket. "Oh, yeah." She pulled out the bracelet Billy had given her and held it out to him. "Here. I can't keep this."

He stared down at the shiny silver bangle reflecting in the sunlight. "I don't want that back. I bought it for you."

"It's not proper for me to take presents from you. We aren't courting."

Billy's eyes narrowed. "You're gonna marry me, even if I have to force you."

Of all the nerve! She jerked her arm, but he wouldn't let go. She'd never been truly afraid of him before, but today, something menacing darkened his blue eyes. Still, she wouldn't be forced to do anything, especially marry him, not when she was within shouting distance of most of the town. She fluffed up her bravado. "No, I'm not. And don't forget my papa is the marshal. He won't take kindly to your threatening me."

He glared back. Then his gaze darted past her. His brows lifted, and he let go and smiled, albeit without his normal charm. "We shall see," he said through clenched teeth.

She needed to tell Luke about Billy's odd behavior, but she kept forgetting. Issuing threats about forcing her to marry was carrying things way too far. Stepping out of his reach, she peered over her shoulder to see what had distracted Billy. A man rode down thc street, watching them. The relief she felt at the stranger's arrival made her knees weak. A beam of sunlight reflected off the star on his vest. A Texas Ranger.

"I gotta go, but this ain't over." Billy swung around and hurried back between the houses.

The ranger stopped his horse beside her and touched the end of his hat in greeting. He glanced in the direction Billy had fled; then his kind gray eyes looked her over. She couldn't see his upper lip because of his large mustache. "You all right, ma'am?"

She nodded and put the bracelet back in her pocket. She couldn't help wondering how forceful Billy might have gotten.

"I'm looking for Marshal Davis. Could you direct me to him?"

Jack smiled. "I sure can. He's my stepfather."

The ranger dismounted. "Martin Carlisle, ma'am. Me and Luke were friends in the army."

"It's a pleasure to meet you, Ranger Carlisle." She waved toward the end of the street. "I reckon you can hear all the noise. We're having a church social and then a wedding."

He fell in step beside her, leading his gray horse. Sweat ringed his old brown hat, and his clothes didn't look a whole lot better than Billy's. "Maybe I can get me a bite to eat at this social."

"I sure hope so. I was just on my way back there and was thinking the same thing."

"It's none of my business, ma'am, but don't let that man get rough with you."

Jack nodded. Billy's harsh grasp on her arm had hurt and reminded her of the times her first pa would sometimes grab hold of her if she didn't obey fast enough. When he was in a fair mood, he never paid her any attention, nor did he ever hug her or bring her a present when he'd been away. He had promised he would, and she always hoped he might, but he never did. Not once. He was a liar—a mean man who hurt women and children. She had a feeling whoever married Billy might suffer the same pain she had as a child.

The ranger walked beside her, leading his horse, his gaze focused on the crowd as they drew near. She glanced at the gun in his holster. Maybe she needed to start carrying a weapon—a derringer—because she'd never let another man treat her like her father had.

Noah stood on the outskirts of the crowd, holding an empty plate and talking to Mr. Mann. At least she didn't have to doubt Noah. She had at first when he wouldn't talk about his past, but many people had things in their past that hurt to remember or they were ashamed of. She rarely ever talked about her first father or what he'd done. At least with Noah being a Christian and a minister, she'd never have to doubt his word.

Carly stood on the edge of the field where folks had laid out their quilts and watched the children playing. The younger ones, their bellies full of their mamas' cooking, played with less enthusiasm than they had when church had first let out. She watched Alan and Abby playing hopscotch for a few minutes, making sure the rambunctious children were behaving. Several older girls sat in a cluster together, chatting and making chains of clover flowers. She'd never once made one. Didn't even know how they hooked those long stems and white flowers together. She swiped her hand in the air at a pesky fly and chased it away.

As far back as she could remember, she had helped her mama wash clothes from sunup to sundown. Hauling water, carving soap chips, squeezing clothes, and hanging them up, then taking them down later to be ironed and folded. Even today, she couldn't resist shuddering when Rachel needed help with the laundry. She'd rather clean a privy.

Would life have been different if she'd had a father? Would her mama still have had to work so hard? Would she?

Pressing her lips together, she blew a heavy breath out her nose. She would never know—and wishing life were different wouldn't change the past. But she could hope the future would be different.

She scanned a crowd of men standing near the horses and wagons and found Garrett beside Luke. They stood with a half dozen others in a rough circle. One man raised his fist, and though she couldn't hear the words, she suspected they were talking about the murder. Everybody had been talking about it. From what Rachel had said, it was the first that had ever taken place in Lookout.

Garrett glanced in her direction and winked. She smiled back, feeling heat warm her cheeks that had nothing to do with the sun. Two women dressed in calico and sunbonnets walked between her and Garrett. One lady glanced at her and scowled, then leaned toward her friend and said something.

Her smile fading, Carly looked away, feeling the brunt of their silent censure. She zigzagged her way through the groups of families, back to the Davises' quilt, wishing Rachel had come or that Jack would return. She smiled a thank-you to Mrs. Castleby for keeping an eye on Emmie while she slept on the quilt.

After sitting and rearranging her skirt, Carly leaned her head back against one of the few trees shading the field. Her eyes drifted shut, and she yawned. Taking a nap right about now would be nice, but the wedding was soon to start. The steady hum of conversation lulled her into a limp state, and her whole body relaxed, her arms felt as heavy as leg irons.

On the other side of the old oak tree, two women chatted about a recipe, but she tried to ignore them. She lifted up a heavy hand and swatted at a mosquito that landed on Emmie's calf. She sighed. If only she knew more people.

"What'dya think about that murder—and those break-ins? Ghastly, aren't they?" one lady behind her said. Carly stiffened.

"Yes, it's getting so that a decent woman's afraid to walk the streets of Lookout these days."

Carly rolled her eyes at the woman's exaggeration.

"Well, if'n you ask me, I think it was that female outlaw. All these appalling things didn't happen until after she came back to Lookout."

Carly gasped, their cruel words breaking her fragile hope. Unable to listen to any more nattering, she pushed up from the quilt. Her heart ached. Would these people never accept her? Couldn't they see she'd changed?

She scooped Emmie up in her arms and looked for Luke. She noticed Garrett instead, talking to Mr. Howard, and made a beeline for him. He smiled in her direction. Mr. Howard turned his head, looking right at her, and one brow lifted. But instead of censure in his gaze she saw surprise, then his mouth curved up in a grin. Too bad Leah had left earlier to go feed her baby. At least she and Carly had something in common.

Garrett leaned toward Mr. Howard, who nodded. Then Garrett walked toward her. His smile dipped. "Is something wrong?"

Carly shrugged, unable to explain her unease. He'd lived in this town his whole life. How could she expect him to understand how badly the woman's unjustified accusations had hurt?

"I thought I'd take Emmie home. The sun is moving toward our quilt, and I don't want her to get a sunburn."

"But what about the wedding?"

Carly shrugged. "I don't know those folks gettin' married, other than she owns the store, and he once hoped to marry Rachel and also your brother's wife—before she married Mark, of course."

Garrett leaned toward her and waggled his blond brows, his blue eyes sparking with mischief, somewhat soothing the pain the callous women had inflicted. "Don't you want to get some ideas for our weddin'?"

"You don't wanna marry me." Tears stung her eyes, frustrating her. She never cried—not even when Luke had hauled her to jail all those years ago. Not even when her brother sat in the cell next to hers, giving her the skunk eye and blaming her for his capture, for hours on end. Only Luke's threats to gag Ty and hog-tie him made him finally shut up.

Garrett grabbed her elbow and hauled her toward the edge of the crowd. Folks gawked at her as if she'd done something wrong or was trying to steal Luke's young'un. Standing between two wagons, so that nobody could see them, he dropped her arm and shoved his hands to his hips. "Why would you say that? I wouldn't have asked to court you if I didn't intend on marryin' you."

Carly shifted Emmie to her other arm. The girl was small, but heavy.

"Let me hold her."

"No, I need to take her home. Could you tell Luke and then help him keep an eye out for Alan and Abby until Jacqueline returns?"

"Don't think I didn't notice you changed the subject."

A horse behind Carly nickered, as if asking for a handout. Why couldn't Garrett just let her go without causing a ruckus? "I prayed and thought God gave me the go-ahead, but I'm foolin' myself to think we could ever marry."

"Why?" His face crinkled up, making him look as if he'd been sucking on lemons. "Am I too old for you? Is that it?"

"What?" Carly blinked, confused at his question. In truth, he didn't look anywhere near forty. His shoulders and arms were muscled from lifting crates of cargo for years, and his blond hair wasn't thinning or turning white. He no longer favored the arm he got shot in or wore the sling. He didn't look overly old at all. "No. I've never thought that."

She nibbled on her lower lip and stared at the closest vehicle. The black paint of the spring wagon was partly worn off, revealing the grayed wood underneath. Stuffing hung out one corner of the padded front bench. Right now, she felt as worn out as the buggy. "It's just that. . .can't I tell you later? Emmie's really getting heavy."

He rubbed his nape, then scratched the back of his head. "I guess so."

"You'll let Luke know I've got Emmie and to watch out for the other young'uns?"

He nodded, but he didn't look too pleased. "Luke's talking

with that ranger over there." He nudged his chin to the right. "Stay here for a minute and let me run and tell him; then I can carry Emmie and escort you back home."

Carly offered him a weak smile. "Thank you, but that isn't necessary. The wedding will be starting soon, and you need to be here."

"Just wait." He held up his hands, palms out, then backed away. "I'll be right back."

Carly watched him jog off, her heart already feeling his loss. She'd dared to dream of marriage and family—of having a permanent home—but she should have known dreams don't come true for people like her. Folks would always think of her as an outlaw. Hadn't those women proved that?

Batting her burning eyes, she wove between the haphazardly parked wagons and buggies, down the street toward the boardinghouse. She shifted Emmie to her shoulder to relieve her shaking arm and patted the child's back.

Maybe it was best for all if she just moved on to another town.

Chapter 29

Jack sat in the church pew for the second time that day, cocooned by her family. Holding Abby, who was nearly asleep, Ma sat on her left, while Alan leaned against Jack's right side, kicking one leg and pouting at having to come back to church again when he'd rather play with his friends. Luke proudly jiggled Andrew, alternating between staring at his newest son and watching the wedding. Even the ranger who'd come to see Luke had decided to attend the wedding after getting his fill of food and sat on the far end of the pew.

A sense of peace—of belonging—wrapped around Jack. How could she even consider leaving her family?

Noah's voice rumbled through the room as he read the vows to Christine Morgan and Rand Kessler, who each recited them in turn. Noah stood straight and tall, his voice confident, but she knew he was nervous about marrying his first couple. She closed her eyes and said the vows along with Mrs. Morgan—only she was saying them to Noah.

Somewhere in the past few days, she'd taken a turn. Dallas no longer held her fascination. Being an ace reporter in the big city had lost most of its attraction, although she hoped to continue to work for Jenny. She had written a letter to the *Dallas Morning News*, declining the job, but she had yet to mail it. Part of her dreaded turning it down. The other part felt at peace with staying in Lookout, but she would continue to pray about it before making a final decision. And how could she possibly think of leaving town until things were settled with Noah?

Was she making a huge mistake? Throwing away her dream just when it was within her reach?

Or had her dream changed? Caring for Noah wasn't something she'd planned or sought after. It just happened—more quickly than she ever would have believed possible. From the first time her eyes had collided with his, she'd felt that connection. Almost as if he'd come to town just for her.

But that was silly. He simply came for the job and had no former knowledge of her.

"Would you please bow your heads as I ask God's blessing on this couple?" Noah's voice pulled her back from her musings. With one hand on Christine Morgan's shoulder and the other on Rand Kessler's, he ducked his head and started praying.

Jack caught a glimpse of the thick black hair on the top of Noah's head, and her fingers moved, aching to touch it. She blew out a heavy sigh. Her ma glanced at her, then closed her eyes again. Jack bowed her head. Why couldn't she concentrate on the wedding instead of Noah?

Because she had to know if she was just having her first severe case of infatuation or if she was truly falling in love. But how could one know the difference?

Noah was kind, brave, handsome, and made her feel things she'd never wanted a man to make her feel. He reminded her of Luke. Both men were honorable, truthful. Tall. But was she only attracted to Noah because he resembled Luke in so many ways?

She needed to talk to someone. Jenny was too jaded. Penny had never been in love. And Tessa—well, she definitely couldn't ask Tessa. Noah said, "Amen," and Jack glanced at her ma. Maybe it was time they had a heart-to-heart talk.

"Mr. Kessler, you may kiss your bride."

Rand's smile was as wide as all of Texas. A rosy red stained Mrs. Kessler's cheeks. The groom ducked down, paused to gaze into his wife's eyes, then kissed her. Masculine cheers resounded throughout the room.

Jack looked at Noah. He was staring directly at her, a gentle smile pulling at one side of his mouth. She'd kissed that mouth. Her pulse leapt. And she hoped to do it again. Was it shameless of her to enjoy kissing him? To feel completely safe and cherished locked within the minister's strong arms?

No, not the minister—the man.

Noah.

The couple quit kissing, but their fervent smiles remained. Noah held out his hand toward the newly married couple. "Ladies and gentlemen, it's my pleasure to present to you Mr. and Mrs. Randall Leland Kessler."

The room filled with cheers and clapping. Abby jerked awake, staring with unfocused eyes. Andrew slept contentedly in his father's arms. Jack, overwhelmed with emotion, hugged Alan, but the boy pulled away.

"Don't we get to eat cake now?" he asked.

Carly changed out of her Sunday dress into her cooler calico. She peeked in the girls' bedroom to check on Emmie. The child slept contentedly, curled on top of her bed. She pulled the door almost shut, in case someone returned with the other children before Emmie woke up; then Carly tiptoed downstairs.

She half-expected Garrett to come knocking on the boarding-house door, but it was probably best he stayed at the wedding. It wouldn't look right for them to be home alone and nobody else around. Carly opened the front door, unable to hold back a contemptuous snort. People could hardly think much worse of her if they were blaming her for thefts and murder. She laid a hand over her chest. Knowing someone believed that about her cut her to the quick.

She dropped down into a rocker below the girls' open window, knowing Emmie would cry out for someone once she woke up. Not a soul walked down Main Street, although as usual, several horses were hitched in front of the Wet Your Whistle.

Closing her eyes, she pushed the rocker into motion and prayed about what to do. She longed to race upstairs, pack her bags, and flee the vicious gossip as if she were running from an angry posse. Faced with the chance of possibly losing Garrett, she knew without a doubt that she wanted to stay, to marry him, and raise a family, but how could she if folks continued to spread rumors? Her husband and children would suffer. Her whole body felt as if she were being split apart.

Tears burned her eyes, frustrating her even more. She swatted at them and wiped her cheek on her shoulder. "What should I do, Lord?"

She spent the next few minutes praying, but no answer came. Maybe she was making too big a deal of things. It had only been the two women talking, after all, and once the marshal figured out who was doing the break-ins and solved the murder, surely talk would die down. Until then, she could stick close to the boardinghouse. There. She felt better thinking things through and praying about the situation.

Loud cheers erupted from the direction of church. So the wedding was over. That meant folks would be walking down the street back to their homes. She opened her eyes, and her heart leapt into her throat.

Two cowboys stood just on the other side of the porch, leering at her. One was leaning on the rail. His mouth lifted in a grin, but his eyes remained cold. "Well, look what we have here, Buck."

The tall, thin man named Buck scowled at the other. "Why'd you have'ta go and use my name, Laredo? That was a dumb thang t'do."

Laredo rolled his gray eyes, then glared at Carly again. For the first time since her return to Lookout, she wished she was armed. But she hadn't carried a gun since her outlaw days.

"If it ain't our local jailbird." Buck smirked, sending shivers racing through her.

Laredo stroked his mustache. "We cain't have her kind in our good town, now can we?"

She pushed up from the rocker and rushed to the front door, nearly tripping as her skirts grabbed her legs. Scuffling sounded behind her, but she didn't look. She twisted the doorknob, then she was jerked into Laredo's arms. With one arm around her waist, he hauled her backward off the porch.

Help me, Lord. She couldn't let him take her and leave Emmie all alone. Her heart fluttered like the wings of a newly caged bird as he dragged her down the steps. She lifted her arm, then brought it down in a swift jab, elbowing him in the side. His breath whooshed past her left ear, but he didn't let go.

"Git her." Buck danced in the street, flapping his arms like a chicken with clipped wings.

Laredo lifted her off the ground, and Carly lifted one leg and kicked back. Laredo cried out and dropped her. The fall jarred her whole body, rattling her teeth. The smooth *shush* of a gun being drawn drew her gaze up. Laredo aimed his pistol at her chest.

Garrett sat in the church, as close to the door as he could. If Rand hadn't been a good friend, he would have skipped the wedding altogether. Why hadn't Carly waited on him? Why had she called off their courting when she'd been happy and hanging on his arm earlier?

Had she become upset because he'd been talking with some of the men instead of sitting on the quilt with her after dinner? Well, tough. He was a man, and men liked to see one another and catch up on the latest news about livestock and new inventions. She'd just have to understand that.

Instantly, he regretted his harsh thought and that he wasn't paying attention. He bowed his head as Noah offered prayer for the couple. Garrett had hoped his wedding would be next. It might have taken him by surprise to realize he had feelings for Carly, but once he did, there was no turning back. He'd just have to figure out how to change her mind.

He winced as he watched Rand kiss his bride. Too bad it wasn't him and Carly up there. He was tired of living alone.

Noah introduced the newly married couple, and everyone stood and cheered. Garrett dashed out the door. He could visit Carly, straighten things out, and then come back and congratulate the Kesslers.

He wove through the bevy of wagons, sending up a prayer.

Lord, You know I believe in You. I don't often ask You for help, but I'm asking today. Change Carly's heart. Let her see I'm serious about this marrying business. I promise we'll be in church each Sunday—'less we're sick.

Eager to see her, he quickened his steps. He cleared the wagons, then noticed a commotion in the street in front of the boardinghouse. Two men were attacking a woman. He sucked in a breath. Not Carly!

Garrett broke into a run. *Help me to help her, Lord.*

He could handle two men—as long as neither pulled a gun. One man had his back to Garrett while the other wrestled with Carly. She elbowed the man, but he didn't let go. She reached up and grabbed hold of the man's hair.

Garrett suddenly darted between Polly's and Dolly's hideous purple house and the Castlebys' fancy home, as if pulled by an invisible hand. He slowed his steps, and an idea forged in his mind. He ran around the banker's home and in the back door of the boardinghouse.

Luke kept a rifle and extra gun in his bedroom. Garrett snatched the gun from its spot on top of the wardrobe where Luke had placed it after he first bought it. He hurried down the hall to the front door and slowly opened it, hating the time he wasted but knowing he needed a weapon if he and Carly were both going to survive.

The men had her almost to the end of the porch. Garrett raced through the parlor and climbed out the open window on the side of the house, then stepped out from behind a bush. Carly sat on the ground, her back to him, staring up at a gun.

"Laredo, look out." The thin man who'd been watching the other man struggle with Carly reached for his gun.

Garrett aimed and fired, completely missing his target. Thank the good Lord the man was a slow draw. Aiming with a steadier hand, he hit the man in the shoulder, just as his gun left his holster. The man yelled and fell to the ground, dropping his gun and grabbing his arm. Garrett's eyes swiveled to the other man, and his heart all but stopped. Laredo held his gun to Carly's head.

"Move, and she's dead, mister."

Chapter 30

Carly's gaze lifted to Garrett's. His beautiful blue eyes held an apology—and more. He was sincerely concerned for her.

The man he'd shot rolled on the ground and howled like a hunting dog. "He'p me, L'rado. I hurt."

She could feel her captor's chest rise and fall as his breathing quickened. With Laredo's arm crushing her just below her breasts, she could barely breathe. He loosened his grip for a second, then hoisted her up, closer to him than before. The gun pressed hard to her temple, forcing it sideways. Hurting. Bruising.

She didn't want to die.

She wanted the dream.

She wanted to live in Lookout and marry Garrett.

"That wedding's over. People will be swarming the streets any minute." Garrett's gaze and his voice hardened. "You'd best just let her go and take your friend and git."

Carly could sense the man's uncertainty. She could almost smell his indecision. She swallowed hard.

"My cousin is the marshal, you know. He won't take kindly to your harming that woman."

"She's nothin' but an outlaw—a jailbird."

Garrett winced, and Carly wondered why. But then she knew. He'd thought the same thing not so long ago. Had his feelings truly changed?

Her gaze snagged his, and she found her answer there. She couldn't explain how it had happened, but he'd come to care for her—and that made her want to livc.

She wouldn't let this man steal her life and her future. She flicked her gaze downward, then back up to Garrett's, and did it again. He frowned. She wiggled one finger of the arm crushed to her side. His gaze dropped down.

Buck groaned. "I'm dyin'. I need a doctor."

"Shut up. It's just a shoulder wound." Laredo's unsympathetic words rushed past Carly's ear. "Get up. And get the horses."

"If he does, I'll shoot him in the leg," Garrett growled.

"Nooo, I cain't walk if'n you do that."

"I'll shoot him myself if he don't git up." Laredo moved the gun away from her head and pointed it at his cohort. "Get up, Buck, and hurry."

With the gun gone, Carly wiggled her finger again. Garrett watched.

She lifted her index finger.

Then the middle one.

And then her ring finger.

Suddenly she went completely limp.

"What the—" Taken off guard, Laredo loosened his hold, and Carly slipped free.

A gun blasted—then another. The stench of gunpowder rent the air, leaving behind a cloud of gray. Laredo yelled and fell back. Carly sat on the ground, head ducked down.

She was afraid to look.

Afraid Garrett would be dead.

Strong, gentle arms lifted her up, and Garrett pressed her against his left side, keeping his gun trained on her attackers. Her arms wrapped around his waist and held tight. He was alive!

"Shh. . .you're safe now." Garrett patted her back and pressed his cheek against her head.

Tears of joy poured from her eyes like a river, dampening his shirt. She never wanted to move.

"You're marrying me, and I won't take no for an answer." Garrett kissed her head. "What happened back at the church that made you say you didn't want to court me?"

She shrugged. He gently set her back from him, and shame made her duck her head. "Two women were talkin'. They said the r–robberies and m–murder were my fault."

Garrett stiffened and lifted her chin with one finger. "You listen to me, Carly. That's a bald-faced lie. People will always talk, but you don't have to take to heart what they say, darlin'. Maybe you were a robber a long time ago, but you've changed. God changed you and set you free from the past. You served your time, and now you're a free woman—in more ways than one."

She studied his face, encouraged by his sincerity. "You're right. I am a child of God. When I gave my heart to Him, He washed me white as snow. It's as if I never sinned."

Pounding footsteps and shouts sounded down the street and drew nearer. Garrett glanced that way, then nodded. "That's right. You're no more of an outlaw than I am."

Buck moaned, but Laredo endured his pain and failure in silence. Carly peeked at them, then saw Luke and a dozen other men running toward them. She hated for this time with Garrett to end.

He pulled her behind the shrub, where they were partially hidden. "It's true that I used to despise you, Carly. I won't lie. Your brother kidnapped Rachel, you pretended to be one of the mail-order brides, and for all I knew, you two planned everything just so you could rob the bank. God changed my heart. I don't know how or when, but He did. I care for you."

He didn't say he loved her, but they hadn't been courting very long. All she knew was that she felt the same. "After I got to know Shannon and Leah, I despised you and your brother for what you'd done to them." She shook her head. "How could you order your cousin three brides?"

Garrett grinned. The footsteps stopped, and the rumble of men's voices floated their way. "I wanted to get his mind off of Rachel, and if only one bride had shown up, he'd have just sent her packing. Besides, I wanted to give him a choice."

"It had the opposite effect, you know. Having those other women competing for him made him realize how much he still loved Rachel." Carly shook her head and smiled. "You're a rascal, you know it?"

"I know."

She smacked him on the chest, but then her heart stilled. He lowered his head and kissed her. Warm sensations zinged through her body, and she tightened her grip on his shirt.

A man cleared his throat, and they jumped apart. Carly lifted her hands to her blazing cheeks.

"Guess I'm going to have to lock you two up for public indecency." Luke grinned. "Care to tell me what happened?"

"We're getting married, and those two"—Garrett waved his gun toward the men on the ground—"tried to break us up."

Luke's brow lifted.

Garrett sobered, all teasing aside. "They attacked Carly. One man looked bent on hauling her off somewhere."

Carly ducked her head. "He said they didn't need my kind here."

Garrett held the gun out to Luke. "Here, thanks for letting me borrow this. I owe you a few bullets, Cuz." He wrapped his arm around Carly and tugged her close. "It's *their* kind we don't need, darlin'."

~

Jack longed to run down the street after the men and see what the gunshots had been about, but she couldn't. She and the rest of the women and children were huddled in a group behind the church, while their menfolk stood guard and waited for Luke and the other half-dozen men to check out what that gunfire had been about. The ladies talked in hushed voices, speculating on what had happened. Tired children fussed, unhappy at being corralled after sitting through church and the wedding.

And the bride stood patiently holding her groom's hand, while in his other hand he held a rifle someone had tossed him.

Jack remembered the stormy day her ma and Luke were married. A tornado hit right after the wedding, sending people scattering, and taking much of the store with it as it roared through town.

Leah Howard stood next to Jack's ma, holding her baby, the rest of her little ones hanging on to her skirt or standing nearby. "What do suppose happened?"

"I don't know, but at least we haven't heard any more gunshots." Her ma lifted Andrew to her shoulder and bounced him.

"Maybe there was another break-in"—Callie Howard leaned toward Jack—"or murder."

"I hope not." Jack studied Callie. She was a pretty girl—only a few years younger than Jack. They'd played together some when they were younger, but Callie had generally been busy tending her siblings and helping her stepmother. Now that Jack had younger brothers and sisters, she had more compassion for the other woman.

Abby suddenly jerked on Jack's hand, trying to get free. "Let go, Sissy."

Ma latched onto Abby's shoulder. "You hold still, young lady, or you'll be in trouble when we get home."

Abby's lower lip popped out. Her brother, holding Jack's other hand, chuckled. Abby lunged toward him. Jack almost jerked her sister's arm out of its socket, trying to keep her away from Alan.

Her ma sighed. Jack knew she'd only planned to come to the wedding because Christine was such a good friend. Most women who'd given birth so recently wouldn't have.

"You look exhausted, Ma." Jack stared at her mother's pinched face. "You want me to hold Andy?"

"I rested all morning at Agatha's, but now that I've been on my feet awhile, I am getting a little tired, and I'm worried about Emmie and Carly."

"Those shots sounded as if they were close." They shared a worried look then went back to watching the road where they'd last seen Luke.

Carrying a rifle, Noah walked around the outside of the crowd with the men who were guarding the women. He looked uncomfortable with the weapon, and Jack wondered if he even knew how to shoot it. She could teach him, if he didn't. Luke had made sure she knew how to protect herself.

Her heart pounded harder, just thinking of standing close and teaching him how to aim a rifle. She thought about his kisses.

They made her feel cherished, special. What would it be like to be married to a kind, gentle man like Noah?

Two men walked past Polly's and Dolly's house, waving their rifles. "All is well," one of them shouted.

The women exhaled a uniform sigh of relief and started moving toward the wagons. Jack was ready to get out of the sun, as she was certain the others were.

Abby jerked again. "I wanna go see Papa."

Ma glanced down. "Stay with your sister. Your father is probably busy."

"Aww. . ." Abby pasted a frown on her face again.

As they passed the Dykstras' purple house, her ma gasped. Jack gazed down the road, her heart nearly jumping from her chest. Luke stood in front of their house, and two men lay in the street. But where was Carly? And Emmie?

She suddenly remembered the time outlaws had kidnapped her ma. Jack dropped her siblings' hands and broke into a run. She had to make sure Emmie was safe.

"Jacqueline!" her mother cried.

"Wait for me, Sissy!" Abby's little feet pounded behind hers.

"What happened, Papa?" Jack skidded to a stop beside Luke. She quickly studied the scene. Two wounded men sat on the ground. Doc Phillips was tending one of them, and the ranger squatted next to the other, questioning him while Jenny took notes. Garrett stood off to the side, pacing. The stench of gunpowder still clung to the air.

Luke snagged Abby's arm as she ran toward one of the strangers. "The children don't need to see this. Take them inside, Half Bit."

Jack winced at Luke's scolding. She should have thought of that herself. "Where's Emmie and Carly? Are they all right?"

"Inside." He nudged his chin toward home. "They're both fine."

She sensed there was more to the story, but maybe Carly could satisfy her curiosity.

"Why's them two men bleedin'?" Abby asked.

Luke passed her to Jack, his brow lifted in an I-told-you-so smirk. She didn't waste time but spun around and headed toward the porch. Alan ran past her, but Ma snapped her fingers, and he jerked to a halt. He glanced back at the men. Luke merely pointed at the house, and Alan's shoulders dropped.

"Ahh. . .can't I watch? I'm gonna be a lawman some day."

"Go inside with your ma, Son."

Alan turned and dragged his toes all the way to the porch, kicking dust on his shoes. Abby wiggled to get down, and Jack set her on the steps. Ma held the door open, not giving either child the option of disobeying.

Jack blew out a breath. She wanted to watch, too, but Jenny would get the story—and Jack really didn't care, other than wanting to know why those men were shot so close to her home. She closed the door.

Carly came down the stairs and lifted a finger to her lips. "Emmie is still asleep."

"If you two wouldn't mind seeing to the other children, it's time for Andrew and me to take a rest." Ma brushed the hair that had come loose from her bun off her forehead with the back of her wrist. She looked exhausted.

"Can I help you with anything?" Jack offered.

Ma shook her head, but then stopped. "If you wouldn't mind changing Andy's diaper and putting him in a fresh gown, I'd appreciate it."

Jack took the baby. "Of course I don't mind."

"I'll tend to the other children. You just get a good rest." Carly took hold of Abby's and Alan's hands and led both children toward the stairs. "Just be mindful that Emmie is sleeping."

The kids clomped up the stairs only slightly less noisily than normal. Jack smiled. "Carly's doing better at getting those two to obey her."

Her ma dropped down onto the bed and exhaled a sigh. She yawned. "I probably should have stayed home today, but I wanted to comfort Agatha and attend the wedding."

Jack laid Andrew on the bed. He raised his fist, brushing his cheek, and his head turned toward it, mouth open. He licked his fist, then scrunched up his face when he didn't find what he wanted. Jack chuckled and quickly fastened on a dry diaper. "I think someone is hungry."

"Not me, that's for sure." Ma shed her Sunday dress and petticoat and climbed into bed. "I hope I can stay awake long enough to feed him."

Jack handed the baby to Ma. "Don't worry about anything, because Carly and I will be here. You can rest all day."

"That sounds nice. Thank you." Ma's eyes shut as Andrew began his lunch.

Jack closed the bedroom door and hurried toward the front of the house. Since Carly and the children were still upstairs, Jack stepped outside and surveyed the scene. In her rush to get home, she'd forgotten the platter and pie tins she was supposed to bring home from the social. She walked over to the crowd that had gathered and watched. Luke had the two men on their feet. The tall, thin man was whining worse than Abby ever did, but the handsomer one kept silent, his head hanging down. She thought she might have seen them around town before, but she wasn't certain.

Knowing she needed to get back to help Carly, she headed toward the church, content to wait to hear the story from Luke. Halfway there, she met the Kesslers coming down the street in their buggy. The engaging smiles on their faces made them both look younger. Tessa sat in the backseat, her face scrunched up in a scowl, arms crossed. She didn't even acknowledge Jack.

"Did you find out what happened?" Rand slowed the buggy.

"No, I had to help with the children, but two men over there have been shot."

"You know 'em?" Rand asked.

Jack shook her head. "Might have seen them in town before, but that's all. I meant to congratulate you two, but then the shooting stirred things up."

"Thank you." Mrs. Kessler turned toward her on the seat. "It was so nice of Rachel to attend after so recently having her baby."

"She wanted to. She is so happy for you both."

Tessa sent Jack a chilly glare.

"Well, guess we'll be on our way." Mrs. Kessler started to face the front then glanced back at Jack. "I'll be in town on Saturdays for a while to open the store—at least until I find a buyer." She peeked at Tessa, as if the thought of having to sell because her children didn't want the mercantile bothered her.

"I'll spread the word."

Rand nodded his thanks, smacked the leather traces on the horse's back, and the buggy rolled forward. Jack couldn't help wishing that she and Noah were the ones riding off together.

Resuming her walk, she shoved her hands in her pocket and felt the forgotten bracelet. *Horse feathers.*

What was she going to do with that thing?

Suddenly an idea burst into her mind.

She spun around and raced to catch the buggy. Thankfully, Rand had stopped it near the crowd of spectators. Jack jogged toward it and stopped on Mrs. Kessler's side of the buggy.

"Mrs. Kessler, I forgot something."

She turned away from the crowd and smiled. "What is it, Jacqueline?"

She pulled the bracelet from her pocket, and the silver glistened in the sunlight. Tessa leaned forward to get a look.

Mrs. Kessler gasped and reached for the bangle. "Where did you get that?"

Luke walked up to Rand and shook his hand but obviously noticed Mrs. Kessler's reaction. He glanced at Jack, brows lifted, probably wondering the same thing.

"Billy gave it to me. He's still trying to get me to marry him, but I told him I can't. I don't care for him the way a woman does her husband. I tried to give it back, but he refused to take it and got angry at me."

Mrs. Kessler fell back against the seat, unable to take her eyes off the bracelet. Jack couldn't imagine what would cause such a reaction.

Rand put his arm around his wife's shoulder. "What's wrong, honey?"

She held out the piece of jewelry. "This was one of the items stolen from the mercantile the morning of the robbery."

Chapter 31

Jack paced the parlor, waiting for her parents to finish tucking in the children for the night. Carly and Garrett had gone out walking, and Noah had been invited to supper with the Manns. She needed to talk to her folks while everyone else was occupied. The newest edition of the *Lookout Ledger* would be available tomorrow afternoon, and she had to tell them about the new hotel.

What would it mean to her family? Would they still have guests come and stay? Would they have to close their doors?

She twisted her hands, hating to be the one to break the news to them.

The railroad coming to town was a good thing, since it would bring growth and new businesses, cut down on travel times, bring more people to town, but the hotel. . .

Too many things were changing. She dropped down on the edge of the chair. Maybe she should get a job where she'd make some decent money. The piddling she got for her occasional articles barely paid for a new dress twice a year.

Her folks entered the parlor and sat down together on the settee. Luke laid his arm around her mother's shoulder, and Jack couldn't help wishing Noah had the freedom to do the same.

"What's on your mind, Half Bit?"

"My guess is a man." A teasing smile danced on her ma's lips.

Luke swung his head toward his wife. "A man!"

Rachel elbowed him in the side. "Stop pretending you haven't noticed how they look at one another."

Luke's mouth turned up on one side, and he scowled.

Jack's heart pounded. She'd tried not to be obvious, but she had a hard time not looking at Noah when he sat across from her during meals. He must be who they were referring to, but then why would that make Luke unhappy? Did he object to her having a relationship with a minister? Who could be a better choice?

"So?" her ma said.

Jack folded her hands then unlocked them and straightened a crease in her skirt. She hated being the bearer of bad news. She glanced at her parents.

Luke leaned forward, knees on his elbows, intensely staring at her. "What's wrong? Did Noah do something that made you uncomfortable?"

"What?" Jack blinked, trying to make sense of his unexpected question. "No! He's never been anything but a gentleman."

"Then tell us. You've got our minds running rampant." Luke relaxed and sat back.

"I overheard something." Jack jumped up and resumed her pacing. "And Jenny's printing the story in tomorrow's paper. I wanted y'all to know ahead of time, so it wouldn't be such a shock."

Luke sat up again. "What did you do?"

Jack grinned and shook her head. "It wasn't me, this time." She thought of how she'd hung from the saloon window and then fallen again but wasn't about to mention that. "The railroad is coming to town. A spur track is being built from Denison to here."

"Oh, that's your news?" Luke exhaled a loud breath. "I already knew that."

"You did? How?"

"The mayor told me. Said he wanted to be prepared for more people coming to town and was going to ask the town council to approve hiring two part-time deputies."

"Truly?" Her ma gazed at Luke. "Then you wouldn't have to work so much." She reached over and squeezed his hand. "I love that idea."

Jack sat down again, stunned that Luke already knew. "Why hasn't the mayor announced it then?"

"He was afraid there'd be a run on land and that prices would soar."

Jack frowned. Had the mayor purposely kept the news quiet so that he could profit? She'd heard he'd recently bought several lots on the east end of town—right where the hotel was going. "Do you already know about the hotel, too?"

Luke rubbed his jaw. "I wouldn't be a very good lawman if I didn't investigate the strangers who pass through my town."

"Why didn't you tell me?" Jack sat back, crossing her arms and pouting, not unlike Tessa.

"Wasn't my news to tell. How did you find out?"

"Uh. . ." Jack swallowed hard. Nope, she couldn't tell him. "I. . . uh. . .used my investigative skills."

This time her ma sat up. "No more rooftops, I hope."

"No." Jack hated how her voice rose unnaturally. Even though she told the truth, guilt needled her for what she'd done. She needed to distract them before they questioned her further. "But if a hotel comes here, won't that put us out of business?"

Luke glanced at her ma, who nodded. "It might. We've been talking about that and have decided it's time to stop taking boarders."

Jack's mouth dropped open. The house would almost feel odd without people coming and going. Where would Noah live? If he moved, she wouldn't see him as much. Wouldn't get to talk to him while he sipped his morning coffee. Wouldn't get to say good night each evening.

She listened to the crickets chirping outside the open window, already missing him.

"What's going on in that creative mind of yours?"

"I'm. . .uh, just shocked—and disappointed that you already know my news. I thought I'd gotten a big scoop—even Jenny was surprised. Who else knows?"

Luke shrugged. "Probably just the town council. Your story will be news to most folks."

Jack settled back in her chair. "Yeah, I suppose. But how will we get by without the additional income?"

"We're not destitute, Half Bit. The house is paid for, plus when your ma and I got married, I had most of my army pay saved and invested. With the railroad coming to town, Garrett's business will slack off. He and I are going to buy some brood mares and a quality stallion and start raising stock horses. We're already looking for a section of land that's not too far from town, where Carly and he can live after they marry." He took a deep breath, then continued. "Your ma has enough to do with just caring for the family and this big home. You sound disappointed."

"No. Just mulling things over." Suddenly a pleasing thought dashed through her mind. "If we aren't taking in boarders, can I have my own room?" She grinned and waggled her eyebrows.

Hope sparked in her ma's eyes, taking Jack by surprise again. "Does that mean you're not going to Dallas?"

They knew? About the letter? Were all her secrets public knowledge? She jumped up, flinging her arms out sideways. "Did Jenny spill the beans? Nobody else knew."

"No." Her ma bit the edge of her lower lip. "I went upstairs to check on Abby yesterday, and she'd gotten in your lap desk. She had the letter and was just getting ready to write on the paper." She ducked her head. "I shouldn't have read your letter, but I was too curious not to. I'm sorry for that, but"—she glanced up with wounded eyes—"how could you even consider such a thing without talking to us? Do you have any idea what it's like in a city that large?"

Luke patted her ma's shoulder. "Now, Rach, I've been to Dallas several times, and it's not a bad town."

The look her ma gave Luke could have boiled frozen water. "Whose side are you on?"

"Nobody's—I mean both of you. Jack's not an ordinary young lady."

"But she *is* a woman—and no woman should go off alone to a big city. Who would protect her?" Her ma blinked her eyes several times, then looked at Jack again with a watery gaze. "What about Noah? I thought something was developing between you two."

Jack fidgeted in her chair. She might have been oblivious to hurting her ma when she was young and half wild, but she didn't like it now. "I was going to tell you. In fact, that was one of the things I wanted to talk about tonight. I've decided to turn down the job offer and stay here."

"Really?" Ma smiled and wiped her eyes with the hanky she'd pulled from her pocket. "I know that must have been a hard decision since you've wanted to be a reporter for so long."

Jack shrugged. In truth, she hadn't made her final decision until she'd seen how upset the thought of her leaving made her ma. What job compared to love of family?

"So, does Noah have anything to do with your staying?" Ma asked.

Jack stared out the window into the twilight. "Maybe."

No, more than maybe—most definitely. But for some reason, she was uncomfortable saying so in front of Luke. He'd grown quiet, which meant he was stewing on something.

"You'd make a good pastor's wife."

"Ma!"

"Rachel!"

Both Jack and Luke spoke at once.

Luke stood and started pacing the room. "Don't you think it's a bit too soon to be talking like that?"

Rachel grinned. "It's springtime, and love is in the air. Look at the Kesslers—and Garrett and Carly."

Luke snorted. "And what about the Lord? Does He still have a say in our lives?"

Rachel fluffed the pillow Luke had been leaning on. "Of course. I've prayed about the man Jacqueline would marry for much of her life. I knew God would bring the right man in His timing."

Jack just stared at her mother. How could she be so confident? Was she actually voicing her approval for a union between her and Noah?

"All that matters is that you've prayed about your relationship with Noah and that you love him."

Luke grunted and ran his hand through his hair. What was wrong with him? She thought he liked Noah.

"I have prayed." Jack's gaze darted to her ma and back to Luke. His behavior was making her uneasy. "I—care for him."

Luke kicked a table leg, whether accidentally or on purpose, she wasn't sure. Her ma gave him a curious glance. "And I believe he cares deeply for you."

"It's too soon," Luke said. "You've only known him a few weeks. How can you care for him that much?"

Jack shrugged again. "I can't explain it. From the first moment I looked into his eyes, I felt something—as if we'd been bound together for a lifetime."

Rachel hugged the pillow. "I know just what you mean. I felt that about Luke when I first met him, too."

"You were in first grade, Rachel. How can you remember that?"

"A woman just does." She batted her lashes and gave him a coy smile.

Luke finally stopped in front of Jack, and she had to lean back to see his puckered brow. "Has Noah talked to you?"

Jack opened her mouth to respond, but paused, baffled by his question. "Uh. . .we talk everyday."

"That's not what I mean." Luke's hand lowered to where his gun normally rested, then he closed his fist. Something was definitely bothering him, but she had no idea what it could be.

Luke squatted and looked her in the eye. "You promise me—before you let your feelings for him grow any more—that you'll have a heart-to-heart talk with him. Tell him he'd better tell you everything—or he'll answer to me."

Jack glanced at her ma, seeing the same confusion she felt. Luke bounced up and strode out of the room and down the hall. What was the "everything" he was referring to?

The front door opened, and Noah strode in, his eyes shining. He shut the door, removed his hat, and noticed them. He walked into the room with a wide grin pulling at his cheeks. "Evening, I just got some rather exciting news—at least it seems that way to me."

Her ma lifted one brow. "Oh, and what is that?"

Noah sat down on the edge of the chair next to Jack's. She

studied each detail of his handsome face. His eye was all healed except for a faint bruise, and a slight red mark remained just above his lip from the cut. His nose was perfectly straight, and dark stubble made him even more appealing. His beautiful eyes beamed. How could this kind-hearted man be hiding a secret so bad that it would send Luke into a tizzy?

Noah leaned toward her. "The Taylors have decided not to return to Lookout. The town council offered me a permanent position and use of the parsonage."

He was staying! Jack's heart leapt for joy. She jumped up and almost hugged him, then remembered her ma was still in the room. "That's wonderful news."

Rachel also stood and clapped her hands. "Yes, that is. I'll miss the Taylors, but I know they've wanted to move back home for a long while. Do you mind if I tell Luke?"

Noah shook his head, and she left the room, leaving them alone. He reached out and took Jackie's hand. "Are you happy?"

She looked happy but not delirious, as he'd hoped. When he first heard the news, he'd wanted to flee the Manns' home and run back here to tell Jackie, but he couldn't. He had to sit quietly and listen to what they expected: no more preaching about pelicans and the discussion about his salary, which was a decent amount plus the offer to use the parsonage. All the time, every part of his being was bouncing.

"I am happy." She squeezed his hand and smiled.

"But?"

She broke his gaze and shrugged.

"Don't you know what this means, Jackie? I have the support of the town council, a home, and a salary that I can support a family on—if we're careful."

"We?" She stared up at him, her blue eyes looking enormous.

Did she not yet know his heart? Or maybe she didn't feel the same. He knew little of women and their ways. Had he misread her?

He closed his eyes. He wanted to obey God and do His work, but if she didn't share his feelings, how could he stay here?

He'd thought God was answering his dream and giving him this opportunity. More than he ever hoped for. Much more than he deserved.

But without her. . .

"I'm thrilled, Noah, but there's something I have to know. What is in your past that you don't want to tell me about?"

The moment he'd dreaded the most was here. He hadn't told the council about his secret yet. He wanted to talk to Luke first about how to approach it. They'd given him a week to decide, but he could tell they weren't happy that he hadn't made an instant decision.

"Noah. If you truly care about me and want a future together, there can be no secrets between us."

He sighed and nodded. "You're right. I'm just. . .scared, I guess."

She took hold of his other hand and gave him a sweet smile, but her eyes held a teasing glint. "You're scared of me?"

You have no idea. "Not exactly." He looked down and studied the floorboards. *How do I tell her, Lord? I don't want to lose her.*

There was no easy way. He captured her gaze, gaining strength from the love he saw there. Ten years had passed. Maybe she didn't even remember Butch.

"You're a good man, Noah. It can't be all that bad. What did you do?"

He shook his head. "It's not what I did but rather who I am."

The confusion in her gaze threatened to steal his boldness. He had to tell her before he lost his nerve. "I lived in Lookout a long time ago, and we went to school together."

Her eyes went wide, and he could almost see her sharp mind racing, trying to figure out the puzzle.

"I—I'm. . .Butch."

She crinkled her brow. Her eyes widened. She dropped his hands and stepped back, forming a chasm between them as wide as the state of Texas. He already felt her loss.

"Not Butch Laird?"

He nodded and ducked his head, hurt with how she'd spewed his name.

"How could you?" With a hand on her chest, she looked as if she couldn't catch her breath. Leaning forward, she narrowed her eyes. "How could you kiss me and not tell mc such a thing? Was this just a cruel game you were playing?"

"No, Jackie—" He ran his hand through his hair, seeing his dream dying. "I care for you—I always have."

"That's a lie." She backed up clear to the piano. "You were mean. You picked fights and—and—you locked me in jail and left me there."

"I'm sorry about the past, but I've changed. Haven't you seen that?"

She shook her head. Tears ran down her cheeks. "Is Noah even your real name? Jeffers sure isn't."

"Yes, Noah is what my ma named me, but my pa never liked it and called me Butch. I adopted my friend Pete's last name when he came to mean more to me than my own pa."

Jack's chin quivered. "You lied to me. More than once, and that's all that matters. I thought you were above such things, but I was wrong. My first pa—he always lied. I told myself I'd never have anything to do with a cruel man or a liar."

She hurried past him, making as wide an arc as possible. He was losing her.

"Jackie—wait."

She skidded to a stop in the hall and looked to her left. His hope took wing. Would she hear him out?

Luke stepped into view.

"You knew!" Jackie's word spewed forth like snake venom.

Luke nodded, sorrow etched in his face.

"Why didn't you say something?"

"It wasn't my place, Half Bit."

Jack swung toward the stairs. She stopped on the fourth one and glared down. "I'll never trust either of you again."

Noah watched her charge upstairs, his dreams dashed. He should have told her sooner.

Much sooner.

Chapter 32

Jack lay in her bed, her aching eyes matching her heart. Her whole body hurt. Her tears were spent. How could he be Butch?

How could he not tell her?

The thing she feared most had come true. She'd lost her heart to a man just like her pa.

She stared up at the half moon. How could she have been so stupid?

How could Luke have betrayed her like that? Wasn't it his job to protect her?

She sucked in a breath and a dose of reality. Luke had tried since she first met him to protect her, but only the Almighty could truly do that.

But hadn't He let her down, too?

Jack sighed and listened to her sisters' breathing as they slept. How could she feel so alone with two others in the room?

Just when Noah had everything he needed to provide for her, she learned the shocking truth—he was Butch Laird, her childhood nemesis. And yet, even knowing that, she still loved him. She bolted up in her bed, her heart pounding. She honestly, truly loved Butch Laird.

The thought should have repulsed her, but it didn't. Hadn't she always been curious about him? Even tried to be friends once?

Noah or Butch—what did it matter when he lied to her?

She could never trust him now. Her tears must have restocked because they started again.

Father God, make this hurt go away.

She wiped her tears on her pillowcase and her nose on her sixth and last hanky. Lying in the dark, she continued to pray. *Show me what to do, Lord.*

How can I stay in Lookout now? I can't bear to see him again.

Should I take the Dallas job?

Jack jerked. She blinked in the darkness and noticed the moon heading toward the horizon. Had she finally fallen asleep?

Her eyes ached, and she lifted her hand to touch their puffiness. Her head hurt as bad as when she'd gotten that concussion, but it was her heart that was shattered.

A metallic *ching* sounded near Emmie's bed. Jack sat up and rubbed her eyes. Something banged and rolled across the floor. Had Emmie awakened?

As her eyes grew used to the darkness, the form of a man's body took shape. "Papa?"

A masculine curse filled the room, and Jack gasped. The man hurled himself toward her. Before she could untangle herself from the sheet, a hand clamped hard over her mouth. Whiskey-laden breath filled her nostrils. "Where's that bracelet?"

Jack's eyes widened in the dark. She turned and could see the man's face in the moonlight. She pulled his hand down. "Billy?"

"I need that bracelet."

"I gave it to your ma."

He sucked in a deep breath. "You stupid. . .you've ruined everything."

He turned away and pulled open a drawer of her dresser—her unmentionables drawer, yanking out one garment after another. She tossed the sheet aside and stood, her nightgown sliding down to cover her legs. "Stop it. I don't have the bracelet anymore."

He grabbed her jaw. "I bought that for you. Why'd you give it to Ma?"

"You're hurting me. Stop it." She grabbed his hand, but he didn't let go.

"Shut up, or I'll hurt you like that fat, ol' lady."

Jack gasped. "You killed Bertha?"

"All I wanted was some money." Suddenly Billy's other hand careened toward her in the moonlight. It crashed into her jaw, knocking her back on the bed. Pain mixed with darkness. She fought to keep a hold on her awareness.

From a distance, someone screamed. Abby. She had to help her sister—as soon as she plowed through this quicksand of darkness.

Noah sat on the edge of the bed, unable to sleep. His heart had broken and fallen in pieces all over the floor. His prayers seemed to fall on deaf ears. He'd had everything he wanted in the palm of his hand for a few minutes—but he'd lost it all.

He'd lost her.

And without her, nothing else mattered.

He jumped up and strode to the window. A cool breeze lifted the curtains, reminding him of things greater than himself. The wind had always put him in mind of God. Something you couldn't see but you knew existed.

"Did I hear You wrong, Lord? Wasn't it Your will for me to come here, to make restitution for my past offenses? To have a chance to start over with Jackie?"

He should have told her the truth from the start. She would have reacted the same, but it wouldn't have hurt so much.

Or maybe it would have.

"What am I going to do, Lord?"

He had to tell the church board who he was. He probably wouldn't have a job after that, but with things like they were now, maybe that was for the best. First thing in the morning, he'd go see them.

He stared at the moon and longed to talk to Pete. The old man always put things in their proper perspective. Noah knew what he'd say, though.

Don't be so hard on yourself.

Talk to your Creator.

Trust the Lord.

But hadn't he done all that and still lost Jackie?

He wanted to throw something. Wanted to get on his horse and ride until he reached the ocean. Wanted things to be like they were when he'd kissed Jackie in the alley.

But they never would be.

A frantic scream broke into his misery. He bolted to the door, stumbling on the chair he'd left out earlier. A sharp pain ratcheted across his knee, but he ignored it when another scream came. He scrambled down the stairs and slid to a stop outside Jack's bedroom door.

He'd overreacted. Abby was just having a bad dream. He could not go in there.

Something thumped hard on the other side of the door, and Abby screamed again. Emmie started crying, and he heard a muffled squeal. "Jackie?"

He reached for the knob. The squeals got louder as if someone called for help. He turned the knob and shoved open the door. Abby's screams reverberated around the room.

His eyes focused on a large shape bending over Jackie's bed—a man's shape. His hand fumbled to light the lamp by the doorway. His eyes rebelled at the sudden brightness, but he rushed forward. Billy Morgan stood over Jack. Her cheek was red, and she glanced at him with a dazed stare. What had Billy done?

All his pain rushed to the surface. In two quick steps he grabbed Billy's arm. Noah hauled the man away from his beloved. He shook Billy hard. "What are you doing in here?"

Without warning, Billy went berserk—kicking, punching, cursing.

Abby's screams continued, and Emmie's wails grew louder. Noah dodged Billy's fist. He didn't want to fight the man again, but he'd crossed a line. He slammed Billy against the wall and held him there by his throat. Billy smashed his fists into Noah's cheeks. Rage filled him.

"Noah, stop it." Jackie's pleas barely pierced his mental armor.

"That's enough, son," Luke's stronger, deeper voice called to him. "Let him go, Noah. I've got my rifle."

He glanced toward Luke and suddenly realized how his rage had overpowered his senses. Just like his pa's always had. He opened his hand, and Billy slid down the wall.

"Papa, he killed Mrs. Boyd." Jackie slid off her bed and rushed to gather Emmie to her then carried her to Abby's bed and cuddled both frightened sisters.

Luke hauled Billy up. "You're under arrest, Mr. Morgan."

Noah took one last glance at Jackie and dashed out of the room. The worst thing he could have imagined had happened—he'd become his father.

The sound of songbirds tickled Jack's ears, and she stretched. She opened her eyes, surprised to see the sun had fully risen and both girls were already up and gone. Suddenly the horrors of last night rushed back.

Noah.

Billy.

What would Billy have done to her if Noah hadn't come to her rescue?

She shivered and sat up. Her eyes felt dry and scratchy—puffy from her hours of crying. And in the end, the result was the same. Noah was Butch—her worst enemy. The man she loved.

How could they be one and the same?

Why hadn't she recognized him?

He had the same black hair. The same dark, probing eyes. And Butch had been tall, but never as well-built as Noah. Somewhere over the years, Butch had lost his pudginess and bad complexion and mean streak and turned into sweet, gentle Noah.

As if someone had snapped together the final piece in a jigsaw puzzle, it all made sense:

That connection she'd felt—as if they had a past history—made sense now.

His familiarity with her—how he knew so much about her

His odd comment about a possible headline: TOWN DELINQUENT RETURNS AS NEW PASTOR

No wonder Noah couldn't stomach pork after his father had raised hogs. As poor as they'd been, it was probably all he'd eaten for years.

Some investigative reporter she turned out to be. The truth was right in front of her. He'd even tossed out clues to his identity like bread crumbs, but she'd acted like an infatuated schoolgirl blinded by reality.

But Noah had lied—and so had Luke.

She longed to do nothing except stay in bed all day, but she couldn't.

Yet how could she face him?

What could she say to him?

Nothing.

She forced herself up and trod to the washroom. She rinsed her face, holding the soothing water on her eyes for a moment. Then she looked in the mirror and gasped.

Her cheek where Billy had hit her was red. Swollen. She worked her jaw, wincing at the pain.

She dressed and brushed her hair, then wandered downstairs, her heart as battered as her face.

She searched for Noah in the parlor, then the dining room, but instead, she found her ma and Carly washing dishes. Emmie sat at the table in her chair, munching on a biscuit, and smiled at her. Jack pulled out a kitchen chair and flopped down, feeling one hundred years old.

Her ma slid a cup of coffee in front of her and sat down. The strong aroma drifted up from the cup, teasing her senses.

"How do you feel?"

"Numb."

"That will pass."

Jack made a derogatory snort. "Maybe in twenty years."

Emmie wrinkled up her nose and snorted, and Jack gave her sister a weak smile.

Her ma squeezed her forearm. Carly set a plate of biscuit, eggs, and bacon in front of her. All she could do was stare at the bacon. It reminded her of Noah. Of Butch.

She was in love with a liar and a man who had come within a hair's inch of bashing Billy to pieces last night—not that he didn't deserve it. Touching the sore place on her cheek, she realized that Noah had never actually hit Billy, but rather just held him away from her until Luke could get there. He wasn't like her pa, after all. He had self-control.

Andrew squeaked from the bedroom then let out a yell. Carly tossed down the towel she'd been drying dishes with. "I'll change his diaper and see if I can make him happy for a bit."

"Where's Luke?" Jack couldn't bring herself to call him papa this morning.

"Down at the jail. He's writing up formal charges against Billy for breaking into his mother's store and also for Bertha's murder. Turns out those two fellows that Garrett shot saw Billy breaking into the store, and they did the other robberies, hoping he would be blamed for all of them." She shook her head. "Billy always was a troublesome boy, but I never expected him to be capable of such things."

"Me neither. Did you know he broke in last night because he wanted the bracelet back that he gave me?"

Ma nodded. "Luke told me. Hardest thing I ever did was staying down here with Andrew when you girls were screaming." She rubbed her palm over the top of Jack's hand. "Luke feels like he let you down. His heart is breaking, you know."

Jack's lowered lip wobbled at causing him pain. "He should have told me."

"He couldn't. It was Noah's place."

"Luke could have said something before I started liking Noah."

"And just when was that? Seems to me you were smitten from the moment you met him."

Her ma didn't play fair. Jack stared into her black coffee—coffee that reminded her of Noah's eyes. She squeezed hers shut and pushed the cup away. "Do you think God sent Noah here for us to be together?"

"I think it's highly possible, but I think God also had another purpose. This town needs a minister."

Jack blew out a mocking breath. "Not one that lies."

"Why are you fighting this so much? You know you love Noah. Are you going to let him get away just because of your stubborn pride?"

Jack glowered at her ma. "He *lied* to me—just like my first pa."

"Everyone lies at one time or another, not that I'm making excuses for him, but when was thc last time you lied?"

Jack winced. "How can I trust him again?"

"I don't condone his lying, but he was scared."

"Of what?"

"Of people rejecting him just because of who he was. Do you honestly think anyone who'd known him as the town bully would receive him as pastor? People harbor long memories of those who hurt their children or destroy their property." Her mother slid the plate of food closer to her.

Something suddenly made sense. "That's why he was chopping wood and painting the store—he was trying to make up for the bad things he'd done." Jack's heart ached. She'd treated him so cruelly.

Ma nodded again. "And I think he waited to tell you who he was because he was afraid of how you'd react."

She hadn't considered that. If she'd known from the start who he was, she probably would have snubbed him—might not have even gone to church—and she'd have missed his thought-provoking messages. She broke off a piece of bacon and put it in her mouth, enjoying the flavor.

"I don't know what to do. I'd be lying if I said I don't care for him, but how can I face him again after how I reacted last night? I wasn't very nice."

"You were hurt—and reacted accordingly." Her mother sighed and played with the corner of the towel she'd used to dry dishes.

"What's wrong?"

The look that engulfed her mother's pretty face scared Jack, but she didn't know what she should be afraid of. "What is it?"

Her ma's pale blue eyes looked straight into Jack's. She swallowed hard, knowing she wouldn't like whatever her ma was going to say.

"I'm sorry, sweetie, but Noah is gone."

A cruel fist squeezed Jack's heart and wouldn't let go. "What do you mean he's gone? Has he already moved to the parsonage?"

"No, he left town."

Jack jumped up so fast the chair fell backward and banged on the floor. "No! Where did he go?"

"Uh-oh," Emmie said and pointed to the chair. Jack picked it up but remained standing.

"Sit down, sweetie."

"I can't. What am I going to do? Why did he leave?"

Her ma stood and came to her, pulling Jack to her chest. "He said it was better for everyone if he did. Better for you."

"I was wrong, Ma. He's a good man."

"Yes, he is. He's not the troubled youth he used to be. God took that wild boy, washed him clean with the blood of Jesus, and formed him into a man of character. A man who loves you."

And she loved him. So help her, she did. How could she have been such a stubborn fool?

She'd let her pride—her refusal to forgive—steal something precious. Her vendetta toward her pa had killed her chances with Noah.

Forgive me, Lord. Help me forgive my pa for all the mean, hurtful things he did.

Jack hugged her ma then stepped back. "You said Noah was headed home? Back to Emporia?"

She nodded. "I think the only person Noah has in the world is Pete, the man who took him in."

Jack backed away, her determination swelling with each breath she took. "No, Ma, he's got us, too."

She spun on her heels and ran into the hall.

"Where are you going?"

"To don my trousers."

Chapter 33

Noah walked his horse down the dusty lane. He was looking forward to seeing Pete again, yet each step Rebel took was a step farther away from Jackie. He missed her with every speck of his mind, body, and soul. He didn't know how he'd go on.

All he'd wanted was a chance to prove he'd changed. He'd fooled himself into believing she loved him, but she never truly had any faith in him—she didn't as a child, and she didn't now.

He'd finally found a place he thought he could call home. People had started accepting and befriending him. Trusting and respecting him.

And he'd lost it all.

Lost his chance to tell the townsfolk of God's love.

Lost the woman he loved.

Tears stung his eyes, and he tilted his head toward the heavens. "I've failed in every way, Lord. Forgive me."

He reined Rebel off the road into a patch of grass and dismounted. Kneeling, he cried out to God. "Forgive me for leaving the town You sent me to. Forgive me for failing You. Make this burning ache go away, Lord."

Yet maybe he deserved the pain. Hadn't he hated his own father? Caused trouble for his schoolmates and the townsfolk each time his pa had beat him? Hadn't his mother and sister died because he'd been too scared to leave them and ride for the doctor?

He was an utter failure.

"No, son, you are forgiven. You are deeply loved. Forgive yourself."

A sob gushed forth from the deepest recesses of his soul as he turned loose of the pain of his past and let the words of God wash over him.

Soothing.

Comforting.

Healing.

He was a child of God. His pain had momentarily blinded him so that he'd listened to the lies of Satan. But he wasn't a failure—he was a man of worth because of Christ's blood, which was shed for him on the cross. He was fully forgiven.

As the reality of the truth set in, Noah relaxed in the peace that only God can bring a troubled man. After the sleepless night before, he closed his eyes, weary from battling his fears but confident now in God's love. He may always love Jackie, but now he could give her to the Lord. He closed his eyes, and sleep overtook him.

The sound of rifle fire jerked him awake.

The rifle shook in Jack's hands. "Get up from there, Reverend."

"Jackie?" Noah stared at her, his eyes still foggy from sleep. "What are you doing?"

"You ran out on me, and I'm not letting you get away that easily." She forced her voice to sound gruff when all she wanted to do was wrap her arms around Noah and kiss him silly.

He lumbered to his feet and rubbed his eyes. "Am I dreaming? Or did you really just shoot at me?"

She could see his apprehension—and no wonder after how she had acted. She slid the rifle into the scabbard that hung from the horse and saddle she'd borrowed from Dan Howard. Bolstering her determination with a quick prayer, she turned back to Noah. "I'm sorry. Your confession last night took me by surprise—and I never liked surprises."

He took a step toward her. "I'm sorry, too. I should have told you sooner, but first I wanted you to get to know me as I am now. I've changed. God changed me."

"I know." She closed the space between them, tears stinging her eyes and making Noah's face blur. "Can you find it in your heart to forgive me?"

He exhaled a cough of disbelief. "Are you serious?"

She smacked him on the arm. "Of course I am. Do you think I'd ride all this way if I wasn't?"

"Yeah, I do, if you were truly bent on shooting me." He grinned and rubbed his arm, something enticing now burning in his gaze. "You pack a wallop for such a little thing."

"I'm an expert shot, too, so don't forget it."

"All right." He ducked his head and toed the dirt. "I'm really sorry, Jackie. I just didn't think you'd give me half a chance if you knew who I was."

"We'll never know now, but I want to put it behind us. Do you have feelings for me or not?" She was tired of mincing words. "And are you going to forgive me or not?"

"Yes." He stepped closer and ran the back of his finger down her cheek.

"Yes, what?"

"Yes, I forgive you, and yes, I love you."

That was all she needed to hear. Jack lunged into his arms, and her lips met his. He lifted her off the ground, nearly squeezing the air from her lungs as he showered her with kisses. The kisses took a turn, desperate, frantic—and then he pulled back, his breath heavy on her cheek.

"I love you, Jackie—I think I always have."

"I love you, too." She ran her hand across his cheek, marveling at its roughness. "It just took me a bit longer to realize it."

Noah's warm smile tickled her stomach. To think she almost gave him up because of her own stubbornness and refusal to forgive. He lowered her so that she could stand.

"Are you ready to go back home?" She fingered a button on his shirt.

"Where is home? I quit my job, you know?"

"I know the marshal real well, and maybe I can persuade him to 'encourage' the council to hire you back."

Noah lifted her off the ground again and kissed her, then he spun her around, hugging her tight. "Thank You, Lord!"

She sent her own prayer winging its way heaven bound. *Thank You, Father, for helping me see past my hurts and for giving me another chance with Noah.*

Epilogue

Jack repeated the vows in her head after Noah stated them. His black eyes caught hers, and he winked, sending shivers of delight through her. In front of the church, Carly gazed at Garrett with adoration and promised to love, honor, and obey him.

Jack winced. She wasn't 100 percent sure about that *obey* stuff, so she skipped that word. Maybe she and Noah could write their own vows before their wedding next month.

She could hardly wait. The two weeks they'd been courting had dragged by slower than a slug. But she'd seen the wisdom in waiting and getting to know each other better—that and they had to wait until another minister could come and marry them. At least Noah had his job back, and most of the town had forgiven him after their initial shock. Nothing stood in their way now—no barriers from the past, no hurt feelings, no unwillingness to forgive.

"Join me in praying for the bride and groom." Noah bowed his head, his deep voice lulling the room into a hushed reverence.

Jack breathed her own prayer, overflowing from her abundantly grateful heart. *Thank You, Lord, for helping me forgive my father and giving me Noah. He's a good man.*

One day soon, she'd finally be a bride.

Discussion Questions for *Finally a Bride*

1. Who was your favorite character in *Finally a Bride*? Why?

2. Jack Davis was determined to get a big story so she could land a job in Dallas as a reporter for a large newspaper. She later realizes that she's been proceeding toward her goal without seeking God's will on the matter. What makes her finally realize her need to seek God?

3. Name a situation where you've moved ahead without asking God's will first. How did it turn out?

4. If Jack goes to Dallas, she'll be there alone, without family and friends. How do you think this could cause her to draw closer to God?

5. Jack's first father was verbally and physically abusive. How did spending her early years in an abusive home affect her as an adult? If you grew up in an abusive home, how does that affect you today?

6. Jack was a rebel of sorts, doing things other females never did, like walking on a rooftop to get her story. What have you done that is out of the norm? Did you learn a specific lesson from it?

7. Both Noah and Carly were good people with bad pasts. Has something you did in your past come back to haunt you later on? How did you deal with it?

8. Carly was apprehensive about returning to Lookout where she'd first pretended to be one of the mail-order brides the Corbett brothers ordered for Luke. When two ladies at the church social gossip about her being an ex-convict and

former outlaw, Carly fled back to the boardinghouse. Do you think she could have handled the situation in a different way? Should she have confronted the women?

9. Garrett looked down on Carly at first because of her past and having been in prison. Has anyone ever looked down on you because of a bad choice you made? How did you deal with that?

10. When Noah first became the town minister, he kept his true identity a secret. Do you think he should have told people right from the start who he was? Would the town—and Jack—have given him a chance to prove he was different?

11. *Finally a Bride* is about allowing God to take you places where you're uncomfortable and trusting him to see you through it. Have you ever been in an uncomfortable situation and relied on God to get you through it?

12. In the whole Texas Boardinghouse Brides series, which character(s) do you think grew the most from the time they were first introduced?

About the Author

Award-winning author Vickie McDonough believes God is the ultimate designer of romance. She loves writing stories in which her characters find true love and grow in their faith. Vickie has published eighteen books. She is an active member of American Christian Fiction Writers and is currently serving as ACFW treasurer. Vickie has been a book reviewer for nine years as well. She is a wife of thirty-five years, mother of four sons, and grandmother to a feisty three-year-old girl. When not writing, she enjoys reading, watching movies, and traveling. Visit Vickie's website at www.vickiemcdonough.com.

About the Author

[illegible]